Cen

CHARLES BROCKDEN BROWN

Charles Brockden Brown

Three Gothic Novels

Wieland
or, The Transformation

Arthur Mervyn
or, Memoirs of the Year 1793

Edgar Huntly
or, Memoirs of a Sleep-Walker

THE LIBRARY OF AMERICA

The paper used in this publication meets the
minimum requirements of the American National Standard for
Information Sciences—Permanence of Paper for Printed
Library Materials, ANSI z39.48—1984.

Distributed to the trade
in the United States by Penguin Putnam Inc.
and in Canada by Penguin Books Canada Ltd.

Library of Congress Catalog Number: 97-46701
For cataloging information, see end of Notes.
ISBN 1–883011–57–4

First Printing
The Library of America—103

Manufactured in the United States of America

SYDNEY J. KRAUSE
WROTE THE NOTES FOR THIS VOLUME

Contents

WIELAND

OR

THE TRANSFORMATION

An American Tale

From Virtue's blissful paths away
The double-tongued are sure to stray;
Good is a forth-right journey still,
And mazy paths but lead to ill.

ADVERTISEMENT

THE following Work is delivered to the world as the first of a series of performances, which the favorable reception of this will induce the Writer to publish. His purpose is neither selfish nor temporary, but aims at the illustration of some important branches of the moral constitution of man. Whether this tale will be classed with the ordinary or frivolous sources of amusement, or be ranked with the few productions whose usefulness secures to them a lasting reputation, the reader must be permitted to decide.

The incidents related are extraordinary and rare. Some of them, perhaps, approach as nearly to the nature of miracles as can be done by that which is not truly miraculous. It is hoped that intelligent readers will not disapprove of the manner in which appearances are solved, but that the solution will be found to correspond with the known principles of human nature. The power which the principal person is said to possess can scarcely be denied to be real. It must be acknowledged to be extremely rare; but no fact, equally uncommon, is supported by the same strength of historical evidence.

Some readers may think the conduct of the younger Wieland impossible. In support of its possibility the Writer must appeal to Physicians and to men conversant with the latent springs and occasional perversions of the human mind. It will not be objected that the instances of similar delusion are rare, because it is the business of moral painters to exhibit their subject in its most instructive and memorable forms. If history furnishes one parallel fact, it is a sufficient vindication of the Writer; but most readers will probably recollect an authentic case, remarkably similar to that of Wieland.

It will be necessary to add, that this narrative is addressed, in an epistolary form, by the Lady whose story it contains, to a small number of friends, whose curiosity, with regard to it, had been greatly awakened. It may likewise be mentioned, that these events took place between the conclusion of the French and the beginning of the revolutionary war. The memoirs of Carwin, alluded to at the conclusion of the work, will be published or suppressed according to the reception which is given to the present attempt.

C.B.B.

September 3, 1798.

Chapter I

I FEEL little reluctance in complying with your request. You know not fully the cause of my sorrows. You are a stranger to the depth of my distresses. Hence your efforts at consolation must necessarily fail. Yet the tale that I am going to tell is not intended as a claim upon your sympathy. In the midst of my despair, I do not disdain to contribute what little I can to the benefit of mankind. I acknowledge your right to be informed of the events that have lately happened in my family. Make what use of the tale you shall think proper. If it be communicated to the world, it will inculcate the duty of avoiding deceit. It will exemplify the force of early impressions, and show the immeasurable evils that flow from an erroneous or imperfect discipline.

My state is not destitute of tranquillity. The sentiment that dictates my feelings is not hope. Futurity has no power over my thoughts. To all that is to come I am perfectly indifferent. With regard to myself, I have nothing more to fear. Fate has done its worst. Henceforth, I am callous to misfortune.

I address no supplication to the Deity. The power that governs the course of human affairs has chosen his path. The decree that ascertained the condition of my life, admits of no recal. No doubt it squares with the maxims of eternal equity. That is neither to be questioned nor denied by me. It suffices that the past is exempt from mutation. The storm that tore up our happiness, and changed into dreariness and desert the blooming scene of our existence, is lulled into grim repose; but not until the victim was transfixed and mangled; till every obstacle was dissipated by its rage; till every remnant of good was wrested from our grasp and exterminated.

How will your wonder, and that of your companions, be excited by my story! Every sentiment will yield to your amazement. If my testimony were without corroborations, you would reject it as incredible. The experience of no human being can furnish a parallel: That I, beyond the rest of mankind, should be reserved for a destiny without alleviation, and without example! Listen to my narrative, and then say what

5

it is that has made me deserve to be placed on this dreadful eminence, if, indeed, every faculty be not suspended in wonder that I am still alive, and am able to relate it.

My father's ancestry was noble on the paternal side; but his mother was the daughter of a merchant. My grand-father was a younger brother, and a native of Saxony. He was placed, when he had reached the suitable age, at a German college. During the vacations, he employed himself in traversing the neighbouring territory. On one occasion it was his fortune to visit Hamburg. He formed an acquaintance with Leonard Weise, a merchant of that city, and was a frequent guest at his house. The merchant had an only daughter, for whom his guest speedily contracted an affection; and, in spite of parental menaces and prohibitions, he, in due season, became her husband.

By this act he mortally offended his relations. Thenceforward he was entirely disowned and rejected by them. They refused to contribute any thing to his support. All intercourse ceased, and he received from them merely that treatment to which an absolute stranger, or detested enemy, would be entitled.

He found an asylum in the house of his new father, whose temper was kind, and whose pride was flattered by this alliance. The nobility of his birth was put in the balance against his poverty. Weise conceived himself, on the whole, to have acted with the highest discretion, in thus disposing of his child. My grand-father found it incumbent on him to search out some mode of independent subsistence. His youth had been eagerly devoted to literature and music. These had hitherto been cultivated merely as sources of amusement. They were now converted into the means of gain. At this period there were few works of taste in the Saxon dialect. My ancestor may be considered as the founder of the German Theatre. The modern poet of the same name is sprung from the same family, and, perhaps, surpasses but little, in the fruitfulness of his invention, or the soundness of his taste, the elder Wieland. His life was spent in the composition of sonatas and dramatic pieces. They were not unpopular, but merely afforded him a scanty subsistence. He died in the bloom of his life, and was quickly followed to the grave by his wife. Their only child was taken under the protection of the merchant. At an early age he was apprenticed to a London trader, and passed seven years of mercantile servitude.

My father was not fortunate in the character of him under whose care he was now placed. He was treated with rigor, and full employment was provided for every hour of his time. His duties were laborious and mechanical. He had been educated with a view to this profession, and, therefore, was not tormented with unsatisfied desires. He did not hold his present occupations in abhorrence, because they withheld him from paths more flowery and more smooth, but he found in unintermitted labour, and in the sternness of his master, sufficient occasions for discontent. No opportunities of recreation were allowed him. He spent all his time pent up in a gloomy apartment, or traversing narrow and crowded streets. His food was coarse, and his lodging humble.

His heart gradually contracted a habit of morose and gloomy reflection. He could not accurately define what was wanting to his happiness. He was not tortured by comparisons drawn between his own situation and that of others. His state was such as suited his age and his views as to fortune. He did not imagine himself treated with extraordinary or unjustifiable rigor. In this respect he supposed the condition of others, bound like himself to mercantile service, to resemble his own; yet every engagement was irksome, and every hour tedious in its lapse.

In this state of mind he chanced to light upon a book written by one of the teachers of the Albigenses, or French Protestants. He entertained no relish for books, and was wholly unconscious of any power they possessed to delight or instruct. This volume had lain for years in a corner of his garret, half buried in dust and rubbish. He had marked it as it lay; had thrown it, as his occasions required, from one spot to another; but had felt no inclination to examine its contents, or even to inquire what was the subject of which it treated.

One Sunday afternoon, being induced to retire for a few minutes to his garret, his eye was attracted by a page of this book, which, by some accident, had been opened and placed full in his view. He was seated on the edge of his bed, and was employed in repairing a rent in some part of his clothes.

His eyes were not confined to his work, but occasionally wandering, lighted at length upon the page. The words "Seek and ye shall find," were those that first offered themselves to his notice. His curiosity was roused by these so far as to prompt him to proceed. As soon as he finished his work, he took up the book and turned to the first page. The further he read, the more inducement he found to continue, and he regretted the decline of the light which obliged him for the present to close it.

The book contained an exposition of the doctrine of the sect of Camissards, and an historical account of its origin. His mind was in a state peculiarly fitted for the reception of devotional sentiments. The craving which had haunted him was now supplied with an object. His mind was at no loss for a theme of meditation. On days of business, he rose at the dawn, and retired to his chamber not till late at night. He now supplied himself with candles, and employed his nocturnal and Sunday hours in studying this book. It, of course, abounded with allusions to the Bible. All its conclusions were deduced from the sacred text. This was the fountain, beyond which it was unnecessary to trace the stream of religious truth; but it was his duty to trace it thus far.

A Bible was easily procured, and he ardently entered on the study of it. His understanding had received a particular direction. All his reveries were fashioned in the same mould. His progress towards the formation of his creed was rapid. Every fact and sentiment in this book were viewed through a medium which the writings of the Camissard apostle had suggested. His constructions of the text were hasty, and formed on a narrow scale. Every thing was viewed in a disconnected position. One action and one precept were not employed to illustrate and restrict the meaning of another. Hence arose a thousand scruples to which he had hitherto been a stranger. He was alternately agitated by fear and by ecstacy. He imagined himself beset by the snares of a spiritual foe, and that his security lay in ceaseless watchfulness and prayer.

His morals, which had never been loose, were now modelled by a stricter standard. The empire of religious duty extended itself to his looks, gestures, and phrases. All levities of speech, and negligences of behaviour, were proscribed. His air was mournful and contemplative. He laboured to keep alive a sentiment of fear, and a belief of the awe-creating presence of the Deity. Ideas foreign to this were sedulously excluded. To suffer their intrusion was a crime against the Divine Majesty inexpiable but by days and weeks of the keenest agonies.

No material variation had occurred in the lapse of two years. Every day confirmed him in his present modes of thinking and acting. It was to be expected that the tide of his emotions would sometimes recede, that intervals of despondency and doubt would occur; but these gradually were more rare, and of shorter duration; and he, at last, arrived at a state considerably uniform in this respect.

His apprenticeship was now almost expired. On his arrival of age he became entitled, by the will of my grand-father, to a small sum. This sum would hardly suffice to set him afloat as a trader in his present situation, and he had nothing to expect from the generosity of his master. Residence in England had, besides, become almost impossible, on account of his religious tenets. In addition to these motives for seeking a new habitation, there was another of the most imperious and irresistable necessity. He had imbibed an opinion that it was his duty to disseminate the truths of the gospel among the unbelieving nations. He was terrified at first by the perils and hardships to which the life of a missionary is exposed. This cowardice made him diligent in the invention of objections and excuses; but he found it impossible wholly to shake off the belief that such was the injunction of his duty. The belief, after every new conflict with his passions, acquired new strength; and, at length, he formed a resolution of complying with what he deemed the will of heaven.

The North-American Indians naturally presented themselves as the first objects for this species of benevolence. As soon as his servitude expired, he converted his little fortune into money, and embarked for Philadelphia. Here his fears were revived, and a nearer survey of savage manners once more shook his resolution. For a while he relinquished his purpose, and purchasing a farm on Schuylkill, within a few miles of the city, set himself down to the cultivation of it. The cheapness of land, and the service of African slaves, which were then in general use, gave him who was poor in Europe all the advantages of wealth. He passed fourteen years in a thrifty and laborious manner. In this time new objects, new employments, and new associates appeared to have nearly obliterated the devout impressions of his youth. He now became acquainted with a woman of a meek and quiet disposition, and of slender acquirements like himself. He proffered his hand and was accepted.

His previous industry had now enabled him to dispense with personal labour, and direct attention to his own concerns. He enjoyed leisure, and was visited afresh by devotional contemplation. The reading of the scriptures, and other religious books, became once more his favorite employment. His ancient belief relative to the conversion of the savage tribes, was revived with uncommon energy. To the former obstacles were now added the pleadings of parental and conjugal love. The struggle was long and vehement; but his sense of duty would not be stifled or enfeebled, and finally triumphed over every impediment.

His efforts were attended with no permanent success. His exhortations had sometimes a temporary power, but more frequently were repelled with insult and derision. In pursuit of this object he encountered the most imminent perils, and underwent incredible fatigues, hunger, sickness, and solitude. The licence of savage passion, and the artifices of his depraved countrymen, all opposed themselves to his progress. His courage did not forsake him till there appeared no reasonable ground to hope for success. He desisted not till his heart was relieved from the supposed obligation to persevere. With a constitution somewhat decayed, he at length returned to his family. An interval of tranquillity succeeded. He was frugal, regular, and strict in the performance of domestic duties. He allied himself with no sect, because he perfectly agreed with none. Social worship is that by which they are all distinguished; but this article found no place in his creed. He rigidly interpreted that precept which enjoins us, when we worship, to retire into solitude, and shut out every species of society. According to him devotion was not only a silent office, but must be performed alone. An hour at noon, and an hour at midnight were thus appropriated.

At the distance of three hundred yards from his house, on

the top of a rock whose sides were steep, rugged, and encumbered with dwarf cedars and stony asperities, he built what to a common eye would have seemed a summer-house. The eastern verge of this precipice was sixty feet above the river which flowed at its foot. The view before it consisted of a transparent current, fluctuating and rippling in a rocky channel, and bounded by a rising scene of cornfields and orchards. The edifice was slight and airy. It was no more than a circular area, twelve feet in diameter, whose flooring was the rock, cleared of moss and shrubs, and exactly levelled, edged by twelve Tuscan columns, and covered by an undulating dome. My father furnished the dimensions and outlines, but allowed the artist whom he employed to complete the structure on his own plan. It was without seat, table, or ornament of any kind.

This was the temple of his Deity. Twice in twenty-four hours he repaired hither, unaccompanied by any human being. Nothing but physical inability to move was allowed to obstruct or postpone this visit. He did not exact from his family compliance with his example. Few men, equally sincere in their faith, were as sparing in their censures and restrictions, with respect to the conduct of others, as my father. The character of my mother was no less devout; but her education had habituated her to a different mode of worship. The loneliness of their dwelling prevented her from joining any established congregation; but she was punctual in the offices of prayer, and in the performance of hymns to her Saviour, after the manner of the disciples of Zinzendorf. My father refused to interfere in her arrangements. His own system was embraced not, accurately speaking, because it was the best, but because it had been expressly prescribed to him. Other modes, if practised by other persons, might be equally acceptable.

His deportment to others was full of charity and mildness. A sadness perpetually overspread his features, but was unmingled with sternness or discontent. The tones of his voice, his gestures, his steps were all in tranquil unison. His conduct was characterised by a certain forbearance and humility, which secured the esteem of those to whom his tenets were most obnoxious. They might call him a fanatic and a dreamer, but they could not deny their veneration to his invincible candour and invariable integrity. His own belief of rectitude was the foundation of his happiness. This, however, was destined to find an end.

Suddenly the sadness that constantly attended him was deepened. Sighs, and even tears, sometimes escaped him. To the expostulations of his wife he seldom answered any thing. When he deigned to be communicative, he hinted that his peace of mind was flown, in consequence of deviation from his duty. A command had been laid upon him, which he had delayed to perform. He felt as if a certain period of hesitation and reluctance had been allowed him, but that this period was passed. He was no longer permitted to obey. The duty assigned to him was transferred, in consequence of his disobedience, to another, and all that remained was to endure the penalty.

He did not describe this penalty. It appeared to be nothing more for some time than a sense of wrong. This was sufficiently acute, and was aggravated by the belief that his offence was incapable of expiation. No one could contemplate the agonies which he seemed to suffer without the deepest compassion. Time, instead of lightening the burthen, appeared to add to it. At length he hinted to his wife, that his end was near. His imagination did not prefigure the mode or the time of his decease, but was fraught with an incurable persuasion that his death was at hand. He was likewise haunted by the belief that the kind of death that awaited him was strange and terrible. His anticipations were thus far vague and indefinite; but they sufficed to poison every moment of his being, and devote him to ceaseless anguish.

Chapter II

EARLY in the morning of a sultry day in August, he left Mettingen, to go to the city. He had seldom passed a day from home since his return from the shores of the Ohio. Some urgent engagements at this time existed, which would not admit of further delay. He returned in the evening, but appeared to be greatly oppressed with fatigue. His silence and dejection were likewise in a more than ordinary degree conspicuous. My mother's brother, whose profession was that of a surgeon, chanced to spend this night at our house. It was from him that I have frequently received an exact account of the mournful catastrophe that followed.

As the evening advanced, my father's inquietudes increased. He sat with his family as usual, but took no part in their conversation. He appeared fully engrossed by his own reflections. Occasionally his countenance exhibited tokens of alarm; he gazed stedfastly and wildly at the ceiling; and the exertions of his companions were scarcely sufficient to interrupt his reverie. On recovering from these fits, he expressed no surprise; but pressing his hand to his head, complained, in a tremulous and terrified tone, that his brain was scorched to cinders. He would then betray marks of insupportable anxiety.

My uncle perceived, by his pulse, that he was indisposed, but in no alarming degree, and ascribed appearances chiefly to the workings of his mind. He exhorted him to recollection and composure, but in vain. At the hour of repose he readily retired to his chamber. At the persuasion of my mother he even undressed and went to bed. Nothing could abate his restlessness. He checked her tender expostulations with some sternness. "Be silent," said he, "for that which I feel there is but one cure, and that will shortly come. You can help me nothing. Look to your own condition, and pray to God to strengthen you under the calamities that await you." "What am I to fear?" she answered. "What terrible disaster is it that you think of?" "Peace—as yet I know it not myself, but come it will, and shortly." She repeated her inquiries and doubts;

but he suddenly put an end to the discourse, by a stern command to be silent.

She had never before known him in this mood. Hitherto all was benign in his deportment. Her heart was pierced with sorrow at the contemplation of this change. She was utterly unable to account for it, or to figure to herself the species of disaster that was menaced.

Contrary to custom, the lamp, instead of being placed on the hearth, was left upon the table. Over it against the wall there hung a small clock, so contrived as to strike a very hard stroke at the end of every sixth hour. That which was now approaching was the signal for retiring to the fane at which he addressed his devotions. Long habit had occasioned him to be always awake at this hour, and the toll was instantly obeyed.

Now frequent and anxious glances were cast at the clock. Not a single movement of the index appeared to escape his notice. As the hour verged towards twelve his anxiety visibly augmented. The trepidations of my mother kept pace with those of her husband; but she was intimidated into silence. All that was left to her was to watch every change of his features, and give vent to her sympathy in tears.

At length the hour was spent, and the clock tolled. The sound appeared to communicate a shock to every part of my father's frame. He rose immediately, and threw over himself a loose gown. Even this office was performed with difficulty, for his joints trembled, and his teeth chattered with dismay. At this hour his duty called him to the rock, and my mother naturally concluded that it was thither he intended to repair. Yet these incidents were so uncommon, as to fill her with astonishment and foreboding. She saw him leave the room, and heard his steps as they hastily descended the stairs. She half resolved to rise and pursue him, but the wildness of the scheme quickly suggested itself. He was going to a place whither no power on earth could induce him to suffer an attendant.

The window of her chamber looked toward the rock. The atmosphere was clear and calm, but the edifice could not be discovered at that distance through the dusk. My mother's anxiety would not allow her to remain where she was. She rose, and seated herself at the window. She strained her sight to get a view of the dome, and of the path that led to it. The first painted itself with sufficient distinctness on her fancy, but was undistinguishable by the eye from the rocky mass on which it was erected. The second could be imperfectly seen; but her husband had already passed, or had taken a different direction.

What was it that she feared? Some disaster impended over her husband or herself. He had predicted evils, but professed himself ignorant of what nature they were. When were they to come? Was this night, or this hour to witness the accomplishment? She was tortured with impatience, and uncertainty. All her fears were at present linked to his person, and she gazed at the clock, with nearly as much eagerness as my father had done, in expectation of the next hour.

An half hour passed away in this state of suspense. Her eyes were fixed upon the rock; suddenly it was illuminated. A light proceeding from the edifice, made every part of the scene visible. A gleam diffused itself over the intermediate space, and instantly a loud report, like the explosion of a mine, followed. She uttered an involuntary shriek, but the new sounds that greeted her ear, quickly conquered her surprise. They were piercing shrieks, and uttered without intermission. The gleams which had diffused themselves far and wide were in a moment withdrawn, but the interior of the edifice was filled with rays.

The first suggestion was that a pistol was discharged, and that the structure was on fire. She did not allow herself time to meditate a second thought, but rushed into the entry and knocked loudly at the door of her brother's chamber. My uncle had been previously roused by the noise, and instantly flew to the window. He also imagined what he saw to be fire. The loud and vehement shrieks which succeeded the first explosion, seemed to be an invocation of succour. The incident was inexplicable; but he could not fail to perceive the propriety of hastening to the spot. He was unbolting the door, when his sister's voice was heard on the outside conjuring him to come forth.

He obeyed the summons with all the speed in his power. He stopped not to question her, but hurried down stairs and across the meadow which lay between the house and the rock.

The shrieks were no longer to be heard; but a blazing light was clearly discernible between the columns of the temple. Irregular steps, hewn in the stone, led him to the summit. On three sides, this edifice touched the very verge of the cliff. On the fourth side, which might be regarded as the front, there was an area of small extent, to which the rude staircase conducted you. My uncle speedily gained this spot. His strength was for a moment exhausted by his haste. He paused to rest himself. Meanwhile he bent the most vigilant attention towards the object before him.

⁓Within the columns he beheld what he could no better describe, than by saying that it resembled a cloud impregnated with light. It had the brightness of flame, but was without its upward motion. It did not occupy the whole area, and rose but a few feet above the floor. No part of the building was on fire. This appearance was astonishing. He approached the temple. As he went forward the light retired, and, when he put his feet within the apartment, utterly vanished. The suddenness of this transition increased the darkness that succeeded in a tenfold degree. Fear and wonder rendered him powerless. An occurrence like this, in a place assigned to devotion, was adapted to intimidate the stoutest heart.

⁓His wandering thoughts were recalled by the groans of one near him. His sight gradually recovered its power, and he was able to discern my father stretched on the floor. At that moment, my mother and servants arrived with a lanthorn, and enabled my uncle to examine more closely this scene. My father, when he left the house, besides a loose upper vest and slippers, wore a shirt and drawers. Now he was naked; his skin throughout the greater part of his body was scorched and bruised. His right arm exhibited marks as of having been struck by some heavy body. His clothes had been removed, and it was not immediately perceived that they were reduced to ashes. His slippers and his hair were untouched.

He was removed to his chamber, and the requisite attention paid to his wounds, which gradually became more painful. A mortification speedily shewed itself in the arm, which had been most hurt. Soon after, the other wounded parts exhibited the like appearance.

Immediately subsequent to this disaster, my father seemed

nearly in a state of insensibility. He was passive under every operation. He scarcely opened his eyes, and was with difficulty prevailed upon to answer the questions that were put to him. By his imperfect account, it appeared, that while engaged in silent orisons, with thoughts full of confusion and anxiety, a faint gleam suddenly shot athwart the apartment. His fancy immediately pictured to itself, a person bearing a lamp. It seemed to come from behind. He was in the act of turning to examine the visitant, when his right arm received a blow from a heavy club. At the same instant, a very bright spark was seen to light upon his clothes. In a moment, the whole was reduced to ashes. This was the sum of the information which he chose to give. There was somewhat in his manner that indicated an imperfect tale. My uncle was inclined to believe that half the truth had been suppressed.

Meanwhile, the disease thus wonderfully generated, betrayed more terrible symptoms. Fever and delirium terminated in lethargic slumber, which, in the course of two hours, gave place to death. Yet not till insupportable exhalations and crawling putrefaction had driven from his chamber and the house every one whom their duty did not detain.

— Such was the end of my father. None surely was ever more mysterious. When we recollect his gloomy anticipations and unconquerable anxiety; the security from human malice which his character, the place, and the condition of the times, might be supposed to confer; the purity and cloudlessness of the atmosphere, which rendered it impossible that lightning was the cause; what are the conclusions that we must form?

The prelusive gleam, the blow upon his arm, the fatal spark, the explosion heard so far, the fiery cloud that environed him, without detriment to the structure though composed of combustible materials, the sudden vanishing of this cloud at my uncle's approach—what is the inference to be drawn from these facts? Their truth cannot be doubted. My uncle's testimony is peculiarly worthy of credit, because no man's temper is more sceptical, and his belief is unalterably attached to natural causes.

I was at this time a child of six years of age. The impressions that were then made upon me, can never be effaced. I was ill qualified to judge respecting what was then passing; but as I advanced in age, and became more fully acquainted with these facts, they oftener became the subject of my thoughts. Their resemblance to recent events revived them with new force in my memory, and made me more anxious to explain them. Was this the penalty of disobedience? this the stroke of a vindictive and invisible hand? Is it a fresh proof that the Divine Ruler interferes in human affairs, meditates an end, selects and commissions his agents, and enforces, by unequivocal sanctions, submission to his will? Or, was it merely the irregular expansion of the fluid that imparts warmth to our heart and our blood, caused by the fatigue of the preceding day, or flowing, by established laws, from the condition of his thoughts?*

*A case, in its symptoms exactly parallel to this, is published in one of the Journals of Florence. See, likewise, similar cases reported by Messrs. Merille and Muraire, in the "Journal de Medicine," for February and May, 1783. The researches of Maffei and Fontana have thrown some light upon this subject.

Chapter III

THE SHOCK which this disastrous occurrence occasioned to my mother, was the foundation of a disease which carried her, in a few months, to the grave. My brother and myself were children at this time, and were now reduced to the condition of orphans. The property which our parents left was by no means inconsiderable. It was entrusted to faithful hands, till we should arrive at a suitable age. Meanwhile, our education was assigned to a maiden aunt who resided in the city, and whose tenderness made us in a short time cease to regret that we had lost a mother.

The years that succeeded were tranquil and happy. Our lives were molested by few of those cares that are incident to childhood. By accident more than design, the indulgence and yielding temper of our aunt was mingled with resolution and stedfastness. She seldom deviated into either extreme of rigour or lenity. Our social pleasures were subject to no unreasonable restraints. We were instructed in most branches of useful knowledge, and were saved from the corruption and tyranny of colleges and boarding schools.

Our companions were chiefly selected from the children of our neighbours. Between one of these and my brother, there quickly grew the most affectionate intimacy. Her name was Catharine Pleyel. She was rich, beautiful, and contrived to blend the most bewitching softness with the most exuberant vivacity. The tie by which my brother and she were united, seemed to add force to the love which I bore her, and which was amply returned. Between her and myself there was every circumstance tending to produce and foster friendship. Our sex and age were the same. We lived within sight of each other's abode. Our tempers were remarkably congenial, and the superintendants of our education not only prescribed to us the same pursuits, but allowed us to cultivate them together.

Every day added strength to the triple bonds that united us. We gradually withdrew ourselves from the society of others, and found every moment irksome that was not devoted to each other. My brother's advance in age made no change in our situation. It was determined that his profession should be agriculture. His fortune exempted him from the necessity of personal labour. The task to be performed by him was nothing more than superintendance. The skill that was demanded by this was merely theoretical, and was furnished by casual inspection, or by closet study. The attention that was paid to this subject did not seclude him for any long time from us, on whom time had no other effect than to augment our impatience in the absence of each other and of him. Our tasks, our walks, our music, were seldom performed but in each other's company.

It was easy to see that Catharine and my brother were born for each other. The passion which they mutually entertained quickly broke those bounds which extreme youth had set to it; confessions were made or extorted, and their union was postponed only till my brother had passed his minority. The previous lapse of two years was constantly and usefully employed.

O my brother! But the task I have set myself let me perform with steadiness. The felicity of that period was marred by no gloomy anticipations. The future, like the present, was serene. Time was supposed to have only new delights in store. I mean not to dwell on previous incidents longer than is necessary to illustrate or explain the great events that have since happened. The nuptial day at length arrived. My brother took possession of the house in which he was born, and here the long protracted marriage was solemnized.

My father's property was equally divided between us. A neat dwelling, situated on the bank of the river, three quarters of a mile from my brother's, was now occupied by me. These domains were called, from the name of the first possessor, Mettingen. I can scarcely account for my refusing to take up my abode with him, unless it were from a disposition to be an economist of pleasure. Self-denial, seasonably exercised, is one means of enhancing our gratifications. I was, beside, desirous of administering a fund, and regulating an household, of my own. The short distance allowed us to exchange visits as often as we pleased. The walk from one mansion to the other was no undelightful prelude to our interviews. I was sometimes their visitant, and they, as frequently, were my guests.

Our education had been modelled by no religious standard. We were left to the guidance of our own understanding, and the casual impressions which society might make upon us. My friend's temper, as well as my own, exempted us from much anxiety on this account. It must not be supposed that we were without religion, but with us it was the product of lively feelings, excited by reflection on our own happiness, and by the grandeur of external nature. We sought not a basis for our faith, in the weighing of proofs, and the dissection of creeds. Our devotion was a mixed and casual sentiment, seldom verbally expressed, or solicitously sought, or carefully retained. In the midst of present enjoyment, no thought was bestowed on the future. As a consolation in calamity religion is dear. But calamity was yet at a distance, and its only tendency was to heighten enjoyments which needed not this addition to satisfy every craving.

My brother's situation was somewhat different. His deportment was grave, considerate, and thoughtful. I will not say whether he was indebted to sublimer views for this disposition. Human life, in his opinion, was made up of changeable elements, and the principles of duty were not easily unfolded. The future, either as anterior, or subsequent to death, was a scene that required some preparation and provision to be made for it. These positions we could not deny, but what distinguished him was a propensity to ruminate on these truths. The images that visited us were blithsome and gay, but those with which he was most familiar were of an opposite hue. They did not generate affliction and fear, but they diffused over his behaviour a certain air of forethought and sobriety. The principal effect of this temper was visible in his features and tones. These, in general, bespoke a sort of thrilling melancholy. I scarcely ever knew him to laugh. He never accompanied the lawless mirth of his companions with more than a smile, but his conduct was the same as ours.

He partook of our occupations and amusements with a zeal not less than ours, but of a different kind. The diversity in our temper was never the parent of discord, and was scarcely a topic of regret. The scene was variegated, but not tarnished or disordered, by it. It hindered the element in which we moved from stagnating. Some agitation and concussion is requisite to the due exercise of human understanding. In his studies, he pursued an austerer and more arduous path. He was much conversant with the history of religious opinions, and took pains to ascertain their validity. He deemed it indispensable to examine the ground of his belief, to settle the relation between motives and actions, the criterion of merit, and the kinds and properties of evidence.

There was an obvious resemblance between him and my father, in their conceptions of the importance of certain topics, and in the light in which the vicissitudes of human life were accustomed to be viewed. Their characters were similar, but the mind of the son was enriched by science, and embellished with literature.

The temple was no longer assigned to its ancient use. From an Italian adventurer, who erroneously imagined that he could find employment for his skill, and sale for his sculptures in America, my brother had purchased a bust of Cicero. He professed to have copied this piece from an antique dug up with his own hands in the environs of Modena. Of the truth of his assertions we were not qualified to judge; but the marble was pure and polished, and we were contented to admire the performance, without waiting for the sanction of connoisseurs. We hired the same artist to hew a suitable pedestal from a neighbouring quarry. This was placed in the temple, and the bust rested upon it. Opposite to this was a harpsichord, sheltered by a temporary roof from the weather. This was the place of resort in the evenings of summer. Here we sung, and talked, and read, and occasionally banqueted. Every joyous and tender scene most dear to my memory, is connected with this edifice. Here the performances of our musical and poetical ancestor were rehearsed. Here my brother's children received the rudiments of their education; here a thousand conversations, pregnant with delight and improvement, took place; and here the social affections were accustomed to expand, and the tear of delicious sympathy to be shed.

My brother was an indefatigable student. The authors whom he read were numerous, but the chief object of his veneration was Cicero. He was never tired of conning and

rehearsing his productions. To understand them was not sufficient. He was anxious to discover the gestures and cadences
with which they ought to be delivered. He was very scrupulous in selecting a true scheme of pronunciation for the Latin
tongue, and in adapting it to the words of his darling writer.
His favorite occupation consisted in embellishing his rhetoric
with all the proprieties of gesticulation and utterance.

Not contented with this, he was diligent in settling and
restoring the purity of the text. For this end, he collected all
the editions and commentaries that could be procured, and
employed months of severe study in exploring and comparing
them. He never betrayed more satisfaction than when he
made a discovery of this kind.

It was not till the addition of Henry Pleyel, my friend's only
brother, to our society, that his passion for Roman eloquence
was countenanced and fostered by a sympathy of tastes. This
young man had been some years in Europe. We had separated
at a very early age, and he was now returned to spend the
remainder of his days among us.

Our circle was greatly enlivened by the accession of a new
member. His conversation abounded with novelty. His gaiety
was almost boisterous, but was capable of yielding to a grave
deportment, when the occasion required it. His discernment
was acute, but he was prone to view every object merely as
supplying materials for mirth. His conceptions were ardent
but ludicrous, and his memory, aided, as he honestly acknowledged, by his invention, was an inexhaustible fund of entertainment.

His residence was at the same distance below the city as
ours was above, but there seldom passed a day without our
being favoured with a visit. My brother and he were endowed
with the same attachment to the Latin writers; and Pleyel was
not behind his friend in his knowledge of the history and
metaphysics of religion. Their creeds, however, were in many
respects opposite. Where one discovered only confirmations
of his faith, the other could find nothing but reasons for
doubt. Moral necessity, and calvinistic inspiration, were the
props on which my brother thought proper to repose. Pleyel
was the champion of intellectual liberty, and rejected all guidance but that of his reason. Their discussions were frequent,

but, being managed with candour as well as with skill, they were always listened to by us with avidity and benefit.

Pleyel, like his new friends, was fond of music and poetry. Henceforth our concerts consisted of two violins, an harpsichord, and three voices. We were frequently reminded how much happiness depends upon society. This new friend, though, before his arrival, we were sensible of no vacuity, could not now be spared. His departure would occasion a void which nothing could fill, and which would produce insupportable regret. Even my brother, though his opinions were hourly assailed, and even the divinity of Cicero contested, was captivated with his friend, and laid aside some part of his ancient gravity at Pleyel's approach.

Chapter IV

Six years of uninterrupted happiness had rolled away, since my brother's marriage. The sound of war had been heard, but it was at such a distance as to enhance our enjoyment by affording objects of comparison. The Indians were repulsed on the one side, and Canada was conquered on the other. Revolutions and battles, however calamitous to those who occupied the scene, contributed in some sort to our happiness, by agitating our minds with curiosity, and furnishing causes of patriotic exultation. Four children, three of whom were of an age to compensate, by their personal and mental progress, the cares of which they had been, at a more helpless age, the objects, exercised my brother's tenderness. The fourth was a charming babe that promised to display the image of her mother, and enjoyed perfect health. To these were added a sweet girl fourteen years old, who was loved by all of us, with an affection more than parental.

Her mother's story was a mournful one. She had come hither from England, when this child was an infant, alone, without friends, and without money. She appeared to have embarked in a hasty and clandestine manner. She passed three years of solitude and anguish under my aunt's protection, and died a martyr to woe; the source of which she could, by no importunities, be prevailed upon to unfold. Her education and manners bespoke her to be of no mean birth. Her last moments were rendered serene, by the assurances she received from my aunt, that her daughter should experience the same protection that had been extended to herself.

On my brother's marriage, it was agreed that she should make a part of his family. I cannot do justice to the attractions of this girl. Perhaps the tenderness she excited might partly originate in her personal resemblance to her mother, whose character and misfortunes were still fresh in our remembrance. She was habitually pensive, and this circumstance tended to remind the spectator of her friendless condition; and yet that epithet was surely misapplied in this case. This being was cherished by those with whom she now resided, with unspeakable fondness. Every exertion was made to enlarge and improve her mind. Her safety was the object of a solicitude that almost exceeded the bounds of discretion. Our affection indeed could scarcely transcend her merits. She never met my eye, or occurred to my reflections, without exciting a kind of enthusiasm. Her softness, her intelligence, her equanimity, never shall I see surpassed. I have often shed tears of pleasure at her approach, and pressed her to my bosom in an agony of fondness.

While every day was adding to the charms of her person, and the stores of her mind, there occurred an event which threatened to deprive us of her. An officer of some rank, who had been disabled by a wound at Quebec, had employed himself, since the ratification of peace, in travelling through the colonies. He remained a considerable period at Philadelphia, but was at last preparing for his departure. No one had been more frequently honoured with his visits than Mrs. Baynton, a worthy lady with whom our family were intimate. He went to her house with a view to perform a farewell visit, and was on the point of taking his leave, when I and my young friend entered the apartment. It is impossible to describe the emotions of the stranger, when he fixed his eyes upon my companion. He was motionless with surprise. He was unable to conceal his feelings, but sat silently gazing at the spectacle before him. At length he turned to Mrs. Baynton, and more by his looks and gestures than by words, besought her for an explanation of the scene. He seized the hand of the girl, who, in her turn, was surprised by his behaviour, and drawing her forward, said in an eager and faultering tone, "Who is she? whence does she come? what is her name?"

The answers that were given only increased the confusion of his thoughts. He was successively told, that she was the daughter of one whose name was Louisa Conway, who arrived among us at such a time, who sedulously concealed her parentage, and the motives of her flight, whose incurable griefs had finally destroyed her, and who had left this child under the protection of her friends. Having heard the tale, he melted into tears, eagerly clasped the young lady in his arms, and called himself her father. When the tumults excited in his breast by this unlooked-for meeting were somewhat subsided, he gratified our curiosity by relating the following incidents.

Miss Conway was the only daughter of a banker in London, who discharged towards her every duty of an affectionate father. He had chanced to fall into her company, had been subdued by her attractions, had tendered her his hand, and been joyfully accepted both by parent and child. His wife had given him every proof of the fondest attachment. Her father, who possessed immense wealth, treated him with distinguished respect, liberally supplied his wants, and had made one condition of his consent to their union, a resolution to take up their abode with him.

They had passed three years of conjugal felicity, which had been augmented by the birth of this child, when his professional duty called him into Germany. It was not without an arduous struggle, that she was persuaded to relinquish the design of accompanying him through all the toils and perils of war. No parting was ever more distressful. They strove to alleviate, by frequent letters, the evils of their lot. Those of his wife, breathed nothing but anxiety for his safety, and impatience of his absence. At length, a new arrangement was made, and he was obliged to repair from Westphalia to Canada. One advantage attended this change. It afforded him an opportunity of meeting his family. His wife anticipated this interview, with no less rapture than himself. He hurried to London, and the moment he alighted from the stage-coach, ran with all speed to Mr. Conway's house.

It was an house of mourning. His father was overwhelmed with grief, and incapable of answering his inquiries. The servants, sorrowful and mute, were equally refractory. He explored the house, and called on the names of his wife and daughter, but his summons was fruitless. At length, this new disaster was explained. Two days before his arrival, his wife's chamber was found empty. No search, however diligent and anxious, could trace her steps. No cause could be assigned for her disappearance. The mother and child had fled away together.

New exertions were made, her chamber and cabinets were ransacked, but no vestige was found serving to inform them as to the motives of her flight, whether it had been voluntary or otherwise, and in what corner of the kingdom or of the world she was concealed. Who shall describe the sorrow and amazement of the husband? His restlessness, his vicissitudes of hope and fear, and his ultimate despair? His duty called him to America. He had been in this city, and had frequently passed the door of the house in which his wife, at that moment, resided. Her father had not remitted his exertions to elucidate this painful mystery, but they had failed. This disappointment hastened his death; in consequence of which, Louisa's father became possessor of his immense property.

This tale was a copious theme of speculation. A thousand questions were started and discussed in our domestic circle, respecting the motives that influenced Mrs. Stuart to abandon her country. It did not appear that her proceeding was involuntary. We recalled and reviewed every particular that had fallen under our own observation. By none of these were we furnished with a clue. Her conduct, after the most rigorous scrutiny, still remained an impenetrable secret. On a nearer view, Major Stuart proved himself a man of most amiable character. His attachment to Louisa appeared hourly to increase. She was no stranger to the sentiments suitable to her new character. She could not but readily embrace the scheme which was proposed to her, to return with her father to England. This scheme his regard for her induced him, however, to postpone. Some time was necessary to prepare her for so great a change and enable her to think without agony of her separation from us.

I was not without hopes of prevailing on her father entirely to relinquish this unwelcome design. Meanwhile, he pursued his travels through the southern colonies, and his daughter continued with us. Louisa and my brother frequently received letters from him, which indicated a mind of no common order. They were filled with amusing details, and profound reflections. While here, he often partook of our evening conversations at the temple; and since his departure, his correspondence had frequently supplied us with topics of discourse.

One afternoon in May, the blandness of the air, and brightness of the verdure, induced us to assemble, earlier than usual, in the temple. We females were busy at the needle, while my brother and Pleyel were bandying quotations and syllogisms. The point discussed was the merit of the oration for Cluentius, as descriptive, first, of the genius of the speaker; and, secondly, of the manners of the times. Pleyel laboured to extenuate both these species of merit, and tasked his ingenuity, to shew that the orator had embraced a bad cause; or, at least, a doubtful one. He urged, that to rely on the exaggerations of an advocate, or to make the picture of a single family a model from which to sketch the condition of a nation, was absurd. The controversy was suddenly diverted into a new channel, by a misquotation. Pleyel accused his companion of saying *"polliceatur"* when he should have said *"polliceretur."* Nothing would decide the contest, but an appeal to the volume. My brother was returning to the house for this purpose, when a servant met him with a letter from Major Stuart. He immediately returned to read it in our company.

Besides affectionate compliments to us, and paternal benedictions on Louisa, his letter contained a description of a waterfall on the Monongahela. A sudden gust of rain falling, we were compelled to remove to the house. The storm passed away, and a radiant moon-light succeeded. There was no motion to resume our seats in the temple. We therefore remained where we were, and engaged in sprightly conversation. The letter lately received naturally suggested the topic. A parallel was drawn between the cataract there described, and one which Pleyel had discovered among the Alps of Glarus. In the state of the former, some particular was mentioned, the truth of which was questionable. To settle the dispute which thence arose, it was proposed to have recourse to the letter. My brother searched for it in his pocket. It was no where to be found. At length, he remembered to have left it in the temple, and he determined to go in search of it. His wife, Pleyel, Louisa, and myself, remained where we were.

In a few minutes he returned. I was somewhat interested in the dispute, and was therefore impatient for his return; yet, as I heard him ascending the stairs, I could not but remark, that he had executed his intention with remarkable dispatch. My eyes were fixed upon him on his entrance. Methought he brought with him looks considerably different from those

with which he departed. Wonder, and a slight portion of anxiety were mingled in them. His eyes seemed to be in search
of some object. They passed quickly from one person to another, till they rested on his wife. She was seated in a careless
attitude on the sofa, in the same spot as before. She had the
same muslin in her hand, by which her attention was chiefly
engrossed.

The moment he saw her, his perplexity visibly increased. He
quietly seated himself, and fixing his eyes on the floor, appeared to be absorbed in meditation. These singularities suspended the inquiry which I was preparing to make respecting
the letter. In a short time, the company relinquished the subject which engaged them, and directed their attention to
Wieland. They thought that he only waited for a pause in the
discourse, to produce the letter. The pause was uninterrupted
by him. At length Pleyel said, "Well, I suppose you have
found the letter."

"No," said he, without any abatement of his gravity, and
looking stedfastly at his wife, "I did not mount the hill."—
"Why not?"—"Catharine, have you not moved from that spot
since I left the room?"—She was affected with the solemnity
of his manner, and laying down her work, answered in a tone
of surprise, "No; Why do you ask that question?"—His eyes
were again fixed upon the floor, and he did not immediately
answer. At length, he said, looking round upon us, "Is it true
that Catharine did not follow me to the hill? That she did not
just now enter the room?"—We assured him, with one voice,
that she had not been absent for a moment, and inquired into
the motive of his questions.

"Your assurances," said he, "are solemn and unanimous;
and yet I must deny credit to your assertions, or disbelieve
the testimony of my senses, which informed me, when I was
half way up the hill, that Catharine was at the bottom."

We were confounded at this declaration. Pleyel rallied him
with great levity on his behaviour. He listened to his friend
with calmness, but without any relaxation of features.

"One thing," said he with emphasis, "is true; either I heard
my wife's voice at the bottom of the hill, or I do not hear
your voice at present."

"Truly," returned Pleyel, "it is a sad dilemma to which you

have reduced yourself. Certain it is, if our eyes can give us certainty, that your wife has been sitting in that spot during every moment of your absence. You have heard her voice, you say, upon the hill. In general, her voice, like her temper, is all softness. To be heard across the room, she is obliged to exert herself. While you were gone, if I mistake not, she did not utter a word. Clara and I had all the talk to ourselves. Still it may be that she held a whispering conference with you on the hill; but tell us the particulars."

"The conference," said he, "was short; and far from being carried on in a whisper. You know with what intention I left the house. Half way to the rock, the moon was for a moment hidden from us by a cloud. I never knew the air to be more bland and more calm. In this interval I glanced at the temple, and thought I saw a glimmering between the columns. It was so faint, that it would not perhaps have been visible, if the moon had not been shrowded. I looked again, but saw nothing. I never visit this building alone, or at night, without being reminded of the fate of my father. There was nothing wonderful in this appearance; yet it suggested something more than mere solitude and darkness in the same place would have done.

"I kept on my way. The images that haunted me were solemn; and I entertained an imperfect curiosity, but no fear, as to the nature of this object. I had ascended the hill little more than half way, when a voice called me from behind. The accents were clear, distinct, powerful, and were uttered, as I fully believed, by my wife. Her voice is not commonly so loud. She has seldom occasion to exert it, but, nevertheless, I have sometimes heard her call with force and eagerness. If my ear was not deceived, it was her voice which I heard.

" 'Stop, go no further. There is danger in your path.' The suddenness and unexpectedness of this warning, the tone of alarm with which it was given, and, above all, the persuasion that it was my wife who spoke, were enough to disconcert and make me pause. I turned and listened to assure myself that I was not mistaken. The deepest silence succeeded. At length, I spoke in my turn. 'Who calls? is it you, Catharine?' I stopped and presently received an answer. 'Yes, it is I; go not up; return instantly; you are wanted at the house.' Still the voice was Catharine's, and still it proceeded from the foot of the stairs.

"What could I do? The warning was mysterious. To be uttered by Catharine at a place, and on an occasion like these, enhanced the mystery. I could do nothing but obey. Accordingly, I trod back my steps, expecting that she waited for me at the bottom of the hill. When I reached the bottom, no one was visible. The moon-light was once more universal and brilliant, and yet, as far as I could see no human or moving figure was discernable. If she had returned to the house, she must have used wonderous expedition to have passed already beyond the reach of my eye. I exerted my voice, but in vain. To my repeated exclamations, no answer was returned.

"Ruminating on these incidents, I returned hither. There was no room to doubt that I had heard my wife's voice; attending incidents were not easily explained; but you now assure me that nothing extraordinary has happened to urge my return, and that my wife has not moved from her seat."

Such was my brother's narrative. It was heard by us with different emotions. Pleyel did not scruple to regard the whole as a deception of the senses. Perhaps a voice had been heard; but Wieland's imagination had misled him in supposing a resemblance to that of his wife, and giving such a signification to the sounds. According to his custom he spoke what he thought. Sometimes, he made it the theme of grave discussion, but more frequently treated it with ridicule. He did not believe that sober reasoning would convince his friend, and gaiety, he thought, was useful to take away the solemnities which, in a mind like Wieland's, an accident of this kind was calculated to produce.

Pleyel proposed to go in search of the letter. He went and speedily returned, bearing it in his hand. He had found it open on the pedestal; and neither voice nor visage had risen to impede his design.

Catharine was endowed with an uncommon portion of good sense; but her mind was accessible, on this quarter, to wonder and panic. That her voice should be thus inexplicably and unwarrantably assumed, was a source of no small disquietude. She admitted the plausibility of the arguments by which Pleyel endeavoured to prove, that this was no more than an auricular deception; but this conviction was sure to be shaken, when she turned her eyes upon her husband, and perceived that Pleyel's logic was far from having produced the same effect upon him.

As to myself, my attention was engaged by this occurrence. I could not fail to perceive a shadowy resemblance between it and my father's death. On the latter event, I had frequently reflected; my reflections never conducted me to certainty, but the doubts that existed were not of a tormenting kind. I could not deny that the event was miraculous, and yet I was invincibly averse to that method of solution. My wonder was excited by the inscrutableness of the cause, but my wonder was unmixed with sorrow or fear. It begat in me a thrilling, and not unpleasing solemnity. Similar to these were the sensations produced by the recent adventure.

But its effect upon my brother's imagination was of chief moment. All that was desirable was, that it should be regarded by him with indifference. The worst effect that could flow, was not indeed very formidable. Yet I could not bear to think that his senses should be the victims of such delusion. It argued a diseased condition of his frame, which might show itself hereafter in more dangerous symptoms. The will is the tool of the understanding, which must fashion its conclusions on the notices of sense. If the senses be depraved, it is impossible to calculate the evils that may flow from the consequent deductions of the understanding.

I said, this man is of an ardent and melancholy character. Those ideas which, in others, are casual or obscure, which are entertained in moments of abstraction and solitude, and easily escape when the scene is changed, have obtained an immoveable hold upon his mind. The conclusions which long habit has rendered familiar, and, in some sort, palpable to his intellect, are drawn from the deepest sources. All his actions and practical sentiments are linked with long and abstruse deductions from the system of divine government and the laws of our intellectual constitution. He is, in some respects, an enthusiast, but is fortified in his belief by innumerable arguments and subtilties.

His father's death was always regarded by him as flowing from a direct and supernatural decree. It visited his meditations oftener than it did mine. The traces which it left were more gloomy and permanent. This new incident had a visible effect in augmenting his gravity. He was less disposed than formerly to converse and reading. When we sifted his thoughts, they were generally found to have a relation, more or less direct, with this incident. It was difficult to ascertain the exact species of impression which it made upon him. He never introduced the subject into conversation, and listened with a silent and half-serious smile to the satirical effusions of Pleyel.

One evening we chanced to be alone together in the temple. I seized that opportunity of investigating the state of his thoughts. After a pause, which he seemed in no wise inclined to interrupt, I spoke to him—"How almost palpable is this dark; yet a ray from above would dispel it." "Ay," said Wieland, with fervor, "not only the physical, but moral night would be dispelled." "But why," said I, "must the Divine Will address its precepts to the eye?" He smiled significantly. "True," said he, "the understanding has other avenues." "You have never," said I, approaching nearer to the point— "you have never told me in what way you considered the late extraordinary incident." "There is no determinate way in which the subject can be viewed. Here is an effect, but the cause is utterly inscrutable. To suppose a deception will not do. Such is possible, but there are twenty other suppositions more probable. They must all be set aside before we reach that point." "What are these twenty suppositions?" "It is needless to mention them. They are only less improbable than Pleyel's. Time may convert one of them into certainty. Till then it is useless to expatiate on them."

Chapter V

SOME TIME had elapsed when there happened another occurrence, still more remarkable. Pleycl, on his return from Europe, brought information of considerable importance to my brother. My ancestors were noble Saxons, and possessed large domains in Lusatia. The Prussian wars had destroyed those persons whose right to these estates precluded my brother's. Pleyel had been exact in his inquiries, and had discovered that, by the law of male-primogeniture, my brother's claims were superior to those of any other person now living. Nothing was wanting but his presence in that country, and a legal application to establish this claim.

Pleyel strenuously recommended this measure. The advantages, he thought, attending it were numerous, and it would argue the utmost folly to neglect them. Contrary to his expectation he found my brother averse to the scheme. Slight efforts, he, at first, thought would subdue his reluctance; but he found this aversion by no means slight. The interest that he took in the happiness of his friend and his sister, and his own partiality to the Saxon soil, from which he had likewise sprung, and where he had spent several years of his youth, made him redouble his exertions to win Wieland's consent. For this end he employed every argument that his invention could suggest. He painted, in attractive colours, the state of manners and government in that country, the security of civil rights, and the freedom of religious sentiments. He dwelt on the privileges of wealth and rank, and drew from the servile condition of one class, an argument in favor of his scheme, since the revenue and power annexed to a German principality afford so large a field for benevolence. The evil flowing from this power, in malignant hands, was proportioned to the good that would arise from the virtuous use of it. Hence, Wieland, in forbearing to claim his own, withheld all the positive felicity that would accrue to his vassals from his success, and hazarded all the misery that would redound from a less enlightened proprietor.

It was easy for my brother to repel these arguments, and to

shew that no spot on the globe enjoyed equal security and liberty to that which he at present inhabited. That if the Saxons had nothing to fear from mis-government, the external causes of havoc and alarm were numerous and manifest. The recent devastations committed by the Prussians furnished a specimen of these. The horrors of war would always impend over them, till Germany were seized and divided by Austrian and Prussian tyrants; an event which he strongly suspected was at no great distance. But setting these considerations aside, was it laudable to grasp at wealth and power even when they were within our reach? Were not these the two great sources of depravity? What security had he, that in this change of place and condition, he should not degenerate into a tyrant and voluptuary? Power and riches were chiefly to be dreaded on account of their tendency to deprave the possessor. He held them in abhorrence, not only as instruments of misery to others, but to him on whom they were conferred. Besides, riches were comparative, and was he not rich already? He lived at present in the bosom of security and luxury. All the instruments of pleasure, on which his reason or imagination set any value, were within his reach. But these he must forego, for the sake of advantages which, whatever were their value, were as yet uncertain. In pursuit of an imaginary addition to his wealth, he must reduce himself to poverty, he must exchange present certainties for what was distant and contingent; for who knows not that the law is a system of expence, delay and uncertainty? If he should embrace this scheme, it would lay him under the necessity of making a voyage to Europe, and remaining for a certain period, separate from his family. He must undergo the perils and discomforts of the ocean; he must divest himself of all domestic pleasures; he must deprive his wife of her companion, and his children of a father and instructor, and all for what? For the ambiguous advantages which overgrown wealth and flagitious tyranny have to bestow? For a precarious possession in a land of turbulence and war? Advantages, which will not certainly be gained, and of which the acquisition, if it were sure, is necessarily distant.

Pleyel was enamoured of his scheme on account of its instrinsic benefits, but, likewise, for other reasons. His abode at Leipsig made that country appear to him like home. He was connected with this place by many social ties. While there he had not escaped the amorous contagion. But the lady, though her heart was impressed in his favor, was compelled to bestow her hand upon another. Death had removed this impediment, and he was now invited by the lady herself to return. This he was of course determined to do, but was anxious to obtain the company of Wieland; he could not bear to think of an eternal separation from his present associates. Their interest, he thought, would be no less promoted by the change than his own. Hence he was importunate and indefatigable in his arguments and solicitations.

He knew that he could not hope for mine or his sister's ready concurrence in this scheme. Should the subject be mentioned to us, we should league our efforts against him, and strengthen that reluctance in Wieland which already was sufficiently difficult to conquer. He, therefore, anxiously concealed from us his purpose. If Wieland were previously enlisted in his cause, he would find it a less difficult task to overcome our aversion. My brother was silent on this subject, because he believed himself in no danger of changing his opinion, and he was willing to save us from any uneasiness. The mere mention of such a scheme and the possibility of his embracing it, he knew, would considerably impair our tranquillity.

One day, about three weeks subsequent to the mysterious call, it was agreed that the family should be my guests. Seldom had a day been passed by us, of more serene enjoyment. Pleyel had promised us his company, but we did not see him till the sun had nearly declined. He brought with him a countenance that betokened disappointment and vexation. He did not wait for our inquiries, but immediately explained the cause. Two days before a packet had arrived from Hamburgh, by which he had flattered himself with the expectation of receiving letters, but no letters had arrived. I never saw him so much subdued by an untoward event. His thoughts were employed in accounting for the silence of his friends. He was seized with the torments of jealousy, and suspected nothing less than the infidelity of her to whom he had devoted his heart. The silence must have been concerted. Her sickness, or absence, or death, would have increased the certainty of some one's having written. No supposition could be formed but that his mistress had grown indifferent, or that she had transferred her affections to another. The miscarriage of a letter was hardly within the reach of possibility. From Leipsig to Hamburgh, and from Hamburgh hither, the conveyance was exposed to no hazard.

He had been so long detained in America chiefly in consequence of Wieland's aversion to the scheme which he proposed. He now became more impatient than ever to return to Europe. When he reflected that, by his delays, he had probably forfeited the affections of his mistress, his sensations amounted to agony. It only remained, by his speedy departure, to repair, if possible, or prevent so intolerable an evil. Already he had half resolved to embark in this very ship which, he was informed, would set out in a few weeks on her return.

Meanwhile he determined to make a new attempt to shake the resolution of Wieland. The evening was somewhat advanced when he invited the latter to walk abroad with him. The invitation was accepted, and they left Catharine, Louisa and me, to amuse ourselves by the best means in our power. During this walk, Pleyel renewed the subject that was nearest his heart. He re-urged all his former arguments, and placed them in more forcible lights.

They promised to return shortly; but hour after hour passed, and they made not their appearance. Engaged in sprightly conversation, it was not till the clock struck twelve that we were reminded of the lapse of time. The absence of our friends excited some uneasy apprehensions. We were expressing our fears, and comparing our conjectures as to what might be the cause, when they entered together. There were indications in their countenances that struck me mute. These were unnoticed by Catharine, who was eager to express her surprize and curiosity at the length of their walk. As they listened to her, I remarked that their surprize was not less than ours. They gazed in silence on each other, and on her. I watched their looks, but could not understand the emotions that were written in them.

These appearances diverted Catharine's inquiries into a new channel. What did they mean, she asked, by their silence, and by their thus gazing wildly at each other, and at her? Pleyel profited by this hint, and assuming an air of indifference,

framed some trifling excuse, at the same time darting significant glances at Wieland, as if to caution him against disclosing
the truth. My brother said nothing, but delivered himself up
to meditation. I likewise was silent, but burned with impatience to fathom this mystery. Presently my brother and his
wife, and Louisa, returned home. Pleyel proposed, of his own
accord, to be my guest for the night. This circumstance, in
addition to those which preceded, gave new edge to my
wonder.

As soon as we were left alone, Pleyel's countenance assumed
an air of seriousness, and even consternation, which I had
never before beheld in him. The steps with which he measured
the floor betokened the trouble of his thoughts. My inquiries
were suspended by the hope that he would give me the information that I wanted without the importunity of questions.
I waited some time, but the confusion of his thoughts appeared in no degree to abate. At length I mentioned the apprehensions which their unusual absence had occasioned, and
which were increased by their behaviour since their return,
and solicited an explanation. He stopped when I began to
speak, and looked stedfastly at me. When I had done, he said,
to me, in a tone which faultered through the vehemence of
his emotions, "How were you employed during our absence?" "In turning over the Della Crusca dictionary, and
talking on different subjects; but just before your entrance,
we were tormenting ourselves with omens and prognosticks
relative to your absence." "Catharine was with you the whole
time?" "Yes." "But are you sure?" "Most sure. She was not
absent a moment." He stood, for a time, as if to assure himself
of my sincerity. Then, clenching his hands, and wildly lifting
them above his head, "Lo," cried he, "I have news to tell
you. The Baroness de Stolberg is dead!"

This was her whom he loved. I was not surprised at the
agitations which he betrayed. But how was the information
procured? How was the truth of this news connected with the
circumstance of Catharine's remaining in our company? He
was for some time inattentive to my questions. When he
spoke, it seemed merely a continuation of the reverie into
which he had been plunged.

"And yet it might be a mere deception. But could both of

us in that case have been deceived? A rare and prodigious coincidence! Barely not impossible. And yet, if the accent be oracular—Theresa is dead. No, no," continued he, covering his face with his hands, and in a tone half broken into sobs, "I cannot believe it. She has not written, but if she were dead, the faithful Bertrand would have given me the earliest information. And yet if he knew his master, he must have easily guessed at the effect of such tidings. In pity to me he was silent.

"Clara, forgive me; to you, this behaviour is mysterious. I will explain as well as I am able. But say not a word to Catharine. Her strength of mind is inferior to your's. She will, besides, have more reason to be startled. She is Wieland's angel."

Pleyel proceeded to inform me, for the first time, of the scheme which he had pressed, with so much earnestness, on my brother. He enumerated the objections which had been made, and the industry with which he had endeavoured to confute them. He mentioned the effect upon his resolutions produced by the failure of a letter. "During our late walk," continued he, "I introduced the subject that was nearest my heart. I re-urged all my former arguments, and placed them in more forcible lights. Wieland was still refractory. He expatiated on the perils of wealth and power, on the sacredness of conjugal and parental duties, and the happiness of mediocrity.

"No wonder that the time passed, unperceived, away. Our whole souls were engaged in this cause. Several times we came to the foot of the rock; as soon as we perceived it, we changed our course, but never failed to terminate our circuitous and devious ramble at this spot. At length your brother observed, 'We seem to be led hither by a kind of fatality. Since we are so near, let us ascend and rest ourselves a while. If you are not weary of this argument we will resume it there.'

"I tacitly consented. We mounted the stairs, and drawing the sofa in front of the river, we seated ourselves upon it. I took up the thread of our discourse where we had dropped it. I ridiculed his dread of the sea, and his attachment to home. I kept on in this strain, so congenial with my disposition, for some time, uninterrupted by him. At length, he said

to me, 'Suppose now that I, whom argument has not convinced, should yield to ridicule, and should agree that your
scheme is eligible; what will you have gained? Nothing. You
have other enemies beside myself to encounter. When you
have vanquished me, your toil has scarcely begun. There are
my sister and wife, with whom it will remain for you to maintain the contest. And trust me, they are adversaries whom all
your force and stratagem will never subdue.' I insinuated that
they would model themselves by his will: that Catharine
would think obedience her duty. He answered, with some
quickness, 'You mistake. Their concurrence is indispensable.
It is not my custom to exact sacrifices of this kind. I live to
be their protector and friend, and not their tyrant and foe. If
my wife shall deem her happiness, and that of her children,
most consulted by remaining where she is, here she shall remain.' 'But,' said I, 'when she knows your pleasure, will she
not conform to it?' Before my friend had time to answer this
question, a negative was clearly and distinctly uttered from
another quarter. It did not come from one side or the other,
from before us or behind. Whence then did it come? By whose
organs was it fashioned?

"If any uncertainty had existed with regard to these particulars, it would have been removed by a deliberate and equally
distinct repetition of the same monosyllable, 'No.' The voice
was my sister's. It appeared to come from the roof. I started
from my seat. 'Catharine,' exclaimed I, 'where are you?' No
answer was returned. I searched the room, and the area before
it, but in vain. Your brother was motionless in his seat. I returned to him, and placed myself again by his side. My astonishment was not less than his.

" 'Well,' said he, at length, 'What think you of this? This is
the self-same voice which I formerly heard; you are now convinced that my ears were well informed.'

" 'Yes,' said I, 'this, it is plain, is no fiction of the fancy.'
We again sunk into mutual and thoughtful silence. A recollection of the hour, and of the length of our absence, made
me at last propose to return. We rose up for this purpose. In
doing this, my mind reverted to the contemplation of my own
condition. 'Yes,' said I aloud, but without particularly addressing myself to Wieland, 'my resolution is taken. I cannot

hope to prevail with my friends to accompany me. They may doze away their days on the banks of Schuylkill, but as to me, I go in the next vessel; I will fly to her presence, and demand the reason of this extraordinary silence.'

"I had scarcely finished the sentence, when the same mysterious voice exclaimed, 'You shall not go. The seal of death is on her lips. Her silence is the silence of the tomb.' Think of the effects which accents like these must have had upon me. I shuddered as I listened. As soon as I recovered from my first amazement, 'Who is it that speaks?' said I, 'whence did you procure these dismal tidings?' I did not wait long for an answer. 'From a source that cannot fail. Be satisfied. She is dead.' You may justly be surprised, that, in the circumstances in which I heard the tidings, and notwithstanding the mystery which environed him by whom they were imparted, I could give an undivided attention to the facts, which were the subject of our dialogue. I eagerly inquired, when and where did she die? What was the cause of her death? Was her death absolutely certain? An answer was returned only to the last of these questions. 'Yes,' was pronounced by the same voice; but it now sounded from a greater distance, and the deepest silence was all the return made to my subsequent interrogatories.

"It was my sister's voice; but it could not be uttered by her; and yet, if not by her, by whom was it uttered? When we returned hither, and discovered you together, the doubt that had previously existed was removed. It was manifest that the intimation came not from her. Yet if not from her, from whom could it come? Are the circumstances attending the imparting of this news proof that the tidings are true? God forbid that they should be true."

Here Pleyel sunk into anxious silence, and gave me leisure to ruminate on this inexplicable event. I am at a loss to describe the sensations that affected me. I am not fearful of shadows. The tales of apparitions and enchantments did not possess that power over my belief which could even render them interesting. I saw nothing in them but ignorance and folly, and was a stranger even to that terror which is pleasing. But this incident was different from any that I had ever before known. Here were proofs of a sensible and intelligent existence, which could not be denied. Here was information obtained and imparted by means unquestionably super-human.

That there are conscious beings, beside ourselves, in existence, whose modes of activity and information surpass our own, can scarcely be denied. Is there a glimpse afforded us into a world of these superior beings? My heart was scarcely large enough to give admittance to so swelling a thought. An awe, the sweetest and most solemn that imagination can conceive, pervaded my whole frame. It forsook me not when I parted from Pleyel and retired to my chamber. An impulse was given to my spirits utterly incompatible with sleep. I passed the night wakeful and full of meditation. I was impressed with the belief of mysterious, but not of malignant agency. Hitherto nothing had occurred to persuade me that this airy minister was busy to evil rather than to good purposes. On the contrary, the idea of superior virtue had always been associated in my mind with that of superior power. The warnings that had thus been heard appeared to have been prompted by beneficent intentions. My brother had been hindered by this voice from ascending the hill. He was told that danger lurked in his path, and his obedience to the intimation had perhaps saved him from a destiny similar to that of my father.

Pleyel had been rescued from tormenting uncertainty, and from the hazards and fatigues of a fruitless voyage, by the same interposition. It had assured him of the death of his Theresa.

This woman was then dead. A confirmation of the tidings, if true, would speedily arrive. Was this confirmation to be deprecated or desired? By her death, the tie that attached him to Europe, was taken away. Henceforward every motive would combine to retain him in his native country, and we were rescued from the deep regrets that would accompany his hopeless absence from us. Propitious was the spirit that imparted these tidings. Propitious he would perhaps have been, if he had been instrumental in producing, as well as in communicating the tidings of her death. Propitious to us, the friends of Pleyel, to whom has thereby been secured the enjoyment of his society; and not unpropitious to himself; for though this object of his love be snatched away, is there not another who is able and willing to console him for her loss?

Twenty days after this, another vessel arrived from the same port. In this interval, Pleyel, for the most part, estranged himself from his old companions. He was become the prey of a gloomy and unsociable grief. His walks were limited to the bank of the Delaware. This bank is an artificial one. Reeds and the river are on one side, and a watery marsh on the other, in that part which bounded his lands, and which extended from the mouth of Hollander's creek to that of Schuylkill. No scene can be imagined less enticing to a lover of the picturesque than this. The shore is deformed with mud, and incumbered with a forest of reeds. The fields, in most seasons, are mire; but when they afford a firm footing, the ditches by which they are bounded and intersected, are mantled with stagnating green, and emit the most noxious exhalations. Health is no less a stranger to those seats than pleasure. Spring and autumn are sure to be accompanied with agues and bilious remittents.

The scenes which environed our dwellings at Mettingen constituted the reverse of this. Schuylkill was here a pure and translucid current, broken into wild and ceaseless music by rocky points, murmuring on a sandy margin, and reflecting on its surface, banks of all varieties of height and degrees of declivity. These banks were chequered by patches of dark verdure and shapeless masses of white marble, and crowned by copses of cedar, or by the regular magnificence of orchards, which, at this season, were in blossom and were prodigal of odours. The ground which receded from the river was scooped into valleys and dales. Its beauties were enhanced by the horticultural skill of my brother, who bedecked this exquisite assemblage of slopes and risings with every species of vegetable ornament, from the giant arms of the oak to the clustering tendrils of the honey-suckle.

To screen him from the unwholesome airs of his own residence, it had been proposed to Pleyel to spend the months of spring with us. He had apparently acquiesced in this proposal; but the late event induced him to change his purpose. He was only to be seen by visiting him in his retirements. His gaiety had flown, and every passion was absorbed in eagerness to procure tidings from Saxony. I have mentioned the arrival of another vessel from the Elbe. He descried her early one morning as he was passing along the skirt of the river. She was easily recognized, being the ship in which he had performed his first voyage to Germany. He immediately went on board, but found no letters directed to him. This omission was, in some degree, compensated by meeting with an old acquaintance among the passengers, who had till lately been a resident in Leipsig. This person put an end to all suspense respecting the fate of Theresa, by relating the particulars of her death and funeral.

Thus was the truth of the former intimation attested. No longer devoured by suspense, the grief of Pleyel was not long in yielding to the influence of society. He gave himself up once more to our company. His vivacity had indeed been damped; but even in this respect he was a more acceptable companion than formerly, since his seriousness was neither incommunicative nor sullen.

These incidents, for a time, occupied all our thoughts. In me they produced a sentiment not unallied to pleasure, and more speedily than in the case of my friends were intermixed with other topics. My brother was particularly affected by them. It was easy to perceive that most of his meditations were tinctured from this source. To this was to be ascribed a design in which his pen was, at this period, engaged, of collecting and investigating the facts which relate to that mysterious personage, the Dæmon of Socrates.

My brother's skill in Greek and Roman learning was exceeded by that of few, and no doubt the world would have accepted a treatise upon this subject from his hand with avidity; but alas! this and every other scheme of felicity and honor, were doomed to sudden blast and hopeless extermination.

Chapter VI

I NOW come to the mention of a person with whose name the most turbulent sensations are connected. It is with a shuddering reluctance that I enter on the province of describing him. Now it is that I begin to perceive the difficulty of the task which I have undertaken; but it would be weakness to shrink from it. My blood is congealed: and my fingers are palsied when I call up his image. Shame upon my cowardly and infirm heart! Hitherto I have proceeded with some degree of composure, but now I must pause. I mean not that dire remembrance shall subdue my courage or baffle my design, but this weakness cannot be immediately conquered. I must desist for a little while.

I have taken a few turns in my chamber, and have gathered strength enough to proceed. Yet have I not projected a task beyond my power to execute? If thus, on the very threshold of the scene, my knees falter and I sink, how shall I support myself, when I rush into the midst of horrors such as no heart has hitherto conceived, nor tongue related? I sicken and recoil at the prospect, and yet my irresolution is momentary. I have not formed this design upon slight grounds, and though I may at times pause and hesitate, I will not be finally diverted from it.

And thou, O most fatal and potent of mankind, in what terms shall I describe thee? What words are adequate to the just delineation of thy character? How shall I detail the means which rendered the secrecy of thy purposes unfathomable? But I will not anticipate. Let me recover if possible, a sober strain. Let me keep down the flood of passion that would render me precipitate or powerless. Let me stifle the agonies that are awakened by thy name. Let me, for a time, regard thee as a being of no terrible attributes. Let me tear myself from contemplation of the evils of which it is but too certain that thou wast the author, and limit my view to those harmless appearances which attended thy entrance on the stage.

One sunny afternoon, I was standing in the door of my

house, when I marked a person passing close to the edge of the bank that was in front. His pace was a careless and lingering one, and had none of that gracefulness and ease which distinguish a person with certain advantages of education from a clown. His gait was rustic and aukward. His form was ungainly and disproportioned. Shoulders broad and square, breast sunken, his head drooping, his body of uniform breadth, supported by long and lank legs, were the ingredients of his frame. His garb was not ill adapted to such a figure. A slouched hat, tarnished by the weather, a coat of thick grey cloth, cut and wrought, as it seemed, by a country tailor, blue worsted stockings, and shoes fastened by thongs, and deeply discoloured by dust, which brush had never disturbed, constituted his dress.

There was nothing remarkable in these appearances; they were frequently to be met with on the road, and in the harvest field. I cannot tell why I gazed upon them, on this occasion, with more than ordinary attention, unless it were that such figures were seldom seen by me, except on the road or field. This lawn was only traversed by men whose views were directed to the pleasures of the walk, or the grandeur of the scenery.

He passed slowly along, frequently pausing, as if to examine the prospect more deliberately, but never turning his eye towards the house, so as to allow me a view of his countenance. Presently, he entered a copse at a small distance, and disappeared. My eye followed him while he remained in sight. If his image remained for any duration in my fancy after his departure, it was because no other object occurred sufficient to expel it.

I continued in the same spot for half an hour, vaguely, and by fits, contemplating the image of this wanderer, and drawing, from outward appearances, those inferences with respect to the intellectual history of this person, which experience affords us. I reflected on the alliance which commonly subsists between ignorance and the practice of agriculture, and indulged myself in airy speculations as to the influence of progressive knowledge in dissolving this alliance, and embodying the dreams of the poets. I asked why the plough and the hoe might not become the trade of every human being, and how this trade might be made conducive to, or, at least, consistent with the acquisition of wisdom and eloquence.

Weary with these reflections, I returned to the kitchen to perform some household office. I had usually but one servant, and she was a girl about my own age. I was busy near the chimney, and she was employed near the door of the apartment, when some one knocked. The door was opened by her, and she was immediately addressed with "Pry'thee, good girl, canst thou supply a thirsty man with a glass of buttermilk?" She answered that there was none in the house. "Aye, but there is some in the dairy yonder. Thou knowest as well as I, though Hermes never taught thee, that though every dairy be an house, every house is not a dairy." To this speech, though she understood only a part of it, she replied by repeating her assurances, that she had none to give. "Well then," rejoined the stranger, "for charity's sweet sake, hand me forth a cup of cold water." The girl said she would go to the spring and fetch it. "Nay, give me the cup, and suffer me to help myself. Neither manacled nor lame, I should merit burial in the maw of carrion crows, if I laid this task upon thee." She gave him the cup, and he turned to go to the spring.

I listened to this dialogue in silence. The words uttered by the person without, affected me as somewhat singular, but what chiefly rendered them remarkable, was the tone that accompanied them. It was wholly new. My brother's voice and Pleyel's were musical and energetic. I had fondly imagined, that, in this respect, they were surpassed by none. Now my mistake was detected. I cannot pretend to communicate the impression that was made upon me by these accents, or to depict the degree in which force and sweetness were blended in them. They were articulated with a distinctness that was unexampled in my experience. But this was not all. The voice was not only mellifluent and clear, but the emphasis was so just, and the modulation so impassioned, that it seemed as if an heart of stone could not fail of being moved by it. It imparted to me an emotion altogether involuntary and incontroulable. When he uttered the words "for charity's sweet sake," I dropped the cloth that I held in my hand, my heart overflowed with sympathy, and my eyes with unbidden tears.

This description will appear to you trifling or incredible. The importance of these circumstances will be manifested in the sequel. The manner in which I was affected on this occasion, was, to my own apprehension, a subject of astonishment. The tones were indeed such as I never heard before; but that they should, in an instant, as it were, dissolve me in tears, will not easily be believed by others, and can scarcely be comprehended by myself.

It will be readily supposed that I was somewhat inquisitive as to the person and demeanour of our visitant. After a moment's pause, I stepped to the door and looked after him. Judge my surprize, when I beheld the self-same figure that had appeared an half hour before upon the bank. My fancy had conjured up a very different image. A form, and attitude, and garb, were instantly created worthy to accompany such elocution; but this person was, in all visible respects, the reverse of this phantom. Strange as it may seem, I could not speedily reconcile myself to this disappointment. Instead of returning to my employment, I threw myself in a chair that was placed opposite the door, and sunk into a fit of musing.

My attention was, in a few minutes, recalled by the stranger, who returned with the empty cup in his hand. I had not thought of the circumstance, or should certainly have chosen a different seat. He no sooner shewed himself, than a confused sense of impropriety, added to the suddenness of the interview, for which, not having foreseen it, I had made no preparation, threw me into a state of the most painful embarrassment. He brought with him a placid brow; but no sooner had he cast his eyes upon me, than his face was as glowingly suffused as my own. He placed the cup upon the bench, stammered out thanks, and retired.

It was some time before I could recover my wonted composure. I had snatched a view of the stranger's countenance. The impression that it made was vivid and indelible. His cheeks were pallid and lank, his eyes sunken, his forehead overshadowed by coarse straggling hairs, his teeth large and irregular, though sound and brilliantly white, and his chin discoloured by a tetter. His skin was of coarse grain, and sallow hue. Every feature was wide of beauty, and the outline of his face reminded you of an inverted cone.

And yet his forehead, so far as shaggy locks would allow it to be seen, his eyes lustrously black, and possessing, in the midst of haggardness, a radiance inexpressibly serene and potent, and something in the rest of his features, which it would be in vain to describe, but which served to betoken a mind of the highest order, were essential ingredients in the portrait. This, in the effects which immediately flowed from it, I count among the most extraordinary incidents of my life. This face, seen for a moment, continued for hours to occupy my fancy, to the exclusion of almost every other image. I had purposed to spend the evening with my brother, but I could not resist the inclination of forming a sketch upon paper of this memorable visage. Whether my hand was aided by any peculiar inspiration, or I was deceived by my own fond conceptions, this portrait, though hastily executed, appeared unexceptionable to my own taste.

I placed it at all distances, and in all lights; my eyes were rivetted upon it. Half the night passed away in wakefulness and in contemplation of this picture. So flexible, and yet so stubborn, is the human mind. So obedient to impulses the most transient and brief, and yet so unalterably observant of the direction which is given to it! How little did I then foresee the termination of that chain, of which this may be regarded as the first link?

Next day arose in darkness and storm. Torrents of rain fell during the whole day, attended with incessant thunder, which reverberated in stunning echoes from the opposite declivity. The inclemency of the air would not allow me to walk out. I had, indeed, no inclination to leave my apartment. I betook myself to the contemplation of this portrait, whose attractions time had rather enhanced than diminished. I laid aside my usual occupations, and seating myself at a window, consumed the day in alternately looking out upon the storm, and gazing at the picture which lay upon a table before me. You will, perhaps, deem this conduct somewhat singular, and ascribe it to certain peculiarities of temper. I am not aware of any such peculiarities. I can account for my devotion to this image no otherwise, than by supposing that its properties were rare and prodigious. Perhaps you will suspect that such were the first inroads of a passion incident to every female heart, and which frequently gains a footing by means even more slight, and more improbable than these. I shall not controvert the reasonableness of the suspicion, but leave you at liberty to draw, from my narrative, what conclusions you please.

Night at length returned, and the storm ceased. The air was once more clear and calm, and bore an affecting contrast to that uproar of the elements by which it had been preceded. I spent the darksome hours, as I spent the day, contemplative and seated at the window. Why was my mind absorbed in thoughts ominous and dreary? Why did my bosom heave with sighs, and my eyes overflow with tears? Was the tempest that had just past a signal of the ruin which impended over me? My soul fondly dwelt upon the images of my brother and his children, yet they only increased the mournfulness of my contemplations. The smiles of the charming babes were as bland as formerly. The same dignity sat on the brow of their father, and yet I thought of them with anguish. Something whispered that the happiness we at present enjoyed was set on mutable foundations. Death must happen to all. Whether our felicity was to be subverted by it to-morrow, or whether it was ordained that we should lay down our heads full of years and of honor, was a question that no human being could solve. At other times, these ideas seldom intruded. I either forbore to reflect upon the destiny that is reserved for all men, or the reflection was mixed up with images that disrobed it of terror; but now the uncertainty of life occurred to me without any of its usual and alleviating accompaniments. I said to myself, we must die. Sooner or later, we must disappear for ever from the face of the earth. Whatever be the links that hold us to life, they must be broken. This scene of existence is, in all its parts, calamitous. The greater number is oppressed with immediate evils, and those, the tide of whose fortunes is full, how small is their portion of enjoyment, since they know that it will terminate.

For some time I indulged myself, without reluctance, in these gloomy thoughts; but at length, the dejection which they produced became insupportably painful. I endeavoured to dissipate it with music. I had all my grand-father's melody as well as poetry by rote. I now lighted by chance on a ballad, which commemorated the fate of a German Cavalier, who fell at the siege of Nice under Godfrey of Bouillon. My choice was unfortunate, for the scenes of violence and carnage which were here wildly but forcibly pourtrayed, only suggested to my thoughts a new topic in the horrors of war.

I sought refuge, but ineffectually, in sleep. My mind was thronged by vivid, but confused images, and no effort that I made was sufficient to drive them away. In this situation I heard the clock, which hung in the room, give the signal for twelve. It was the same instrument which formerly hung in my father's chamber, and which, on account of its being his workmanship, was regarded, by every one of our family, with veneration. It had fallen to me, in the division of his property, and was placed in this asylum. The sound awakened a series of reflections, respecting his death. I was not allowed to pursue them; for scarcely had the vibrations ceased, when my attention was attracted by a whisper, which, at first, appeared to proceed from lips that were laid close to my ear.

No wonder that a circumstance like this startled me. In the first impulse of my terror, I uttered a slight scream, and shrunk to the opposite side of the bed. In a moment, however, I recovered from my trepidation. I was habitually indifferent to all the causes of fear, by which the majority are afflicted. I entertained no apprehension of either ghosts or robbers. Our security had never been molested by either, and I made use of no means to prevent or counterwork their machinations. My tranquillity, on this occasion, was quickly retrieved. The whisper evidently proceeded from one who was posted at my bed-side. The first idea that suggested itself was, that it was uttered by the girl who lived with me as a servant. Perhaps, somewhat had alarmed her, or she was sick, and had come to request my assistance. By whispering in my ear, she intended to rouse without alarming me.

Full of this persuasion, I called; "Judith," said I, "is it you? What do you want? Is there any thing the matter with you?" No answer was returned. I repeated my inquiry, but equally in vain. Cloudy as was the atmosphere, and curtained as my bed was, nothing was visible. I withdrew the curtain, and leaning my head on my elbow, I listened with the deepest attention to catch some new sound. Meanwhile, I ran over in my thoughts, every circumstance that could assist my conjectures.

My habitation was a wooden edifice, consisting of two stories. In each story were two rooms, separated by an entry, or middle passage, with which they communicated by opposite doors. The passage, on the lower story, had doors at the two ends, and a stair-case. Windows answered to the doors on the upper story. Annexed to this, on the eastern side, were wings, divided, in like manner, into an upper and lower room; one of them comprized a kitchen, and chamber above it for the servant, and communicated, on both stories, with the parlour adjoining it below, and the chamber adjoining it above. The opposite wing is of smaller dimensions, the rooms not being above eight feet square. The lower of these was used as a depository of household implements, the upper was a closet in which I deposited my books and papers. They had but one inlet, which was from the room adjoining. There was no window in the lower one, and in the upper, a small aperture which communicated light and air, but would scarcely admit the body. The door which led into this, was close to my bed-head, and was always locked, but when I myself was within. The avenues below were accustomed to be closed and bolted at nights.

The maid was my only companion, and she could not reach my chamber without previously passing through the opposite chamber, and the middle passage, of which, however, the doors were usually unfastened. If she had occasioned this noise, she would have answered my repeated calls. No other conclusion, therefore, was left me, but that I had mistaken the sounds, and that my imagination had transformed some casual noise into the voice of a human creature. Satisfied with this solution, I was preparing to relinquish my listening attitude, when my ear was again saluted with a new and yet louder whispering. It appeared, as before, to issue from lips that touched my pillow. A second effort of attention, however, clearly shewed me, that the sounds issued from within the closet, the door of which was not more than eight inches from my pillow.

This second interruption occasioned a shock less vehement than the former. I started, but gave no audible token of alarm.

I was so much mistress of my feelings, as to continue listening to what should be said. The whisper was distinct, hoarse, and uttered so as to shew that the speaker was desirous of being heard by some one near, but, at the same time, studious to avoid being overheard by any other.

"Stop, stop, I say; madman as you are! there are better means than that. Curse upon your rashness! There is no need to shoot."

Such were the words uttered in a tone of eagerness and anger, within so small a distance of my pillow. What construction could I put upon them? My heart began to palpitate with dread of some unknown danger. Presently, another voice, but equally near me, was heard whispering in answer. "Why not? I will draw a trigger in this business, but perdition be my lot if I do more." To this, the first voice returned, in a tone which rage had heightened in a small degree above a whisper, "Coward! stand aside, and see me do it. I will grasp her throat; I will do her business in an instant; she shall not have time so much as to groan." What wonder that I was petrified by sounds so dreadful! Murderers lurked in my closet. They were planning the means of my destruction. One resolved to shoot, and the other menaced suffocation. Their means being chosen, they would forthwith break the door. Flight instantly suggested itself as most eligible in circumstances so perilous. I deliberated not a moment; but, fear adding wings to my speed, I leaped out of bed, and scantily robed as I was, rushed out of the chamber, down stairs, and into the open air. I can hardly recollect the process of turning keys, and withdrawing bolts. My terrors urged me forward with almost a mechanical impulse. I stopped not till I reached my brother's door. I had not gained the threshold, when, exhausted by the violence of my emotions, and by my speed, I sunk down in a fit.

How long I remained in this situation I know not. When I recovered, I found myself stretched on a bed, surrounded by my sister and her female servants. I was astonished at the scene before me, but gradually recovered the recollection of what had happened. I answered their importunate inquiries as well as I was able. My brother and Pleyel, whom the storm of the preceding day chanced to detain here, informing themselves of every particular, proceeded with lights and weapons to my deserted habitation. They entered my chamber and my closet, and found every thing in its proper place and customary order. The door of the closet was locked, and appeared not to have been opened in my absence. They went to Judith's apartment. They found her asleep and in safety. Pleyel's caution induced him to forbear alarming the girl; and finding her wholly ignorant of what had passed, they directed her to return to her chamber. They then fastened the doors, and returned.

My friends were disposed to regard this transaction as a dream. That persons should be actually immured in this closet, to which, in the circumstances of the time, access from without or within was apparently impossible, they could not seriously believe. That any human beings had intended murder, unless it were to cover a scheme of pillage, was incredible; but that no such design had been formed, was evident from the security in which the furniture of the house and the closet remained.

I revolved every incident and expression that had occurred. My senses assured me of the truth of them, and yet their abruptness and improbability made me, in my turn, somewhat incredulous. The adventure had made a deep impression on my fancy, and it was not till after a week's abode at my brother's, that I resolved to resume the possession of my own dwelling.

There was another circumstance that enhanced the mysteriousness of this event. After my recovery it was obvious to inquire by what means the attention of the family had been drawn to my situation. I had fallen before I had reached the threshold, or was able to give any signal. My brother related, that while this was transacting in my chamber, he himself was awake, in consequence of some slight indisposition, and lay, according to his custom, musing on some favorite topic. Suddenly the silence, which was remarkably profound, was broken by a voice of most piercing shrillness, that seemed to be uttered by one in the hall below his chamber. "Awake! arise!" it exclaimed: "hasten to succour one that is dying at your door."

This summons was effectual. There was no one in the house who was not roused by it. Pleyel was the first to obey, and my brother overtook him before he reached the hall. What was the general astonishment when your friend was discovered stretched upon the grass before the door, pale, ghastly, and with every mark of death!

This was the third instance of a voice, exerted for the benefit of this little community. The agent was no less inscrutable in this, than in the former case. When I ruminated upon these events, my soul was suspended in wonder and awe. Was I really deceived in imagining that I heard the closet conversation? I was no longer at liberty to question the reality of those accents which had formerly recalled my brother from the hill; which had imparted tidings of the death of the German lady to Pleyel; and which had lately summoned them to my assistance.

But how was I to regard this midnight conversation? Hoarse and manlike voices conferring on the means of death, so near my bed, and at such an hour! How had my ancient security vanished! That dwelling, which had hitherto been an inviolate asylum, was now beset with danger to my life. That solitude, formerly so dear to me, could no longer be endured. Pleyel, who had consented to reside with us during the months of spring, lodged in the vacant chamber, in order to quiet my alarms. He treated my fears with ridicule, and in a short time very slight traces of them remained: but as it was wholly indifferent to him whether his nights were passed at my house or at my brother's, this arrangement gave general satisfaction.

Chapter VII

I WILL NOT enumerate the various inquiries and conjectures which these incidents occasioned. After all our efforts, we came no nearer to dispelling the mist in which they were involved; and time, instead of facilitating a solution, only accumulated our doubts.

In the midst of thoughts excited by these events, I was not unmindful of my interview with the stranger. I related the particulars, and shewed the portrait to my friends. Pleyel recollected to have met with a figure resembling my description in the city; but neither his face or garb made the same impression upon him that it made upon me. It was a hint to rally me upon my prepossessions, and to amuse us with a thousand ludicrous anecdotes which he had collected in his travels. He made no scruple to charge me with being in love; and threatened to inform the swain, when he met him, of his good fortune.

Pleyel's temper made him susceptible of no durable impressions. His conversation was occasionally visited by gleams of his ancient vivacity; but, though his impetuosity was sometimes inconvenient, there was nothing to dread from his malice. I had no fear that my character or dignity would suffer in his hands, and was not heartily displeased when he declared his intention of profiting by his first meeting with the stranger to introduce him to our acquaintance.

Some weeks after this I had spent a toilsome day, and, as the sun declined, found myself disposed to seek relief in a walk. The river bank is, at this part of it, and for some considerable space upward, so rugged and steep as not to be easily descended. In a recess of this declivity, near the southern verge of my little demesne, was placed a slight building, with seats and lattices. From a crevice of the rock, to which this edifice was attached, there burst forth a stream of the purest water, which, leaping from ledge to ledge, for the space of sixty feet, produced a freshness in the air, and a murmur, the most delicious and soothing imaginable. These, added to the odours of the cedars which embowered it, and of the honey-suckle which clustered among the lattices, rendered this my favorite retreat in summer.

On this occasion I repaired hither. My spirits drooped through the fatigue of long attention, and I threw myself upon a bench, in a state, both mentally and personally, of the utmost supineness. The lulling sounds of the waterfall, the fragrance and the dusk combined to becalm my spirits, and, in a short time, to sink me into sleep. Either the uneasiness of my posture, or some slight indisposition molested my repose with dreams of no cheerful hue. After various incoherences had taken their turn to occupy my fancy, I at length imagined myself walking, in the evening twilight, to my brother's habitation. A pit, methought, had been dug in the path I had taken, of which I was not aware. As I carelessly pursued my walk, I thought I saw my brother, standing at some distance before me, beckoning and calling me to make haste. He stood on the opposite edge of the gulph. I mended my pace, and one step more would have plunged me into this abyss, had not some one from behind caught suddenly my arm, and exclaimed, in a voice of eagerness and terror, "Hold! hold!"

The sound broke my sleep, and I found myself, at the next moment, standing on my feet, and surrounded by the deepest darkness. Images so terrific and forcible disabled me, for a time, from distinguishing between sleep and wakefulness, and withheld from me the knowledge of my actual condition. My first panics were succeeded by the perturbations of surprize, to find myself alone in the open air, and immersed in so deep a gloom. I slowly recollected the incidents of the afternoon, and how I came hither. I could not estimate the time, but saw the propriety of returning with speed to the house. My faculties were still too confused, and the darkness too intense, to allow me immediately to find my way up the steep. I sat down, therefore, to recover myself, and to reflect upon my situation.

This was no sooner done, than a low voice was heard from behind the lattice, on the side where I sat. Between the rock and the lattice was a chasm not wide enough to admit a human body; yet, in this chasm he that spoke appeared to be stationed. "Attend! attend! but be not terrified."

I started and exclaimed, "Good heavens! what is that? Who are you?"

"A friend; one come, not to injure, but to save you; fear nothing."

This voice was immediately recognized to be the same with one of those which I had heard in the closet; it was the voice of him who had proposed to shoot, rather than to strangle, his victim. My terror made me, at once, mute and motionless. He continued, "I leagued to murder you. I repent. Mark my bidding, and be safe. Avoid this spot. The snares of death encompass it. Elsewhere danger will be distant; but this spot, shun it as you value your life. Mark me further; profit by this warning, but divulge it not. If a syllable of what has passed escape you, your doom is sealed. Remember your father, and be faithful."

Here the accents ceased, and left me overwhelmed with dismay. I was fraught with the persuasion, that during every moment I remained here, my life was endangered; but I could not take a step without hazard of falling to the bottom of the precipice. The path, leading to the summit, was short, but rugged and intricate. Even star-light was excluded by the umbrage, and not the faintest gleam was afforded to guide my steps. What should I do? To depart or remain was equally and eminently perilous.

In this state of uncertainty, I perceived a ray flit across the gloom and disappear. Another succeeded, which was stronger, and remained for a passing moment. It glittered on the shrubs that were scattered at the entrance, and gleam continued to succeed gleam for a few seconds, till they, finally, gave place to unintermitted darkness.

The first visitings of this light called up a train of horrors in my mind; destruction impended over this spot; the voice which I had lately heard had warned me to retire, and had menaced me with the fate of my father if I refused. I was desirous, but unable, to obey; these gleams were such as preluded the stroke by which he fell; the hour, perhaps, was the same—I shuddered as if I had beheld, suspended over me, the exterminating sword.

Presently a new and stronger illumination burst through the lattice on the right hand, and a voice, from the edge of the

precipice above, called out my name. It was Pleyel. Joyfully
did I recognize his accents; but such was the tumult of my
thoughts that I had not power to answer him till he had frequently repeated his summons. I hurried, at length, from the
fatal spot, and, directed by the lanthorn which he bore, ascended the hill.

Pale and breathless, it was with difficulty I could support
myself. He anxiously inquired into the cause of my affright,
and the motive of my unusual absence. He had returned from
my brother's at a late hour, and was informed by Judith, that
I had walked out before sun-set, and had not yet returned.
This intelligence was somewhat alarming. He waited some
time; but, my absence continuing, he had set out in search of
me. He had explored the neighbourhood with the utmost
care, but, receiving no tidings of me, he was preparing to
acquaint my brother with this circumstance, when he recollected the summer-house on the bank, and conceived it possible that some accident had detained me there. He again
inquired into the cause of this detention, and of that confusion and dismay which my looks testified.

I told him that I had strolled hither in the afternoon, that
sleep had overtaken me as I sat, and that I had awakened a
few minutes before his arrival. I could tell him no more. In
the present impetuosity of my thoughts, I was almost dubious,
whether the pit, into which my brother had endeavoured to
entice me, and the voice that talked through the lattice, were
not parts of the same dream. I remembered, likewise, the
charge of secrecy, and the penalty denounced, if I should
rashly divulge what I had heard. For these reasons, I was silent
on that subject, and shutting myself in my chamber, delivered
myself up to contemplation.

What I have related will, no doubt, appear to you a fable.
You will believe that calamity has subverted my reason, and
that I am amusing you with the chimeras of my brain, instead
of facts that have really happened. I shall not be surprized or
offended, if these be your suspicions. I know not, indeed, how
you can deny them admission. For, if to me, the immediate
witness, they were fertile of perplexity and doubt, how must
they affect another to whom they are recommended only by

my testimony? It was only by subsequent events, that I was fully and incontestibly assured of the veracity of my senses.

Meanwhile what was I to think? I had been assured that a design had been formed against my life. The ruffians had leagued to murder me. Whom had I offended? Who was there with whom I had ever maintained intercourse, who was capable of harbouring such atrocious purposes?

My temper was the reverse of cruel and imperious. My heart was touched with sympathy for the children of misfortune. But this sympathy was not a barren sentiment. My purse, scanty as it was, was ever open, and my hands ever active, to relieve distress. Many were the wretches whom my personal exertions had extricated from want and disease, and who rewarded me with their gratitude. There was no face which lowered at my approach, and no lips which uttered imprecations in my hearing. On the contrary, there was none, over whose fate I had exerted any influence, or to whom I was known by reputation, who did not greet me with smiles, and dismiss me with proofs of veneration; yet did not my senses assure me that a plot was laid against my life?

I am not destitute of courage. I have shewn myself deliberative and calm in the midst of peril. I have hazarded my own life, for the preservation of another, but now was I confused and panic-struck. I have not lived so as to fear death, yet to perish by an unseen and secret stroke, to be mangled by the knife of an assassin, was a thought at which I shuddered; what had I done to deserve to be made the victim of malignant passions?

But soft! was I not assured, that my life was safe in all places but one? And why was the treason limited to take effect in this spot? I was every where equally defenceless. My house and chamber were, at all times, accessible. Danger still impended over me; the bloody purpose was still entertained, but the hand that was to execute it, was powerless in all places but one!

Here I had remained for the last four or five hours, without the means of resistance or defence, yet I had not been attacked. A human being was at hand, who was conscious of my presence, and warned me hereafter to avoid this retreat.

His voice was not absolutely new, but had I never heard it but once before? But why did he prohibit me from relating this incident to others, and what species of death will be awarded if I disobey?

He talked of my father. He intimated, that disclosure would pull upon my head, the same destruction. Was then the death of my father, portentous and inexplicable as it was, the consequence of human machinations? It should seem, that this being is apprised of the true nature of this event, and is conscious of the means that led to it. Whether it shall likewise fall upon me, depends upon the observance of silence. Was it the infraction of a similar command, that brought so horrible a penalty upon my father?

Such were the reflections that haunted me during the night, and which effectually deprived me of sleep. Next morning, at breakfast, Pleyel related an event which my disappearance had hindered him from mentioning the night before. Early the preceding morning, his occasions called him to the city; he had stepped into a coffee-house to while away an hour; here he had met a person whose appearance instantly bespoke him to be the same whose hasty visit I have mentioned, and whose extraordinary visage and tones had so powerfully affected me. On an attentive survey, however, he proved, likewise, to be one with whom my friend had had some intercourse in Europe. This authorised the liberty of accosting him, and after some conversation, mindful, as Pleyel said, of the footing which this stranger had gained in my heart, he had ventured to invite him to Mettingen. The invitation had been cheerfully accepted, and a visit promised on the afternoon of the next day.

This information excited no sober emotions in my breast. I was, of course, eager to be informed as to the circumstances of their ancient intercourse. When, and where had they met? What knew he of the life and character of this man?

In answer to my inquiries, he informed me that, three years before, he was a traveller in Spain. He had made an excursion from Valencia to Murviedro, with a view to inspect the remains of Roman magnificence, scattered in the environs of that town. While traversing the scite of the theatre of old Saguntum, he lighted upon this man, seated on a stone, and deeply engaged in perusing the work of the deacon Marti. A short conversation ensued, which proved the stranger to be English. They returned to Valencia together.

His garb, aspect, and deportment, were wholly Spanish. A residence of three years in the country, indefatigable attention to the language, and a studious conformity with the customs of the people, had made him indistinguishable from a native, when he chose to assume that character. Pleyel found him to be connected, on the footing of friendship and respect, with many eminent merchants in that city. He had embraced the catholic religion, and adopted a Spanish name instead of his own, which was CARWIN, and devoted himself to the literature and religion of his new country. He pursued no profession, but subsisted on remittances from England.

While Pleyel remained in Valencia, Carwin betrayed no aversion to intercourse, and the former found no small attractions in the society of this new acquaintance. On general topics he was highly intelligent and communicative. He had visited every corner of Spain, and could furnish the most accurate details respecting its ancient and present state. On topics of religion and of his own history, previous to his *transformation* into a Spaniard, he was invariably silent. You could merely gather from his discourse that he was English, and that he was well acquainted with the neighbouring countries.

His character excited considerable curiosity in this observer. It was not easy to reconcile his conversion to the Romish faith, with those proofs of knowledge and capacity that were exhibited by him on different occasions. A suspicion was, sometimes, admitted, that his belief was counterfeited for some political purpose. The most careful observation, however, produced no discovery. His manners were, at all times, harmless and inartificial, and his habits those of a lover of contemplation and seclusion. He appeared to have contracted an affection for Pleyel, who was not slow to return it.

My friend, after a month's residence in this city, returned into France, and, since that period, had heard nothing concerning Carwin till his appearance at Mettingen.

On this occasion Carwin had received Pleyel's greeting with a certain distance and solemnity to which the latter had not been accustomed. He had waved noticing the inquiries of

Pleyel respecting his desertion of Spain, in which he had formerly declared that it was his purpose to spend his life. He had assiduously diverted the attention of the latter to indifferent topics, but was still, on every theme, as eloquent and judicious as formerly. Why he had assumed the garb of a rustic, Pleyel was unable to conjecture. Perhaps it might be poverty, perhaps he was swayed by motives which it was his interest to conceal, but which were connected with consequences of the utmost moment.

Such was the sum of my friend's information. I was not sorry to be left alone during the greater part of this day. Every employment was irksome which did not leave me at liberty to meditate. I had now a new subject on which to exercise my thoughts. Before evening I should be ushered into his presence, and listen to those tones whose magical and thrilling power I had already experienced. But with what new images would he then be accompanied?

Carwin was an adherent to the Romish faith, yet was an Englishman by birth, and, perhaps, a protestant by education. He had adopted Spain for his country, and had intimated a design to spend his days there, yet now was an inhabitant of this district, and disguised by the habiliments of a clown! What could have obliterated the impressions of his youth, and made him abjure his religion and his country? What subsequent events had introduced so total a change in his plans? In withdrawing from Spain, had he reverted to the religion of his ancestors; or was it true, that his former conversion was deceitful, and that his conduct had been swayed by motives which it was prudent to conceal?

Hours were consumed in revolving these ideas. My meditations were intense; and, when the series was broken, I began to reflect with astonishment on my situation. From the death of my parents, till the commencement of this year, my life had been serene and blissful, beyond the ordinary portion of humanity; but, now, my bosom was corroded by anxiety. I was visited by dread of unknown dangers, and the future was a scene over which clouds rolled, and thunders muttered. I compared the cause with the effect, and they seemed disproportioned to each other. All unaware, and in a manner which

I had no power to explain, I was pushed from my immoveable and lofty station, and cast upon a sea of troubles.

I determined to be my brother's visitant on this evening, yet my resolves were not unattended with wavering and reluctance. Pleyel's insinuations that I was in love, affected, in no degree, my belief, yet the consciousness that this was the opinion of one who would, probably, be present at our introduction to each other, would excite all that confusion which the passion itself is apt to produce. This would confirm him in his error, and call forth new railleries. His mirth, when exerted upon this topic, was the source of the bitterest vexation. Had he been aware of its influence upon my happiness, his temper would not have allowed him to persist; but this influence, it was my chief endeavour to conceal. That the belief of my having bestowed my heart upon another, produced in my friend none but ludicrous sensations, was the true cause of my distress; but if this had been discovered by him, my distress would have been unspeakably aggravated.

Chapter VIII

As soon as evening arrived, I performed my visit. Carwin made one of the company, into which I was ushered. Appearances were the same as when I before beheld him. His garb was equally negligent and rustic. I gazed upon his countenance with new curiosity. My situation was such as to enable me to bestow upon it a deliberate examination. Viewed at more leisure, it lost none of its wonderful properties. I could not deny my homage to the intelligence expressed in it, but was wholly uncertain, whether he were an object to be dreaded or adored, and whether his powers had been exerted to evil or to good.

He was sparing in discourse; but whatever he said was pregnant with meaning, and uttered with rectitude of articulation, and force of emphasis, of which I had entertained no conception previously to my knowledge of him. Notwithstanding the uncouthness of his garb, his manners were not unpolished. All topics were handled by him with skill, and without pedantry or affectation. He uttered no sentiment calculated to produce a disadvantageous impression: on the contrary, his observations denoted a mind alive to every generous and heroic feeling. They were introduced without parade, and accompanied with that degree of earnestness which indicates sincerity.

He parted from us not till late, refusing an invitation to spend the night here, but readily consented to repeat his visit. His visits were frequently repeated. Each day introduced us to a more intimate acquaintance with his sentiments, but left us wholly in the dark, concerning that about which we were most inquisitive. He studiously avoided all mention of his past or present situation. Even the place of his abode in the city he concealed from us.

Our sphere, in this respect, being somewhat limited, and the intellectual endowments of this man being indisputably great, his deportment was more diligently marked, and copiously commented on by us, than you, perhaps, will think the circumstances warranted. Not a gesture, or glance, or accent, that was not, in our private assemblies, discussed, and infer-

ences deduced from it. It may well be thought that he modelled his behaviour by an uncommon standard, when, with all
our opportunities and accuracy of observation, we were able,
for a long time, to gather no satisfactory information. He
afforded us no ground on which to build even a plausible
conjecture.

There is a degree of familiarity which takes place between
constant associates, that justifies the negligence of many rules
of which, in an earlier period of their intercourse, politeness
requires the exact observance. Inquiries into our condition are
allowable when they are prompted by a disinterested concern
for our welfare; and this solicitude is not only pardonable, but
may justly be demanded from those who chuse us for their
companions. This state of things was more slow to arrive on
this occasion than on most others, on account of the gravity
and loftiness of this man's behaviour.

Pleyel, however, began, at length, to employ regular means
for this end. He occasionally alluded to the circumstances in
which they had formerly met, and remarked the incongru-
ousness between the religion and habits of a Spaniard, with
those of a native of Britain. He expressed his astonishment at
meeting our guest in this corner of the globe, especially as,
when they parted in Spain, he was taught to believe that
Carwin should never leave that country. He insinuated, that
a change so great must have been prompted by motives of a
singular and momentous kind.

No answer, or an answer wide of the purpose, was generally
made to these insinuations. Britons and Spaniards, he said, are
votaries of the same Deity, and square their faith by the same
precepts; their ideas are drawn from the same fountains of
literature, and they speak dialects of the same tongue; their
government and laws have more resemblances than differences; they were formerly provinces of the same civil, and till
lately, of the same religious, Empire.

As to the motives which induce men to change the place of
their abode, these must unavoidably be fleeting and mutable.
If not bound to one spot by conjugal or parental ties, or by
the nature of that employment to which we are indebted for
subsistence, the inducements to change are far more numerous and powerful, than opposite inducements.

He spoke as if desirous of shewing that he was not aware
of the tendency of Pleyel's remarks; yet, certain tokens were
apparent, that proved him by no means wanting in penetration. These tokens were to be read in his countenance, and
not in his words. When any thing was said, indicating curiosity
in us, the gloom of his countenance was deepened, his eyes
sunk to the ground, and his wonted air was not resumed without visible struggle. Hence, it was obvious to infer, that some
incidents of his life were reflected on by him with regret; and
that, since these incidents were carefully concealed, and even
that regret which flowed from them laboriously stifled, they
had not been merely disastrous. The secrecy that was observed
appeared not designed to provoke or baffle the inquisitive, but
was prompted by the shame, or by the prudence of guilt.

These ideas, which were adopted by Pleyel and my brother,
as well as myself, hindered us from employing more direct
means for accomplishing our wishes. Questions might have
been put in such terms, that no room should be left for the
pretence of misapprehension, and if modesty merely had been
the obstacle, such questions would not have been wanting;
but we considered, that, if the disclosure were productive of
pain or disgrace, it was inhuman to extort it.

Amidst the various topics that were discussed in his presence, allusions were, of course, made to the inexplicable
events that had lately happened. At those times, the words
and looks of this man were objects of my particular attention.
The subject was extraordinary; and any one whose experience
or reflections could throw any light upon it, was entitled to
my gratitude. As this man was enlightened by reading and
travel, I listened with eagerness to the remarks which he
should make.

At first, I entertained a kind of apprehension, that the tale
would be heard by him with incredulity and secret ridicule. I
had formerly heard stories that resembled this in some of their
mysterious circumstances, but they were, commonly, heard by
me with contempt. I was doubtful, whether the same impression would not now be made on the mind of our guest; but
I was mistaken in my fears.

He heard them with seriousness, and without any marks
either of surprize or incredulity. He pursued, with visible

pleasure, that kind of disquisition which was naturally suggested by them. His fancy was eminently vigorous and prolific, and if he did not persuade us, that human beings are, sometimes, admitted to a sensible intercourse with the author of nature, he, at least, won over our inclination to the cause. He merely deduced, from his own reasonings, that such intercourse was probable; but confessed that, though he was acquainted with many instances somewhat similar to those which had been related by us, none of them were perfectly exempted from the suspicion of human agency.

On being requested to relate these instances, he amused us with many curious details. His narratives were constructed with so much skill, and rehearsed with so much energy, that all the effects of a dramatic exhibition were frequently produced by them. Those that were most coherent and most minute, and, of consequence, least entitled to credit, were yet rendered probable by the exquisite art of this rhetorician. For every difficulty that was suggested, a ready and plausible solution was furnished. Mysterious voices had always a share in producing the catastrophe, but they were always to be explained on some known principles, either as reflected into a focus, or communicated through a tube. I could not but remark that his narratives, however complex or marvellous, contained no instance sufficiently parallel to those that had befallen ourselves, and in which the solution was applicable to our own case.

My brother was a much more sanguine reasoner than our guest. Even in some of the facts which were related by Carwin, he maintained the probability of celestial interference, when the latter was disposed to deny it, and had found, as he imagined, footsteps of an human agent. Pleyel was by no means equally credulous. He scrupled not to deny faith to any testimony but that of his senses, and allowed the facts which had lately been supported by this testimony, not to mould his belief, but merely to give birth to doubts.

It was soon observed that Carwin adopted, in some degree, a similar distinction. A tale of this kind, related by others, he would believe, provided it was explicable upon known principles; but that such notices were actually communicated by beings of an higher order, he would believe only when his own ears were assailed in a manner which could not be oth-erwise accounted for. Civility forbad him to contradict my brother or myself, but his understanding refused to acquiesce in our testimony. Besides, he was disposed to question whether the voices heard in the temple, at the foot of the hill, and in my closet, were not really uttered by human organs. On this supposition he was desired to explain how the effect was produced.

He answered, that the power of mimickry was very common. Catharine's voice might easily be imitated by one at the foot of the hill, who would find no difficulty in eluding, by flight, the search of Wieland. The tidings of the death of the Saxon lady were uttered by one near at hand, who overheard the conversation, who conjectured her death, and whose conjecture happened to accord with the truth. That the voice appeared to come from the cieling was to be considered as an illusion of the fancy. The cry for help, heard in the hall on the night of my adventure, was to be ascribed to an human creature, who actually stood in the hall when he uttered it. It was of no moment, he said, that we could not explain by what motives he that made the signal was led hither. How imperfectly acquainted were we with the condition and designs of the beings that surrounded us? The city was near at hand, and thousands might there exist whose powers and purposes might easily explain whatever was mysterious in this transaction. As to the closet dialogue, he was obliged to adopt one of two suppositions, and affirm either that it was fashioned in my own fancy, or that it actually took place between two persons in the closet.

Such was Carwin's mode of explaining these appearances. It is such, perhaps, as would commend itself as most plausible to the most sagacious minds, but it was insufficient to impart conviction to us. As to the treason that was meditated against me, it was doubtless just to conclude that it was either real or imaginary; but that it was real was attested by the mysterious warning in the summer-house, the secret of which I had hitherto locked up in my own breast.

A month passed away in this kind of intercourse. As to Carwin, our ignorance was in no degree enlightened respecting his genuine character and views. Appearances were uniform.

No man possessed a larger store of knowledge, or a greater degree of skill in the communication of it to others: Hence he was regarded as an inestimable addition to our society. Considering the distance of my brother's house from the city, he was frequently prevailed upon to pass the night where he spent the evening. Two days seldom elapsed without a visit from him; hence he was regarded as a kind of inmate of the house. He entered and departed without ceremony. When he arrived he received an unaffected welcome, and when he chose to retire, no importunities were used to induce him to remain.

The temple was the principal scene of our social enjoyments; yet the felicity that we tasted when assembled in this asylum, was but the gleam of a former sun-shine. Carwin never parted with his gravity. The inscrutableness of his character, and the uncertainty whether his fellowship tended to good or to evil, were seldom absent from our minds. This circumstance powerfully contributed to sadden us.

My heart was the seat of growing disquietudes. This change in one who had formerly been characterized by all the exuberances of soul, could not fail to be remarked by my friends. My brother was always a pattern of solemnity. My sister was clay, moulded by the circumstances in which she happened to be placed. There was but one whose deportment remains to be described as being of importance to our happiness. Had Pleyel likewise dismissed his vivacity?

He was as whimsical and jestful as ever, but he was not happy. The truth, in this respect, was of too much importance to me not to make me a vigilant observer. His mirth was easily perceived to be the fruit of exertion. When his thoughts wandered from the company, an air of dissatisfaction and impatience stole across his features. Even the punctuality and frequency of his visits were somewhat lessened. It may be supposed that my own uneasiness was heightened by these tokens; but, strange as it may seem, I found, in the present state of my mind, no relief but in the persuasion that Pleyel was unhappy.

That unhappiness, indeed, depended, for its value, in my eyes, on the cause that produced it. It did not arise from the death of the Saxon lady: it was not a contagious emanation from the countenances of Wieland or Carwin. There was but one other source whence it could flow. A nameless ecstacy thrilled through my frame when any new proof occurred that the ambiguousness of my behaviour was the cause.

Chapter IX

MY BROTHER had received a new book from Germany. It was a tragedy, and the first attempt of a Saxon poet, of whom my brother had been taught to entertain the highest expectations. The exploits of Zisca, the Bohemian hero, were woven into a dramatic series and connection. According to German custom, it was minute and diffuse, and dictated by an adventurous and lawless fancy. It was a chain of audacious acts, and unheard-of disasters. The moated fortress, and the thicket; the ambush and the battle; and the conflict of head-long passions, were pourtrayed in wild numbers, and with terrific energy. An afternoon was set apart to rehearse this performance. The language was familiar to all of us but Carwin, whose company, therefore, was tacitly dispensed with.

The morning previous to this intended rehearsal, I spent at home. My mind was occupied with reflections relative to my own situation. The sentiment which lived with chief energy in my heart, was connected with the image of Pleyel. In the midst of my anguish, I had not been destitute of consolation. His late deportment had given spring to my hopes. Was not the hour at hand, which should render me the happiest of human creatures? He suspected that I looked with favorable eyes upon Carwin. Hence arose disquietudes, which he struggled in vain to conceal. He loved me, but was hopeless that his love would be compensated. Is it not time, said I, to rectify this error? But by what means is this to be effected? It can only be done by a change of deportment in me; but how must I demean myself for this purpose?

I must not speak. Neither eyes, nor lips, must impart the information. He must not be assured that my heart is his, previous to the tender of his own; but he must be convinced that it has not been given to another; he must be supplied with space whereon to build a doubt as to the true state of my affections; he must be prompted to avow himself. The line of delicate propriety; how hard it is, not to fall short, and not to overleap it!

This afternoon we shall meet at the temple. We shall not

separate till late. It will be his province to accompany me home. The airy expanse is without a speck. This breeze is usually stedfast, and its promise of a bland and cloudless evening, may be trusted. The moon will rise at eleven, and at that hour, we shall wind along this bank. Possibly that hour may decide my fate. If suitable encouragement be given, Pleyel will reveal his soul to me; and I, ere I reach this threshold, will be made the happiest of beings. And is this good to be mine? Add wings to thy speed, sweet evening; and thou, moon, I charge thee, shroud thy beams at the moment when my Pleyel whispers love. I would not for the world, that the burning blushes, and the mounting raptures of that moment, should be visible.

But what encouragement is wanting? I must be regardful of insurmountable limits. Yet when minds are imbued with a genuine sympathy, are not words and looks superfluous? Are not motion and touch sufficient to impart feelings such as mine? Has he not eyed me at moments, when the pressure of his hand has thrown me into tumults, and was it possible that he mistook the impetuosities of love, for the eloquence of indignation?

But the hastening evening will decide. Would it were come! And yet I shudder at its near approach. An interview that must thus terminate, is surely to be wished for by me; and yet it is not without its terrors. Would to heaven it were come and gone!

I feel no reluctance, my friends to be thus explicit. Time was, when these emotions would be hidden with immeasurable solicitude, from every human eye. Alas! these airy and fleeting impulses of shame are gone. My scruples were preposterous and criminal. They are bred in all hearts, by a perverse and vicious education, and they would still have maintained their place in my heart, had not my portion been set in misery. My errors have taught me thus much wisdom; that those sentiments which we ought not to disclose, it is criminal to harbour.

It was proposed to begin the rehearsal at four o'clock; I counted the minutes as they passed; their flight was at once too rapid and too slow; my sensations were of an excruciating kind; I could taste no food, nor apply to any task, nor enjoy a moment's repose: when the hour arrived, I hastened to my brother's.

Pleyel was not there. He had not yet come. On ordinary occasions, he was eminent for punctuality. He had testified great eagerness to share in the pleasures of this rehearsal. He was to divide the task with my brother, and, in tasks like these, he always engaged with peculiar zeal. His elocution was less sweet than sonorous; and, therefore, better adapted than the mellifluences of his friend, to the outrageous vehemence of this drama.

What could detain him? Perhaps he lingered through forgetfulness. Yet this was incredible. Never had his memory been known to fail upon even more trivial occasions. Not less impossible was it, that the scheme had lost its attractions, and that he staid, because his coming would afford him no gratification. But why should we expect him to adhere to the minute?

An half hour elapsed, but Pleyel was still at a distance. Perhaps he had misunderstood the hour which had been proposed. Perhaps he had conceived that to-morrow, and not to-day, had been selected for this purpose: but no. A review of preceding circumstances demonstrated that such misapprehension was impossible; for he had himself proposed this day, and this hour. This day, his attention would not otherwise be occupied; but to-morrow, an indispensible engagement was foreseen, by which all his time would be engrossed: his detention, therefore, must be owing to some unforeseen and extraordinary event. Our conjectures were vague, tumultuous, and sometimes fearful. His sickness and his death might possibly have detained him.

Tortured with suspense, we sat gazing at each other, and at the path which led from the road. Every horseman that passed was, for a moment, imagined to be him. Hour succeeded hour, and the sun, gradually declining, at length, disappeared. Every signal of his coming proved fallacious, and our hopes were at length dismissed. His absence affected my friends in no insupportable degree. They should be obliged, they said, to defer this undertaking till the morrow; and, perhaps, their impatient curiosity would compel them to dispense entirely with his presence. No doubt, some harmless occurrence had diverted him from his purpose; and they trusted that they should receive a satisfactory account of him in the morning.

It may be supposed that this disappointment affected me in a very different manner. I turned aside my head to conceal my tears. I fled into solitude, to give vent to my reproaches, without interruption or restraint. My heart was ready to burst with indignation and grief. Pleyel was not the only object of my keen but unjust upbraiding. Deeply did I execrate my own folly. Thus fallen into ruins was the gay fabric which I had reared! Thus had my golden vision melted into air!

How fondly did I dream that Pleyel was a lover! If he were, would he have suffered any obstacle to hinder his coming? Blind and infatuated man! I exclaimed. Thou sportest with happiness. The good that is offered thee, thou hast the insolence and folly to refuse. Well, I will henceforth intrust my felicity to no one's keeping but my own.

The first agonies of this disappointment would not allow me to be reasonable or just. Every ground on which I had built the persuasion that Pleyel was not unimpressed in my favor, appeared to vanish. It seemed as if I had been misled into this opinion, by the most palpable illusions.

I made some trifling excuse, and returned, much earlier than I expected, to my own house. I retired early to my chamber, without designing to sleep. I placed myself at a window, and gave the reins to reflection.

The hateful and degrading impulses which had lately controuled me were, in some degree, removed. New dejection succeeded, but was now produced by contemplating my late behaviour. Surely that passion is worthy to be abhorred which obscures our understanding, and urges us to the commission of injustice. What right had I to expect his attendance? Had I not demeaned myself like one indifferent to his happiness, and as having bestowed my regards upon another? His absence might be prompted by the love which I considered his absence as a proof that he wanted. He came not because the sight of me, the spectacle of my coldness or aversion, contributed to his despair. Why should I prolong, by hypocrisy or silence, his misery as well as my own? Why not deal with him explicitly, and assure him of the truth?

You will hardly believe that, in obedience to this suggestion,

I rose for the purpose of ordering a light, that I might instantly make this confession in a letter. A second thought shewed me the rashness of this scheme, and I wondered by what infirmity of mind I could be betrayed into a momentary approbation of it. I saw with the utmost clearness that a confession like that would be the most remediless and unpardonable outrage upon the dignity of my sex, and utterly unworthy of that passion which controuled me.

I resumed my seat and my musing. To account for the absence of Pleyel became once more the scope of my conjectures. How many incidents might occur to raise an insuperable impediment in his way? When I was a child, a scheme of pleasure, in which he and his sister were parties, had been, in like manner, frustrated by his absence; but his absence, in that instance, had been occasioned by his falling from a boat into the river, in consequence of which he had run the most imminent hazard of being drowned. Here was a second disappointment endured by the same persons, and produced by his failure. Might it not originate in the same cause? Had he not designed to cross the river that morning to make some necessary purchases in Jersey? He had preconcerted to return to his own house to dinner; but, perhaps, some disaster had befallen him. Experience had taught me the insecurity of a canoe, and that was the only kind of boat which Pleyel used: I was, likewise, actuated by an hereditary dread of water. These circumstances combined to bestow considerable plausibility on this conjecture; but the consternation with which I began to be seized was allayed by reflecting, that if this disaster had happened my brother would have received the speediest information of it. The consolation which this idea imparted was ravished from me by a new thought. This disaster might have happened, and his family not be apprized of it. The first intelligence of his fate may be communicated by the livid corpse which the tide may cast, many days hence, upon the shore.

Thus was I distressed by opposite conjectures: thus was I tormented by phantoms of my own creation. It was not always thus. I cannot ascertain the date when my mind became the victim of this imbecility; perhaps it was coeval with the inroad of a fatal passion; a passion that will never rank me in the number of its eulogists; it was alone sufficient to the extermination of my peace: it was itself a plenteous source of calamity, and needed not the concurrence of other evils to take away the attractions of existence, and dig for me an untimely grave.

The state of my mind naturally introduced a train of reflections upon the dangers and cares which inevitably beset an human being. By no violent transition was I led to ponder on the turbulent life and mysterious end of my father. I cherished, with the utmost veneration, the memory of this man, and every relique connected with his fate was preserved with the most scrupulous care. Among these was to be numbered a manuscript, containing memoirs of his own life. The narrative was by no means recommended by its eloquence; but neither did all its value flow from my relationship to the author. Its stile had an unaffected and picturesque simplicity. The great variety and circumstantial display of the incidents, together with their intrinsic importance, as descriptive of human manners and passions, made it the most useful book in my collection. It was late; but being sensible of no inclination to sleep, I resolved to betake myself to the perusal of it.

To do this it was requisite to procure a light. The girl had long since retired to her chamber: it was therefore proper to wait upon myself. A lamp, and the means of lighting it, were only to be found in the kitchen. Thither I resolved forthwith to repair; but the light was of use merely to enable me to read the book. I knew the shelf and the spot where it stood. Whether I took down the book, or prepared the lamp, in the first place, appeared to be a matter of no moment. The latter was preferred, and, leaving my seat, I approached the closet in which, as I mentioned formerly, my books and papers were deposited.

Suddenly the remembrance of what had lately passed in this closet occurred. Whether midnight was approaching, or had passed, I knew not. I was, as then, alone, and defenceless. The wind was in that direction in which, aided by the deathlike repose of nature, it brought to me the murmur of the water-fall. This was mingled with that solemn and enchanting sound, which a breeze produces among the leaves of pines. The words of that mysterious dialogue, their fearful import, and the wild excess to which I was transported by my terrors, filled my imagination anew. My steps faultered, and I stood a moment to recover myself.

I prevailed on myself at length to move towards the closet. I touched the lock, but my fingers were powerless; I was visited afresh by unconquerable apprehensions. A sort of belief darted into my mind, that some being was concealed within, whose purposes were evil. I began to contend with these fears, when it occurred to me that I might, without impropriety, go for a lamp previously to opening the closet. I receded a few steps; but before I reached my chamber door my thoughts took a new direction. Motion seemed to produce a mechanical influence upon me. I was ashamed of my weakness. Besides, what aid could be afforded me by a lamp?

My fears had pictured to themselves no precise object. It would be difficult to depict, in words, the ingredients and hues of that phantom which haunted me. An hand invisible and of preternatural strength, lifted by human passions, and selecting my life for its aim, were parts of this terrific image. All places were alike accessible to this foe, or if his empire were restricted by local bounds, those bounds were utterly inscrutable by me. But had I not been told by some one in league with this enemy, that every place but the recess in the bank was exempt from danger?

I returned to the closet, and once more put my hand upon the lock. O! may my ears lose their sensibility, ere they be again assailed by a shriek so terrible! Not merely my understanding was subdued by the sound: it acted on my nerves like an edge of steel. It appeared to cut asunder the fibres of my brain, and rack every joint with agony.

The cry, loud and piercing as it was, was nevertheless human. No articulation was ever more distinct. The breath which accompanied it did not fan my hair, yet did every circumstance combine to persuade me that the lips which uttered it touched my very shoulder.

"Hold! Hold!" were the words of this tremendous prohibition, in whose tone the whole soul seemed to be rapt up, and every energy converted into eagerness and terror.

Shuddering, I dashed myself against the wall, and by the same involuntary impulse, turned my face backward to examine the mysterious monitor. The moon-light streamed into each window, and every corner of the room was conspicuous, and yet I beheld nothing!

The interval was too brief to be artificially measured, between the utterance of these words, and my scrutiny directed to the quarter whence they came. Yet if a human being had been there, could he fail to have been visible? Which of my senses was the prey of a fatal illusion? The shock which the sound produced was still felt in every part of my frame. The sound, therefore, could not but be a genuine commotion. But that I had heard it, was not more true than that the being who uttered it was stationed at my right ear; yet my attendant was invisible.

I cannot describe the state of my thoughts at that moment. Surprize had mastered my faculties. My frame shook, and the vital current was congealed. I was conscious only to the vehemence of my sensations. This condition could not be lasting. Like a tide, which suddenly mounts to an overwhelming height, and then gradually subsides, my confusion slowly gave place to order, and my tumults to a calm. I was able to deliberate and move. I resumed my feet, and advanced into the midst of the room. Upward, and behind, and on each side, I threw penetrating glances. I was not satisfied with one examination. He that hitherto refused to be seen, might change his purpose, and on the next survey be clearly distinguishable.

Solitude imposes least restraint upon the fancy. Dark is less fertile of images than the feeble lustre of the moon. I was alone, and the walls were chequered by shadowy forms. As the moon passed behind a cloud and emerged, these shadows seemed to be endowed with life, and to move. The apartment was open to the breeze, and the curtain was occasionally blown from its ordinary position. This motion was not unaccompanied with sound. I failed not to snatch a look, and to listen when this motion and this sound occurred. My belief that my monitor was posted near, was strong, and instantly converted these appearances to tokens of his presence, and yet I could discern nothing.

When my thoughts were at length permitted to revert to the past, the first idea that occurred was the resemblance between the words of the voice which I had just heard, and those which had terminated my dream in the summer-house. There are means by which we are able to distinguish a substance from a shadow, a reality from the phantom of a dream. The pit, my brother beckoning me forward, the seizure of my arm, and the voice behind, were surely imaginary. That these incidents were fashioned in my sleep, is supported by the same indubitable evidence that compels me to believe myself awake at present; yet the words and the voice were the same. Then, by some inexplicable contrivance, I was aware of the danger, while my actions and sensations were those of one wholly unacquainted with it. Now, was it not equally true that my actions and persuasions were at war? Had not the belief, that evil lurked in the closet, gained admittance, and had not my actions betokened an unwarrantable security? To obviate the effects of my infatuation, the same means had been used.

In my dream, he that tempted me to my destruction, was my brother. Death was ambushed in my path. From what evil was I now rescued? What minister or implement of ill was shut up in this recess? Who was it whose suffocating grasp I was to feel, should I dare to enter it? What monstrous conception is this? my brother!

No; protection, and not injury is his province. Strange and terrible chimera! Yet it would not be suddenly dismissed. It was surely no vulgar agency that gave this form to my fears. He to whom all parts of time are equally present, whom no contingency approaches, was the author of that spell which now seized upon me. Life was dear to me. No consideration was present that enjoined me to relinquish it. Sacred duty combined with every spontaneous sentiment to endear to me my being. Should I not shudder when my being was endangered? But what emotion should possess me when the arm lifted against me was Wieland's?

Ideas exist in our minds that can be accounted for by no established laws. Why did I dream that my brother was my foe? Why but because an omen of my fate was ordained to be communicated? Yet what salutary end did it serve? Did it arm me with caution to elude, or fortitude to bear the evils to which I was reserved? My present thoughts were, no doubt, indebted for their hue to the similitude existing between these incidents and those of my dream. Surely it was phrenzy that dictated my deed. That a ruffian was hidden in the closet, was

an idea, the genuine tendency of which was to urge me to
flight. Such had been the effect formerly produced. Had my
mind been simply occupied with this thought at present, no
doubt, the same impulse would have been experienced; but
now it was my brother whom I was irresistably persuaded to
regard as the contriver of that ill of which I had been forewarned. This persuasion did not extenuate my fears or my
danger. Why then did I again approach the closet and withdraw the bolt? My resolution was instantly conceived, and executed without faultering.

The door was formed of light materials. The lock, of simple
structure, easily forewent its hold. It opened into the room,
and commonly moved upon its hinges, after being unfastened,
without any effort of mine. This effort, however, was bestowed upon the present occasion. It was my purpose to open
it with quickness, but the exertion which I made was ineffectual. It refused to open.

At another time, this circumstance would not have looked
with a face of mystery. I should have supposed some casual
obstruction, and repeated my efforts to surmount it. But now
my mind was accessible to no conjecture but one. The door
was hindered from opening by human force. Surely, here was
new cause for affright. This was confirmation proper to decide
my conduct. Now was all ground of hesitation taken away.
What could be supposed but that I deserted the chamber and
the house? that I at least endeavoured no longer to withdraw
the door?

Have I not said that my actions were dictated by phrenzy?
My reason had forborne, for a time, to suggest or to sway my
resolves. I reiterated my endeavours. I exerted all my force to
overcome the obstacle, but in vain. The strength that was
exerted to keep it shut, was superior to mine.

A casual observer might, perhaps, applaud the audacious-
ness of this conduct. Whence, but from an habitual defiance
of danger, could my perseverance arise? I have already assigned, as distinctly as I am able, the cause of it. The frantic
conception that my brother was within, that the resistance
made to my design was exerted by him, had rooted itself in
my mind. You will comprehend the height of this infatuation,
when I tell you, that, finding all my exertions vain, I betook

myself to exclamations. Surely I was utterly bereft of understanding.

Now had I arrived at the crisis of my fate. "O! hinder not the door to open," I exclaimed, in a tone that had less of fear than of grief in it. "I know you well. Come forth, but harm me not. I beseech you come forth."

I had taken my hand from the lock, and removed to a small distance from the door. I had scarcely uttered these words, when the door swung upon its hinges, and displayed to my view the interior of the closet. Whoever was within, was shrouded in darkness. A few seconds passed without interruption of the silence. I knew not what to expect or to fear. My eyes would not stray from the recess. Presently, a deep sigh was heard. The quarter from which it came heightened the eagerness of my gaze. Some one approached from the farther end. I quickly perceived the outlines of a human figure. Its steps were irresolute and slow. I recoiled as it advanced.

By coming at length within the verge of the room, his form was clearly distinguishable. I had prefigured to myself a very different personage. The face that presented itself was the last that I should desire to meet at an hour, and in a place like this. My wonder was stifled by my fears. Assassins had lurked in this recess. Some divine voice warned me of danger, that at this moment awaited me. I had spurned the intimation, and challenged my adversary.

I recalled the mysterious countenance and dubious character of Carwin. What motive but atrocious ones could guide his steps hither? I was alone. My habit suited the hour, and the place, and the warmth of the season. All succour was remote. He had placed himself between me and the door. My frame shook with the vehemence of my apprehensions.

Yet I was not wholly lost to myself: I vigilantly marked his demeanour. His looks were grave, but not without perturbation. What species of inquietude it betrayed, the light was not strong enough to enable me to discover. He stood still; but his eyes wandered from one object to another. When these powerful organs were fixed upon me, I shrunk into myself. At length, he broke silence. Earnestness, and not embarrassment, was in his tone. He advanced close to me while he spoke.

"What voice was that which lately addressed you?"

He paused for an answer; but observing my trepidation, he resumed, with undiminished solemnity: "Be not terrified. Whoever he was, he hast done you an important service. I need not ask you if it were the voice of a companion. That sound was beyond the compass of human organs. The knowledge that enabled him to tell you who was in the closet, was obtained by incomprehensible means.

"You knew that Carwin was there. Were you not apprized of his intents? The same power could impart the one as well as the other. Yet, knowing these, you persisted. Audacious girl! but, perhaps, you confided in his guardianship. Your confidence was just. With succour like this at hand you may safely defy me.

"He is my eternal foe; the baffler of my best concerted schemes. Twice have you been saved by his accursed interposition. But for him I should long ere now have borne away the spoils of your honor."

He looked at me with greater stedfastness than before. I became every moment more anxious for my safety. It was with difficulty I stammered out an entreaty that he would instantly depart, or suffer me to do so. He paid no regard to my request, but proceeded in a more impassioned manner.

"What is it you fear? Have I not told you, you are safe? Has not one in whom you more reasonably place trust assured you of it? Even if I execute my purpose, what injury is done? Your prejudices will call it by that name, but it merits it not.

"I was impelled by a sentiment that does you honor; a sentiment, that would sanctify my deed; but, whatever it be, you are safe. Be this chimera still worshipped; I will do nothing to pollute it." Here he stopped.

The accents and gestures of this man left me drained of all courage. Surely, on no other occasion should I have been thus pusillanimous. My state I regarded as a hopeless one. I was wholly at the mercy of this being. Whichever way I turned my eyes, I saw no avenue by which I might escape. The resources of my personal strength, my ingenuity, and my eloquence, I estimated at nothing. The dignity of virtue, and the force of truth, I had been accustomed to celebrate; and had frequently vaunted of the conquests which I should make with their assistance.

I used to suppose that certain evils could never befall a being in possession of a sound mind; that true virtue supplies us with energy which vice can never resist; that it was always in our power to obstruct, by his own death, the designs of an enemy who aimed at less than our life. How was it that a sentiment like despair had now invaded me, and that I trusted to the protection of chance, or to the pity of my persecutor?

His words imparted some notion of the injury which he had meditated. He talked of obstacles that had risen in his way. He had relinquished his design. These sources supplied me with slender consolation. There was no security but in his absence. When I looked at myself, when I reflected on the hour and the place, I was overpowered by horror and dejection.

He was silent, museful, and inattentive to my situation, yet made no motion to depart. I was silent in my turn. What could I say? I was confident that reason in this contest would be impotent. I must owe my safety to his own suggestions. Whatever purpose brought him hither, he had changed it. Why then did he remain? His resolutions might fluctuate, and the pause of a few minutes restore to him his first resolutions.

Yet was not this the man whom we had treated with unwearied kindness? Whose society was endeared to us by his intellectual elevation and accomplishments? Who had a thousand times expatiated on the usefulness and beauty of virtue? Why should such a one be dreaded? If I could have forgotten the circumstances in which our interview had taken place, I might have treated his words as jests. Presently, he resumed:

"Fear me not: the space that severs us is small, and all visible succour is distant. You believe yourself completely in my power; that you stand upon the brink of ruin. Such are your groundless fears. I cannot lift a finger to hurt you. Easier it would be to stop the moon in her course than to injure you. The power that protects you would crumble my sinews, and reduce me to a heap of ashes in a moment, if I were to harbour a thought hostile to your safety.

"Thus are appearances at length solved. Little did I expect that they originated hence. What a portion is assigned to you? Scanned by the eyes of this intelligence, your path will be without pits to swallow, or snares to entangle you. Environed by the arms of this protection, all artifices will be frustrated, and all malice repelled."

Here succeeded a new pause. I was still observant of every gesture and look. The tranquil solemnity that had lately possessed his countenance gave way to a new expression. All now was trepidation and anxiety.

"I must be gone," said he in a faltering accent. "Why do I linger here? I will not ask your forgiveness. I see that your terrors are invincible. Your pardon will be extorted by fear, and not dictated by compassion. I must fly from you forever. He that could plot against your honor, must expect from you and your friends persecution and death. I must doom myself to endless exile."

Saying this, he hastily left the room. I listened while he descended the stairs, and, unbolting the outer door, went forth. I did not follow him with my eyes, as the moon-light would have enabled me to do. Relieved by his absence, and exhausted by the conflict of my fears, I threw myself on a chair, and resigned myself to those bewildering ideas which incidents like these could not fail to produce.

Chapter X

ORDER could not readily be introduced into my thoughts. The voice still rung in my ears. Every accent that was uttered by Carwin was fresh in my remembrance. His unwelcome approach, the recognition of his person, his hasty departure, produced a complex impression on my mind which no words can delineate. I strove to give a slower motion to my thoughts, and to regulate a confusion which became painful; but my efforts were nugatory. I covered my eyes with my hand, and sat, I know not how long, without power to arrange or utter my conceptions.

I had remained for hours, as I believed, in absolute solitude. No thought of personal danger had molested my tranquillity. I had made no preparation for defence. What was it that suggested the design of perusing my father's manuscript? If, instead of this, I had retired to bed, and to sleep, to what fate might I not have been reserved? The ruffian, who must almost have suppressed his breathings to screen himself from discovery, would have noticed this signal, and I should have awakened only to perish with affright, and to abhor myself. Could I have remained unconscious of my danger? Could I have tranquilly slept in the midst of so deadly a snare?

And who was he that threatened to destroy me? By what means could he hide himself in this closet? Surely he is gifted with supernatural power. Such is the enemy of whose attempts I was forewarned. Daily I had seen him and conversed with him. Nothing could be discerned through the impenetrable veil of his duplicity. When busied in conjectures, as to the author of the evil that was threatened, my mind did not light, for a moment, upon his image. Yet has he not avowed himself my enemy? Why should he be here if he had not meditated evil?

He confesses that this has been his second attempt. What was the scene of his former conspiracy? Was it not he whose whispers betrayed him? Am I deceived; or was there not a faint resemblance between the voice of this man and that which talked of grasping my throat, and extinguishing my life in a moment? Then he had a colleague in his crime; now he is alone. Then death was the scope of his thoughts; now an injury unspeakably more dreadful. How thankful should I be to the power that has interposed to save me!

That power is invisible. It is subject to the cognizance of one of my senses. What are the means that will inform me of what nature it is? He has set himself to counterwork the machinations of this man, who had menaced destruction to all that is dear to me, and whose cunning had surmounted every human impediment. There was none to rescue me from his grasp. My rashness even hastened the completion of his scheme, and precluded him from the benefits of deliberation. I had robbed him of the power to repent and forbear. Had I been apprized of the danger, I should have regarded my conduct as the means of rendering my escape from it impossible. Such, likewise, seem to have been the fears of my invisible protector. Else why that startling intreaty to refrain from opening the closet? By what inexplicable infatuation was I compelled to proceed?

Yet my conduct was wise. Carwin, unable to comprehend my folly, ascribed my behaviour to my knowledge. He conceived himself previously detected, and such detection being possible to flow only from *my* heavenly friend, and *his* enemy, his fears acquired additional strength.

He is apprized of the nature and intentions of this being. Perhaps he is a human agent. Yet, on that supposition his atchievements are incredible. Why should I be selected as the object of his care; or, if a mere mortal, should I not recognize some one, whom, benefits imparted and received had prompted to love me? What were the limits and duration of his guardianship? Was the genius of my birth entrusted by divine benignity with this province? Are human faculties adequate to receive stronger proofs of the existence of unfettered and beneficent intelligences than I have received?

But who was this man's coadjutor? The voice that acknowledged an alliance in treachery with Carwin warned me to avoid the summer-house. He assured me that there only my safety was endangered. His assurance, as it now appears, was fallacious. Was there not deceit in his admonition? Was his compact really annulled? Some purpose was, perhaps, to be accomplished by preventing my future visits to that spot. Why was I enjoined silence to others, on the subject of this admonition, unless it were for some unauthorized and guilty purpose?

No one but myself was accustomed to visit it. Backward, it was hidden from distant view by the rock, and in front, it was screened from all examination, by creeping plants, and the branches of cedars. What recess could be more propitious to secrecy? The spirit which haunted it formerly was pure and rapturous. It was a fane sacred to the memory of infantile days, and to blissful imaginations of the future! What a gloomy reverse had succeeded since the ominous arrival of this stranger! Now, perhaps, it is the scene of his meditations. Purposes fraught with horror, that shun the light, and contemplate the pollution of innocence, are here engendered, and fostered, and reared to maturity.

Such were the ideas that, during the night, were tumultuously revolved by me. I reviewed every conversation in which Carwin had borne a part. I studied to discover the true inferences deducible from his deportment and words with regard to his former adventures and actual views. I pondered on the comments which he made on the relation which I had given of the closet dialogue. No new ideas suggested themselves in the course of this review. My expectation had, from the first, been disappointed on the small degree of surprize which this narrative excited in him. He never explicitly declared his opinion as to the nature of those voices, or decided whether they were real or visionary. He recommended no measures of caution or prevention.

But what measures were now to be taken? Was the danger which threatened me at an end? Had I nothing more to fear? I was lonely, and without means of defence. I could not calculate the motives and regulate the footsteps of this person. What certainty was there, that he would not re-assume his purposes, and swiftly return to the execution of them?

This idea covered me once more with dismay. How deeply did I regret the solitude in which I was placed, and how ardently did I desire the return of day! But neither of these inconveniencies were susceptible of remedy. At first, it occurred to me to summon my servant, and make her spend the

night in my chamber; but the inefficacy of this expedient to
enhance my safety was easily seen. Once I resolved to leave
the house, and retire to my brother's, but was deterred by
reflecting on the unseasonableness of the hour, on the alarm
which my arrival, and the account which I should be obliged
to give, might occasion, and on the danger to which I might
expose myself in the way thither. I began, likewise, to consider
Carwin's return to molest me as exceedingly improbable. He
had relinquished, of his own accord, his design, and departed
without compulsion.

Surely, said I, there is omnipotence in the cause that
changed the views of a man like Carwin. The divinity that
shielded me from his attempts will take suitable care of my
future safety. Thus to yield to my fears is to deserve that they
should be realized.

Scarcely had I uttered these words, when my attention was
startled by the sound of footsteps. They denoted some one
stepping into the piazza in front of my house. My new-born
confidence was extinguished in a moment. Carwin, I thought,
had repented his departure, and was hastily returning. The
possibility that his return was prompted by intentions consistent with my safety, found no place in my mind. Images of
violation and murder assailed me anew, and the terrors which
succeeded almost incapacitated me from taking any measures
for my defence. It was an impulse of which I was scarcely
conscious, that made me fasten the lock and draw the bolts
of my chamber door. Having done this, I threw myself on a
seat; for I trembled to a degree which disabled me from standing, and my soul was so perfectly absorbed in the act of listening, that almost the vital motions were stopped.

The door below creaked on its hinges. It was not again
thrust to, but appeared to remain open. Footsteps entered,
traversed the entry, and began to mount the stairs. How I
detested the folly of not pursuing the man when he withdrew,
and bolting after him the outer door! Might he not conceive
this omission to be a proof that my angel had deserted me,
and be thereby fortified in guilt?

Every step on the stairs, which brought him nearer to my
chamber, added vigor to my desperation. The evil with which
I was menaced was to be at any rate eluded. How little did I

preconceive the conduct which, in an exigence like this, I should be prone to adopt. You will suppose that deliberation and despair would have suggested the same course of action, and that I should have, unhesitatingly, resorted to the best means of personal defence within my power. A penknife lay open upon my table. I remembered that it was there, and seized it. For what purpose you will scarcely inquire. It will be immediately supposed that I meant it for my last refuge, and that if all other means should fail, I should plunge it into the heart of my ravisher.

I have lost all faith in the stedfastness of human resolves. It was thus that in periods of calm I had determined to act. No cowardice had been held by me in greater abhorrence than that which prompted an injured female to destroy, not her injurer ere the injury was perpetrated, but herself when it was without remedy. Yet now this penknife appeared to me of no other use than to baffle my assailant, and prevent the crime by destroying myself. To deliberate at such a time was impossible; but among the tumultuous suggestions of the moment, I do not recollect that it once occurred to me to use it as an instrument of direct defence.

The steps had now reached the second floor. Every footfall accelerated the completion, without augmenting the certainty of evil. The consciousness that the door was fast, now that nothing but that was interposed between me and danger, was a source of some consolation. I cast my eye towards the window. This, likewise, was a new suggestion. If the door should give way, it was my sudden resolution to throw myself from the window. Its height from the ground, which was covered beneath by a brick pavement, would insure my destruction; but I thought not of that.

When opposite to my door the footsteps ceased. Was he listening whether my fears were allayed, and my caution were asleep? Did he hope to take me by surprise? Yet, if so, why did he allow so many noisy signals to betray his approach? Presently the steps were again heard to approach the door. An hand was laid upon the lock, and the latch pulled back. Did he imagine it possible that I should fail to secure the door? A slight effort was made to push it open, as if all bolts being withdrawn, a slight effort only was required.

I no sooner perceived this, than I moved swiftly towards the window. Carwin's frame might be said to be all muscle. His strength and activity had appeared, in various instances, to be prodigious. A slight exertion of his force would demolish the door. Would not that exertion be made? Too surely it would; but, at the same moment that this obstacle should yield, and he should enter the apartment, my determination was formed to leap from the window. My senses were still bound to this object. I gazed at the door in momentary expectation that the assault would be made. The pause continued. The person without was irresolute and motionless.

Suddenly, it occurred to me that Carwin might conceive me to have fled. That I had not betaken myself to flight was, indeed, the least probable of all conclusions. In this persuasion he must have been confirmed on finding the lower door unfastened, and the chamber door locked. Was it not wise to foster this persuasion? Should I maintain deep silence, this, in addition to other circumstances, might encourage the belief, and he would once more depart. Every new reflection added plausibility to this reasoning. It was presently more strongly enforced, when I noticed footsteps withdrawing from the door. The blood once more flowed back to my heart, and a dawn of exultation began to rise: but my joy was short lived. Instead of descending the stairs, he passed to the door of the opposite chamber, opened it, and having entered, shut it after him with a violence that shook the house.

How was I to interpret this circumstance? For what end could he have entered this chamber? Did the violence with which he closed the door testify the depth of his vexation? This room was usually occupied by Pleyel. Was Carwin aware of his absence on this night? Could he be suspected of a design so sordid as pillage? If this were his view there were no means in my power to frustrate it. It behoved me to seize the first opportunity to escape; but if my escape were supposed by my enemy to have been already effected, no asylum was more secure than the present. How could my passage from the house be accomplished without noises that might incite him to pursue me?

Utterly at a loss to account for his going into Pleyel's chamber, I waited in instant expectation of hearing him come forth.

All, however, was profoundly still. I listened in vain for a considerable period, to catch the sound of the door when it should again be opened. There was no other avenue by which he could escape, but a door which led into the girl's chamber. Would any evil from this quarter befall the girl?

Hence arose a new train of apprehensions. They merely added to the turbulence and agony of my reflections. Whatever evil impended over her, I had no power to avert it. Seclusion and silence were the only means of saving myself from the perils of this fatal night. What solemn vows did I put up, that if I should once more behold the light of day, I would never trust myself again within the threshold of this dwelling!

Minute lingered after minute, but no token was given that Carwin had returned to the passage. What, I again asked, could detain him in this room? Was it possible that he had returned, and glided, unperceived, away? I was speedily aware of the difficulty that attended an enterprize like this; and yet, as if by that means I were capable of gaining any information on that head, I cast anxious looks from the window.

The object that first attracted my attention was an human figure standing on the edge of the bank. Perhaps my penetration was assisted by my hopes. Be that as it will, the figure of Carwin was clearly distinguishable. From the obscurity of my station, it was impossible that I should be discerned by him, and yet he scarcely suffered me to catch a glimpse of him. He turned and went down the steep, which, in this part, was not difficult to be scaled.

My conjecture then had been right. Carwin has softly opened the door, descended the stairs, and issued forth. That I should not have overheard his steps, was only less incredible than that my eyes had deceived me. But what was now to be done? The house was at length delivered from this detested inmate. By one avenue might he again re-enter. Was it not wise to bar the lower door? Perhaps he had gone out by the kitchen door. For this end, he must have passed through Judith's chamber. These entrances being closed and bolted, as great security was gained as was compatible with my lonely condition.

The propriety of these measures was too manifest not to make me struggle successfully with my fears. Yet I opened my own door with the utmost caution, and descended as if I were afraid that Carwin had been still immured in Pleyel's chamber. The outer door was a-jar. I shut, with trembling eagerness, and drew every bolt that appended to it. I then passed with light and less cautious steps through the parlour, but was sur-prized to discover that the kitchen door was secure. I was compelled to acquiesce in the first conjecture that Carwin had escaped through the entry.

My heart was now somewhat eased of the load of appre-hension. I returned once more to my chamber, the door of which I was careful to lock. It was no time to think of repose. The moon-light began already to fade before the light of the day. The approach of morning was betokened by the usual signals. I mused upon the events of this night, and determined to take up my abode henceforth at my brother's. Whether I should inform him of what had happened was a question which seemed to demand some consideration. My safety un-questionably required that I should abandon my present habitation.

As my thoughts began to flow with fewer impediments, the image of Pleyel, and the dubiousness of his condition, again recurred to me. I again ran over the possible causes of his absence on the preceding day. My mind was attuned to mel-ancholy. I dwelt, with an obstinacy for which I could not ac-count, on the idea of his death. I painted to myself his struggles with the billows, and his last appearance. I imagined myself a midnight wanderer on the shore, and to have stum-bled on his corpse, which the tide had cast up. These dreary images affected me even to tears. I endeavoured not to re-strain them. They imparted a relief which I had not antici-pated. The more copiously they flowed, the more did my general sensations appear to subside into calm, and a certain restlessness give way to repose.

Perhaps, relieved by this effusion, the slumber so much wanted might have stolen on my senses, had there been no new cause of alarm.

Chapter XI

I WAS aroused from this stupor by sounds that evidently arose in the next chamber. Was it possible that I had been mistaken in the figure which I had seen on the bank? or had Carwin, by some inscrutable means, penetrated once more into this chamber? The opposite door opened; footsteps came forth, and the person, advancing to mine, knocked.

So unexpected an incident robbed me of all presence of mind, and, starting up, I involuntarily exclaimed, "Who is there?" An answer was immediately given. The voice, to my inexpressible astonishment, was Pleyel's.

"It is I. Have you risen? If you have not, make haste; I want three minutes conversation with you in the parlour—I will wait for you there." Saying this he retired from the door.

Should I confide in the testimony of my ears? If that were true, it was Pleyel that had been hitherto immured in the opposite chamber: he whom my rueful fancy had depicted in so many ruinous and ghastly shapes: he whose footsteps had been listened to with such inquietude! What is man, that knowledge is so sparingly conferred upon him! that his heart should be wrung with distress, and his frame be exanimated with fear, though his safety be encompassed with impregnable walls! What are the bounds of human imbecility! He that warned me of the presence of my foe refused the intimation by which so many racking fears would have been precluded.

Yet who would have imagined the arrival of Pleyel at such an hour? His tone was desponding and anxious. Why this unseasonable summons? and why this hasty departure? Some tidings he, perhaps, bears of mysterious and unwelcome import.

My impatience would not allow me to consume much time in deliberation: I hastened down. Pleyel I found standing at a window, with eyes cast down as in meditation, and arms folded on his breast. Every line in his countenance was pregnant with sorrow. To this was added a certain wanness and air of fatigue. The last time I had seen him appearances had been the reverse of these. I was startled at the change. The first impulse was to question him as to the cause. This impulse was supplanted by some degree of confusion, flowing from a consciousness that love had too large, and, as it might prove, a perceptible share in creating this impulse. I was silent.

Presently he raised his eyes and fixed them upon me. I read in them an anguish altogether ineffable. Never had I witnessed a like demeanour in Pleyel. Never, indeed, had I observed an human countenance in which grief was more legibly inscribed. He seemed struggling for utterance; but his struggles being fruitless, he shook his head and turned away from me.

My impatience would not allow me to be longer silent: "What," said I, "for heaven's sake, my friend, what is the matter?"

He started at the sound of my voice. His looks, for a moment, became convulsed with an emotion very different from grief. His accents were broken with rage.

"The matter—O wretch!—thus exquisitely fashioned—on whom nature seemed to have exhausted all her graces; with charms so awful and so pure! how art thou fallen! From what height fallen! A ruin so complete—so unheard of!"

His words were again choked by emotion. Grief and pity were again mingled in his features. He resumed, in a tone half suffocated by sobs:

"But why should I upbraid thee? Could I restore to thee what thou has lost; efface this cursed stain; snatch thee from the jaws of this fiend; I would do it. Yet what will avail my efforts? I have not arms with which to contend with so consummate, so frightful a depravity.

"Evidence less than this would only have excited resentment and scorn. The wretch who should have breathed a suspicion injurious to thy honor, would have been regarded without anger; not hatred or envy could have prompted him; it would merely be an argument of madness. That my eyes, that my ears, should bear witness to thy fall! By no other way could detestible conviction be imparted.

"Why do I summon thee to this conference? Why expose myself to thy derision? Here admonition and entreaty are vain. Thou knowest him already, for a murderer and thief. I had thought to have been the first to disclose to thee his infamy; to have warned thee of the pit to which thou art hastening;

but thy eyes are open in vain. O foul and insupportable disgrace!

"There is but one path. I know you will disappear together. In thy ruin, how will the felicity and honor of multitudes be involved! But it must come. This scene shall not be blotted by his presence. No doubt thou wilt shortly see thy detested paramour. This scene will be again polluted by a midnight assignation. Inform him of his danger; tell him that his crimes are known; let him fly far and instantly from this spot, if he desires to avoid the fate which menaced him in Ireland.

"And wilt thou not stay behind?—But shame upon my weakness. I know not what I would say.—I have done what I purposed. To stay longer, to expostulate, to beseech, to enumerate the consequences of thy act—what end can it serve but to blazon thy infamy and embitter our woes? And yet, O think, think ere it be too late, on the distresses which thy flight will entail upon us; on the base, grovelling, and atrocious character of the wretch to whom thou hast sold thy honor. But what is this? Is not thy effrontery impenetrable, and thy heart thoroughly cankered? O most specious, and most profligate of women!"

Saying this, he rushed out of the house. I saw him in a few moments hurrying along the path which led to my brother's. I had no power to prevent his going, or to recall, or to follow him. The accents I had heard were calculated to confound and bewilder. I looked around me to assure myself that the scene was real. I moved that I might banish the doubt that I was awake. Such enormous imputations from the mouth of Pleyel! To be stigmatized with the names of wanton and profligate! To be charged with the sacrifice of honor! with midnight meetings with a wretch known to be a murderer and thief! with an intention to fly in his company!

What I had heard was surely the dictate of phrenzy, or it was built upon some fatal, some incomprehensible mistake. After the horrors of the night, after undergoing perils so imminent from this man, to be summoned to an interview like this; to find Pleyel fraught with a belief that, instead of having chosen death as a refuge from the violence of this man, I had hugged his baseness to my heart, had sacrificed for him my purity, my spotless name, my friendships, and my fortune! that even madness could engender accusations like these was not to be believed.

What evidence could possibly suggest conceptions so wild? After the unlooked-for interview with Carwin in my chamber, he retired. Could Pleyel have observed his exit? It was not long after that Pleyel himself entered. Did he build on this incident, his odious conclusions? Could the long series of my actions and sentiments grant me no exemption from suspicions so foul? Was it not more rational to infer that Carwin's designs had been illicit; that my life had been endangered by the fury of one whom, by some means, he had discovered to be an assassin and robber; that my honor had been assailed, not by blandishments, but by violence?

He has judged me without hearing. He has drawn from dubious appearances, conclusions the most improbable and unjust. He has loaded me with all outrageous epithets. He has ranked me with prostitutes and thieves. I cannot pardon thee, Pleyel, for this injustice. Thy understanding must be hurt. If it be not, if thy conduct was sober and deliberate, I can never forgive an outrage so unmanly, and so gross.

These thoughts gradually gave place to others. Pleyel was possessed by some momentary phrenzy: appearances had led him into palpable errors. Whence could his sagacity have contracted this blindness? Was it not love? Previously assured of my affection for Carwin, distracted with grief and jealousy, and impelled hither at that late hour by some unknown instigation, his imagination transformed shadows into monsters, and plunged him into these deplorable errors.

This idea was not unattended with consolation. My soul was divided between indignation at his injustice, and delight on account of the source from which I conceived it to spring. For a long time they would allow admission to no other thoughts. Surprize is an emotion that enfeebles, not invigorates. All my meditations were accompanied with wonder. I rambled with vagueness, or clung to one image with an obstinacy which sufficiently testified the maddening influence of late transactions.

Gradually I proceeded to reflect upon the consequences of Pleyel's mistake, and on the measures I should take to guard myself against future injury from Carwin. Should I suffer this mistake to be detected by time? When his passion should subside, would he not perceive the flagrancy of his injustice, and hasten to atone for it? Did it not become my character to testify resentment for language and treatment so opprobrious? Wrapt up in the consciousness of innocence, and confiding in the influence of time and reflection to confute so groundless a charge, it was my province to be passive and silent.

As to the violences meditated by Carwin, and the means of eluding them, the path to be taken by me was obvious. I resolved to tell the tale to my brother, and regulate myself by his advice. For this end, when the morning was somewhat advanced, I took the way to his house. My sister was engaged in her customary occupations. As soon as I appeared, she remarked a change in my looks. I was not willing to alarm her by the information which I had to communicate. Her health was in that condition which rendered a disastrous tale particularly unsuitable. I forbore a direct answer to her inquiries, and inquired, in my turn, for Wieland.

"Why," said she, "I suspect something mysterious and unpleasant has happened this morning. Scarcely had we risen when Pleyel dropped among us. What could have prompted him to make us so early and so unseasonable a visit I cannot tell. To judge from the disorder of his dress, and his countenance, something of an extraordinary nature has occurred. He permitted me merely to know that he had slept none, nor even undressed, during the past night. He took your brother to walk with him. Some topic must have deeply engaged them, for Wieland did not return till the breakfast hour was passed, and returned alone. His disturbance was excessive; but he would not listen to my importunities, or tell me what had happened. I gathered from hints which he let fall, that your situation was, in some way, the cause: yet he assured me that you were at your own house, alive, in good health, and in perfect safety. He scarcely ate a morsel, and immediately after breakfast went out again. He would not inform me whither he was going, but mentioned that he probably might not return before night."

I was equally astonished and alarmed by this information. Pleyel had told his tale to my brother, and had, by a plausible and exaggerated picture, instilled into him unfavorable thoughts of me. Yet would not the more correct judgment of Wieland perceive and expose the fallacy of his conclusions? Perhaps his uneasiness might arise from some insight into the character of Carwin, and from apprehensions for my safety. The appearances by which Pleyel had been misled, might induce him likewise to believe that I entertained an indiscreet, though not dishonorable affection for Carwin. Such were the conjectures rapidly formed. I was inexpressibly anxious to change them into certainty. For this end an interview with my brother was desirable. He was gone, no one knew whither, and was not expected speedily to return. I had no clue by which to trace his footsteps.

My anxieties could not be concealed from my sister. They heightened her solicitude to be acquainted with the cause. There were many reasons persuading me to silence: at least, till I had seen my brother, it would be an act of inexcusable temerity to unfold what had lately passed. No other expedient for eluding her importunities occurred to me, but that of returning to my own house. I recollected my determination to become a tenant of this roof. I mentioned it to her. She joyfully acceded to this proposal, and suffered me, with less reluctance, to depart, when I told her that it was with a view to collect and send to my new dwelling what articles would be immediately useful to me.

Once more I returned to the house which had been the scene of so much turbulence and danger. I was at no great distance from it when I observed my brother coming out. On seeing me he stopped, and after ascertaining, as it seemed, which way I was going, he returned into the house before me. I sincerely rejoiced at this event, and I hastened to set things, if possible, on their right footing.

His brow was by no means expressive of those vehement emotions with which Pleyel had been agitated. I drew a favorable omen from this circumstance. Without delay I began the conversation.

"I have been to look for you," said I, "but was told by Catharine that Pleyel had engaged you on some important and disagreeable affair. Before his interview with you he spent a few minutes with me. These minutes he employed in upbraiding me for crimes and intentions with which I am by no means chargeable. I believe him to have taken up his opinions on very insufficient grounds. His behaviour was in the highest degree precipitate and unjust, and, until I receive some atonement, I shall treat him, in my turn, with that contempt which he justly merits: meanwhile I am fearful that he has prejudiced my brother against me. That is an evil which I most anxiously deprecate, and which I shall indeed exert myself to remove. Has he made me the subject of this morning's conversation?"

My brother's countenance testified no surprize at my address. The benignity of his looks were no wise diminished.

"It is true," said he, "your conduct was the subject of our discourse. I am your friend, as well as your brother. There is no human being whom I love with more tenderness, and whose welfare is nearer my heart. Judge then with what emotions I listened to Pleyel's story. I expect and desire you to vindicate yourself from aspersions so foul, if vindication be possible."

The tone with which he uttered the last words affected me deeply. "If vindication be possible!" repeated I. "From what you know, do you deem a formal vindication necessary? Can you harbour for a moment the belief of my guilt?"

He shook his head with an air of acute anguish. "I have struggled," said he, "to dismiss that belief. You speak before a judge who will profit by any pretence to acquit you: who is ready to question his own senses when they plead against you."

These words incited a new set of thoughts in my mind. I began to suspect that Pleyel had built his accusations on some foundation unknown to me. "I may be a stranger to the grounds of your belief. Pleyel loaded me with indecent and virulent invectives, but he withheld from me the facts that generated his suspicions. Events took place last night of which some of the circumstances were of an ambiguous nature. I conceived that these might possibly have fallen under his cognizance, and that, viewed through the mists of prejudice and passion, they supplied a pretence for his conduct, but believed that your more unbiassed judgment would estimate them at their just value. Perhaps his tale has been different from what I suspect it to be. Listen then to my narrative. If there be any thing in his story inconsistent with mine, his story is false."

I then proceeded to a circumstantial relation of the incidents of the last night. Wieland listened with deep attention. Having finished, "This," continued I, "is the truth; you see in what circumstances an interview took place between Carwin and me. He remained for hours in my closet, and for some minutes in my chamber. He departed without haste or interruption. If Pleyel marked him as he left the house, and it is not impossible that he did, inferences injurious to my character might suggest themselves to him. In admitting them, he gave proofs of less discernment and less candor than I once ascribed to him."

"His proofs," said Wieland, after a considerable pause, "are different. That he should be deceived, is not possible. That he himself is not the deceiver, could not be believed, if his testimony were not inconsistent with yours; but the doubts which I entertained are now removed. Your tale, some parts of it, is marvellous; the voice which exclaimed against your rashness in approaching the closet, your persisting notwithstanding that prohibition, your belief that I was the ruffian, and your subsequent conduct, are believed by me, because I have known you from childhood, because a thousand instances have attested your veracity, and because nothing less than my own hearing and vision would convince me, in opposition to her own assertions, that my sister had fallen into wickedness like this."

I threw my arms around him, and bathed his cheek with my tears. "That," said I, "is spoken like my brother. But what are the proofs?"

He replied—"Pleyel informed me that, in going to your house, his attention was attracted by two voices. The persons speaking sat beneath the bank out of sight. These persons, judging by their voices, were Carwin and you. I will not repeat the dialogue. If my sister was the female, Pleyel was justified in concluding you to be, indeed, one of the most profligate of women. Hence, his accusations of you, and his efforts to obtain my concurrence to a plan by which an eternal separation should be brought about between my sister and this man."

I made Wieland repeat this recital. Here, indeed, was a tale to fill me with terrible foreboding. I had vainly thought that my safety could be sufficiently secured by doors and bars, but this is a foe from whose grasp no power of divinity can save me! His artifices will ever lay my fame and happiness at his mercy. How shall I counterwork his plots, or detect his co-adjutor? He has taught some vile and abandoned female to mimic my voice. Pleyel's ears were the witnesses of my dishonor. This is the midnight assignation to which he alluded. Thus is the silence he maintained when attempting to open the door of my chamber, accounted for. He supposed me absent, and meant, perhaps, had my apartment been accessible, to leave in it some accusing memorial.

Pleyel was no longer equally culpable. The sincerity of his anguish, the depth of his despair, I remembered with some tendencies to gratitude. Yet was he not precipitate? Was the conjecture that my part was played by some mimic so utterly untenable? Instances of this faculty are common. The wickedness of Carwin must, in his opinion, have been adequate to such contrivances, and yet the supposition of my guilt was adopted in preference to that.

But how was this error to be unveiled? What but my own assertion had I to throw in the balance against it? Would this be permitted to outweigh the testimony of his senses? I had no witnesses to prove my existence in another place. The real events of that night are marvellous. Few, to whom they should be related, would scruple to discredit them. Pleyel is sceptical in a transcendant degree. I cannot summon Carwin to my bar, and make him the attestor of my innocence, and the accuser of himself.

My brother saw and comprehended my distress. He was unacquainted, however, with the full extent of it. He knew not by how many motives I was incited to retrieve the good opinion of Pleyel. He endeavored to console me. Some new event, he said, would occur to disentangle the maze. He did not question the influence of my eloquence, if I thought proper to exert it. Why not seek an interview with Pleyel, and exact from him a minute relation, in which something may be met with serving to destroy the probability of the whole?

I caught, with eagerness, at this hope; but my alacrity was

damped by new reflections. Should I, perfect in this respect, and unblemished as I was, thrust myself, uncalled, into his presence, and make my felicity depend upon his arbitrary verdict?

"If you chuse to seek an interview," continued Wieland, "you must make haste, for Pleyel informed me of his intention to set out this evening or to-morrow on a long journey."

No intelligence was less expected or less welcome than this. I had thrown myself in a window seat; but now, starting on my feet, I exclaimed, "Good heavens! what is it you say? a journey? whither? when?"

"I cannot say whither. It is a sudden resolution I believe. I did not hear of it till this morning. He promises to write to me as soon as he is settled."

I needed no further information as to the cause and issue of this journey. The scheme of happiness to which he had devoted his thoughts was blasted by the discovery of last night. My preference of another, and my unworthiness to be any longer the object of his adoration, were evinced by the same act and in the same moment. The thought of utter desertion, a desertion originating in such a cause, was the prelude to distraction. That Pleyel should abandon me forever, because I was blind to his excellence, because I coveted pollution, and wedded infamy, when, on the contrary, my heart was the shrine of all purity, and beat only for his sake, was a destiny which, as long as my life was in my own hands, I would by no means consent to endure.

I remembered that this evil was still preventable; that this fatal journey it was still in my power to procrastinate, or, perhaps, to occasion it to be laid aside. There were no impediments to a visit: I only dreaded lest the interview should be too long delayed. My brother befriended my impatience, and readily consented to furnish me with a chaise and servant to attend me. My purpose was to go immediately to Pleyel's farm, where his engagements usually detained him during the day.

Chapter XII

MY WAY lay through the city. I had scarcely entered it when I was seized with a general sensation of sickness. Every object grew dim and swam before my sight. It was with difficulty I prevented myself from sinking to the bottom of the carriage. I ordered myself to be carried to Mrs. Baynton's, in hope that an interval of repose would invigorate and refresh me. My distracted thoughts would allow me but little rest. Growing somewhat better in the afternoon, I resumed my journey.

My contemplations were limited to a few objects. I regarded my success, in the purpose which I had in view, as considerably doubtful. I depended, in some degree, on the suggestions of the moment, and on the materials which Pleyel himself should furnish me. When I reflected on the nature of the accusation, I burned with disdain. Would not truth, and the consciousness of innocence, render me triumphant? Should I not cast from me, with irresistible force, such atrocious imputations?

What an entire and mournful change has been effected in a few hours! The gulf that separates man from insects is not wider than that which severs the polluted from the chaste among women. Yesterday and to-day I am the same. There is a degree of depravity to which it is impossible for me to sink; yet, in the apprehension of another, my ancient and intimate associate, the perpetual witness of my actions, and partaker of my thoughts, I had ceased to be the same. My integrity was tarnished and withered in his eyes. I was the colleague of a murderer, and the paramour of a thief!

His opinion was not destitute of evidence: yet what proofs could reasonably avail to establish an opinion like this? If the sentiments corresponded not with the voice that was heard, the evidence was deficient; but this want of correspondence would have been supposed by me if I had been the auditor and Pleyel the criminal. But mimicry might still more plausibly have been employed to explain the scene. Alas! it is the fate of Clara Wieland to fall into the hands of a precipitate and inexorable judge.

But what, O man of mischief! is the tendency of thy thoughts? Frustrated in thy first design, thou wilt not forego the immolation of thy victim. To exterminate my reputation was all that remained to thee, and this my guardian has permitted. To dispossess Pleyel of this prejudice may be impossible; but if that be effected, it cannot be supposed that thy wiles are exhausted; thy cunning will discover innumerable avenues to the accomplishment of thy malignant purpose.

Why should I enter the lists against thee? Would to heaven I could disarm thy vengeance by my deprecations! When I think of all the resources with which nature and education have supplied thee; that thy form is a combination of steely fibres and organs of exquisite ductility and boundless compass, actuated by an intelligence gifted with infinite endowments, and comprehending all knowledge, I perceive that my doom is fixed. What obstacle will be able to divert thy zeal or repel thy efforts? That being who has hitherto protected me has borne testimony to the formidableness of thy attempts, since nothing less than supernatural interference could check thy career.

Musing on these thoughts, I arrived, towards the close of the day, at Pleyel's house. A month before, I had traversed the same path; but how different were my sensations! Now I was seeking the presence of one who regarded me as the most degenerate of human kind. I was to plead the cause of my innocence, against witnesses the most explicit and unerring, of those which support the fabric of human knowledge. The nearer I approached the crisis, the more did my confidence decay. When the chaise stopped at the door, my strength refused to support me, and I threw myself into the arms of an ancient female domestic. I had not courage to inquire whether her master was at home. I was tormented with fears that the projected journey was already undertaken. These fears were removed, by her asking me whether she should call her young master, who had just gone into his own room. I was somewhat revived by this intelligence, and resolved immediately to seek him there.

In my confusion of mind, I neglected to knock at the door,

but entered his apartment without previous notice. This abruptness was altogether involuntary. Absorbed in reflections of such unspeakable moment, I had no leisure to heed the niceties of punctilio. I discovered him standing with his back towards the entrance. A small trunk, with its lid raised, was before him, in which it seemed as if he had been busy in packing his clothes. The moment of my entrance, he was employed in gazing at something which he held in his hand.

I imagined that I fully comprehended this scene. The image which he held before him, and by which his attention was so deeply engaged, I doubted not to be my own. These preparations for his journey, the cause to which it was to be imputed, the hopelessness of success in the undertaking on which I had entered, rushed at once upon my feelings, and dissolved me into a flood of tears.

Startled by this sound, he dropped the lid of the trunk and turned. The solemn sadness that previously overspread his countenance, gave sudden way to an attitude and look of the most vehement astonishment. Perceiving me unable to uphold myself, he stepped towards me without speaking, and supported me by his arm. The kindness of this action called forth a new effusion from my eyes. Weeping was a solace to which, at that time, I had not grown familiar, and which, therefore, was peculiarly delicious. Indignation was no longer to be read in the features of my friend. They were pregnant with a mixture of wonder and pity. Their expression was easily interpreted. This visit, and these tears, were tokens of my penitence. The wretch whom he had stigmatized as incurably and obdurately wicked, now shewed herself susceptible of remorse, and had come to confess her guilt.

This persuasion had no tendency to comfort me. It only shewed me, with new evidence, the difficulty of the task which I had assigned myself. We were mutually silent. I had less power and less inclination than ever to speak. I extricated myself from his hold, and threw myself on a sofa. He placed himself by my side, and appeared to wait with impatience and anxiety for some beginning of the conversation. What could I say? If my mind had suggested any thing suitable to the occasion, my utterance was suffocated by tears.

Frequently he attempted to speak, but seemed deterred by

some degree of uncertainty as to the true nature of the scene. At length, in faltering accents he spoke:

"My friend! would to heaven I were still permitted to call you by that name. The image that I once adored existed only in my fancy; but though I cannot hope to see it realized, you may not be totally insensible to the horrors of that gulf into which you are about to plunge. What heart is forever exempt from the goadings of compunction and the influx of laudable propensities?

"I thought you accomplished and wise beyond the rest of women. Not a sentiment you uttered, not a look you assumed, that were not, in my apprehension, fraught with the sublimities of rectitude and the illuminations of genius. Deceit has some bounds. Your education could not be without influence. A vigorous understanding cannot be utterly devoid of virtue; but you could not counterfeit the powers of invention and reasoning. I was rash in my invectives. I will not, but with life, relinquish all hopes of you. I will shut out every proof that would tell me that your heart is incurably diseased.

"You come to restore me once more to happiness; to convince me that you have torn her mask from vice, and feel nothing but abhorrence for the part you have hitherto acted."

At these words my equanimity forsook me. For a moment I forgot the evidence from which Pleyel's opinions were derived, the benevolence of his remonstrances, and the grief which his accents bespoke; I was filled with indignation and horror at charges so black; I shrunk back and darted at him a look of disdain and anger. My passion supplied me with words.

"What detestable infatuation was it that led me hither! Why do I patiently endure these horrible insults! My offences exist only in your own distempered imagination: you are leagued with the traitor who assailed my life: you have vowed the destruction of my peace and honor. I deserve infamy for listening to calumnies so base!"

These words were heard by Pleyel without visible resentment. His countenance relapsed into its former gloom; but he did not even look at me. The ideas which had given place to my angry emotions returned, and once more melted me into tears. "O!" I exclaimed, in a voice broken by sobs, "what a task is mine! Compelled to hearken to charges which I feel to be false, but which I know to be believed by him that utters them; believed too not without evidence, which, though fallacious, is not unplausible.

"I came hither not to confess, but to vindicate. I know the source of your opinions. Wieland has informed me on what your suspicions are built. These suspicions are fostered by you as certainties; the tenor of my life, of all my conversations and letters, affords me no security; every sentiment that my tongue and my pen have uttered, bear testimony to the rectitude of my mind; but this testimony is rejected. I am condemned as brutally profligate: I am classed with the stupidly and sordidly wicked.

"And where are the proofs that must justify so foul and so improbable an accusation? You have overheard a midnight conference. Voices have saluted your ear, in which you imagine yourself to have recognized mine, and that of a detected villain. The sentiments expressed were not allowed to outweigh the casual or concerted resemblance of voice. Sentiments the reverse of all those whose influence my former life had attested, denoting a mind polluted by grovelling vices, and entering into compact with that of a thief and a murderer. The nature of these sentiments did not enable you to detect the cheat, did not suggest to you the possibility that my voice had been counterfeited by another.

"You were precipitate and prone to condemn. Instead of rushing on the impostors, and comparing the evidence of sight with that of hearing, you stood aloof, or you fled. My innocence would not now have stood in need of vindication, if this conduct had been pursued. That you did not pursue it, your present thoughts incontestibly prove. Yet this conduct might surely have been expected from Pleyel. That he would not hastily impute the blackest of crimes, that he would not couple my name with infamy, and cover me with ruin for inadequate or slight reasons, might reasonably have been expected." The sobs which convulsed my bosom would not suffer me to proceed.

Pleyel was for a moment affected. He looked at me with

some expression of doubt; but this quickly gave place to a mournful solemnity. He fixed his eyes on the floor as in reverie, and spoke:

"Two hours hence I am gone. Shall I carry away with me the sorrow that is now my guest? or shall that sorrow be accumulated tenfold? What is she that is now before me? Shall every hour supply me with new proofs of a wickedness beyond example? Already I deem her the most abandoned and detestable of human creatures. Her coming and her tears imparted a gleam of hope, but that gleam has vanished."

He now fixed his eyes upon me, and every muscle in his face trembled. His tone was hollow and terrible—"Thou knowest that I was a witness of your interview, yet thou comest hither to upbraid me for injustice! Thou canst look me in the face and say that I am deceived!—An inscrutable providence has fashioned thee for some end. Thou wilt live, no doubt, to fulfil the purposes of thy maker, if he repent not of his workmanship, and send not his vengeance to exterminate thee, ere the measure of thy days be full. Surely nothing in the shape of man can vie with thee!

"But I thought I had stifled this fury. I am not constituted thy judge. My office is to pity and amend, and not to punish and revile. I deemed myself exempt from all tempestuous passions. I had almost persuaded myself to weep over thy fall; but I am frail as dust, and mutable as water; I am calm, I am compassionate only in thy absence.—Make this house, this room, thy abode as long as thou wilt, but forgive me if I prefer solitude for the short time during which I shall stay." Saying this, he motioned as if to leave the apartment.

The stormy passions of this man affected me by sympathy. I ceased to weep. I was motionless and speechless with agony. I sat with my hands clasped, mutely gazing after him as he withdrew. I desired to detain him, but was unable to make any effort for that purpose, till he had passed out of the room. I then uttered an involuntary and piercing cry—"Pleyel! Art thou gone? Gone forever?"

At this summons he hastily returned. He beheld me wild, pale, gasping for breath, and my head already sinking on my bosom. A painful dizziness seized me, and I fainted away.

When I recovered, I found myself stretched on a bed in the

outer apartment, and Pleyel, with two female servants, standing beside it. All the fury and scorn which the countenance of the former lately expressed, had now disappeared, and was succeeded by the most tender anxiety. As soon as he perceived that my senses were returned to me, he clasped his hands, and exclaimed, "God be thanked! you are once more alive. I had almost despaired of your recovery. I fear I have been precipitate and unjust. My senses must have been the victims of some inexplicable and momentary phrenzy. Forgive me, I beseech you, forgive my reproaches. I would purchase conviction of your purity, at the price of my existence here and hereafter."

He once more, in a tone of the most fervent tenderness, besought me to be composed, and then left me to the care of the women.

Chapter XIII

HERE was wrought a surprizing change in my friend. What was it that had shaken conviction so firm? Had any thing occurred during my fit, adequate to produce so total an alteration? My attendants informed me that he had not left my apartment; that the unusual duration of my fit, and the failure, for a time, of all the means used for my recovery, had filled him with grief and dismay. Did he regard the effect which his reproaches had produced as a proof of my sincerity?

In this state of mind, I little regarded my languors of body. I rose and requested an interview with him before my departure, on which I was resolved, notwithstanding his earnest solicitation to spend the night at his house. He complied with my request. The tenderness which he had lately betrayed, had now disappeared, and he once more relapsed into a chilling solemnity.

I told him that I was preparing to return to my brother's; that I had come hither to vindicate my innocence from the foul aspersions which he had cast upon it. My pride had not taken refuge in silence or distance. I had not relied upon time, or the suggestions of his cooler thoughts, to confute his charges. Conscious as I was that I was perfectly guiltless, and entertaining some value for his good opinion, I could not prevail upon myself to believe that my efforts to make my innocence manifest, would be fruitless. Adverse appearances might be numerous and specious, but they were unquestionably false. I was willing to believe him sincere, that he made no charges which he himself did not believe; but these charges were destitute of truth. The grounds of his opinion were fallacious; and I desired an opportunity of detecting their fallacy. I entreated him to be explicit, and to give me a detail of what he had heard, and what he had seen.

At these words, my companion's countenance grew darker. He appeared to be struggling with his rage. He opened his lips to speak, but his accents died away ere they were formed. This conflict lasted for some minutes, but his fortitude was finally successful. He spoke as follows:

"I would fain put an end to this hateful scene: what I shall say, will be breath idly and unprofitably consumed. The clearest narrative will add nothing to your present knowledge. You are acquainted with the grounds of my opinion, and yet you avow yourself innocent: Why then should I rehearse these grounds? You are apprized of the character of Carwin: Why then should I enumerate the discoveries which I have made respecting him? Yet, since it is your request; since, considering the limitedness of human faculties, some error may possibly lurk in those appearances which I have witnessed, I will briefly relate what I know.

"Need I dwell upon the impressions which your conversation and deportment originally made upon me? We parted in childhood; but our intercourse, by letter, was copious and uninterrupted. How fondly did I anticipate a meeting with one whom her letters had previously taught me to consider as the first of women, and how fully realized were the expectations that I had formed!

"Here, said I, is a being, after whom sages may model their transcendent intelligence, and painters, their ideal beauty. Here is exemplified, that union between intellect and form, which has hitherto existed only in the conceptions of the poet. I have watched your eyes; my attention has hung upon your lips. I have questioned whether the enchantments of your voice were more conspicuous in the intricacies of melody, or the emphasis of rhetoric. I have marked the transitions of your discourse, the felicities of your expression, your refined argumentation, and glowing imagery; and been forced to acknowledge, that all delights were meagre and contemptible, compared with those connected with the audience and sight of you. I have contemplated your principles, and been astonished at the solidity of their foundation, and the perfection of their structure. I have traced you to your home. I have viewed you in relation to your servants, to your family, to your neighbours, and to the world. I have seen by what skilful arrangements you facilitate the performance of the most arduous and complicated duties; what daily accessions of strength your judicious discipline bestowed upon your memory; what correctness and abundance of knowledge was daily experienced by your unwearied application to books, and to writing. If she that possesses so much in the bloom of youth, will go on accumulating her stores, what, said I, is the picture she will display at a mature age?

"You know not the accuracy of my observation. I was desirous that others should profit by an example so rare. I therefore noted down, in writing, every particular of your conduct. I was anxious to benefit by an opportunity so seldom afforded us. I laboured not to omit the slightest shade, or the most petty line in your portrait. Here there was no other task incumbent on me but to copy; there was no need to exaggerate or overlook, in order to produce a more unexceptionable pattern. Here was a combination of harmonies and graces, incapable of diminution or accession without injury to its completeness.

"I found no end and no bounds to my task. No display of a scene like this could be chargeable with redundancy or superfluity. Even the colour of a shoe, the knot of a ribband, or your attitude in plucking a rose, were of moment to be recorded. Even the arrangements of your breakfast-table and your toilet have been amply displayed.

"I know that mankind are more easily enticed to virtue by example than by precept. I know that the absoluteness of a model, when supplied by invention, diminishes its salutary influence, since it is useless, we think, to strive after that which we know to be beyond our reach. But the picture which I drew was not a phantom; as a model, it was devoid of imperfection; and to aspire to that height which had been really attained, was by no means unreasonable. I had another and more interesting object in view. One existed who claimed all my tenderness. Here, in all its parts, was a model worthy of assiduous study, and indefatigable imitation. I called upon her, as she wished to secure and enhance my esteem, to mould her thoughts, her words, her countenance, her actions, by this pattern.

"The task was exuberant of pleasure, and I was deeply engaged in it, when an imp of mischief was let loose in the form of Carwin. I admired his powers and accomplishments. I did not wonder that they were admired by you. On the rectitude of your judgment, however, I relied to keep this admiration within discreet and scrupulous bounds. I assured myself, that the strangeness of his deportment, and the obscurity of his life, would teach you caution. Of all errors, my knowledge of your character informed me that this was least likely to befall you.

"You were powerfully affected by his first appearance; you were bewitched by his countenance and his tones; your description was ardent and pathetic: I listened to you with some emotions of surprize. The portrait you drew in his absence, and the intensity with which you mused upon it, were new and unexpected incidents. They bespoke a sensibility somewhat too vivid; but from which, while subjected to the guidance of an understanding like yours, there was nothing to dread.

"A more direct intercourse took place between you. I need not apologize for the solicitude which I entertained for your safety. He that gifted me with perception of excellence, compelled me to love it. In the midst of danger and pain, my contemplations have ever been cheered by your image. Every object in competition with you, was worthless and trivial. No price was too great by which your safety could be purchased. For that end, the sacrifice of ease, of health, and even of life, would cheerfully have been made by me. What wonder then, that I scrutinized the sentiments and deportment of this man with ceaseless vigilance; that I watched your words and your looks when he was present; and that I extracted cause for the deepest inquietudes, from every token which you gave of having put your happiness into this man's keeping?

"I was cautious in deciding. I recalled the various conversations in which the topics of love and marriage had been discussed. As a woman, young, beautiful, and independent, it behoved you to have fortified your mind with just principles on this subject. Your principles were eminently just. Had not their rectitude and their firmness been attested by your treatment of that specious seducer Dashwood? These principles, I was prone to believe, exempted you from danger in this new state of things. I was not the last to pay my homage to the unrivalled capacity, insinuation, and eloquence of this man. I have disguised, but could never stifle the conviction, that his eyes and voice had a witchcraft in them, which rendered him truly formidable: but I reflected on the ambiguous expression of his countenance—an ambiguity which you were the first to remark; on the cloud which obscured his character; and on the suspicious nature of that concealment which he studied; and concluded you to be safe. I denied the obvious construction to appearances. I referred your conduct to some principle which had not been hitherto disclosed, but which was reconcileable with those already known.

"I was not suffered to remain long in this suspense. One evening, you may recollect, I came to your house, where it was my purpose, as usual, to lodge, somewhat earlier than ordinary. I spied a light in your chamber as I approached from the outside, and on inquiring of Judith, was informed that you were writing. As your kinsman and friend, and fellow-lodger, I thought I had a right to be familiar. You were in your chamber, but your employment and the time were such as to make it no infraction of decorum to follow you thither. The spirit of mischievous gaiety possessed me. I proceeded on tiptoe. You did not perceive my entrance; and I advanced softly till I was able to overlook your shoulder.

"I had gone thus far in error, and had no power to recede. How cautiously should we guard against the first inroads of temptation! I knew that to pry into your papers was criminal; but I reflected that no sentiment of yours was of a nature which made it your interest to conceal it. You wrote much more than you permitted your friends to peruse. My curiosity was strong, and I had only to throw a glance upon the paper, to secure its gratification. I should never have deliberately committed an act like this. The slightest obstacle would have repelled me; but my eye glanced almost spontaneously upon the paper. I caught only parts of sentences; but my eyes comprehended more at a glance, because the characters were short-hand. I lighted on the words *summer-house*, *midnight*, and made out a passage which spoke of the propriety and of the effects to be expected from *another* interview. All this passed in less than a moment. I then checked myself, and made myself known to you, by a tap upon your shoulder.

"I could pardon and account for some trifling alarm; but your trepidation and blushes were excessive. You hurried the paper out of sight, and seemed too anxious to discover whether I knew the contents to allow yourself to make any inquiries. I wondered at these appearances of consternation, but did not reason on them until I had retired. When alone, these incidents suggested themselves to my reflections anew.

"To what scene, or what interview, I asked, did you allude? Your disappearance on a former evening, my tracing you to the recess in the bank, your silence on my first and second call, your vague answers and invincible embarrassment, when you, at length, ascended the hill, I recollected with new sur-prize. Could this be the summer-house alluded to? A certain timidity and consciousness had generally attended you, when this incident and this recess had been the subjects of conver-sation. Nay, I imagined that the last time that adventure was mentioned, which happened in the presence of Carwin, the countenance of the latter betrayed some emotion. Could the interview have been with him?

"This was an idea calculated to rouse every faculty to con-templation. An interview at that hour, in this darksome re-treat, with a man of this mysterious but formidable character; a clandestine interview, and one which you afterwards endea-voured with so much solicitude to conceal! It was a fearful and portentous occurrence. I could not measure his power, or fathom his designs. Had he rifled from you the secret of your love, and reconciled you to concealment and nocturnal meetings? I scarcely ever spent a night of more inquietude.

"I knew not how to act. The ascertainment of this man's character and views seemed to be, in the first place, necessary. Had he openly preferred his suit to you, we should have been impowered to make direct inquiries; but since he had chosen this obscure path, it seemed reasonable to infer that his char-acter was exceptionable. It, at least, subjected us to the ne-cessity of resorting to other means of information. Yet the improbability that you should commit a deed of such rashness, made me reflect anew upon the insufficiency of those grounds on which my suspicions had been built, and almost to con-demn myself for harbouring them.

"Though it was mere conjecture that the interview spoken of had taken place with Carwin, yet two ideas occurred to involve me in the most painful doubts. This man's reasonings might be so specious, and his artifices so profound, that, aided by the passion which you had conceived for him, he had finally succeeded; or his situation might be such as to justify the secrecy which you maintained. In neither case did my wildest reveries suggest to me, that your honor had been forfeited.

"I could not talk with you on this subject. If the imputation was false, its atrociousness would have justly drawn upon me your resentment, and I must have explained by what facts it had been suggested. If it were true, no benefit would follow from the mention of it. You had chosen to conceal it for some reasons, and whether these reasons were true or false, it was proper to discover and remove them in the first place. Finally, I acquiesced in the least painful supposition, trammelled as it was with perplexities, that Carwin was upright, and that, if the reasons of your silence were known, they would be found to be just.

Chapter XIV

"THREE DAYS have elapsed since this occurrence. I have been haunted by perpetual inquietude. To bring myself to regard Carwin without terror, and to acquiesce in the belief of your safety, was impossible. Yet to put an end to my doubts, seemed to be impracticable. If some light could be reflected on the actual situation of this man, a direct path would present itself. If he were, contrary to the tenor of his conversation, cunning and malignant, to apprize you of this, would be to place you in security. If he were merely unfortunate and innocent, most readily would I espouse his cause; and if his intentions were upright with regard to you, most eagerly would I sanctify your choice by my approbation.

"It would be vain to call upon Carwin for an avowal of his deeds. It was better to know nothing, than to be deceived by an artful tale. What he was unwilling to communicate, and this unwillingness had been repeatedly manifested, could never be extorted from him. Importunity might be appeased, or imposture effected by fallacious representations. To the rest of the world he was unknown. I had often made him the subject of discourse; but a glimpse of his figure in the street was the sum of their knowledge who knew most. None had ever seen him before, and received as new, the information which my intercourse with him in Valencia, and my present intercourse, enabled me to give.

"Wieland was your brother. If he had really made you the object of his courtship, was not a brother authorized to interfere and demand from him the confession of his views? Yet what were the grounds on which I had reared this supposition? Would they justify a measure like this? Surely not.

"In the course of my restless meditations, it occurred to me, at length, that my duty required me to speak to you, to confess the indecorum of which I had been guilty, and to state the reflections to which it had led me. I was prompted by no mean or selfish views. The heart within my breast was not more precious than your safety: most cheerfully would I have interposed my life between you and danger. Would you cherish resentment at my conduct? When acquainted with the motive which produced it, it would not only exempt me from censure, but entitle me to gratitude.

"Yesterday had been selected for the rehearsal of the newly-imported tragedy. I promised to be present. The state of my thoughts but little qualified me for a performer or auditor in such a scene; but I reflected that, after it was finished, I should return home with you, and should then enjoy an opportunity of discoursing with you fully on this topic. My resolution was not formed without a remnant of doubt, as to its propriety. When I left this house to perform the visit I had promised, my mind was full of apprehension and despondency. The dubiousness of the event of our conversation, fear that my interference was too late to secure your peace, and the uncertainty, to which hope gave birth, whether I had not erred in believing you devoted to this man, or, at least, in imagining that he had obtained your consent to midnight conferences, distracted me with contradictory opinions, and repugnant emotions.

"I can assign no reason for calling at Mrs. Baynton's. I had seen her in the morning, and knew her to be well. The concerted hour had nearly arrived, and yet I turned up the street which leads to her house, and dismounted at her door. I entered the parlour and threw myself in a chair. I saw and inquired for no one. My whole frame was overpowered by dreary and comfortless sensations. One idea possessed me wholly; the inexpressible importance of unveiling the designs and character of Carwin, and the utter improbability that this ever would be effected. Some instinct induced me to lay my hand upon a newspaper. I had perused all the general intelligence it contained in the morning, and at the same spot. The act was rather mechanical than voluntary.

"I threw a languid glance at the first column that presented itself. The first words which I read, began with the offer of a reward of three hundred guineas for the apprehension of a convict under sentence of death, who had escaped from Newgate prison in Dublin. Good heaven! how every fibre of my frame tingled when I proceeded to read that the name of the criminal was Francis Carwin!

"The descriptions of his person and address were minute.

His stature, hair, complexion, the extraordinary position and arrangement of his features, his aukward and disproportionate form, his gesture and gait, corresponded perfectly with those of our mysterious visitant. He had been found guilty in two indictments. One for the murder of the Lady Jane Conway, and the other for a robbery committed on the person of the honorable Mr. Ludloe.

"I repeatedly perused this passage. The ideas which flowed in upon my mind, affected me like an instant transition from death to life. The purpose dearest to my heart was thus effected, at a time and by means the least of all others within the scope of my foresight. But what purpose? Carwin was detected. Acts of the blackest and most sordid guilt had been committed by him. Here was evidence which imparted to my understanding the most luminous certainty. The name, visage, and deportment, were the same. Between the time of his escape, and his appearance among us, there was a sufficient agreement. Such was the man with whom I suspected you to maintain a clandestine correspondence. Should I not haste to snatch you from the talons of this vulture? Should I see you rushing to the verge of a dizzy precipice, and not stretch forth a hand to pull you back? I had no need to deliberate. I thrust the paper in my pocket, and resolved to obtain an immediate conference with you. For a time, no other image made its way to my understanding. At length, it occurred to me, that though the information I possessed was, in one sense, sufficient, yet if more could be obtained, more was desirable. This passage was copied from a British paper; part of it only, perhaps, was transcribed. The printer was in possession of the original.

"Towards his house I immediately turned my horse's head. He produced the paper, but I found nothing more than had already been seen. While busy in perusing it, the printer stood by my side. He noticed the object of which I was in search. 'Aye,' said he, 'that is a strange affair. I should never have met with it, had not Mr. Hallet sent to me the paper, with a particular request to republish that advertisement.'

"Mr. Hallet! What reasons could he have for making this request? Had the paper sent to him been accompanied by any information respecting the convict? Had he personal or extraordinary reasons for desiring its republication? This was to be known only in one way. I speeded to his house. In answer to my interrogations, he told me that Ludloe had formerly been in America, and that during his residence in this city, considerable intercourse had taken place between them. Hence a confidence arose, which has since been kept alive by occasional letters. He had lately received a letter from him, enclosing the newspaper from which this extract had been made. He put it into my hands, and pointed out the passages which related to Carwin.

"Ludloe confirms the facts of his conviction and escape; and adds, that he had reason to believe him to have embarked for America. He describes him in general terms, as the most incomprehensible and formidable among men; as engaged in schemes, reasonably suspected to be, in the highest degree, criminal, but such as no human intelligence is able to unravel: that his ends are pursued by means which leave it in doubt whether he be not in league with some infernal spirit: that his crimes have hitherto been perpetrated with the aid of some unknown but desperate accomplices: that he wages a perpetual war against the happiness of mankind, and sets his engines of destruction at work against every object that presents itself.

"This is the substance of the letter. Hallet expressed some surprize at the curiosity which was manifested by me on this occasion. I was too much absorbed by the ideas suggested by this letter, to pay attention to his remarks. I shuddered with the apprehension of the evil to which our indiscreet familiarity with this man had probably exposed us. I burnt with impatience to see you, and to do what in me lay to avert the calamity which threatened us. It was already five o'clock. Night was hastening, and there was no time to be lost. On leaving Mr. Hallet's house, who should meet me in the street, but Bertrand, the servant whom I left in Germany. His appearance and accoutrements bespoke him to have just alighted from a toilsome and long journey. I was not wholly without expectation of seeing him about this time, but no one was then more distant from my thoughts. You know what reasons I have for anxiety respecting scenes with which this man was conversant. Carwin was for a moment forgotten. In answer to my vehement inquiries, Bertrand produced a copious packet.

I shall not at present mention its contents, nor the measures which they obliged me to adopt. I bestowed a brief perusal on these papers, and having given some directions to Bertrand, resumed my purpose with regard to you. My horse I was obliged to resign to my servant, he being charged with a commission that required speed. The clock had struck ten, and Mettingen was five miles distant. I was to journey thither on foot. These circumstances only added to my expedition.

"As I passed swiftly along, I reviewed all the incidents accompanying the appearance and deportment of that man among us. Late events have been inexplicable and mysterious beyond any of which I have either read or heard. These events were coeval with Carwin's introduction. I am unable to explain their origin and mutual dependance; but I do not, on that account, believe them to have a supernatural original. Is not this man the agent? Some of them seem to be propitious; but what should I think of those threats of assassination with which you were lately alarmed? Bloodshed is the trade, and horror is the element of this man. The process by which the sympathies of nature are extinguished in our hearts, by which evil is made our good, and by which we are made susceptible of no activity but in the infliction, and no joy but in the spectacle of woes, is an obvious process. As to an alliance with evil geniuses, the power and the malice of dæmons have been a thousand times exemplified in human beings. There are no devils but those which are begotten upon selfishness, and reared by cunning.

"Now, indeed, the scene was changed. It was not his secret poniard that I dreaded. It was only the success of his efforts to make you a confederate in your own destruction, to make your will the instrument by which he might bereave you of liberty and honor.

"I took, as usual, the path through your brother's ground. I ranged with celerity and silence along the bank. I approached the fence, which divides Wieland's estate from yours. The recess in the bank being near this line, it being necessary for me to pass near it, my mind being tainted with inveterate suspicions concerning you; suspicions which were indebted for their strength to incidents connected with this spot; what wonder that it seized upon my thoughts!

"I leaped on the fence; but before I descended on the opposite side, I paused to survey the scene. Leaves dropping with dew, and glistening in the moon's rays, with no moving object to molest the deep repose, filled me with security and hope. I left the station at length, and tended forward. You were probably at rest. How should I communicate without alarming you, the intelligence of my arrival? An immediate interview was to be procured. I could not bear to think that a minute should be lost by remissness or hesitation. Should I knock at the door? or should I stand under your chamber windows, which I perceived to be open, and awaken you by my calls?

"These reflections employed me, as I passed opposite to the summer-house. I had scarcely gone by, when my ear caught a sound unusual at this time and place. It was almost too faint and too transient to allow me a distinct perception of it. I stopped to listen; presently it was heard again, and now it was somewhat in a louder key. It was laughter; and unquestionably produced by a female voice. That voice was familiar to my senses. It was yours.

"Whence it came, I was at first at a loss to conjecture; but this uncertainty vanished when it was heard the third time. I threw back my eyes towards the recess. Every other organ and limb was useless to me. I did not reason on the subject. I did not, in a direct manner, draw my conclusions from the hour, the place, the hilarity which this sound betokened, and the circumstance of having a companion, which it no less incontestably proved. In an instant, as it were, my heart was invaded with cold, and the pulses of life at a stand.

"Why should I go further? Why should I return? Should I not hurry to a distance from a sound, which, though formerly so sweet and delectable, was now more hideous than the shrieks of owls?

"I had no time to yield to this impulse. The thought of approaching and listening occurred to me. I had no doubt of which I was conscious. Yet my certainty was capable of increase. I was likewise stimulated by a sentiment that partook of rage. I was governed by an half-formed and tempestuous resolution to break in upon your interview, and strike you dead with my upbraiding.

"I approached with the utmost caution. When I reached the edge of the bank immediately above the summer-house, I thought I heard voices from below, as busy in conversation. The steps in the rock are clear of bushy impediments. They allowed me to descend into a cavity beside the building without being detected. Thus to lie in wait could only be justified by the momentousness of the occasion."

Here Pleyel paused in his narrative, and fixed his eyes upon me. Situated as I was, my horror and astonishment at this tale gave way to compassion for the anguish which the countenance of my friend betrayed. I reflected on his force of understanding. I reflected on the powers of my enemy. I could easily divine the substance of the conversation that was overheard. Carwin had constructed his plot in a manner suited to the characters of those whom he had selected for his victims. I saw that the convictions of Pleyel were immutable. I forbore to struggle against the storm, because I saw that all struggles would be fruitless. I was calm; but my calmness was the torpor of despair, and not the tranquillity of fortitude. It was calmness invincible by any thing that his grief and his fury could suggest to Pleyel. He resumed—

"Woman! wilt thou hear me further? Shall I go on to repeat the conversation? Is it shame that makes thee tongue-tied? Shall I go on? or art thou satisfied with what has been already said?"

I bowed my head. "Go on," said I. "I make not this request in the hope of undeceiving you. I shall no longer contend with my own weakness. The storm is let loose, and I shall peaceably submit to be driven by its fury. But go on. This conference will end only with affording me a clearer foresight of my destiny; but that will be some satisfaction, and I will not part without it."

Why, on hearing these words, did Pleyel hesitate? Did some unlooked-for doubt insinuate itself into his mind? Was his belief suddenly shaken by my looks, or my words, or by some newly recollected circumstance? Whencesoever it arose, it could not endure the test of deliberation. In a few minutes the flame of resentment was again lighted up in his bosom. He proceeded with his accustomed vehemence—

"I hate myself for this folly. I can find no apology for this tale. Yet I am irresistibly impelled to relate it. She that hears me is apprized of every particular. I have only to repeat to her her own words. She will listen with a tranquil air, and the spectacle of her obduracy will drive me to some desperate act. Why then should I persist! yet persist I must."

Again he paused. "No," said he, "it is impossible to repeat your avowals of love, your appeals to former confessions of your tenderness, to former deeds of dishonor, to the circumstances of the first interview that took place between you. It was on that night when I traced you to this recess. Thither had he enticed you, and there had you ratified an unhallowed compact by admitting him—

"Great God! Thou witnessedst the agonies that tore my bosom at that moment! Thou witnessedst my efforts to repel the testimony of my ears! It was in vain that you dwelt upon the confusion which my unlooked-for summons excited in you; the tardiness with which a suitable excuse occurred to you; your resentment that my impertinent intrusion had put an end to that charming interview: A disappointment for which you endeavoured to compensate yourself, by the frequency and duration of subsequent meetings.

"In vain you dwelt upon incidents of which you only could be conscious; incidents that occurred on occasions on which none beside your own family were witnesses. In vain was your discourse characterized by peculiarities inimitable of sentiment and language. My conviction was effected only by an accumulation of the same tokens. I yielded not but to evidence which took away the power to withhold my faith.

"My sight was of no use to me. Beneath so thick an umbrage, the darkness was intense. Hearing was the only avenue to information, which the circumstances allowed to be open. I was couched within three feet of you. Why should I approach nearer? I could not contend with your betrayer. What could be the purpose of a contest? You stood in no need of a protector. What could I do, but retire from the spot overwhelmed with confusion and dismay? I sought my chamber, and endeavoured to regain my composure. The door of the house, which I found open, your subsequent entrance, closing, and fastening it and going into your chamber, which had been thus long deserted, were only confirmations of the truth.

"Why should I paint the tempestuous fluctuation of my thoughts between grief and revenge, between rage and despair? Why should I repeat my vows of eternal implacability and persecution, and the speedy recantation of these vows?

"I have said enough. You have dismissed me from a place in your esteem. What I think, and what I feel, is of no importance in your eyes. May the duty which I owe myself enable me to forget your existence. In a few minutes I go hence. Be the maker of your fortune, and may adversity instruct you in that wisdom, which education was unable to impart to you."

These were the last words which Pleyel uttered. He left the room, and my new emotions enabled me to witness his departure without any apparent loss of composure. As I sat alone, I ruminated on these incidents. Nothing was more evident than that I had taken an eternal leave of happiness. Life was a worthless thing, separate from that good which had now been wrested from me; yet the sentiment that now possessed me had no tendency to palsy my exertions, and overbear my strength. I noticed that the light was declining, and perceived the propriety of leaving this house. I placed myself again in the chaise, and returned slowly towards the city.

Chapter XV

BEFORE I reached the city it was dusk. It was my purpose to spend the night at Mettingen. I was not solicitous, as long as I was attended by a faithful servant, to be there at an early hour. My exhausted strength required me to take some refreshment. With this view, and in order to pay respect to one whose affection for me was truly maternal, I stopped at Mrs. Baynton's. She was absent from home; but I had scarcely entered the house when one of her domestics presented me a letter. I opened and read as follows:

"To Clara Wieland,

"What shall I say to extenuate the misconduct of last night? It is my duty to repair it to the utmost of my power, but the only way in which it can be repaired, you will not, I fear, be prevailed on to adopt. It is by granting me an interview, at your own house, at eleven o'clock this night. I have no means of removing any fears that you may entertain of my designs, but my simple and solemn declarations. These, after what has passed between us, you may deem unworthy of confidence. I cannot help it. My folly and rashness has left me no other resource. I will be at your door by that hour. If you chuse to admit me to a conference, provided that conference has no witnesses, I will disclose to you particulars, the knowledge of which is of the utmost importance to your happiness. Farewell.

CARWIN."

What a letter was this! A man known to be an assassin and robber; one capable of plotting against my life and my fame; detected lurking in my chamber, and avowing designs the most flagitious and dreadful, now solicits me to grant him a midnight interview! To admit him alone into my presence! Could he make this request with the expectation of my compliance? What had he seen in me, that could justify him in admitting so wild a belief? Yet this request is preferred with the utmost gravity. It is not unaccompanied by an appearance of uncommon earnestness. Had the misconduct to which he alludes been a slight incivility, and the interview requested to take place in the midst of my friends, there would have been no extravagance in the tenor of this letter; but, as it was, the writer had surely been bereft of his reason.

I perused this epistle frequently. The request it contained might be called audacious or stupid, if it had been made by a different person; but from Carwin, who could not be unaware of the effect which it must naturally produce, and of the manner in which it would unavoidably be treated, it was perfectly inexplicable. He must have counted on the success of some plot, in order to extort my assent. None of those motives by which I am usually governed would ever have persuaded me to meet any one of his sex, at the time and place which he had prescribed. Much less would I consent to a meeting with a man, tainted with the most detestable crimes, and by whose arts my own safety had been so imminently endangered, and my happiness irretrievably destroyed. I shuddered at the idea that such a meeting was possible. I felt some reluctance to approach a spot which he still visited and haunted.

Such were the ideas which first suggested themselves on the perusal of the letter. Meanwhile, I resumed my journey. My thoughts still dwelt upon the same topic. Gradually from ruminating on this epistle, I reverted to my interview with Pleyel. I recalled the particulars of the dialogue to which he had been an auditor. My heart sunk anew on viewing the inextricable complexity of this deception, and the inauspicious concurrence of events, which tended to confirm him in his error. When he approached my chamber door, my terror kept me mute. He put his ear, perhaps, to the crevice, but it caught the sound of nothing human. Had I called, or made any token that denoted some one to be within, words would have ensued; and as omnipresence was impossible, this discovery, and the artless narrative of what had just passed, would have saved me from his murderous invectives. He went into his chamber, and after some interval, I stole across the entry and down the stairs, with inaudible steps. Having secured the outer doors, I returned with less circumspection. He heard me not when I descended; but my returning steps were easily distinguished. Now, he thought, was the guilty interview at an end. In what other way was it possible for him to construe these signals?

How fallacious and precipitate was my decision! Carwin's plot owed its success to a coincidence of events scarcely credible. The balance was swayed from its equipoise by a hair. Had I even begun the conversation with an account of what befel me in my chamber, my previous interview with Wieland would have taught him to suspect me of imposture; yet, if I were discoursing with this ruffian, when Pleyel touched the lock of my chamber door, and when he shut his own door with so much violence, how, he might ask, should I be able to relate these incidents? Perhaps he had withheld the knowledge of these circumstances from my brother, from whom, therefore, I could not obtain it, so that my innocence would have thus been irresistibly demonstrated.

The first impulse which flowed from these ideas was to return upon my steps, and demand once more an interview; but he was gone: his parting declarations were remembered.

Pleyel, I exclaimed, thou art gone for ever! Are thy mistakes beyond the reach of detection? Am I helpless in the midst of this snare? The plotter is at hand. He even speaks in the style of penitence. He solicits an interview which he promises shall end in the disclosure of something momentous to my happiness. What can he say which will avail to turn aside this evil? But why should his remorse be feigned? I have done him no injury. His wickedness is fertile only of despair; and the billows of remorse will some time overbear him. Why may not this event have already taken place? Why should I refuse to see him?

This idea was present, as it were, for a moment. I suddenly recoiled from it, confounded at that frenzy which could give even momentary harbour to such a scheme; yet presently it returned. At length I even conceived it to deserve deliberation. I questioned whether it was not proper to admit, at a lonely spot, in a sacred hour, this man of tremendous and inscrutable attributes, this performer of horrid deeds, and whose presence was predicted to call down unheard-of and unutterable horrors.

What was it that swayed me? I felt myself divested of the power to will contrary to the motives that determined me to seek his presence. My mind seemed to be split into separate parts, and these parts to have entered into furious and implacable contention. These tumults gradually subsided. The reasons why I should confide in that interposition which had hitherto defended me; in those tokens of compunction which this letter contained; in the efficacy of this interview to restore its spotlessness to my character, and banish all illusions from the mind of my friend, continually acquired new evidence and new strength.

What should I fear in his presence? This was unlike an artifice intended to betray me into his hands. If it were an artifice, what purpose would it serve? The freedom of my mind was untouched, and that freedom would defy the assaults of blandishments or magic. Force was I not able to repel. On the former occasion my courage, it is true, had failed at the imminent approach of danger; but then I had not enjoyed opportunities of deliberation; I had foreseen nothing; I was sunk into imbecility by my previous thoughts; I had been the victim of recent disappointments and anticipated ills: Witness my infatuation in opening the closet in opposition to divine injunctions.

Now, perhaps, my courage was the offspring of a no less erring principle. Pleyel was for ever lost to me. I strove in vain to assume his person, and suppress my resentment; I strove in vain to believe in the assuaging influence of time, to look forward to the birth-day of new hopes, and the re-exaltation of that luminary, of whose effulgencies I had so long and so liberally partaken.

What had I to suffer worse than was already inflicted?

Was not Carwin my foe? I owed my untimely fate to his treason. Instead of flying from his presence, ought I not to devote all my faculties to the gaining of an interview, and compel him to repair the ills of which he has been the author? Why should I suppose him impregnable to argument? Have I not reason on my side, and the power of imparting conviction? Cannot he be made to see the justice of unravelling the maze in which Pleyel is bewildered?

He may, at least, be accessible to fear. Has he nothing to fear from the rage of an injured woman? But suppose him inaccessible to such inducements; suppose him to persist in all his flagitious purposes; are not the means of defence and resistance in my power?

In the progress of such thoughts, was the resolution at last formed. I hoped that the interview was sought by him for a laudable end; but, be that as it would, I trusted that, by energy of reasoning or of action, I should render it auspicious, or, at least, harmless.

Such a determination must unavoidably fluctuate. The poet's chaos was no unapt emblem of the state of my mind. A torment was awakened in my bosom, which I foresaw would end only when this interview was past, and its consequences fully experienced. Hence my impatience for the arrival of the hour which had been prescribed by Carwin.

Meanwhile, my meditations were tumultuously active. New impediments to the execution of the scheme were speedily suggested. I had apprized Catharine of my intention to spend this and many future nights with her. Her husband was informed of this arrangement, and had zealously approved it. Eleven o'clock exceeded their hour of retiring. What excuse should I form for changing my plan? Should I shew this letter to Wieland, and submit myself to his direction? But I knew in what way he would decide. He would fervently dissuade me from going. Nay, would he not do more? He was apprized of the offences of Carwin, and of the reward offered for his apprehension. Would he not seize this opportunity of executing justice on a criminal?

This idea was new. I was plunged once more into doubt. Did not equity enjoin me thus to facilitate his arrest? No. I disdained the office of betrayer. Carwin was unapprized of his danger, and his intentions were possibly beneficent. Should I station guards about the house, and make an act, intended perhaps for my benefit, instrumental to his own destruction? Wieland might be justified in thus employing the knowledge which I should impart, but I, by imparting it, should pollute myself with more hateful crimes than those undeservedly imputed to me. This scheme, therefore, I unhesitatingly rejected. The views with which I should return to my own house, it would therefore be necessary to conceal. Yet some pretext must be invented. I had never been initiated into the trade of lying. Yet what but falsehood was a deliberate suppression of the truth? To deceive by silence or by words is the same.

Yet what would a lie avail me? What pretext would justify

this change in my plan? Would it not tend to confirm the imputations of Pleyel? That I should voluntarily return to an house in which honor and life had so lately been endangered, could be explained in no way favorable to my integrity.

These reflections, if they did not change, at least suspended my decision. In this state of uncertainty I alighted at the *Hut*. We gave this name to the house tenanted by the farmer and his servants, and which was situated on the verge of my brother's ground, and at a considerable distance from the mansion. The path to the mansion was planted by a double row of walnuts. Along this path I proceeded alone. I entered the parlour, in which was a light just expiring in the socket. There was no one in the room. I perceived by the clock that stood against the wall, that it was near eleven. The lateness of the hour startled me. What had become of the family? They were usually retired an hour before this; but the unextinguished taper, and the unbarred door were indications that they had not retired. I again returned to the hall, and passed from one room to another, but still encountered not a human being.

I imagined that, perhaps, the lapse of a few minutes would explain these appearances. Meanwhile I reflected that the preconcerted hour had arrived. Carwin was perhaps waiting my approach. Should I immediately retire to my own house, no one would be apprized of my proceeding. Nay, the interview might pass, and I be enabled to return in half an hour. Hence no necessity would arise for dissimulation.

I was so far influenced by these views that I rose to execute this design; but again the unusual condition of the house occurred to me, and some vague solicitude as to the condition of the family. I was nearly certain that my brother had not retired; but by what motives he could be induced to desert his house thus unseasonably, I could by no means divine. Louisa Conway, at least, was at home, and had, probably, retired to her chamber; perhaps she was able to impart the information I wanted.

I went to her chamber, and found her asleep. She was delighted and surprized at my arrival, and told me with how much impatience and anxiety my brother and his wife had waited my coming. They were fearful that some mishap had

befallen me, and had remained up longer than the usual period. Notwithstanding the lateness of the hour, Catharine
would not resign the hope of seeing me. Louisa said she had
left them both in the parlour, and she knew of no cause for
their absence.

As yet I was not without solicitude on account of their personal safety. I was far from being perfectly at ease on that
head, but entertained no distinct conception of the danger
that impended over them. Perhaps to beguile the moments of
my long protracted stay, they had gone to walk upon the
bank. The atmosphere, though illuminated only by the star-
light, was remarkably serene. Meanwhile the desireableness of
an interview with Carwin again returned, and I finally resolved
to seek it.

I passed with doubting and hasty steps along the path. My
dwelling, seen at a distance, was gloomy and desolate. It had
no inhabitant, for my servant, in consequence of my new arrangement, had gone to Mettingen. The temerity of this attempt began to shew itself in more vivid colours to my
understanding. Whoever has pointed steel is not without
arms; yet what must have been the state of my mind when I
could meditate, without shuddering, on the use of a murderous weapon, and believe myself secure merely because I was
capable of being made so by the death of another? Yet this
was not my state. I felt as if I was rushing into deadly toils,
without the power of pausing or receding.

Chapter XVI

As soon as I arrived in sight of the front of the house, my attention was excited by a light from the window of my own chamber. No appearance could be less explicable. A meeting was expected with Carwin, but that he pre-occupied my chamber, and had supplied himself with light, was not to be believed. What motive could influence him to adopt this conduct? Could I proceed until this was explained? Perhaps, if I should proceed to a distance in front, some one would be visible. A sidelong but feeble beam from the window, fell upon the piny copse which skirted the bank. As I eyed it, it suddenly became mutable, and after flitting to and fro, for a short time, it vanished. I turned my eye again toward the window, and perceived that the light was still there; but the change which I had noticed was occasioned by a change in the position of the lamp or candle within. Hence, that some person was there was an unavoidable inference.

I paused to deliberate on the propriety of advancing. Might I not advance cautiously, and, therefore, without danger? Might I not knock at the door, or call, and be apprized of the nature of my visitant before I entered? I approached and listened at the door, but could hear nothing. I knocked at first timidly, but afterwards with loudness. My signals were unnoticed. I stepped back and looked, but the light was no longer discernible. Was it suddenly extinguished by a human agent? What purpose but concealment was intended? Why was the illumination produced, to be thus suddenly brought to an end? And why, since some one was there, had silence been observed?

These were questions, the solution of which may be readily supposed to be entangled with danger. Would not this danger, when measured by a woman's fears, expand into gigantic dimensions? Menaces of death; the stunning exertions of a warning voice; the known and unknown attributes of Carwin; our recent interview in this chamber; the pre-appointment of a meeting at this place and hour, all thronged into my memory. What was to be done?

Courage is no definite or stedfast principle. Let that man who shall purpose to assign motives to the actions of another, blush at his folly and forbear. Not more presumptuous would it be to attempt the classification of all nature, and the scanning of supreme intelligence. I gazed for a minute at the window, and fixed my eyes, for a second minute, on the ground. I drew forth from my pocket, and opened, a penknife. This, said I, be my safe-guard and avenger. The assailant shall perish, or myself shall fall.

I had locked up the house in the morning, but had the key of the kitchen door in my pocket. I, therefore, determined to gain access behind. Thither I hastened, unlocked and entered. All was lonely, darksome, and waste. Familiar as I was with every part of my dwelling, I easily found my way to a closet, drew forth a taper, a flint, tinder, and steel, and, in a moment, as it were, gave myself the guidance and protection of light.

What purpose did I meditate? Should I explore my way to my chamber, and confront the being who had dared to intrude into this recess, and had laboured for concealment? By putting out the light did he seek to hide himself, or mean only to circumvent my incautious steps? Yet was it not more probable that he desired my absence by thus encouraging the supposition that the house was unoccupied? I would see this man in spite of all impediments; ere I died, I would see his face, and summon him to penitence and retribution; no matter at what cost an interview was purchased. Reputation and life might be wrested from me by another, but my rectitude and honor were in my own keeping, and were safe.

I proceeded to the foot of the stairs. At such a crisis my thoughts may be supposed at no liberty to range; yet vague images rushed into my mind, of the mysterious interposition which had been experienced on the last night. My case, at present, was not dissimilar; and, if my angel were not weary of fruitless exertions to save, might not a new warning be expected? Who could say whether his silence were ascribable to the absence of danger, or to his own absence?

In this state of mind, no wonder that a shivering cold crept through my veins; that my pause was prolonged; and, that a fearful glance was thrown backward.

Alas! my heart droops, and my fingers are enervated; my

ideas are vivid, but my language is faint; now know I what it is to entertain incommunicable sentiments. The chain of subsequent incidents is drawn through my mind, and being linked with those which forewent, by turns rouse up agonies and sink me into hopelessness.

Yet I will persist to the end. My narrative may be invaded by inaccuracy and confusion; but if I live no longer, I will, at least, live to complete it. What but ambiguities, abruptnesses, and dark transitions, can be expected from the historian who is, at the same time, the sufferer of these disasters?

I have said that I cast a look behind. Some object was expected to be seen, or why should I have gazed in that direction? Two senses were at once assailed. The same piercing exclamation of *"hold! hold!"* was uttered within the same distance of my ear. This it was that I heard. The airy undulation, and the shock given to my nerves, were real. Whether the spectacle which I beheld existed in my fancy or without, might be doubted.

I had not closed the door of the apartment I had just left. The stair-case, at the foot of which I stood, was eight or ten feet from the door, and attached to the wall through which the door led. My view, therefore, was sidelong, and took in no part of the room.

Through this aperture was an head thrust and drawn back with so much swiftness, that the immediate conviction was, that thus much of a form, ordinarily invisible, had been unshrouded. The face was turned towards me. Every muscle was tense; the forehead and brows were drawn into vehement expression; the lips were stretched as in the act of shrieking; and the eyes emitted sparks, which, no doubt, if I had been unattended by a light, would have illuminated like the corruscations of a meteor. The sound and the vision were present, and departed together at the same instant; but the cry was blown into my ear, while the face was many paces distant.

This face was well suited to a being whose performances exceeded the standard of humanity, and yet its features were akin to those I had before seen. The image of Carwin was blended in a thousand ways with the stream of my thoughts. This visage was, perhaps, pourtrayed by my fancy. If so, it will excite no surprize that some of his lineaments were now discovered. Yet affinities were few and unconspicuous, and were lost amidst the blaze of opposite qualities.

What conclusion could I form? Be the face human or not, the intimation was imparted from above. Experience had evinced the benignity of that being who gave it. Once he had interposed to shield me from harm, and subsequent events demonstrated the usefulness of that interposition. Now was I again warned to forbear. I was hurrying to the verge of the same gulf, and the same power was exerted to recall my steps. Was it possible for me not to obey? Was I capable of holding on in the same perilous career? Yes. Even of this I was capable!

The intimation was imperfect: it gave no form to my danger, and prescribed no limits to my caution. I had formerly neglected it, and yet escaped. Might I not trust to the same issue? This idea might possess, though imperceptibly, some influence. I persisted; but it was not merely on this account. I cannot delineate the motives that led me on. I now speak as if no remnant of doubt existed in my mind as to the supernal origin of these sounds; but this is owing to the imperfection of my language, for I only mean that the belief was more permanent, and visited more frequently my sober meditations than its opposite. The immediate effects served only to undermine the foundations of my judgment and precipitate my resolutions.

I must either advance or return. I chose the former, and began to ascend the stairs. The silence underwent no second interruption. My chamber door was closed, but unlocked, and, aided by vehement efforts of my courage, I opened and looked in.

No hideous or uncommon object was discernible. The danger, indeed, might easily have lurked out of sight, have sprung upon me as I entered, and have rent me with his iron talons; but I was blind to this fate, and advanced, though cautiously, into the room.

Still every thing wore its accustomed aspect. Neither lamp nor candle was to be found. Now, for the first time, suspicions were suggested as to the nature of the light which I had seen. Was it possible to have been the companion of that supernatural visage; a meteorous refulgence producible at the will of him to whom that visage belonged, and partaking of the nature of that which accompanied my father's death?

The closet was near, and I remembered the complicated horrors of which it had been productive. Here, perhaps, was inclosed the source of my peril, and the gratification of my curiosity. Should I adventure once more to explore its recesses? This was a resolution not easily formed. I was suspended in thought: when glancing my eye on a table, I perceived a written paper. Carwin's hand was instantly recognized, and snatching up the paper, I read as follows:—

"There was folly in expecting your compliance with my invitation. Judge how I was disappointed in finding another in your place. I have waited, but to wait any longer would be perilous. I shall still seek an interview, but it must be at a different time and place: meanwhile, I will write this—How will you bear—How inexplicable will be this transaction!—An event so unexpected—a sight so horrible!"

Such was this abrupt and unsatisfactory script. The ink was yet moist, the hand was that of Carwin. Hence it was to be inferred that he had this moment left the apartment, or was still in it. I looked back, on the sudden expectation of seeing him behind me.

What other did he mean? What transaction had taken place adverse to my expectations? What sight was about to be exhibited? I looked around me once more, but saw nothing which indicated strangeness. Again I remembered the closet, and was resolved to seek in that the solution of these mysteries. Here, perhaps, was inclosed the scene destined to awaken my horrors and baffle my foresight.

I have already said, that the entrance into this closet was beside my bed, which, on two sides, was closely shrouded by curtains. On that side nearest the closet, the curtain was raised. As I passed along I cast my eye thither. I started, and looked again. I bore a light in my hand, and brought it nearer my eyes, in order to dispel any illusive mists that might have hovered before them. Once more I fixed my eyes upon the bed, in hope that this more stedfast scrutiny would annihilate the object which before seemed to be there.

This then was the sight which Carwin had predicted! This was the event which my understanding was to find inexplicable! This was the fate which had been reserved for me, but which, by some untoward chance, had befallen on another!

I had not been terrified by empty menaces. Violation and death awaited my entrance into this chamber. Some inscrutable chance had led *her* hither before me, and the merciless fangs of which I was designed to be the prey, had mistaken their victim, and had fixed themselves in *her* heart. But where was my safety? Was the mischief exhausted or flown? The steps of the assassin had just been here; they could not be far off; in a moment he would rush into my presence, and I should perish under the same polluting and suffocating grasp!

My frame shook, and my knees were unable to support me. I gazed alternately at the closet door and at the door of my room. At one of these avenues would enter the exterminator of my honor and my life. I was prepared for defence; but now that danger was imminent, my means of defence, and my power to use them were gone. I was not qualified, by education and experience, to encounter perils like these: or, perhaps, I was powerless because I was again assaulted by surprize, and had not fortified my mind by foresight and previous reflection against a scene like this.

Fears for my own safety again yielded place to reflections on the scene before me. I fixed my eyes upon her countenance. My sister's well-known and beloved features could not be concealed by convulsion or lividness. What direful illusion led thee hither? Bereft of thee, what hold on happiness remains to thy offspring and thy spouse? To lose thee by a common fate would have been sufficiently hard; but thus suddenly to perish—to become the prey of this ghastly death! How will a spectacle like this be endured by Wieland? To die beneath his grasp would not satisfy thy enemy. This was mercy to the evils which he previously made thee suffer! After these evils death was a boon which thou besoughtest him to grant. He entertained no enmity against thee: I was the object of his treason; but by some tremendous mistake his fury was misplaced. But how camest thou hither? and where was Wieland in thy hour of distress?

I approached the corpse: I lifted the still flexible hand, and kissed the lips which were breathless. Her flowing drapery was discomposed. I restored it to order, and seating myself on the bed, again fixed stedfast eyes upon her countenance. I cannot distinctly recollect the ruminations of that moment. I saw confusedly, but forcibly, that every hope was extinguished with the life of _Catharine_. All happiness and dignity must henceforth be banished from the house and name of Wieland: all that remained was to linger out in agonies a short existence; and leave to the world a monument of blasted hopes and changeable fortune. Pleyel was already lost to me; yet, while Catharine lived life was not a detestable possession: but now, severed from the companion of my infancy, the partaker of all my thoughts, my cares, and my wishes, I was like one set afloat upon a stormy sea, and hanging his safety upon a plank; night was closing upon him, and an unexpected surge had torn him from his hold and overwhelmed him forever.

Chapter XVII

I HAD no inclination nor power to move from this spot. For more than an hour, my faculties and limbs seemed to be deprived of all activity. The door below creaked on its hinges, and steps ascended the stairs. My wandering and confused thoughts were instantly recalled by these sounds, and dropping the curtain of the bed, I moved to a part of the room where any one who entered should be visible; such are the vibrations of sentiment, that notwithstanding the seeming fulfilment of my fears, and increase of my danger, I was conscious, on this occasion, to no turbulence but that of curiosity.

At length he entered the apartment, and I recognized my brother. It was the same Wieland whom I had ever seen. Yet his features were pervaded by a new expression. I supposed him unacquainted with the fate of his wife, and his appearance confirmed this persuasion. A brow expanding into exultation I had hitherto never seen in him, yet such a brow did he now wear. Not only was he unapprized of the disaster that had happened, but some joyous occurrence had betided. What a reverse was preparing to annihilate his transitory bliss! No husband ever doated more fondly, for no wife ever claimed so boundless a devotion. I was not uncertain as to the effects to flow from the discovery of her fate. I confided not at all in the efforts of his reason or his piety. There were few evils which his modes of thinking would not disarm of their sting; but here, all opiates to grief, and all compellers of patience were vain. This spectacle would be unavoidably followed by the outrages of desperation, and a rushing to death.

For the present, I neglected to ask myself what motive brought him hither. I was only fearful of the effects to flow from the sight of the dead. Yet could it be long concealed from him? Some time and speedily he would obtain this knowledge. No stratagems could considerably or usefully prolong his ignorance. All that could be sought was to take away the abruptness of the change, and shut out the confusion of despair, and the inroads of madness: but I knew my brother, and knew that all exertions to console him would be fruitless.

What could I say? I was mute, and poured forth those tears on his account, which my own unhappiness had been unable to extort. In the midst of my tears, I was not unobservant of his motions. These were of a nature to rouse some other sentiment than grief, or, at least, to mix with it a portion of astonishment.

His countenance suddenly became troubled. His hands were clasped with a force that left the print of his nails in his flesh. His eyes were fixed on my feet. His brain seemed to swell beyond its continent. He did not cease to breathe, but his breath was stifled into groans. I had never witnessed the hurricane of human passions. My element had, till lately, been all sunshine and calm. I was unconversant with the altitudes and energies of sentiment, and was transfixed with inexplicable horror by the symptoms which I now beheld.

After a silence and a conflict which I could not interpret, he lifted his eyes to heaven, and in broken accents exclaimed, "This is too much! Any victim but this, and thy will be done. Have I not sufficiently attested my faith and my obedience? She that is gone, they that have perished, were linked with my soul by ties which only thy command would have broken; but here is sanctity and excellence surpassing human. This workmanship is thine, and it cannot be thy will to heap it into ruins."

Here suddenly unclasping his hands, he struck one of them against his forehead, and continued—"Wretch! who made thee quicksighted in the councils of thy Maker? Deliverance from mortal fetters is awarded to this being, and thou art the minister of this decree."

So saying, Wieland advanced towards me. His words and his motions were without meaning, except on one supposition. The death of Catharine was already known to him, and that knowledge, as might have been suspected, had destroyed his reason. I had feared nothing less; but now that I beheld the extinction of a mind the most luminous and penetrating that ever dignified the human form, my sensations were fraught with new and insupportable anguish.

I had not time to reflect in what way my own safety would be affected by this revolution, or what I had to dread from the wild conceptions of a mad-man. He advanced towards me.

Some hollow noises were wafted by the breeze. Confused clamours were succeeded by many feet traversing the grass, and then crowding into the piazza.

These sounds suspended my brother's purpose, and he stood to listen. The signals multiplied and grew louder; perceiving this, he turned from me, and hurried out of my sight. All about me was pregnant with motives to astonishment. My sister's corpse, Wieland's frantic demeanour, and, at length, this crowd of visitants so little accorded with my foresight, that my mental progress was stopped. The impulse had ceased which was accustomed to give motion and order to my thoughts.

Footsteps thronged upon the stairs, and presently many faces shewed themselves within the door of my apartment. These looks were full of alarm and watchfulness. They pryed into corners as if in search of some fugitive; next their gaze was fixed upon me, and betokened all the vehemence of terror and pity. For a time I questioned whether these were not shapes and faces like that which I had seen at the bottom of the stairs, creatures of my fancy or airy existences.

My eye wandered from one to another, till at length it fell on a countenance which I well knew. It was that of Mr. Hallet. This man was a distant kinsman of my mother, venerable for his age, his uprightness, and sagacity. He had long discharged the functions of a magistrate and good citizen. If any terrors remained, his presence was sufficient to dispel them.

He approached, took my hand with a compassionate air, and said in a low voice, "Where, my dear Clara, are your brother and sister?" I made no answer, but pointed to the bed. His attendants drew aside the curtain, and while their eyes glared with horror at the spectacle which they beheld, those of Mr. Hallet overflowed with tears.

After considerable pause, he once more turned to me. "My dear girl, this sight is not for you. Can you confide in my care, and that of Mrs. Baynton's? We will see performed all that circumstances require."

I made strenuous opposition to this request. I insisted on remaining near her till she were interred. His remonstrances, however, and my own feelings, shewed me the propriety of a temporary dereliction. Louisa stood in need of a comforter, and my brother's children of a nurse. My unhappy brother was himself an object of solicitude and care. At length, I consented to relinquish the corpse, and go to my brother's, whose house, I said, would need a mistress, and his children a parent.

During this discourse, my venerable friend struggled with his tears, but my last intimation called them forth with fresh violence. Meanwhile, his attendants stood round in mournful silence, gazing on me and at each other. I repeated my resolution, and rose to execute it; but he took my hand to detain me. His countenance betrayed irresolution and reluctance. I requested him to state the reason of his opposition to this measure. I entreated him to be explicit. I told him that my brother had just been there, and that I knew his condition. This misfortune had driven him to madness, and his offspring must not want a protector. If he chose, I would resign Wieland to his care; but his innocent and helpless babes stood in instant need of nurse and mother, and these offices I would by no means allow another to perform while I had life.

Every word that I uttered seemed to augment his perplexity and distress. At last he said, "I think, Clara, I have entitled myself to some regard from you. You have professed your willingness to oblige me. Now I call upon you to confer upon me the highest obligation in your power. Permit Mrs. Baynton to have the management of your brother's house for two or three days; then it shall be yours to act in it as you please. No matter what are my motives in making this request: perhaps I think your age, your sex, or the distress which this disaster must occasion, incapacitates you for the office. Surely you have no doubt of Mrs. Baynton's tenderness or discretion."

New ideas now rushed into my mind. I fixed my eyes stedfastly on Mr. Hallet. "Are they well?" said I. "Is Louisa well? Are Benjamin, and William, and Constantine, and Little Clara, are they safe? Tell me truly, I beseech you!"

"They are well," he replied; "they are perfectly safe."

"Fear no effeminate weakness in me: I can bear to hear the truth. Tell me truly, are they well?"

He again assured me that they were well.

"What then," resumed I, "do you fear? Is it possible for any calamity to disqualify me for performing my duty to these helpless innocents? I am willing to divide the care of them with Mrs. Baynton; I shall be grateful for her sympathy and aid; but what should I be to desert them at an hour like this!"

I will cut short this distressful dialogue. I still persisted in my purpose, and he still persisted in his opposition. This excited my suspicions anew; but these were removed by solemn declarations of their safety. I could not explain this conduct in my friend; but at length consented to go to the city, provided I should see them for a few minutes at present, and should return on the morrow.

Even this arrangement was objected to. At length he told me they were removed to the city. Why were they removed, I asked, and whither? My importunities would not now be eluded. My suspicions were roused, and no evasion or artifice was sufficient to allay them. Many of the audience began to give vent to their emotions in tears. Mr. Hallet himself seemed as if the conflict were too hard to be longer sustained. Something whispered to my heart that havoc had been wider than I now witnessed. I suspected this concealment to arise from apprehensions of the effects which a knowledge of the truth would produce in me. I once more entreated him to inform me truly of their state. To enforce my entreaties, I put on an air of insensibility. "I can guess," said I, "what has happened—They are indeed beyond the reach of injury, for they are dead! Is it not so?" My voice faltered in spite of my courageous efforts.

"Yes," said he, "they are dead! Dead by the same fate, and by the same hand, with their mother!"

"Dead!" replied I; "what, all?"

"All!" replied he: "he spared *not one*!"

Allow me, my friends, to close my eyes upon the after-scene. Why should I protract a tale which I already begin to feel is too long? Over this scene at least let me pass lightly. Here, indeed, my narrative would be imperfect. All was tempestuous commotion in my heart and in my brain. I have no memory for ought but unconscious transitions and rueful sights. I was ingenious and indefatigable in the invention of torments. I would not dispense with any spectacle adapted to exasperate my grief. Each pale and mangled form I crushed to my bosom. Louisa, whom I loved with so ineffable a passion, was denied to me at first, but my obstinacy conquered their reluctance.

They led the way into a darkened hall. A lamp pendant from the ceiling was uncovered, and they pointed to a table. The assassin had defrauded me of my last and miserable consolation. I sought not in her visage, for the tinge of the morning, and the lustre of heaven. These had vanished with life; but I hoped for liberty to print a last kiss upon her lips. This was denied me; for such had been the merciless blow that destroyed her, that *not a lineament remained*!

I was carried hence to the city. Mrs. Hallet was my companion and my nurse. Why should I dwell upon the rage of fever, and the effusions of delirium? Carwin was the phantom that pursued my dreams, the giant oppressor under whose arm I was for ever on the point of being crushed. Strenuous muscles were required to hinder my flight, and hearts of steel to withstand the eloquence of my fears. In vain I called upon them to look upward, to mark his sparkling rage and scowling contempt. All I sought was to fly from the stroke that was lifted. Then I heaped upon my guards the most vehement reproaches, or betook myself to wailings on the haplessness of my condition.

This malady, at length, declined, and my weeping friends began to look for my restoration. Slowly, and with intermitted beams, memory revisited me. The scenes that I had witnessed were revived, became the theme of deliberation and deduction, and called forth the effusions of more rational sorrow.

Chapter XVIII

I HAD imperfectly recovered my strength, when I was informed of the arrival of my mother's brother, Thomas Cambridge. Ten years since, he went to Europe, and was a surgeon in the British forces in Germany during the whole of the late war. After its conclusion, some connection that he had formed with an Irish officer, made him retire into Ireland. Intercourse had been punctually maintained by letters with his sister's children, and hopes were given that he would shortly return to his native country, and pass his old age in our society. He was now in an evil hour arrived.

I desired an interview with him for numerous and urgent reasons. With the first returns of my understanding I had anxiously sought information of the fate of my brother. During the course of my disease I had never seen him; and vague and unsatisfactory answers were returned to all my inquiries. I had vehemently interrogated Mrs. Hallet and her husband, and solicited an interview with this unfortunate man; but they mysteriously insinuated that his reason was still unsettled, and that his circumstances rendered an interview impossible. Their reserve on the particulars of this destruction, and the author of it, was equally invincible.

For some time, finding all my efforts fruitless, I had desisted from direct inquiries and solicitations, determined, as soon as my strength was sufficiently renewed, to pursue other means of dispelling my uncertainty. In this state of things my uncle's arrival and intention to visit me were announced. I almost shuddered to behold the face of this man. When I reflected on the disasters that had befallen us, I was half unwilling to witness that dejection and grief which would be disclosed in his countenance. But I believed that all transactions had been thoroughly disclosed to him, and confided in my importunity to extort from him the knowledge that I sought.

I had no doubt as to the person of our enemy; but the motives that urged him to perpetrate these horrors, the means that he used, and his present condition, were totally unknown. It was reasonable to expect some information on this head, from my uncle. I therefore waited his coming with impatience. At length, in the dusk of the evening, and in my solitary chamber, this meeting took place.

This man was our nearest relation, and had ever treated us with the affection of a parent. Our meeting, therefore, could not be without overflowing tenderness and gloomy joy. He rather encouraged than restrained the tears that I poured out in his arms, and took upon himself the task of comforter. Allusions to recent disasters could not be long omitted. One topic facilitated the admission of another. At length, I mentioned and deplored the ignorance in which I had been kept respecting my brother's destiny, and the circumstances of our misfortunes. I entreated him to tell me what was Wieland's condition, and what progress had been made in detecting or punishing the author of this unheard-of devastation.

"The author!" said he; "Do you know the author?"

"Alas!" I answered, "I am too well acquainted with him. The story of the grounds of my suspicions would be painful and too long. I am not apprized of the extent of your present knowledge. There are none but Wieland, Pleyel, and myself, who are able to relate certain facts."

"Spare yourself the pain," said he. "All that Wieland and Pleyel can communicate, I know already. If any thing of moment has fallen within your own exclusive knowledge, and the relation be not too arduous for your present strength, I confess I am desirous of hearing it. Perhaps you allude to one by the name of Carwin. I will anticipate your curiosity by saying, that since these disasters, no one has seen or heard of him. His agency is, therefore, a mystery still unsolved."

I readily complied with his request, and related as distinctly as I could, though in general terms, the events transacted in the summer-house and my chamber. He listened without apparent surprize to the tale of Pleyel's errors and suspicions, and with augmented seriousness, to my narrative of the warnings and inexplicable vision, and the letter found upon the table. I waited for his comments.

"You gather from this," said he, "that Carwin is the author of all this misery."

"Is it not," answered I, "an unavoidable inference? But what know you respecting it? Was it possible to execute this mischief without witness or coadjutor? I beseech you to relate to me, when and why Mr. Hallet was summoned to the scene, and by whom this disaster was first suspected or discovered. Surely, suspicion must have fallen upon some one, and pursuit was made."

My uncle rose from his seat, and traversed the floor with hasty steps. His eyes were fixed upon the ground, and he seemed buried in perplexity. At length he paused, and said with an emphatic tone, "It is true; the instrument is known. Carwin may have plotted, but the execution was another's. That other is found, and his deed is ascertained."

"Good heaven!" I exclaimed, "what say you? Was not Carwin the assassin? Could any hand but his have carried into act this dreadful purpose?"

"Have I not said," returned he, "that the performance was another's? Carwin, perhaps, or heaven, or insanity, prompted the murderer; but Carwin is unknown. The actual performer has, long since, been called to judgment and convicted, and is, at this moment, at the bottom of a dungeon loaded with chains."

I lifted my hands and eyes. "Who then is this assassin? By what means, and whither was he traced? What is the testimony of his guilt?"

"His own, corroborated with that of a servant-maid who spied the murder of the children from a closet where she was concealed. The magistrate returned from your dwelling to your brother's. He was employed in hearing and recording the testimony of the only witness, when the criminal himself, unexpected, unsolicited, unsought, entered the hall, acknowledged his guilt, and rendered himself up to justice.

"He has since been summoned to the bar. The audience was composed of thousands whom rumours of this wonderful event had attracted from the greatest distance. A long and impartial examination was made, and the prisoner was called upon for his defence. In compliance with this call he delivered an ample relation of his motives and actions." There he stopped.

I besought him to say who this criminal was, and what the instigations that compelled him. My uncle was silent. I urged this inquiry with new force. I reverted to my own knowledge, and sought in this some basis to conjecture. I ran over the scanty catalogue of the men whom I knew; I lighted on no one who was qualified for ministering to malice like this. Again I resorted to importunity. Had I ever seen the criminal? Was it sheer cruelty, or diabolical revenge that produced this overthrow?

He surveyed me, for a considerable time, and listened to my interrogations in silence. At length he spoke: "Clara, I have known thee by report, and in some degree by observation. Thou art a being of no vulgar sort. Thy friends have hitherto treated thee as a child. They meant well, but, perhaps, they were unacquainted with thy strength. I assure myself that nothing will surpass thy fortitude.

"Thou art anxious to know the destroyer of thy family, his actions, and his motives. Shall I call him to thy presence, and permit him to confess before thee? Shall I make him the narrator of his own tale?"

I started on my feet, and looked round me with fearful glances, as if the murderer was close at hand. "What do you mean?" said I; "put an end, I beseech you, to this suspence."

"Be not alarmed; you will never more behold the face of this criminal, unless he be gifted with supernatural strength, and sever like threads the constraint of links and bolts. I have said that the assassin was arraigned at the bar, and that the trial ended with a summons from the judge to confess or to vindicate his actions. A reply was immediately made with significance of gesture, and a tranquil majesty, which denoted less of humanity than god-head. Judges, advocates and auditors were panic-struck and breathless with attention. One of the hearers faithfully recorded the speech. There it is," continued he, putting a roll of papers in my hand, "you may read it at your leisure."

With these words my uncle left me alone. My curiosity refused me a moment's delay. I opened the papers, and read as follows.

Chapter XIX

THEODORE WIELAND, the prisoner at the bar, was now called upon for his defence. He looked around him for some time in silence, and with a mild countenance. At length he spoke:

"It is strange; I am known to my judges and my auditors. Who is there present a stranger to the character of Wieland? who knows him not as an husband—as a father—as a friend? yet here am I arraigned as a criminal. I am charged with diabolical malice; I am accused of the murder of my wife and my children!

"It is true, they were slain by me; they all perished by my hand. The task of vindication is ignoble. What is it that I am called to vindicate? and before whom?

"You know that they are dead, and that they were killed by me. What more would you have? Would you extort from me a statement of my motives? Have you failed to discover them already? You charge me with malice; but your eyes are not shut; your reason is still vigorous; your memory has not forsaken you. You know whom it is that you thus charge. The habits of his life are known to you; his treatment of his wife and his offspring is known to you; the soundness of his integrity, and the unchangeableness of his principles, are familiar to your apprehension; yet you persist in this charge! You lead me hither manacled as a felon; you deem me worthy of a vile and tormenting death!

"Who are they whom I have devoted to death? My wife—the little ones that drew their being from me—that creature who, as she surpassed them in excellence, claimed a larger affection than those whom natural affinities bound to my heart. Think ye that malice could have urged me to this deed? Hide your audacious fronts from the scrutiny of heaven. Take refuge in some cavern unvisited by human eyes. Ye may deplore your wickedness or folly, but ye cannot expiate it.

"Think not that I speak for your sakes. Hug to your hearts this detestable infatuation. Deem me still a murderer, and drag me to untimely death. I make not an effort to dispel your illusion: I utter not a word to cure you of your sanguinary folly: but there are probably some in this assembly who have come from far: for their sakes, whose distance has disabled them from knowing me, I will tell what I have done, and why.

"It is needless to say that God is the object of my supreme passion. I have cherished, in his presence, a single and upright heart. I have thirsted for the knowledge of his will. I have burnt with ardour to approve my faith and my obedience.

"My days have been spent in searching for the revelation of that will; but my days have been mournful, because my search failed. I solicited direction: I turned on every side where glimmerings of light could be discovered. I have not been wholly uninformed; but my knowledge has always stopped short of certainty. Dissatisfaction has insinuated itself into all my thoughts. My purposes have been pure; my wishes indefatigable; but not till lately were these purposes thoroughly accomplished, and these wishes fully gratified.

"I thank thee, my father, for thy bounty; that thou didst not ask a less sacrifice than this; that thou placedst me in a condition to testify my submission to thy will! What have I withheld which it was thy pleasure to exact? Now may I, with dauntless and erect eye, claim my reward, since I have given thee the treasure of my soul.

"I was at my own house: it was late in the evening: my sister had gone to the city, but proposed to return. It was in expectation of her return that my wife and I delayed going to bed beyond the usual hour; the rest of the family, however, were retired.

"My mind was contemplative and calm; not wholly devoid of apprehension on account of my sister's safety. Recent events, not easily explained, had suggested the existence of some danger; but this danger was without a distinct form in our imagination, and scarcely ruffled our tranquillity.

"Time passed, and my sister did not arrive; her house is at some distance from mine, and though her arrangements had been made with a view to residing with us, it was possible that, through forgetfulness, or the occurrence of unforeseen emergencies, she had returned to her own dwelling.

"Hence it was conceived proper that I should ascertain the truth by going thither. I went. On my way my mind was full

of those ideas which related to my intellectual condition. In
the torrent of fervid conceptions, I lost sight of my purpose.
Some times I stood still; some times I wandered from my
path, and experienced some difficulty, on recovering from my
fit of musing, to regain it.

"The series of my thoughts is easily traced. At first every
vein beat with raptures known only to the man whose parental
and conjugal love is without limits, and the cup of whose
desires, immense as it is, overflows with gratification. I know
not why emotions that were perpetual visitants should now
have recurred with unusual energy. The transition was not
new from sensations of joy to a consciousness of gratitude.
The author of my being was likewise the dispenser of every
gift with which that being was embellished. The service to
which a benefactor like this was entitled, could not be circum-
scribed. My social sentiments were indebted to their alliance
with devotion for all their value. All passions are base, all joys
feeble, all energies malignant, which are not drawn from this
source.

"For a time, my contemplations soared above earth and its
inhabitants. I stretched forth my hands; I lifted my eyes, and
exclaimed, O! that I might be admitted to thy presence; that
mine were the supreme delight of knowing thy will, and of
performing it! The blissful privilege of direct communication
with thee, and of listening to the audible enunciation of thy
pleasure!

"What task would I not undertake, what privation would I
not cheerfully endure, to testify my love of thee? Alas! thou
hidest thyself from my view: glimpses only of thy excellence
and beauty are afforded me. Would that a momentary emanation from thy glory would visit me! that some unambiguous
token of thy presence would salute my senses!

"In this mood, I entered the house of my sister. It was
vacant. Scarcely had I regained recollection of the purpose
that brought me hither. Thoughts of a different tendency had
such absolute possession of my mind, that the relations of
time and space were almost obliterated from my understanding. These wanderings, however, were restrained, and I ascended to her chamber.

"I had no light, and might have known by external observation, that the house was without any inhabitant. With this, however, I was not satisfied. I entered the room, and the object of my search not appearing, I prepared to return.

"The darkness required some caution in descending the stair. I stretched my hand to seize the balustrade by which I might regulate my steps. How shall I describe the lustre, which, at that moment, burst upon my vision!

"I was dazzled. My organs were bereaved of their activity. My eye-lids were half-closed, and my hands withdrawn from the balustrade. A nameless fear chilled my veins, and I stood motionless. This irradiation did not retire or lessen. It seemed as if some powerful effulgence covered me like a mantle.

"I opened my eyes and found all about me luminous and glowing. It was the element of heaven that flowed around. Nothing but a fiery stream was at first visible; but, anon, a shrill voice from behind called upon me to attend.

"I turned: It is forbidden to describe what I saw: Words, indeed, would be wanting to the task. The lineaments of that being, whose veil was now lifted, and whose visage beamed upon my sight, no hues of pencil or of language can pourtray.

"As it spoke, the accents thrilled to my heart. 'Thy prayers are heard. In proof of thy faith, render me thy wife. This is the victim I chuse. Call her hither, and here let her fall.'—The sound, and visage, and light vanished at once.

"What demand was this? The blood of Catharine was to be shed! My wife was to perish by my hand! I sought opportunity to attest my virtue. Little did I expect that a proof like this would have been demanded.

"'My wife!' I exclaimed: 'O God! substitute some other victim. Make me not the butcher of my wife. My own blood is cheap. This will I pour out before thee with a willing heart; but spare, I beseech thee, this precious life, or commission some other than her husband to perform the bloody deed.'

"In vain. The conditions were prescribed; the decree had gone forth, and nothing remained but to execute it. I rushed out of the house and across the intermediate fields, and stopped not till I entered my own parlour.

"My wife had remained here during my absence, in anxious expectation of my return with some tidings of her sister. I had none to communicate. For a time, I was breathless with my speed: This, and the tremors that shook my frame, and the wildness of my looks, alarmed her. She immediately suspected some disaster to have happened to her friend, and her own speech was as much overpowered by emotion as mine.

"She was silent, but her looks manifested her impatience to hear what I had to communicate. I spoke, but with so much precipitation as scarcely to be understood; catching her, at the same time, by the arm, and forcibly pulling her from her seat.

" 'Come along with me: fly: waste not a moment: time will be lost, and the deed will be omitted. Tarry not; question not; but fly with me!'

"This deportment added afresh to her alarms. Her eyes pursued mine, and she said, 'What is the matter? For God's sake what is the matter? Where would you have me go?'

"My eyes were fixed upon her countenance while she spoke. I thought upon her virtues; I viewed her as the mother of my babes; as my wife: I recalled the purpose for which I thus urged her attendance. My heart faltered, and I saw that I must rouse to this work all my faculties. The danger of the least delay was imminent.

"I looked away from her, and again exerting my force, drew her towards the door—'You must go with me—indeed you must.'

"In her fright she half-resisted my efforts, and again exclaimed, 'Good heaven! what is it you mean? Where go? What has happened? Have you found Clara?'

" 'Follow me, and you will see,' I answered, still urging her reluctant steps forward.

" 'What phrenzy has seized you? Something must needs have happened. Is she sick? Have you found her?'

" 'Come and see. Follow me, and know for yourself.'

"Still she expostulated and besought me to explain this mysterious behaviour. I could not trust myself to answer her; to look at her; but grasping her arm, I drew her after me. She hesitated, rather through confusion of mind than from unwillingness to accompany me. This confusion gradually abated, and she moved forward, but with irresolute footsteps, and continual exclamations of wonder and terror. Her interrogations of what was the matter? and whither was I going? were ceaseless and vehement.

"It was the scope of my efforts not to think; to keep up a conflict and uproar in my mind in which all order and distinctness should be lost; to escape from the sensations produced by her voice. I was, therefore, silent. I strove to abridge this interval by my haste, and to waste all my attention in furious gesticulations.

"In this state of mind we reached my sister's door. She looked at the windows and saw that all was desolate—'Why come we here? There is no body here. I will not go in.'

"Still I was dumb; but opening the door, I drew her into the entry. This was the allotted scene: here she was to fall. I let go her hand, and pressing my palms against my forehead, made one mighty effort to work up my soul to the deed.

"In vain; it would not be; my courage was appalled; my arms nerveless: I muttered prayers that my strength might be aided from above. They availed nothing.

"Horror diffused itself over me. This conviction of my cowardice, my rebellion, fastened upon me, and I stood rigid and cold as marble. From this state I was somewhat relieved by my wife's voice, who renewed her supplications to be told why we came hither, and what was the fate of my sister.

"What could I answer? My words were broken and inarticulate. Her fears naturally acquired force from the observation of these symptoms; but these fears were misplaced. The only inference she deduced from my conduct was, that some terrible mishap had befallen Clara.

"She wrung her hands, and exclaimed in an agony, 'O tell me, where is she? What has become of her? Is she sick? Dead? Is she in her chamber? O let me go thither and know the worst!'

"This proposal set my thoughts once more in motion. Perhaps what my rebellious heart refused to perform here, I might obtain strength enough to execute elsewhere.

" 'Come then,' said I, 'let us go.'

" 'I will, but not in the dark. We must first procure a light.'

" 'Fly then and procure it; but I charge you, linger not. I will await for your return.'

"While she was gone, I strode along the entry. The fellness of a gloomy hurricane but faintly resembled the discord that reigned in my mind. To omit this sacrifice must not be; yet my sinews had refused to perform it. No alternative was offered. To rebel against the mandate was impossible; but obedience would render me the executioner of my wife. My will was strong, but my limbs refused their office.

"She returned with a light; I led the way to the chamber; she looked round her; she lifted the curtain of the bed; she saw nothing.

"At length, she fixed inquiring eyes upon me. The light now enabled her to discover in my visage what darkness had hitherto concealed. Her cares were now transferred from my sister to myself, and she said in a tremulous voice, 'Wieland! you are not well: What ails you? Can I do nothing for you?'

"That accents and looks so winning should disarm me of my resolution, was to be expected. My thoughts were thrown anew into anarchy. I spread my hand before my eyes that I might not see her, and answered only by groans. She took my other hand between her's, and pressing it to her heart, spoke with that voice which had ever swayed my will, and wafted away sorrow.

" 'My friend! my soul's friend! tell me thy cause of grief. Do I not merit to partake with thee in thy cares? Am I not thy wife?'

"This was too much. I broke from her embrace, and retired to a corner of the room. In this pause, courage was once more infused into me. I resolved to execute my duty. She followed me, and renewed her passionate entreaties to know the cause of my distress.

"I raised my head and regarded her with stedfast looks. I muttered something about death, and the injunctions of my duty. At these words she shrunk back, and looked at me with a new expression of anguish. After a pause, she clasped her hands, and exclaimed—

" 'O Wieland! Wieland! God grant that I am mistaken; but surely something is wrong. I see it: it is too plain: thou art undone—lost to me and to thyself.' At the same time she gazed on my features with intensest anxiety, in hope that different symptoms would take place. I replied to her with vehemence—

" 'Undone! No; my duty is known, and I thank my God that my cowardice is now vanquished, and I have power to fulfil it. Catharine! I pity the weakness of thy nature: I pity thee, but must not spare. Thy life is claimed from my hands: thou must die!'

"Fear was now added to her grief. 'What mean you? Why talk you of death? Bethink yourself, Wieland: bethink yourself, and this fit will pass. O why came I hither! Why did you drag me hither?'

" 'I brought thee hither to fulfil a divine command. I am appointed thy destroyer, and destroy thee I must.' Saying this I seized her wrists. She shrieked aloud, and endeavoured to free herself from my grasp; but her efforts were vain.

" 'Surely, surely Wieland, thou dost not mean it. Am I not thy wife? and wouldst thou kill me? Thou wilt not; and yet—I see—thou art Wieland no longer! A fury resistless and horrible possesses thee—Spare me—spare—help—help——'

"Till her breath was stopped she shrieked for help—for mercy. When she could speak no longer, her gestures, her looks appealed to my compassion. My accursed hand was irresolute and tremulous. I meant thy death to be sudden, thy struggles to be brief. Alas! my heart was infirm; my resolves mutable. Thrice I slackened my grasp, and life kept its hold, though in the midst of pangs. Her eye-balls started from their sockets. Grimness and distortion took place of all that used to bewitch me into transport, and subdue me into reverence.

"I was commissioned to kill thee, but not to torment thee with the foresight of thy death; not to multiply thy fears, and prolong thy agonies. Haggard, and pale, and lifeless, at length thou ceasedst to contend with thy destiny.

"This was a moment of triumph. Thus had I successfully subdued the stubbornness of human passions: the victim which had been demanded was given: the deed was done past recal.

"I lifted the corpse in my arms and laid it on the bed. I gazed upon it with delight. Such was the elation of my thoughts, that I even broke into laughter. I clapped my hands and exclaimed, 'It is done! My sacred duty is fulfilled! To that I have sacrificed, O my God! thy last and best gift, my wife!'

"For a while I thus soared above frailty. I imagined I had set myself forever beyond the reach of selfishness; but my imaginations were false. This rapture quickly subsided. I looked again at my wife. My joyous ebullitions vanished, and

I asked myself who it was whom I saw? Methought it could not be Catharine. It could not be the woman who had lodged for years in my heart; who had slept, nightly, in my bosom; who had borne in her womb, who had fostered at her breast, the beings who called me father; whom I had watched with delight, and cherished with a fondness ever new and perpetually growing: it could not be the same.

"Where was her bloom! These deadly and blood-suffused orbs but ill resemble the azure and exstatic tenderness of her eyes. The lucid stream that meandered over that bosom, the glow of love that was wont to sit upon that cheek, are much unlike these livid stains and this hideous deformity. Alas! these were the traces of agony; the gripe of the assassin had been here!

"I will not dwell upon my lapse into desperate and outrageous sorrow. The breath of heaven that sustained me was withdrawn, and I sunk into *mere man*. I leaped from the floor: I dashed my head against the wall: I uttered screams of horror: I panted after torment and pain. Eternal fire, and the bickerings of hell, compared with what I felt, were music and a bed of roses.

"I thank my God that this degeneracy was transient, that he deigned once more to raise me aloft. I thought upon what I had done as a sacrifice to duty, and *was calm*. My wife was dead; but I reflected, that though this source of human consolation was closed, yet others were still open. If the transports of an husband were no more, the feelings of a father had still scope for exercise. When remembrance of their mother should excite too keen a pang, I would look upon them, and *be comforted*.

"While I revolved these ideas, new warmth flowed in upon my heart—I was wrong. These feelings were the growth of selfishness. Of this I was not aware, and to dispel the mist that obscured my perceptions, a new effulgence and a new mandate were necessary.

"From these thoughts I was recalled by a ray that was shot into the room. A voice spake like that which I had before heard—'Thou hast done well; but all is not done—the sacrifice is incomplete—thy children must be offered—they must perish with their mother!—' "

Chapter XX

WILL YOU wonder that I read no farther? Will you not rather be astonished that I read thus far? What power supported me through such a task I know not. Perhaps the doubt from which I could not disengage my mind, that the scene here depicted was a dream, contributed to my perseverance. In vain the solemn introduction of my uncle, his appeals to my fortitude, and allusions to something monstrous in the events he was about to disclose; in vain the distressful perplexity, the mysterious silence and ambiguous answers of my attendants, especially when the condition of my brother was the theme of my inquiries, were remembered. I recalled the interview with Wieland in my chamber, his preternatural tranquillity succeeded by bursts of passion and menacing actions. All these coincided with the tenor of this paper.

Catharine and her children, and Louisa were dead. The act that destroyed them was, in the highest degree, inhuman. It was worthy of savages trained to murder, and exulting in agonies.

Who was the performer of the deed? Wieland! My brother! The husband and the father! That man of gentle virtues and invincible benignity! placable and mild—an idolator of peace! Surely, said I, it is a dream. For many days have I been vexed with frenzy. Its dominion is still felt; but new forms are called up to diversify and augment my torments.

The paper dropped from my hand, and my eyes followed it. I shrunk back, as if to avoid some petrifying influence that approached me. My tongue was mute; all the functions of nature were at a stand, and I sunk upon the floor lifeless.

The noise of my fall, as I afterwards heard, alarmed my uncle, who was in a lower apartment, and whose apprehensions had detained him. He hastened to my chamber, and administered the assistance which my condition required. When I opened my eyes I beheld him before me. His skill as a reasoner as well as a physician, was exerted to obviate the injurious effects of this disclosure; but he had wrongly estimated the strength of my body or of my mind. This new shock brought me once more to the brink of the grave, and my malady was much more difficult to subdue than at first.

I will not dwell upon the long train of dreary sensations, and the hideous confusion of my understanding. Time slowly restored its customary firmness to my frame, and order to my thoughts. The images impressed upon my mind by this fatal paper were somewhat effaced by my malady. They were obscure and disjointed like the parts of a dream. I was desirous of freeing my imagination from this chaos. For this end I questioned my uncle, who was my constant companion. He was intimidated by the issue of his first experiment, and took pains to elude or discourage my inquiry. My impetuosity some times compelled him to have resort to misrepresentations and untruths.

Time effected that end, perhaps, in a more beneficial manner. In the course of my meditations the recollections of the past gradually became more distinct. I revolved them, however, in silence, and being no longer accompanied with surprize, they did not exercise a death-dealing power. I had discontinued the perusal of the paper in the midst of the narrative; but what I read, combined with information elsewhere obtained, threw, perhaps, a sufficient light upon these detestable transactions; yet my curiosity was not inactive. I desired to peruse the remainder.

My eagerness to know the particulars of this tale was mingled and abated by my antipathy to the scene which would be disclosed. Hence I employed no means to effect my purpose. I desired knowledge, and, at the same time, shrunk back from receiving the boon.

One morning, being left alone, I rose from my bed, and went to a drawer where my finer clothing used to be kept. I opened it, and this fatal paper saluted my sight. I snatched it involuntarily, and withdrew to a chair. I debated, for a few minutes, whether I should open and read. Now that my fortitude was put to trial, it failed. I felt myself incapable of deliberately surveying a scene of so much horror. I was prompted to return it to its place, but this resolution gave way, and I determined to peruse some part of it. I turned over the leaves till I came near the conclusion. The narrative of the criminal was finished. The verdict of *guilty* reluctantly pronounced by the jury, and the accused interrogated why sentence of death should not pass. The answer was brief, solemn, and emphatical.

"No. I have nothing to say. My tale has been told. My motives have been truly stated. If my judges are unable to discern the purity of my intentions, or to credit the statement of them, which I have just made; if they see not that my deed was enjoined by heaven; that obedience was the test of perfect virtue, and the extinction of selfishness and error, they must pronounce me a murderer.

"They refuse to credit my tale; they impute my acts to the influence of dæmons; they account me an example of the highest wickedness of which human nature is capable; they doom me to death and infamy. Have I power to escape this evil? If I have, be sure I will exert it. I will not accept evil at their hand, when I am entitled to good; I will suffer only when I cannot elude suffering.

"You say that I am guilty. Impious and rash! thus to usurp the prerogatives of your Maker! to set up your bounded views and halting reason, as the measure of truth!

"Thou, Omnipotent and Holy! Thou knowest that my actions were conformable to thy will. I know not what is crime; what actions are evil in their ultimate and comprehensive tendency or what are good. Thy knowledge, as thy power, is unlimited. I have taken thee for my guide, and cannot err. To the arms of thy protection, I entrust my safety. In the awards of thy justice, I confide for my recompense.

"Come death when it will, I am safe. Let calumny and abhorrence pursue me among men; I shall not be defrauded of my dues. The peace of virtue, and the glory of obedience, will be my portion hereafter."

Here ended the speaker. I withdrew my eyes from the page; but before I had time to reflect on what I had read, Mr. Cambridge entered the room. He quickly perceived how I had been employed, and betrayed some solicitude respecting the condition of my mind.

His fears, however, were superfluous. What I had read, threw me into a state not easily described. Anguish and fury, however, had no part in it. My faculties were chained up in wonder and awe. Just then, I was unable to speak. I looked at my friend with an air of inquisitiveness, and pointed at the roll. He comprehended my inquiry, and answered me with looks of gloomy acquiescence. After some time, my thoughts found their way to my lips.

"Such then were the acts of my brother. Such were his words. For this he was condemned to die: To die upon the gallows! A fate, cruel and unmerited! And is it so?" continued I, struggling for utterance, which this new idea made difficult; "is he—dead!"

"No. He is alive. There could be no doubt as to the cause of these excesses. They originated in sudden madness; but that madness continues, and he is condemned to perpetual imprisonment."

"Madness, say you? Are you sure? Were not these sights, and these sounds, really seen and heard?"

My uncle was surprized at my question. He looked at me with apparent inquietude. "Can you doubt," said he, "that these were illusions? Does heaven, think you, interfere for such ends?"

"O no; I think it not. Heaven cannot stimulate to such unheard-of outrage. The agent was not good, but evil."

"Nay, my dear girl," said my friend, "lay aside these fancies. Neither angel nor devil had any part in this affair."

"You misunderstand me," I answered; "I believe the agency to be external and real, but not supernatural."

"Indeed!" said he, in an accent of surprize. "Whom do you then suppose to be the agent?"

"I know not. All is wildering conjecture. I cannot forget Carwin. I cannot banish the suspicion that he was the setter of these snares. But how can we suppose it to be madness? Did insanity ever before assume this form?"

"Frequently. The illusion, in this case, was more dreadful in its consequences, than any that has come to my knowledge; but, I repeat that similar illusions are not rare. Did you never hear of an instance which occurred in your mother's family?"

"No. I beseech you relate it. My grandfather's death I have understood to have been extraordinary, but I know not in what respect. A brother, to whom he was much attached, died in his youth, and this, as I have heard, influenced, in some remarkable way, the fate of my grandfather; but I am unacquainted with particulars."

"On the death of that brother," resumed my friend, "my father was seized with dejection, which was found to flow from two sources. He not only grieved for the loss of a friend, but entertained the belief that his own death would be inevitably consequent on that of his brother. He waited from day to day in expectation of the stroke which he predicted was speedily to fall upon him. Gradually, however, he recovered his cheerfulness and confidence. He married, and performed his part in the world with spirit and activity. At the end of twenty-one years it happened that he spent the summer with his family at an house which he possessed on the sea coast in Cornwall. It was at no great distance from a cliff which overhung the ocean, and rose into the air to a great height. The summit was level and secure, and easily ascended on the land side. The company frequently repaired hither in clear weather, invited by its pure airs and extensive prospects. One evening in June my father, with his wife and some friends, chanced to be on this spot. Every one was happy, and my father's imagination seemed particularly alive to the grandeur of the scenery.

"Suddenly, however, his limbs trembled and his features betrayed alarm. He threw himself into the attitude of one listening. He gazed earnestly in a direction in which nothing was visible to his friends. This lasted for a minute; then turning to his companions, he told them that his brother had just delivered to him a summons, which must be instantly obeyed. He then took an hasty and solemn leave of each person, and, before their surprize would allow them to understand the scene, he rushed to the edge of the cliff, threw himself headlong, and was seen no more.

"In the course of my practice in the German army, many cases, equally remarkable, have occurred. Unquestionably the illusions were maniacal, though the vulgar thought otherwise. They are all reducible to one class,* and are not more difficult of explication and cure than most affections of our frame."

*Mania Mutabilis. See Darwin's Zoonomia, vol. ii. Class III. 1. 2. where similar cases are stated.

This opinion my uncle endeavoured, by various means, to impress upon me. I listened to his reasonings and illustrations with silent respect. My astonishment was great on finding proofs of an influence of which I had supposed there were no examples; but I was far from accounting for appearances in my uncle's manner. Ideas thronged into my mind which I was unable to disjoin or to regulate. I reflected that this madness, if madness it were, had affected Pleyel and myself as well as Wieland. Pleyel had heard a mysterious voice. I had seen and heard. A form had showed itself to me as well as to Wieland. The disclosure had been made in the same spot. The appearance was equally complete and equally prodigious in both instances. Whatever supposition I should adopt, had I not equal reason to tremble? What was my security against influences equally terrific and equally irresistable?

It would be vain to attempt to describe the state of mind which this idea produced. I wondered at the change which a moment had effected in my brother's condition. Now was I stupified with tenfold wonder in contemplating myself. Was I not likewise transformed from rational and human into a creature of nameless and fearful attributes? Was I not transported to the brink of the same abyss? Ere a new day should come, my hands might be embrued in blood, and my remaining life be consigned to a dungeon and chains.

With moral sensibility like mine, no wonder that this new dread was more insupportable than the anguish I had lately endured. Grief carries its own antidote along with it. When thought becomes merely a vehicle of pain, its progress must be stopped. Death is a cure which nature or ourselves must administer: To this cure I now looked forward with gloomy satisfaction.

My silence could not conceal from my uncle the state of my thoughts. He made unwearied efforts to divert my attention from views so pregnant with danger. His efforts, aided by time, were in some measure successful. Confidence in the strength of my resolution, and in the healthful state of my faculties, was once more revived. I was able to devote my thoughts to my brother's state, and the causes of this disasterous proceeding.

My opinions were the sport of eternal change. Some times

I conceived the apparition to be more than human. I had no grounds on which to build a disbelief. I could not deny faith to the evidence of my religion; the testimony of men was loud and unanimous: both these concurred to persuade me that evil spirits existed, and that their energy was frequently exerted in the system of the world.

These ideas connected themselves with the image of Carwin. Where is the proof, said I, that dæmons may not be subjected to the controul of men? This truth may be distorted and debased in the minds of the ignorant. The dogmas of the vulgar, with regard to this subject, are glaringly absurd; but though these may justly be neglected by the wise, we are scarcely justified in totally rejecting the possibility that men may obtain supernatural aid.

The dreams of superstition are worthy of contempt. Witchcraft, its instruments and miracles, the compact ratified by a bloody signature, the apparatus of sulpherous smells and thundering explosions, are monstrous and chimerical. These have no part in the scene over which the genius of Carwin presides. That conscious beings, dissimilar from human, but moral and voluntary agents as we are, some where exist, can scarcely be denied. That their aid may be employed to benign or malignant purposes, cannot be disproved.

Darkness rests upon the designs of this man. The extent of his power is unknown; but is there not evidence that it has been now exerted?

I recurred to my own experience. Here Carwin had actually appeared upon the stage; but this was in a human character. A voice and a form were discovered; but one was apparently exerted, and the other disclosed, not to befriend, but to counteract Carwin's designs. There were tokens of hostility, and not of alliance, between them. Carwin was the miscreant whose projects were resisted by a minister of heaven. How can this be reconciled to the stratagem which ruined my brother? There the agency was at once preternatural and malignant.

The recollection of this fact led my thoughts into a new channel. The malignity of that influence which governed my brother had hitherto been no subject of doubt. His wife and children were destroyed; they had expired in agony and fear;

yet was it indisputably certain that their murderer was criminal? He was acquitted at the tribunal of his own conscience;
his behaviour at his trial and since, was faithfully reported to
me; appearances were uniform; not for a moment did he lay
aside the majesty of virtue; he repelled all invectives by appealing to the deity, and to the tenor of his past life; surely
there was truth in this appeal: none but a command from
heaven could have swayed his will; and nothing but unerring
proof of divine approbation could sustain his mind in its present elevation.

Chapter XXI

SUCH, for some time, was the course of my meditations. My weakness, and my aversion to be pointed at as an object of surprize or compassion, prevented me from going into public. I studiously avoided the visits of those who came to express their sympathy, or gratify their curiosity. My uncle was my principal companion. Nothing more powerfully tended to console me than his conversation.

With regard to Pleyel, my feelings seemed to have undergone a total revolution. It often happens that one passion supplants another. Late disasters had rent my heart, and now that the wound was in some degree closed, the love which I had cherished for this man seemed likewise to have vanished.

Hitherto, indeed, I had had no cause for despair. I was innocent of that offence which had estranged him from my presence. I might reasonably expect that my innocence would at some time be irresistably demonstrated, and his affection for me be revived with his esteem. Now my aversion to be thought culpable by him continued, but was unattended with the same impatience. I desired the removal of his suspicions, not for the sake of regaining his love, but because I delighted in the veneration of so excellent a man, and because he himself would derive pleasure from conviction of my integrity.

My uncle had early informed me that Pleyel and he had seen each other, since the return of the latter from Europe. Amidst the topics of their conversation, I discovered that Pleyel had carefully omitted the mention of those events which had drawn upon me so much abhorrence. I could not account for his silence on this subject. Perhaps time or some new discovery had altered or shaken his opinion. Perhaps he was unwilling, though I were guilty, to injure me in the opinion of my venerable kinsman. I understood that he had frequently visited me during my disease, had watched many successive nights by my bedside, and manifested the utmost anxiety on my account.

The journey which he was preparing to take, at the termination of our last interview, the catastrophe of the ensuing night induced him to delay. The motives of this journey I had, till now, totally mistaken. They were explained to me by my uncle, whose tale excited my astonishment without awakening my regret. In a different state of mind, it would have added unspeakably to my distress, but now it was more a source of pleasure than pain. This, perhaps, is not the least extraordinary of the facts contained in this narrative. It will excite less wonder when I add, that my indifference was temporary, and that the lapse of a few days shewed me that my feelings were deadened for a time, rather than finally extinguished.

Theresa de Stolberg was alive. She had conceived the resolution of seeking her lover in America. To conceal her flight, she had caused the report of her death to be propagated. She put herself under the conduct of Bertrand, the faithful servant of Pleyel. The pacquet which the latter received from the hands of his servant, contained the tidings of her safe arrival at Boston, and to meet her there was the purpose of his journey.

This discovery had set this man's character in a new light. I had mistaken the heroism of friendship for the phrenzy of love. He who had gained my affections, may be supposed to have previously entitled himself to my reverence; but the levity which had formerly characterized the behaviour of this man, tended to obscure the greatness of his sentiments. I did not fail to remark, that since this lady was still alive, the voice in the temple which asserted her death, must either have been intended to deceive, or have been itself deceived. The latter supposition was inconsistent with the notion of a spiritual, and the former with that of a benevolent being.

When my disease abated, Pleyel had forborne his visits, and had lately set out upon this journey. This amounted to a proof that my guilt was still believed by him. I was grieved for his errors, but trusted that my vindication would, sooner or later, be made.

Meanwhile, tumultuous thoughts were again set afloat by a proposal made to me by my uncle. He imagined that new airs would restore my languishing constitution, and a varied succession of objects tend to repair the shock which my mind had received. For this end, he proposed to me to take up my abode with him in France or Italy.

At a more prosperous period, this scheme would have pleased for its own sake. Now my heart sickened at the prospect of nature. The world of man was shrowded in misery and blood, and constituted a loathsome spectacle. I willingly closed my eyes in sleep, and regretted that the respite it afforded me was so short. I marked with satisfaction the progress of decay in my frame, and consented to live, merely in the hope that the course of nature would speedily relieve me from the burthen. Nevertheless, as he persisted in his scheme, I concurred in it merely because he was entitled to my gratitude, and because my refusal gave him pain.

No sooner was he informed of my consent, than he told me I must make immediate preparation to embark, as the ship in which he had engaged a passage would be ready to depart in three days. This expedition was unexpected. There was an impatience in his manner when he urged the necessity of dispatch that excited my surprize. When I questioned him as to the cause of this haste, he generally stated reasons which, at that time, I could not deny to be plausible; but which, on the review, appeared insufficient. I suspected that the true motives were concealed, and believed that these motives had some connection with my brother's destiny.

I now recollected that the information respecting Wieland which had, from time to time, been imparted to me, was always accompanied with airs of reserve and mysteriousness. What had appeared sufficiently explicit at the time it was uttered, I now remembered to have been faltering and ambiguous. I was resolved to remove my doubts, by visiting the unfortunate man in his dungeon.

Heretofore the idea of this visit had occurred to me; but the horrors of his dwelling-place, his wild yet placid physiognomy, his neglected locks, the fetters which constrained his limbs, terrible as they were in description, how could I endure to behold!

Now, however, that I was preparing to take an everlasting farewell of my country, now that an ocean was henceforth to separate me from him, how could I part without an interview? I would examine his situation with my own eyes. I would know whether the representations which had been made to me were true. Perhaps the sight of the sister whom he was wont to love with a passion more than fraternal, might have an auspicious influence on his malady.

Having formed this resolution, I waited to communicate it to Mr. Cambridge. I was aware that, without his concurrence, I could not hope to carry it into execution; and could discover no objection to which it was liable. If I had not been deceived as to his condition, no inconvenience could arise from this proceeding. His consent, therefore, would be the test of his sincerity.

I seized this opportunity to state my wishes on this head. My suspicions were confirmed by the manner in which my request affected him. After some pause, in which his countenance betrayed every mark of perplexity, he said to me, "Why would you pay this visit? What useful purpose can it serve?"

"We are preparing," said I, "to leave the country forever: What kind of being should I be to leave behind me a brother in calamity without even a parting interview? Indulge me for three minutes in the sight of him. My heart will be much easier after I have looked at him, and shed a few tears in his presence."

"I believe otherwise. The sight of him would only augment your distress, without contributing, in any degree, to his benefit."

"I know not that," returned I. "Surely the sympathy of his sister, proofs that her tenderness is as lively as ever, must be a source of satisfaction to him. At present he must regard all mankind as his enemies and calumniators. His sister he, probably, conceives to partake in the general infatuation, and to join in the cry of abhorrence that is raised against him. To be undeceived in this respect, to be assured that, however I may impute his conduct to delusion, I still retain all my former affection for his person, and veneration for the purity of his motives, cannot but afford him pleasure. When he hears that I have left the country, without even the ceremonious attention of a visit, what will he think of me? His magnanimity may hinder him from repining, but he will surely consider my behaviour as savage and unfeeling. Indeed, dear Sir, I must pay this visit. To embark with you without paying it, will be impossible. It may be of no service to him, but will enable me to acquit myself of what I cannot but esteem a duty. Besides," continued I, "if it be a mere fit of insanity that has seized him, may not my presence chance to have a salutary influence? The mere sight of me, it is not impossible, may rectify his perceptions."

"Ay," said my uncle, with some eagerness; "it is by no means impossible that your interview may have that effect; and for that reason, beyond all others, would I dissuade you from it."

I expressed my surprize at this declaration. "Is it not to be desired that an error so fatal as this should be rectified?"

"I wonder at your question. Reflect on the consequences of this error. Has he not destroyed the wife whom he loved, the children whom he idolized? What is it that enables him to bear the remembrance, but the belief that he acted as his duty enjoined? Would you rashly bereave him of this belief? Would you restore him to himself, and convince him that he was instigated to this dreadful outrage by a perversion of his organs, or a delusion from hell?

"Now his visions are joyous and elate. He conceives himself to have reached a loftier degree of virtue, than any other human being. The merit of his sacrifice is only enhanced in the eyes of superior beings, by the detestation that pursues him here, and the sufferings to which he is condemned. The belief that even his sister has deserted him, and gone over to his enemies, adds to his sublimity of feelings, and his confidence in divine approbation and future recompense.

"Let him be undeceived in this respect, and what floods of despair and of horror will overwhelm him! Instead of glowing approbation and serene hope, will he not hate and torture himself? Self-violence, or a phrenzy far more savage and destructive than this, may be expected to succeed. I beseech you, therefore, to relinquish this scheme. If you calmly reflect upon it, you will discover that your duty lies in carefully shunning him."

Mr. Cambridge's reasonings suggested views to my understanding, that had not hitherto occurred. I could not but admit their validity, but they shewed, in a new light, the depth of that misfortune in which my brother was plunged. I was silent and irresolute.

Presently, I considered, that whether Wieland was a maniac,

a faithful servant of his God, the victim of hellish illusions, or the dupe of human imposture, was by no means certain. In this state of my mind it became me to be silent during the visit that I projected. This visit should be brief: I should be satisfied merely to snatch a look at him. Admitting that a change in his opinions were not to be desired, there was no danger, from the conduct which I should pursue, that this change should be wrought.

But I could not conquer my uncle's aversion to this scheme. Yet I persisted, and he found that to make me voluntarily relinquish it, it was necessary to be more explicit than he had hitherto been. He took both my hands, and anxiously examining my countenance as he spoke, "Clara," said he, "this visit must not be paid. We must hasten with the utmost expedition from this shore. It is folly to conceal the truth from you, and, since it is only by disclosing the truth that you can be prevailed upon to lay aside this project, the truth shall be told.

"O my dear girl!" continued he with increasing energy in his accent, "your brother's phrenzy is, indeed, stupendous and frightful. The soul that formerly actuated his frame has disappeared. The same form remains; but the wise and benevolent Wieland is no more. A fury that is rapacious of blood, that lifts his strength almost above that of mortals, that bends all his energies to the destruction of whatever was once dear to him, possesses him wholly.

"You must not enter his dungeon; his eyes will no sooner be fixed upon you, than an exertion of his force will be made. He will shake off his fetters in a moment, and rush upon you. No interposition will then be strong or quick enough to save you.

"The phantom that has urged him to the murder of Catharine and her children is not yet appeased. Your life, and that of Pleyel, are exacted from him by this imaginary being. He is eager to comply with this demand. Twice he has escaped from his prison. The first time, he no sooner found himself at liberty, than he hasted to Pleyel's house. It being midnight, the latter was in bed. Wieland penetrated unobserved to his chamber, and opened his curtain. Happily, Pleyel awoke at the critical moment, and escaped the fury of his kinsman, by leaping from his chamber-window into the court. Happily, he reached the ground without injury. Alarms were given, and after diligent search, your brother was found in a chamber of your house, whither, no doubt, he had sought you.

"His chains, and the watchfulness of his guards, were re-doubled; but again, by some miracle, he restored himself to liberty. He was now incautiously apprized of the place of your abode: and had not information of his escape been instantly given, your death would have been added to the number of his atrocious acts.

"You now see the danger of your project. You must not only forbear to visit him, but if you would save him from the crime of embruing his hands in your blood, you must leave the country. There is no hope that his malady will end but with his life, and no precaution will ensure your safety, but that of placing the ocean between you.

"I confess I came over with an intention to reside among you, but these disasters have changed my views. Your own safety and my happiness require that you should accompany me in my return, and I entreat you to give your cheerful con-currence to this measure."

After these representations from my uncle, it was impossible to retain my purpose. I readily consented to seclude myself from Wieland's presence. I likewise acquiesced in the proposal to go to Europe; not that I ever expected to arrive there, but because, since my principles forbad me to assail my own life, change had some tendency to make supportable the few days which disease should spare to me.

What a tale had thus been unfolded! I was hunted to death, not by one whom my misconduct had exasperated, who was conscious of illicit motives, and who sought his end by cir-cumvention and surprize; but by one who deemed himself commissioned for this act by heaven, who regarded this career of horror as the last refinement of virtue, whose implacability was proportioned to the reverence and love which he felt for me, and who was inaccessible to the fear of punishment and ignominy!

In vain should I endeavour to stay his hand by urging the claims of a sister or friend: these were his only reasons for pursuing my destruction. Had I been a stranger to his blood;

had I been the most worthless of human kind; my safety had not been endangered.

Surely, said I, my fate is without example. The phrenzy which is charged upon my brother, must belong to myself. My foe is manacled and guarded; but I derive no security from these restraints. I live not in a community of savages; yet, whether I sit or walk, go into crouds, or hide myself in solitude, my life is marked for a prey to inhuman violence; I am in perpetual danger of perishing; of perishing under the grasp of a brother!

I recollected the omens of this destiny; I remembered the gulf to which my brother's invitation had conducted me; I remembered that, when on the brink of danger, the author of my peril was depicted by my fears in his form: Thus realized, were the creatures of prophetic sleep, and of wakeful terror!

These images were unavoidably connected with that of Carwin. In this paroxysm of distress, my attention fastened on him as the grand deceiver; the author of this black conspiracy; the intelligence that governed in this storm.

Some relief is afforded in the midst of suffering, when its author is discovered or imagined; and an object found on which we may pour out our indignation and our vengeance. I ran over the events that had taken place since the origin of our intercourse with him, and reflected on the tenor of that description which was received from Ludloe. Mixed up with notions of supernatural agency, were the vehement suspicions which I entertained, that Carwin was the enemy whose machinations had destroyed us.

I thirsted for knowledge and for vengeance. I regarded my hasty departure with reluctance, since it would remove me from the means by which this knowledge might be obtained, and this vengeance gratified. This departure was to take place in two days. At the end of two days I was to bid an eternal adieu to my native country. Should I not pay a parting visit to the scene of these disasters? Should I not bedew with my tears the graves of my sister and her children? Should I not explore their desolate habitation, and gather from the sight of its walls and furniture food for my eternal melancholy?

This suggestion was succeeded by a secret shuddering. Some disastrous influence appeared to overhang the scene.

How many memorials should I meet with serving to recall the images of those I had lost!

I was tempted to relinquish my design, when it occurred to me that I had left among my papers a journal of transactions in short-hand. I was employed in this manuscript on that night when Pleyel's incautious curiosity tempted him to look over my shoulder. I was then recording my adventure in *the recess*, an imperfect sight of which led him into such fatal errors.

I had regulated the disposition of all my property. This manuscript, however, which contained the most secret transactions of my life, I was desirous of destroying. For this end I must return to my house, and this I immediately determined to do.

I was not willing to expose myself to opposition from my friends, by mentioning my design; I therefore bespoke the use of Mr. Hallet's chaise, under pretence of enjoying an airing, as the day was remarkably bright.

This request was gladly complied with, and I directed the servant to conduct me to Mettingen. I dismissed him at the gate, intending to use, in returning, a carriage belonging to my brother.

Chapter XXII

The inhabitants of the *Hut* received me with a mixture of joy and surprize. Their homely welcome, and their artless sympathy, were grateful to my feelings. In the midst of their inquiries, as to my health, they avoided all allusions to the source of my malady. They were honest creatures, and I loved them well. I participated in the tears which they shed when I mentioned to them my speedy departure for Europe, and promised to acquaint them with my welfare during my long absence.

They expressed great surprize when I informed them of my intention to visit my cottage. Alarm and foreboding overspread their features, and they attempted to dissuade me from visiting an house which they firmly believed to be haunted by a thousand ghastly apparitions.

These apprehensions, however, had no power over my conduct. I took an irregular path which led me to my own house. All was vacant and forlorn. A small enclosure, near which the path led, was the burying-ground belonging to the family. This I was obliged to pass. Once I had intended to enter it, and ponder on the emblems and inscriptions which my uncle had caused to be made on the tombs of Catharine and her children; but now my heart faltered as I approached, and I hastened forward, that distance might conceal it from my view.

When I approached the recess, my heart again sunk. I averted my eyes, and left it behind me as quickly as possible. Silence reigned through my habitation and a darkness, which closed doors and shutters produced. Every object was connected with mine or my brother's history. I passed the entry, mounted the stair, and unlocked the door of my chamber. It was with difficulty that I curbed my fancy and smothered my fears. Slight movements and casual sounds were transformed into beckoning shadows and calling shapes.

I proceeded to the closet. I opened and looked round it with fearfulness. All things were in their accustomed order. I sought and found the manuscript where I was used to deposit it. This being secured, there was nothing to detain me; yet I stood and contemplated awhile the furniture and walls of my chamber. I remembered how long this apartment had been a sweet and tranquil asylum; I compared its former state with its present dreariness, and reflected that I now beheld it for the last time.

Here it was that the incomprehensible behaviour of Carwin was witnessed: this the stage on which that enemy of man shewed himself for a moment unmasked. Here the menaces of murder were wafted to my ear; and here these menaces were executed.

These thoughts had a tendency to take from me my self-command. My feeble limbs refused to support me, and I sunk upon a chair. Incoherent and half-articulate exclamations escaped my lips. The name of Carwin was uttered, and eternal woes, woes like that which his malice had entailed upon us, were heaped upon him. I invoked all-seeing heaven to drag to light and to punish this betrayer, and accused its providence for having thus long delayed the retribution that was due to so enormous a guilt.

I have said that the window shutters were closed. A feeble light, however, found entrance through the crevices. A small window illuminated the closet, and the door being closed, a dim ray streamed through the key-hole. A kind of twilight was thus created, sufficient for the purposes of vision; but, at the same time, involving all minuter objects in obscurity.

This darkness suited the colour of my thoughts. I sickened at the remembrance of the past. The prospect of the future excited my loathing. I muttered in a low voice, Why should I live longer? Why should I drag on a miserable being? All, for whom I ought to live, have perished. Am I not myself hunted to death?

At that moment, my despair suddenly became vigorous. My nerves were no longer unstrung. My powers, that had long been deadened, were revived. My bosom swelled with a sudden energy, and the conviction darted through my mind, that to end my torments was, at once, practicable and wise.

I knew how to find way to the recesses of life. I could use a lancet with some skill, and could distinguish between vein and artery. By piercing deep into the latter, I should shun the evils which the future had in store for me, and take refuge from my woes in quiet death.

I started on my feet, for my feebleness was gone, and hasted to the closet. A lancet and other small instruments were preserved in a case which I had deposited here. Inattentive as I was to foreign considerations, my ears were still open to any sound of mysterious import that should occur. I thought I heard a step in the entry. My purpose was suspended, and I cast an eager glance at my chamber door, which was open. No one appeared, unless the shadow which I discerned upon the floor, was the outline of a man. If it were, I was authorized to suspect that some one was posted close to the entrance, who possibly had overheard my exclamations.

My teeth chattered, and a wild confusion took place of my momentary calm. Thus it was when a terrific visage had disclosed itself on a former night. Thus it was when the evil destiny of Wieland assumed the lineaments of something human. What horrid apparition was preparing to blast my sight?

Still I listened and gazed. Not long, for the shadow moved; a foot, unshapely and huge, was thrust forward; a form advanced from its concealment, and stalked into the room. It was Carwin!

While I had breath I shrieked. While I had power over my muscles, I motioned with my hand that he should vanish. My exertions could not last long; I sunk into a fit.

O that this grateful oblivion had lasted for ever! Too quickly I recovered my senses. The power of distinct vision was no sooner restored to me, than this hateful form again presented itself, and I once more relapsed.

A second time, untoward nature recalled me from the sleep of death. I found myself stretched upon the bed. When I had power to look up, I remembered only that I had cause to fear. My distempered fancy fashioned to itself no distinguishable image. I threw a languid glance round me; once more my eyes lighted upon Carwin.

He was seated on the floor, his back rested against the wall, his knees were drawn up, and his face was buried in his hands. That his station was at some distance, that his attitude was not menacing, that his ominous visage was concealed, may account for my now escaping a shock, violent as those which were past. I withdrew my eyes, but was not again deserted by my senses.

On perceiving that I had recovered my sensibility, he lifted his head. This motion attracted my attention. His countenance was mild, but sorrow and astonishment sat upon his features. I averted my eyes and feebly exclaimed—"O! fly—fly far and for ever!—I cannot behold you and live!"

He did not rise upon his feet, but clasped his hands, and said in a tone of deprecation—"I will fly. I am become a fiend, the sight of whom destroys. Yet tell me my offence! You have linked curses with my name; you ascribe to me a malice monstrous and infernal. I look around; all is loneliness and desert! This house and your brother's are solitary and dismantled! You die away at the sight of me! My fear whispers that some deed of horror has been perpetrated; that I am the undesigning cause."

What language was this? Had he not avowed himself a ravisher? Had not this chamber witnessed his atrocious purposes? I besought him with new vehemence to go.

He lifted his eyes—"Great heaven! what have I done? I think I know the extent of my offences. I have acted, but my actions have possibly effected more than I designed. This fear has brought me back from my retreat. I come to repair the evil of which my rashness was the cause, and to prevent more evil. I come to confess my errors."

"Wretch!" I cried when my suffocating emotions would permit me to speak, "the ghosts of my sister and her children, do they not rise to accuse thee? Who was it that blasted the intellects of Wieland? Who was it that urged him to fury, and guided him to murder? Who, but thou and the devil, with whom thou art confederated?"

At these words a new spirit pervaded his countenance. His eyes once more appealed to heaven. "If I have memory, if I have being, I am innocent. I intended no ill; but my folly, indirectly and remotely, may have caused it; but what words are these! Your brother lunatic! His children dead!"

What should I infer from this deportment? Was the ignorance which these words implied real or pretended?—Yet how could I imagine a mere human agency in these events? But if the influence was preternatural or maniacal in my brother's case, they must be equally so in my own. Then I remembered that the voice exerted, was to save me from Carwin's attempts. These ideas tended to abate my abhorrence of this man, and to detect the absurdity of my accusations.

"Alas!" said I, "I have no one to accuse. Leave me to my fate. Fly from a scene stained with cruelty; devoted to despair."

Carwin stood for a time musing and mournful. At length he said, "What has happened? I came to expiate my crimes: let me know them in their full extent. I have horrible forebodings! What has happened?"

I was silent; but recollecting the intimation given by this man when he was detected in my closet, which implied some knowledge of that power which interfered in my favor, I eagerly inquired, "What was that voice which called upon me to hold when I attempted to open the closet? What face was that which I saw at the bottom of the stairs? Answer me truly."

"I came to confess the truth. Your allusions are horrible and strange. Perhaps I have but faint conceptions of the evils which my infatuation has produced; but what remains I will perform. It was *my voice* that you heard! It was *my face* that you saw!"

For a moment I doubted whether my remembrance of events were not confused. How could he be at once stationed at my shoulder and shut up in my closet? How could he stand near me and yet be invisible? But if Carwin's were the thrilling voice and the fiery visage which I had heard and seen, then was he the prompter of my brother, and the author of these dismal outrages.

Once more I averted my eyes and struggled for speech. "Begone! thou man of mischief! Remorseless and implacable miscreant! begone!"

"I will obey," said he in a disconsolate voice; "yet, wretch as I am, am I unworthy to repair the evils that I have committed? I came as a repentant criminal. It is you whom I have injured, and at your bar am I willing to appear, and confess and expiate my crimes. I have deceived you: I have sported with your terrors: I have plotted to destroy your reputation.

I come now to remove your errors; to set you beyond the reach of similar fears; to rebuild your fame as far as I am able.

"This is the amount of my guilt, and this the fruit of my remorse. Will you not hear me? Listen to my confession, and then denounce punishment. All I ask is a patient audience."

"What!" I replied, "was not thine the voice that commanded my brother to imbrue his hands in the blood of his children—to strangle that angel of sweetness his wife? Has he not vowed my death, and the death of Pleyel, at thy bidding? Hast thou not made him the butcher of his family; changed him who was the glory of his species into worse than brute; robbed him of reason; and consigned the rest of his days to fetters and stripes?"

Carwin's eyes glared, and his limbs were petrified at this intelligence. No words were requisite to prove him guiltless of these enormities: at the time, however, I was nearly insensible to these exculpatory tokens. He walked to the farther end of the room, and having recovered some degree of composure, he spoke—

"I am not this villain; I have slain no one; I have prompted none to slay; I have handled a tool of wonderful efficacy without malignant intentions, but without caution; ample will be the punishment of my temerity, if my conduct has contributed to this evil." He paused.—

I likewise was silent. I struggled to command myself so far as to listen to the tale which he should tell. Observing this, he continued—

"You are not apprized of the existence of a power which I possess. I know not by what name to call it.* It enables me to mimic exactly the voice of another, and to modify th

---

*Biloquium, or vetrilocution. Sound is varied according to the variatio direction and distance. The art of the ventriloquist consists in modifyi voice according to all these variations, without changing his place. S work of the Abbe de la Chappelle, in which are accurately recorded formances of one of these artists, and some ingenious, though unsa speculations are given on the means by which the effects are prod power is, perhaps, given by nature, but is doubtless improvable quirable, by art. It may, possibly, consist in an unusual flexibilit of the bottom of the tongue and the uvula. That speech is prod alone must be granted, since anatomists mention two insta speaking without a tongue. In one case, the organ was origir

sound so that it shall appear to come from what quarter, and be uttered at what distance I please.

"I know not that every one possesses this power. Perhaps, though a casual position of my organs in my youth shewed me that I possessed it, it is an art which may be taught to all. Would to God I had died unknowing of the secret! It has produced nothing but degradation and calamity.

"For a time the possession of so potent and stupendous an endowment elated me with pride. Unfortified by principle, subjected to poverty, stimulated by headlong passions, I made this powerful engine subservient to the supply of my wants, and the gratification of my vanity. I shall not mention how diligently I cultivated this gift, which seemed capable of unlimited improvement; nor detail the various occasions on which it was successfully exerted to lead superstition, conquer avarice, or excite awe.

"I left America, which is my native soil, in my youth. I have been engaged in various scenes of life, in which my peculiar talent has been exercised with more or less success. I was finally betrayed by one who called himself my friend, into acts which cannot be justified, though they are susceptible of apology.

"The perfidy of this man compelled me to withdraw from Europe. I returned to my native country, uncertain whether silence and obscurity would save me from his malice. I resided in the purlieus of the city. I put on the garb and assumed the manners of a clown.

"My chief recreation was walking. My principal haunts were the lawns and gardens of Mettingen. In this delightful region the luxuriances of nature had been chastened by judicious art, and each successive contemplation unfolded new enchantments.

---

its place was supplied by a small tubercle, and the uvula was perfect. In the other, the tongue was destroyed by disease, but probably a small part of it remained.

This power is difficult to explain, but the fact is undeniable. Experience shews that the human voice can imitate the voice of all men and of all inferior animals. The sound of musical instruments, and even noises from the contact of inanimate substances, have been accurately imitated. The mimicry of animals is notorious; and Dr. Burney (Musical Travels) mentions one who imitated a flute and violin, so as to deceive even his ears.

"I was studious of seclusion: I was satiated with the intercourse of mankind, and discretion required me to shun their intercourse. For these reasons I long avoided the observation of your family, and chiefly visited these precincts at night.

"I was never weary of admiring the position and ornaments of *the temple*. Many a night have I passed under its roof, revolving no pleasing meditations. When, in my frequent rambles, I perceived this apartment was occupied, I gave a different direction to my steps. One evening, when a shower had just passed, judging by the silence that no one was within, I ascended to this building. Glancing carelessly round, I perceived an open letter on the pedestal. To read it was doubtless an offence against politeness. Of this offence, however, I was guilty.

"Scarcely had I gone half through when I was alarmed by the approach of your brother. To scramble down the cliff on the opposite side was impracticable. I was unprepared to meet a stranger. Besides the aukwardness attending such an interview in these circumstances, concealment was necessary to my safety. A thousand times had I vowed never again to employ the dangerous talent which I possessed; but such was the force of habit and the influence of present convenience, that I used this method of arresting his progress and leading him back to the house, with his errand, whatever it was, unperformed. I had often caught parts, from my station below, of your conversation in this place, and was well acquainted with the voice of your sister.

"Some weeks after this I was again quietly seated in this recess. The lateness of the hour secured me, as I thought, from all interruption. In this, however, I was mistaken, for Wieland and Pleyel, as I judged by their voices, earnest in dispute, ascended the hill.

"I was not sensible that any inconvenience could possibly have flowed from my former exertion; yet it was followed with compunction, because it was a deviation from a path which I had assigned to myself. Now my aversion to this means of escape was enforced by an unauthorized curiosity, and by the knowledge of a bushy hollow on the edge of the hill, where I should be safe from discovery. Into this hollow I thrust myself.

"The propriety of removal to Europe was the question eagerly discussed. Pleyel intimated that his anxiety to go was augmented by the silence of Theresa de Stolberg. The temptation to interfere in this dispute was irresistible. In vain I contended with inveterate habits. I disguised to myself the impropriety of my conduct, by recollecting the benefits which it might produce. Pleyel's proposal was unwise, yet it was enforced with plausible arguments and indefatigable zeal. Your brother might be puzzled and wearied, but could not be convinced. I conceived that to terminate the controversy in favor of the latter was conferring a benefit on all parties. For this end I profited by an opening in the conversation, and assured them of Catharine's irreconcilable aversion to the scheme, and of the death of the Saxon baroness. The latter event was merely a conjecture, but rendered extremely probable by Pleyel's representations. My purpose, you need not be told, was effected.

"My passion for mystery, and a species of imposture, which I deemed harmless, was thus awakened afresh. This second lapse into error made my recovery more difficult. I cannot convey to you an adequate idea of the kind of gratification which I derived from these exploits; yet I meditated nothing. My views were bounded to the passing moment, and commonly suggested by the momentary exigence.

"I must not conceal any thing. Your principles teach you to abhor a voluptuous temper; but, with whatever reluctance, I acknowledge this temper to be mine. You imagine your servant Judith to be innocent as well as beautiful; but you took her from a family where hypocrisy, as well as licentiousness, was wrought into a system. My attention was captivated by her charms, and her principles were easily seen to be flexible.

"Deem me not capable of the iniquity of seduction. Your servant is not destitute of feminine and virtuous qualities; but she was taught that the best use of her charms consists in the sale of them. My nocturnal visits to Mettingen were now prompted by a double view, and my correspondence with your servant gave me, at all times, access to your house.

"The second night after our interview, so brief and so little foreseen by either of us, some dæmon of mischief seized me. According to my companion's report, your perfections were little less than divine. Her uncouth but copious narratives converted you into an object of worship. She chiefly dwelt upon your courage, because she herself was deficient in that quality. You held apparitions and goblins in contempt. You took no precautions against robbers. You were just as tranquil and secure in this lonely dwelling, as if you were in the midst of a crowd.

"Hence a vague project occurred to me, to put this courage to the test. A woman capable of recollection in danger, of warding off groundless panics, of discerning the true mode of proceeding, and profiting by her best resources, is a prodigy. I was desirous of ascertaining whether you were such an one.

"My expedient was obvious and simple: I was to counterfeit a murderous dialogue; but this was to be so conducted that another, and not yourself, should appear to be the object. I was not aware of the possibility that you should appropriate these menaces to yourself. Had you been still and listened, you would have heard the struggles and prayers of the victim, who would likewise have appeared to be shut up in the closet, and whose voice would have been Judith's. This scene would have been an appeal to your compassion; and the proof of cowardice or courage which I expected from you, would have been your remaining inactive in your bed, or your entering the closet with a view to assist the sufferer. Some instances which Judith related of your fearlessness and promptitude made me adopt the latter supposition with some degree of confidence.

"By the girl's direction I found a ladder, and mounted to your closet window. This is scarcely large enough to admit the head, but it answered my purpose too well.

"I cannot express my confusion and surprise at your abrupt and precipitate flight. I hastily removed the ladder; and, after some pause, curiosity and doubts of your safety induced me to follow you. I found you stretched on the turf before your brother's door, without sense or motion. I felt the deepest regret at this unlooked-for consequence of my scheme. I knew not what to do to procure you relief. The idea of awakening the family naturally presented itself. This emergency was critical, and there was no time to deliberate. It was a sudden thought that occurred. I put my lips to the key-hole, and sounded an alarm which effectually roused the sleepers. My organs were naturally forcible, and had been improved by long and assiduous exercise.

"Long and bitterly did I repent of my scheme. I was somewhat consoled by reflecting that my purpose had not been evil, and renewed my fruitless vows never to attempt such dangerous experiments. For some time I adhered, with laudable forbearance, to this resolution.

"My life has been a life of hardship and exposure. In the summer I prefer to make my bed of the smooth turf, or, at most, the shelter of a summer-house suffices. In all my rambles I never found a spot in which so many picturesque beauties and rural delights were assembled as at Mettingen. No corner of your little domain unites fragrance and secrecy in so perfect a degree as the recess in the bank. The odour of its leaves, the coolness of its shade, and the music of its waterfall, had early attracted my attention. Here my sadness was converted into peaceful melancholy—here my slumbers were sound, and my pleasures enhanced.

"As most free from interruption, I chose this as the scene of my midnight interviews with Judith. One evening, as the sun declined, I was seated here, when I was alarmed by your approach. It was with difficulty that I effected my escape unnoticed by you.

"At the customary hour, I returned to your habitation, and was made acquainted by Judith, with your unusual absence. I half suspected the true cause, and felt uneasiness at the danger there was that I should be deprived of my retreat; or, at least, interrupted in the possession of it. The girl, likewise, informed me, that among your other singularities, it was not uncommon for you to leave your bed, and walk forth for the sake of night-airs and starlight contemplations.

"I desired to prevent this inconvenience. I found you easily swayed by fear. I was influenced, in my choice of means, by the facility and certainty of that to which I had been accustomed. All that I foresaw was, that, in future, this spot would be cautiously shunned by you.

"I entered the recess with the utmost caution, and discovered, by your breathings, in what condition you were. The unexpected interpretation which you placed upon my former proceeding, suggested my conduct on the present occasion. The mode in which heaven is said by the poet, to interfere for the prevention of crimes,* was somewhat analogous to my province, and never failed to occur to me at seasons like this. It was requisite to break your slumbers, and for this end I uttered the powerful monosyllable, 'hold! hold!' My purpose was not prescribed by duty, yet surely it was far from being atrocious and inexpiable. To effect it, I uttered what was false, but it was well suited to my purpose. Nothing less was intended, than to injure you. Nay, the evil resulting from my former act, was partly removed by assuring you that in all places but this you were safe.

*—Peeps through the blanket of the dark, and cries
   Hold! Hold!—   SHAKESPEARE

Chapter XXIII

"MY MORALS will appear to you far from rigid, yet my conduct will fall short of your suspicions. I am now to confess actions less excusable, and yet surely they will not entitle me to the name of a desperate or sordid criminal.

"Your house was rendered, by your frequent and long absences, easily accessible to my curiosity. My meeting with Pleyel was the prelude to direct intercourse with you. I had seen much of the world, but your character exhibited a specimen of human powers that was wholly new to me. My intercourse with your servant furnished me with curious details of your domestic management. I was of a different sex: I was not your husband; I was not even your friend; yet my knowledge of you was of that kind, which conjugal intimacies can give, and, in some respects, more accurate. The observation of your domestic was guided by me.

"You will not be surprised that I should sometimes profit by your absence, and adventure to examine with my own eyes, the interior of your chamber. Upright and sincere, you used no watchfulness, and practised no precautions. I scrutinized every thing, and pried every where. Your closet was usually locked, but it was once my fortune to find the key on a bureau. I opened and found new scope for my curiosity in your books. One of these was manuscript, and written in characters which essentially agreed with a short-hand system which I had learned from a Jesuit missionary.

"I cannot justify my conduct, yet my only crime was curiosity. I perused this volume with eagerness. The intellect which it unveiled, was brighter than my limited and feeble organs could bear. I was naturally inquisitive as to your ideas respecting my deportment, and the mysteries that had lately occurred.

"You know what you have written. You know that in this volume the key to your inmost soul was contained. If I had been a profound and malignant impostor, what plenteous materials were thus furnished me of stratagems and plots!

"The coincidence of your dream in the summer-house with

my exclamation, was truly wonderful. The voice which warned you to forbear was, doubtless, mine; but mixed by a common process of the fancy, with the train of visionary incidents.

"I saw in a stronger light than ever, the dangerousness of that instrument which I employed, and renewed my resolutions to abstain from the use of it in future; but I was destined perpetually to violate my resolutions. By some perverse fate, I was led into circumstances in which the exertion of my powers was the sole or the best means of escape.

"On that memorable night on which our last interview took place, I came as usual to Mettingen. I was apprized of your engagement at your brother's, from which you did not expect to return till late. Some incident suggested the design of visiting your chamber. Among your books which I had not examined, might be something tending to illustrate your character, or the history of your family. Some intimation had been dropped by you in discourse, respecting a performance of your father, in which some important transaction in his life was recorded.

"I was desirous of seeing this book; and such was my habitual attachment to mystery, that I preferred the clandestine perusal of it. Such were the motives that induced me to make this attempt. Judith had disappeared, and finding the house unoccupied, I supplied myself with a light, and proceeded to your chamber.

"I found it easy, on experiment, to lock and unlock your closet door without the aid of a key. I shut myself in this recess, and was busily exploring your shelves, when I heard some one enter the room below. I was at a loss who it could be, whether you or your servant. Doubtful, however, as I was, I conceived it prudent to extinguish the light. Scarcely was this done, when some one entered the chamber. The footsteps were easily distinguished to be yours.

"My situation was now full of danger and perplexity. For some time, I cherished the hope that you would leave the room so long as to afford me an opportunity of escaping. As the hours passed, this hope gradually deserted me. It was plain that you had retired for the night.

"I knew not how soon you might find occasion to enter the closet. I was alive to all the horrors of detection, and ruminated without ceasing, on the behaviour which it would be proper, in case of detection, to adopt. I was unable to discover any consistent method of accounting for my being thus immured.

"It occurred to me that I might withdraw you from your chamber for a few minutes, by counterfeiting a voice from without. Some message from your brother might be delivered, requiring your presence at his house. I was deterred from this scheme by reflecting on the resolution I had formed, and on the possible evils that might result from it. Besides, it was not improbable that you would speedily retire to bed, and then, by the exercise of sufficient caution, I might hope to escape unobserved.

"Meanwhile I listened with the deepest anxiety to every motion from without. I discovered nothing which betokened preparation for sleep. Instead of this I heard deep-drawn sighs, and occasionally an half-expressed and mournful ejaculation. Hence I inferred that you were unhappy. The true state of your mind with regard to Pleyel your own pen had disclosed; but I supposed you to be framed of such materials, that, though a momentary sadness might affect you, you were impregnable to any permanent and heartfelt grief. Inquietude for my own safety was, for a moment, suspended by sympathy with your distress.

"To the former consideration I was quickly recalled by a motion of yours which indicated I knew not what. I fostered the persuasion that you would now retire to bed; but presently you approached the closet, and detection seemed to be inevitable. You put your hand upon the lock. I had formed no plan to extricate myself from the dilemma in which the opening of the door would involve me. I felt an irreconcilable aversion to detection. Thus situated, I involuntarily seized the door with a resolution to resist your efforts to open it.

"Suddenly you receded from the door. This deportment was inexplicable, but the relief it afforded me was quickly gone. You returned, and I once more was thrown into perplexity. The expedient that suggested itself was precipitate and inartificial. I exerted my organs and called upon you to *hold*.

"That you should persist in spite of this admonition, was a subject of astonishment. I again resisted your efforts; for the first expedient having failed, I knew not what other to resort to. In this state, how was my astonishment increased when I heard your exclamations!

"It was now plain that you knew me to be within. Further resistance was unavailing and useless. The door opened, and I shrunk backward. Seldom have I felt deeper mortification, and more painful perplexity. I did not consider that the truth would be less injurious than any lie which I could hastily frame. Conscious as I was of a certain degree of guilt, I conceived that you would form the most odious suspicions. The truth would be imperfect, unless I were likewise to explain the mysterious admonition which had been given; but that explanation was of too great moment, and involved too extensive consequences to make me suddenly resolve to give it.

"I was aware that this discovery would associate itself in your mind, with the dialogue formerly heard in this closet. Thence would your suspicions be aggravated, and to escape from these suspicions would be impossible. But the mere truth would be sufficiently opprobrious, and deprive me for ever of your good opinion.

"Thus was I rendered desperate, and my mind rapidly passed to the contemplation of the use that might be made of previous events. Some good genius would appear to you to have interposed to save you from injury intended by me. Why, I said, since I must sink in her opinion, should I not cherish this belief? Why not personate an enemy, and pretend that celestial interference has frustrated my schemes? I must fly, but let me leave wonder and fear behind me. Elucidation of the mystery will always be practicable. I shall do no injury, but merely talk of evil that was designed, but is now past.

"Thus I extenuated my conduct to myself, but I scarcely expect that this will be to you a sufficient explication of the scene that followed. Those habits which I have imbibed, the rooted passion which possesses me for scattering around me amazement and fear, you enjoy no opportunities of knowing. That a man should wantonly impute to himself the most flagitious designs, will hardly be credited, even though you reflect that my reputation was already, by my own folly, irretrievably ruined; and that it was always in my power to communicate the truth, and rectify the mistake.

"I left you to ponder on this scene. My mind was full of rapid and incongruous ideas. Compunction, self-upbraiding, hopelessness, satisfaction at the view of those effects likely to flow from my new scheme, misgivings as to the beneficial result of this scheme, took possession of my mind, and seemed to struggle for the mastery.

"I had gone too far to recede. I had painted myself to you as an assassin and ravisher, withheld from guilt only by a voice from heaven. I had thus reverted into the path of error, and now, having gone thus far, my progress seemed to be irrevocable. I said to myself, I must leave these precincts for ever. My acts have blasted my fame in the eyes of the Wielands. For the sake of creating a mysterious dread, I have made myself a villain. I may complete this mysterious plan by some new imposture, but I cannot aggravate my supposed guilt.

"My resolution was formed, and I was swiftly ruminating on the means for executing it, when Pleyel appeared in sight. This incident decided my conduct. It was plain that Pleyel was a devoted lover, but he was, at the same time, a man of cold resolves and exquisite sagacity. To deceive him would be the sweetest triumph I had ever enjoyed. The deception would be momentary, but it would likewise be complete. That his delusion would so soon be rectified, was a recommendation to my scheme, for I esteemed him too much to desire to entail upon him lasting agonies.

"I had no time to reflect further, for he proceeded, with a quick step, towards the house. I was hurried onward involuntarily and by a mechanical impulse. I followed him as he passed the recess in the bank, and shrowding myself in that spot, I counterfeited sounds which I knew would arrest his steps.

"He stopped, turned, listened, approached, and overheard a dialogue whose purpose was to vanquish his belief in a point where his belief was most difficult to vanquish. I exerted all my powers to imitate your voice, your general sentiments, and your language. Being master, by means of your journal, of your personal history and most secret thoughts, my efforts were the more successful. When I reviewed the tenor of this dialogue, I cannot believe but that Pleyel was deluded. When I think of your character, and of the inferences which this dialogue was intended to suggest, it seems incredible that this delusion should be produced.

"I spared not myself. I called myself murderer, thief, guilty of innumerable perjuries and misdeeds: that you had debased yourself to the level of such an one, no evidence, methought, would suffice to convince him who knew you so thoroughly as Pleyel; and yet the imposture amounted to proof which the most jealous scrutiny would find to be unexceptionable.

"He left his station precipitately and resumed his way to the house. I saw that the detection of his error would be instantaneous, since, not having gone to bed, an immediate interview would take place between you. At first this circumstance was considered with regret; but as time opened my eyes to the possible consequences of this scene, I regarded it with pleasure.

"In a short time the infatuation which had led me thus far began to subside. The remembrance of former reasonings and transactions was renewed. How often I had repented this kind of exertion; how many evils were produced by it which I had not foreseen; what occasions for the bitterest remorse it had administered, now passed through my mind. The black catalogue of stratagems was now increased. I had inspired you with the most vehement terrors: I had filled your mind with faith in shadows and confidence in dreams: I had depraved the imagination of Pleyel: I had exhibited you to his understanding as devoted to brutal gratifications and consummate in hypocrisy. The evidence which accompanied this delusion would be irresistible to one whose passion had perverted his judgment, whose jealousy with regard to me had already been excited, and who, therefore, would not fail to overrate the force of this evidence. What fatal act of despair or of vengeance might not this error produce?

"With regard to myself, I had acted with a phrenzy that surpassed belief. I had warred against my peace and my fame: I had banished myself from the fellowship of vigorous and pure minds: I was self-expelled from a scene which the munificence of nature had adorned with unrivalled beauties, and from haunts in which all the muses and humanities had taken refuge.

"I was thus torn by conflicting fears and tumultuous regrets. The night passed away in this state of confusion; and next morning in the gazette left at my obscure lodging, I read a description and an offer of reward for the apprehension of my person. I was said to have escaped from an Irish prison, in which I was confined as an offender convicted of enormous and complicated crimes.

"This was the work of an enemy, who, by falsehood and stratagem, had procured my condemnation. I was, indeed, a prisoner, but escaped, by the exertion of my powers, the fate to which I was doomed, but which I did not deserve. I had hoped that the malice of my foe was exhausted; but I now perceived that my precautions had been wise, for that the intervention of an ocean was insufficient for my security.

"Let me not dwell on the sensations which this discovery produced. I need not tell by what steps I was induced to seek an interview with you, for the purpose of disclosing the truth, and repairing, as far as possible, the effects of my misconduct. It was unavoidable that this gazette would fall into your hands, and that it would tend to confirm every erroneous impression.

"Having gained this interview, I purposed to seek some retreat in the wilderness, inaccessible to your inquiry and to the malice of my foe, where I might henceforth employ myself in composing a faithful narrative of my actions. I designed it as my vindication from the aspersions that had rested on my character, and as a lesson to mankind on the evils of credulity on the one hand, and of imposture on the other.

"I wrote you a billet, which was left at the house of your friend, and which I knew would, by some means, speedily come to your hands. I entertained a faint hope that my invitation would be complied with. I knew not what use you would make of the opportunity which this proposal afforded you of procuring the seizure of my person; but this fate I was determined to avoid, and I had no doubt but due circumspection, and the exercise of the faculty which I possessed, would enable me to avoid it.

"I lurked, through the day, in the neighbourhood of Mettingen: I approached your habitation at the appointed hour: I entered it in silence, by a trap-door which led into the cellar. This had formerly been bolted on the inside, but Judith had, at an early period in our intercourse, removed this impediment. I ascended to the first floor, but met with no one, nor any thing that indicated the presence of an human being.

"I crept softly up stairs, and at length perceived your chamber door to be opened, and a light to be within. It was of moment to discover by whom this light was accompanied. I was sensible of the inconveniencies to which my being discovered at your chamber door by any one within would subject me; I therefore called out in my own voice, but so modified that it should appear to ascend from the court below, 'Who is in the chamber? Is it Miss Wieland?'

"No answer was returned to this summons. I listened, but no motion could be heard. After a pause I repeated my call, but no less ineffectually.

"I now approached nearer the door, and adventured to look in. A light stood on the table, but nothing human was discernible. I entered cautiously, but all was solitude and stillness.

"I knew not what to conclude. If the house were inhabited, my call would have been noticed; yet some suspicion insinuated itself that silence was studiously kept by persons who intended to surprize me. My approach had been wary, and the silence that ensued my call had likewise preceded it; a circumstance that tended to dissipate my fears.

"At length it occurred to me that Judith might possibly be in her own room. I turned my steps thither; but she was not to be found. I passed into other rooms, and was soon convinced that the house was totally deserted. I returned to your chamber, agitated by vain surmises and opposite conjectures. The appointed hour had passed, and I dismissed the hope of an interview.

"In this state of things I determined to leave a few lines on your toilet, and prosecute my journey to the mountains. Scarcely had I taken the pen when I laid it aside, uncertain in what manner to address you. I rose from the table and walked across the floor. A glance thrown upon the bed acquainted me with a spectacle to which my conceptions of horror had not yet reached.

"In the midst of shuddering and trepidation, the signal of your presence in the court below recalled me to myself. The deed was newly done: I only was in the house: what had lately happened justified any suspicions, however enormous. It was plain that this catastrophe was unknown to you: I thought upon the wild commotion which the discovery would awaken in your breast: I found the confusion of my own thoughts unconquerable, and perceived that the end for which I sought an interview was not now to be accomplished.

"In this state of things it was likewise expedient to conceal my being within. I put out the light and hurried down stairs. To my unspeakable surprize, notwithstanding every motive to fear, you lighted a candle and proceeded to your chamber.

"I retired to that room below from which a door leads into the cellar. This door concealed me from your view as you passed. I thought upon the spectacle which was about to present itself. In an exigence so abrupt and so little foreseen, I was again subjected to the empire of mechanical and habitual impulses. I dreaded the effects which this shocking exhibition, bursting on your unprepared senses, might produce.

"Thus actuated, I stept swiftly to the door, and thrusting my head forward, once more pronounced the mysterious interdiction. At that moment, by some untoward fate, your eyes were cast back, and you saw me in the very act of utterance. I fled through the darksome avenue at which I entered, covered with the shame of this detection.

"With diligence, stimulated by a thousand ineffable emotions, I pursued my intended journey. I have a brother whose farm is situated in the bosom of a fertile desert, near the sources of the Leheigh, and thither I now repaired.

Chapter XXIV

"DEEPLY did I ruminate on the occurrences that had just passed. Nothing excited my wonder so much as the means by which you discovered my being in the closet. This discovery appeared to be made at the moment when you attempted to open it. How could you have otherwise remained so long in the chamber apparently fearless and tranquil? And yet, having made this discovery, how could you persist in dragging me forth: persist in defiance of an interdiction so emphatical and solemn?

"But your sister's death was an event detestable and ominous. She had been the victim of the most dreadful species of assassination. How, in a state like yours, the murderous intention could be generated, was wholly inconceivable.

"I did not relinquish my design of confessing to you the part which I had sustained in your family, but I was willing to defer it till the task which I had set myself was finished. That being done, I resumed the resolution. The motives to incite me to this continually acquired force. The more I revolved the events happening at Mettingen, the more insupportable and ominous my terrors became. My waking hours and my sleep were vexed by dismal presages and frightful intimations.

"Catharine was dead by violence. Surely my malignant stars had not made me the cause of her death; yet had I not rashly set in motion a machine, over whose progress I had no controul, and which experience had shewn me was infinite in power? Every day might add to the catalogue of horrors of which this was the source, and a seasonable disclosure of the truth might prevent numberless ills.

"Fraught with this conception, I have turned my steps hither. I find your brother's house desolate: the furniture removed, and the walls stained with damps. Your own is in the same situation. Your chamber is dismantled and dark, and you exhibit an image of incurable grief, and of rapid decay.

"I have uttered the truth. This is the extent of my offences. You tell me an horrid tale of Wieland being led to the destruction of his wife and children, by some mysterious agent. You charge me with the guilt of this agency; but I repeat that the amount of my guilt has been truly stated. The perpetrator of Catharine's death was unknown to me till now; nay, it is still unknown to me."

At that moment, the closing of a door in the kitchen was distinctly heard by us. Carwin started and paused. "There is some one coming. I must not be found here by my enemies, and need not, since my purpose is answered."

I had drunk in, with the most vehement attention, every word that he had uttered. I had no breath to interrupt his tale by interrogations or comments. The power that he spoke of was hitherto unknown to me: its existence was incredible; it was susceptible of no direct proof.

He owns that his were the voice and face which I heard and saw. He attempts to give an human explanation of these phantasms; but it is enough that he owns himself to be the agent; his tale is a lie, and his nature devilish. As he deceived me, he likewise deceived my brother, and now do I behold the author of all our calamities!

Such were my thoughts when his pause allowed me to think. I should have bad him begone if the silence had not been interrupted; but now I feared no more for myself; and the milkiness of my nature was curdled into hatred and rancour. Some one was near, and this enemy of God and man might possibly be brought to justice. I reflected not that the preternatural power which he had hitherto exerted, would avail to rescue him from any toils in which his feet might be entangled. Meanwhile, looks, and not words of menace and abhorrence, were all that I could bestow.

He did not depart. He seemed dubious, whether, by passing out of the house, or by remaining somewhat longer where he was, he should most endanger his safety. His confusion increased when steps of one barefoot were heard upon the stairs. He threw anxious glances sometimes at the closet, sometimes at the window, and sometimes at the chamber door, yet he was detained by some inexplicable fascination. He stood as if rooted to the spot.

As to me, my soul was bursting with detestation and revenge. I had no room for surmises and fears respecting him that approached. It was doubtless a human being, and would befriend me so far as to aid me in arresting this offender.

The stranger quickly entered the room. My eyes and the eyes of Carwin were, at the same moment, darted upon him. A second glance was not needed to inform us who he was. His locks were tangled, and fell confusedly over his forehead and ears. His shirt was of coarse stuff, and open at the neck and breast. His coat was once of bright and fine texture, but now torn and tarnished with dust. His feet, his legs, and his arms were bare. His features were the seat of a wild and tranquil solemnity, but his eyes bespoke inquietude and curiosity.

He advanced with firm step, and looking as in search of some one. He saw me and stopped. He bent his sight on the floor, and clenching his hands, appeared suddenly absorbed in meditation. Such were the figure and deportment of Wieland! Such, in his fallen state, were the aspect and guise of my brother!

Carwin did not fail to recognize the visitant. Care for his own safety was apparently swallowed up in the amazement which this spectacle produced. His station was conspicuous, and he could not have escaped the roving glances of Wieland; yet the latter seemed totally unconscious of his presence.

Grief at this scene of ruin and blast was at first the only sentiment of which I was conscious. A fearful stillness ensued. At length Wieland, lifting his hands, which were locked in each other, to his breast, exclaimed, "Father! I thank thee. This is thy guidance. Hither thou hast led me, that I might perform thy will: yet let me not err: let me hear again thy messenger!"

He stood for a minute as if listening; but recovering from his attitude, he continued—"It is not needed. Dastardly wretch! thus eternally questioning the behests of thy Maker! weak in resolution! wayward in faith!"

He advanced to me, and, after another pause, resumed: "Poor girl! a dismal fate has set its mark upon thee. Thy life is demanded as a sacrifice. Prepare thee to die. Make not my office difficult by fruitless opposition. Thy prayers might subdue stones; but none but he who enjoined my purpose can shake it."

These words were a sufficient explication of the scene. The

nature of his phrenzy, as described by my uncle, was remembered. I who had sought death, was now thrilled with horror because it was near. Death in this form, death from the hand of a brother, was thought upon with undescribable repugnance.

In a state thus verging upon madness, my eye glanced upon Carwin. His astonishment appeared to have struck him motionless and dumb. My life was in danger, and my brother's hand was about to be embrued in my blood. I firmly believed that Carwin's was the instigation. I could rescue me from this abhorred fate; I could dissipate this tremendous illusion; I could save my brother from the perpetration of new horrors, by pointing out the devil who seduced him; to hesitate a moment was to perish. These thoughts gave strength to my limbs, and energy to my accents: I started on my feet.

"O brother! spare me, spare thyself: There is thy betrayer. He counterfeited the voice and face of an angel, for the purpose of destroying thee and me. He has this moment confessed it. He is able to speak where he is not. He is leagued with hell, but will not avow it; yet he confesses that the agency was his."

My brother turned slowly his eyes, and fixed them upon Carwin. Every joint in the frame of the latter trembled. His complexion was paler than a ghost's. His eye dared not meet that of Wieland, but wandered with an air of distraction from one space to another.

"Man," said my brother, in a voice totally unlike that which he had used to me, "what art thou? The charge has been made. Answer it. The visage—the voice—at the bottom of these stairs—at the hour of eleven—To whom did they belong? To thee?"

Twice did Carwin attempt to speak, but his words died away upon his lips. My brother resumed in a tone of greater vehemence—

"Thou falterest; faltering is ominous; say yes or no: one word will suffice; but beware of falsehood. Was it a stratagem of hell to overthrow my family? Wast thou the agent?"

I now saw that the wrath which had been prepared for me was to be heaped upon another. The tale that I heard from him, and his present trepidations, were abundant testimonies of his guilt. But what if Wieland should be undeceived! What if he shall find his acts to have proceeded not from an heavenly prompter, but from human treachery! Will not his rage mount into whirlwind? Will not he tear limb from limb this devoted wretch?

Instinctively I recoiled from this image, but it gave place to another. Carwin may be innocent, but the impetuosity of his judge may misconstrue his answers into a confession of guilt. Wieland knows not that mysterious voices and appearances were likewise witnessed by me. Carwin may be ignorant of those which misled my brother. Thus may his answers unwarily betray himself to ruin.

Such might be the consequences of my frantic precipitation, and these, it was necessary, if possible, to prevent. I attempted to speak, but Wieland, turning suddenly upon me, commanded silence, in a tone furious and terrible. My lips closed, and my tongue refused its office.

"What art thou?" he resumed, addressing himself to Carwin. "Answer me; whose form—whose voice—was it thy contrivance? Answer me."

The answer was now given, but confusedly and scarcely articulated. "I meant nothing—I intended no ill—if I understand—if I do not mistake you—it is too true—I did appear —in the entry—did speak. The contrivance was mine, but—"

These words were no sooner uttered, than my brother ceased to wear the same aspect. His eyes were downcast: he was motionless: his respiration became hoarse, like that of a man in the agonies of death. Carwin seemed unable to say more. He might have easily escaped, but the thought which occupied him related to what was horrid and unintelligible in this scene, and not to his own danger.

Presently the faculties of Wieland, which, for a time, were chained up, were seized with restlessness and trembling. He broke silence. The stoutest heart would have been appalled by the tone in which he spoke. He addressed himself to Carwin.

"Why art thou here? Who detains thee? Go and learn better. I will meet thee, but it must be at the bar of thy Maker. There shall I bear witness against thee."

Perceiving that Carwin did not obey, he continued; "Dost

thou wish me to complete the catalogue by thy death? Thy life is a worthless thing. Tempt me no more. I am but a man, and thy presence may awaken a fury which may spurn my controul. Begone!"

Carwin, irresolute, striving in vain for utterance, his complexion pallid as death, his knees beating one against another, slowly obeyed the mandate and withdrew.

Chapter XXV

A FEW WORDS more and I lay aside the pen for ever. Yet why should I not relinquish it now? All that I have said is preparatory to this scene, and my fingers, tremulous and cold as my heart, refuse any further exertion. This must not be. Let my last energies support me in the finishing of this task. Then will I lay down my head in the lap of death. Hushed will be all my murmurs in the sleep of the grave.

Every sentiment has perished in my bosom. Even friendship is extinct. Your love for me has prompted me to this task; but I would not have complied if it had not been a luxury thus to feast upon my woes. I have justly calculated upon my remnant of strength. When I lay down the pen the taper of life will expire: my existence will terminate with my tale.

Now that I was left alone with Wieland, the perils of my situation presented themselves to my mind. That this paroxysm should terminate in havock and rage it was reasonable to predict. The first suggestion of my fears had been disproved by my experience. Carwin had acknowledged his offences, and yet had escaped. The vengeance which I had harboured had not been admitted by Wieland, and yet the evils which I had endured, compared with those inflicted on my brother, were as nothing. I thirsted for his blood, and was tormented with an insatiable appetite for his destruction; yet my brother was unmoved, and had dismissed him in safety. Surely thou wast more than man, while I am sunk below the beasts.

Did I place a right construction on the conduct of Wieland? Was the error that misled him so easily rectified? Were views so vivid and faith so strenuous thus liable to fading and to change? Was there not reason to doubt the accuracy of my perceptions? With images like these was my mind thronged, till the deportment of my brother called away my attention.

I saw his lips move and his eyes cast up to heaven. Then would he listen and look back, as if in expectation of some one's appearance. Thrice he repeated these gesticulations and this inaudible prayer. Each time the mist of confusion and doubt seemed to grow darker and to settle on his understanding. I guessed at the meaning of these tokens. The words of Carwin had shaken his belief, and he was employed in summoning the messenger who had formerly communed with him, to attest the value of these new doubts. In vain the summons was repeated, for his eye met nothing but vacancy, and not a sound saluted his ear.

He walked to the bed, gazed with eagerness at the pillow which had sustained the head of the breathless Catharine, and then returned to the place where I sat. I had no power to lift my eyes to his face: I was dubious of his purpose: this purpose might aim at my life.

Alas! nothing but subjection to danger, and exposure to temptation, can show us what we are. By this test was I now tried, and found to be cowardly and rash. Men can deliberately untie the thread of life, and of this I had deemed myself capable; yet now that I stood upon the brink of fate, that the knife of the sacrificer was aimed at my heart, I shuddered and betook myself to any means of escape, however monstrous.

Can I bear to think—can I endure to relate the outrage which my heart meditated? Where were my means of safety? Resistance was vain. Not even the energy of despair could set me on a level with that strength which his terrific prompter had bestowed upon Wieland. Terror enables us to perform incredible feats; but terror was not then the state of my mind: where then were my hopes of rescue?

Methinks it is too much. I stand aside, as it were, from myself; I estimate my own deservings; a hatred, immortal and inexorable, is my due. I listen to my own pleas, and find them empty and false: yes, I acknowledge that my guilt surpasses that of all mankind: I confess that the curses of a world, and the frowns of a deity, are inadequate to my demerits. Is there a thing in the world worthy of infinite abhorrence? It is I.

What shall I say! I was menaced, as I thought, with death, and, to elude this evil, my hand was ready to inflict death upon the menacer. In visiting my house, I had made provision against the machinations of Carwin. In a fold of my dress an open penknife was concealed. This I now seized and drew forth. It lurked out of view; but I now see that my state of mind would have rendered the deed inevitable if my brother had lifted his hand. This instrument of my preservation would have been plunged into his heart.

O, insupportable remembrance! hide thee from my view for a time; hide it from me that my heart was black enough to meditate the stabbing of a brother! a brother thus supreme in misery; thus towering in virtue!

He was probably unconscious of my design, but presently drew back. This interval was sufficient to restore me to myself. The madness, the iniquity of that act which I had purposed rushed upon my apprehension. For a moment I was breathless with agony. At the next moment I recovered my strength, and threw the knife with violence on the floor.

The sound awoke my brother from his reverie. He gazed alternately at me and at the weapon. With a movement equally solemn he stooped and took it up. He placed the blade in different positions, scrutinizing it accurately, and maintaining, at the same time, a profound silence.

Again he looked at me, but all that vehemence and loftiness of spirit which had so lately characterized his features, were flown. Fallen muscles, a forehead contracted into folds, eyes dim with unbidden drops, and a ruefulness of aspect which no words can describe, were now visible.

His looks touched into energy the same sympathies in me, and I poured forth a flood of tears. This passion was quickly checked by fear, which had now, no longer my own, but his safety for their object. I watched his deportment in silence. At length he spoke:

"Sister," said he, in an accent mournful and mild, "I have acted poorly my part in this world. What thinkest thou? Shall I not do better in the next?"

I could make no answer. The mildness of his tone astonished and encouraged me. I continued to regard him with wistful and anxious looks.

"I think," resumed he, "I will try. My wife and my babes have gone before. Happy wretches! I have sent you to repose, and ought not to linger behind."

These words had a meaning sufficiently intelligible. I looked at the open knife in his hand and shuddered, but knew not how to prevent the deed which I dreaded. He quickly noticed my fears, and comprehended them. Stretching towards me his hand, with an air of increasing mildness: "Take it," said he: "Fear not for thy own sake, nor for mine. The cup is gone by, and its transient inebriation is succeeded by the soberness of truth.

"Thou angel whom I was wont to worship! fearest thou, my sister, for thy life? Once it was the scope of my labours to destroy thee, but I was prompted to the deed by heaven; such, at least, was my belief. Thinkest thou that thy death was sought to gratify malevolence? No. I am pure from all stain. I believed that my God was my mover!

"Neither thee nor myself have I cause to injure. I have done my duty, and surely there is merit in having sacrificed to that, all that is dear to the heart of man. If a devil has deceived me, he came in the habit of an angel. If I erred, it was not my judgment that deceived me, but my senses. In thy sight, being of beings! I am still pure. Still will I look for my reward in thy justice!"

Did my ears truly report these sounds? If I did not err, my brother was restored to just perceptions. He knew himself to have been betrayed to the murder of his wife and children, to have been the victim of infernal artifice; yet he found consolation in the rectitude of his motives. He was not devoid of sorrow, for this was written on his countenance; but his soul was tranquil and sublime.

Perhaps this was merely a transition of his former madness into a new shape. Perhaps he had not yet awakened to the memory of the horrors which he had perpetrated. Infatuated wretch that I was! To set myself up as a model by which to judge of my heroic brother! My reason taught me that his conclusions were right; but conscious of the impotence of reason over my own conduct; conscious of my cowardly rashness and my criminal despair, I doubted whether any one could be stedfast and wise.

Such was my weakness, that even in the midst of these thoughts, my mind glided into abhorrence of Carwin, and I uttered in a low voice, "O! Carwin! Carwin! What hast thou to answer for!"

My brother immediately noticed the involuntary exclamation: "Clara!" said he, "be thyself. Equity used to be a theme for thy eloquence. Reduce its lessons to practice, and be just to that unfortunate man. The instrument has done its work, and I am satisfied.

"I thank thee, my God, for this last illumination! My enemy is thine also. I deemed him to be man, the man with whom I have often communed; but now thy goodness has unveiled to me his true nature. As the performer of thy behests, he is my friend."

My heart began now to misgive me. His mournful aspect had gradually yielded place to a serene brow. A new soul appeared to actuate his frame, and his eyes to beam with preternatural lustre. These symptoms did not abate, and he continued:

"Clara! I must not leave thee in doubt. I know not what brought about thy interview with the being whom thou callest Carwin. For a time, I was guilty of thy error, and deduced from his incoherent confessions that I had been made the victim of human malice. He left us at my bidding, and I put up a prayer that my doubts should be removed. Thy eyes were shut, and thy ears sealed to the vision that answered my prayer.

"I was indeed deceived. The form thou hast seen was the incarnation of a dæmon. The visage and voice which urged me to the sacrifice of my family, were his. Now he personates a human form: then he was invironed with the lustre of heaven.—

"Clara," he continued, advancing closer to me, "thy death must come. This minister is evil, but he from whom his commission was received is God. Submit then with all thy wonted resignation to a decree that cannot be reversed or resisted. Mark the clock. Three minutes are allowed to thee, in which to call up thy fortitude, and prepare thee for thy doom." There he stopped.

Even now, when this scene exists only in memory, when life and all its functions have sunk into torpor, my pulse throbs, and my hairs uprise: my brows are knit, as then; and I gaze around me in distraction. I was unconquerably averse to death; but death, imminent and full of agony as that which was threatened, was nothing. This was not the only or chief inspirer of my fears.

For him, not for myself, was my soul tormented. I might die, and no crime, surpassing the reach of mercy, would pursue me to the presence of my Judge; but my assassin would survive to contemplate his deed, and that assassin was Wieland!

Wings to bear me beyond his reach I had not. I could not vanish with a thought. The door was open, but my murderer was interposed between that and me. Of self-defence I was incapable. The phrenzy that lately prompted me to blood was gone; my state was desperate; my rescue was impossible.

The weight of these accumulated thoughts could not be borne. My sight became confused; my limbs were seized with convulsion; I spoke, but my words were half-formed: —

"Spare me, my brother! Look down, righteous Judge! snatch me from this fate! take away this fury from him, or turn it elsewhere!"

Such was the agony of my thoughts, that I noticed not steps entering my apartment. Supplicating eyes were cast upward, but when my prayer was breathed, I once more wildly gazed at the door. A form met my sight: I shuddered as if the God whom I invoked were present. It was Carwin that again intruded, and who stood before me, erect in attitude, and stedfast in look!

The sight of him awakened new and rapid thoughts. His recent tale was remembered: his magical transitions and mysterious energy of voice: Whether he were infernal, or miraculous, or human, there was no power and no need to decide. Whether the contriver or not of this spell, he was able to unbind it, and to check the fury of my brother. He had ascribed to himself intentions not malignant. Here now was afforded a test of his truth. Let him interpose, as from above; revoke the savage decree which the madness of Wieland has assigned to heaven; and extinguish for ever this passion for blood!

My mind detected at a glance this avenue to safety. The recommendations it possessed thronged as it were together, and made but one impression on my intellect. Remoter effects and collateral dangers I saw not. Perhaps the pause of an instant had sufficed to call them up. The improbability that the influence which governed Wieland was external or human; the tendency of this stratagem to sanction so fatal an error, or substitute a more destructive rage in place of this; the sufficiency of Carwin's mere muscular forces to counteract the efforts, and restrain the fury of Wieland, might, at a second glance, have been discovered; but no second glance was allowed. My first thought hurried me to action, and, fixing my eyes upon Carwin I exclaimed—

"O wretch! once more hast thou come? Let it be to abjure thy malice; to counterwork this hellish stratagem; to turn from me and from my brother, this desolating rage!

"Testify thy innocence or thy remorse: exert the powers which pertain to thee, whatever they be, to turn aside this ruin. Thou art the author of these horrors! What have I done to deserve thus to die? How have I merited this unrelenting persecution? I adjure thee, by that God whose voice thou hast dared to counterfeit, to save my life!

"Wilt thou then go? leave me! Succourless!"

Carwin listened to my intreaties unmoved, and turned from me. He seemed to hesitate a moment: then glided through the door. Rage and despair stifled my utterance. The interval of respite was passed; the pangs reserved for me by Wieland, were not to be endured; my thoughts rushed again into anarchy. Having received the knife from his hand, I held it loosely and without regard; but now it seized again my attention, and I grasped it with force.

He seemed to notice not the entrance or exit of Carwin. My gesture and the murderous weapon appeared to have escaped his notice. His silence was unbroken; his eye, fixed upon the clock for a time, was now withdrawn; fury kindled in every feature; all that was human in his face gave way to an expression supernatural and tremendous. I felt my left arm within his grasp.—

Even now I hesitated to strike. I shrunk from his assault, but in vain.—

Here let me desist. Why should I rescue this event from oblivion? Why should I paint this detestable conflict? Why not terminate at once this series of horrors?—hurry to the verge of the precipice, and cast myself for ever beyond remembrance and beyond hope?

Still I live: with this load upon my breast; with this phantom to pursue my steps; with adders lodged in my bosom, and stinging me to madness: still I consent to live!

Yes, I will rise above the sphere of mortal passions: I will spurn at the cowardly remorse that bids me seek impunity in silence, or comfort in forgetfulness. My nerves shall be new strung to the task. Have I not resolved? I will die. The gulph before me is inevitable and near. I will die, but then only when my tale is at an end.

Chapter XXVI

MY RIGHT HAND, grasping the unseen knife, was still disengaged. It was lifted to strike. All my strength was exhausted, but what was sufficient to the performance of this deed. Already was the energy awakened, and the impulse given, that should bear the fatal steel to his heart, when— Wieland shrunk back: his hand was withdrawn. Breathless with affright and desperation, I stood, freed from his grasp; unassailed; untouched.

Thus long had the power which controuled the scene forborne to interfere; but now his might was irresistible, and Wieland in a moment was disarmed of all his purposes. A voice, louder than human organs could produce, shriller than language can depict, burst from the ceiling, and commanded him—to *hold!*

Trouble and dismay succeeded to the stedfastness that had lately been displayed in the looks of Wieland. His eyes roved from one quarter to another, with an expression of doubt. He seemed to wait for a further intimation.

Carwin's agency was here easily recognized. I had besought him to interpose in my defence. He had flown. I had imagined him deaf to my prayer, and resolute to see me perish: yet he disappeared merely to devise and execute the means of my relief.

Why did he not forbear when this end was accomplished? Why did his misjudging zeal and accursed precipitation overpass that limit? Or meant he thus to crown the scene, and conduct his inscrutable plots to this consummation?

Such ideas were the fruit of subsequent contemplation. This moment was pregnant with fate. I had no power to reason. In the career of my tempestuous thoughts, rent into pieces, as my mind was, by accumulating horrors, Carwin was unseen and unsuspected. I partook of Wieland's credulity, shook with his amazement, and panted with his awe.

Silence took place for a moment; so much as allowed the attention to recover its post. Then new sounds were uttered from above.

"Man of errors! cease to cherish thy delusion: not heaven or hell, but thy senses have misled thee to commit these acts. Shake off thy phrenzy, and ascend into rational and human. Be lunatic no longer."

My brother opened his lips to speak. His tone was terrific and faint. He muttered an appeal to heaven. It was not difficult to comprehend the theme of his inquiries. They implied doubt as to the nature of the impulse that hitherto had guided him, and questioned whether he had acted in consequence of insane perceptions.

To these interrogatories the voice, which now seemed to hover at his shoulder, loudly answered in the affirmative. Then uninterrupted silence ensued.

Fallen from his lofty and heroic station; now finally restored to the perception of truth; weighed to earth by the recollection of his own deeds; consoled no longer by a consciousness of rectitude, for the loss of offspring and wife—a loss for which he was indebted to his own misguided hand; Wieland was transformed at once into the *man of sorrows!*

He reflected not that credit should be as reasonably denied to the last, as to any former intimation; that one might as justly be ascribed to erring or diseased senses as the other. He saw not that this discovery in no degree affected the integrity of his conduct; that his motives had lost none of their claims to the homage of mankind; that the preference of supreme good, and the boundless energy of duty, were undiminished in his bosom.

It is not for me to pursue him through the ghastly changes of his countenance. Words he had none. Now he sat upon the floor, motionless in all his limbs, with his eyes glazed and fixed; a monument of woe.

Anon a spirit of tempestuous but undesigning activity seized him. He rose from his place and strode across the floor, tottering and at random. His eyes were without moisture, and gleamed with the fire that consumed his vitals. The muscles of his face were agitated by convulsion. His lips moved, but no sound escaped him.

That nature should long sustain this conflict was not to be believed. My state was little different from that of my brother. I entered, as it were, into his thought. My heart was visited and rent by his pangs—Oh that thy phrenzy had never been cured! that thy madness, with its blissful visions, would return! or, if that must not be, that thy scene would hasten to a close! that death would cover thee with his oblivion!

What can I wish for thee? Thou who hast vied with the great preacher of thy faith in sanctity of motives, and in elevation above sensual and selfish! Thou whom thy fate has changed into paricide and savage! Can I wish for the continuance of thy being? No.

For a time his movements seemed destitute of purpose. If he walked; if he turned; if his fingers were entwined with each other; if his hands were pressed against opposite sides of his head with a force sufficient to crush it into pieces; it was to tear his mind from self-contemplation; to waste his thoughts on external objects.

Speedily this train was broken. A beam appeared to be darted into his mind, which gave a purpose to his efforts. An avenue to escape presented itself; and now he eagerly gazed about him: when my thoughts became engaged by his demeanour, my fingers were stretched as by a mechanical force, and the knife, no longer heeded or of use, escaped from my grasp, and fell unperceived on the floor. His eye now lighted upon it; he seized it with the quickness of thought.

I shrieked aloud, but it was too late. He plunged it to the hilt in his neck; and his life instantly escaped with the stream that gushed from the wound. He was stretched at my feet; and my hands were sprinkled with his blood as he fell.

Such was thy last deed, my brother! For a spectacle like this was it my fate to be reserved! Thy eyes were closed—thy face ghastly with death—thy arms, and the spot where thou liedest, floated in thy life's blood! These images have not, for a moment, forsaken me. Till I am breathless and cold, they must continue to hover in my sight.

Carwin, as I said, had left the room, but he still lingered in the house. My voice summoned him to my aid; but I scarcely noticed his re-entrance, and now faintly recollect his terrified looks, his broken exclamations, his vehement avowals of innocence, the effusions of his pity for me, and his offers of assistance.

I did not listen—I answered him not—I ceased to upbraid

or accuse. His guilt was a point to which I was indifferent. Ruffian or devil, black as hell or bright as angels, thenceforth he was nothing to me. I was incapable of sparing a look or a thought from the ruin that was spread at my feet.

When he left me, I was scarcely conscious of any variation in the scene. He informed the inhabitants of the *Hut* of what had passed, and they flew to the spot. Careless of his own safety, he hasted to the city to inform my friends of my condition.

My uncle speedily arrived at the house. The body of Wieland was removed from my presence, and they supposed that I would follow it; but no, my home is ascertained; here I have taken up my rest, and never will I go hence, till, like Wieland, I am borne to my grave.

Importunity was tried in vain: they threatened to remove me by violence—nay, violence was used; but my soul prizes too dearly this little roof to endure to be bereaved of it. Force should not prevail when the hoary locks and supplicating tears of my uncle were ineffectual. My repugnance to move gave birth to ferociousness and phrenzy when force was employed, and they were obliged to consent to my return.

They besought me—they remonstrated—they appealed to every duty that connected me with him that made me, and with my fellow-men—in vain. While I live I will not go hence. Have I not fulfilled my destiny?

Why will ye torment me with your reasonings and reproofs? Can ye restore to me the hope of my better days? Can ye give me back Catharine and her babes? Can ye recall to life him who died at my feet?

I will eat—I will drink—I will lie down and rise up at your bidding—all I ask is the choice of my abode. What is there unreasonable in this demand? Shortly will I be at peace. This is the spot which I have chosen in which to breathe my last sigh. Deny me not, I beseech you, so slight a boon.

Talk not to me, O my revered friend! of Carwin. He has told thee his tale, and thou exculpatest him from all direct concern in the fate of Wieland. This scene of havock was produced by an illusion of the senses. Be it so: I care not from what source these disasters have flowed; it suffices that they have swallowed up our hopes and our existence.

What his agency began, his agency conducted to a close. He intended, by the final effort of his power, to rescue me and to banish his illusions from my brother. Such is his tale, concerning the truth of which I care not. Henceforth I foster but one wish—I ask only quick deliverance from life and all the ills that attend it.—

Go wretch! torment me not with thy presence and thy prayers.—Forgive thee? Will that avail thee when thy fateful hour shall arrive? Be thou acquitted at thy own tribunal, and thou needest not fear the verdict of others. If thy guilt be capable of blacker hues, if hitherto thy conscience be without stain, thy crime will be made more flagrant by thus violating my retreat. Take thyself away from my sight if thou wouldest not behold my death!

Thou art gone! murmuring and reluctant! And now my repose is coming—my work is done!

Chapter XXVII

[*Written three years after the foregoing, and dated at Montpellier.*]

I IMAGINED that I had forever laid aside the pen; and that I should take up my abode in this part of the world, was of all events the least probable. My destiny I believed to be accomplished, and I looked forward to a speedy termination of my life with the fullest confidence.

Surely I had reason to be weary of existence, to be impatient of every tie which held me from the grave. I experienced this impatience in its fullest extent. I was not only enamoured of death, but conceived, from the condition of my frame, that to shun it was impossible, even though I had ardently desired it; yet here am I, a thousand leagues from my native soil, in full possession of life and of health, and not destitute of happiness.

Such is man. Time will obliterate the deepest impressions. Grief the most vehement and hopeless, will gradually decay and wear itself out. Arguments may be employed in vain: every moral prescription may be ineffectually tried: remonstrances, however cogent or pathetic, shall have no power over the attention, or shall be repelled with disdain; yet, as day follows day, the turbulence of our emotions shall subside, and our fluctuations be finally succeeded by a calm.

Perhaps, however, the conquest of despair was chiefly owing to an accident which rendered my continuance in my own house impossible. At the conclusion of my long, and, as I then supposed, my last letter to you, I mentioned my resolution to wait for death in the very spot which had been the principal scene of my misfortunes. From this resolution my friends exerted themselves with the utmost zeal and perseverance to make me depart. They justly imagined that to be thus surrounded by memorials of the fate of my family, would tend to foster my disease. A swift succession of new objects, and the exclusion of every thing calculated to remind me of my loss, was the only method of cure.

I refused to listen to their exhortations. Great as my calamity was, to be torn from this asylum was regarded by me as an aggravation of it. By a perverse constitution of mind, he was considered as my greatest enemy who sought to withdraw me from a scene which supplied eternal food to my melancholy, and kept my despair from languishing.

In relating the history of these disasters I derived a similar species of gratification. My uncle earnestly dissuaded me from this task; but his remonstrances were as fruitless on this head as they had been on others. They would have withheld from me the implements of writing; but they quickly perceived that to withstand would be more injurious than to comply with my wishes. Having finished my tale, it seemed as if the scene were closing. A fever lurked in my veins, and my strength was gone. Any exertion, however slight, was attended with difficulty, and, at length, I refused to rise from my bed.

I now see the infatuation and injustice of my conduct in its true colours. I reflect upon the sensations and reasonings of that period with wonder and humiliation. That I should be insensible to the claims and tears of my friends; that I should overlook the suggestions of duty, and fly from that post in which only I could be instrumental to the benefit of others; that the exercise of the social and beneficent affections, the contemplation of nature and the acquisition of wisdom should not be seen to be means of happiness still within my reach, is, at this time, scarcely credible.

It is true that I am now changed; but I have not the consolation to reflect that my change was owing to my fortitude or to my capacity for instruction. Better thoughts grew up in my mind imperceptibly. I cannot but congratulate myself on the change, though, perhaps, it merely argues a fickleness of temper, and a defect of sensibility.

After my narrative was ended I betook myself to my bed, in the full belief that my career in this world was on the point of finishing. My uncle took up his abode with me, and performed for me every office of nurse, physician and friend. One night, after some hours of restlessness and pain, I sunk into deep sleep. Its tranquillity, however, was of no long duration. My fancy became suddenly distempered, and my brain was turned into a theatre of uproar and confusion. It would not be easy to describe the wild and phantastical incongruities that pestered me. My uncle, Wieland, Pleyel and Carwin were successively and momently discerned amidst the storm. Sometimes I was swallowed up by whirlpools, or caught up in the air by half-seen and gigantic forms, and thrown upon pointed rocks, or cast among the billows. Sometimes gleams of light were shot into a dark abyss, on the verge of which I was standing, and enabled me to discover, for a moment, its enormous depth and hideous precipices. Anon, I was transported to some ridge of Ætna, and made a terrified spectator of its fiery torrents and its pillars of smoke.

However strange it may seem, I was conscious, even during my dream, of my real situation. I knew myself to be asleep, and struggled to break the spell, by muscular exertions. These did not avail, and I continued to suffer these abortive creations till a loud voice, at my bed side, and some one shaking me with violence, put an end to my reverie. My eyes were unsealed, and I started from my pillow.

My chamber was filled with smoke, which, though in some degree luminous, would permit me to see nothing, and by which I was nearly suffocated. The crackling of flames, and the deafening clamour of voices without, burst upon my ears. Stunned as I was by this hubbub, scorched with heat, and nearly choaked by the accumulating vapours, I was unable to think or act for my own preservation; I was incapable, indeed, of comprehending my danger.

I was caught up, in an instant, by a pair of sinewy arms, borne to the window, and carried down a ladder which had been placed there. My uncle stood at the bottom and received me. I was not fully aware of my situation till I found myself sheltered in the *Hut*, and surrounded by its inhabitants.

By neglect of the servant, some unextinguished embers had been placed in a barrel in the cellar of the building. The barrel had caught fire; this was communicated to the beams of the lower floor, and thence to the upper part of the structure. It was first discovered by some persons at a distance, who hastened to the spot and alarmed my uncle and the servants. The flames had already made considerable progress, and my condition was overlooked till my escape was rendered nearly impossible.

My danger being known, and a ladder quickly procured,

one of the spectators ascended to my chamber, and effected my deliverance in the manner before related.

This incident, disastrous as it may at first seem, had, in reality, a beneficial effect upon my feelings. I was, in some degree, roused from the stupor which had seized my faculties. The monotonous and gloomy series of my thoughts was broken. My habitation was levelled with the ground, and I was obliged to seek a new one. A new train of images, disconnected with the fate of my family, forced itself on my attention, and a belief insensibly sprung up, that tranquillity, if not happiness, was still within my reach. Notwithstanding the shocks which my frame had endured, the anguish of my thoughts no sooner abated than I recovered my health.

I now willingly listened to my uncle's solicitations to be the companion of his voyage. Preparations were easily made, and after a tedious passage, we set our feet on the shore of the ancient world. The memory of the past did not forsake me; but the melancholy which it generated, and the tears with which it filled my eyes, were not unprofitable. My curiosity was revived, and I contemplated, with ardour, the spectacle of living manners and the monuments of past ages.

In proportion as my heart was reinstated in the possession of its ancient tranquillity, the sentiment which I had cherished with regard to Pleyel returned. In a short time he was united to the Saxon woman, and made his residence in the neighbourhood of Boston. I was glad that circumstances would not permit an interview to take place between us. I could not desire their misery; but I reaped no pleasure from reflecting on their happiness. Time, and the exertions of my fortitude, cured me, in some degree, of this folly. I continued to love him, but my passion was disguised to myself; I considered it merely as a more tender species of friendship, and cherished it without compunction.

Through my uncle's exertions a meeting was brought about between Carwin and Pleyel, and explanations took place which restored me at once to the good opinion of the latter. Though separated so widely our correspondence was punctual and frequent, and paved the way for that union which can only end with the death of one of us.

In my letters to him I made no secret of my former sentiments. This was a theme on which I could talk without painful, though not without delicate emotions. That knowledge which I should never have imparted to a lover, I felt little scruple to communicate to a friend.

A year and an half elapsed, when Theresa was snatched from him by death, in the hour in which she gave him the first pledge of their mutual affection. This event was borne by him with his customary fortitude. It induced him, however, to make a change in his plans. He disposed of his property in America, and joined my uncle and me, who had terminated the wanderings of two years at Montpellier, which will henceforth, I believe, be our permanent abode.

If you reflect upon that entire confidence which had subsisted from our infancy between Pleyel and myself; on the passion that I had contracted, and which was merely smothered for a time; and on the esteem which was mutual, you will not, perhaps, be surprized that the renovation of our intercourse should give birth to that union which at present subsists. When the period had elapsed necessary to weaken the remembrance of Theresa, to whom he had been bound by ties more of honor than of love, he tendered his affections to me. I need not add that the tender was eagerly accepted.

Perhaps you are somewhat interested in the fate of Carwin. He saw, when too late, the danger of imposture. So much affected was he by the catastrophe to which he was a witness, that he laid aside all regard to his own safety. He sought my uncle, and confided to him the tale which he had just related to me. He found a more impartial and indulgent auditor in Mr. Cambridge, who imputed to maniacal illusion the conduct of Wieland, though he conceived the previous and unseen agency of Carwin, to have indirectly but powerfully predisposed him to this deplorable perversion of mind.

It was easy for Carwin to elude the persecutions of Ludloe. It was merely requisite to hide himself in a remote district of Pennsylvania. This, when he parted from us, he determined to do. He is now probably engaged in the harmless pursuits of agriculture, and may come to think, without insupportable remorse, on the evils to which his fatal talents have given birth. The innocence and usefulness of his future life may, in some degree, atone for the miseries so rashly or so thoughtlessly inflicted.

More urgent considerations hindered me from mentioning, in the course of my former mournful recital, any particulars respecting the unfortunate father of Louisa Conway. That man surely was reserved to be a monument of capricious fortune. His southern journies being finished, he returned to Philadelphia. Before he reached the city he left the highway, and alighted at my brother's door. Contrary to his expectation, no one came forth to welcome him, or hail his approach. He attempted to enter the house, but bolted doors, barred windows, and a silence broken only by unanswered calls, shewed him that the mansion was deserted.

He proceeded thence to my habitation, which he found, in like manner, gloomy and tenantless. His surprize may be easily conceived. The rustics who occupied the *Hut* told him an imperfect and incredible tale. He hasted to the city, and extorted from Mrs. Baynton a full disclosure of late disasters.

He was inured to adversity, and recovered, after no long time, from the shocks produced by this disappointment of his darling scheme. Our intercourse did not terminate with his departure from America. We have since met with him in France, and light has at length been thrown upon the motives which occasioned the disappearance of his wife, in the manner which I formerly related to you.

I have dwelt upon the ardour of their conjugal attachment, and mentioned that no suspicion had ever glanced upon her purity. This, though the belief was long cherished, recent discoveries have shewn to be questionable. No doubt her integrity would have survived to the present moment, if an extraordinary fate had not befallen her.

Major Stuart had been engaged, while in Germany, in a contest of honor with an Aid de Camp of the Marquis of Granby. His adversary had propagated a rumour injurious to his character. A challenge was sent; a meeting ensued; and Stuart wounded and disarmed the calumniator. The offence was atoned for, and his life secured by suitable concessions.

Maxwell, that was his name, shortly after, in consequence of succeeding to a rich inheritance, sold his commission and

returned to London. His fortune was speedily augmented by
an opulent marriage. Interest was his sole inducement to this
marriage, though the lady had been swayed by a credulous
affection. The true state of his heart was quickly discovered,
and a separation, by mutual consent, took place. The lady
withdrew to an estate in a distant county, and Maxwell continued to consume his time and fortune in the dissipation of
the capital.

Maxwell, though deceitful and sensual, possessed great
force of mind and specious accomplishments. He contrived to
mislead the generous mind of Stuart, and to regain the esteem
which his misconduct, for a time, had forfeited. He was recommended by her husband to the confidence of Mrs. Stuart.
Maxwell was stimulated by revenge, and by a lawless passion,
to convert this confidence into a source of guilt.

The education and capacity of this woman, the worth of
her husband, the pledge of their alliance which time had produced, her maturity in age and knowledge of the world—all
combined to render this attempt hopeless. Maxwell, however,
was not easily discouraged. The most perfect being, he believed, must owe his exemption from vice to the absence of
temptation. The impulses of love are so subtile, and the influence of false reasoning, when enforced by eloquence and passion, so unbounded, that no human virtue is secure from
degeneracy. All arts being tried, every temptation being summoned to his aid, dissimulation being carried to its utmost
bound, Maxwell, at length, nearly accomplished his purpose.
The lady's affections were withdrawn from her husband and
transferred to him. She could not, as yet, be reconciled to
dishonor. All efforts to induce her to elope with him were
ineffectual. She permitted herself to love, and to avow her
love; but at this limit she stopped, and was immoveable.

Hence this revolution in her sentiments was productive only
of despair. Her rectitude of principle preserved her from actual
guilt, but could not restore to her her ancient affection, or
save her from being the prey of remorseful and impracticable
wishes. Her husband's absence produced a state of suspense.
This, however, approached to a period, and she received tidings of his intended return. Maxwell, being likewise apprized
of this event, and having made a last and unsuccessful effort

to conquer her reluctance to accompany him in a journey to Italy, whither he pretended an invincible necessity of going, left her to pursue the measures which despair might suggest. At the same time she received a letter from the wife of Maxwell, unveiling the true character of this man, and revealing facts which the artifices of her seducer had hitherto concealed from her. Mrs. Maxwell had been prompted to this disclosure by a knowledge of her husband's practices, with which his own impetuosity had made her acquainted.

This discovery, joined to the delicacy of her scruples and the anguish of remorse, induced her to abscond. This scheme was adopted in haste, but effected with consummate prudence. She fled, on the eve of her husband's arrival, in the disguise of a boy, and embarked at Falmouth in a packet bound for America.

The history of her disastrous intercourse with Maxwell, the motives inducing her to forsake her country, and the measures she had taken to effect her design, were related to Mrs. Maxwell, in reply to her communication. Between these women an ancient intimacy and considerable similitude of character subsisted. This disclosure was accompanied with solemn injunctions of secrecy, and these injunctions were, for a long time, faithfully observed.

Mrs. Maxwell's abode was situated on the banks of the Wey. Stuart was her kinsman; their youth had been spent together; and Maxwell was in some degree indebted to the man whom he betrayed, for his alliance with this unfortunate lady. Her esteem for the character of Stuart had never been diminished. A meeting between them was occasioned by a tour which the latter had undertaken, in the year after his return from America, to Wales and the western counties. This interview produced pleasure and regret in each. Their own transactions naturally became the topics of their conversation; and the untimely fate of his wife and daughter were related by the guest.

Mrs. Maxwell's regard for her friend, as well as for the safety of her husband, persuaded her to concealment; but the former being dead, and the latter being out of the kingdom, she ventured to produce Mrs. Stuart's letter, and to communicate her own knowledge of the treachery of Maxwell. She had previously extorted from her guest a promise not to pursue any scheme of vengeance; but this promise was made while ignorant of the full extent of Maxwell's depravity, and his passion refused to adhere to it.

At this time my uncle and I resided at Avignon. Among the English resident there, and with whom we maintained a social intercourse, was Maxwell. This man's talents and address rendered him a favorite both with my uncle and myself. He had even tendered me his hand in marriage; but this being refused, he had sought and obtained permission to continue with us the intercourse of friendship. Since a legal marriage was impossible, no doubt, his views were flagitious. Whether he had relinquished these views I was unable to judge.

He was one in a large circle at a villa in the environs, to which I had likewise been invited, when Stuart abruptly entered the apartment. He was recognized with genuine satisfaction by me, and with seeming pleasure by Maxwell. In a short time, some affair of moment being pleaded, which required an immediate and exclusive interview, Maxwell and he withdrew together. Stuart and my uncle had been known to each other in the German army; and the purpose contemplated by the former in this long and hasty journey, was confided to his old friend.

A defiance was given and received, and the banks of a rivulet, about a league from the city, was selected as the scene of this contest. My uncle, having exerted himself in vain to prevent an hostile meeting, consented to attend them as a surgeon.—Next morning, at sun-rise, was the time chosen.

I returned early in the evening to my lodgings. Preliminaries being settled between the combatants, Stuart had consented to spend the evening with us, and did not retire till late. On the way to his hotel he was exposed to no molestation, but just as he stepped within the portico, a swarthy and malignant figure started from behind a column, and plunged a stiletto into his body.

The author of this treason could not certainly be discovered; but the details communicated by Stuart, respecting the history of Maxwell, naturally pointed him out as an object of suspicion. No one expressed more concern, on account of this disaster, than he; and he pretended an ardent zeal to vindicate his character from the aspersions that were cast upon it.

Thenceforth, however, I denied myself to his visits; and shortly after he disappeared from this scene.

Few possessed more estimable qualities, and a better title to happiness and the tranquil honors of long life, than the mother and father of Louisa Conway: yet they were cut off in the bloom of their days; and their destiny was thus accomplished by the same hand. Maxwell was the instrument of their destruction, though the instrument was applied to this end in so different a manner.

I leave you to moralize on this tale. That virtue should become the victim of treachery is, no doubt, a mournful consideration; but it will not escape your notice, that the evils of which Carwin and Maxwell were the authors, owed their existence to the errors of the sufferers. All efforts would have been ineffectual to subvert the happiness or shorten the existence of the Stuarts, if their own frailty had not seconded these efforts. If the lady had crushed her disastrous passion in the bud, and driven the seducer from her presence, when the tendency of his artifices was seen; if Stuart had not admitted the spirit of absurd revenge, we should not have had to deplore this catastrophe. If Wieland had framed juster notions of moral duty, and of the divine attributes; or if I had been gifted with ordinary equanimity or foresight, the double-tongued deceiver would have been baffled and repelled.

ARTHUR MERVYN

OR

MEMOIRS OF THE YEAR 1793

PREFACE

T HE evils of pestilence by which this city has lately been afflicted will probably form an aera in its history. The schemes of reformation and improvement to which they will give birth, or, if no efforts of human wisdom can avail to avert the periodical visitations of this calamity, the change in manners and population which they will produce, will be, in the highest degree, memorable. They have already supplied new and copious materials for reflection to the physician and the political economist. They have not been less fertile of instruction to the moral observer, to whom they have furnished new displays of the influence of human passions and motives.

Amidst the medical and political discussions which are now afloat in the community relative to this topic, the author of these remarks has ventured to methodize his own reflections, and to weave into an humble narrative, such incidents as appeared to him most instructive and remarkable among those which came within the sphere of his own observation. It is every one's duty to profit by all opportunities of inculcating on mankind the lessons of justice and humanity. The influences of hope and fear, the trials of fortitude and constancy, which took place in this city, in the autumn of 1793, have, perhaps, never been exceeded in any age. It is but just to snatch some of these from oblivion, and to deliver to posterity a brief but faithful sketch of the condition of this metropolis during that calamitous period. Men only require to be made acquainted with distress for their compassion and their charity to be awakened. He that depicts, in lively colours, the evils of disease and poverty, performs an eminent service to the sufferers, by calling forth benevolence in those who are able to afford relief, and he who pourtrays examples of disinterestedness and intrepidity, confers on virtue the notoriety and homage that are due to it, and rouses in the spectators, the spirit of salutary emulation.

In the following tale a particular series of adventures is brought to a close; but these are necessarily connected with the events which happened subsequent to the period here described. These events are not less memorable than those which form the subject of the present volume, and may hereafter be published either separately or in addition to this.

C.B.B.

Chapter I

I WAS resident in this city during the year 1793. Many motives contributed to detain me, though departure was easy and commodious, and my friends were generally solicitous for me to go. It is not my purpose to enumerate these motives, or to dwell on my present concerns and transactions, but merely to compose a narrative of some incidents with which my situation made me acquainted.

Returning one evening, somewhat later than usual, to my own house, my attention was attracted, just as I entered the porch, by the figure of a man, reclining against the wall at a few paces distant. My sight was imperfectly assisted by a far-off lamp; but the posture in which he sat, the hour, and the place immediately suggested the idea of one disabled by sickness. It was obvious to conclude that his disease was pestilential. This did not deter me from approaching and examining him more closely.

He leaned his head against the wall, his eyes were shut, his hands clasped in each other, and his body seemed to be sustained in an upright position merely by the cellar door against which he rested his left shoulder. The lethargy into which he was sunk seemed scarcely interrupted by my feeling his hand and his forehead. His throbbing temples and burning skin indicated a fever, and his form, already emaciated, seemed to prove that it had not been of short duration.

There was only one circumstance that hindered me from forming an immediate determination in what manner this person should be treated. My family consisted of my wife and a young child. Our servant maid had been seized three days before by the reigning malady, and, at her own request, had been conveyed to the hospital. We ourselves enjoyed good health, and were hopeful of escaping with our lives. Our measures for this end had been cautiously taken and carefully adhered to. They did not consist in avoiding the receptacles of infection, for my office required me to go daily into the midst of them; nor in filling the house with the exhalations of gun-powder, vinegar, or tar. They consisted in cleanliness, reasonable exercise, and wholesome diet. Custom had likewise blunted the edge of our apprehensions. To take this person into my house, and bestow upon him the requisite attendance was the scheme that first occurred to me. In this, however, the advice of my wife was to govern me.

I mentioned the incident to her. I pointed out the danger which was to be dreaded from such an inmate. I desired her to decide with caution and mentioned my resolution to conform myself implicitly to her decision. Should we refuse to harbour him, we must not forget that there was an hospital to which he would, perhaps, consent to be carried, and where he would be accommodated in the best manner the times would admit.

Nay, said she, talk not of hospitals. At least let him have his choice. I have no fear about me for my part, in a case where the injunctions of duty are so obvious. Let us take the poor unfortunate wretch into our protection and care, and leave the consequences to Heaven.

I expected and was pleased with this proposal. I returned to the sick man, and on rousing him from his stupor found him still in possession of his reason. With a candle near, I had opportunity of viewing him more accurately.

His garb was plain, careless, and denoted rusticity: His aspect was simple and ingenuous, and his decayed visage still retained traces of uncommon, but manlike beauty. He had all the appearances of mere youth, unspoiled by luxury and uninured to misfortune. I scarcely ever beheld an object which laid so powerful and sudden a claim to my affection and succour.

You are sick, said I, in as cheerful a tone as I could assume. Cold bricks and night airs are comfortless attendants for one in your condition. Rise, I pray you, and come into the house. We will try to supply you with accommodations a little more suitable.

At this address he fixed his languid eyes upon me. What would you have? said he. I am very well as I am. While I breathe, which will not be long, I shall breathe with more freedom here than elsewhere. Let me alone—I am very well as I am.

Nay, said I, this situation is unsuitable to a sick man. I only ask you to come into my house and receive all the kindness that it is in our power to bestow. Pluck up courage and I will answer for your recovery, provided you submit to directions, and do as we would have you. Rise, and come along with me. We will find you a physician and a nurse, and all we ask in return is good spirits and compliance.

Do you not know, he replied, what my disease is? Why should you risk your safety for the sake of one, whom your kindness cannot benefit, and who has nothing to give in return?

There was something in the style of this remark, that heightened my prepossession in his favour and made me pursue my purpose with more zeal. Let us try what we can do for you, I answered. If we save your life, we shall have done you some service, and as for recompence, we will look to that.

It was with considerable difficulty that he was persuaded to accept our invitation. He was conducted to a chamber, and the criticalness of his case requiring unusual attention, I spent the night at his bed-side.

My wife was encumbered with the care both of her infant and her family. The charming babe was in perfect health, but her mother's constitution was frail and delicate. We simplified the houshould duties as much as possible; but still these duties were considerably burthensome to one not used to the performance, and luxuriously educated. The addition of a sick man, was likely to be productive of much fatigue. My engagements would not allow me to be always at home, and the state of my patient and the remedies necessary to be prescribed were attended with many noxious and disgustful circumstances. My fortune would not allow me to hire assistance. My wife, with a feeble frame and a mind shrinking, on ordinary occasions, from such offices with fastidious scrupulousness, was to be his only or principal nurse.

My neighbours were fervent in their well-meant zeal, and loud in their remonstrances on the imprudence and rashness of my conduct. They called me presumptuous and cruel in exposing my wife and child as well as myself to such imminent hazard, for the sake of one too who most probably was worthless, and whose disease had doubtless been, by negligence or mistreatment, rendered incurable.

I did not turn a deaf ear to these censurers. I was aware of all the inconveniencies and perils to which I thus spontaneously exposed myself. No one knew better the value of that woman whom I called mine, or set an higher price upon her life, her health, and her ease. The virulence and activity of this contagion, the dangerous condition of my patient, and the dubiousness of his character, were not forgotten by me; but still my conduct in this affair received my own entire approbation. All objections on the score of my friend were removed by her own willingness and even solicitude to undertake the province. I had more confidence than others in the vincibility of this disease, and in the success of those measures which we had used for our defence against it. But, whatever were the evils to accrue to us, we were sure of one thing; namely, that the consciousness of having neglected this unfortunate person would be a source of more unhappiness than could possibly redound from the attendance and care that he would claim.

The more we saw of him, indeed, the more did we congratulate ourselves on our proceeding. His torments were acute and tedious, but in the midst even of delirium, his heart seemed to overflow with gratitude, and to be actuated by no wish but to alleviate our toil and our danger. He made prodigious exertions to perform necessary offices for himself. He suppressed his feelings and struggled to maintain a cheerful tone and countenance, that he might prevent that anxiety which the sight of his sufferings produced in us. He was perpetually furnishing reasons why his nurse should leave him alone, and betrayed dissatisfaction whenever she entered his apartment.

In a few days there were reasons to conclude him out of danger; and in a fortnight, nothing but exercise and nourishment were wanting to complete his restoration. Meanwhile nothing was obtained from him but general information, that his place of abode was Chester County, and that some momentous engagement induced him to hazard his safety by coming to the city in the height of the epidemic.

He was far from being talkative. His silence seemed to be

the joint result of modesty and unpleasing remembrances. His features were characterised by pathetic seriousness, and his deportment by a gravity very unusual at his age. According to his own representation, he was no more than eighteen years old, but the depth of his remarks indicated a much greater advance. His name was Arthur Mervyn. He described himself as having passed his life at the plough-tail and the threshing floor: as being destitute of all scholastic instruction; and as being long since bereft of the affectionate regards of parents and kinsmen.

When questioned as to the course of life which he meant to pursue, upon his recovery, he professed himself without any precise object. He was willing to be guided by the advice of others, and by the lights which experience should furnish. The country was open to him, and he supposed that there was no part of it in which food could not be purchased by his labour. He was unqualified, by his education, for any liberal profession. His poverty was likewise an insuperable impediment. He could afford to spend no time in the acquisition of a trade. He must labour not for future emolument but for immediate subsistence. The only pursuit which his present circumstances would allow him to adopt was that which, he was inclined to believe, was likewise the most eligible. Without doubt, his experience was slender, and it seemed absurd to pronounce concerning that of which he had no direct knowledge; but so it was, he could not outroot from his mind the persuasion that to plow, to sow, and to reap were employments most befitting a reasonable creature, and from which the truest pleasure and the least pollution would flow. He contemplated no other scheme than to return as soon as his health should permit, into the country, seek employment where it was to be had, and acquit himself in his engagements with fidelity and diligence.

I pointed out to him various ways in which the city might furnish employment to one with his qualifications. He had said that he was somewhat accustomed to the pen. There were stations in which the possession of a legible hand was all that was requisite. He might add to this a knowledge of accompts and thereby procure himself a post in some mercantile or public office.

To this he objected, that experience had shewn him unfit for the life of a penman. This had been his chief occupation for a little while, and he found it wholly incompatible with his health. He must not sacrifice the end for the means. Starving was a disease preferable to consumption. Besides, he laboured merely for the sake of living, and he lived merely for the sake of pleasure. If his tasks should enable him to live, but at the same time, bereave him of all satisfaction, they inflicted injury and were to be shunned as worse evils than death.

I asked to what species of pleasure he alluded, with which the business of a clerk was inconsistent.

He answered, that he scarcely knew how to describe it. He read books when they came in his way. He had lighted upon few, and perhaps the pleasure they afforded him was owing to their fewness; yet he confessed that a mode of life which entirely forbade him to read, was by no means to his taste. But this was trivial. He knew how to value the thoughts of other people, but he could not part with the privilege of observing and thinking for himself. He wanted business which would suffer at least nine tenths of his attention to go free. If it afforded agreeable employment to that part of his attention which it applied to its own use, so much the better; but if it did not, he should not repine. He should be content with a life whose pleasures were to its pains as nine are to one. He had tried the trade of a copyist, and in circumstances more favourable than it was likely he should ever again have an opportunity of trying it, and he had found that it did not fulfil the requisite conditions. Whereas the trade of plowman was friendly to health, liberty, and pleasure.

The pestilence, if it may so be called, was now declining. The health of my young friend allowed him to breathe the fresh air and to walk.—A friend of mine, by name Wortley, who had spent two months from the city, and to whom, in the course of a familiar correspondence, I had mentioned the foregoing particulars, returned from his rural excursion. He was posting, on the evening of the day of his arrival, with a friendly expedition, to my house, when he overtook Mervyn going in the same direction. He was surprised to find him go before him into my dwelling, and to discover, which he speedily did, that this was the youth whom I had so frequently mentioned to him. I was present at their meeting.

There was a strange mixture in the countenance of Wortley, when they were presented to each other. His satisfaction was mingled with surprise, and his surprise with anger. Mervyn, in his turn, betrayed considerable embarrassment. Wortley's thoughts were too earnest on some topic to allow him to converse. He shortly made some excuse for taking leave and, rising, addressed himself to the youth with a request that he would walk home with him. This invitation, delivered in a tone which left it doubtful whether a compliment or menace were meant, augmented Mervyn's confusion. He complied without speaking, and they went out together;—my wife and I were left to comment upon the scene.

It could not fail to excite uneasiness. They were evidently no strangers to each other. The indignation that flashed from the eyes of Wortley, and the trembling consciousness of Mervyn were unwelcome tokens. The former was my dearest friend, and venerable for his discernment and integrity: The latter appeared to have drawn upon himself the anger and disdain of this man. We already anticipated the shock which the discovery of his unworthiness would produce.

In an half hour Mervyn returned. His embarrassment had given place to dejection. He was always serious, but his features were now overcast by the deepest gloom. The anxiety which I felt would not allow me to hesitate long.

Arthur, said I, something is the matter with you. Will you not disclose it to us? Perhaps you have brought yourself into some dilemma out of which we may help you to escape. Has any thing of an unpleasant nature passed between you and Wortley?

The youth did not readily answer. He seemed at a loss for a suitable reply. At length he said, That something disagreeable had indeed passed between him and Wortley. He had had the misfortune to be connected with a man by whom Wortley, conceived himself to be injured. He had borne no part in inflicting this injury, but had nevertheless been threatened with ill treatment if he did not make disclosures which indeed it was in his power to make, but which he was bound by every sanction to withhold. This disclosure would be of no benefit to Wortley. It would rather operate injuriously than otherwise; yet it was endeavoured to be wrested from him by the heaviest menaces.—There he paused.

We were naturally inquisitive as to the scope of these menaces; but Mervyn intreated us to forbear any further discussion of this topic. He foresaw the difficulties to which his silence would subject him. One of its most fearful consequences would be the loss of our good opinion. He knew not what he had to dread from the enmity of Wortley. Mr. Wortley's violence was not without excuse. It was his mishap to be exposed to suspicions which could only be obviated by breaking his faith. But, indeed, he knew not, whether any degree of explicitness would confute the charges that were made against him; whether, by trampling on his sacred promise, he should not multiply his perils instead of lessening their number. A difficult part had been assigned to him: by much too difficult for one, young, improvident, and inexperienced as he was.

Sincerity, perhaps, was the best course. Perhaps, after having had an opportunity for deliberation, he should conclude to adopt it; meanwhile he intreated permission to retire to his chamber. He was unable to exclude from his mind ideas which yet could, with no propriety, at least at present, be made the theme of conversation.

These words were accompanied with simplicity and pathos, and with tokens of unaffected distress.

Arthur, said I, you are master of your actions and time in this house. Retire when you please; but you will naturally suppose us anxious to dispel this mystery. Whatever shall tend to obscure or malign your character will of course excite our solicitude. Wortley is not short-sighted or hasty to condemn. So great is my confidence in his integrity that I will not promise my esteem to one who has irrecoverably lost that of Wortley. I am not acquainted with your motives to concealment or what it is you conceal, but take the word of one who possesses that experience which you complain of wanting, that sincerity is always safest.

As soon as he had retired, my curiosity prompted me to pay an immediate visit to Wortley. I found him at home. He was no less desirous of an interview, and answered my enquiries with as much eagerness as they were made.

You know, said he, my disastrous connection with Thomas Welbeck. You recollect his sudden disappearance last July, by which I was reduced to the brink of ruin. Nay, I am, even now, far from certain that I shall survive that event. I spoke to you about the youth who lived with him, and by what means that youth was discovered to have crossed the river in his company on the night of his departure. This is that very youth.

This will account for my emotion at meeting him at your house: I brought him out with me. His confusion sufficiently indicated his knowledge of transactions between Welbeck and me. I questioned him as to the fate of that man. To own the truth, I expected some well digested lie; but he merely said, that he had promised secrecy on that subject, and must therefore be excused from giving me any information. I asked him if he knew, that his master, or accomplice, or whatever was his relation to him, absconded in my debt? He answered that he knew it well; but still pleaded a promise of inviolable secrecy as to his hiding place. This conduct justly exasperated me and I treated him with the severity which he deserved. I am half ashamed to confess the excesses of my passion; I even went so far as to strike him. He bore my insults with the utmost patience. No doubt the young villain is well instructed in his lesson. He knows that he may safely defy my power.— From threats I descended to entreaties. I even endeavoured to wind the truth from him by artifice. I promised him a part of the debt if he would enable me to recover the whole. I offered him a considerable reward if he would merely afford me a clue by which I might trace him to his retreat; but all was insufficient. He merely put on an air of perplexity and shook his head in token of non-compliance.

Such was my friend's account of this interview. His suspicions were unquestionably plausible; but I was disposed to put a more favourable construction on Mervyn's behaviour. I recollected the desolate and pennyless condition in which I found him, and the uniform complacency and rectitude of his deportment for the period during which we had witnessed it. These ideas had considerable influence on my judgment, and indisposed me to follow the advice of my friend, which was to turn him forth from my doors that very night.

My wife's prepossessions were still more powerful advocates of this youth. She would vouch, she said, before any tribunal, for his innocence; but she willingly concurred with me in allowing him the continuance of our friendship, on no other condition than that of a disclosure of the truth. To entitle ourselves to this confidence we were willing to engage, in our turn, for the observance of secrecy, so far that no detriment should accrue from this disclosure to himself or his friend.

Next morning at breakfast, our guest appeared with a countenance less expressive of embarrassment than on the last evening. His attention was chiefly engaged by his own thoughts, and little was said till the breakfast was removed. I then reminded him of the incidents of the former day, and mentioned that the uneasiness which thence arose to us had rather been encreased than diminished by time.

It is in your power, my young friend, continued I, to add still more to this uneasiness or to take it entirely away. I had no personal acquaintance with Thomas Welbeck. I have been informed by others that his character for a certain period was respectable, but that, at length, he contracted large debts and instead of paying them absconded. You, it seems, lived with him. On the night of his departure you are known to have accompanied him across the river, and this, it seems, is the first of your re-appearance on the stage. Welbeck's conduct was dishonest. He ought doubtless to be pursued to his asylum and be compelled to refund his winnings. You confess yourself to know his place of refuge, but urge a promise of secrecy. Know you not that to assist, or connive at, the escape of this man was wrong? To have promised to favour his concealment and impunity by silence was only an aggravation of this wrong. That, however, is past. Your youth, and circumstances, hitherto unexplained, may apologize for that misconduct, but it is certainly your duty to repair it to the utmost of your power. Think whether by disclosing what you know, you will not repair it.

I have spent most of last night, said the youth, in reflecting on this subject. I had come to a resolution, before you spoke, of confiding to you my simple tale. I perceive in what circumstances I am placed, and that I can keep my hold of your good opinion only by a candid deportment. I have indeed given a promise which it was wrong or rather absurd in another to exact and in me to give; yet none but considerations of the highest importance would persuade me to break my promise. No injury will accrue from my disclosure to Welbeck. If there should, dishonest as he was, that would be a sufficient reason for my silence. Wortley will not, in any degree, be benefited by any communication that I can make. Whether I grant or withhold information my conduct will have influence only on my own happiness, and that influence will justify me in granting it.

I received your protection when I was friendless and forlorn. You have a right to know whom it is that you protected. My own fate is connected with the fate of Welbeck, and that connection, together with the interest you are pleased to take in my concerns because they are mine, will render a tale worthy of attention which will not be recommended by variety of facts or skill in the display of them.

Wortley, though passionate, and, with regard to me, unjust, may yet be a good man; but I have no desire to make him one of my auditors. You, Sir, may, if you think proper, relate to him afterwards what particulars concerning Welbeck it may be of importance for him to know; but at present it will be well if your indulgence shall support me to the end of a tedious but humble tale.

The eyes of my Eliza sparkled with delight at this proposal. She regarded this youth with a sisterly affection and considered his candour, in this respect, as an unerring test of his rectitude. She was prepared to hear and to forgive the errors of inexperience and precipitation. I did not fully participate in her satisfaction, but was nevertheless most zealously disposed to listen to his narrative.

My engagements obliged me to postpone this rehearsal till late in the evening. Collected then round a cheerful hearth, exempt from all likelihood of interruption from without, and our babe's unpractised senses shut up in the sweetest and profoundest sleep, Mervyn, after a pause of recollection, began.

Chapter II

MY NATAL SOIL is Chester County. My father had a small farm on which he has been able, by industry, to maintain himself and a numerous family. He has had many children, but some defect in the constitution of our mother has been fatal to all of them but me. They died successively as they attained the age of nineteen or twenty, and since I have not yet reached that age I may reasonably look for the same premature fate. In the spring of last year my mother followed her fifth child to the grave, and three months afterwards died herself.

My constitution has always been frail, and, till the death of my mother I enjoyed unlimited indulgence. I cheerfully sustained my portion of labour, for that necessity prescribed; but the intervals were always at my own disposal, and in whatever manner I thought proper to employ them, my plans were encouraged and assisted. Fond appellations, tones of mildness, solicitous attendance when I was sick, deference to my opinions, and veneration for my talents compose the image which I still retain of my mother. I had the thoughtlessness and presumption of youth, and now that she is gone my compunction is awakened by a thousand recollections of my treatment of her. I was indeed guilty of no flagrant acts of contempt or rebellion. Perhaps her deportment was inevitably calculated to instil into me a froward and refractory spirit. My faults, however, were speedily followed by repentance, and in the midst of impatience and passion, a look of tender upbraiding from her was always sufficient to melt me into tears and make me ductile to her will. If sorrow for her loss be any atonement for the offences which I committed during her life, ample atonement has been made.

My father is a man of slender capacity but of a temper easy and flexible. He was sober and industrious by habit. He was content to be guided by the superior intelligence of his wife. Under this guidance he prospered; but when that was withdrawn, his affairs soon began to betray marks of unskilfulness and negligence. My understanding, perhaps, qualified me to counsel and assist my father, but I was wholly unaccustomed to the task of superintendence. Besides, gentleness and fortitude did not descend to me from my mother, and these were indispensable attributes in a boy who desires to dictate to his grey-headed parent. Time perhaps might have conferred dexterity on me, or prudence on him, had not a most unexpected event given a different direction to my views.

Betty Lawrence was a wild girl from the pine forests of New Jersey. At the age of ten years she became a bond servant in this city, and, after the expiration of her time, came into my father's neighbourhood in search of employment. She was hired in our family as milk-maid and market woman. Her features were coarse, her frame robust, her mind totally unlettered, and her morals defective in that point in which female excellence is supposed chiefly to consist. She possessed superabundant health and good humour, and was quite a supportable companion in the hay-field or the barn-yard.

On the death of my mother, she was exalted to a somewhat higher station. The same tasks fell to her lot; but the time and manner of performing them were, in some degree, submitted to her own choice. The cows and the dairy were still her province; but in this no one interfered with her or pretended to prescribe her measures. For this province she seemed not unqualified, and as long as my father was pleased with her management, I had nothing to object.

This state of things continued, without material variation for several months. There were appearances in my father's deportment to Betty, which excited my reflections, but not my fears. The deference which was occasionally paid to the advice or the claims of this girl, was accounted for by that feebleness of mind which degraded my father, in whatever scene he should be placed, to be the tool of others. I had no conception that her claims extended beyond a temporary or superficial gratification.

At length, however, a visible change took place in her manners. A scornful affectation and awkward dignity began to be assumed. A greater attention was paid to dress, which was of gayer hues and more fashionable texture. I rallied her on these tokens of a sweetheart, and amused myself with expatiating to her on the qualifications of her lover. A clownish fellow was frequently her visitant. His attentions did not appear to be discouraged. He therefore was readily supposed to be the man. When pointed out as the favourite, great resentment was expressed, and obscure insinuations were made that her aim was not quite so low as that. These denials I supposed to be customary on such occasions, and considered the continuance of his visits as a sufficient confutation of them.

I frequently spoke of Betty, her newly acquired dignity, and of the probable cause of her change of manners to my father. When this theme was started, a certain coldness and reserve overspread his features. He dealt in monosyllables and either laboured to change the subject or made some excuse for leaving me. This behaviour, though it occasioned surprise, was never very deeply reflected on. My father was old, and the mournful impressions which were made upon him by the death of his wife, the lapse of almost half a year seemed scarcely to have weakened. Betty had chosen her partner and I was in daily expectation of receiving a summons to the wedding.

One afternoon this girl dressed herself in the gayest manner and seemed making preparations for some momentous ceremony. My father had directed me to put the horse to the chaise. On my enquiring whither he was going he answered me in general terms that he had some business at a few miles distance. I offered to go in his stead, but he said that was impossible. I was proceeding to ascertain the possibility of this when he left me to go to a field where his workmen were busy, directing me to inform him when the chaise was ready, and to supply his place, while absent, in overlooking the workmen.

This office was performed; but before I called him from the field I exchanged a few words with the milk-maid, who sat on a bench, in all the primness of expectation and decked with the most gaudy plumage. I rated her imaginary lover for his tardiness, and vowed eternal hatred to them both for not making me a bride's attendant. She listened to me with an air in which embarrassment was mingled sometimes with exultation and sometimes with malice. I left her at length, and returned to the house not till a late hour. As soon as I entered, my father presented Betty to me as his wife, and desired she might receive that treatment from me which was due to a mother.

It was not till after repeated and solemn declarations from both of them that I was prevailed upon to credit this event. Its effect upon my feelings may be easily conceived. I knew the woman to be rude, ignorant, and licentious. Had I suspected this event I might have fortified my father's weakness and enabled him to shun the gulf to which he was tending; but my presumption had been careless of the danger. To think that such an one should take the place of my revered mother was intolerable.

To treat her in any way not squaring with her real merits; to hinder anger and scorn from rising at the sight of her in her new condition, was not in my power. To be degraded to the rank of her servant; to become the sport of her malice and her artifices was not to be endured. I had no independent provision; but I was the only child of my father, and had reasonably hoped to succeed to his patrimony. On this hope I had built a thousand agreeable visions. I had meditated innumerable projects which the possession of this estate would enable me to execute. I had no wish beyond the trade of agriculture, and beyond the opulence which an hundred acres would give.

These visions were now at an end. No doubt her own interest would be to this woman the supreme law, and this interest would be considered as irreconcilably hostile to mine. My father would easily be moulded to her purpose and that act easily extorted from him which should reduce me to beggary. She had a gross and perverse taste. She had a numerous kindred, indigent and hungry. On these his substance would speedily be lavished. Me she hated because she was conscious of having injured me, because she knew that I held her in contempt, and because I had detected her in an illicit intercourse with the son of a neighbour.

The house in which I lived was no longer my own, nor even my father's. Hitherto I had thought and acted in it with the freedom of a master, but now I was become, in my own conceptions, an alien and an enemy to the roof under which I was born. Every tie which had bound me to it was dissolved or converted into something which repelled me to a distance from it. I was a guest whose presence was borne with anger and impatience.

I was fully impressed with the necessity of removal, but I knew not whither to go or what kind of subsistence to seek. My father had been a Scottish emigrant, and had no kindred on this side of the ocean. My mother's family lived in New Hampshire, and long separation had extinguished all the rights of relationship in her offspring. Tilling the earth was my only profession, and to profit by my skill in it, it would be necessary to become a day-labourer in the service of strangers; but this was a destiny to which I, who had so long enjoyed the pleasures of independence and command, could not suddenly reconcile myself. It occurred to me that the city might afford me an asylum. A short day's journey would transport me into it. I had been there twice or thrice in my life, but only for a few hours each time. I knew not an human face, and was a stranger to its modes and dangers. I was qualified for no employment, compatible with a town-life, but that of the pen. This indeed had ever been a favourite tool with me, and though it may appear somewhat strange, it is no less true that I had had nearly as much practice at the quill as at the mattock. But the sum of my skill lay in tracing distinct characters. I had used it merely to transcribe what others had written, or to give form to my own conceptions. Whether the city would afford me employment, as a mere copyist, sufficiently lucrative, was a point on which I possessed no means of information.

My determination was hastened by the conduct of my new mother. My conjectures as to the course she would pursue with regard to me had not been erroneous. My father's deportment in a short time grew sullen and austere. Directions were given in a magisterial tone, and any remissness in the execution of his orders was rebuked with an air of authority. At length these rebukes were followed by certain intimations that I was now old enough to provide for myself; that it was time to think of some employment by which I might secure a livelihood; that it was a shame for me to spend my youth in idleness; that what he had gained was by his own labour; and I must be indebted for my living to the same source.

These hints were easily understood. At first, they excited indignation and grief. I knew the source whence they sprung and was merely able to suppress the utterance of my feelings in her presence. My looks, however, were abundantly significant, and my company became hourly more insupportable. Abstracted from these considerations, my father's remonstrances were not destitute of weight. He gave me being but sustenance ought surely to be my own gift. In the use of that for which he had been indebted to his own exertions, he might reasonably consult his own choice. He assumed no control over me; he merely did what he would with his own, and so far from fettering my liberty, he exhorted me to use it for my benefit and to make provision for myself.

I now reflected that there were other manual occupations besides that of the plough. Among these none had fewer disadvantages than that of carpenter or cabinet-maker. I had no knowledge of this art; but, neither custom, nor law, nor the impenetrableness of the mystery required me to serve a seven years' apprenticeship to it. A master in this trade might possibly be persuaded to take me under his tuition: two or three years would suffice to give me the requisite skill. Meanwhile my father would, perhaps, consent to bear the cost of my maintenance. Nobody could live upon less than I was willing to do.

I mentioned these ideas to my father; but he merely commended my intentions without offering to assist me in the execution of them. He had full employment, he said, for all the profits of his ground. No doubt if I would bind myself to serve four or five years, my master would be at the expence of my subsistence. Be that as it would, I must look for nothing from him. I had shewn very little regard for his happiness: I had refused all marks of respect to a woman who was entitled to it from her relation to him. He did not see why he should treat as a son one who refused what was due to him as a father. He thought it right that I should henceforth maintain myself. He did not want my services on the farm, and the sooner I quitted his house the better.

I retired from this conference with a resolution to follow the advice that was given. I saw that henceforth I must be my own protector, and wondered at the folly that detained me so long under this roof. To leave it was now become indispensable, and there could be no reason for delaying my departure for a single hour. I determined to bend my course to the city. The scheme foremost in my mind was to apprentice myself to some mechanical trade. I did not overlook the evils of constraint and the dubiousness as to the character of the master I should choose. I was not without hopes that accident would suggest a different expedient and enable me to procure an immediate subsistence without forfeiting my liberty.

I determined to commence my journey the next morning. No wonder the prospect of so considerable a change in my condition should deprive me of sleep. I spent the night ruminating on the future and in painting to my fancy the adventures which I should be likely to meet. The foresight of man is in proportion to his knowledge. No wonder that in my state of profound ignorance, not the faintest preconception should be formed of the events that really befel me. My temper was inquisitive, but there was nothing in the scene to which I was going from which my curiosity expected to derive gratification. Discords and evil smells, unsavoury food, unwholesome labour, and irksome companions, were, in my opinion, the unavoidable attendants of a city.

My best clothes were of the homeliest texture and shape. My whole stock of linen consisted of three check shirts. Part of my winter evening's employment since the death of my mother consisted in knitting my own stockings. Of these I had three pair, one of which I put on and the rest I formed, together with two shirts, into a bundle. Three quarter-dollar pieces composed my whole fortune in money.

Chapter III

I ROSE at the dawn, and without asking or bestowing a blessing, sallied forth into the high road to the city which passed near the house. I left nothing behind, the loss of which I regretted. I had purchased most of my own books with the product of my own separate industry, and their number being, of course, small, I had, by incessant application, gotten the whole of them by rote. They had ceased, therefore, to be of any further use. I left them, without reluctance, to the fate for which I knew them to be reserved, that of affording food and habitation to mice.

I trod this unwonted path with all the fearlessness of youth. In spite of the motives to despondency and apprehension, incident to my state, my heels were light and my heart joyous. Now, said I, I am mounted into man. I must build a name and a fortune for myself. Strange if this intellect and these hands will not supply me with an honest livelihood. I will try the city in the first place; but if that should fail, resources are still left to me. I will resume my post in the corn-field and threshing-floor, to which I shall always have access, and where I shall always be happy.

I had proceeded some miles on my journey, when I began to feel the inroads of hunger. I might have stopped at any farm house, and have breakfasted for nothing. It was prudent to husband, with the utmost care, my slender stock; but I felt reluctance to beg as long as I had the means of buying, and I imagined that coarse bread and a little milk would cost little even at a tavern, when any farmer was willing to bestow them for nothing. My resolution was farther influenced by the appearance of a sign-post. What excuse could I make for begging a breakfast with an inn at hand and silver in my pocket?

I stopped accordingly and breakfasted. The landlord was remarkably attentive and obliging, but his bread was stale, his milk sour, and his cheese the greenest imaginable. I disdained to animadvert on these defects, naturally supposing that his house could furnish no better.

Having finished my meal, I put, without speaking, one of

my pieces into his hand. This deportment I conceived to be highly becoming, and to indicate a liberal and manly spirit. I always regarded with contempt a scrupulous maker of bargains. He received the money with a complaisant obeisance. Right, said he. *Just* the money, Sir. You are on foot, Sir. A pleasant way of travelling, Sir. I wish you a good day, Sir.— So saying he walked away.

This proceeding was wholly unexpected. I conceived myself entitled to at least three-fourths of it in change. The first impulse was to call him back, and contest the equity of his demand, but a moment's reflection shewed me the absurdity of such conduct. I resumed my journey with spirits somewhat depressed. I have heard of voyagers and wanderers in deserts who were willing to give a casket of gems for a cup of cold water. I had not supposed my own condition to be, in any respect, similar; yet I had just given one third of my estate for a breakfast.

I stopped at noon at another inn. I had counted on purchasing a dinner for the same price, since I meant to content myself with the same fare. A large company was just sitting down to a smoking banquet. The landlord invited me to join them. I took my place at the table, but was furnished with bread and milk. Being prepared to depart, I took him aside. What is to pay? said I.—Did you drink any thing, Sir?—Certainly. I drank the milk which was furnished.—But any liquors, Sir?—No.

He deliberated a moment and then assuming an air of disinterestedness, 'Tis our custom to charge dinner and club, but as you drank nothing, we'll let the club go. A mere dinner is half-a-dollar, Sir.

He had no leisure to attend to my fluctuations. After debating with myself on what was to be done, I concluded that compliance was best, and leaving the money at the bar, resumed my way.

I had not performed more than half my journey, yet my purse was entirely exhausted. This was a specimen of the cost incurred by living at an inn. If I entered the city, a tavern must, at least for some time, be my abode, but I had not a farthing remaining to defray my charges. My father had formerly entertained a boarder for a dollar per week, and, in a case of need, I was willing to subsist upon coarser fare, and lie on an harder bed than those with which our guest had been supplied. These facts had been the foundation of my negligence on this occasion.

What was now to be done? To return to my paternal mansion was impossible. To relinquish my design of entering the city and to seek a temporary asylum, if not permanent employment, at some one of the plantations, within view, was the most obvious expedient. These deliberations did not slacken my pace. I was almost unmindful of my way, when I found I had passed Schuylkill at the upper bridge. I was now within the precincts of the city and night was hastening. It behoved me to come to a speedy decision.

Suddenly I recollected that I had not paid the customary toll at the bridge: neither had I money wherewith to pay it. A demand of payment would have suddenly arrested my progress; and so slight an incident would have precluded that wonderful destiny to which I was reserved. The obstacle that would have hindered my advance, now prevented my return. Scrupulous honesty did not require me to turn back and awaken the vigilance of the toll-gatherer. I had nothing to pay, and by returning I should only double my debt. Let it stand, said I, where it does. All that honour enjoins is to pay when I am able.

I adhered to the cross ways, till I reached Market street. Night had fallen, and a triple row of lamps presented a spectacle enchanting and new. My personal cares were, for a time, lost in the tumultuous sensations with which I was now engrossed. I had never visited the city at this hour. When my last visit was paid I was a mere child. The novelty which environed every object was, therefore, nearly absolute. I proceeded with more cautious steps, but was still absorbed in attention to passing objects. I reached the market-house, and entering it, indulged myself in new delight and new wonder.

I need not remark that our ideas of magnificence and splendour are merely comparative; yet you may be prompted to smile when I tell you that, in walking through this avenue, I for a moment conceived myself transported to the hall "pendent with many a row of starry lamps and blazing crescents fed by naphtha and asphaltos." That this transition from my homely and quiet retreat, had been effected in so few hours, wore the aspect of miracle or magic.

I proceeded from one of these buildings to another, till I reached their termination in Front street. Here my progress was checked, and I sought repose to my weary limbs by seating myself on a stall. No wonder some fatigue was felt by me, accustomed as I was to strenuous exertions, since, exclusive of the minutes spent at breakfast and dinner, I had travelled fifteen hours and forty-five miles.

I began now to reflect, with some earnestness, on my condition. I was a stranger, friendless, and moneyless. I was unable to purchase food and shelter, and was wholly unused to the business of begging. Hunger was the only serious inconvenience to which I was immediately exposed. I had no objection to spend the night in the spot where I then sat. I had no fear that my visions would be troubled by the officers of police. It was no crime to be without a home; but how should I supply my present cravings and the cravings of to-morrow?

At length it occurred to me that one of our country neighbours was probably at this time in the city. He kept a store as well as cultivated a farm. He was a plain and well meaning man, and should I be so fortunate as to meet him, his superior knowledge of the city might be of essential benefit to me in my present forlorn circumstances. His generosity might likewise induce him to lend me so much as would purchase one meal. I had formed the resolution to leave the city next day and was astonished at the folly that had led me into it; but, meanwhile, my physical wants must be supplied.

Where should I look for this man? In the course of conversation I recollected him to have referred to the place of his temporary abode. It was an inn, but the sign or the name of the keeper, for some time withstood all my efforts to recall them.

At length I lighted on the last. It was Lesher's tavern. I immediately set out in search of it. After many enquiries I at last arrived at the door. I was preparing to enter the house when I perceived that my bundle was gone. I had left it on the stall where I had been sitting. People were perpetually passing to and fro. It was scarcely possible not to have been noticed. No one that observed it would fail to make it his prey. Yet it was of too much value to me, to allow me to be governed by a bare probability. I resolved to lose not a moment in returning.

With some difficulty I retraced my steps, but the bundle had disappeared. The clothes were, in themselves, of small value, but they constituted the whole of my wardrobe; and I now reflected that they were capable of being transmuted, by the pawn or sale of them, into food. There were other wretches as indigent as I was, and I consoled myself by thinking that my shirts and stockings might furnish a seasonable covering to their nakedness; but there was a relique concealed within this bundle, the loss of which could scarcely be endured by me. It was the portrait of a young man who died three years ago at my father's house, drawn by his own hand.

He was discovered one morning in the orchard with many marks of insanity upon him. His air and dress bespoke some elevation of rank and fortune. My mother's compassion was excited, and, as his singularities were harmless, an asylum was afforded him, though he was unable to pay for it. He was constantly declaiming in an incoherent manner, about some mistress who had proved faithless. His speeches seemed, however, like the rantings of an actor, to be rehearsed by rote, or for the sake of exercise. He was totally careless of his person and health, and by repeated negligences of this kind, at last contracted a fever of which he speedily died. The name which he assumed was Clavering.

He gave no distinct account of his family, but stated in loose terms that they were residents in England, high born and wealthy. That they had denied him the woman whom he loved and banished him to America under penalty of death if he should dare to return, and that they had refused him all means of subsistence in a foreign land. He predicted, in his wild and declamatory way, his own death. He was very skilful at the pencil and drew this portrait a short time before his dissolution, presented it to me, and charged me to preserve it in remembrance of him. My mother loved the youth because he was amiable and unfortunate, and chiefly because she fancied a very powerful resemblance between his countenance and mine. I was too young to build affection on any rational foundation. I loved him, for whatever reason, with an ardour unusual at my age, and which this portrait had contributed to prolong and to cherish.

In thus finally leaving my home, I was careful not to leave this picture behind. I wrapt it in paper in which a few elegiac stanzas were inscribed in my own hand and with my utmost elegance of penmanship. I then placed it in a leathern case, which, for greater security, was deposited in the centre of my bundle. It will occur to you, perhaps, that it would be safer in some fold or pocket of the clothes which I wore. I was of a different opinion and was now to endure the penalty of my error.

It was in vain to heap execrations on my negligence, or to consume the little strength left to me in regrets. I returned once more to the tavern and made enquiries for Mr. Capper, the person whom I have just mentioned as my father's neighbour. I was informed that Capper was now in town; that he had lodged, on the last-night, at this house; that he had expected to do the same to-night, but a gentleman had called ten minutes ago, whose invitation to lodge with him to-night had been accepted. They had just gone out together. Who, I asked, was the gentleman? The landlord had no knowledge of him: He knew neither his place of abode nor his name. . . . Was Mr. Capper expected to return hither in the morning? —No, he had heard the stranger propose to Mr. Capper to go with him into the country to-morrow, and Mr. Capper, he believed, had assented.

This disappointment was peculiarly severe. I had lost, by my own negligence, the only opportunity that would offer of meeting my friend. Had even the recollection of my loss been postponed for three minutes, I should have entered the house, and a meeting would have been secured. I could discover no other expedient to obviate the present evil. My heart began now, for the first time, to droop. I looked back, with nameless emotions, on the days of my infancy. I called up the image of my mother. I reflected on the infatuation of my surviving parent, and the usurpation of the detestable Betty with horror. I viewed myself as the most calamitous and desolate of human beings.

At this time I was sitting in the common room. There were others in the same apartment, lounging, or whistling, or singing. I noticed them not, but leaning my head upon my hand, I delivered myself up to painful and intense meditation. From this I was roused by some one placing himself on the bench near me and addressing me thus: Pray Sir, if you will excuse me, who was the person whom you were looking for just now? Perhaps I can give you the information you want. If I can, you will be very welcome to it.—I fixed my eyes with some eagerness on the person that spoke. He was a young man, expensively and fashionably dressed, whose mien was considerably prepossessing, and whose countenance bespoke some portion of discernment. I described to him the man whom I sought. I am in search of the same man myself, said he, but I expect to meet him here. He may lodge elsewhere, but he promised to meet me here at half after nine. I have no doubt he will fulfil his promise, so that you will meet the gentleman.

I was highly gratified by this information, and thanked my informant with some degree of warmth. My gratitude he did not notice but continued: In order to beguile expectation, I have ordered supper: Will you do me the favour to partake with me, unless indeed you have supped already? I was obliged, somewhat awkwardly, to decline his invitation, conscious as I was that the means of payment were not in my power. He continued however to urge my compliance, till at length it was, though reluctantly, yielded. My chief motive was the certainty of seeing Capper.

My new acquaintance was exceedingly conversible, but his conversation was chiefly characterized by frankness and good humour. My reserves gradually diminished, and I ventured to inform him, in general terms, of my former condition and present views. He listened to my details with seeming attention, and commented on them with some judiciousness. His statements, however, tended to discourage me from remaining in the city.

Meanwhile the hour passed and Capper did not appear. I noticed this circumstance to him with no little solicitude. He said that possibly he might have forgotten or neglected his engagement. His affair was not of the highest importance, and might be readily postponed to a future opportunity. He perceived that my vivacity was greatly damped by this intelligence. He importuned me to disclose the cause. He made himself very merry with my distress, when it was at length discovered. As to the expence of supper, I had partaken of it at his invitation, he therefore should of course be charged with it. As to lodging, he had a chamber and a bed which he would insist upon my sharing with him.

My faculties were thus kept upon the stretch of wonder. Every new act of kindness in this man surpassed the fondest expectation that I had formed. I saw no reason why I should be treated with benevolence. I should have acted in the same manner if placed in the same circumstances; yet it appeared incongruous and inexplicable. I know not whence my ideas of human nature were derived. They certainly were not the offspring of my own feelings. These would have taught me that interest and duty were blended in every act of generosity.

I did not come into the world without my scruples and suspicions. I was more apt to impute kindnesses to sinister and hidden than to obvious and laudable motives. I paused to reflect upon the possible designs of this person. What end could be served by this behaviour? I was no subject of violence or fraud. I had neither trinket nor coin to stimulate the treachery of others. What was offered was merely lodging for the night. Was this an act of such transcendent disinterestedness as to be incredible? My garb was meaner than that of my companion, but my intellectual accomplishments were at least upon a level with his. Why should he be supposed to be insensible to my claims upon his kindness. I was a youth, destitute of experience, money, and friends; but I was not devoid of all mental and personal endowments. That my merit should be discovered, even on such slender intercourse, had surely nothing in it that shocked belief.

While I was thus deliberating, my new friend was earnest in his solicitations for my company. He remarked my hesitation but ascribed it to a wrong cause. Come, said he, I can guess your objections and can obviate them. You are afraid of being ushered into company; and people who have passed their lives like you have a wonderful antipathy to strange faces; but this is bed-time with our family, so that we can defer your introduction to them till to-morrow. We may go to our chamber without being seen by any but servants.

I had not been aware of this circumstance. My reluctance

flowed from a different cause, but now that the inconveniences of ceremony were mentioned, they appeared to me of considerable weight. I was well pleased that they should thus be avoided, and consented to go along with him.

We passed several streets and turned several corners. At last we turned into a kind of court which seemed to be chiefly occupied by stables. We will go, said he, by the back way into the house. We shall thus save ourselves the necessity of entering the parlour, where some of the family may still be.

My companion was as talkative as ever, but said nothing from which I could gather any knowledge of the number, character, and condition of his family.

Chapter IV

W E ARRIVED at a brick wall through which we passed by a gate into an extensive court or yard. The darkness would allow me to see nothing but outlines. Compared with the pigmy dimensions of my father's wooden hovel, the buildings before me were of gigantic loftiness. The horses were here far more magnificently accommodated than I had been. By a large door we entered an elevated hall. Stay here, said he, just while I fetch a light.

He returned, bearing a candle, before I had time to ponder on my present situation.

We now ascended a stair-case, covered with painted canvas. No one whose inexperience is less than mine, can imagine to himself the impressions made upon me by surrounding objects. The height to which this stair ascended, its dimensions, and its ornaments, appeared to me a combination of all that was pompous and superb.

We stopped not till we had reached the third story. Here my companion unlocked and led the way into a chamber. This, said he, is my room: Permit me to welcome you into it.

I had no time to examine this room before, by some accident, the candle was extinguished. Curse upon my carelessness, said he. I must go down again and light the candle. I will return in a twinkling. Meanwhile you may undress yourself and go to bed. He went out, and, as I afterwards recollected, locked the door behind him.

I was not indisposed to follow his advice, but my curiosity would first be gratified by a survey of the room. Its height and spaciousness were imperfectly discernible by star-light, and by gleams from a street lamp. The floor was covered with a carpet, the walls with brilliant hangings; the bed and windows were shrouded by curtains of a rich texture and glossy hues. Hitherto I had merely read of these things. I knew them to be the decorations of opulence, and yet as I viewed them, and remembered where and what I was on the same hour the preceding day, I could scarcely believe myself awake or that my senses were not beguiled by some spell.

Where, said I, will this adventure terminate? I rise on the morrow with the dawn and speed into the country. When this night is remembered, how like a vision will it appear! If I tell the tale by a kitchen fire, my veracity will be disputed. I shall be ranked with the story tellers of Shirauz and Bagdad.

Though busied in these reflections, I was not inattentive to the progress of time. Methought my companion was remarkably dilatory. He went merely to re-light his candle, but certainly he might, during this time, have performed the operation ten times over. Some unforeseen accident might occasion his delay.

Another interval passed and no tokens of his coming. I began now to grow uneasy. I was unable to account for his detention. Was not some treachery designed? I went to the door and found that it was locked. This heightened my suspicions. I was alone, a stranger, in an upper room of the house. Should my conductor have disappeared, by design or by accident, and some one of the family should find me here, what would be the consequence? Should I not be arrested as a thief and conveyed to prison? My transition from the street to this chamber would not be more rapid than my passage hence to a gaol.

These ideas struck me with panick. I revolved them anew, but they only acquired greater plausibility. No doubt I had been the victim of malicious artifice. Inclination, however, conjured up opposite sentiments and my fears began to subside. What motive, I asked, could induce an human being to inflict wanton injury? I could not account for his delay, but how numberless were the contingencies, that might occasion it?

I was somewhat comforted by these reflections, but the consolation they afforded was short-lived. I was listening with the utmost eagerness to catch the sound of a foot, when a noise was indeed heard, but totally unlike a step. It was human breath struggling, as it were, for passage. On the first effort of attention it appeared like a groan. Whence it arose I could not tell. He that uttered it was near; perhaps in the room.

Presently the same noise was again heard, and now I perceived that it came from the bed. It was accompanied with a motion like some one changing his posture. What I at first conceived to be a groan, appeared now to be nothing more than the expiration of a sleeping man. What should I infer from this incident? My companion did not apprize me that the apartment was inhabited. Was his imposture a jestful or a wicked one?

There was no need to deliberate. There were no means of concealment or escape. The person would sometime awaken and detect me. The interval would only be fraught with agony and it was wise to shorten it. Should I not withdraw the curtain, awake the person, and encounter at once all the consequences of my situation? I glided softly to the bed, when the thought occurred, May not the sleeper be a female?

I cannot describe the mixture of dread and of shame which glowed in my veins. The light in which such a visitant would be probably regarded by a woman's fears, the precipitate alarms that might be given, the injury which I might unknowingly inflict or undeservedly suffer, threw my thoughts into painful confusion. My presence might pollute a spotless reputation or furnish fuel to jealousy.

Still, though it were a female, would not least injury be done by gently interrupting her slumber? But the question of sex still remained to be decided. For this end I once more approached the bed and drew aside the silk. The sleeper was a babe. This I discovered by the glimmer of a street lamp.

Part of my solicitudes were now removed. It was plain that this chamber belonged to a nurse or a mother. She had not yet come to bed. Perhaps it was a married pair and their approach might be momently expected. I pictured to myself their entrance and my own detection. I could imagine no consequence that was not disastrous and horrible, and from which I would not, at any price, escape. I again examined the door, and found that exit by this avenue was impossible. There were other doors in this room. Any practicable expedient in this extremity was to be pursued. One of these was bolted. I unfastened it and found a considerable space within. Should I immure myself in this closet? I saw no benefit that would finally result from it. I discovered that there was a bolt on the inside which would somewhat contribute to security. This being drawn no one could enter without breaking the door.

I had scarcely paused when the long expected sound of footsteps were heard in the entry. Was it my companion or a stranger? If it were the latter, I had not yet mustered courage sufficient to meet him. I cannot applaud the magnanimity of my proceeding, but no one can expect intrepid or judicious measures from one in my circumstances. I stepped into the closet and closed the door. Some one immediately after, unlocked the chamber door. He was unattended with a light. The footsteps, as they moved along the carpet, could scarcely be heard.

I waited impatiently for some token by which I might be governed. I put my ear to the key-hole, and at length heard a voice, but not that of my companion, exclaim, somewhat above a whisper, Smiling cherub! safe and sound, I see. Would to God my experiment may succeed and that thou mayest find a mother where I have found a wife! There he stopped. He appeared to kiss the babe and presently retiring locked the door after him.

These words were capable of no consistent meaning. They served, at least, to assure me that I had been treacherously dealt with. This chamber it was manifest, did not belong to my companion. I put up prayers to my deity that he would deliver me from these toils. What a condition was mine! Immersed in palpable darkness! shut up in this unknown recess! lurking like a robber!

My meditations were disturbed by new sounds. The door was unlocked, more than one person entered the apartment, and light streamed through the key-hole. I looked; but the aperture was too small and the figures passed too quickly to permit me the sight of them. I bent my ear and this imparted some more authentic information.

The man, as I judged by the voice, was the same who had just departed. Rustling of silk denoted his companion to be female. Some words being uttered by the man in too low a key to be overheard, the lady burst into a passion of tears. He strove to comfort her by soothing tones and tender appellations. How can it be helped, said he. It is time to resume your courage. Your duty to yourself and to me requires you to subdue this unreasonable grief.

He spoke frequently in this strain, but all he said seemed to have little influence in pacifying the lady. At length, however, her sobs began to lessen in vehemence and frequency.

He exhorted her to seek for some repose. Apparently she prepared to comply, and conversation was, for a few minutes, intermitted.

I could not but advert to the possibility that some occasion to examine the closet in which I was immured, might occur. I knew not in what manner to demean myself if this should take place. I had no option at present. By withdrawing myself from view I had lost the privilege of an upright deportment. Yet the thought of spending the night in this spot was not to be endured.

Gradually I began to view the project of bursting from the closet, and trusting to the energy of truth and of an artless tale, with more complacency. More than once my hand was placed upon the bolt, but withdrawn by a sudden faltering of resolution. When one attempt failed, I recurred once more to such reflections as were adapted to renew my purpose.

I preconcerted the address which I should use. I resolved to be perfectly explicit: To withhold no particular of my adventures from the moment of my arrival. My description must necessarily suit some person within their knowledge. All I should want was liberty to depart; but if this were not allowed, I might at least hope to escape any ill treatment, and to be confronted with my betrayer. In that case I did not fear to make him the attester of my innocence.

Influenced by these considerations, I once more touched the lock. At that moment the lady shrieked, and exclaimed Good God! What is here? An interesting conversation ensued. The object that excited her astonishment was the child. I collected from what passed that the discovery was wholly unexpected by her. Her husband acted as if equally unaware of this event. He joined in all her exclamations of wonder and all her wild conjectures. When these were somewhat exhausted he artfully insinuated the propriety of bestowing care upon the little foundling. I now found that her grief had been occasioned by the recent loss of her own offspring. She was, for some time, averse to her husband's proposal, but at length was persuaded to take the babe to her bosom and give it nourishment.

This incident had diverted my mind from its favourite project, and filled me with speculations on the nature of the scene. One explication was obvious, that the husband was the parent of this child and had used this singular expedient to procure for it the maternal protection of his wife. It would soon claim from her all the fondness which she entertained for her own progeny. No suspicion probably had yet, or would hereafter, occur with regard to its true parent. If her character be distinguished by the usual attributes of women, the knowledge of this truth may convert her love into hatred. I reflected with amazement on the slightness of that thread by which human passions are led from their true direction. With no less amazement did I remark the complexity of incidents by which I had been empowered to communicate to her this truth. How baseless are the structures of falsehood, which we build in opposition to the system of eternal nature. If I should escape undetected from this recess, it will be true that I never saw the face of either of these persons, and yet I am acquainted with the most secret transaction of their lives.

My own situation was now more critical than before. The lights were extinguished and the parties had sought repose. To issue from the closet now would be eminently dangerous. My councils were again at a stand and my designs frustrated. Meanwhile the persons did not drop their discourse, and I thought myself justified in listening. Many facts of the most secret and momentous nature were alluded to. Some allusions were unintelligible. To others I was able to affix a plausible meaning, and some were palpable enough. Every word that was uttered on that occasion is indelibly imprinted on my memory. Perhaps the singularity of my circumstances and my previous ignorance of what was passing in the world, contributed to render me a greedy listener. Most that was said I shall overlook, but one part of the conversation it will be necessary to repeat.

A large company had assembled that evening at their house. They criticised the character and manners of several. At last the husband said, What think you of the Nabob? Especially when he talked about riches? How artfully he encourages the notion of his poverty! Yet not a soul believes him. I cannot for my part account for that scheme of his. I half suspect that his wealth flows from a bad source, since he is so studious of concealing it.

Perhaps, after all, said the lady, you are mistaken as to his wealth.

Impossible, exclaimed the other. Mark how he lives. Have I not seen his bank account. His deposits, since he has been here, amount to not less than half a million.

Heaven grant that it be so, said the lady with a sigh. I shall think with less aversion of your scheme. If poor Tom's fortune be made, and he not the worse, or but little the worse on that account, I shall think it on the whole best.

That, replied he, is what reconciles me to the scheme. To him thirty thousand are nothing.

But will he not suspect you of some hand in it?

How can he? Will I not appear to lose as well as himself? Tom is my brother, but who can be supposed to answer for a brother's integrity: but he cannot suspect either of us. Nothing less than a miracle can bring our plot to light. Besides, this man is not what he ought to be. He will some time or other, come out to be a grand impostor. He makes money by other arts than bargain and sale. He has found his way, by some means, to the Portuguese treasury.

Here the conversation took a new direction, and, after some time, the silence of sleep ensued.

Who, thought I, is this nabob who counts his dollars by half millions, and on whom, it seems, as if some fraud was intended to be practised. Amidst their wariness and subtlety how little are they aware that their conversation has been overheard! By means as inscrutable as those which conducted me hither, I may hereafter be enabled to profit by this detection of a plot. But, meanwhile, what was I to do? How was I to effect my escape from this perilous asylum?

After much reflection it occurred to me that to gain the street without exciting their notice was not utterly impossible. Sleep does not commonly end of itself, unless at a certain period. What impediments were there between me and liberty which I could not remove, and remove with so much caution as to escape notice. Motion and sound inevitably go together, but every sound is not attended to. The doors of the closet and the chamber did not creak upon their hinges. The latter might be locked. This I was able to ascertain only by experiment. If it were so, yet the key was probably in the lock and might be used without much noise.

I waited till their slow and hoarser inspirations shewed them to be both asleep. Just then, on changing my position, my head struck against some things which depended from the ceiling of the closet. They were implements of some kind which rattled against each other in consequence of this unlucky blow. I was fearful lest this noise should alarm, as the closet was little distant from the bed. The breathing of one instantly ceased, and a motion was made as if the head were lifted from the pillow. This motion, which was made by the husband, awaked his companion, who exclaimed, What is the matter?

Something, I believe, replied he, in the closet. If I was not dreaming, I heard the pistols strike against each other as if some one was taking them down.

This intimation was well suited to alarm the lady. She besought him to ascertain the matter. This to my utter dismay he at first consented to do, but presently observed that probably his ears had misinformed him. It was hardly possible that the sound proceeded from them. It might be a rat, or his own fancy might have fashioned it.—It is not easy to describe my trepidations while this conference was holding. I saw how easily their slumber was disturbed. The obstacles to my escape were less surmountable than I had imagined.

In a little time all was again still. I waited till the usual tokens of sleep were distinguishable. I once more resumed my attempt. The bolt was withdrawn with all possible slowness; but I could by no means prevent all sound. My state was full of inquietude and suspense; my attention being painfully divided between the bolt and the condition of the sleepers. The difficulty lay in giving that degree of force which was barely sufficient. Perhaps not less than fifteen minutes were consumed in this operation. At last it was happily effected and the door was cautiously opened.

Emerging as I did from utter darkness, the light admitted into three windows, produced, to my eyes, a considerable illumination. Objects which on my first entrance into this apartment were invisible, were now clearly discerned. The bed was

shrowded by curtains, yet I shrunk back into my covert, fearful of being seen. To facilitate my escape I put off my shoes.
My mind was so full of objects of more urgent moment that
the propriety of taking them along with me never occurred.
I left them in the closet.

I now glided across the apartment to the door. I was not a
little discouraged by observing that the key was wanting. My
whole hope depended on the omission to lock it. In my haste
to ascertain this point, I made some noise which again roused
one of the sleepers. He started and cried Who is there?

I now regarded my case as desperate and detection as inevitable. My apprehensions, rather than my caution, kept me
mute. I shrunk to the wall, and waited in a kind of agony for
the moment that should decide my fate.

The lady was again roused. In answer to her enquiries, her
husband said that some one he believed was at the door, but
there was no danger of their entering, for he had locked it
and the key was in his pocket.

My courage was completely annihilated by this piece of intelligence. My resources were now at an end. I could only
remain in this spot, till the morning light, which could be at
no great distance, should discover me. My inexperience disabled me from estimating all the perils of my situation. Perhaps I had no more than temporary inconveniences to dread.
My intention was innocent, and I had been betrayed into my
present situation, not by my own wickedness but the wickedness of others.

I was deeply impressed with the ambiguousness which
would necessarily rest upon my motives, and the scrutiny to
which they would be subjected. I shuddered at the bare possibility of being ranked with thieves. These reflections again
gave edge to my ingenuity in search of the means of escape.
I had carefully attended to the circumstances of their entrance.
Possibly the act of locking had been unnoticed; but was it not
likewise possible that this person had been mistaken? The key
was gone. Would this have been the case if the door were
unlocked?

My fears rather than my hopes, impelled me to make the
experiment. I drew back the latch and, to my unspeakable joy,
the door opened.

I passed through and explored my way to the stair-case. I descended till I reached the bottom. I could not recollect with accuracy the position of the door leading into the court, but by carefully feeling along the wall with my hands, I at length, discovered it. It was fastened by several bolts and a lock. The bolts were easily withdrawn, but the key was removed. I knew not where it was deposited. I thought I had reached the threshold of liberty but here was an impediment that threatened to be insurmountable.

But if doors could not be passed, windows might be unbarred. I remembered that my companion had gone into a door on the left hand, in search of a light. I searched for this door. Fortunately it was fastened only by a bolt. It admitted me into a room which I carefully explored till I reached a window. I will not dwell on my efforts to unbar this entrance. Suffice it to say that, after much exertion and frequent mistakes, I at length found my way into the yard, and thence passed into the court.

Chapter V

Now I was once more on public ground. By so many anxious efforts had I disengaged myself from the perilous precincts of private property. As many stratagems as are usually made to enter an house, had been employed by me to get out of it. I was urged to the use of them by my fears; yet so far from carrying off spoil, I had escaped with the loss of an essential part of my dress.

I had now leisure to reflect. I seated myself on the ground and reviewed the scenes through which I had just passed. I began to think that my industry had been misemployed. Suppose I had met the person on his first entrance into his chamber. Was the truth so utterly wild as not to have found credit? Since the door was locked, and there was no other avenue; what other statement but the true one would account for my being found there? This deportment had been worthy of an honest purpose. My betrayer probably expected that this would be the issue of his jest. My rustic simplicity, he might think, would suggest no more ambiguous or elaborate expedient. He might likewise have predetermined to interfere if my safety had been really endangered.

On the morrow the two doors of the chamber and the window below would be found unclosed. They will suspect a design to pillage, but their searches will terminate in nothing but in the discovery of a pair of clumsy and dusty shoes in the closet. Now that I was safe I could not help smiling at the picture which my fancy drew of their anxiety and wonder. These thoughts, however, gave place to more momentous considerations.

I could not image to myself a more perfect example of indigence than I now exhibited. There was no being in the city on whose kindness I had any claim. Money I had none and what I then wore comprised my whole stock of moveables. I had just lost my shoes, and this loss rendered my stockings of no use. My dignity remonstrated against a barefoot pilgrimage, but to this, necessity now reconciled me. I threw my stockings between the bars of a stable window, belonging, as I thought, to the mansion I had just left. These, together with my shoes, I left to pay the cost of my entertainment.

I saw that the city was no place for *me*. The end that I had had in view, of procuring some mechanical employment, could only be obtained by the use of means, but what means to pursue I knew not. This night's perils and deceptions gave me a distaste to a city life, and my ancient occupations rose to my view enhanced by a thousand imaginary charms. I resolved forthwith to strike into the country.

The day began now to dawn. It was Sunday, and I was desirous of eluding observation. I was somewhat recruited by rest though the languors of sleeplessness oppressed me. I meant to throw myself on the first lap of verdure I should meet, and indulge in sleep that I so much wanted. I knew not the direction of the streets; but followed that which I first entered from the court, trusting that, by adhering steadily to one course, I should sometime reach the fields. This street, as I afterwards found, tended to Schuylkill, and soon extricated me from houses. I could not cross this river without payment of toll. It was requisite to cross it in order to reach that part of the country whither I was desirous of going, but how should I effect my passage? I knew of no ford, and the smallest expence exceeded my capacity. Ten thousand guineas and a farthing were equally remote from nothing, and nothing was the portion allotted to me.

While my mind was thus occupied, I turned up one of the streets which tend northward. It was, for some length, uninhabited and unpaved. Presently I reached a pavement, and a painted fence, along which a row of poplars was planted. It bounded a garden into which a knot hole permitted me to pry. The enclosure was a charming green, which I saw appended to an house of the loftiest and most stately order. It seemed like a recent erection, had all the gloss of novelty, and exhibited, to my unpracticed eyes, the magnificence of palaces. My father's dwelling did not equal the height of one story, and might be easily comprised in one fourth of those buildings which here were designed to accommodate the menials. My heart dictated the comparison between my own condition and that of the proprietors of this domain. How wide and

how impassible was the gulf by which we were separated! This
fair inheritance had fallen to one who, perhaps, would only
abuse it to the purposes of luxury, while I, with intentions
worthy of the friend of mankind, was doomed to wield the
flail and the mattock.

I had been entirely unaccustomed to this strain of reflection. My books had taught me the dignity and safety of the
middle path and my darling writer abounded with encomiums
on rural life. At a distance from luxury and pomp I viewed
them, perhaps, in a just light. A nearer scrutiny confirmed my
early prepossessions, but at the distance at which I now stood,
the lofty edifices, the splendid furniture, and the copious accommodations of the rich, excited my admiration and my
envy.

I relinquished my station and proceeded, in an heartless
mood, along the fence. I now came to the mansion itself. The
principal door was entered by a stair-case of marble. I had
never seen the stone of Carrara, and wildly supposed this to
have been dug from Italian quarries. The beauty of the poplars, the coolness exhaled from the dew-besprent bricks, the
commodiousness of the seat which these steps afforded, and
the uncertainty into which I was plunged respecting my future
conduct, all combined to make me pause. I sat down on the
lower step and began to meditate.

By some transition it occurred to me that the supply of my
most urgent wants, might be found in some inhabitant of this
house. I needed at present a few cents; and what were a few
cents to the tenant of a mansion like this. I had an invincible
aversion to the calling of a beggar, but I regarded with still
more antipathy the vocation of a thief; to this alternative,
however, I was now reduced. I must either steal or beg; unless, indeed, assistance could be procured under the notion of
a loan. Would a stranger refuse to lend the pittance that I
wanted? Surely not, when the urgency of my wants were explained.

I recollected other obstacles. To summon the master of the
house from his bed, perhaps, for the sake of such an application, would be preposterous. I should be in more danger of
provoking his anger than exciting his benevolence. This request might, surely, with more propriety be preferred to a

passenger. I should, probably, meet several before I should arrive at Schuylkill.

A servant just then appeared at the door, with bucket and brush. This obliged me, much sooner than I intended, to decamp. With some reluctance I rose and proceeded.—This house occupied the corner of the street, and I now turned this corner, towards the country. A person, at some distance before me, was approaching in an opposite direction.

Why, said I, may I not make my demand of the first man I meet? This person exhibits tokens of ability to lend. There is nothing chilling or austere in his demeanour.

The resolution to address this passenger was almost formed; but the nearer he advanced, my resolves grew less firm. He noticed me not till he came within a few paces. He seemed busy in reflection, and had not my figure caught his eye; or had he merely bestowed a passing glance upon me, I should not have been sufficiently courageous to have detained him. The event however was widely different.

He looked at me and started. For an instant, as it were, and till he had time to dart at me a second glance, he checked his pace. This behaviour decided mine, and he stopped on perceiving tokens of a desire to address him. I spoke, but my accents and air sufficiently denoted my embarrassments.

I am going to solicit a favour, which my situation makes of the highest importance to me, and which I hope it will be easy for you, Sir, to grant. It is not an alms but a loan that I seek; a loan that I will repay the moment I am able to do it. I am going to the country, but have not wherewith to pay my passage over Schuylkill, or to buy a morsel of bread. May I venture to request of you, Sir, the loan of six pence? As I told you, it is my intention to repay it.

I delivered this address, not without some faltering, but with great earnestness. I laid particular stress upon my intention to refund the money. He listened with a most inquisitive air. His eye perused me from head to foot.

After some pause, he said, in a very emphatic manner. Why into the country? Have you family? Kindred? Friends?

No, answered I, I have neither. I go in search of the means of subsistence. I have passed my life upon a farm, and propose to die in the same condition.

Whence have you come?

I came yesterday from the country, with a view to earn my bread in some way, but have changed my plan and propose now to return.

Why have you changed it? In what way are you capable of earning your bread?

I hardly know, said I. I can, as yet, manage no tool, that can be managed in the city, but the pen. My habits have, in some small degree, qualified me for a writer. I would willingly accept employment of that kind.

He fixed his eyes upon the earth, and was silent for some minutes. At length, recovering himself, he said, Follow me to my house. Perhaps something may be done for you. If not, I will lend you six pence.

It may be supposed that I eagerly complied with the invitation. My companion said no more, his air bespeaking him to be absorbed by his own thoughts, till we reached his house, which proved to be that at the door of which I had been seated. We entered a parlour together.

Unless you can assume my ignorance and my simplicity, you will be unable to conceive the impressions that were made by the size and ornaments of this apartment. I shall omit these impressions, which, indeed, no descriptions could adequately convey, and dwell on incidents of greater moment. He asked me to give him a specimen of my penmanship. I told you that I had bestowed very great attention upon this art. Implements were brought and I sat down to the task. By some inexplicable connection a line in Shakspeare occurred to me, and I wrote

"My poverty, but not my will consents."

The sentiment conveyed in this line powerfully affected him, but in a way which I could not then comprehend. I collected from subsequent events that the inference was not unfavourable to my understanding or my morals. He questioned me as to my history. I related my origin and my inducements to desert my father's house. With respect to last night's adventures I was silent. I saw no useful purpose that could be answered by disclosure, and I half suspected that my companion would refuse credit to my tale.

There were frequent intervals of abstraction and reflection

between his questions. My examination lasted not much less than an hour. At length he said, I want an amanuensis or copyist: On what terms will you live with me?

I answered that I knew not how to estimate the value of my services. I knew not whether these services were agreeable or healthful. My life had hitherto been active. My constitution was predisposed to diseases of the lungs and the change might be hurtful. I was willing however to try and to content myself for a month or a year, with so much as would furnish me with food, clothing, and lodging.

'Tis well, said he. You remain with me as long and no longer than both of us please. You shall lodge and eat in this house. I will supply you with clothing, and your task will be to write what I dictate. Your person, I see, has not shared much of your attention. It is in my power to equip you instantly in the manner which becomes a resident in this house. Come with me.

He led the way into the court behind and thence into a neat building, which contained large wooden vessels and a pump. There, said he, you may wash yourself, and when that is done, I will conduct you to your chamber and your wardrobe.

This was speedily performed and he accordingly led the way to the chamber. It was an apartment in the third story, finished and furnished in the same costly and superb style, with the rest of the house. He opened closets and drawers which overflowed with clothes and linen of all and of the best kinds. These are yours, said he, as long as you stay with me. Dress yourself as likes you best. Here is every thing your nakedness requires. When dressed you may descend to breakfast. With these words he left me.

The clothes were all in the French style, as I afterwards, by comparing my garb with that of others, discovered. They were fitted to my shape with the nicest precision. I bedecked myself with all my care. I remembered the style of dress, used by my beloved Clavering. My locks were of shining auburn, flowing and smooth like his. Having wrung the wet from them, and combed, I tied them carelessly in a black riband. Thus equipped I surveyed myself in a mirror.

You may imagine, if you can, the sensations which this instantaneous transformation produced. Appearances are

wonderfully influenced by dress. Check shirt, buttoned at the
neck, an awkward fustian coat, check trowsers, and bare feet
were now supplanted by linen and muslin, nankeen coat,
striped with green, a white silk waistcoat, elegantly needle-
wrought, casimer pantaloons, stockings of variegated silk, and
shoes that in their softness, pliancy, and polished surface vied
with sattin. I could scarcely forbear looking back to see
whether the image in the glass, so well proportioned, so gal-
ant, and so graceful, did not belong to another. I could
scarcely recognize any lineaments of my own. I walked to the
window. Twenty minutes ago, said I, I was traversing that
path a barefoot beggar; now I am thus. Again I surveyed myself. Surely some insanity has fastened on my understanding.
My senses are the sport of dreams. Some magic that disdains
the cumbrousness of nature's progress, has wrought this
change. I was roused from these doubts by a summons to
breakfast, obsequiously delivered by a black servant.

I found Welbeck, (for I shall henceforth call him by his true
name) at the breakfast table. A superb equipage of silver and
china was before him. He was startled at my entrance. The
change in my dress seemed for a moment to have deceived
him. His eye was frequently fixed upon me, with unusual
steadfastness. At these times there was inquietude and wonder
in his features.

I had now an opportunity of examining my host. There was
nicety but no ornament in his dress. His form was of the
middle height, spare, but vigorous and graceful. His face was
cast, I thought, in a foreign mould. His forehead receded beyond the usual degree in visages which I had seen. His eyes
large and prominent, but imparting no marks of benignity and
habitual joy. The rest of his face forcibly suggested the idea
of a convex edge. His whole figure impressed me with emotions of veneration and awe. A gravity that almost amounted
to sadness invariably attended him when we were alone together.

He whispered the servant that waited, who immediately retired. He then said, turning to me, A lady will enter presently,
whom you are to treat with the respect due to my daughter.
You must not notice any emotion she may betray at the sight
of you, nor expect her to converse with you; for she does not

understand your language. He had scarcely spoken when she entered. I was seized with certain misgivings and flutterings which a clownish education may account for. I so far conquered my timidity, however, as to snatch a look at her. I was not born to execute her portrait. Perhaps the turban that wreathed her head, the brilliant texture and inimitable folds of her drapery, and nymphlike port, more than the essential attributes of her person, gave splendour to the celestial vision. Perhaps it was her snowy hues and the cast, rather than the position of her features, that were so prolific of enchantment: or perhaps the wonder originated only in my own ignorance.

She did not immediately notice me. When she did she almost shrieked with surprise. She held up her hands, and gazing upon me, uttered various exclamations which I could not understand. I could only remark that her accents were thrillingly musical. Her perturbations refused to be stilled. It was with difficulty that she withdrew her regards from me. Much conversation passed between her and Welbeck, but I could comprehend no part of it. I was at liberty to animadvert on the visible part of their intercourse. I diverted some part of my attention from my own embarrassments, and fixed it on their looks.

In this art, as in most others, I was an unpracticed simpleton. In the countenance of Welbeck, there was somewhat else than sympathy with the astonishment and distress of the lady; but I could not interpret these additional tokens. When her attention was engrossed by Welbeck, her eyes were frequently vagrant or downcast; her cheeks contracted a deeper hue; and her breathing was almost prolonged into a sigh. These were marks on which I made no comments at the time. My own situation was calculated to breed confusion in my thoughts and awkwardness in my gestures. Breakfast being finished, the lady apparently at the request of Welbeck, sat down to a piano forte.

Here again I must be silent. I was not wholly destitute of musical practice and musical taste. I had that degree of knowledge which enabled me to estimate the transcendent skill of this performer. As if the pathos of her touch were insufficient, I found after some time that the lawless jarrings of the keys were chastened by her own more liquid notes. She played without a book, and though her base might be preconcerted, it was plain that her right-hand notes were momentary and spontaneous inspirations. Meanwhile Welbeck stood, leaning his arms on the back of a chair near her, with his eyes fixed on her face. His features were fraught with a meaning which I was eager to interpret but unable.

I have read of transitions effected by magic: I have read of palaces and deserts which were subject to the dominion of spells: Poets may sport with their power, but I am certain that no transition was ever conceived more marvellous and more beyond the reach of foresight, than that which I had just experienced. Heaths vexed by a midnight storm may be changed into an hall of choral nymphs and regal banqueting; forest glades may give sudden place to colonnades and carnivals, but he whose senses are deluded finds himself still on his natal earth. These miracles are contemptible when compared with that which placed me under this roof and gave me to partake in this audience. I know that my emotions are in danger of being regarded as ludicrous by those who cannot figure to themselves the consequences of a limited and rustic education.

Chapter VI

I N A SHORT TIME the lady retired. I naturally expected that some comments would be made on her behaviour, and that the cause of her surprise and distress on seeing me, would be explained, but Welbeck said nothing on that subject. When she had gone, he went to the window and stood for some time occupied, as it seemed, with his own thoughts. Then he turned to me and, calling me by my name, desired me to accompany him up stairs. There was neither cheerfulness nor mildness in his address, but neither was there any thing domineering or arrogant.

We entered an apartment on the same floor with my chamber, but separated from it by a spacious entry. It was supplied with bureaus, cabinets, and book-cases. This, said he, is your room and mine; but we must enter it and leave it together. I mean to act not as your master but your friend. My maimed hand so saying he shewed me his right hand, the forefinger of which was wanting, will not allow me to write accurately or copiously. For this reason I have required your aid, in a work of some moment. Much haste will not be requisite, and as to the hours and duration of employment, these will be seasonable and short.

Your present situation is new to you and we will therefore defer entering on our business. Meanwhile you may amuse yourself in what manner you please. Consider this house as your home and make yourself familiar with it. Stay within or go out, be busy or be idle, as your fancy shall prompt: Only you will conform to our domestic system as to eating and sleep: the servants will inform you of this. Next week we will enter on the task for which I designed you. You may now withdraw.

I obeyed this mandate with some awkwardness and hesitation. I went into my own chamber not displeased with an opportunity of loneliness. I threw myself on a chair and resigned myself to those thoughts which would naturally arise in this situation. I speculated on the character and views of Welbeck. I saw that he was embosomed in tranquility and

grandeur. Riches, therefore, were his; but in what did his opulence consist, and whence did it arise? What were the limits
by which it was confined, and what its degree of permanence?
I was unhabituated to ideas of floating or transferable wealth.
The rent of houses and lands was the only species of property
which was, as yet, perfectly intelligible: My previous ideas led
me to regard Welbeck as the proprietor of this dwelling and
of numerous houses and farms. By the same cause I was fain
to suppose him enriched by inheritance, and that his life had
been uniform.

I next adverted to his social condition. This mansion appeared to have but two inhabitants beside servants. Who was
the nymph who had hovered for a moment in my sight? Had
he not called her his daughter? The apparent difference in
their ages would justify this relation; but her guise, her features, and her accents were foreign. Her language I suspected
strongly to be that of Italy. How should he be the father of
an Italian? But were there not some foreign lineaments in his
countenance?

This idea seemed to open a new world to my view. I had
gained from my books, confused ideas of European govern-
ments and manners. I knew that the present was a period of
revolution and hostility. Might not these be illustrious fugitives from Provence or the Milanese? Their portable wealth,
which may reasonably be supposed to be great, they have
transported hither. Thus may be explained the sorrow that
veils their countenance. The loss of estates and honours; the
untimely death of kindred, and perhaps of his wife, may furnish eternal food for regrets. Welbeck's utterance, though
rapid and distinct, partook as I conceived, in some very slight
degree of a foreign idiom.

Such was the dream that haunted my undisciplined and
unenlightened imagination. The more I revolved it the more
plausible it seemed. On this supposition every appearance that
I had witnessed was easily solved—unless it were their treatment of me. This, at first, was a source of hopeless perplexity.
Gradually, however, a clue seemed to be afforded. Welbeck
had betrayed astonishment on my first appearance. The lady's
wonder was mingled with distress. Perhaps they discovered a
remarkable resemblance between me and one who stood in

the relation of son to Welbeck and of brother to the lady. This youth might have perished on the scaffold or in war. These, no doubt were his clothes. This chamber might have been reserved for him, but his death left it to be appropriated to another.

I had hitherto been unable to guess at the reason why all this kindness had been lavished on me. Will not this conjecture sufficiently account for it? No wonder that this resemblance was enhanced by assuming his dress.

Taking all circumstances into view, these ideas were not, perhaps, destitute of probability. Appearances naturally suggested them to me. They were, also, powerfully enforced by inclination. They threw me into transports of wonder and hope. When I dwelt upon the incidents of my past life, and traced the chain of events from the death of my mother to the present moment, I almost acquiesced in the notion that some beneficent and ruling genius had prepared my path for me. Events which, when foreseen, would most ardently have been deprecated, and when they happened were accounted, in the highest degree luckless, were now seen to be propitious. Hence I inferred the infatuation of despair and the folly of precipitate conclusions.

But what was the fate reserved for me? Perhaps Welbeck would adopt me for his own son. Wealth has ever been capriciously distributed. The mere physical relation of birth is all that intitles us to manors and thrones. Identity itself frequently depends upon a casual likeness or an old nurse's imposture. Nations have risen in arms, as in the case of the Stewarts, in the cause of one, the genuineness of whose birth has been denied and can never be proved. But if the cause be trivial and fallacious, the effects are momentous and solid. It ascertains our portion of felicity and usefulness, and fixes our lot among peasants or princes.

Something may depend upon my own deportment. Will it not behove me to cultivate all my virtues and eradicate all my defects? I see that the abilities of this man are venerable. Perhaps he will not lightly or hastily decide in my favour. He will be governed by the proofs that I shall give of discernment and integrity. I had always been exempt from temptation and was therefore undepraved, but this view of things had a wonderful tendency to invigorate my virtuous resolutions. All within me was exhilaration and joy.

There was but one thing wanting to exalt me to a dizzy height and give me place among the stars of heaven. My resemblance to her brother had forcibly affected this lady: but I was not her brother. I was raised to a level with her and made a tenant of the same mansion. Some intercourse would take place between us: Time would lay level impediments and establish familiarity, and this intercourse might foster love and terminate in—*marriage!*

These images were of a nature too glowing and expansive to allow me to be longer inactive. I sallied forth into the open air. This tumult of delicious thoughts in some time subsided and gave way to images relative to my present situation. My curiosity was awake. As yet I had seen little of the city, and this opportunity for observation was not to be neglected. I therefore coursed through several streets, attentively examining the objects that successively presented themselves.

At length, it occurred to me to search out the house in which I had lately been immured. I was not without hopes that at some future period I should be able to comprehend the allusions and brighten the obscurities that hung about the dialogue of last night.

The house was easily discovered. I reconnoitred the court and gate through which I had passed. The mansion was of the first order in magnitude and decoration. This was not the bound of my present discovery, for I was gifted with that confidence which would make me set on foot inquiries in the neighbourhood. I looked around for a suitable medium of intelligence. The opposite and adjoining houses were small and apparently occupied by persons of an indigent class. At one of these was a sign denoting it to be the residence of a taylor. Seated on a bench at the door was a young man, with coarse, uncombed locks, breeches knee-unbound, stockings ungartered, shoes slip-shod and unbuckled, and a face unwashed, gazing stupidly from hollow eyes. His aspect was embellished with good nature though indicative of ignorance.

This was the only person in sight. He might be able to say something concerning his opulent neighbour. To him, therefore, I resolved to apply. I went up to him and, pointing to the house in question, asked him who lived there?

He answered, Mr. Mathews.

What is his profession: his way of life?

A gentleman. He does nothing but walk about.

How long has he been married?

Married! He is not married as I know on. He never has been married. He is a bachelor.

This intelligence was unexpected. It made me pause to reflect whether I had not mistaken the house. This, however, seemed impossible. I renewed my questions.

A bachelor, say you? Are you not mistaken?

No. It would be an odd thing if he was married. An old fellow, with one foot in the grave—Comical enough for him to *git* a *vife*.

An old man? Does he live alone? What is his family?

No he does not live alone. He has a niece that lives with him. She is married and her husband lives there too.

What is his name?

I don't know: I never heard it as I know on.

What is his trade?

He's a marchant: he keeps a store somewhere or other; but I don't know where.

How long has he been married?

About two years. They lost a child lately. The young woman was in a huge taking about it. They says she was quite crazy some days for the death of the child: And she is not quite out of *the dumps* yet. To be sure the child was a sweet little thing; but they need not make such a rout about it. I'll warn they'll have enough of them before they die.

What is the character of the young man? Where was he born and educated? Has he parents or brothers?

My companion was incapable of answering these questions, and I left him with little essential addition to the knowledge I already possessed.

Chapter VII

A FTER VIEWING various parts of the city; intruding into churches; and diving into alleys, I returned. The rest of the day I spent chiefly in my chamber, reflecting on my new condition; surveying my apartment, its presses and closets; and conjecturing the causes of appearances.

At dinner and supper I was alone. Venturing to inquire of the servant where his master and mistress were, I was answered that they were engaged. I did not question him as to the nature of their engagement, though it was a fertile source of curiosity.

Next morning, at breakfast, I again met Welbeck and the lady. The incidents were nearly those of the preceding morning, if it were not that the lady exhibited tokens of somewhat greater uneasiness. When she left us Welbeck sank into apparent meditation. I was at a loss whether to retire or remain where I was. At last, however, I was on the point of leaving the room, when he broke silence and began a conversation with me.

He put questions to me, the obvious scope of which was to know my sentiments on moral topics. I had no motives to conceal my opinions, and therefore delivered them with frankness. At length he introduced allusions to my own history, and made more particular inquiries on that head. Here I was not equally frank: yet I did not fain any thing, but merely dealt in generals. I had acquired notions of propriety on this head, perhaps somewhat fastidious. Minute details, respecting our own concerns, are apt to weary all but the narrator himself. I said thus much and the truth of my remark was eagerly assented to.

With some marks of hesitation and after various preliminaries, my companion hinted that my own interest, as well as his, enjoined upon me silence to all but himself, on the subject of my birth and early adventures. It was not likely, that while in his service, my circle of acquaintance would be large or my intercourse with the world frequent; but in my communication with others he requested me to speak rather of others than of myself. This request, he said, might appear singular to me, but he had his reasons for making it, which it was not necessary, at present, to disclose, though, when I should know them, I should readily acknowledge their validity.

I scarcely knew what answer to make. I was willing to oblige him. I was far from expecting that any exigence would occur, making disclosure my duty. The employment was productive of pain more than of pleasure, and the curiosity that would uselessly seek a knowledge of my past life, was no less impertinent than the loquacity that would uselessly communicate that knowledge. I readily promised, therefore, to adhere to his advice.

This assurance afforded him evident satisfaction; yet it did not seem to amount to quite as much as he wished. He repeated, in stronger terms, the necessity there was for caution. He was far from suspecting me to possess an impertinent and talkative disposition, or that in my eagerness to expatiate on my own concerns, I should overstep the limits of politeness: But this was not enough. I was to govern myself by a persuasion that the interests of my friend and myself would be materially affected by my conduct.

Perhaps I ought to have allowed these insinuations to breed suspicion in my mind: but conscious as I was of the benefits which I had received from this man; prone, from my inexperience, to rely upon professions and confide in appearances; and unaware that I could be placed in any condition, in which mere silence respecting myself could be injurious or criminal, I made no scruple to promise compliance with his wishes. Nay, I went farther than this: I desired to be accurately informed as to what it was proper to conceal. He answered that my silence might extend to every thing anterior to my arrival in the city, and my being incorporated with his family. Here our conversation ended and I retired to ruminate on what had passed.

I derived little satisfaction from my reflections. I began now to perceive inconveniencies that might arise from this precipitate promise. Whatever should happen in consequence of my being immured in the chamber, and of the loss of my clothes and of the portrait of my friend, I had bound myself to silence. These inquietudes, however, were transient. I trusted that these events would operate auspiciously; but my curiosity was now awakened as to the motives which *Welbeck* could have for exacting from me this concealment? To act under the guidance of another, and to wander in the dark, ignorant whither my path tended, and what effects might flow from my agency was a new and irksome situation.

From these thoughts I was recalled by a message from Welbeck. He gave me a folded paper which he requested me to carry to No. . . . South Fourth Street. Inquire, said he, for Mrs. Wentworth, in order, merely to ascertain the house, for you need not ask to see her: merely give the letter to the servant and retire. Excuse me for imposing this service upon you. It is of too great moment to be trusted to a common messenger: I usually perform it myself, but am at present otherwise engaged.

I took the letter and set out to deliver it. This was a trifling circumstance, yet my mind was full of reflections on the consequences that might flow from it. I remembered the directions that were given, but construed them in a manner different, perhaps, from Welbeck's expectations or wishes. He had charged me to leave the billet with the servant who happened to answer my summons; but had he not said that the message was important, insomuch that it could not be intrusted to common hands? He had permitted, rather than enjoined, me to dispense with seeing the lady, and this permission I conceived to be dictated merely by regard to my convenience. It was incumbent on me, therefore, to take some pains to deliver the script into her own hands.

I arrived at the house and knocked. A female servant appeared. Her mistress was up stairs: she would tell her if I wished to see her, and meanwhile invited me to enter the parlour: I did so; and the girl retired to inform her mistress that one waited for her.—I ought to mention that my departure from the directions which I had received was, in some degree, owing to an inquisitive temper: I was eager after knowledge, and was disposed to profit by every opportunity to survey the interior of dwellings and converse with their inhabitants.

I scanned the walls, the furniture, the pictures. Over the fire place was a portrait in oil of a female. She was elderly and matron-like. Perhaps she was the mistress of this habitation and the person to whom I should immediately be introduced. Was it a casual suggestion, or was there an actual resemblance between the strokes of the pencil which executed this portrait and that of Clavering? However that be, the sight of this picture revived the memory of my friend and called up a fugitive suspicion that this was the production of his skill.

I was busily revolving this idea when the lady herself entered. It was the same whose portrait I had been examining. She fixed scrutinizing and powerful eyes upon me. She looked at the superscription of the letter which I presented, and immediately resumed her examination of me. I was somewhat abashed by the closeness of her observation and gave tokens of this state of mind which did not pass unobserved. They seemed instantly to remind her that she behaved with too little regard to civility. She recovered herself and began to peruse the letter. Having done this, her attention was once more fixed upon me. She was evidently desirous of entering into some conversation, but seemed at a loss in what manner to begin. This situation was new to me and was productive of no small embarrassment. I was preparing to take my leave when she spoke, though not without considerable hesitation.

This letter is from Mr. Welbeck—you are his friend—I presume—perhaps—a relation?

I was conscious that I had no claim to either of these titles, and that I was no more than his servant. My pride would not allow me to acknowledge this, and I merely said—I live with him at present Madam.

I imagined that this answer did not perfectly satisfy her; yet she received it with a certain air of acquiescence. She was silent for a few minutes, and then, rising, said—Excuse me, Sir, for a few minutes. I will write a few words to Mr. Welbeck.—So saying she withdrew.

I returned to the contemplation of the picture. From this, however, my attention was quickly diverted by a paper that lay on the mantle. A single glance was sufficient to put my blood into motion. I started and laid my hand upon the well-known pacquet. It was that which inclosed the portrait of Clavering!

I unfolded and examined it with eagerness. By what miracle

came it hither? It was found, together with my bundle, two nights before. I had despaired of ever seeing it again, and yet, here was the same portrait inclosed in the self-same paper! I have forborne to dwell upon the regret, amounting to grief, with which I was affected in consequence of the loss of this precious relique. My joy on thus speedily and unexpectedly regaining it, is not easily described.

For a time I did not reflect that to hold it thus in my hand was not sufficient to intitle me to repossession. I must acquaint this lady with the history of this picture, and convince her of my ownership. But how was this to be done? Was she connected in any way, by friendship or by consanguinity, with that unfortunate youth. If she were, some information as to his destiny would be anxiously sought. I did not, just then, perceive any impropriety in imparting it. If it came into her hands by accident still it will be necessary to relate the mode in which it was lost in order to prove my title to it.

I now heard her descending footsteps and hastily replaced the picture on the mantle. She entered and, presenting me a letter, desired me to deliver it to Mr. Welbeck. I had no pretext for deferring my departure; but was unwilling to go without obtaining possession of the portrait. An interval of silence and irresolution succeeded. I cast significant glances at the spot where it lay and at length, mustering up my strength of mind, and pointing to the paper—Madam, said I, *there* is something which I recognize to be mine—I know not how it came into your possession, but so lately as the day before yesterday, it was in mine. I lost it by a strange accident, and as I deem it of inestimable value, I hope you will have no objection to restore it.—

During this speech the lady's countenance exhibited marks of the utmost perturbation—Your picture! she exclaimed, You lost it! How? Where? Did you know that person? What has become of him?—

I knew him well, said I. That picture was executed by himself. He gave it to me with his own hands; and, till the moment I unfortunately lost it, it was my dear and perpetual companion.

Good Heaven! she exclaimed with increasing vehemence,

where did you meet with him? What has become of him? Is he dead or alive?

These appearances sufficiently shewed me that Clavering and this lady were connected by some ties of tenderness. I answered that he was dead; that my mother and myself were his attendants and nurses, and that this portrait was his legacy to me.

This intelligence melted her into tears, and it was some time before she recovered strength enough to resume the conversation. She then inquired When and where was it that he died? How did you lose this portrait? It was found wrapt in some coarse clothes, lying in a stall in the market house, on Saturday evening. Two negro women, servants of one of my friends, strolling through the market, found it and brought it to their mistress, who, recognizing the portrait, sent it to me. To whom did that bundle belong? Was it yours?

These questions reminded me of the painful predicament in which I now stood. I had promised Welbeck to conceal from every one my former condition: but to explain in what manner this bundle was lost, and how my intercourse with Clavering had taken place was to violate this promise. It was possible, perhaps, to escape the confession of the truth by equivocation. Falsehoods were easily invented, and might lead her far away from my true condition: but I was wholly unused to equivocation. Never yet had a lie polluted my lips. I was not weak enough to be ashamed of my origin. This lady had an interest in the fate of Clavering, and might justly claim all the information which I was able to impart. Yet to forget the compact which I had so lately made, and an adherence to which might possibly be in the highest degree, beneficial to me and to Welbeck—I was willing to adhere to it, provided falsehood could be avoided.

These thoughts rendered me silent. The pain of my embarrassment amounted almost to agony. I felt the keenest regret at my own precipitation in claiming the picture. Its value to me was altogether imaginary. The affection which this lady had borne the original, whatever was the source of that affection, would prompt her to cherish the copy, and, however precious it was in my eyes, I should cheerfully resign it to her.

In the confusion of my thoughts an expedient suggested itself sufficiently inartificial and bold—It is true, Madam; what I have said. I saw him breathe his last. This is his only legacy. If you wish it I willingly resign it; but this is all that I can now disclose. I am placed in circumstances which render it improper to say more.

These words were uttered not very distinctly, and the lady's vehemence hindered her from noticing them. She again repeated her interrogations, to which I returned the same answer.

At first she expressed the utmost surprise at my conduct. From this she descended to some degree of asperity. She made rapid allusions to the history of Clavering. He was the son of the gentleman who owned the house in which Welbeck resided. He was the object of immeasurable fondness and indulgence. He had sought permission to travel, and this being refused by the absurd timidity of his parents, he had twice been frustrated in attempting to embark for Europe clandestinely. They ascribed his disappearance to a third and successful attempt of this kind, and had exercised anxious and unwearied diligence in endeavouring to trace his footsteps. All their efforts had failed. One motive for their returning to Europe was the hope of discovering some traces of him, as they entertained no doubt of his having crossed the ocean. The vehemence of Mrs. Wentworth's curiosity as to those particulars of his life and death may be easily conceived. My refusal only heightened this passion.

Finding me refractory to all her efforts she at length dismissed me in anger.

Chapter VIII

THIS extraordinary interview was now passed. Pleasure as well as pain attended my reflections on it. I adhered to the promise I had improvidently given to Welbeck, but had excited displeasure, and perhaps suspicion in the lady. She would find it hard to account for my silence. She would probably impute it to perverseness, or imagine it to flow from some incident connected with the death of Clavering, calculated to give a new edge to her curiosity.

It was plain that some connection subsisted between her and Welbeck. Would she drop the subject at the point which it had now attained? Would she cease to exert herself to extract from me the desired information, or would she not rather make Welbeck a party in the cause, and prejudice my new friend against me? This was an evil proper, by all lawful means, to avoid. I knew of no other expedient than to confess to him the truth, with regard to Clavering, and explain to him the dilemma in which my adherence to my promise had involved me.

I found him on my return home and delivered him the letter with which I was charged. At the sight of it surprise, mingled with some uneasiness, appeared in his looks. What! said he, in a tone of disappointment, you then saw the lady?

I now remembered his directions to leave my message at the door, and apologized for my neglecting them by telling my reasons. His chagrin vanished, but not without an apparent effort, and he said that all was well; the affair was of no moment.

After a pause of preparation, I intreated his attention to something which I had to relate. I then detailed the history of Clavering and of my late embarrassments. As I went on his countenance betokened increasing solicitude. His emotion was particularly strong when I came to the interrogatories of Mrs. Wentworth in relation to Clavering; but this emotion gave way to profound surprise when I related the manner in which I had eluded her inquiries. I concluded with observing, that when I promised forbearance on the subject of my own adventures, I had not foreseen any exigence which would make an adherence to my promise difficult or inconvenient: that, if his interest was promoted by my silence, I was still willing to maintain it and requested his directions how to conduct myself on this occasion.

He appeared to ponder deeply and with much perplexity on what I had said. When he spoke there was hesitation in his manner and circuity in his expressions, that proved him to have something in his thoughts which he knew not how to communicate. He frequently paused; but my answers and remarks, occasionally given, appeared to deter him from the revelation of his purpose. Our discourse ended, for the present, by his desiring me to persist in my present plan; I should suffer no inconveniencies from it, since it would be my own fault if an interview again took place between the lady and me; meanwhile he should see her and effectually silence her inquiries.

I ruminated not superficially or briefly on this dialogue. By what means would he silence her inquiries? He surely meant not to mislead her by fallacious representations. Some inquietude now crept into my thoughts. I began to form conjectures as to the nature of the scheme to which my suppression of the truth was to be thus made subservient. It seemed as if I were walking in the dark and might rush into snares or drop into pits before I was aware of my danger. Each moment accumulated my doubts and I cherished a secret foreboding that the event would prove my new situation to be far less fortunate than I had, at first, fondly believed. The question now occurred with painful repetition, Who and what was Welbeck? What was his relation to this foreign lady? What was the service for which I was to be employed?

I could not be contented without a solution of these mysteries. Why should I not lay my soul open before my new friend? Considering my situation, would he regard my fears and my surmises as criminal? I felt that they originated in laudable habits and views. My peace of mind depended on the favourable verdict which conscience should pass on my proceedings. I saw the emptiness of fame and luxury when put in the balance against the recompense of virtue. Never would I purchase the blandishments of adulation and the glare of opulence at the price of my honesty.

Amidst these reflections the dinner-hour arrived. The lady and Welbeck were present. A new train of sentiments now occupied my mind. I regarded them both with inquisitive eyes. I cannot well account for the revolution which had taken place in my mind. Perhaps it was a proof of the capriciousness of my temper, or it was merely the fruit of my profound ignorance of life and manners. Whence ever it arose, certain it is that I contemplated the scene before me with altered eyes. Its order and pomp was no longer the parent of tranquility and awe. My wild reveries of inheriting this splendour and appropriating the affections of this nymph, I now regarded as lunatic hope and childish folly. Education and nature had qualified me for a different scene. This might be the mask of misery and the structure of vice.

My companions as well as myself were silent during the meal. The lady retired as soon as it was finished. My inexplicable melancholy increased. It did not pass unnoticed by Welbeck, who inquired, with an air of kindness, into the cause of my visible dejection. I am almost ashamed to relate to what extremes my folly transported me. Instead of answering him I was weak enough to shed tears.

This excited afresh his surprise and his sympathy. He renewed his inquiries: my heart was full, but how to disburthen it I knew not. At length, with some difficulty, I expressed my wishes to leave his house and return into the country.

What, he asked, had occurred to suggest this new plan? What motive could incite me to bury myself in rustic obscurity? How did I purpose to dispose of myself? Had some new friend sprung up more able or more willing to benefit me than he had been?

No, I answered, I have no relation who would own me, or friend who would protect. If I went into the country it would be to the toilsome occupations of a day-labourer: but even that was better than my present situation.

This opinion, he observed, must be newly formed. What was there irksome or offensive in my present mode of life?

That this man condescended to expostulate with me; to dissuade me from my new plan; and to enumerate the benefits which he was willing to confer, penetrated my heart with gratitude. I could not but acknowledge that leisure and literature,

copious and elegant accommodation were valuable for their
own sake: that all the delights of sensation and refinements of
intelligence were comprised within my present sphere; and
would be nearly wanting in that to which I was going; I felt
temporary compunction for my folly, and determined to adopt
a different deportment. I could not prevail upon myself to
unfold the true cause of my dejection and permitted him
therefore to ascribe it to a kind of homesickness; to inexperience; and to that ignorance which, on being ushered into a
new scene, is oppressed with a sensation of forlornness. He
remarked that these chimeras would vanish before the influence of time, and company, and occupation. On the next week
he would furnish me with employment; meanwhile he would
introduce me into company where intelligence and vivacity
would combine to dispel my glooms.

As soon as we separated, my disquietudes returned. I contended with them in vain and finally resolved to abandon my
present situation. When and how this purpose was to be effected I knew not. That was to be the theme of future deliberation.

Evening having arrived, Welbeck proposed to me to accompany him on a visit to one of his friends. I cheerfully accepted
the invitation and went with him to your friend Mr. Wortley's.
A numerous party was assembled, chiefly of the female sex. I
was introduced by Welbeck by the title of *a young friend of
his.* Notwithstanding my embarrassment I did not fail to attend to what passed on this occasion. I remarked that the
utmost deference was paid to my companion, on whom his
entrance into this company appeared to operate like magic.
His eye sparkled; his features expanded into a benign serenity;
and his wonted reserve gave place to a torrent-like and overflowing elocution.

I marked this change in his deportment with the utmost
astonishment. So great was it, that I could hardly persuade
myself that it was the same person. A mind thus susceptible
of new impressions must be, I conceived, of a wonderful texture. Nothing was further from my expectations than that this
vivacity was mere dissimulation and would take its leave of
him when he left the company: yet this I found to be the case.

The door was no sooner closed after him than his accustomed solemnity returned. He spake little, and that little was delivered with emphatical and monosyllabic brevity.

We returned home at a late hour, and I immediately retired to my chamber, not so much from the desire of repose as in order to enjoy and pursue my own reflections without interruption.

The condition of my mind was considerably remote from happiness. I was placed in a scene that furnished fuel to my curiosity. This passion is a source of pleasure, provided its gratification be practicable. I had no reason, in my present circumstances, to despair of knowledge; yet suspicion and anxiety beset me. I thought upon the delay and toil which the removal of my ignorance would cost and reaped only pain and fear from the reflection.

The air was remarkably sultry. Lifted sashes and lofty ceilings were insufficient to attemper it. The perturbation of my thoughts affected my body, and the heat which oppressed me, was aggravated, by my restlessness, almost into fever. Some hours were thus painfully past, when I recollected that the bath, erected in the court below, contained a sufficient antidote to the scorching influence of the atmosphere.

I rose, and descended the stairs softly, that I might not alarm Welbeck and the lady, who occupied the two rooms on the second floor. I proceeded to the bath, and filling the reservoir with water, speedily dissipated the heat that incommoded me. Of all species of sensual gratification, that was the most delicious; and I continued for a long time, laving my limbs and moistening my hair. In the midst of this amusement, I noticed the approach of day, and immediately saw the propriety of returning to my chamber. I returned with the same caution which I had used in descending; my feet were bare, so that it was easy to proceed unattended by the smallest signal of my progress.

I had reached the carpetted stair-case, and was slowly ascending, when I heard, within the chamber that was occupied by the lady, a noise, as of some one moving. Though not conscious of having acted improperly, yet I felt reluctance to be seen. There was no reason to suppose that this sound was connected with the detection of me, in this situation; yet I acted as if this reason existed, and made haste to pass the door and gain the second flight of steps.

I was unable to accomplish my design, when the chamber door slowly opened, and Welbeck, with a light in his hand, came out. I was abashed and disconcerted at this interview. He started at seeing me; but discovering in an instant who it was, his face assumed an expression in which shame and anger were powerfully blended. He seemed on the point of opening his mouth to rebuke me; but suddenly checking himself, he said, in a tone of mildness, How is this?—Whence come you?

His emotion seemed to communicate itself, with an electrical rapidity, to my heart. My tongue faltered while I made some answer. I said, I had been seeking relief from the heat of the weather, in the bath. He heard my explanation in silence: and, after a moment's pause, passed into his own room, and shut himself in. I hastened to my chamber.

A different observer might have found in these circumstances no food for his suspicion or his wonder. To me, however, they suggested vague and tumultuous ideas.

As I strode across the room I repeated, This woman is his daughter. What proof have I of that? He once asserted it; and has frequently uttered allusions and hints from which no other inference could be drawn. The chamber from which he came, in an hour devoted to sleep, was hers. For what end could a visit like this be paid? A parent may visit his child at all seasons, without a crime. On seeing me, methought his features indicated more than surprise. A keen interpreter would be apt to suspect a consciousness of wrong. What if this woman be not his child! How shall their relationship be ascertained?

I was summoned at the customary hour to breakfast. My mind was full of ideas connected with this incident. I was not endowed with sufficient firmness to propose the cool and systematic observation of this man's deportment. I felt as if the state of my mind could not but be evident to him; and experienced in myself all the confusion which this discovery was calculated to produce in him. I would have willingly excused myself from meeting him; but that was impossible.

At breakfast, after the usual salutations, nothing was said. For a time I scarcely lifted my eyes from the table. Stealing a glance at Welbeck, I discovered in his features nothing but his wonted gravity. He appeared occupied with thoughts that had no relation to last night's adventure. This encouraged me; and I gradually recovered my composure. Their inattention to me allowed me occasionally to throw scrutinizing and comparing glances at the face of each.

The relationship of parent and child is commonly discoverable in the visage; but the child may resemble either of its parents, yet have no feature in common with both. Here outlines, surfaces, and hues were in absolute contrariety. That kindred subsisted between them was possible, notwithstanding this dissimilitude: but this circumstance contributed to envenom my suspicions.

Breakfast being finished, Welbeck cast an eye of invitation to the piano forte. The lady rose to comply with his request. My eye chanced to be, at that moment, fixed on her. In stepping to the instrument some motion or appearance awakened a thought in my mind, which affected my feelings like the shock of an earthquake.

I have too slight acquaintance with the history of the passions to truly explain the emotion which now throbbed in my veins. I had been a stranger to what is called love. From subsequent reflection, I have contracted a suspicion, that the sentiment with which I regarded this lady was not untinctured from this source, and that hence arose the turbulence of my feelings, on observing what I construed into marks of pregnancy. The evidence afforded me was slight; yet it exercised an absolute sway over my belief.

It was well that this suspicion had not been sooner excited. Now civility did not require my stay in the apartment, and nothing but flight could conceal the state of my mind. I hastened, therefore, to a distance, and shrowded myself in the friendly secrecy of my own chamber.

The constitution of my mind is doubtless singular and perverse; yet that opinion, perhaps, is the fruit of my ignorance. It may by no means be uncommon for men to *fashion* their conclusions in opposition to evidence and *probability*, and so as to feed their malice and subvert their happiness. Thus it was, in an eminent degree, in my case. The simple fact was connected, in my mind, with a train of the most hateful consequences. The depravity of Welbeck was inferred from it. The charms of this angelic woman were tarnished and withered. I had formerly surveyed her as a precious and perfect monument, but now it was a scene of ruin and blast.

This had been a source of sufficient anguish; but this was not all. I recollected that the claims of a parent had been urged. Will you believe that these claims were now admitted, and that they heightened the iniquity of Welbeck into the blackest and most stupendous of all crimes? These ideas were necessarily transient. Conclusions more conformable to appearances succeeded. This lady might have been lately reduced to widowhood. The recent loss of a beloved companion would sufficiently account for her dejection, and make her present situation compatible with duty.

By this new train of ideas I was somewhat comforted. I saw the folly of precipitate inferences, and the injustice of my atrocious imputations, and acquired some degree of patience in my present state of uncertainty. My heart was lightened of its wonted burthen, and I laboured to invent some harmless explication of the scene that I had witnessed the preceding night.

At dinner Welbeck appeared as usual, but not the lady. I ascribed her absence to some casual indisposition, and ventured to inquire into the state of her health. My companion said she was well, but that she had left the city for a month or two, finding the heat of summer inconvenient where she was. This was no unplausible reason for retirement. A candid mind would have acquiesced in this representation, and found in it nothing inconsistent with a supposition respecting the cause of appearances, favourable to her character; but otherwise was I affected. The uneasiness which had flown for a moment returned, and I sunk into gloomy silence.

From this I was roused by my patron, who requested me to deliver a billet, which he put into my hand, at the countinghouse of Mr. Thetford, and to bring him an answer. This message was speedily performed. I entered a large building by the river side. A spacious apartment presented itself, well furnished with pipes and hogsheads. In one corner was a smaller room, in which a gentleman was busy at writing. I advanced to the door of the room, but was there met by a young person, who received my paper, and delivered it to him within. I stood still at the door; but was near enough to overhear what would pass between them.

The letter was laid upon the desk, and presently he that sat at it lifted his eyes, and glanced at the superscription. He scarcely spoke above a whisper, but his words, nevertheless, were clearly distinguishable. I did not call to mind the sound of his voice, but his words called up a train of recollections.

Lo! said he, carelessly, this from the *Nabob!*

An incident so slight as this was sufficient to open a spacious scene of meditation. This little word, half whispered in a thoughtless mood, was a key to unlock an extensive cabinet of secrets. Thetford was probably indifferent whether his exclamation were overheard. Little did he think on the inferences which would be built upon it.

The Nabob! By this appellation had some one been denoted in the chamber-dialogue, of which I had been an unsuspected auditor. The man who pretended poverty, and yet gave proofs of inordinate wealth; whom it was pardonable to defraud of thirty thousand dollars; first, because the loss of that sum would be trivial to one opulent as he; and secondly, because he was imagined to have acquired this opulence by other than honest methods. Instead of forthwith returning home, I wandered into the fields, to indulge myself in the new thoughts which were produced by this occurrence.

I entertained no doubt that the person alluded to was my patron. No new light was thrown upon his character; unless something were deducible from the charge vaguely made, that his wealth was the fruit of illicit practices. He was opulent, and the sources of his wealth were unknown, if not to the rest of the community, at least to Thetford. But here had a plot been laid. The fortune of Thetford's brother was to rise from the success of artifices, of which the credulity of Welbeck was to be the victim. To detect and to counterwork this plot was obviously my duty. My interference might now indeed be too late to be useful; but this was at least to be ascertained by experiment.

How should my intention be effected? I had hitherto concealed from Welbeck my adventures at Thetford's house. These it was now necessary to disclose, and to mention the

recent occurrence. My deductions, in consequence of my ignorance, might be erroneous; but of their truth his knowledge
of his own affairs would enable him to judge. It was possible
that Thetford and he, whose chamber-conversation I had
overheard, were different persons. I endeavoured in vain to
ascertain their identity by a comparison of their voices. The
words lately heard, my remembrance did not enable me certainly to pronounce to be uttered by the same organs.

This uncertainty was of little moment. It sufficed that Welbeck was designated by this appellation, and that therefore he
was proved to be the subject of some fraudulent proceeding.
The information that I possessed it was my duty to communicate as expeditiously as possible. I was resolved to employ
the first opportunity that offered for this end.

My meditations had been ardently pursued, and, when I
recalled my attention, I found myself bewildered among fields
and fences. It was late before I extricated myself from unknown paths, and reached home.

I entered the parlour; but Welbeck was not there. A table,
with tea-equipage for one person was set; from which I inferred that Welbeck was engaged abroad. This belief was confirmed by the report of the servant. He could not inform me
where his master was, but merely that he should not take tea
at home. This incident was a source of vexation and impatience. I knew not but that delay would be of the utmost
moment to the safety of my friend. Wholly unacquainted as I
was with the nature of his contracts with Thetford, I could
not decide whether a single hour would not avail to obviate
the evils that threatened him. Had I known whither to trace
his footsteps, I should certainly have sought an immediate
interview; but, as it was, I was obliged to wait with what patience I could collect for his return to his own house.

I waited hour after hour in vain. The sun declined, and
the shades of evening descended; but Welbeck was still at a
distance.

Chapter IX

WELBECK did not return tho' hour succeeded hour till the clock struck ten. I inquired of the servants, who informed me that their master was not accustomed to stay out so late. I seated myself at a table, in the parlour, on which there stood a light, and listened for the signal of his coming, either by the sound of steps on the pavement without, or by a peal from the bell. The silence was uninterrupted and profound, and each minute added to my sum of impatience and anxiety.

To relieve myself from the heat of the weather, which was aggravated by the condition of my thoughts, as well as to beguile this tormenting interval, it occurred to me to betake myself to the bath. I left the candle where it stood, and imagined that even in the bath, I should hear the sound of the bell which would be rung upon his arrival at the door.

No such signal occurred, and, after taking this refreshment, I prepared to return to my post. The parlour was still unoccupied, but this was not all: The candle I had left upon the table was gone. This was an inexplicable circumstance. On my promise to wait for their master, the servants had retired to bed. No signal of any one's entrance had been given. The street door was locked and the key hung at its customary place, upon the wall. What was I to think? It was obvious to suppose that the candle had been removed by a domestic; but their footsteps could not be traced, and I was not sufficiently acquainted with the house to find the way, especially immersed in darkness, to their chamber. One measure, however, it was evidently proper to take, which was to supply myself, anew, with a light. This was instantly performed; but what was next to be done?

I was weary of the perplexities in which I was embroiled. I saw no avenue to escape from them but that which led me to the bosom of nature and to my ancient occupations. For a moment I was tempted to resume my rustic garb, and, on that very hour, to desert this habitation. One thing only detained me; the desire to apprize my patron of the treachery of Thetford. For this end I was anxious to obtain an interview; but now I reflected that this information, could, by other means be imparted. Was it not sufficient to write him briefly these particulars, and leave him to profit by the knowledge? Thus, I might, likewise, acquaint him with my motives for thus abruptly and unseasonably deserting his service.

To the execution of this scheme pen and paper were necessary. The business of writing was performed in the chamber on the third story. I had been hitherto denied access to this room: In it was a show of papers and books. Here it was that the task, for which I had been retained, was to be performed; but I was to enter it and leave it only in company with Welbeck. For what reasons, I asked, was this procedure to be adopted?

The influence of prohibitions and an appearance of disguise in awakening curiosity, are well known. My mind fastened upon the idea of this room with an unusual degree of intenseness. I had seen it but for a moment. Many of Welbeck's hours were spent in it. It was not to be inferred that they were consumed in idleness: What then was the nature of his employment over which a veil of such impenetrable secrecy was cast?

Will you wonder that the design of entering this recess was insensibly formed? Possibly it was locked, but its accessibleness was likewise possible. I meant not the commission of any crime. My principal purpose was to procure the implements of writing, which were elsewhere not to be found. I should neither unseal papers nor open drawers. I would merely take a survey of the volumes and attend to the objects that spontaneously presented themselves to my view. In this there surely was nothing criminal or blameworthy. Meanwhile I was not unmindful of the sudden disappearance of the candle. This incident filled my bosom with the inquietudes of fear and the perturbations of wonder.

Once more I paused to catch any sound that might arise from without. All was still. I seized the candle and prepared to mount the stairs. I had not reached the first landing when I called to mind my midnight meeting with Welbeck at the door of his daughter's chamber. The chamber was now desolate: perhaps it was accessible: if so no injury was done by entering it. My curiosity was strong, but it pictured to itself no precise object. Three steps would bear me to the door. The trial, whether it was fastened, might be made in a moment; and I readily imagined that something might be found within to reward the trouble of examination. The door yielded to my hand and I entered.

No remarkable object was discoverable. The apartment was supplied with the usual furniture. I bent my steps towards a table over which a mirror was suspended. My glances which roved with swiftness from one object to another, shortly lighted on a miniature portrait that hung near. I scrutinized it with eagerness. It was impossible to overlook its resemblance to my own visage. This was so great that, for a moment, I imagined myself to have been the original from which it had been drawn. This flattering conception yielded place to a belief merely of similitude between me and the genuine original.

The thoughts which this opinion was fitted to produce were suspended by a new object. A small volume, that had, apparently, been much used, lay upon the toilet. I opened it, and found it to contain some of the Dramas of Apostolo Zeno. I turned over the leaves: a written paper saluted my sight. A single glance informed me that it was English. For the present I was insensible to all motives that would command me to forbear. I seized the paper with an intention to peruse it.

At that moment a stunning report was heard. It was loud enough to shake the walls of the apartment, and abrupt enough to throw me into tremours. I dropped the book and yielded for a moment to confusion and surprise. From what quarter it came, I was unable accurately to determine: but there could be no doubt, from its loudness, that it was near, and even in the house. It was no less manifest that the sound arose from the discharge of a pistol. Some hand must have drawn the trigger. I recollected the disappearance of the candle from the room below. Instantly a supposition darted into my mind which made my hair rise and my teeth chatter.

This, I said, is the deed of Welbeck. He entered while I was absent from the room; he hied to his chamber; and, prompted by some unknown instigation, has inflicted on himself death! This idea had a tendency to palsy my limbs and my thoughts.

Some time past in painful and tumultuous fluctuation. My aversion to this catastrophe, rather than a belief of being, by that means, able to prevent or repair the evil, induced me to attempt to enter his chamber. It was possible that my conjectures were erroneous.

The door of his room was locked. I knocked: I demanded entrance in a low voice: I put my eye and my ear to the key-hole and the crevices: nothing could be heard or seen. It was unavoidable to conclude that no one was within; yet the effluvia of gun-powder was perceptible.

Perhaps the room above had been the scene of this catastrophe. I ascended the second flight of stairs. I approached the door. No sound could be caught by my most vigilant attention. I put out the light that I carried, and was then able to perceive that there was light within the room. I scarcely knew how to act. For some minutes I paused at the door. I spoke, and requested permission to enter. My words were succeeded by a death-like stillness. At length I ventured softly to withdraw the bolt; to open, and to advance within the room. Nothing could exceed the horror of my expectation; yet I was startled by the scene that I beheld.

In a chair, whose back was placed against the front wall, sat Welbeck. My entrance alarmed him not, nor roused him from the stupor into which he was plunged. He rested his hands upon his knees, and his eyes were rivetted to something that lay, at the distance of a few feet before him, on the floor. A second glance was sufficient to inform me of what nature this object was. It was the body of a man, bleeding, ghastly, and still exhibiting the marks of convulsion and agony!

I shall omit to describe the shock which a spectacle like this communicated to my unpractised senses. I was nearly as panic-struck and powerless as Welbeck himself. I gazed, without power of speech, at one time, at Welbeck: Then I fixed terrified eyes on the distorted features of the dead. At length, Welbeck, recovering from his reverie, looked up, as if to see who it was that had entered. No surprise, no alarm, was betrayed by him on seeing me. He manifested no desire or intention to interrupt the fearful silence.

My thoughts wandered in confusion and terror. The first impulse was to fly from the scene; but I could not be long insensible to the exigencies of the moment. I saw that affairs must not be suffered to remain in their present situation. The insensibility or despair of Welbeck required consolation and succour. How to communicate my thoughts, or offer my assistance, I knew not. What led to this murderous catastrophe; who it was whose breathless corpse was before me; what concern Welbeck had in producing his death; were as yet unknown.

At length he rose from his seat, and strode at first with faltering, and then with more steadfast steps, across the floor. This motion seemed to put him in possession of himself. He seemed now, for the first time, to recognize my presence. He turned to me and said, in a tone of severity:

How now! What brings you here?

This rebuke was unexpected. I stammered out in reply, that the report of the pistol had alarmed me, and that I came to discover the cause of it.

He noticed not my answer, but resumed his perturbed steps, and his anxious, but abstracted looks. Suddenly he checked himself, and glancing a furious eye at the corse, he muttered, Yes, the die is cast. This worthless and miserable scene shall last no longer. I will at once get rid of life and all its humiliations.

Here succeeded a new pause. The course of his thoughts seemed now to become once more tranquil. Sadness, rather than fury, overspread his features; and his accent, when he spoke to me, was not faltering, but solemn.

Mervyn, said he, you comprehend not this scene. Your youth and inexperience make you a stranger to a deceitful and flagitious world. You know me not. It is time that this ignorance should vanish. The knowledge of me and of my actions may be of use to you. It may teach you to avoid the shoals on which my virtue and my peace have been wrecked; but to the rest of mankind it can be of no use. The ruin of my fame is, perhaps, irretrievable; but the height of my iniquity need not be known. I perceive in you a rectitude and firmness worthy to be trusted; promise me, therefore, that not a syllable of what I tell you shall ever pass your lips.

I had lately experienced the inconvenience of a promise; but I was now confused, embarrassed, ardently inquisitive as to the nature of this scene, and unapprized of the motives that might afterwards occur, persuading or compelling me to disclosure. The promise which he exacted was given. He resumed:

I have detained you in my service, partly for your own benefit, but chiefly for mine. I intended to inflict upon you injury, and to do you good. Neither of these ends can I now accomplish, unless the lessons which my example may inculcate shall inspire you with fortitude, and arm you with caution.

What it was that made me thus, I know not. I am not destitute of understanding. My thirst of knowledge, though irregular, is ardent. I can talk and can feel as virtue and justice prescribe; yet the tenor of my actions has been uniform. One tissue of iniquity and folly has been my life; while my thoughts have been familiar with enlightened and disinterested principles. Scorn and detestation I have heaped upon myself. Yesterday is remembered with remorse. To-morrow is contemplated with anguish and fear; yet every day is productive of the same crimes and of the same follies.

I was left, by the insolvency of my father (a trader of Liverpool), without any means of support, but such as labour should afford me. Whatever could generate pride, and the love of independence, was my portion. Whatever can incite to diligence was the growth of my condition; yet my indolence was a cureless disease; and there were no arts too sordid for me to practise.

I was content to live on the bounty of a kinsman. His family was numerous, and his revenue small. He forbore to upbraid me, or even to insinuate the propriety of providing for myself; but he empowered me to pursue any liberal or mechanical profession which might suit my taste. I was insensible to every generous motive. I laboured to forget my dependent and disgraceful condition, because the remembrance was a source of anguish, without being able to inspire me with a steady resolution to change it.

I contracted an acquaintance with a woman who was unchaste, perverse, and malignant. Me, however, she found it no difficult task to deceive. My uncle remonstrated against the union. He took infinite pain to unveil my error, and to convince me that wedlock was improper for one destitute, as I was, of the means of support, even if the object of my choice were personally unexceptionable.

His representations were listened to with anger. That he thwarted my will, in this respect, even by affectionate expostulation, cancelled all that debt of gratitude which I owed to him. I rewarded him for all his kindness by invective and disdain, and hastened to complete my ill-omened marriage. I had deceived the woman's father by assertions of possessing secret resources. To gratify my passion I descended to dissimulation and falsehood. He admitted me into his family, as the husband of his child; but the character of my wife and the fallacy of my assertions were quickly discovered. He denied me accommodation under his roof, and I was turned forth to the world to endure the penalty of my rashness and my indolence.

Temptation would have moulded me into any villainous shape. My virtuous theories and comprehensive erudition would not have saved me from the basest of crimes. Luckily for me, I was, for the present, exempted from temptation. I had formed an acquaintance with a young American captain. On being partially informed of my situation, he invited me to embark with him for his own country. My passage was gratuitous. I arrived, in a short time, at Charleston, which was the place of his abode.

He introduced me to his family, every member of which was, like himself, embued with affection and benevolence. I was treated like their son and brother. I was hospitably entertained until I should be able to select some path of lucrative industry. Such was my incurable depravity, that I made no haste to select my pursuit. An interval of inoccupation succeeded, which I applied to the worst purposes.

My friend had a sister, who was married; but, during the absence of her husband, resided with her family. Hence originated our acquaintance. The purest of human hearts and the most vigorous understanding were hers. She idolized her husband, who well deserved to be the object of her adoration. Her affection for him, and her general principles, appeared to be confirmed beyond the power to be shaken. I sought her intercourse without illicit views: I delighted in the effusions of her candour and the flashes of her intelligence: I conformed, by a kind of instinctive hypocrisy, to her views: I spoke and felt from the influence of immediate and momentary conviction. She imagined she had found in me a friend worthy to partake in all her sympathies, and forward all her wishes. We were mutually deceived. She was the victim of self-delusion; but I must charge myself with practising deceit both upon myself and her.

I reflect with astonishment and horror on the steps which led to her degradation and to my calamity. In the high career of passion all consequences were overlooked. She was the dupe of the most audacious sophistry and the grossest delusion. I was the slave of sensual impulses and voluntary blindness. The effect may be easily conceived. Not till symptoms of pregnancy began to appear were our eyes opened to the ruin which impended over us.

Then I began to revolve the consequences, which the mist of passion had hitherto concealed. I was tormented by the pangs of remorse, and pursued by the phantom of ingratitude. To complete my despair, this unfortunate lady was apprized of my marriage with another woman; a circumstance which I had anxiously concealed from her. She fled from her father's house at a time when her husband and brother were hourly expected. What became of her I knew not. She left behind her a letter to her father, in which the melancholy truth was told.

Shame and remorse had no power over my life. To elude the storm of invective and upbraiding; to quiet the uproar of my mind, I did not betake myself to voluntary death. My pusillanimity still clung to this wretched existence. I abruptly retired from the scene, and, repairing to the port, embarked in the first vessel which appeared. The ship chanced to belong to Wilmington, in Delaware, and here I sought out an obscure and cheap abode.

I possessed no means of subsistence. I was unknown to my neighbours, and desired to remain unknown. I was unqualified for manual labour by all the habits of my life; but there was no choice between penury and diligence—between honest labour and criminal inactivity. I mused incessantly on the forlornness of my condition. Hour after hour passed, and the horrors of want began to encompass me. I sought with eagerness for an avenue by which I might escape from it. The perverseness of my nature led me on from one guilty thought to another. I took refuge in my customary sophistries, and reconciled myself at length to a scheme of—*forgery!*

Chapter X

HAVING ascertained my purpose, it was requisite to search out the means by which I might effect it. These were not clearly or readily suggested. The more I contemplated my project, the more numerous and arduous its difficulties appeared. I had no associates in my undertaking. A due regard to my safety and the unextinguished sense of honour deterred me from seeking auxiliaries and co-agents. The esteem of mankind was the spring of all my activity, the parent of all my virtue and all my vice. To preserve this, it was necessary that my guilty projects should have neither witness nor partaker.

I quickly discovered that to execute this scheme demanded time, application and money, none of which my present situation would permit me to devote to it. At first, it appeared that an attainable degree of skill and circumspection would enable me to arrive, by means of counterfeit bills, to the pinnacle of affluence and honour. My error was detected by a closer scrutiny, and I, finally, saw nothing in this path but enormous perils and insurmountable impediments.

Yet what alternative was offered me. To maintain myself by the labour of my hands, to perform any toilsome or prescribed task, was incompatible with my nature. My habits debarred me from country occupations. My pride regarded as vile and ignominious drudgery any employment which the town could afford. Meanwhile, my wants were as urgent as ever and my funds were exhausted.

There are few, perhaps, whose external situation resembled mine, who would have found in it any thing but incitements to industry and invention. A thousand methods of subsistence, honest but laborious, were at my command, but to these I entertained an irreconcilable aversion. Ease and the respect attendant upon opulence I was willing to purchase at the price of ever-wakeful suspicion and eternal remorse; but, even at this price, the purchase was impossible.

The desperateness of my condition became hourly more apparent. The further I extended my view, the darker grew the clouds which hung over futurity. Anguish and infamy appeared to be the inseparable conditions of my existence. There was one mode of evading the evils that impended. To free myself from self-upbraiding and to shun the persecutions of my fortune was possible only by shaking off life itself.

One evening, as I traversed the bank of the creek, these dismal meditations were uncommonly intense. They at length terminated in a resolution to throw myself into the stream. The first impulse was to rush instantly to my death, but the remembrance of papers, lying at my lodgings, which might unfold more than I desired to the curiosity of survivors, induced me to postpone this catastrophe till the next morning.

My purpose being formed, I found my heart lightened of its usual weight. By you it will be thought strange, but it is nevertheless true, that I derived from this new prospect, not only tranquility but cheerfulness. I hastened home. As soon as I entered, my land-lord informed me that a person had been searching for me in my absence. This was an unexampled incident and forboded me no good. I was strongly persuaded that my visitant had been led hither not by friendly, but hostile purposes. This persuasion was confirmed by the description of the stranger's guize and demeanour given by my land-lord. My fears instantly recognized the image of Watson, the man by whom I had been so eminently benefitted, and whose kindness I had compensated by the ruin of his sister and the confusion of his family.

An interview with this man was less to be endured than to look upon the face of an avenging deity. I was determined to avoid this interview, and for this end, to execute my fatal purpose within the hour. My papers were collected with a tremulous hand, and consigned to the flames. I then bade my land-lord inform all visitants that I should not return till the next day, and once more hastened towards the river.

My way led past the Inn where one of the stages from Baltimore was accustomed to stop. I was not unaware that Watson had possibly been brought in the coach which had recently arrived, and which now stood before the door of the Inn. The danger of my being descried or encountered by him as I passed did not fail to occur. This was to be eluded by deviating from the main street.

Scarcely had I turned a corner for this purpose when I was

accosted by a young man whom I knew to be an inhabitant of the town, but with whom I had hitherto had no intercourse but what consisted in a transient salutation. He apologized for the liberty of addressing me, and, at the same time, inquired if I understood the French language.

Being answered in the affirmative, he proceeded to tell me, that in the stage, just arrived, had come a passenger, a youth who appeared to be French, who was wholly unacquainted with our language, and who had been seized with a violent disease.

My informant had felt compassion for the forlorn condition of the stranger, and had just been seeking me at my lodgings, in hope that my knowledge of French would enable me to converse with the sick man, and obtain from him a knowledge of his situation and views.

The apprehensions I had precipitately formed, were thus removed and I readily consented to perform this service. The youth was, indeed, in a deplorable condition. Besides the pains of his disease, he was overpowered by dejection. The inn-keeper, was extremely anxious for the removal of his guest. He was by no means willing to sustain the trouble and expense of a sick or a dying man, for which it was, scarcely probable that he should ever be reimbursed. The traveller had no baggage and his dress betokened the pressure of many wants.

My compassion for this stranger was powerfully awakened. I was in possession of a suitable apartment, for which I had no power to pay the rent that was accruing, but my inability in this respect was unknown, and I might enjoy my lodgings unmolested for some weeks. The fate of this youth would be speedily decided, and I should be left at liberty to execute my first intentions before my embarrassments should be visibly increased.

After a moment's pause, I conducted the stranger to my home, placed him in my own bed, and became his nurse. His malady was such as is known in the tropical islands, by the name of the Yellow or Malignant Fever, and the physician who was called, speedily pronounced his case desperate.

It was my duty to warn him of the death that was hastening, and to promise the fulfillment of any of his wishes, not inconsistent with my present situation. He received my intelligence with fortitude, and appeared anxious to communicate some information respecting his own state. His pangs and his weakness scarcely allowed him to be intelligible. From his feeble efforts and broken narrative I collected thus much concerning his family and fortune.

His father's name was Vincentio Lodi. From a Merchant at Leghorn, he had changed himself into a planter in the Island of Guadaloupe. His Son, had been sent, at an early age, for the benefits of education to Europe. The young Vincentio was, at length, informed by his father, that, being weary of his present mode of existence, he had determined to sell his property, and transport himself to the United States. The son was directed to hasten home, that he might embark, with his father, on this voyage.

The summons was cheerfully obeyed. The youth on his arrival at the Island found preparation making for the funeral of his father. It appeared that the elder Lodi had flattered one of his slaves with the prospect of his freedom, but had, nevertheless, included this slave in the sale that he had made of his estate. Actuated by revenge, the slave assassinated Lodi in the open street and resigned himself, without a struggle, to the punishment which the law had provided for such a deed.

The property had been recently transferred, and the price was now presented to young Vincentio by the purchaser. He was, by no means, inclined to adopt his father's project, and was impatient, to return with his inheritance, to France. Before this could be done, the conduct of his father had rendered a voyage to the continent indispensable.

Lodi had a daughter, whom, a few weeks previous to his death, he had intrusted to an American Captain, for whom, he had contracted a friendship. The vessel was bound to Philadelphia, but the conduct she was to pursue, and the abode she was to select, on her arrival, were known only to the father, whose untimely death involved the son in considerable uncertainty, with regard to his sister's fate. His anxiety on this account induced him to seize the first conveyance that offered. In a short time he landed at Baltimore.

As soon as he recovered from the fatigues of his voyage, he prepared to go to Philadelphia. Thither his baggage was im-

mediately sent under the protection of a passenger and coun-
tryman. His money consisted in Portuguese gold, which, in
pursuance of advice, he had changed into Bank-notes. He besought me, in pathetic terms, to search out his sister, whose
youth and poverty and ignorance of the language and manners
of the country might expose her to innumerable hardships.
At the same time, he put a pocket-book and small volume
into my hand, indicating, by his countenance and gestures, his
desire that I would deliver them to his sister.

His obsequies being decently performed, I had leisure to
reflect upon the change in my condition which this incident
had produced. In the pocket-book were found bills to the
amount of twenty thousand dollars. The volume proved to be
a manuscript, written by the elder Lodi in Italian, and contained memoirs of the Ducal house of Visconti, from whom
the writer believed himself to have lineally descended.

Thus had I arrived, by an avenue so much beyond my foresight, at the possession of wealth. The evil which impelled me
to the brink of suicide, and which was the source, though not
of all, yet of the larger portion of my anguish, was now removed. What claims to honour or to ease were consequent
on riches, were, by an extraordinary fortune, now conferred
upon me.

Such, for a time, were my new born but transitory raptures.
I forgot that this money was not mine. That it had been received under every sanction of fidelity, for another's use. To
retain it was equivalent to robbery. The sister of the deceased
was the rightful claimant: it was my duty to search her out,
and perform my tacit, but sacred obligations, by putting the
whole into her possession.

This conclusion was too adverse to my wishes, not to be
strenuously combatted. I asked, what it was that gave man the
power of ascertaining the successor to his property? During
his life, he might transfer the actual possession, but if vacant
at his death, he, into whose hands accident should cast it, was
the genuine proprietor. It is true, that the law had sometimes
otherwise decreed, but in law, there was no validity, further
than it was able by investigation and punishment, to enforce
its decrees; But would the law extort this money from me?

It was rather by gesture than by words that the will of Lodi was imparted. It was the topic of remote inferences and vague conjecture rather than of explicit and unerring declarations. Besides if the lady were found, would not prudence dictate the reservation of her fortune to be administered by me, for her benefit? Of this her age and education had disqualified herself. It was sufficient for the maintenance of both. She would regard me as her benefactor and protector. By supplying all her wants and watching over her safety without apprizing her of the means, by which I shall be enabled to do this, I shall lay irresistible claims to her love and her gratitude.

Such were the sophistries by which reason was seduced and my integrity annihilated. I hastened away from my present abode. I easily traced the baggage of the deceased to an inn, and gained possession of it. It contained nothing but clothes and books. I then instituted the most diligent search after the young lady. For a time, my exertions were fruitless.

Meanwhile, the possessor of this house thought proper to embark with his family for Europe. The sum which he demanded for his furniture, though enormous, was precipitately paid by me. His servants were continued in their former stations, and in the day, at which he relinquished the mansion, I entered on possession.

There was no difficulty in persuading the world that Welbeck was a personage of opulence and rank. My birth and previous adventures it was proper to conceal. The facility with which mankind are misled in their estimate of characters, their proneness to multiply inferences and conjectures will not be readily conceived by one destitute of my experience. My sudden appearance on the stage, my stately reserve, my splendid habitation and my circumspect deportment were sufficient to intitle me to homage. The artifices that were used to unveil the truth, and the guesses that were current respecting me, were adapted to gratify my ruling passion.

I did not remit my diligence to discover the retreat of Mademoiselle Lodi; I found her, at length, in the family of a kinsman of the Captain under whose care she had come to America. Her situation was irksome and perilous. She had already experienced the evils of being protectorless and indigent, and my seasonable interference snatched her from impending and less supportable ills.

I could safely unfold all that I knew of her brother's history, except the legacy which he had left. I ascribed the diligence with which I had sought her to his death-bed injunctions, and prevailed upon her to accept from me the treatment which she would have received from her brother, if he had continued to live, and if his power to benefit had been equal to my own.

Though less can be said in praise of the understanding, than of the sensibilities of this woman, she is one, whom, no one could refrain from loving, though placed in situations far less favourable to the generation of that sentiment, than mine. In habits of domestic and incessant intercourse, in the perpetual contemplation of features animated by boundless gratitude and ineffable sympathies, it could not be expected that either she or I should escape enchantment.

The poison was too sweet not to be swallowed with avidity by me. Too late I remembered that I was already enslaved by inextricable obligations. It was easy to have hidden this impediment from the eyes of my companion, but here my integrity refused to yield. I can, indeed, lay claim to little merit on account of this forbearance. If there had been no alternative between deceit and the frustration of my hopes, I should doubtless have dissembled the truth with as little scruple on this, as on a different occasion, but I could not be blind to the weakness of her with whom I had to contend.

Chapter XI

MEANWHILE large deductions had been made from my stock of money, and the remnant would be speedily consumed by my present mode of life. My expences far exceeded my previous expectations. In no long time I should be reduced to my ancient poverty, which the luxurious existence that I now enjoyed, and the regard due to my beloved and helpless companion, would render more irksome than ever. Some scheme to rescue me from this fate, was indispensable; but my aversion to labour, to any pursuit, the end of which was merely gain, and which would require application and attention continued undiminished.

I was plunged anew into dejection and perplexity. From this I was somewhat relieved by a plan suggested by Mr. Thetford. I thought I had experience of his knowledge and integrity, and the scheme that he proposed seemed liable to no possibility of miscarriage. A ship was to be purchased, supplied with a suitable cargo, and dispatched to a port in the West-Indies. Loss from storms and enemies was to be precluded by insurance. Every hazard was to be enumerated, and the ship and cargo valued at the highest rate. Should the voyage be safely performed, the profits would be double the original expense. Should the ship be taken or wrecked, the insurers would have bound themselves to make ample, speedy, and certain indemnification—Thetford's brother, a wary and experienced trader, was to be the supercargo.

All my money was laid out upon this scheme. Scarcely enough was reserved to supply domestic and personal wants. Large debts were likewise incurred. Our caution had, as we conceived, annihilated every chance of failure. Too much could not be expended on a project so infallible; and the vessel, amply fitted and freighted, departed on her voyage.

An interval, not devoid of suspense and anxiety, succeeded. My mercantile inexperience made me distrust the clearness of my own discernment, and I could not but remember, that my utter and irretrievable destruction was connected with the failure of my scheme. Time added to my distrust and apprehensions. The time, at which tidings of the ship were to be expected, elapsed without affording any information of her destiny. My anxieties, however, were to be carefully hidden from the world. I had taught mankind to believe, that this project had been adopted more for amusement than gain; and the debts which I had contracted, seemed to arise from willingness to adhere to established maxims, more than from the pressure of necessity.

Month succeeded month, and intelligence was still withheld. The notes which I had given for one third of the cargo, and for the premium of insurance, would shortly become due. For the payment of the former, and the cancelling of the latter, I had relied upon the expeditious return, or the demonstrated loss of the vessel. Neither of these events had taken place.

My cares were augmented from another quarter. My companion's situation now appeared to be such, as, if our intercourse had been sanctified by wedlock, would have been regarded with delight. As it was, no symptoms were equally to be deplored. Consequences, as long as they were involved in uncertainty, were extenuated or overlooked; but now, when they became apparent and inevitable, were fertile of distress and upbraiding.

Indefinable fears, and a desire to monopolize all the meditations and affections of this being, had induced me to perpetuate her ignorance of any but her native language, and debar her from all intercourse with the world. My friends were of course inquisitive respecting her character, adventures, and particularly her relation to me. The consciousness how much the truth redounded to my dishonour, made me solicitous to lead conjecture astray. For this purpose I did not discountenance the conclusion that was adopted by some, that she was my daughter. I reflected, that all dangerous surmizes would be effectually precluded by this belief.

These precautions afforded me some consolation in my present difficulties. It was requisite to conceal the lady's condition from the world. If this should be ineffectual, it would not be difficult to divert suspicion from my person. The secrecy that I had practised would be justified, in the apprehension of those to whom the personal condition of Clemenza should be disclosed, by the feelings of a father.

Meanwhile, it was an obvious expedient to remove the unhappy lady to a distance from impertinent observers. A rural retreat, lonely, and sequestered, was easily procured, and hither she consented to repair. This arrangement being concerted, I had leisure to reflect upon the evils which every hour brought nearer, and which threatened to exterminate me.

My inquietudes forbade me to sleep, and I was accustomed to rise before day, and seek some respite in the fields. Returning from one of these unseasonable rambles, I chanced to meet you. Your resemblance to the deceased Lodi, in person and visage, is remarkable. When you first met my eye, this similitude startled me. Your subsequent appeal to my compassion was cloathed in such terms, as formed a powerful contrast with your dress, and prepossessed me greatly in favour of your education and capacity.

In my present hopeless condition, every incident, however trivial, was attentively considered, with a view to extract from it some means of escaping from my difficulties. My love for the Italian girl, in spite of all my efforts to keep it alive, had begun to languish. Marriage was impossible; and had now, in some degree, ceased to be desirable. We are apt to judge of others by ourselves. The passion, I now found myself disposed to ascribe chiefly to fortuitous circumstances; to the impulse of gratitude, and the exclusion of competitors; and believed that your resemblance to her brother, your age, and personal accomplishments, might, after a certain time, and in consequence of suitable contrivances, on my part, give a new direction to her feelings. To gain your concurrence, I relied upon your simplicity, your gratitude, and your susceptibility to the charms of this bewitching creature.

I contemplated, likewise, another end. Mrs. Wentworth is rich. A youth who was once her favourite, and designed to inherit her fortunes, has disappeared, for some years, from the scene. His death is most probable, but of that there is no satisfactory information. The life of this person, whose name is Clavering, is an obstacle to some designs which had occurred to me in relation to this woman. My purposes were crude and scarcely formed. I need not swell the catalogue of my errors by expatiating upon them. Suffice it to say, that the peculiar circumstances of your introduction to me, led me to reflections on the use that might be made of your agency, in procuring this lady's acquiescence in my schemes. You were to be ultimately persuaded to confirm in her the belief that her nephew was dead. To this consummation it was indispensible to lead you by slow degrees, and circuitous paths. Meanwhile, a profound silence, with regard to your genuine history, was to be observed; and to this forbearance, your consent was obtained with more readiness than I expected.

There was an additional motive for the treatment you received from me. My personal projects and cares had hitherto prevented me from reading Lodi's manuscript; a slight inspection, however, was sufficient to prove that the work was profound and eloquent. My ambition has panted, with equal avidity, after the reputation of literature and opulence. To claim the authorship of this work was too harmless and specious a stratagem, not to be readily suggested. I meant to translate it into English, and to enlarge it by enterprising incidents of my own invention. My scruples to assume the merit of the original composer, might thus be removed. For this end, your assistance as an amanuensis would be necessary.

You will perceive, that all these projects depended on the seasonable arrival of intelligence from . . . . The delay of another week would seal my destruction. The silence might arise from the foundering of the ship, and the destruction of all on board. In this case, the insurance was not forfeited, but payment could not be obtained within a year. Meanwhile, the premium and other debts must be immediately discharged, and this was beyond my power. Meanwhile I was to live in a manner that would not belie my pretensions; but my coffers were empty.

I cannot adequately paint the anxieties with which I have been haunted. Each hour has added to the burthen of my existence, till, in consequence of the events of this day, it has become altogether insupportable. Some hours ago, I was summoned by Thetford to his house. The messenger informed me that tidings had been received of my ship. In answer to my eager interrogations, he could give no other information than that she had been captured by the British. He was unable to relate particulars.

News of her safe return would, indeed, have been far more acceptable; but even this information was a source of infinite congratulation. It precluded the demand of my insurers. The payment of other debts might be postponed for a month, and my situation be the same as before the adoption of this successless scheme. Hope and joy were reinstated in my bosom, and I hasted to Thetford's compting house.

He received me with an air of gloomy dissatisfaction. I accounted for his sadness by supposing him averse to communicate information, which was less favourable than our wishes had dictated. He confirmed, with visible reluctance, the news of her capture. He had just received letters from his brother, acquainting him with all particulars, and containing the official documents of this transaction.

This had no tendency to damp my satisfaction, and I proceeded to peruse with eagerness, the papers which he put into my hand. I had not proceeded far when my joyous hopes vanished. Two French mulattoes had, after much solicitation, and the most solemn promises to carry with them no articles which the laws of war decree to be contraband, obtained a passage in the vessel. She was speedily encountered by a privateer, by whom every receptacle was ransacked. In a chest, belonging to the Frenchmen, and which they had affirmed to contain nothing but their clothes, were found two sabres, and other accoutrements of an officer of cavalry. Under this pretence, the vessel was captured and condemned, and this was a cause of forfeiture, which had not been provided against in the contract of insurance.

By this untoward event my hopes were irreparably blasted. The utmost efforts were demanded to conceal my thoughts from my companion. The anguish that preyed upon my heart was endeavoured to be masked by looks of indifference. I pretended to have been previously informed by the messenger, not only of the capture, but of the cause that led to it, and forbore to expatiate upon my loss, or to execrate the authors of my disappointment. My mind, however, was the theatre of discord and agony, and I waited with impatience for an opportunity to leave him.

For want of other topics, I asked by whom this information had been brought. He answered, that the bearer was Captain Amos Watson, whose vessel had been forfeited, at the same time, under a different pretence. He added, that my name being mentioned, accidentally, to Watson, the latter had betrayed marks of great surprise, and been very earnest in his inquiries respecting my situation. Having obtained what knowledge Thetford was able to communicate, the captain had departed, avowing a former acquaintance with me, and declaring his intention of paying me a visit.

These words operated on my frame like lightning. All within me was tumult and terror, and I rushed precipitately out of the house. I went forward with unequal steps, and at random. Some instinct led me into the fields, and I was not apprized of the direction of my steps, till, looking up, I found myself upon the shore of Schuylkill.

Thus was I, a second time, overborne by hopeless and incurable evils. An interval of motley feelings, of specious artifice, and contemptible imposture, had elapsed since my meeting with the stranger at Wilmington. Then my forlorn state had led me to the brink of suicide. A brief and feverish respite had been afforded me, but now was I transported to the verge of the same abyss.

Amos Watson was the brother of the angel whom I had degraded and destroyed. What but fiery indignation and unappeasable vengeance, could lead him into my presence? With what heart could I listen to his invectives? How could I endure to look upon the face of one, whom I had loaded with such atrocious and intolerable injuries?

I was acquainted with his loftiness of mind: his detestation of injustice, and the whirl-wind passions that ingratitude and villainy like mine were qualified to awaken in his bosom. I dreaded not his violence. The death that he might be prompted to inflict, was no object of aversion. It was poverty and disgrace, the detection of my crimes, the looks and voice of malediction and upbraiding, from which my cowardice shrunk.

Why should I live? I must vanish from that stage which I had lately trodden. My flight must be instant and precipitate. To be a fugitive from exasperated creditors, and from the industrious revenge of Watson, was an easy undertaking; but whither could I fly, where I should not be pursued by the phantoms of remorse, by the dread of hourly detection, by the necessities of hunger and thirst? In what scene should I be exempt from servitude and drudgery? Was my existence embellished with enjoyments that would justify my holding it, encumbered with hardships, and immersed in obscurity?

There was no room for hesitation. To rush into the stream before me, and to put an end at once to my life and the miseries inseparably linked with it, was the only proceeding which fate had left to my choice. My muscles were already exerted for this end, when the helpless condition of Clemenza was remembered. What provision could I make against the evils that threatened her? Should I leave her utterly forlorn and friendless? Mrs. Wentworth's temper was forgiving and compassionate. Adversity had taught her to participate, and her wealth enabled her to relieve distress. Who was there by whom such powerful claims to succour and protection could be urged as by this desolate girl? Might I not state her situation in a letter to this lady, and urge irresistible pleas for the extension of her kindness to this object?

These thoughts made me suspend my steps. I determined to seek my habitation once more, and having written and deposited this letter, to return to the execution of my fatal purpose. I had scarcely reached my own door, when some one approached along the pavement. The form, at first, was undistinguishable, but by coming, at length, within the illumination of a lamp, it was perfectly recognized.

To avoid this detested interview was now impossible. Watson approached and accosted me. In this conflict of tumultuous feelings I was still able to maintain an air of intrepidity. His demeanour was that of a man who struggles with his rage. His accents were hurried, and scarcely articulate. I have ten words to say to you, said he: lead into the house, and to some private room. My business with you will be dispatched in a breath.

I made him no answer, but led the way into my house, and to my study. On entering this room, I put the light upon the table, and turning to my visitant, prepared, silently to hear, what he had to unfold. He struck his clenched hand against the table with violence. His motion was of that tempestuous kind, as to overwhelm the power of utterance, and found it easier to vent itself in gesticulations than in words. At length, he exclaimed,

It is well. Now has the hour, so long, and so impatiently demanded by my vengeance, arrived. Welbeck! Would that my first words could strike thee dead! They will so, if thou hast any title to the name of man.

My sister is dead: dead of anguish and a broken heart. Remote from her friends; in a hovel; the abode of indigence and misery.

Her husband is no more. He returned after long absence, a tedious navigation, and vicissitudes of hardships. He flew to the bosom of his love; of his wife. She was gone; lost to him, and to virtue. In a fit of desperation, he retired to his chamber, and dispatched himself. This is the instrument with which the deed was performed.

Saying this, Watson took a pistol from his pocket, and held it to my head. I lifted not my hand to turn aside the weapon. I did not shudder at the spectacle, or shrink from his approaching hand. With fingers clasped together, and eyes fixed upon the floor, I waited till his fury was exhausted. He continued:

All passed in a few hours. The elopement of his daughter—the death of his son. O! my father! Most loved, and most venerable of men! To see thee changed into a maniac! Haggard and wild! Deterred from outrage on thyself and those around thee, by fetters and stripes! What was it that saved me from a like fate? To view this hideous ruin, and to think by whom it was occasioned! Yet not to become frantic like thee, my father; or not destroy myself like thee, my brother! My friend!—

No. For this hour was I reserved: to avenge your wrongs and mine in the blood of this ungrateful villain.

There, continued he, producing a second pistol, and tendering it to me, there is thy defence. Take we opposite sides of this table, and fire at the same instant.

During this address I was motionless. He tendered the pistol, but I unclasped not my hands to receive it.

Why do you hesitate? resumed he. Let the chance between us be equal, or fire you first.

No, said I, I am ready to die by your hand. I wish it. It will preclude the necessity of performing the office for myself. I have injured you, and merit all that your vengeance can inflict. I know your nature too well, to believe that my death will be perfect expiation. When the gust of indignation is past, the remembrance of your deed will only add to your sum of misery: yet I do not love you well enough to wish that you would forbear. I desire to die, and to die by another's hand rather than my own.

Coward! exclaimed Watson, with augmented vehemence. You know me too well, to believe me capable of assassination. Vile subterfuge! Contemptible plea! Take the pistol and defend yourself. You want not the power or the will; but, knowing that I spurn at murder, you think your safety will be found in passiveness. Your refusal will avail you little. Your fame, if not your life, is at my mercy. If you faulter now, I will allow you to live, but only till I have stabbed your reputation.

I now fixed my eyes stedfastly upon him, and spoke: How much a stranger are you to the feelings of Welbeck! How poor a judge of his cowardice! I take your pistol, and consent to your conditions.

We took opposite sides of the table. Are you ready? he cried, fire!

Both triggers were drawn at the same instant. Both pistols were discharged. Mine was negligently raised. Such is the untoward chance that presides over human affairs: such is the malignant destiny by which my steps have ever been pursued. The bullet whistled harmlessly by me. Levelled by an eye that never before failed, and with so small an interval between us. I escaped, but my blind and random shot took place in his heart.

There is the fruit of this disastrous meeting. The catalogue of death is thus completed. Thou sleepest Watson! Thy sister is at rest, and so art thou. Thy vows of vengeance are at an end. It was not reserved for thee to be thy own and thy sister's avenger. Welbeck's measure of transgressions is now full, and his own hand must execute the justice that is due to him.

Chapter XII

SUCH was Welbeck's tale listened to by me with an eagerness in which every faculty was absorbed. How adverse to my dreams were the incidents that had just been related! The curtain was lifted, and a scene of guilt and ignominy disclosed where my rash and inexperienced youth had suspected nothing but loftiness and magnanimity.

For a while the wondrousness of this tale kept me from contemplating the consequences that awaited us. My unfledged fancy had not hitherto soared to this pitch. All was astounding by its novelty, or terrific by its horror. The very scene of these offences partook, to my rustic apprehension, of fairy splendour, and magical abruptness. My understanding was bemazed, and my senses were taught to distrust their own testimony.

From this musing state I was recalled by my companion, who said to me in solemn accents. Mervyn! I have but two requests to make. Assist me to bury these remains, and then accompany me across the river. I have no power to compel your silence on the acts that you have witnessed. I have meditated to benefit, as well as to injure you; but I do not desire that your demeanour should conform to any other standard than justice. You have promised, and to that promise I trust.

If you chuse to fly from this scene, to withdraw yourself from what you may conceive to be a theatre of guilt or peril, the avenues are open; retire unmolested and in silence. If you have a man-like spirit, if you are grateful for the benefits bestowed upon you, if your discernment enables you to see that compliance with my request will intangle you in no guilt, and betray you into no danger, stay, and aid me in hiding these remains from human scrutiny.

Watson is beyond the reach of further injury. I never intended him harm, though I have torn from him his sister and friend, and have brought his life to an untimely close. To provide him a grave, is a duty that I owe to the dead and to the living. I shall quickly place myself beyond the reach of inquisitors and judges, but would willingly rescue from molestation or suspicion those whom I shall leave behind.

What would have been the fruit of deliberation, if I had had the time or power to deliberate, I know not. My thoughts flowed with tumult and rapidity. To shut this spectacle from my view was the first impulse; but to desert this man, in a time of so much need, appeared a thankless and dastardly deportment. To remain where I was, to conform implicitly to his direction, required no effort. Some fear was connected with his presence, and with that of the dead; but, in the tremulous confusion of my present thoughts, solitude would conjure up a thousand phantoms.

I made no preparation to depart. I did not verbally assent to his proposal. He interpreted my silence into acquiescence. He wrapt the body in the carpet, and then lifting one end, cast at me a look which indicated his expectations, that I would aid him in lifting this ghastly burthen. During this process, the silence was unbroken.

I knew not whither he intended to convey the corpse. He had talked of burial, but no receptacle had been provided. How far safety might depend upon his conduct in this particular, I was unable to estimate. I was in too heartless a mood to utter my doubts. I followed his example in raising the corpse from the floor.

He led the way into the passage and down stairs. Having reached the first floor, he unbolted a door which led into the cellar. The stairs and passage were illuminated by lamps, that hung from the ceiling, and were accustomed to burn during the night. Now, however, we were entering darksome and murky recesses.

Return, said he, in a tone of command, and fetch the light. I will wait for you.

I obeyed. As I returned with the light, a suspicion stole into my mind, that Welbeck had taken this opportunity to fly; and that on regaining the foot of the stairs, I should find the spot deserted by all but the dead. My blood was chilled by this image. The momentary resolution it inspired was to follow the example of the fugitive, and leave the persons, whom the ensuing day might convene on this spot, to form their own conjectures as to the cause of this catastrophe.

Meanwhile, I cast anxious eyes forward. Welbeck was discovered in the same place and posture in which he had been left; lifting the corpse and its shroud in his arms he directed me to follow him. The vaults beneath were lofty and spacious. He passed from one to the other till we reached a small and remote cell. Here he cast his burthen on the ground. In the fall, the face of Watson chanced to be disengaged from its covering. Its closed eyes and sunken muscles were rendered, in a tenfold degree, ghastly and rueful by the feeble light which the candle shed upon it.

This object did not escape the attention of Welbeck. He leaned against the wall and folding his arms resigned himself to reverie. He gazed upon the countenance of Watson but his looks denoted his attention to be elsewhere employed.

As to me, my state will not be easily described. My eye roved fearfully from one object to another. By turns it was fixed upon the murdered person and the murderer. The narrow cell in which we stood, its rudely fashioned walls and arches, destitute of communication with the external air, and its palpable dark scarcely penetrated by the rays of a solitary candle, added to the silence which was deep and universal, produced an impression on my fancy which no time will obliterate.

Perhaps my imagination was distempered by terror. The incident which I am going to relate may appear to have existed only in my fancy. Be that as it may, I experienced all the effects which the fullest belief is adapted to produce. Glancing vaguely at the countenance of Watson, my attention was arrested by a convulsive motion in the eye-lids. This motion increased, till, at length the eyes opened, and a glance, languid but wild, was thrown around. Instantly they closed, and the tremulous appearance vanished.

I started from my place and was on the point of uttering some involuntary exclamation. At the same moment, Welbeck seemed to recover from his reverie.

How is this! said he. Why do we linger here? Every moment is precious. We cannot dig for him a grave with our hands. Wait here, while I go in search of a spade.

Saying this, he snatched the candle from my hand, and hasted away. My eye followed the light as its gleams shifted their place upon the walls and ceilings, and gradually vanishing, gave place to unrespited gloom. This proceeding was so unexpected and abrupt, that I had no time to remonstrate against it. Before I retreived the power of reflection, the light had disappeared and the foot-steps were no longer to be heard.

I was not, on ordinary occasions, destitute of equanimity, but, perhaps the imagination of man is naturally abhorrent of death, until tutored into indifference by habit. Every circumstance combined to fill me with shuddering and panick. For a while, I was enabled to endure my situation by the exertions of my reason. That the lifeless remains of an human being are powerless to injure or benefit, I was thoroughly persuaded. I summoned this belief to my aid, and was able, if not to subdue, yet to curb my fears. I listened to catch the sound of the returning foot-steps of Welbeck, and hoped that every new moment would terminate my solitude.

No signal of his coming was afforded. At length it occurred to me that Welbeck had gone with no intention to return: That his malice had seduced me hither, to encounter the consequences of his deed. He had fled and barred every door behind him. This suspicion may well be supposed to overpower my courage, and to call forth desperate efforts for my deliverance.

I extended my hands and went forward. I had been too little attentive to the situation and direction of these vaults and passages, to go forward with undeviating accuracy. My fears likewise tended to confuse my perceptions and bewilder my steps. Notwithstanding the danger of encountering obstructions, I rushed towards the entrance with precipitation.

My temerity was quickly punished. In a moment, I was repelled by a jutting angle of the wall, with such force that I staggered backward and fell. The blow was stunning, and when I recovered my senses, I perceived that a torrent of blood was gushing from my nostrils. My clothes were moistened with this unwelcome effusion, and I could not but reflect on the hazard which I should incur by being detected in this recess, covered by these accusing stains.

This reflection once more set me on my feet, and incited my exertions. I now proceeded with greater wariness and caution. I had lost all distinct notions of my way. My motions were at random. All my labour was to shun obstructions and to advance whenever the vacuity would permit. By this means, the entrance was at length found, and after various efforts, I arrived, beyond my hopes, at the foot of the stair-case.

I ascended, but quickly encountered an insuperable impediment. The door at the stair-head, was closed and barred. My utmost strength was exerted in vain, to break the lock or the hinges. Thus were my direst apprehensions fulfilled. Welbeck had left me to sustain the charge of murder: to obviate suspicions the most atrocious and plausible that the course of human events is capable of producing.

Here I must remain till the morrow: till some one can be made to overhear my calls and come to my deliverance. What effects will my appearance produce on the spectator! Terrified by phantoms and stained with blood shall I not exhibit the tokens of a maniac as well as an assassin?

The corpse of Watson will quickly be discovered. If previous to this disclosure I should change my blood-stained garments and withdraw into the country, shall I not be pursued by the most vehement suspicions and, perhaps, hunted to my obscurest retreat by the ministers of justice? I am innocent, but my tale however circumstantial or true, will scarcely suffice for my vindication. My flight will be construed into a proof of incontestable guilt.

While harassed by these thoughts my attention was attracted by a faint gleam cast upon the bottom of the stair-case. It grew stronger, hovered for a moment in my sight, and then disappeared. That it proceeded from a lamp or candle, borne by some one along the passages was no untenable opinion, but was far less probable than that the effulgence was meteorous. I confided in the latter supposition and fortified myself anew against the dread of preternatural dangers. My thoughts reverted to the contemplation of the hazards and suspicions which flowed from my continuance in this spot.

In the midst of my perturbed musing, my attention was again recalled by an illumination like the former. Instead of hovering and vanishing, it was permanent. No ray could be more feeble, but the tangible obscurity to which it succeeded rendered it conspicuous as an electrical flash. For a while I eyed it without moving from my place, and in momentary expectation of its disappearance.

Remarking its stability, the propriety of scrutinizing it more nearly, and of ascertaining the source whence it flowed, was at length suggested. Hope, as well as curiosity, was the parent of my conduct. Though utterly at a loss to assign the cause of this appearance, I was willing to believe some connection between that cause and the means of my deliverance.

I had scarcely formed the resolution of descending the stair, when my hope was extinguished by the recollection that the cellar had narrow and grated windows, through which light from the street might possibly have found access. A second recollection supplanted this belief, for in my way to this stair-case, my attention would have been solicited, and my steps, in some degree, been guided by light coming through these avenues.

Having returned to the bottom of the stair, I perceived every part of the long drawn passage illuminated. I threw a glance forward, to the quarter whence the rays seemed to proceed, and beheld, at a considerable distance, Welbeck in the cell which I had left, turning up the earth with a spade.

After a pause of astonishment, the nature of the error which I had committed, rushed upon apprehension. I now perceived that the darkness had misled me to a different stair-case from that which I had originally descended. It was apparent that Welbeck intended me no evil, but had really gone in search of the instrument which he had mentioned.

This discovery overwhelmed me with contrition and shame, though it freed from the terrors of imprisonment and accusation. To return to the cell which I had left, and where Welbeck was employed in his disastrous office, was the expedient which regards to my own safety unavoidably suggested.

Welbeck paused at my approach, and betrayed a momentary consternation at the sight of my ensanguined visage. The blood, by some inexplicable process of nature, perhaps by the counteracting influence of fear, had quickly ceased to flow. Whether the cause of my evasion, and of my flux of blood, was guessed, or whether his attention was withdrawn, by more momentous objects, from my condition, he proceeded in his task in silence.

A shallow bed, and a slight covering of clay was provided for the hapless Watson. Welbeck's movements were hurried and tremulous. His countenance betokened a mind engrossed by a single purpose, in some degree, foreign to the scene before him. An intensity and fixedness of features, that were conspicuous, led me to suspect the subversion of his reason.

Having finished the task, he threw aside his impliment. He then put into my hand a pocket-book, saying it belonged to Watson, and might contain something serviceable to the living. I might make what use of it I thought proper. He then remounted the stairs and, placing the candle on a table in the hall, opened the principal door and went forth. I was driven, by a sort of mechanical impulse, in his foot-steps. I followed him because it was agreeable to him and because I knew not whither else to direct my steps.

The streets were desolate and silent. The watchman's call remotely and faintly heard, added to the general solemnity. I followed my companion in a state of mind not easily described. I had no spirit even to inquire whither he was going. It was not till we arrived at the water's edge that I persuaded myself to break silence. I then began to reflect on the degree in which his present schemes might endanger Welbeck or myself. I had acted long enough a servile and mechanical part; and been guided by blind and foreign impulses. It was time to lay aside my fetters, and demand to know whither the path tended in which I was importuned to walk.

Meanwhile I found myself intangled among boats and shipping. I am unable to describe the spot by any indisputable tokens. I know merely that it was the termination of one of the principal streets. Here Welbeck selected a boat and prepared to enter it. For a moment I hesitated to comply with his apparent invitation. I stammered out an interrogation. Why is this? Why should we cross the river? What service can I do for you? I ought to know the purpose of my voyage before I enter it.

He checked himself and surveyed me for a minute in silence. What do you fear? said he. Have I not explained my wishes? Merely cross the river with me, for I cannot navigate a boat by myself. Is there any thing arduous or mysterious in this undertaking? We part on the Jersey shore, and I shall leave you to your destiny. All I shall ask from you will be silence, and to hide from mankind what you know concerning me.

He now entered the boat and urged me to follow his example. I reluctantly complied. I perceived that the boat contained but one oar and that was a small one. He seemed startled and thrown into great perplexity by this discovery. It will be impossible, said he, in a tone of panic and vexation, to procure another at this hour; what is to be done?

This impediment was by no means insuperable. I had sinewy arms and knew well how to use an oar for the double purpose of oar and rudder. I took my station at the stern, and quickly extricated the boat from its neighbours and from the wharves. I was wholly unacquainted with the river. The bar, by which it was incumbered, I knew to exist, but in what direction and to what extent it existed, and how it might be avoided in the present state of the tide I knew not. It was probable, therefore, unknowing as I was of the proper tract, that our boat would speedily have grounded.

My attention, meanwhile, was fixed upon the oar. My companion sat at the prow and was in a considerable degree unnoticed. I cast eyes occasionally at the scene which I had left. Its novelty, joined with the incidents of my condition, threw me into a state of suspense and wonder which frequently slackened my hand, and left the vessel to be driven by the downward current. Lights were sparingly seen, and these were perpetually fluctuating, as masts, yards, and hulls were interposed, and passed before them. In proportion as we receded from the shore, the clamours seemed to multiply, and the suggestion that the city was involved in confusion and uproar, did not easily give way to maturer thoughts. *Twelve* was the hour cried, and this ascended at once from all quarters, and was mingled with the baying of dogs, so as to produce trepidation and alarm.

From this state of magnificent and awful feeling, I was suddenly called by the conduct of Welbeck. We had scarcely moved two hundred yards from the shore, when he plunged into the water. The first conception was that some implement or part of the boat had fallen overboard. I looked back and perceived that his seat was vacant. In my first astonishment I loosened my hold of the oar, and it floated away. The surface was smooth as glass and the eddy occasioned by his sinking was scarcely visible. I had not time to determine whether this was designed or accidental. Its suddenness deprived me of the power to exert myself for his succour. I wildly gazed around me in hopes of seeing him rise. After some time my attention was drawn, by the sound of agitation in the water, to a considerable distance.

It was too dark for any thing to be distinctly seen. There was no cry for help. The noise was like that of one vigorously struggling for a moment, and then sinking to the bottom. I listened with painful eagerness, but was unable to distinguish a third signal. He sunk to rise no more.

I was, for a time, inattentive to my own situation. The dreadfulness, and unexpectedness of this catastrophe occupied me wholly. The quick motion of the lights upon the shore, shewed me that I was borne rapidly along with the tide. How to help myself, how to impede my course, or to regain either shore, since I had lost the oar, I was unable to tell. I was no less at a loss to conjecture whither the current, if suffered to control my vehicle, would finally transport me.

The disappearance of lights and buildings, and the diminution of the noises, acquainted me that I had passed the town. It was impossible longer to hesitate. The shore was to be regained by one way only, which was swimming. To any exploit of this kind, my strength and my skill were adequate. I threw away my loose gown; put the pocket-book of the unfortunate Watson in my mouth, to preserve it from being injured by moisture; and committed myself to the stream.

I landed in a spot incommoded with mud and reeds. I sunk knee-deep into the former, and was exhausted by the fatigue of extricating myself. At length I recovered firm ground, and threw myself on the turf to repair my wasted strength, and to reflect on the measures which my future welfare enjoined me to pursue.

What condition was ever parallel to mine? The transactions of the last three days, resembled the monstrous creations of delirium. They were painted with vivid hues on my memory; but so rapid and incongruous were these transitions, that I almost denied belief to their reality. They exercised a bewildering and stupifying influence on my mind, from which the meditations of an hour were scarcely sufficient to relieve me.

Gradually I recovered the power of arranging my ideas, and forming conclusions.

Welbeck was dead. His property was swallowed up, and his creditors left to wonder at his disappearance. All that was left, was the furniture of his house, to which Mrs. Wentworth would lay claim, in discharge of the unpaid rent. What now was the destiny that awaited the lost and friendless Mademoiselle Lodi. Where was she concealed? Welbeck had dropped no intimation by which I might be led to suspect the place of her abode. If my power, in other respects, could have contributed aught to her relief, my ignorance of her asylum had utterly disabled me.

But what of the murdered person? He had suddenly vanished from the face of the earth. His fate and the place of his interment would probably be suspected and ascertained. Was I sure to escape from the consequences of this deed? Watson had relatives and friends. What influence on their state and happiness his untimely and mysterious fate would possess, it was obvious to inquire. This idea led me to the recollection of his pocket-book. Some papers might be there explanatory of his situation.

I resumed my feet. I knew not where to direct my steps. I was dropping with wet, and shivering with the cold. I was destitute of habitation and friend. I had neither money, nor any valuable thing in my possession. I moved forward, mechanically and at random. Where I landed was at no great distance from the verge of the town. In a short time I discovered the glimmering of a distant lamp. To this I directed my steps, and here I paused to examine the contents of the pocket-book.

I found three bank-notes, each of fifty dollars, inclosed in a piece of blank paper. Beside these were three letters, apparently written by his wife, and dated at Baltimore. They were brief, but composed in a strain of great tenderness, and containing affecting allusions to their child. I could gather from their date and tenor, that they were received during his absence on his recent voyage; that her condition was considerably necessitous, and surrounded by wants which their prolonged separation had increased.

The fourth letter was open, and seemed to have been very lately written. It was directed to Mrs. Mary Watson. He informed her in it of his arrival at Philadelphia from St. Domingo; of the loss of his ship and cargo; and of his intention to hasten home with all possible expedition. He told her that all was lost but one hundred and fifty dollars, the greater part of which he should bring with him, to relieve her more pressing wants. The letter was signed, and folded, and superscribed, but unsealed.

A little consideration shewed me, in what manner it became me, on this occasion, to demean myself. I put the bank-notes in the letter, and sealed it with a wafer, a few of which were found in the pocket-book. I hesitated sometime whether I should add any thing to the information which the letter contained, by means of a pencil which offered itself to my view; but I concluded to forbear. I could select no suitable terms in which to communicate the mournful truth. I resolved to deposit this letter at the post-office, where I knew letters could be left at all hours.

My reflections at length, reverted to my own condition. What was the fate reserved for me? How far my safety might be affected by remaining in the city, in consequence of the disappearance of Welbeck, and my known connection with the fugitive, it was impossible to foresee. My fears readily suggested innumerable embarrassments and inconveniences which would flow from this source. Besides, on what pretence should I remain? To whom could I apply for protection or employment? All avenues, even to subsistence, were shut against me. The country was my sole asylum. Here, in exchange for my labour, I could at least purchase food, safety, and repose. But if my choice pointed to the country, there was no reason for a moment's delay. It would be prudent to regain the fields, and be far from this detested city before the rising of the sun.

Meanwhile I was chilled and chaffed by the clothes that I wore. To change them for others, was absolutely necessary to my ease. The clothes which I wore were not my own, and were extremely unsuitable to my new condition. My rustic and homely garb was deposited in my chamber at Welbeck's. These thoughts suggested the design of returning thither. I considered, that, probably, the servants had not been alarmed. That the door was unfastened, and the house was accessible. It would be easy to enter and retire without notice; and this, not without some waverings and misgivings, I presently determined to do.

Having deposited my letter at the office, I proceeded to my late abode. I approached, and lifted the latch with caution. There were no appearances of any one having been disturbed. I procured a light in the kitchen, and hied softly and with dubious foot-steps to my chamber. There I disrobed, and resumed my check shirt, and trowsers, and fustian coat. This change being accomplished, nothing remained but that I should strike into the country with the utmost expedition.

In a momentary review which I took of the past, the design for which Welbeck professed to have originally detained me in his service, occurred to my mind. I knew the danger of reasoning loosely on the subject of property. To any trinket, or piece of furniture in this house, I did not allow myself to question the right of Mrs. Wentworth; a right accruing to her in consequence of Welbeck's failure in the payment of his rent; but there was one thing which I felt an irresistible desire, and no scruples which should forbid me, to possess, and that was, the manuscript to which Welbeck had alluded, as having been written by the deceased Lodi.

I was well instructed in Latin, and knew the Tuscan language to be nearly akin to it. I despaired not of being at sometime able to cultivate this language, and believed that the possession of this manuscript might essentially contribute to this end, as well as to many others equally beneficial. It was easy to conjecture that the volume was to be found among his printed books, and it was scarcely less easy to ascertain the truth of this conjecture. I entered, not without tremulous sensations, into the apartment which had been the scene of the disastrous interview between Watson and Welbeck. At every step I almost dreaded to behold the spectre of the former rise before me.

Numerous and splendid volumes were arranged on mahogany shelves, and screened by doors of glass. I ran swiftly over their names, and was at length so fortunate as to light upon the book of which I was in search. I immediately secured it, and leaving the candle extinguished on a table in the parlour, I once more issued forth into the street. With light steps and palpitating heart I turned my face towards the country. My necessitous condition I believed would justify me in passing without payment the Schuylkill bridge, and the eastern sky began to brighten with the dawn of morning not till I had gained the distance of nine miles from the city.

Such is the tale which I proposed to relate to you. Such are the memorable incidents of five days of my life; from which I have gathered more instruction than from the whole tissue of my previous existence. Such are the particulars of my knowledge respecting the crimes and misfortunes of Welbeck; which the insinuations of Wortley, and my desire to retain your good opinion, have induced me to unfold.

Chapter XIII

MERVYN'S pause allowed his auditors to reflect on the particulars of his narration, and to compare them with the facts, with a knowledge of which, their own observation had supplied them. My profession introduced me to the friendship of Mrs. Wentworth, by whom, after the disappearance of Welbeck, many circumstances respecting him had been mentioned. She particularly dwelt upon the deportment and appearance of this youth, at the single interview which took place between them, and her representations were perfectly conformable to those which Mervyn had himself delivered.

Previously to this interview Welbeck had insinuated to her that a recent event had put him in possession of the truth respecting the destiny of Clavering. A kinsman of his, had arrived from Portugal, by whom this intelligence had been brought. He dexterously eluded her intreaties to be furnished with minuter information, or to introduce this kinsman to her acquaintance. As soon as Mervyn was ushered into her presence, she suspected him to be the person to whom Welbeck had alluded, and this suspicion his conversation had confirmed. She was at a loss to comprehend the reasons of the silence which he so pertinaciously maintained.

Her uneasiness, however, prompted her to renew her solicitations. On the day, subsequent to the catastrophe related by Mervyn, she sent a messenger to Welbeck, with a request to see him. Gabriel, the black servant, informed the messenger that his master had gone into the country for a week. At the end of the week, a messenger was again dispatched with the same errand. He called and knocked, but no one answered his signals. He examined the entrance by the kitchen, but every avenue was closed. It appeared that the house was wholly deserted.

These appearances naturally gave birth to curiosity and suspicion. The house was repeatedly examined, but the solitude and silence within continued the same. The creditors of Welbeck were alarmed by these appearances, and their claims to the property remaining in the house were precluded by Mrs.

Wentworth, who, as owner of the mansion, was legally entitled to the furniture, in place of the rent which Welbeck had
suffered to accumulate.

On examining the dwelling, all that was valuable and portable, particularly linen and plate, was removed. The remainder
was distrained, but the tumults of pestilence succeeded, and
hindered it from being sold. Things were allowed to continue
in their former situation, and the house was carefully secured.
We had no leisure to form conjectures on the causes of this
desertion. An explanation was afforded us by the narrative of
this youth. It is probable that the servants, finding their master's absence continue, had pillaged the house and fled.

Meanwhile, though our curiosity with regard to Welbeck
was appeased, it was obvious to inquire by what series of inducements and events Mervyn was reconducted to the city
and led to the spot where I first met with him. We intimated
our wishes in this respect, and our young friend readily consented to take up the thread of his story and bring it down
to the point that was desired. For this purpose, the ensuing
evening was selected. Having, at an early hour, shut ourselves
up from all intruders and visitors, he continued as follows:

I have mentioned that, by sun-rise, I had gained the distance of many miles from the city. My purpose was to stop at
the first farm-house, and seek employment as a day-labourer.
The first person whom I observed was a man of placid mien
and plain garb. Habitual benevolence was apparent amidst the
wrinkles of age. He was traversing his buck-wheat field and
measuring, as it seemed, the harvest that was now nearly ripe.

I accosted him with diffidence, and explained my wishes.
He listened to my tale with complacency, inquired into my
name and family, and into my qualifications for the office to
which I aspired. My answers were candid and full.

Why, said he, I believe thou and I can make a bargain. We
will, at least, try each other for a week or two. If it does not
suit our mutual convenience we can change. The morning is
damp and cool, and thy plight does not appear the most comfortable that can be imagined. Come to the house and eat
some breakfast.

The behaviour of this good man filled me with gratitude
and joy. Methought I could embrace him as a father, and

entrance into his house, appeared like return to a long-lost and much-loved home. My desolate and lonely condition appeared to be changed for paternal regards and the tenderness of friendship.

These emotions were confirmed and heightened by every object that presented itself under this roof. The family consisted of Mrs. Hadwin, two simple and affectionate girls, his daughters, and servants. The manners of this family, quiet, artless, and cordial, the occupations allotted me, the land by which the dwelling was surrounded, its pure airs, romantic walks, and exhaustless fertility, constituted a powerful contrast to the scenes which I had left behind, and were congenial with every dictate of my understanding and every sentiment that glowed in my heart.

My youth, mental cultivation, and circumspect deportment entitled me to deference and confidence. Each hour confirmed me in the good opinion of Mr. Hadwin, and in the affections of his daughters. In the mind of my employer, the simplicity of the husbandman and the devotion of the Quaker, were blended with humanity and intelligence. The sisters, Susan and Eliza, were unacquainted with calamity and vice, through the medium of either observation or books. They were strangers to the benefits of an elaborate education, but they were endowed with curiosity and discernment, and had not suffered their slender means of instruction to remain unimproved.

The sedateness of the elder formed an amusing contrast with the laughing eye and untamable vivacity of the younger: but they smiled and they wept in unison. They thought and acted in different but not discordant keys. On all momentous occasions, they reasoned and felt alike. In ordinary cases, they separated, as it were, into different tracks; but this diversity was productive, not of jarring, but of harmony.

A romantic and untutored disposition like mine, may be supposed liable to strong impressions from perpetual converse with persons of their age and sex. The elder was soon discovered to have already disposed of her affections. The younger was free, and somewhat that is more easily conceived than named, stole insensibly upon my heart. The images that haunted me at home and abroad, in her absence and her presence, gradually coalesced into one shape, and gave birth to an incessant train of latent palpitations and indefinable hopes. My days were little else than uninterrupted reveries, and night only called up phantoms more vivid and equally enchanting.

The memorable incidents which had lately happened scarcely counterpoised my new sensations or diverted my contemplations from the present. My views were gradually led to rest upon futurity, and in that I quickly found cause of circumspection and dread. My present labours were light and were sufficient for my subsistence in a single state; but wedlock was the parent of new wants and of new cares. Mr. Hadwin's possessions were adequate to his own frugal maintenance, but divided between his children would be too scanty for either. Besides this division could only take place at his death, and that was an event whose speedy occurrence was neither desirable nor probable.

Another obstacle was now remembered. Hadwin was the consciencious member of a sect, which forbade the marriage of its votaries with those of a different communion. I had been trained in an opposite creed, and imagined it impossible that I should ever become a proselyte to Quakerism. It only remained for me to feign conversion, or to root out the opinions of my friend, and win her consent to a secret marriage. Whether hypocrisy was eligible was no subject of deliberation. If the possession of all that ambition can conceive, were added to the transports of union with Eliza Hadwin, and offered as the price of dissimulation, it would have been instantly rejected. My external goods were not abundant nor numerous, but the consciousness of rectitude was mine, and, in competition with this, the luxury of the heart and of the senses, the gratifications of boundless ambition and inexhaustible wealth were contemptible and frivolous.

The conquest of Eliza's errors was easy; but to introduce discord and sorrow into this family, was an act of the utmost ingratitude and profligacy. It was only requisite for my understanding clearly to discern, to be convinced of the insuperability of this obstacle. It was manifest, therefore, that the point to which my wishes tended was placed beyond my reach.

To foster my passion, was to foster a disease destructive either of my integrity or my existence. It was indispensable to fix my thoughts upon a different object, and to debar myself even from her intercourse. To ponder on themes foreign to my darling image, and to seclude myself from her society, at hours which had usually been spent with her, were difficult tasks. The latter was the least practicable. I had to contend with eyes, which alternately wondered at, and upbraided me for my unkindness. She was wholly unaware of the nature of her own feelings, and this ignorance made her less scrupulous in the expression of her sentiments.

Hitherto I had needed not employment beyond myself and my companions. Now my new motives made me eager to discover some means of controlling and beguiling my thoughts. In this state, the manuscript of Lodi occurred to me. In my way hither, I had resolved to make the study of the language of this book, and the translation of its contents into English, the business and solace of my leisure. Now this resolution was revived with new force.

My project was perhaps singular. The ancient language of Italy possessed a strong affinity with the modern. My knowledge of the former, was my only means of gaining the latter. I had no grammar or vocabulary to explain how far the meanings and inflections of Tuscan words varied from the Roman dialect. I was to ponder on each sentence and phrase; to select among different conjectures the most plausible, and to ascertain the true, by patient and repeated scrutiny.

This undertaking, phantastic and impracticable as it may seem, proved upon experiment, to be within the compass of my powers. The detail of my progress would be curious and instructive. What impediments, in the attainment of a darling purpose, human ingenuity and patience are able to surmount; how much may be done by strenuous and solitary efforts; how the mind, unassisted, may draw forth the principles of inflection and arrangement; may profit by remote, analogous, and latent similitudes, would be forcibly illustrated by my example; but the theme, however attractive, must, for the present, be omitted.

My progress was slow; but the perception of hourly improvement afforded me unspeakable pleasure. Having arrived near the last pages, I was able to pursue, with little interruption, the thread of an eloquent narration. The triumph of a leader of out-laws over the popular enthusiasm of the Milanese, and the claims of neighbouring potentates, were about to be depicted. The *Condottiere* Sforza, had taken refuge from his enemies in a tomb, accidentally discovered amidst the ruins of a Roman fortress in the Apennine. He had sought this recess for the sake of concealment, but found in it a treasure, by which he would be enabled to secure the wavering and venal faith of that crew of ruffians that followed his standard, provided he fell not into the hands of the enemies who were now in search of him.

My tumultuous curiosity was suddenly checked by the following leaves being glewed together at the edges. To dissever them without injury to the written spaces, was by no means easy. I proceeded to the task, not without precipitation. The edges were torn away, and the leaves parted.

It may be thought that I took up the thread where it had been broken; but no. The object that my eyes encountered, and which the cemented leaves had so long concealed, was beyond the power of the most capricious or lawless fancy to have prefigured; yet it bore a shadowy resemblance to the images with which my imagination was previously occupied. I opened, and beheld—*a bank-note!*

To the first transports of surprise, the conjecture succeeded that the remaining leaves, cemented together in the same manner, might inclose similar bills. They were hastily separated, and the conjecture was verified. My sensations, at this discovery, were of an inexplicable kind. I gazed at the notes in silence. I moved my finger over them; held them in different positions; read and re-read the name of each sum, and the signature; added them together, and repeated to myself—*Twenty thousand dollars!* They are mine, and by such means!

This sum would have redeemed the falling fortunes of Welbeck. The dying Lodi was unable to communicate all the contents of this inestimable volume. He had divided his treasure, with a view to its greater safety, between this volume and his pocket-book. Death hasted upon him too suddenly to allow him to explain his precautions. Welbeck had placed the book in his collection, purposing sometime to peruse it; but deterred by anxieties, which the perusal would have dissipated, he rushed to desperation and suicide, from which some evanescent contingency, by unfolding this treasure to his view, would have effectually rescued him.

But was this event to be regretted? This sum, like the former, would probably have been expended in the same pernicious prodigality. His career would have continued sometime longer, but his inveterate habits would have finally conducted his existence to the same criminal and ignominious close.

But the destiny of Welbeck was accomplished. The money was placed, without guilt or artifice, in my possession. My fortune had been thus unexpectedly and wonderously propitious. How was I to profit by her favour? Would not this sum enable me to gather round me all the instruments of pleasure? Equipage, and palace, and a multitude of servants; polished mirrors, splendid hangings, banquets, and flatterers, were equally abhorrent to my taste, and my principles. The accumulation of knowledge, and the diffusion of happiness, in which riches may be rendered eminently instrumental, were the only precepts of duty, and the only avenues to genuine felicity.

But what, said I, is my title to this money? By retaining it, shall I not be as culpable as Welbeck? It came into his possession as it came into mine, without a crime; but my knowledge of the true proprietor is equally certain, and the claims of the unfortunate stranger are as valid as ever. Indeed, if utility, and not law, be the measure of justice, her claim, desolate and indigent as she is, unfitted, by her past life, by the softness and the prejudices of her education, for contending with calamity, is incontestible.

As to me, health and diligence will give me, not only the competence which I seek, but the power of enjoying it. If my present condition be unchangeable, I shall not be unhappy. My occupations are salutary and meritorious; I am a stranger to the cares as well as to the enjoyment of riches; abundant means of knowledge are possessed by me, as long as I have eyes to gaze at man and at nature, as they are exhibited in their original forms or in books. The precepts of my duty cannot be mistaken. The lady must be sought and the money be restored to her.

Certain obstacles existed to the immediate execution of this scheme. How should I conduct my search? What apology should I make for withdrawing thus abruptly, and contrary to the terms of an agreement into which I had lately entered, from the family and service of my friend and benefactor, Hadwin?

My thoughts were called away from pursuing these inquiries by a rumour, which had gradually swelled to formidable dimensions; and which, at length, reached us in our quiet retreats. The city, we were told, was involved in confusion and panick, for a pestilential disease had begun its destructive progress. Magistrates and citizens were flying to the country. The numbers of the sick multiplied beyond all example; even in the pest affected cities of the Levant. The malady was malignant, and unsparing.

The usual occupations and amusements of life were at an end. Terror had exterminated all the sentiments of nature. Wives were deserted by husbands, and children by parents. Some had shut themselves in their houses, and debarred themselves from all communication with the rest of mankind. The consternation of others had destroyed their understanding, and their misguided steps hurried them into the midst of the danger which they had previously laboured to shun. Men were seized by this disease in the streets; passengers fled from them; entrance into their own dwellings was denied to them; they perished in the public ways.

The chambers of disease were deserted, and the sick left to die of negligence. None could be found to remove the lifeless bodies. Their remains, suffered to decay by piece-meal, filled the air with deadly exhalations, and added tenfold to the devastation.

Such was the tale, distorted and diversified a thousand ways, by the credulity and exaggeration of the tellers. At first I listened to the story with indifference or mirth. Methought it was confuted by its own extravagance. The enormity and variety of such an evil made it unworthy to be believed. I expected that every new day would detect the absurdity and fallacy of such representations. Every new day, however, added to the number of witnesses, and the consistency of the tale, till, at length, it was not possible to withhold my faith.

Chapter XIV

THIS RUMOUR was of a nature to absorb and suspend the whole soul. A certain sublimity is connected with enormous dangers, that imparts to our consternation or our pity, a tincture of the pleasing. This, at least, may be experienced by those who are beyond the verge of peril. My own person was exposed to no hazard. I had leisure to conjure up terrific images, and to personate the witnesses and sufferers of this calamity. This employment was not enjoined upon me by necessity, but was ardently pursued, and must therefore have been recommended by some nameless charm.

Others were very differently affected. As often as the tale was embellished with new incidents, or inforced by new testimony, the hearer grew pale, his breath was stifled by inquietudes, his blood was chilled and his stomach was bereaved of its usual energies. A temporary indisposition was produced in many. Some were haunted by a melancholy bordering upon madness, and some, in consequence of sleepless panics, for which no cause could be assigned, and for which no opiates could be found, were attacked by lingering or mortal diseases.

Mr. Hadwin was superior to groundless apprehensions. His daughters, however, partook in all the consternation which surrounded them. The eldest had, indeed, abundant reason for her terror. The youth to whom she was betrothed, resided in the city. A year previous to this, he had left the house of Mr. Hadwin, who was his uncle, and had removed to Philadelphia, in pursuit of fortune.

He made himself clerk to a merchant, and by some mercantile adventures in which he had successfully engaged, began to flatter himself with being able, in no long time, to support a family. Meanwhile, a tender and constant correspondence was maintained between him and his beloved Susan. This girl was a soft enthusiast, in whose bosom devotion and love glowed with an ardour that has seldom been exceeded.

The first tidings of the *yellow fever*, was heard by her with unspeakable perturbation. Wallace was interrogated, by letter, respecting its truth. For a time, he treated it as a vague report. At length, a confession was extorted from him that there existed a pestilential disease in the city, but, he added, that it was hitherto confined to one quarter, distant from the place of his abode.

The most pathetic intreaties, were urged by her that he would withdraw into the country. He declared his resolution to comply when the street in which he lived should become infected, and his stay should be attended with real danger. He stated how much his interests depended upon the favour of his present employer, who had used the most powerful arguments to detain him, but declared that, when his situation should become, in the least degree, perillous, he would slight every consideration of gratitude and interest, and fly to *Malverton*. Meanwhile, he promised to communicate tidings of his safety, by every opportunity.

Belding, Mr. Hadwin's next neighbour, though not uninfected by the general panic, persisted to visit the city daily with his *market-cart*. He set out by sun-rise, and usually returned by noon. By him a letter was punctually received by Susan. As the hour of Belding's return approached, her impatience and anxiety increased. The daily epistle was received and read, in a transport of eagerness. For a while, her emotion subsided, but returned with augmented vehemence at noon on the ensuing day.

These agitations were too vehement for a feeble constitution like her's. She renewed her supplications to Wallace to quit the city. He repeated his assertions of being, hitherto, secure, and his promise of coming when the danger should be imminent. When Belding returned, and, instead of being accompanied by Wallace, merely brought a letter from him, the unhappy Susan would sink into fits of lamentation and weeping, and repel every effort to console her with an obstinacy that partook of madness. It was, at length, manifest, that Wallace's delays would be fatally injurious to the health of his mistress.

Mr. Hadwin had hitherto been passive. He conceived that the intreaties and remonstrances of his daughter were more likely to influence the conduct of Wallace, than any representations which he could make. Now, however, he wrote the contumacious Wallace a letter, in which he laid his commands upon him to return in company with Belding, and declared that by a longer delay, the youth would forfeit his favour.

The malady had, at this time, made considerable progress. Belding's interest at length yielded to his fears, and this was the last journey which he proposed to make. Hence our impatience for the return of Wallace was augmented; since, if this opportunity were lost, no suitable conveyance might again be offered him.

Belding set out, as usual, at the dawn of day. The customary interval between his departure and return, was spent by Susan, in a tumult of hopes and fears. As noon approached her suspense arose to a pitch of wildness and agony. She could scarcely be restrained from running along the road, many miles, towards the city; that she might, by meeting Belding half way, the sooner ascertain the fate of her lover. She stationed herself at a window which overlooked the road along which Belding was to pass.

Her sister, and her father, though less impatient, marked, with painful eagerness, the first sound of the approaching vehicle. They snatched a look at it as soon as it appeared in sight. Belding was without a companion.

This confirmation of her fears, overwhelmed the unhappy Susan. She sunk into a fit, from which, for a long time, her recovery was hopeless. This was succeeded by paroxysms of a furious insanity, in which she attempted to snatch any pointed implement which lay within her reach, with a view to destroy herself. These being carefully removed, or forcibly wrested from her, she resigned herself to sobs and exclamations.

Having interrogated Belding, he informed us that he occupied his usual post in the market place; that heretofore, Wallace had duly sought him out, and exchanged letters; but, that on this morning, the young man had not made his appearance; though Belding had been induced, by his wish to see him, to prolong his stay in the city, much beyond the usual period.

That some other cause than sickness had occasioned this omission, was barely possible. There was scarcely room for the most sanguine temper to indulge an hope. Wallace was without kindred, and probably without friends, in the city. The merchant, in whose service he had placed himself, was connected with him by no consideration but that of interest. What then must be his situation when seized with a malady which all believed to be contagious; and the fear of which, was able to dissolve the strongest ties that bind human beings together?

I was personally a stranger to this youth. I had seen his letters, and they bespoke, not indeed any great refinement or elevation of intelligence, but a frank and generous spirit, to which I could not refuse my esteem; but his chief claim to my affection consisted in his consanguinity to Mr. Hadwin, and his place in the affections of Susan. His welfare was essential to the happiness of those, whose happiness had become essential to mine. I witnessed the outrages of despair in the daughter, and the symptoms of a deep, but less violent grief, in the sister and parent. Was it not possible for me to alleviate their pangs? Could not the fate of Wallace be ascertained?

This disease assailed men with different degrees of malignity. In its worst form perhaps it was incurable; but in some of its modes, it was doubtless conquerable by the skill of physicians, and the fidelity of nurses. In its least formidable symptoms, negligence and solitude would render it fatal.

Wallace might, perhaps, experience this pest in its most lenient degree: but the desertion of all mankind; the want, not only of medicines, but of food, would irrevocably seal his doom. My imagination was incessantly pursued by the image of this youth, perishing alone, and in obscurity; calling on the name of distant friends, or invoking, ineffectually, the succour of those who were near.

Hitherto distress had been contemplated at a distance, and through the medium of a fancy delighting to be startled by the wonderful, or transported by sublimity. Now the calamity had entered my own doors, imaginary evils were supplanted by real, and my heart was the seat of commiseration and horror.

I found myself unfit for recreation or employment. I shrouded myself in the gloom of the neighbouring forest, or lost myself in the maze of rocks and dells. I endeavoured, in vain, to shut out the phantoms of the dying Wallace, and to forget the spectacle of domestic woes. At length, it occurred to me to ask, May not this evil be obviated, and the felicity of the Hadwins re-established? Wallace is friendless and suc- courless; but cannot I supply to him the place of protector and nurse? Why not hasten to the city, search out his abode, and ascertain whether he be living or dead? If he still retain life, may I not, by consolation and attendance, contribute to the restoration of his health, and conduct him once more to the bosom of his family?

With what transports will his arrival be hailed! How amply will their impatience and their sorrow be compensated by his return! In the spectacle of their joys, how rapturous and pure will be my delight! Do the benefits which I have received from the Hadwins demand a less retribution than this?

It is true, that my own life will be endangered; but my danger will be proportioned to the duration of my stay in this seat of infection. The death or the flight of Wallace may ab- solve me from the necessity of spending one night in the city. The rustics who daily frequent the market are, as experience proves, exempt from this disease; in consequence, perhaps, of limiting their continuance in the city to a few hours. May I not, in this respect, conform to their example, and enjoy a similar exemption?

My stay, however, may be longer than the day. I may be condemned to share in the common destiny. What then? Life is dependent on a thousand contingencies, not to be com- puted or foreseen. The seeds of an early and lingering death are sown in my constitution. It is vain to hope to escape the malady by which my mother and my brothers have died. We are a race, whose existence some inherent property has limited to the short space of twenty years. We are exposed, in com- mon with the rest of mankind, to innumerable casualities; but if these be shunned, we are unalterably fated to perish by *con- sumption*. Why then should I scruple to lay down my life in the cause of virtue and humanity? It is better to die, in the consciousness of having offered an heroic sacrifice; to die by a speedy stroke, than by the perverseness of nature, in igno- minious inactivity, and lingering agonies.

These considerations determined me to hasten to the city. To mention my purpose to the Hadwins would be useless or pernicious. It would only augment the sum of their present anxieties. I should meet with a thousand obstacles in the tenderness and terror of Eliza, and in the prudent affection of her father. Their arguments I should be condemned to hear, but should not be able to confute; and should only load myself with imputations of perverseness and temerity.

But how else should I explain my absence? I had hitherto preserved my lips untainted by prevarication or falsehood. Perhaps there was no occasion which would justify an untruth; but here, at least, it was superfluous or hurtful. My disappearance, if effected without notice or warning, will give birth to speculation and conjecture; but my true motives will never be suspected, and therefore will excite no fears. My conduct will not be charged with guilt. It will merely be thought upon with some regret, which will be alleviated by the opinion of my safety, and the daily expectation of my return.

But, since my purpose was to search out Wallace, I must be previously furnished with directions to the place of his abode, and a description of his person. Satisfaction on this head was easily obtained from Mr. Hadwin; who was prevented from suspecting the motives of my curiosity, by my questions being put in a manner apparently casual. He mentioned the street, and the number of the house.

I listened with surprise. It was an house with which I was already familiar. He resided, it seems, with a merchant. Was it possible for me to be mistaken?

What, I asked, was the merchant's name?

Thetford.

This was a confirmation of my first conjecture. I recollected the extraordinary means by which I had gained access to the house and bed-chamber of this gentleman. I recalled the person and appearance of the youth by whose artifices I had been intangled in the snare. These artifices implied some domestic or confidential connection between Thetford and my guide. Wallace was a member of the family. Could it be he by whom I was betrayed?

Suitable questions easily obtained from Hadwin a description of the person and carriage of his nephew. Every circumstance evinced the identity of their persons. Wallace, then, was the engaging and sprightly youth whom I had encountered at

Lesher's; and who, for purposes not hitherto discoverable, had led me into a situation so romantic and perilous.

I was far from suspecting that these purposes were criminal. It was easy to infer that his conduct proceeded from juvenile wantonness, and a love of sport. My resolution was unaltered by this disclosure; and having obtained all the information which I needed, I secretly began my journey.

My reflections, on the way, were sufficiently employed in tracing the consequences of my project; in computing the inconveniences and dangers to which I was preparing to subject myself; in fortifying my courage against the influence of rueful sights and abrupt transitions; and in imagining the measures which it would be proper to pursue in every emergency.

Connected as these views were with the family and character of Thetford, I could not but sometimes advert to those incidents which formerly happened. The mercantile alliance between him and Welbeck was remembered; the allusions which were made to the condition of the latter in the chamber conversation, of which I was an unsuspected auditor; and the relation which these allusions might possess with subsequent occurrences. Welbeck's property was forfeited. It had been confided to the care of Thetford's brother. Had the case of this forfeiture been truly or thoroughly explained? Might not contraband articles have been admitted through the management, or under the connivance of the brothers; and might not the younger Thetford be furnished with the means of purchasing the captured vessel and her cargo; which, as usual, would be sold by auction at a fifth or tenth of its real value?

Welbeck was not alive to profit by the detection of this artifice, admitting these conclusions to be just. My knowledge will be useless to the world; for by what motives can I be influenced to publish the truth; or by whom will my single testimony be believed, in opposition to that plausible exterior, and, perhaps, to that general integrity which Thetford has maintained? To myself it will not be unprofitable. It is a lesson on the principles of human nature; on the delusiveness of appearances; on the perviousness of fraud; and on the power with which nature has invested human beings over the thoughts and actions of each other.

Thetford and his frauds were dismissed from my thoughts, to give place to considerations relative to Clemenza Lodi, and the money which chance had thrown into my possession. Time had only confirmed my purpose to restore these bills to the rightful proprietor, and heightened my impatience to discover her retreat. I reflected, that the means of doing this were more likely to suggest themselves at the place to which I was going than elsewhere. I might, indeed, perish before my views, in this respect, could be accomplished. Against these evils, I had at present no power to provide. While I lived, I would bear perpetually about me the volume and its precious contents. If I died, a superior power must direct the course of this as of all other events.

Chapter XV

THESE MEDITATIONS did not enfeeble my resolution, or slacken my pace. In proportion as I drew near the city, the tokens of its calamitous condition became more apparent. Every farm-house was filled with supernumerary tenants; fugitives from home, and haunting the skirts of the road, eager to detain every passenger with inquiries after news. The passengers were numerous; for the tide of emigration was by no means exhausted. Some were on foot, bearing in their countenances the tokens of their recent terror, and filled with mournful reflections on the forlornness of their state. Few had secured to themselves an asylum; some were without the means of paying for victuals or lodging for the coming night; others, who were not thus destitute, yet knew not whither to apply for entertainment, every house being already overstocked with inhabitants, or barring its inhospitable doors at their approach.

Families of weeping mothers, and dismayed children, attended with a few pieces of indispensable furniture, were carried in vehicles of every form. The parent or husband had perished; and the price of some moveable, or the pittance handed forth by public charity, had been expended to purchase the means of retiring from this theatre of disasters; though uncertain and hopeless of accommodation in the neighbouring districts.

Between these and the fugitives whom curiosity had led to the road, dialogues frequently took place, to which I was suffered to listen. From every mouth the tale of sorrow was repeated with new aggravations. Pictures of their own distress, or of that of their neighbours, were exhibited in all the hues which imagination can annex to pestilence and poverty.

My preconceptions of the evil now appeared to have fallen short of the truth. The dangers into which I was rushing, seemed more numerous and imminent than I had previously imagined. I wavered not in my purpose. A panick crept to my heart, which more vehement exertions were necessary to subdue or control; but I harboured not a momentary doubt that the course which I had taken was prescribed by duty. There was no difficulty or reluctance in proceeding. All for which my efforts were demanded, was to walk in this path without tumult or alarm.

Various circumstances had hindered me from setting out upon this journey as early as was proper. My frequent pauses to listen to the narratives of travellers, contributed likewise to procrastination. The sun had nearly set before I reached the precincts of the city. I pursued the track which I had formerly taken, and entered High-street after night-fall. Instead of equipages and a throng of passengers, the voice of levity and glee, which I had formerly observed, and which the mildness of the season would, at other times, have produced, I found nothing but a dreary solitude.

The market-place, and each side of this magnificent avenue were illuminated, as before, by lamps; but between the verge of Schuylkill and the heart of the city, I met not more than a dozen figures; and these were ghost-like, wrapt in cloaks, from behind which they cast upon me glances of wonder and suspicion; and, as I approached, changed their course, to avoid touching me. Their clothes were sprinkled with vinegar; and their nostrils defended from contagion by some powerful perfume.

I cast a look upon the houses, which I recollected to have formerly been, at this hour, brilliant with lights, resounding with lively voices, and thronged with busy faces. Now they were closed, above and below; dark, and without tokens of being inhabited. From the upper windows of some, a gleam sometimes fell upon the pavement I was traversing, and shewed that their tenants had not fled, but were secluded or disabled.

These tokens were new, and awakened all my panicks. Death seemed to hover over this scene, and I dreaded that the floating pestilence had already lighted on my frame. I had scarcely overcome these tremors, when I approached an house, the door of which was open, and before which stood a vehicle, which I presently recognized to be an *hearse*.

The driver was seated on it. I stood still to mark his visage, and to observe the course which he proposed to take. Presently a coffin, borne by two men, issued from the house. The

driver was a negro, but his companions were white. Their features were marked by ferocious indifference to danger or pity.
One of them as he assisted in thrusting the coffin into the
cavity provided for it, said, I'll be damned if I think the poor
dog was quite dead. It wasn't the *fever* that ailed him, but the
sight of the girl and her mother on the floor. I wonder how
they all got into that room. What carried them there?

The other surlily muttered, Their legs to be sure.

But what should they hug together in one room for?

To save us trouble to be sure.

And I thank them with all my heart; but damn it, it wasn't
right to put him in his coffin before the breath was fairly gone.
I thought the last look he gave me, told me to stay a few
minutes.

Pshaw! He could not live. The sooner dead the better for
him; as well as for us. Did you mark how he eyed us, when
we carried away his wife and daughter? I never cried in my
life, since I was knee-high, but curse me if I ever felt in better
tune for the business than just then. Hey! continued he, looking up, and observing me standing a few paces distant, and
listening to their discourse, What's wanted? Any body dead?

I stayed not to answer or parly, but hurried forward. My
joints trembled, and cold drops stood on my forehead. I was
ashamed of my own infirmity; and by vigorous efforts of my
reason, regained some degree of composure. The evening had
now advanced, and it behoved me to procure accommodation
at some of the inns.

These were easily distinguished by their *signs*, but many
were without inhabitants. At length, I lighted upon one, the
hall of which was open, and the windows lifted. After knocking for some time, a young girl appeared, with many marks
of distress. In answer to my question, she answered that both
her parents were sick, and that they could receive no one. I
inquired, in vain, for any other tavern at which strangers
might be accommodated. She knew of none such; and left
me, on some one's calling to her from above, in the midst of
my embarrassment. After a moment's pause, I returned, dis-
comforted and perplexed, to the street.

I proceeded, in a considerable degree, at random. At
length, I reached a spacious building, in Fourth-street, which

the sign-post shewed me to be an inn. I knocked loudly and often at the door. At length, a female opened the window of the second story, and, in a tone of peevishness, demanded what I wanted? I told her that I wanted lodging.

Go hunt for it somewhere else, said she; you'll find none here. I began to expostulate; but she shut the window with quickness, and left me to my own reflections.

I began now to feel some regret at the journey I had taken. Never, in the depth of caverns or forests, was I equally conscious of loneliness. I was surrounded by the habitations of men; but I was destitute of associate or friend. I had money, but an horse shelter, or a morsel of food, could not be purchased. I came for the purpose of relieving others, but stood in the utmost need myself. Even in health my condition was helpless and forlorn; but what would become of me, should this fatal malady be contracted. To hope that an asylum would be afforded to a sick man, which was denied to one in health, was unreasonable.

The first impulse which flowed from these reflections, was to hasten back to *Malverton*; which, with sufficient diligence, I might hope to regain before the morning light. I could not, methought, return upon my steps with too much speed. I was prompted to run, as if the pest was rushing upon me, and could be eluded only by the most precipitate flight.

This impulse was quickly counteracted by new ideas. I thought with indignation and shame on the imbecility of my proceeding. I called up the images of Susan Hadwin, and of Wallace. I reviewed the motives which had led me to the undertaking of this journey. Time had, by no means, diminished their force. I had, indeed, nearly arrived at the accomplishment of what I had intended. A few steps would carry me to Thetford's habitation. This might be the critical moment, when succour was most needed, and would be most efficacious.

I had previously concluded to defer going thither till the ensuing morning; but why should I allow myself a moment's delay? I might at least gain an external view of the house, and circumstances might arise, which would absolve me from the obligation of remaining an hour longer in the city. All for which I came might be performed; the destiny of Wallace be ascertained; and I be once more safe within the precincts of *Malverton* before the return of day.

I immediately directed my steps towards the habitation of Thetford. Carriages bearing the dead were frequently discovered. A few passengers likewise occurred, whose hasty and perturbed steps, denoted their participation in the common distress. The house, of which I was in quest, quickly appeared. Light, from an upper window, indicated that it was still inhabited.

I paused a moment to reflect in what manner it became me to proceed. To ascertain the existence and condition of Wallace was the purpose of my journey. He had inhabited this house; and whether he remained in it, was now to be known. I felt repugnance to enter, since my safety might, by entering, be unawares and uselessly endangered. Most of the neighbouring houses were apparently deserted. In some there were various tokens of people being within. Might I not inquire, at one of these, respecting the condition of Thetford's family? Yet why should I disturb them by inquiries so impertinent, at this unseasonable hour? To knock at Thetford's door, and put my questions to him who should obey the signal, was the obvious method.

I knocked dubiously and lightly. No one came. I knocked again, and more loudly; I likewise drew the bell. I distinctly heard its distant peals. If any were within, my signal could not fail to be noticed. I paused, and listened, but neither voice nor foot-steps could be heard. The light, though obscured by window curtains, which seemed to be drawn close, was still perceptible.

I ruminated on the causes that might hinder my summons from being obeyed. I figured to myself nothing but the helplessness of disease, or the insensibility of death. These images only urged me to persist in endeavouring to obtain admission. Without weighing the consequences of my act, I involuntarily lifted the latch. The door yielded to my hand, and I put my feet within the passage.

Once more I paused. The passage was of considerable extent, and at the end of it I perceived light as from a lamp or candle. This impelled me to go forward, till I reached the foot of a stair-case. A candle stood upon the lowest step.

This was a new proof that the house was not deserted. I struck my heel against the floor with some violence; but this, like my former signals, was unnoticed. Having proceeded thus far, it would have been absurd to retire with my purpose uneffected. Taking the candle in my hand, I opened a door that was near. It led into a spacious parlour, furnished with profusion and splendour. I walked to and fro, gazing at the objects which presented themselves; and involved in perplexity, I knocked with my heel louder than ever; but no less ineffectually.

Notwithstanding the lights which I had seen, it was possible that the house was uninhabited. This I was resolved to ascertain, by proceeding to the chamber which I had observed, from without, to be illuminated. This chamber, as far as the comparison of circumstances would permit me to decide, I believed to be the same in which I had passed the first night of my late abode in the city. Now was I, a second time, in almost equal ignorance of my situation, and of the consequences which impended exploring my way to the same recess.

I mounted the stair. As I approached the door of which I was in search, a vapour, infectious and deadly, assailed my senses. It resembled nothing of which I had ever before been sensible. Many odours had been met with, even since my arrival in the city, less insupportable than this. I seemed not so much to smell as to taste the element that now encompassed me. I felt as if I had inhaled a poisonous and subtle fluid, whose power instantly bereft my stomach of all vigour. Some fatal influence appeared to seize upon my vitals; and the work of corrosion and decomposition to be busily begun.

For a moment, I doubted whether imagination had not some share in producing my sensation; but I had not been previously panick-struck; and even now I attended to my own sensations without mental discomposure. That I had imbibed this disease was not to be questioned. So far the chances in my favour were annihilated. The lot of sickness was drawn.

Whether my case would be lenient or malignant; whether I should recover or perish, was to be left to the decision of the future. This incident, instead of appalling me, tended rather to invigorate my courage. The danger which I feared had come. I might enter with indifference, on this theatre of pestilence. I might execute without faultering, the duties that my circumstances might create. My state was no longer hazardous; and my destiny would be totally uninfluenced by my future conduct.

The pang with which I was first seized, and the momentary inclination to vomit, which it produced, presently subsided. My wholesome feelings, indeed, did not revisit me, but strength to proceed was restored to me. The effluvia became more sensible as I approached the door of the chamber. The door was ajar; and the light within was perceived. My belief, that those within were dead, was presently confuted by a sound, which I first supposed to be that of steps moving quickly and timorously across the floor. This ceased, and was succeeded by sounds of different, but inexplicable import.

Having entered the apartment, I saw a candle on the hearth. A table was covered with vials and other apparatus of a sick chamber. A bed stood on one side, the curtain of which was dropped at the foot, so as to conceal any one within. I fixed my eyes upon this object. There were sufficient tokens that some one lay upon the bed. Breath, drawn at long intervals; mutterings scarcely audible; and a tremulous motion in the bedstead, were fearful and intelligible indications.

If my heart faultered, it must not be supposed that my trepidations arose from any selfish considerations. Wallace only, the object of my search, was present to my fancy. Pervaded with remembrance of the Hadwins; of the agonies which they had already endured; of the despair which would overwhelm the unhappy Susan, when the death of her lover should be ascertained; observant of the lonely condition of this house, whence I could only infer that the sick had been denied suitable attendance; and reminded by the symptoms that appeared, that this being was struggling with the agonies of death; a sickness of the heart, more insupportable than that which I had just experienced stole upon me.

My fancy readily depicted the progress and completion of this tragedy. Wallace was the first of the family on whom the pestilence had seized. Thetford had fled from his habitation. Perhaps, as a father and husband, to shun the danger attending his stay, was the injunction of his duty. It was questionless the conduct which selfish regards would dictate. Wallace was left to perish alone; or, perhaps, which indeed was a supposition somewhat justified by appearances, he had been left to the tendence of mercenary wretches; by whom, at this desperate moment he had been abandoned.

I was not mindless of the possibility that these forebodings, specious as they were, might be false. The dying person might be some other than Wallace. The whispers of my hope were, indeed, faint; but they, at least, prompted me to snatch a look at the expiring man. For this purpose, I advanced and thrust my head within the curtain.

Chapter XVI

THE FEATURES of one whom I had seen so transiently as Wallace, may be imagined to be not easily recognized, especially when those features were tremulous and deathful. Here, however, the differences were too conspicuous to mislead me. I beheld one to whom I could recollect none that bore resemblance. Though ghastly and livid, the traces of intelligence and beauty were undefaced. The life of Wallace was of more value to a feeble individual, but surely the being that was stretched before me and who was hastening to his last breath was precious to thousands.

Was he not one in whose place I would willingly have died? The offering was too late. His extremities were already cold. A vapour, noisome and contagious, hovered over him. The flutterings of his pulse had ceased. His existence was about to close amidst convulsion and pangs.

I withdrew my gaze from this object, and walked to a table. I was nearly unconscious of my movements. My thoughts were occupied with contemplations of the train of horrors and disasters that pursue the race of man. My musings were quickly interrupted by the sight of a small cabinet the hinges of which were broken and the lid half-raised. In the present state of my thoughts, I was prone to suspect the worst. Here were traces of pillage. Some casual or mercenary attendant, had not only contributed to hasten the death of the patient, but had rifled his property and fled.

This suspicion would, perhaps, have yielded to mature reflections, if I had been suffered to reflect. A moment scarcely elapsed, when some appearance in the mirror, which hung over the table, called my attention. It was a human figure, nothing could be briefer than the glance that I fixed upon this apparition, yet there was room enough for the vague conception to suggest itself, that the dying man had started from his bed and was approaching me. This belief was, at the same instant, confuted, by the survey of his form and garb. One eye, a scar upon his cheek, a tawny skin, a form grotesquely misproportioned, brawny as Hercules, and habited in livery, composed, as it were, the parts of one view.

To perceive, to fear, and to confront this apparition were blended into one sentiment. I turned towards him with the swiftness of lightning, but my speed was useless to my safety. A blow upon my temple was succeeded by an utter oblivion of thought and of feeling. I sunk upon the floor prostrate and senseless.

My insensibility might be mistaken by observers for death, yet some part of this interval was haunted by a fearful dream. I conceived myself lying on the brink of a pit whose bottom the eye could not reach. My hands and legs were fettered, so as to disable me from resisting two grim and gigantic figures, who stooped to lift me from the earth. Their purpose methought was to cast me into this abyss. My terrors were unspeakable, and I struggled with such force, that my bonds snapt and I found myself at liberty. At this moment my senses returned and I opened my eyes.

The memory of recent events was, for a time, effaced by my visionary horrors. I was conscious of transition from one state of being to another, but my imagination was still filled with images of danger. The bottomless gulf and my gigantic persecutors were still dreaded. I looked up with eagerness. Beside me I discovered three figures, whose character or office were explained by a coffin of pine-boards which lay upon the floor. One stood with hammer and nails in his hand, as ready to replace and fasten the lid of the coffin, as soon as its burthen should be received.

I attempted to rise from the floor, but my head was dizzy and my sight confused. Perceiving me revive, one of the men, assisted me to regain my feet. The mist and confusion presently vanished, so as to allow me to stand unsupported and to move. I once more gazed at my attendants, and recognized the three men, whom I had met in High-street, and whose conversation I have mentioned that I overheard. I looked again upon the coffin. A wavering recollection of the incidents that led me hither and of the stunning blow which I had received, occurred to me. I saw into what error, appearances had misled these men, and shuddered to reflect, by what hairbreadth means I had escaped being buried alive.

Before the men had time to interrogate me, or to comment upon my situation, one entered the apartment whose habit and mein tended to incourage me. The stranger was characterised by an aspect full of composure and benignity, a face in which the serious lines of age were blended with the ruddiness and smoothness of youth, and a garb that bespoke that religious profession, with whose benevolent doctrines the example of Hadwin had rendered me familiar.

On observing me on my feet, he betrayed marks of surprise and satisfaction. He addressed me in a tone of mildness.

Young man, said he, what is thy condition? Art thou sick? If thou art, thou must consent to receive the best treatment which the times will afford. These men will convey thee to the hospital at Bush-Hill.

The mention of that contagious and abhorred receptacle, inspired me with some degree of energy. No, said I, I am not sick, a violent blow reduced me to this situation. I shall presently recover strength enough to leave this spot, without assistance.

He looked at me, with an incredulous but compassionate air: I fear thou dost deceive thyself or me. The necessity of going to the hospital is much to be regretted, but on the whole it is best. Perhaps, indeed, thou hast kindred or friends who will take care of thee.

No, said I; neither kindred nor friends. I am a stranger in the city. I do not even know a single being.

Alas! returned the stranger with a sigh, thy state is sorrowful—but how camest thou hither? continued he, looking around him, and whence comest thou?

I came from the country. I reached the city, a few hours ago. I was in search of a friend who lived in this house.

Thy undertaking was strangely hazardous and rash: but who is the friend thou seekest? Was it he who died in that bed, and whose corpse has just been removed?

The men now betrayed some impatience; and inquired of the last comer, whom they called Mr. Estwick, what they were to do. He turned to me, and asked if I were willing to be conducted to the hospital?

I assured him that I was free from disease, and stood in no need of assistance; adding, that my feebleness was owing to a stunning blow received from a ruffian on my temple. The marks of this blow were conspicuous, and after some hesitation he dismissed the men; who, lifting the empty coffin on their shoulders, disappeared.

He now invited me to descend into the parlour: for, said he, the air of this room is deadly. I feel already as if I should have reason to repent of having entered it.

He now inquired into the cause of those appearances which he had witnessed. I explained my situation as clearly and succinctly as I was able.

After pondering, in silence, on my story:—I see how it is, said he: the person whom thou sawest in the agonies of death was a stranger. He was attended by his servant and an hired nurse. His master's death being certain, the nurse was dispatched by the servant to procure a coffin. He probably chose that opportunity to rifle his master's trunk, that stood upon the table. Thy unseasonable entrance interrupted him; and he designed, by the blow which he gave thee, to secure his retreat before the arrival of an hearse. I know the man, and the apparition thou hast so well described, was his. Thou sayest that a friend of thine lived in this house—Thou hast come too late to be of service. The whole family have perished—Not one was suffered to escape.

This intelligence was fatal to my hopes. It required some efforts to subdue my rising emotions. Compassion not only for Wallace, but for Thetford, his father, his wife and his child, caused a passionate effusion of tears. I was ashamed of this useless and child-like sensibility; and attempted to apologize to my companion. The sympathy, however, had proved contagious, and the stranger turned away his face to hide his own tears.

Nay, said he, in answer to my excuses, there is no need to be ashamed of thy emotion. Merely to have known this family, and to have witnessed their deplorable fate, is sufficient to melt the most obdurate heart. I suspect that thou wast united to some one of this family, by ties of tenderness like those which led the unfortunate *Maravegli* hither.

This suggestion was attended, in relation to myself, with some degree of obscurity; but my curiosity was somewhat excited by the name that he had mentioned. I inquired into the character and situation of this person, and particularly respecting his connection with this family.

Maravegli, answered he, was the lover of the eldest daughter and already betrothed to her. The whole family, consisting of helpless females, had placed themselves under his peculiar guardianship. Mary Walpole and her children enjoyed in him an husband and a father.

The name of Walpole, to which I was a stranger, suggested doubts which I hastened to communicate. I am in search, said I, not of a female friend, though not devoid of interest in the welfare of Thetford and his family. My principal concern is for a youth, by name, Wallace.

He looked at me with surprise. Thetford! this is not his abode. He changed his habitation some weeks previous to the *fever*. Those who last dwelt under this roof were an English woman, and seven daughters.

This detection of my error somewhat consoled me. It was still possible that Wallace was alive and in safety. I eagerly inquired whither Thetford had removed, and whether he had any knowledge of his present condition.

They had removed to number . . . , in Market-street. Concerning their state he knew nothing. His acquaintance with Thetford was imperfect. Whether he had left the city or had remained, he was wholly uninformed.

It became me to ascertain the truth in these respects. I was preparing to offer my parting thanks to the person by whom I had been so highly benefitted; since, as he now informed, it was by his interposition that I was hindered from being inclosed alive in a coffin. He was dubious of my true condition, and peremptorily commanded the followers of the hearse to desist. A delay of twenty minutes, and some medical application, would, he believed, determine whether my life was extinguished or suspended. At the end of this time, happily, my senses were recovered.

Seeing my intention to depart he inquired why, and whither I was going? Having heard my answer, Thy design resumed he, is highly indiscrete and rash. Nothing will sooner generate this fever than fatigue and anxiety. Thou hast scarcely recovered from the blow so lately received. Instead of being useful to others this precipitation will only disable thyself. Instead of roaming the streets and inhaling this unwholesome air, thou hadst better betake thyself to bed and try to obtain some sleep. In the morning, thou wilt be better qualified to ascertain the fate of thy friend, and afford him the relief which he shall want.

I could not but admit the reasonableness of these remonstrances, but where should a chamber and bed be sought? It was not likely that a new attempt to procure accommodation at the Inns would succeed better than the former.

Thy state, replied he, is sorrowful. I have no house to which I can lead thee. I divide my chamber and even my bed with another, and my landlady could not be prevailed upon to admit a stranger. What thou wilt do, I know not. This house has no one to defend it. It was purchased and furnished by the last possessor, but the whole family, including mistress, children and servants, were cut off in a single week. Perhaps, no one in America can claim the property. Meanwhile plunderers are numerous and active. An house thus totally deserted, and replenished with valuable furniture will, I fear, become their prey. To night, nothing can be done towards rendering it secure, but staying in it. Art thou willing to remain here till the morrow?

Every bed in the house has probably sustained a dead person. It would not be proper, therefore, to lie in any one of them. Perhaps, thou mayest find some repose upon this carpet. It is, at least, better than the harder pavement, and the open air.

This proposal, after some hesitation, I embraced. He was preparing to leave me, promising, if life were spared to him, to return early in the morning. My curiosity respecting the person whose dying agonies I had witnessed, prompted me to detain him a few minutes.

Ah! said he, this perhaps, is the only one of many victims to this pestilence whose loss the remotest generations may have reason to deplore. He was the only descendent of an illustrious house of Venice. He has been devoted from his childhood to the acquisition of knowledge and the practice of virtue. He came hither, as an enlightened observer, and after traversing the country, conversing with all the men in it eminent for their talents or their office; and collecting a fund of observations, whose solidity and justice have seldom been paralleled, he embarked, three months ago, for Europe.

Previously to his departure, he formed a tender connection with the eldest daughter of this family. The mother and her children had recently arrived from England. So many faultless women, both mentally and personally considered, it was not my fortune to meet with before. This youth well deserved to be adopted into this family. He proposed to return with the utmost expedition to his native country, and after the settlement of his affairs, to hasten back to America, and ratify his contract with Fanny Walpole.

The ship in which he embarked, had scarcely gone twenty leagues to sea, before she was disabled by a storm, and obliged to return to port. He posted to New-York, to gain a passage in a packet shortly to sail. Meanwhile this malady prevailed among us. Mary Walpole was hindered by her ignorance of the nature of that evil which assailed us, and the counsel of injudicious friends, from taking the due precautions for her safety. She hesitated to fly till flight was rendered impracticable. Her death added to the helplessness and distraction of the family. They were successively seized and destroyed by the same pest.

Maravegli was apprised of their danger. He allowed the packet to depart without him, and hastened to the rescue of the Walpoles from the perils which encompassed them. He arrived in this city time enough to witness the interment of the last survivor. In the same hour he was seized himself by this disease: the catastrophe is known to thee.

I will now leave thee to thy repose. Sleep is no less needful to myself than to thee: for this is the second night which has past without it—Saying this, my companion took his leave.

I now enjoyed leisure to review my situation. I experienced no inclination to sleep. I lay down for a moment, but my comfortless sensations and restless contemplations would not permit me to rest. Before I entered this roof, I was tormented with hunger, but my craving had given place to inquietude and loathing. I paced, in thoughtful and anxious mood, across the floor of the apartment.

I mused upon the incidents related by Estwick, upon the exterminating nature of this pestilence, and on the horrors of which it was productive. I compared the experience of the last hours, with those pictures which my imagination had drawn in the retirements of *Malverton*. I wondered at the contrariety that exists between the scenes of the city and the country; and fostered with more zeal than ever, the resolution to avoid those seats of depravity and danger.

Concerning my own destiny, however, I entertained no doubt. My new sensations assured me that my stomach had received this corrosive poison. Whether I should die or live was easily decided. The sickness which assiduous attendance and powerful prescriptions might remove, would, by negligence and solitude, be rendered fatal: but from whom could I expect medical or friendly treatment?

I had indeed a roof over my head. I should not perish in the public way: but what was my ground for hoping to continue under this roof? My sickness being suspected, I should be dragged in a cart to the hospital; where I should, indeed die; but not with the consolation of loneliness and silence. Dying groans were the only music, and livid corpses were the only spectacle to which I should there be introduced.

Immured in these dreary meditations, the night passed away. The light glancing through the window awakened in my bosom a gleam of cheerfulness. Contrary to my expectations, my feelings were not more distempered, notwithstanding my want of sleep, than on the last evening. This was a token that my state was far from being so desperate as I suspected. It was possible, I thought, that this was the worst indisposition to which I was liable.

Meanwhile the coming of Estwick was impatiently expected. The sun arose, and the morning advanced, but he came not. I remembered that he talked of having reason to repent his visit to this house. Perhaps, he likewise, was sick, and that this was the cause of his delay. This man's kindness had even my love. If I had known the way to his dwelling, I should have hastened thither, to inquire into his condition, and to perform for him every office that humanity might enjoin, but he had not afforded me any information on that head.

Chapter XVII

IT WAS now incumbent on me to seek the habitation of Thetford. To leave this house accessible to every passenger appeared to be imprudent. I had no key by which I might lock the principal door. I therefore bolted it on the inside, and passed through a window, the shutters of which I closed, though I could not fasten, after me. This led me into a spacious court, at the end of which was a brick wall, over which I leaped into the street. This was the means by which I had formerly escaped from the same precincts.

The streets, as I passed, were desolate and silent. The largest computation made the number of fugitives two-thirds of the whole people; yet, judging by the universal desolation, it seemed, as if the solitude were nearly absolute. That so many of the houses were closed, I was obliged to ascribe to the cessation of traffic, which made the opening of their windows useless, and the terror of infection, which made the inhabitants seclude themselves from the observation of each other.

I proceeded to search out the house to which Estwick had directed me, as the abode of Thetford. What was my consternation when I found it to be the same, at the door of which the conversation took place, of which I had been an auditor on the last evening.

I recalled the scene, of which a rude sketch had been given by the *hearse-men*. If such were the fate of the master of the family, abounding with money and friends, what could be hoped for the moneyless and friendless Wallace? The house appeared to be vacant and silent; but these tokens might deceive. There was little room for hope; but certainty was wanting, and might, perhaps, be obtained by entering the house. In some of the upper rooms a wretched being might be immured; by whom the information, so earnestly desired, might be imparted, and to whom my presence might bring relief; not only from pestilence, but famine. For a moment, I forgot my own necessitous condition; and reflected not that abstinence had already undermined my strength.

I proceeded to knock at the door. That my signal was un-

noticed, produced no surprize. The door was unlocked, and
I opened. At this moment my attention was attracted by the
opening of another door near me. I looked, and perceived a
man issuing forth from an house at a small distance.

It now occurred to me, that the information which I sought
might possibly be gained from one of Thetford's neighbours.
This person was aged, but seemed to have lost neither cheerfulness nor vigour. He had an air of intrepidity and calmness.
It soon appeared that I was the object of his curiosity. He
had, probably, marked my deportment through some window
of his dwelling, and had come forth to make inquiries into
the motives of my conduct.

He courteously saluted me. You seem, said he, to be in
search of some one. If I can afford you the information you
want, you will be welcome to it.

Encouraged by this address, I mentioned the name of
Thetford; and added my fears that he had not escaped the
general calamity.

It is true, said he. Yesterday himself, his wife, and his child
were in an hopeless condition. I saw them in the evening, and
expected not to find them alive this morning. As soon as it
was light, however, I visited the house again; but found it
empty. I suppose they must have died, and been removed in
the night.

Though anxious to ascertain the destiny of Wallace, I was
unwilling to put direct questions. I shuddered, while I longed
to know the truth.

Why, said I, falteringly, did he not seasonably withdraw
from the city? Surely he had the means of purchasing an asylum in the country.

I can scarcely tell you, he answered. Some infatuation appeared to have seized him. No one was more timorous; but
he seemed to think himself safe, as long as he avoided contact
with infected persons. He was likewise, I believe, detained by
a regard to his interest. His flight would not have been more
injurious to his affairs, than it was to those of others; but gain
was, in his eyes, the supreme good. He intended ultimately
to withdraw; but his escape to-day, gave him new courage to
encounter the perils of to-morrow. He deferred his departure
from day to day, till it ceased to be practicable.

His family, said I, was numerous. It consisted of more than his wife and children. Perhaps these retired in sufficient season.

Yes, said he; his father left the house at an early period. One or two of the servants likewise forsook him. One girl, more faithful and heroic than the rest, resisted the remonstrances of her parents and friends, and resolved to adhere to him in every fortune. She was anxious that the family should fly from danger, and would willingly have fled in their company; but while they stayed, it was her immovable resolution not to abandon them.

Alas, poor girl! She knew not of what stuff the heart of Thetford was made. Unhappily, she was the first to become sick. I question much whether her disease was pestilential. It was, probably, a slight indisposition; which, in a few days, would have vanished of itself, or have readily yielded to suitable treatment.

Thetford was transfixed with terror. Instead of summoning a physician, to ascertain the nature of her symptoms, he called a negro and his cart from Bush-hill. In vain the neighbours interceded for this unhappy victim. In vain she implored his clemency, and asserted the lightness of her indisposition. She besought him to allow her to send to her mother, who resided a few miles in the country, who would hasten to her succour, and relieve him and his family from the danger and trouble of nursing her.

The man was lunatic with apprehension. He rejected her intreaties, though urged in a manner that would have subdued an heart of flint. The girl was innocent, and amiable, and courageous, but entertained an unconquerable dread of the hospital. Finding intreaties ineffectual, she exerted all her strength in opposition to the man who lifted her into the cart.

Finding that her struggles availed nothing, she resigned herself to despair. In going to the hospital, she believed herself led to certain death, and to the sufferance of every evil which the known inhumanity of its attendants could inflict. This state of mind, added to exposure to a noon-day sun, in an open vehicle, moving, for a mile, over a rugged pavement, was sufficient to destroy her. I was not surprised to hear that she died the next day.

This proceeding was sufficiently iniquitous; yet it was not the worst act of this man. The rank and education of the young woman, might be some apology for negligence; but his clerk, a youth who seemed to enjoy his confidence, and to be treated by his family, on the footing of a brother or son, fell sick on the next night, and was treated in the same manner.

These tidings struck me to the heart. A burst of indignation and sorrow filled my eyes. I could scarcely stifle my emotion sufficiently to ask, Of whom, sir, do you speak? Was the name of the youth—his name—was—

His name was Wallace. I see that you have some interest in his fate. He was one whom I loved. I would have given half my fortune to procure him accommodation under some hospitable roof. His attack was violent; but still, his recovery, if he had been suitably attended, was possible. That he should survive removal to the hospital, and the treatment he must receive when there, was not to be hoped.

The conduct of Thetford was as absurd as it was wicked. To imagine this disease to be contagious was the height of folly; to suppose himself secure, merely by not permitting a sick man to remain under his roof, was no less stupid; but Thetford's fears had subverted his understanding. He did not listen to arguments or supplications. His attention was incapable of straying from one object. To influence him by words was equivalent to reasoning with the deaf.

Perhaps the wretch was more to be pitied than hated. The victims of his implacable caution, could scarcely have endured agonies greater than those which his pusillanimity inflicted on himself. Whatever be the amount of his guilt, the retribution has been adequate. He witnessed the death of his wife and child, and last night was the close of his own existence. Their sole attendant was a black woman; whom, by frequent visits, I endeavoured, with little success, to make diligent in the performance of her duty.

Such, then, was the catastrophe of Wallace. The end for which I journeyed hither was accomplished. His destiny was ascertained; and all that remained was to fulfil the gloomy predictions of the lovely, but unhappy Susan. To tell them all the truth, would be needlessly to exasperate her sorrow. Time, aided by the tenderness and sympathy of friendship, may banish her despair, and relieve her from all but the witcheries of melancholy.

Having disengaged my mind from these reflections, I explained to my companion in general terms, my reasons for visiting the city, and my curiosity respecting Thetford. He inquired into the particulars of my journey, and the time of my arrival. When informed that I had come in the preceding evening, and had passed the subsequent hours without sleep or food, he expressed astonishment and compassion.

Your undertaking, said he, has certainly been hazardous. There is poison in every breath which you draw, but this hazard has been greatly increased by abstaining from food and sleep. My advice is to hasten back into the country; but you must first take some repose and some victuals. If you pass Schuylkill before night-fall, it will be sufficient.

I mentioned the difficulty of procuring accommodation on the road. It would be most prudent to set out upon my journey so as to reach *Malverton* at night. As to food and sleep they were not to be purchased in this city.

True, answered my companion, with quickness, they are not to be bought, but I will furnish you with as much as you desire of both for nothing. That is my abode, continued he, pointing to the house, which he had lately left. I reside with a widow lady and her daughter, who took my counsel, and fled in due season. I remain to moralize upon the scene, with only a faithful black, who makes my bed, prepares my coffee, and bakes my loaf. If I am sick, all that a physician can do, I will do for myself, and all that a nurse can perform, I expect to be performed by *Austin*.

Come with me, drink some coffee, rest a while on my matrass, and then fly, with my benedictions on your head.

These words were accompanied by features disembarrassed and benevolent. My temper is alive to social impulses, and I accepted his invitation, not so much because I wished to eat or to sleep, but because I felt reluctance to part so soon with a being, who possessed so much fortitude and virtue.

He was surrounded by neatness and plenty. Austin added dexterity to submissiveness. My companion, whose name I now found to be Medlicote, was prone to converse, and commented on the state of the city like one whose reading had been extensive and experience large. He combatted an opinion which I had casually formed, respecting the origin of this epidemic, and imputed it, not to infected substances imported from the east or west, but to a morbid constitution of the atmosphere, owing wholly, or in part to filthy streets, airless habitations and squalid persons.

As I talked with this man, the sense of danger was obliterated, I felt confidence revive in my heart, and energy revisit my stomach. Though far from my wonted health, my sensation grew less comfortless, and I found myself to stand in no need of repose.

Breakfast being finished, my friend pleaded his daily engagements as reasons for leaving me. He counselled me to strive for some repose, but I was conscious of incapacity to sleep. I was desirous of escaping, as soon as possible, from this tainted atmosphere and reflected whether any thing remained to be done respecting Wallace.

It now occurred to me that this youth must have left some clothes and papers, and, perhaps, books. The property of these was now vested in the Hadwins. I might deem myself, without presumtion, their representative or agent. Might I not take some measures for obtaining possession, or at least, for the security of these articles?

The house and its furniture was tenantless and unprotected. It was liable to be ransacked and pillaged by those desperate ruffians, of whom many were said to be hunting for spoil, even at a time like this. If these should overlook this dwelling, Thetford's unknown successor or heir might appropriate the whole. Numberless accidents might happen to occasion the destruction or embezzlement of what belonged to Wallace, which might be prevented by the conduct which I should now pursue.

Immersed in these perplexities, I remained bewildered and motionless. I was at length roused by some one knocking at the door. Austin obeyed the signal, and instantly returned, leading in—Mr. Hadwin!

I know not whether this unlooked-for interview excited on my part, most grief or surprize. The motive of his coming was easily divined. His journey was on two accounts superfluous.

He whom he sought was dead. The duty of ascertaining his condition, I had assigned to myself.

I now perceived and deplored the error of which I had been guilty, in concealing my intended journey from my patron. Ignorant of the part I had acted, he had rushed into the jaws of this pest, and endangered a life unspeakably valuable to his children and friends. I should doubtless have obtained his grateful consent to the project which I had conceived; but my wretched policy had led me into this clandestine path. Secrecy may seldom be a crime. A virtuous intention may produce it; but surely it is always erroneous and pernicious.

My friend's astonishment at the sight of me, was not inferior to my own. The causes which led to this unexpected interview were mutually explained. To soothe the agonies of his child, he consented to approach the city, and endeavour to procure intelligence of Wallace. When he left his house, he intended to stop in the environs, and hire some emissary, whom an ample reward might tempt to enter the city, and procure the information which was needed.

No one could be prevailed upon to execute so dangerous a service. Averse to return without performing his commission, he concluded to examine for himself. Thetford's removal to this street was known to him; but, being ignorant of my purpose, he had not mentioned this circumstance to me, during our last conversation.

I was sensible of the danger which Hadwin had incurred by entering the city. Perhaps, my knowledge or the inexpressible importance of his life, to the happiness of his daughters, made me aggravate his danger. I knew that the longer he lingered in this tainted air, the hazard was increased. A moment's delay was unnecessary. Neither Wallace nor myself were capable of being benefitted by his presence.

I mentioned the death of his nephew, as a reason for hastening his departure. I urged him in the most vehement terms to remount his horse and to fly; I endeavoured to preclude all inquiries respecting myself or Wallace; promising to follow him immediately, and answer all his questions at *Malverton*. My importunities were inforced by his own fears, and after a moment's hesitation, he rode away.

The emotions produced by this incident, were, in the present critical state of my frame, eminently hurtful. My morbid indications suddenly returned. I had reason to ascribe my condition to my visit to the chamber of Maravegli, but this, and its consequences, to myself, as well as the journey of Hadwin, were the fruits of my unhappy secrecy.

I had always been accustomed to perform my journeys on foot. This, on ordinary occasions, was the preferable method, but now I ought to have adopted the easiest and swiftest means. If Hadwin had been acquainted with my purpose he would not only have approved, but would have allowed me the use of an horse. These reflections were rendered less pungent by the recollection that my motives were benevolent, and that I had endeavoured the benefit of others by means, which appeared to me most suitable.

Meanwhile, how was I to proceed? What hindered me from pursuing the foot-steps of Hadwin with all the expedition which my uneasiness, of brain and stomach would allow? I conceived that to leave any thing undone, with regard to Wallace, would be absurd. His property might be put under the care of my new friend. But how was it to be distinguished from the property of others? It was, probably, contained in trunks, which was designated by some label or mark. I was unacquainted with his chamber, but, by passing from one to the other, I might finally discover it. Some token, directing my foot-steps, might occur, though at present unforeseen.

Actuated by these considerations, I once more entered Thetford's habitation. I regretted that I had not procured the counsel or attendance of my new friend, but some engagements, the nature of which he did not explain, occasioned him to leave me as soon as breakfast was finished.

Chapter XVIII

I WANDERED over this deserted mansion, in a considerable degree, at random. Effluvia of a pestilential nature, assailed me from every corner. In the front room of the second story, I imagined that I discovered vestiges of that catastrophe which the past night had produced. The bed appeared as if some one had recently been dragged from it. The sheets were tinged with yellow, and with that substance which is said to be characteristic of this disease, the gangrenous or black vomit. The floor exhibited similar stains.

There are many, who will regard my conduct as the last refinement of temerity, or of heroism. Nothing, indeed, more perplexes me than a review of my own conduct. Not, indeed, that death is an object always to be dreaded, or that my motive did not justify my actions; but of all dangers, those allied to pestilence, by being mysterious and unseen, are the most formidable. To disarm them of their terrors, requires the longest familiarity. Nurses and physicians soonest become intrepid or indifferent; but the rest of mankind recoil from the scene with unconquerable loathing.

I was sustained, not by confidence of safety, and a belief of exemption from this malady, or by the influence of habit, which inures us to all that is detestable or perilous, but by a belief that this was as eligible an avenue to death as any other; and that life is a trivial sacrifice in the cause of duty.

I passed from one room to the other. A portmanteau, marked with the initials of Wallace's name, at length attracted my notice. From this circumstance I inferred, that this apartment had been occupied by him. The room was neatly arranged, and appeared as if no one had lately used it. There were trunks and drawers. That which I have mentioned, was the only one that bore marks of Wallace's ownership. This I lifted in my arms with a view to remove it to Medlicote's house.

At that moment, methought I heard a foot-step slowly and lingeringly ascending the stair. I was disconcerted at this incident. The foot-step had in it a ghost-like solemnity and tardiness. This phantom vanished in a moment, and yielded place to more humble conjectures. A human being approached, whose office and commission were inscrutable. That we were strangers to each other was easily imagined; but how would my appearance, in this remote chamber, and loaded with another's property, be interpreted? Did he enter the house after me, or was he the tenant of some chamber hitherto unvisited; whom my entrance had awakened from his trance and called from his couch?

In the confusion of my mind, I still held my burthen uplifted. To have placed it on the floor, and encountered this visitant, without this equivocal token about me, was the obvious proceeding. Indeed, time only could decide whether these foot-steps tended to this, or to some other apartment.

My doubts were quickly dispelled. The door opened, and a figure glided in. The portmanteau dropped from my arms, and my heart's-blood was chilled. If an apparition of the dead were possible, and that possibility I could not deny, this was such an apparition. A hue, yellowish and livid; bones, uncovered with flesh; eyes, ghastly, hollow, woe-begone, and fixed in an agony of wonder upon me; and locks, matted and negligent, constituted the image which I now beheld. My belief of somewhat preternatural in this appearance, was confirmed by recollection of resemblances between these features and those of one who was dead. In this shape and visage, shadowy and death-like as they were, the lineaments of Wallace, of him who had misled my rustic simplicity on my first visit to this city, and whose death I had conceived to be incontestably ascertained, were forcibly recognized.

This recognition, which at first alarmed my superstition, speedily led to more rational inferences. Wallace had been dragged to the hospital. Nothing was less to be suspected than that he would return alive from that hideous receptacle, but this was by no means impossible. The figure that stood before me, had just risen from the bed of sickness, and from the brink of the grave. The crisis of his malady had passed, and he was once more entitled to be ranked among the living.

This event, and the consequences which my imagination connected with it, filled me with the liveliest joy. I thought not of his ignorance of the causes of my satisfaction, of the doubts to which the circumstances of our interview would give birth, respecting the integrity of my purpose. I forgot the artifices by which I had formerly been betrayed, and the embarrassments which a meeting with the victim of his artifices would excite in him; I thought only of the happiness which his recovery would confer upon his uncle and his cousins.

I advanced towards him with an air of congratulation, and offered him my hand. He shrunk back, and exclaimed in a feeble voice, Who are you? What business have you here?

I am the friend of Wallace, if he will allow me to be so. I am a messenger from your uncle and cousins at *Malverton*. I came to know the cause of your silence, and to afford you any assistance in my power.

He continued to regard me with an air of suspicion and doubt. These I endeavoured to remove by explaining the motives that led me hither. It was with difficulty that he seemed to credit my representations. When thoroughly convinced of the truth of my assertions, he inquired with great anxiety and tenderness concerning his relations; and expressed his hope that they were ignorant of what had befallen him.

I could not encourage his hopes. I regretted my own precipitation in adopting the belief of his death. This belief, had been uttered with confidence, and without stating my reasons for embracing it, to Mr. Hadwin. These tidings would be borne to his daughters, and their grief would be exasperated to a deplorable, and, perhaps, to a fatal degree.

There was but one method of repairing or eluding this mischief. Intelligence ought to be conveyed to them of his recovery. But where was the messenger to be found? No one's attention could be found disengaged from his own concerns. Those who were able or willing to leave the city had sufficient motives for departure, in relation to themselves. If vehicle or horse were procurable for money, ought it not to be secured for the use of Wallace himself, whose health required the easiest and speediest conveyance from this theatre of death?

My companion was powerless in mind as in limbs. He seemed unable to consult upon the means of escaping from the inconveniences by which he was surrounded. As soon as sufficient strength was regained, he had left the hospital. To repair to *Malverton* was the measure which prudence obviously dictated; but he was hopeless of effecting it. The city was close at hand; this was his usual home; and hither his tottering, and almost involuntary steps had conducted him.

He listened to my representations and councils, and acknowledged their propriety. He put himself under my protection and guidance, and promised to conform implicitly to my directions. His strength had sufficed to bring him thus far, but was now utterly exhausted. The task of searching for a carriage and horse devolved upon me.

In effecting this purpose, I was obliged to rely upon my own ingenuity and diligence. Wallace, though so long a resident in the city, knew not to whom I could apply, or by whom carriages were let to hire. My own reflections taught me, that this accommodation was most likely to be furnished by innkeepers, or that some of those might at least inform me of the best measures to be taken. I resolved to set out immediately on this search. Meanwhile, Wallace was persuaded to take refuge in Medlicote's apartments; and to make, by the assistance of Austin, the necessary preparation for his journey.

The morning had now advanced. The rays of a sultry sun had a sickening and enfeebling influence, beyond any which I had ever experienced. The drought of unusual duration had bereft the air and the earth of every particle of moisture. The element which I breathed appeared to have stagnated into noxiousness and putrifaction. I was astonished at observing the enormous diminution of my strength. My brows were heavy, my intellects benumbed, my sinews enfeebled, and my sensations universally unquiet.

These prognostics were easily interpreted. What I chiefly dreaded was, that they would disable me from executing the task which I had undertaken. I summoned up all my resolution, and cherished a disdain of yielding to this ignoble destiny. I reflected that the source of all energy, and even of life, is seated in thought; that nothing is arduous to human efforts; that the external frame will seldom languish, while actuated by an unconquerable soul.

I fought against my dreary feelings, which pulled me to the earth. I quickened my pace, raised my drooping eye-lids, and hummed a cheerful and favourite air. For all that I accomplished during this day, I believe myself indebted to the strenuousness and ardour of my resolutions.

I went from one tavern to another. One was deserted; in another the people were sick, and their attendants refused to hearken to my inquiries or offers; at a third, their horses were engaged. I was determined to prosecute my search as long as an inn or a livery-stable remained unexamined, and my strength would permit.

To detail the events of this expedition, the arguments and supplications which I used to overcome the dictates of avarice and fear, the fluctuation of my hopes and my incessant disappointments, would be useless. Having exhausted all my expedients ineffectually, I was compelled to turn my weary steps once more to Medlicote's lodgings.

My meditations were deeply engaged by the present circumstances of my situation. Since the means which were first suggested, were impracticable, I endeavoured to investigate others. Wallace's debility made it impossible for him to perform this journey on foot: but would not his strength and his resolution suffice to carry him beyond Schuylkill? A carriage or horse, though not to be obtained in the city, could, without difficulty, be procured, in the country. Every farmer had beasts for burthen and draught. One of these might be hired at no immoderate expense, for half a day.

This project appeared so practicable and so specious, that I deeply regretted the time and the efforts which had already been so fruitlessly expended. If my project, however, had been mischievous, to review it with regret, was only to prolong and to multiply its mischiefs. I trusted that time and strength would not be wanting to the execution of this new design.

On entering Medlicote's house, my looks, which, in spite of my languors, were sprightly and confident, flattered Wallace with the belief that my exertions had succeeded. When acquainted with their failure, he sunk as quickly into hopelessness. My new expedient was heard by him with no marks of satisfaction. It was impossible, he said, to move from this spot by his own strength. All his powers were exhausted by his walk from Bush-hill.

I endeavoured, by arguments and railleries, to revive his courage. The pure air of the country would exhilirate him into new life. He might stop at every fifty yards, and rest upon the green sod. If overtaken by the night, we would procure a lodging, by address and importunity; but if every door should be shut against us, we should at least, enjoy the shelter of some barn, and might diet wholsomely upon the new-laid eggs that we should find there. The worst treatment we could meet with, was better than continuance in the city.

These remonstrances had some influence, and he at length consented to put his ability to the test. First, however, it was necessary to invigorate himself by a few hours rest. To this, though with infinite reluctance, I consented.

This interval allowed him to reflect upon the past, and to inquire into the fate of Thetford and his family. The intelligence, which Medlicote had enabled me to afford him, was heard with more satisfaction than regret. The ingratitude and cruelty with which he had been treated, seemed to have extinguished every sentiment, but hatred and vengeance. I was willing to profit by this interval to know more of Thetford, than I already possessed. I inquired why Wallace, had so perversely neglected the advice of his uncle and cousin, and persisted to brave so many dangers when flight was so easy.

I cannot justify my conduct, answered he. It was in the highest degree, thoughtless and perverse. I was confident and unconcerned as long as our neighbourhood was free from disease, and as long as I forbore any communication with the sick; yet I should have withdrawn to Malverton, merely to gratify my friends, if Thetford had not used the most powerful arguments to detain me. He laboured to extenuate the danger.

Why not stay, said he, as long as I and my family stay? Do you think that we would linger here, if the danger were imminent. As soon as it becomes so, we will fly. You know that we have a country-house prepared for our reception. When we go, you shall accompany us. Your services at this time are indispensable to my affairs. If you will not desert me, your salary next year shall be double; and that will enable you to marry your cousin immediately. Nothing is more improbable than that any of us should be sick, but if this should happen to you, I plight my honour that you shall be carefully and faithfully attended.

These assurances were solemn and generous. To make Susan Hadwin my wife, was the scope of all my wishes and labours. By staying I should hasten this desirable event, and incur little hazard. By going, I should alienate the affections of Thetford; by whom, it is but justice to acknowledge, that I had hitherto been treated with unexampled generosity and kindness; and blast all the schemes I had formed for rising into wealth.

My resolution was by no means stedfast. As often as a letter from *Malverton* arrived, I felt myself disposed to hasten away, but this inclination was combated by new arguments and new intreaties of Thetford.

In this state of suspense, the girl by whom Mrs. Thetford's infant was nursed, fell sick. She was an excellent creature, and merited better treatment than she received. Like me, she resisted the persuasions of her friends, but her motives for remaining were disinterested and heroic.

No sooner did her indisposition appear, than she was hurried to the hospital. I saw that no reliance could be placed upon the assurances of Thetford. Every consideration gave way to his fear of death. After the girl's departure, though he knew that she was led by his means to execution,—yet he consoled himself with repeating and believing her assertions, that her disease was not *the fever*.

I was now greatly alarmed for my own safety. I was determined to encounter his anger and repel his persuasions; and to depart with the market-man, next morning. That night, however, I was seized with a violent fever. I knew in what manner patients were treated at the hospital, and removal thither was to the last degree abhorred.

The morning arrived, and my situation was discovered. At the first intimation, Thetford rushed out of the house, and refused to re-enter it till I was removed. I knew not my fate, till three ruffians made their appearance at my bed-side, and communicated their commission.

I called on the name of Thetford and his wife. I intreated a moment's delay, till I had seen these persons, and endeavoured to procure a respite from my sentence. They were deaf to my intreaties, and prepared to execute their office by force. I was delirious with rage and with terror. I heaped the bitterest

execrations on my murderer; and by turns, invoked the compassion, and poured a torrent of reproaches on, the wretches
whom he had selected for his ministers. My struggles and outcries were vain.

I have no perfect recollection of what passed till my arrival
at the hospital. My passions combined with my disease, to
make me frantic and wild. In a state like mine, the slightest
motion could not be indured without agony. What then must
I have felt, scorched and dazled by the sun, sustained by hard
boards, and borne for miles over a rugged pavement?

I cannot make you comprehend the anguish of my feelings.
To be disjointed and torn piece-meal by the rack, was a torment inexpressibly inferior to this. Nothing excites my wonder, but that I did not expire before the cart had moved three
paces.

I knew not how, or by whom I was moved from this vehicle.
Insensibility came at length to my relief. After a time I opened
my eyes, and slowly gained some knowledge of my situation.
I lay upon a mattress, whose condition proved that an half-
decayed corpse had recently been dragged from it. The room
was large, but it was covered with beds like my own. Between
each, there was scarcely the interval of three feet. Each sustained a wretch, whose groans and distortions, bespoke the
desperateness of his condition.

The atmosphere was loaded by mortal stenches. A vapour,
suffocating and malignant, scarcely allowed me to breathe. No
suitable receptacle was provided for the evacuations produced
by medicine or disease. My nearest neighbour was struggling
with death, and my bed, casually extended, was moist with
the detestable matter which had flowed from his stomach.

You will scarcely believe that, in this scene of horrors, the
sound of laughter should be overheard. While the upper
rooms of this building, are filled with the sick and the dying,
the lower apartments are the scene of carrousals and mirth.
The wretches who are hired, at enormous wages, to tend the
sick and convey away the dead, neglect their duty and consume the cordials, which are provided for the patients, in debauchery and riot.

A female visage, bloated with malignity and drunkenness,
occasionally looked in. Dying eyes were cast upon her, in-

voking the boon, perhaps, of a drop of cold water, or her assistance to change a posture which compelled him to behold the ghastly writhings or deathful *smile* of his neighbour.

The visitant had left the banquet for a moment, only to see who was dead. If she entered the room, blinking eyes and reeling steps, shewed her to be totally unqualified for ministering the aid that was needed. Presently, she disappeared and others ascended the stair-case, a coffin was deposited at the door, the wretch, whose heart still quivered, was seized by rude hands, and dragged along the floor into the passage.

O! how poor are the conceptions which are formed, by the fortunate few, of the sufferings to which millions of their fellow beings are condemned. This misery was more frightful, because it was seen to flow from the depravity of the attendants. My own eyes only would make me credit the existence of wickedness so enormous. No wonder that to die in garrets and cellars and stables, unvisited and unknown, had, by so many, been preferred to being brought hither.

A physician cast an eye upon my state. He gave some directions to the person who attended him. I did not comprehend them, they were never executed by the nurses, and if the attempt had been made, I should probably have refused to receive what was offered. Recovery was equally beyond my expectations and my wishes. The scene which was hourly displayed before me, the entrance of the sick, most of whom perished in a few hours, and their departure to the graves prepared for them, reminded me of the fate to which I, also, was reserved.

Three days passed away, in which every hour was expected to be the last. That, amidst an atmosphere so contagious and deadly, amidst causes of distruction hourly accumulating, I should yet survive, appears to me nothing less than miraculous. That of so many conducted to this house, the only one who passed out of it alive, should be myself, almost surpasses my belief.

Some inexplicable principle rendered harmless those potent enemies of human life. My fever subsided and vanished. My strength was revived, and the first use that I made of my limbs, was to bear me far from the contemplation and sufferance of those evils.

Chapter XIX

HAVING gratified my curiosity in this respect, Wallace proceeded to remind me of the circumstances of our first interview. He had entertained doubts whether I was the person, whom he had met at Lesher's. I acknowledged myself to be the same, and inquired, in my turn, into the motives of his conduct on that occasion.

I confess, said he, with some hesitation, I meant only to sport with your simplicity and ignorance. You must not imagine, however, that my stratagem was deep-laid and deliberately executed. My professions at the tavern were sincere. I meant not to injure but to serve you. It was not till I reached the head of the stair-case, that the mischievous contrivance occurred. I foresaw nothing, at the moment, but ludicrous mistakes and embarrassment. The scheme was executed almost at the very moment it occurred.

After I had returned to the parlour, Thetford charged me with the delivery of a message in a distant quarter of the city. It was not till I had performed this commission, and had set out on my return, that I fully revolved the consequences likely to flow from my project.

That Thetford and his wife would detect you in their bed-chamber was unquestionable. Perhaps, weary of my long delay, you would have fairly undressed and gone to bed. The married couple would have made preparation to follow you, and when the curtain was undrawn, would discover a robust youth, fast asleep, in their place. These images, which had just before excited my laughter, now produced a very different emotion. I dreaded some fatal catastrophe from the fiery passions of Thetford. In the first transports of his fury he might pistol you, or, at least, might command you to be dragged to prison.

I now heartily repented of my jest and hastened home that I might prevent, as far as possible, the evil effects that might flow from it. The acknowledgment of my own agency in this affair, would at least, transfer Thetford's indignation to myself to whom it was equitably due.

The married couple had retired to their chamber, and no alarm or confusion had followed. This was an inexplicable circumstance. I waited with impatience till the morning should furnish a solution of the difficulty. The morning arrived. A strange event, had, indeed, taken place in their bed-chamber. They found an infant asleep in their bed. Thetford had been roused twice in the night, once by a noise in the closet and, afterwards, by a noise at the door.

Some connection between these sounds and the foundling, was naturally suspected. In the morning the closet was examined, and a coarse pair of shoes was found on the floor. The chamber door, which Thetford had locked in the evening, was discovered to be open, as likewise a window in the kitchen.

These appearances were a source of wonder and doubt to others, but were perfectly intelligible to me. I rejoiced that my stratagem had no more dangerous consequence, and admired the ingenuity and perseverance with which you had extricated yourself from so critical a state.

This narrative was only the verification of my own guesses. Its facts were quickly supplanted in my thoughts by the disastrous picture he had drawn of the state of the hospital. I was confounded and shocked by the magnitude of this evil. The cause of it was obvious. The wretches whom money could purchase, were of course, licentious and unprincipled; superintended and controlled they might be useful instruments, but that superintendence could not be bought.

What qualities were requisite in the governor of such an institution? He must have zeal, diligence and perseverance. He must act from lofty and pure motives. He must be mild and firm, intrepid and compliant. One perfectly qualified for the office it is desirable, but not possible, to find. A dispassionate and honest zeal in the cause of duty and humanity, may be of eminent utility. Am I not endowed with this zeal? Cannot my feeble efforts obviate some portion of this evil?

No one has hitherto claimed this disgustful and perillous situation. My powers and discernment are small, but if they be honestly exerted they cannot fail to be somewhat beneficial.

The impulse, produced by these reflections, was to hasten

to the City-hall, and make known my wishes. This impulse was controlled by recollections of my own indisposition, and of the state of Wallace. To deliver this youth to his friends was the strongest obligation. When this was discharged, I might return to the city, and acquit myself of more comprehensive duties.

Wallace had now enjoyed a few hours rest, and was persuaded to begin the journey. It was now noon-day, and the sun darted insupportable rays. Wallace was more sensible than I of their unwholesome influence. We had not reached the suburbs, when his strength was wholly exhausted, and had I not supported him, he would have sunk upon the pavement.

My limbs were scarcely less weak, but my resolutions were much more strenuous than his. I made light of his indisposition, and endeavoured to persuade him that his vigour would return in proportion to his distance from the city. The moment we should reach a shade, a short respite would restore us to health and cheerfulness.

Nothing could revive his courage or induce him to go on. To return or to proceed was equally impracticable. But, should he be able to return, where should he find a retreat! The danger of relapse was imminent: his own chamber at Thetford's was unoccupied. If he could regain this house, might I not procure him a physician and perform for him the part of nurse.

His present situation was critical and mournful. To remain in the street, exposed to the malignant fervours of the sun, was not to be endured. To carry him in my arms, exceeded my strength. Should I not claim the assistance of the first passenger that appeared?

At that moment a horse and chaise passed us. The vehicle proceeded at a quick pace. He that rode in it might afford us the succour that we needed. He might be persuaded to deviate from his course and convey the helpless Wallace to the house we had just left.

This thought instantly impelled me forward. Feeble as I was, I even ran with speed, in order to overtake the vehicle. My purpose was effected with the utmost difficulty. It fortunately happened that the carriage contained but one person, who stopped at my request. His countenance and guise was mild and encouraging.

Good friend, I exclaimed, here is a young man too indisposed to walk. I want him carried to his lodgings. Will you, for money or for charity, allow him a place in your chaise, and set him down where I shall direct? Observing tokens of hesitation, I continued, you need have no fears to perform this office. He is not sick, but merely feeble. I will not ask twenty minutes, and you may ask what reward you think proper.

Still he hesitated to comply. His business, he said, had not led him into the city. He merely passed along the skirts of it, whence he conceived that no danger would arise. He was desirous of helping the unfortunate, but he could not think of risqueing his own life, in the cause of a stranger, when he had a wife and children depending on his existence and exertions, for bread. It gave him pain to refuse, but he thought his duty to himself and to others required that he should not hazard his safety by compliance.

This plea was irresistable. The mildness of his manner shewed, that he might have been overpowered by persuasion or tempted by reward. I would not take advantage of his tractability; but should have declined his assistance, even if it had been spontaneously offered. I turned away from him in silence, and prepared to return to the spot where I had left my friend. The man prepared to resume his way.

In this perplexity, the thought occurred to me, that, since this person was going into the country, he might, possibly, consent to carry Wallace along with him. I confided greatly in the salutary influence of rural airs. I believed that debility constituted the whole of his complaint; that continuance in the city might occasion his relapse, or, at least, procrastinate his restoration.

I once more addressed myself to the traveller, and inquired in what direction, and how far he was going. To my unspeakable satisfaction, his answer informed me, that his home lay beyond Mr. Hadwin's, and that his road carried him directly past that gentleman's door. He was willing to receive Wallace into his chaise, and to leave him at his uncle's.

This joyous and auspicious occurrence surpassed my fondest

hopes. I hurried with the pleasing tidings to Wallace, who eagerly consented to enter the carriage. I thought not at the moment of myself, or how far the same means of escaping from my danger might be used. The stranger could not be anxious on my account; and Wallace's dejection and weakness may apologize for his not soliciting my company, or expressing his fears for my safety. He was no sooner seated, than the traveller hurried away. I gazed after them, motionless and mute, till the carriage turning a corner, passed beyond my sight.

I had now leisure to revert to my own condition, and to ruminate on that series of abrupt and diversified events that had happened, during the few hours which had been passed in the city: the end of my coming was thus speedily and satisfactorily accomplished. My hopes and fears had rapidly fluctuated; but, respecting this young man, had now subsided into calm and propitious certainty. Before the decline of the sun, he would enter his paternal roof, and diffuse ineffable joy throughout that peaceful and chaste asylum.

This contemplation, though rapturous and soothing speedily gave way to reflections on the conduct which my duty required, and the safe departure of Wallace, afforded me liberty to pursue. To offer myself as a superintendent of the hospital was still my purpose. The languors of my frame might terminate in sickness, but this event it was useless to anticipate. The lofty scite and pure airs of Bush-hill might tend to dissipate my languors and restore me to health. At least, while I had power, I was bound to exert it to the wisest purposes. I resolved to seek the City-hall immediately, and, for that end, crossed the intermediate fields which separated Sassafras from Chesnut-street.

More urgent considerations had diverted my attention from the money which I bore about me, and from the image of the desolate lady to whom it belonged. My intentions, with regard to her, were the same as ever; but now it occurred to me, with new force, that my death might preclude an interview between us, and that it was prudent to dispose, in some useful way, of the money which would otherwise be left to the sport of chance.

The evils which had befallen this city were obvious and

enormous. Hunger and negligence had exasperated the malignity and facilitated the progress of the pestilence. Could this
money be more usefully employed than in alleviating these
evils? During my life, I had no power over it, but my death
would justify me in prescribing the course which it should
take.

How was this course to be pointed out? How might I place
it, so that I should effect my intentions without relinquishing
the possession during my life.

These thoughts were superseded by a tide of new sensations. The weight that incommoded my brows and my stomach was suddenly increased. My brain was usurped by some
benumbing power, and my limbs refused to support me. My
pulsations were quickened, and the prevalence of fever could
no longer be doubted.

Till now, I had entertained a faint hope, that my indisposition would vanish of itself. This hope was at an end. The
grave was before me, and my projects of curiosity or benevolence were to sink into oblivion. I was not bereaved of the
powers of reflection. The consequences of lying in the road,
friendless and unprotected, were sure. The first passenger
would notice me, and hasten to summon one of those carriages which are busy night and day, in transporting its victims
to the hospital.

This fate was, beyond all others, abhorrent to my imagination. To hide me under some roof, where my existence
would be unknown and unsuspected, and where I might perish unmolested and in quiet, was my present wish. Thetford's
or Medlicote's might afford me such an asylum, if it were
possible to reach it.

I made the most strenuous exertions; but they could not
carry me forward more than an hundred paces. Here I rested
on steps, which, on looking up, I perceived to belong to
Welbeck's house.

This incident was unexpected. It led my reflections into a
new train. To go farther, in the present condition of my frame,
was impossible. I was well acquainted with this dwelling. All
its avenues were closed. Whether it had remained unoccupied
since my flight from it, I could not decide. It was evident that,
at present, it was without inhabitants. Possibly it might have

continued in the same condition in which Welbeck had left it. Beds or sofas might be found, on which a sick man might rest, and be fearless of intrusion.

This inference was quickly overturned by the obvious supposition, that every avenue was bolted and locked. This, however, might not be the condition of the bath-house, in which there was nothing that required to be guarded with unusual precautions. I was suffocated by inward, and scorched by external heat; and the relief of bathing and drinking, appeared inestimable.

The value of this prize, in addition to my desire to avoid the observation of passengers, made me exert all my remnant of strength. Repeated efforts at length enabled me to mount the wall; and placed me, as I imagined, in security. I swallowed large draughts of water as soon as I could reach the well.

The effect was, for a time, salutary and delicious. My fervours were abated, and my faculties relieved from the weight which had lately oppressed them. My present condition was unspeakably more advantageous than the former. I did not believe that it could be improved, till, casting my eye vaguely over the building, I happened to observe the shutters of a lower window partly opened.

Whether this was occasioned by design or by accident there was no means of deciding. Perhaps, in the precipitation of the latest possessor, this window had been overlooked. Perhaps it had been unclosed by violence, and afforded entrance to a robber. By what means soever it had happened, it undoubtedly afforded ingress to me. I felt no scruple in profiting by this circumstance. My purposes were not dishonest. I should not injure or purloin any thing. It was laudable to seek a refuge from the well-meant persecutions of those who governed the city. All I sought was the privilege of dying alone.

Having gotten in at the window, I could not but remark that the furniture and its arrangements had undergone no alteration in my absence. I moved softly from one apartment to another, till at length I entered, that which had formerly been Welbeck's bed-chamber.

The bed was naked of covering. The cabinets and closets exhibited their fastenings broken. Their contents were gone. Whether these appearances had been produced by midnight

robbers or by the ministers of law, and the rage of the creditors of Welbeck, was a topic of fruitless conjecture.

My design was now effected. This chamber should be the
scene of my disease and my refuge from the charitable cruelty
of my neighbours. My new sensations, conjured up the hope
that my indisposition might prove a temporary evil. Instead
of pestilential or malignant fever it might be an harmless in-
termittent. Time would ascertain its true nature; meanwhile I
would turn the carpet into a coverlet, supplying my pitcher
with water, and administer without sparing, and without fear,
that remedy which was placed within my reach.

Chapter XX

I LAID myself on the bed and wrapped my limbs in the folds of the carpet. My thoughts were restless and perturbed. I was once more busy in reflecting on the conduct which I ought to pursue, with regard to the bank-bills. I weighed with scrupulous attention, every circumstance that might influence my decision. I could not conceive any more beneficial application of this property, than to the service of the indigent, at this season of multiplied distress, but I considered that if my death were unknown, the house would not be opened or examined till the pestilence had ceased, and the benefits of this application would thus be partly or wholly precluded.

This season of disease, however, would give place to a season of scarcity. The number and wants of the poor, during the ensuing winter, would be deplorably aggravated. What multitudes might be rescued from famine and nakedness by the judicious application of this sum?

But how should I secure this application? To inclose the bills in a letter, directed to some eminent citizen or public officer, was the obvious proceeding. Both of these conditions were fulfilled in the person of the present chief magistrate. To him, therefore, the packet was to be sent.

Paper and the implements of writing were necessary for this end. Would they be found, I asked, in the upper room? If that apartment, like the rest which I had seen, and its furniture had remained untouched, my task would be practicable, but if the means of writing were not to be immediately procured, my purpose, momentous and dear as it was, must be relinquished.

The truth, in this respect, was easily, and ought immediately to be ascertained. I rose from the bed which I had lately taken, and proceeded to the *study*. The entries and stair cases were illuminated by a pretty strong twilight. The rooms, in consequence of every ray being excluded by the closed shutters, were nearly as dark as if it had been midnight. The rooms into which I had already passed, were locked, but its key was in each lock. I flattered myself that the entrance into the *study* would be found in the same condition. The door was shut but no key was to be seen. My hopes were considerably damped by this appearance, but I conceived it to be still possible to enter, since, by chance or by design, the door might be unlocked.

My fingers touched the lock, when a sound was heard as if a bolt, appending to the door on the inside, had been drawn. I was startled by this incident. It betokened that the room was already occupied by some other, who desired to exclude a visitor. The unbarred shutter below was remembered, and associated itself with this circumstance. That this house should be entered by the same avenue, at the same time, and this room should be sought, by two persons was a mysterious concurrence.

I began to question whether I had heard distinctly. Numberless inexplicable noises are apt to assail the ear in an empty dwelling. The very echoes of our steps are unwonted and new. This perhaps was some such sound. Resuming courage, I once more applied to the lock. The door, in spite of my repeated efforts, would not open.

My design was too momentous to be readily relinquished. My curiosity and my fears likewise were awakened. The marks of violence, which I had seen on the closets and cabinets below, seemed to indicate the presence of plunderers. Here was one who laboured for seclusion and concealment.

The pillage was not made upon my property. My weakness would disable me from encountering or mastering a man of violence. To solicit admission into this room would be useless. To attempt to force my way would be absurd. These reflections prompted me to withdraw from the door, but the uncertainty of the conclusions I had drawn, and the importance of gaining access to this apartment, combined to check my steps.

Perplexed as to the means I should employ, I once more tried the lock. This attempt was as fruitless as the former. Though hopeless of any information to be gained by that means, I put my eye to the key-hole. I discovered a light different from what was usually met with at this hour. It was

not the twilight which the sun, imperfectly excluded, produces, but gleams, as from a lamp; yet gleams were fainter and
obscurer than a lamp generally imparts.

Was this a confirmation of my first conjecture? Lamp-light
at noon-day, in a mansion thus deserted, and in a room which
had been the scene of memorable and disastrous events, was
ominous. Hitherto no direct proof had been given of the presence of an human being. How to ascertain his presence, or
whether it were eligible by any means, to ascertain it, were
points on which I had not deliberated.

I had no power to deliberate. My curiosity, impelled me to
call—Is there any one within? Speak.

These words were scarcely uttered, when some one exclaimed, in a voice, vehement but half-smothered—Good
God!—

A deep pause succeeded. I waited for an answer: for somewhat to which this emphatic invocation might be a prelude.
Whether the tones were expressive of surprise or pain, or grief,
was, for a moment dubious. Perhaps the motives which led
me to this house, suggested the suspicion, which, presently
succeeded to my doubts, that the person within was disabled
by sickness. The circumstances of my own condition took
away the improbability from this belief. Why might not another be induced like me to hide himself in this desolate retreat? Might not a servant, left to take care of the house, a
measure usually adopted by the opulent at this time, be seized
by the reigning malady? Incapacitated for exertion, or fearing
to be dragged to the hospital, he has shut himself in this apartment. The robber, it may be, who came to pillage, was overtaken and detained by disease. In either case, detection or
intrusion would be hateful, and would be assiduously eluded.

These thoughts had no tendency to weaken or divert my
efforts to obtain access to this room. The person was a brother
in calamity, whom it was my duty to succour and cherish to
the utmost of my power. Once more I spoke:—

Who is within? I beseech you answer me. Whatever you be,
I desire to do you good and not injury. Open the door and
let me know your condition. I will try to be of use to you.

I was answered by a deep groan, and by a sob counteracted
and devoured as it were by a mighty effort. This token of

distress thrilled to my heart. My terrors wholly disappeared, and gave place to unlimited compassion. I again intreated to be admitted, promising all the succour or consolation which my situation allowed me to afford.

Answers were made in tones of anger and impatience, blended with those of grief—I want no succour—vex me not with your entreaties and offers. Fly from this spot: Linger not a moment lest you participate my destiny and rush upon your death.

These, I considered merely as the effusions of delirium, or the dictates of despair. The style and articulation denoted the speaker to be superior to the class of servants. Hence my anxiety to see and to aid him was increased. My remonstrances were sternly and pertinaciously repelled. For a time, incoherent and impassioned exclamations flowed from him. At length, I was only permitted to hear strong aspirations and sobs, more eloquent and more indicative of grief than any language.

This deportment filled me with no less wonder than commiseration. By what views this person was led hither, by what motives induced to deny himself to my intreaties, was wholly incomprehensible. Again, though hopeless of success, I repeated my request to be admitted.

My perseverance seemed now to have exhausted all his patience, and he exclaimed, in a voice of thunder—Arthur Mervyn! Begone. Linger but a moment and my rage, tygerlike, will rush upon you and rend you limb from limb.

This address petrified me. The voice that uttered this sanguinary menace, was strange to my ears. It suggested no suspicion of ever having heard it before. Yet my accents had betrayed me to him. He was familiar with my name. Notwithstanding the improbability of my entrance into this dwelling, I was clearly recognized and unhesitatingly named!

My curiosity and compassion were in no wise diminished, but I found myself compelled to give up my purpose—I withdrew reluctantly from the door, and once more threw myself upon my bed. Nothing was more necessary in the present condition of my frame, than sleep; and sleep had, perhaps, been possible, if the scene around me had been less pregnant with causes of wonder and panic.

Once more I tasked my memory in order to discover, in
the persons with whom I had hitherto conversed, some resemblance in voice or tones, to him whom I had just heard.
This process was effectual. Gradually my imagination called
up an image, which now, that it was clearly seen, I was astonished had not instantly occurred. Three years ago, a man, by
name Colvill, came on foot, and with a knapsack on his back,
into the district where my father resided. He had learning and
genius, and readily obtained the station for which only he
deemed himself qualified; that of a schoolmaster.

His demeanour was gentle and modest; his habits, as to
sleep, food, and exercise, abstemious and regular. Meditation
in the forest, or reading in his closet, seemed to constitute,
together with attention to his scholars, his sole amusement
and employment. He estranged himself from company, not
because society afforded no pleasure, but because studious seclusion afforded him chief satisfaction.

No one was more idolized by his unsuspecting neighbours.
His scholars revered him as a father, and made under his tuition a remarkable proficiency. His character seemed open to
boundless inspection, and his conduct was pronounced by all
to be faultless.

At the end of a year the scene was changed. A daughter of
one of his patrons, young, artless and beautiful, appeared to
have fallen a prey to the arts of some detestable seducer. The
betrayer was gradually detected, and successive discoveries
shewed that the same artifices had been practised, with the
same success upon many others. Colvill was the arch-villain.
He retired from the storm of vengeance that was gathering
over him, and had not been heard of since that period.

I saw him rarely, and for a short time, and I was a mere
boy. Hence, the failure to recollect his voice, and to perceive
that the voice of him, immured in the room above, was the
same with that of Colvill. Though I had slight reasons for
recognizing his features, or accents, I had abundant cause to
think of him with detestation, and pursue him with implacable
revenge, for the victim of his arts, she whose ruin was first
detected, was—*my sister.*

This unhappy girl, escaped from the upbraidings of her parents, from the contumelies of the world, from the goadings

of remorse, and the anguish flowing from the perfidy and desertion of Colvill, in a voluntary death. She was innocent and lovely. Previous to this evil, my soul was linked with her's by a thousand resemblances and sympathies, as well as by perpetual intercourse from infancy, and by the fraternal relation. She was my sister, my preceptress and friend, but she died—her end was violent, untimely, and criminal!—I cannot think of her without heart-bursting grief, of her destroyer, without a rancour which I know to be wrong, but which I cannot subdue.

When the image of Colvill rushed, upon this occasion, on my thought, I almost started on my feet. To meet him, after so long a separation, here, and in these circumstances, was so unlooked-for and abrupt an event, and revived a tribe of such hateful impulses and agonizing recollections, that a total revolution seemed to have been effected in my frame. His recognition of my person, his aversion to be seen, his ejaculation of terror and surprise on first hearing my voice, all contributed to strengthen my belief.

How was I to act? My feeble frame could but illy second my vengeful purposes; but vengeance, though it sometimes occupied my thoughts, was hindered by my reason, from leading me in any instance, to outrage or even to upbraiding.

All my wishes with regard to this man, were limited to expelling his image from my memory, and to shunning a meeting with him. That he had not opened the door at my bidding, was now a topic of joy. To look upon some bottomless pit, into which I was about to be cast headlong, and alive, was less to be abhorred than to look upon the face of Colvill. Had I known that he had taken refuge in this house, no power should have compelled me to enter it. To be immersed in the infection of the hospital, and to be hurried, yet breathing and observant, to my grave, was a more supportable fate.

I dwell, with self-condemnation and shame, upon this part of my story. To feel extraordinary indignation at vice, merely because we have partaken in an extraordinary degree, of its mischiefs, is unjustifiable. To regard the wicked with no emotion but pity, to be active in reclaiming them, in controlling their malevolence, and preventing or repairing the ills which they produce, is the only province of duty. This lesson, as well as a thousand others, I have yet to learn; but I despair of living long enough for that or any beneficial purpose.

My emotions with regard to Colvill, were erroneous, but omnipotent. I started from my bed, and prepared to rush into the street. I was careless of the lot that should befal me, since no fate could be worse than that of abiding under the same roof with a wretch spotted with so many crimes.

I had not set my feet upon the floor before my precipitation was checked by a sound from above. The door of the study was cautiously and slowly opened. This incident admitted only of one construction, supposing all obstructions removed. Colvill was creeping from his hiding place, and would probably fly with speed from the house. My belief of his sickness was now confuted. An illicit design was congenial with his character and congruous with those appearances already observed.

I had no power or wish to obstruct his flight. I thought of it with transport and once more threw myself upon the bed, and wrapped my averted face in the carpet. He would probably pass this door, unobservant of me, and my muffled face would save me from the agonies connected with the sight of him.

The foot-steps above were distinguishable, though it was manifest that they moved with lightsomeness and circumspection. They reached the stair and descended. The room in which I lay, was, like the rest, obscured by the closed shutters. This obscurity now gave way to a light, resembling that glimmering and pale reflection which I had noticed in the study. My eyes, though averted from the door, were disengaged from the folds which covered the rest of my head, and observed these tokens of Colvill's approach, flitting on the wall.

My feverish perturbations increased as he drew nearer. He reached the door, and stopped. The light rested for a moment. Presently he entered the apartment. My emotions suddenly rose to an height that would not be controlled. I imagined that he approached the bed, and was gazing upon me. At the same moment, by an involuntary impulse, I threw off my covering, and, turning my face, fixed my eyes upon my visitant.

It was as I suspected. The figure, lifting in his right hand a candle, and gazing at the bed, with lineaments and attitude, bespeaking fearful expectation and tormenting doubts, was now beheld. One glance communicated to my senses all the parts of this terrific vision. A sinking at my heart, as if it had been penetrated by a dagger, seized me. This was not enough. I uttered a shriek, too rueful and loud not to have startled the attention of the passengers, if any had, at that moment been passing the street.

Heaven seemed to have decreed that this period should be filled with trials of my equanimity and fortitude. The test of my courage was once more employed to cover me with humiliation and remorse. This second time, my fancy conjured up a spectre, and I shuddered as if the grave were forsaken and the unquiet dead haunted my pillow.

The visage and the shape had indeed preternatural attitudes, but they belonged, not to Colvill, but to—WELBECK.

Chapter XXI

H E WHOM I had accompanied to the midst of the river; whom I had imagined that I saw sink to rise no more, was now before me. Though incapable of precluding the groundless belief of preternatural visitations, I was able to banish the phantom almost at the same instant at which it appeared. Welbeck had escaped from the stream alive; or had, by some inconceivable means, been restored to life.

The first was the most plausible conclusion. It instantly engendered a suspicion, that his plunging into the water was an artifice, intended to establish a belief of his death. His own tale had shewn him to be versed in frauds, and flexible to evil. But was he not associated with Colvill; and what, but a compact in iniquity, could bind together such men?

While thus musing, Welbeck's countenance and gesture displayed emotions too vehement for speech. The glances that he fixed upon me were unstedfast and wild. He walked along the floor, stopping at each moment, and darting looks of eagerness upon me. A conflict of passions kept him mute. At length, advancing to the bed, on the side of which I was now sitting, he addressed me.

What is this? Are you here? In defiance of pestilence, are you actuated by some demon to haunt me, like the ghost of my offences, and cover me with shame? What have I to do with that dauntless, yet guileless front? With that foolishly, confiding, and obsequious, yet erect and unconquerable spirit? Is there no means of evading your pursuit? Must I dip my hands, a second time, in blood; and dig for you a grave by the side of Watson?

These words were listened to with calmness. I suspected and pitied the man, but I did not fear him. His words and his looks were indicative less of cruelty than madness. I looked at him with an air compassionate and wistful. I spoke with mildness and composure.

Mr. Welbeck, you are unfortunate and criminal. Would to God I could restore you to happiness and virtue; but though my desire be strong, I have no power to change your habits or rescue you from misery.

I believed you to be dead. I rejoice to find myself mistaken. While you live, there is room to hope that your errors will be cured; and the turmoils, and inquietudes that have hitherto beset your guilty progress, will vanish by your reverting into better paths.

From me you have nothing to fear. If your welfare will be promoted by my silence on the subject of your history, my silence shall be inviolate. I deem not lightly of my promises. They are given and shall not be recalled.

This meeting was casual. Since I believed you to be dead, it could not be otherwise. You err, if you suppose that any injury will accrue to you from my life; but you need not discard that error. Since my death is coming, I am not averse to your adopting the belief that the event is fortunate to you.

Death is the inevitable and universal lot. When or how it comes, is of little moment. To stand, when so many thousands are falling around me, is not to be expected. I have acted an humble and obscure part in the world, and my career has been short; but I murmur not at the decree that makes it so.

The pestilence is now upon me. The chances of recovery are too slender to deserve my confidence. I came hither to die unmolested, and at peace. All I ask of you is to consult your own safety by immediate flight; and not to disappoint my hopes of concealment, by disclosing my condition to the agents of the hospital.

Welbeck listened with the deepest attention. The wildness of his air disappeared, and gave place to perplexity and apprehension.

You are sick, said he, in a tremulous tone, in which terror was mingled with affection. You know this, and expect not to recover. No mother, nor sister, nor friend will be near to administer food, or medicine, or comfort; yet you can talk calmly; can be thus considerate of others—of me; whose guilt has been so deep, and who has merited so little at your hands!

Wretched coward! Thus miserable as I am, and expect to be, I cling to life. To comply with your heroic counsel, and to fly; to leave you thus desolate and helpless, is the strongest impulse. Fain would I resist it but cannot.

To desert you would be flagitious and dastardly beyond all

former acts, yet to stay with you is to contract the disease and to perish after you.

Life, burthened as it is, with guilt and ignominy, is still dear—yet you exhort me to go; you dispense with my assistance. Indeed, I could be of no use, I should injure myself and profit you nothing. I cannot go into the city and procure a physician or attendant. I must never more appear in the streets of this city. I must leave you then—He hurried to the door. Again, he hesitated. I renewed my intreaties that he would leave me; and encouraged his belief that his presence might endanger himself without conferring the slightest benefit upon me.

Whither should I fly? The wide world contains no asylum for me. I lived but on one condition. I came hither to find what would save me from ruin—from death. I find it not. It has vanished. Some audacious and fortunate hand has snatched it from its place, and now my ruin is complete. My last hope is extinct.

Yes. Mervyn! I will stay with you. I will hold your head. I will put water to your lips. I will watch night and day by your side. When you die, I will carry you by night to the neighbouring field: will bury you, and water your grave with those tears that are due to your incomparable worth and untimely destiny. Then I will lay myself in your bed and wait for the same oblivion.

Welbeck seemed now no longer to be fluctuating between opposite purposes. His tempestuous features subsided into calm. He put the candle, still lighted on the table, and paced the floor with less disorder than at his first entrance.

His resolution was seen to be the dictate of despair. I hoped that it would not prove invincible to my remonstrances. I was conscious that his attendance might preclude, in some degree, my own exertions, and alleviate the pangs of death; but these consolations might be purchased too dear. To receive them at the hazard of his life would be to make them odious.

But if he should remain, what conduct would his companion pursue? Why did he continue in the study when Welbeck had departed? By what motives were those men led hither? I addressed myself to Welbeck.

Your resolution to remain is hasty and rash. By persisting

in it, you will add to the miseries of my condition; you will take away the only hope that I cherished. But, however you may act, Colvill or I must be banished from this roof. What is the league between you? Break it, I conjure you; before his frauds have involved you in inextricable destruction.

Welbeck looked at me with some expression of doubt.

I mean, continued I, the man whose voice I heard above. He is a villain and betrayer. I have manifold proofs of his guilt. Why does he linger behind you? However you may decide, it is fitting that he should vanish.

Alas! said Welbeck, I have no companion; none to partake with me in good or evil. I came hither alone.

How? exclaimed I. Whom did I hear in the room above? Some one answered my interrogations and intreaties, whom I too certainly recognized. Why does he remain?

You heard no one but myself. The design that brought me hither, was to be accomplished without a witness. I desired to escape detection, and repelled your solicitations for admission in a counterfeited voice.

That voice belonged to one from whom I had lately parted. What his merits or demerits are, I know not. He found me wandering in the forests of New-Jersey. He took me to his home. When seized by a lingering malady, he nursed me with fidelity, and tenderness. When somewhat recovered, I speeded hither; but our ignorance of each other's character and views was mutual and profound.

I deemed it useful to assume a voice different from my own. This was the last which I had heard, and this arbitrary and casual circumstance decided my choice.

This imitation was too perfect, and had influenced my fears too strongly, to be easily credited. I suspected Welbeck of some new artifice to baffle my conclusions and mislead my judgment. This suspicion, however, yielded to his earnest and repeated declarations. If Colvill were not here, where had he made his abode? How came friendship and intercourse between Welbeck and him? By what miracle escaped the former from the river, into which I had imagined him forever sunk?

I will answer you, said he, with candour. You know already too much for me to have any interest in concealing any part of my life. You have discovered my existence, and the causes that rescued me from destruction may be told without detriment to my person or fame.

When I leaped into the river, I intended to perish. I harboured no previous doubts of my ability to execute my fatal purpose. In this respect I was deceived. Suffocation would not come at my bidding. My muscles and limbs rebelled against my will. There was a mechanical repugnance to the loss of life which I could not vanquish. My struggles might thrust me below the surface, but my lips were spontaneously shut and excluded the torrent from my lungs. When my breath was exhausted, the efforts that kept me at the bottom were involuntarily remitted, and I rose to the surface.

I cursed my own pusillanimity. Thrice I plunged to the bottom and as often rose again. My aversion to life swiftly diminished, and at length, I consented to make use of my skill in swimming, which has seldom been exceeded, to prolong my existence. I landed in a few minutes on the Jersey shore.

This scheme being frustrated, I sunk into dreariness and inactivity. I felt as if no dependence could be placed upon my courage, as if any effort I should make for self-destruction would be fruitless; yet existence was as void as ever of enjoyment and embellishment. My means of living were annihilated. I saw no path before me. To shun the presence of mankind was my sovereign wish. Since I could not die, by my own hands, I must be content to crawl upon the surface, till a superior fate should permit me to perish.

I wandered into the centre of the wood. I stretched myself on the mossy verge of a brook, and gazed at the stars till they disappeared. The next day was spent with little variation. The cravings of hunger were felt, and the sensation was a joyous one, since it afforded me the practicable means of death. To refrain from food was easy, since some efforts would be needful to procure it, and these efforts should not be made. Thus was the sweet oblivion for which I so earnestly panted, placed within my reach.

Three days of abstinence, and reverie, and solitude succeeded. On the evening of the fourth, I was seated on a rock, with my face buried in my hands. Some one laid his hand upon my shoulder. I started and looked up. I beheld a face, beaming with compassion and benignity. He endeavoured to extort from me the cause of my solitude and sorrow. I disregarded his intreaties, and was obstinately silent.

Finding me invincible in this respect, he invited me to his cottage, which was hard by. I repelled him at first, with impatience and anger, but he was not to be discouraged or intimidated. To elude his persuasions I was obliged to comply. My strength was gone and the vital fabric was crumbling into pieces. A fever raged in my veins, and I was consoled by reflecting that my life was at once assailed by famine and disease.

Meanwhile, my gloomy meditations experienced no respite. I incessantly ruminated on the events of my past life. The long series of my crimes arose daily and afresh to my imagination. The image of Lodi was recalled, his expiring looks and the directions which were mutually given respecting his sister and his property.

As I perpetually revolved these incidents, they assumed new forms, and were linked with new assocations. The volume written by his father, and transferred to me by tokens, which were now remembered to be more emphatic than the nature of the composition seemed to justify, was likewise remembered. It came attended by recollections respecting a volume which I filled, when a youth, with extracts from the Roman and Greek poets. Besides this literary purpose I likewise used to preserve the bank-bills, with the keeping or carriage of which I chanced to be intrusted. This image led me back to the leather-case containing Lodi's property, which was put into my hands at the same time with the volume.

These images now gave birth to a third conception, which darted on my benighted understanding like an electrical flash. Was it possible that part of Lodi's property might be inclosed within the leaves of this volume? In hastily turning it over, I recollected to have noticed leaves whose edges by accident or design adhered to each other. Lodi, in speaking of the sale of his father's West-Indian property, mentioned that the sum obtained for it, was forty thousand dollars. Half only of this sum had been discovered by me. How had the remainder been appropriated? Surely this volume contained it.

The influence of this thought was like the infusion of a new soul into my frame. From torpid and desperate, from inflexible aversion to medicine and food, I was changed in a moment into vivacity and hope, into ravenous avidity for whatever could contribute to my restoration to health.

I was not without pungent regrets and racking fears. That this volume would be ravished away by creditors or plunderers, was possible. Every hour might be that which decided my fate. The first impulse was to seek my dwelling and search for this precious deposit.

Meanwhile, my perturbations and impatience only exasperated my disease. While chained to my bed, the rumour of pestilence was spread abroad. This event, however generally calamitous, was propitious to me, and was hailed with satisfaction. It multiplied the chances that my house and its furniture would be unmolested.

My friend was assiduous and indefatigable in his kindness. My deportment, before and subsequent to the revival of my hopes, was incomprehensible, and argued nothing less than insanity. My thoughts were carefully concealed from him, and all that he witnessed was contradictory and unintelligible.

At length, my strength was sufficiently restored. I resisted all my protector's importunities, to postpone my departure till the perfect confirmation of my health. I designed to enter the city at midnight, that prying eyes might be eluded; to bear with me a candle and the means of lighting it, to explore my way to my ancient study, and to ascertain my future claim to existence and felicity.

I crossed the river this morning. My impatience would not suffer me to wait till evening. Considering the desolation of the city, I thought I might venture to approach thus near, without hazard of detection. The house, at all its avenues was closed. I stole into the back-court. A window-shutter proved to be unfastened. I entered, and discovered closets and cabinets, unfastened and emptied of all their contents. At this spectacle my heart sunk. My books, doubtless, had shared the common destiny. My blood throbbed with painful vehemence as I approached the study and opened the door.

My hopes, that languished for a moment, were revived by the sight of my shelves, furnished as formerly. I had lighted my candle below, for I desired not to awaken observation and suspicion, by unclosing the windows. My eye eagerly sought the spot where I remembered to have left the volume. Its place was empty. The object of all my hopes had eluded my grasp, and disappeared forever.

To paint my confusion, to repeat my execrations on the infatuation, which had rendered, during so long a time, that it was in my possession, this treasure useless to me, and my curses of the fatal interference which had snatched away this prize, would be only aggravations of my disappointment and my sorrow. You found me in this state, and know what followed.

Chapter XXII

THIS NARRATIVE threw new light on the character of Welbeck. If accident had given him possession of this treasure, it was easy to predict on what schemes of luxury and selfishness it would have been expended. The same dependence on the world's erroneous estimation, the same devotion to imposture, and thoughtlessness of futurity, would have constituted the picture of his future life, as had distinguished the past.

This money was another's. To retain it for his own use was criminal. Of this crime he appeared to be as insensible as ever. His own gratification was the supreme law of his actions. To be subjected to the necessity of honest labour, was the heaviest of all evils, and one from which he was willing to escape by the commission of suicide.

The volume which he sought was mine. It was my duty to restore it to the rightful owner, or, if the legal claimant could not be found, to employ it in the promotion of virtue and happiness. To give it to Welbeck was to consecrate it to the purpose of selfishness and misery. My right, legally considered, was as valid as his.

But if I intended not to resign it to him, was it proper to disclose the truth, and explain by whom the volume was purloined from the shelf? The first impulse was to hide this truth: but my understanding had been taught, by recent occurrences, to question the justice, and deny the usefulness of secrecy in any case. My principles were true; my motives were pure: Why should I scruple to avow my principles, and vindicate my actions?

Welbeck had ceased to be dreaded or revered. That awe which was once created by his superiority of age, refinement of manners and dignity of garb, had vanished. I was a boy in years, an indigent and uneducated rustic, but I was able to discern the illusions of power and riches, and abjured every claim to esteem that was not founded on integrity. There was no tribunal before which I should faulter in asserting the truth, and no species of martyrdom which I would not cheerfully embrace in its cause.

After some pause, I said: cannot you conjecture in what way this volume has disappeared?

No: he answered with a sigh. Why, of all his volumes, this only should have vanished, was an inexplicable enigma.

Perhaps, said I, it is less important to know how it was removed, than by whom it is now possessed.

Unquestionably: and yet, unless that knowledge enables me to regain the possession it will be useless.

Useless then it will be, for the present possessor will never return it to you.

Indeed, replied he, in a tone of dejection, your conjecture is most probable. Such a prize is of too much value to be given up.

What I have said, flows not from conjecture, but from knowledge. I know that it will never be restored to you.

At these words, Welbeck looked at me with anxiety and doubt—You *know* that it will not! Have you any knowledge of the book? Can you tell me what has become of it?

Yes, after our separation on the river, I returned to this house. I found this volume and secured it; you rightly suspected its contents. The money was there.

Welbeck started as if he had trodden on a mine of gold. His first emotion was rapturous, but was immediately chastised by some degree of doubt. What has become of it? Have you got it? Is it entire? Have you it with you?

It is unimpaired. I have got it, and shall hold it as a sacred trust for the rightful proprietor.

The tone with which this declaration was accompanied, shook the new born confidence of Welbeck. The rightful Proprietor! true, but I am he. To me only it belongs and to me, you are, doubtless, willing to restore it.

Mr. Welbeck! It is not my desire to give you perplexity or anguish; to sport with your passions. On the supposition of your death, I deemed it no infraction of justice to take this manuscript. Accident unfolded its contents. I could not hesitate to chuse my path. The natural and legal successor of Vincentio Lodi is his sister. To her, therefore, this property belongs, and to her only will I give it.

Presumptuous boy! And this is your sage decision. I tell you that I am the owner, and to me you shall render it. Who is this girl! childish and ignorant! Unable to consult and to act for herself on the most trivial occasion. Am I not, by the appointment of her dying brother, her protector and guardian? Her age produces a legal incapacity of property. Do you imagine that so obvious an expedient, as that of procuring my legal appointment as her guardian, was overlooked by me? If it were neglected, still my title to provide her subsistance and enjoyment is unquestionable.

Did I not rescue her from poverty and prostitution and infamy? Have I not supplied all her wants with incessant solicitude? Whatever her condition required has been plenteously supplied. This dwelling and its furniture, was hers, as far as a rigid jurisprudence would permit. To prescribe her expences and govern her family, was the province of her guardian.

You have heard the tale of my anguish and despair. Whence did they flow but from the frustration of schemes, projected for her benefit, as they were executed with her money and by means which the authority of her guardian fully justified. Why have I encountered this contagious atmosphere, and explored my way, like a thief, to this recess, but with a view to rescue her from poverty and restore to her, her own?

Your scruples are ridiculous and criminal. I treat them with less severity, because your youth is raw and your conceptions crude. But if, after this proof of the justice of my claim, you hesitate to restore the money, I shall treat you as a robber, who has plundered my cabinet and refused to refund his spoil.

These reasonings were powerful and new. I was acquainted with the rights of guardianship. Welbeck had, in some respects, acted as the friend of this lady. To vest himself with this office, was the conduct which her youth and helplessness prescribed to her friend. His title to this money, as her guardian, could not be denied.

But how was this statement compatible with former representations? No mention had then been made of guardianship. By thus acting, he would have thwarted all his schemes for winning the esteem of mankind, and fostering the belief which the world entertained of his opulence and independence.

I was thrown, by these thoughts, into considerable perplexity. If his statement were true, his claim to this money was established, but I questioned its truth. To intimate my doubts of his veracity, would be to provoke abhorrence and outrage.

His last insinuation was peculiarly momentous. Suppose him the fraudulent possessor of this money, shall I be justified in taking it away by violence under pretence of restoring it to the genuine proprietor, who, for aught I know, may be dead, or with whom, at least, I may never procure a meeting? But will not my behaviour on this occasion, be deemed illicit? I entered Welbeck's habitation at midnight, proceeded to his closet, possessed myself of portable property, and retired unobserved. Is not guilt imputable to an action like this?

Welbeck waited with impatience for a conclusion to my pause. My perplexity and indecision did not abate, and my silence continued. At length, he repeated his demands, with new vehemence. I was compelled to answer. I told him, in few words, that his reasonings had not convinced me of the equity of his claim, and that my determination was unaltered.

He had not expected this inflexibility from one in my situation. The folly of opposition, when my feebleness and loneliness were contrasted with his activity and resources, appeared to him monstrous and glaring, but his contempt was converted into rage and fear when he reflected that this folly might finally defeat his hopes. He had probably determined to obtain the money, let the purchase cost what it would, but was willing to exhaust pacific expedients before he should resort to force. He might likewise question whether the money was within his reach: I had told him that I had it, but whether it was now about me, was somewhat dubious; yet, though he used no direct inquiries, he chose to proceed on the supposition of its being at hand. His angry tones were now changed into those of remonstrance and persuasion.

Your present behaviour, Mervyn, does not justify the expectation I had formed of you. You have been guilty of a base theft. To this you have added the deeper crime of ingratitude, but your infatuation and folly are, at least, as glaring as your guilt. Do you think I can credit your assertions that you keep this money for another, when I recollect that six weeks have passed since you carried it off? Why have you not sought the owner and restored it to her? If your intentions had been honest, would you have suffered so long a time to elapse without doing this? It is plain, that you designed to keep it for your own use.

But whether this were your purpose or not, you have no longer power to restore it or retain it. You say that you came hither to die. If so, what is to be the fate of the money? In your present situation you cannot gain access to the lady. Some other must inherit this wealth. Next to *Signora Lodi*, whose right can be put in competition with mine? But if you will not give it to me, on my own account, let it be given in trust for her. Let me be the bearer of it to her own hands. I have already shewn you that my claim to it, as her guardian, is legal and incontrovertible, but this claim, I wave. I will merely be the executor of your will. I will bind myself to comply with your directions by any oath, however solemn and tremendous, which you shall prescribe.

As long as my own heart acquitted me, these imputations of dishonesty affected me but little. They excited no anger, because they originated in ignorance, and were rendered plausible to Welbeck, by such facts as were known to him. It was needless to confute the charge by elaborate and circumstantial details.

It was true that my recovery was, in the highest degree, improbable, and that my death would put an end to my power over this money; but had I not determined to secure its useful application, in case of my death? This project was obstructed by the presence of Welbeck, but I hoped that his love of life would induce him to fly. He might wrest this volume from me by violence, or he might wait till my death should give him peaceable possession. But these, though probable events, were not certain, and would, by no means, justify the voluntary surrender. His strength, if employed for this end, could not be resisted; but then it would be a sacrifice, not to choice, but necessity.

Promises were easily given, but were surely not to be confided in. Welbeck's own tale, in which it could not be imagined that he had aggravated his defects, attested the frailty of his virtue. To put into his hands, a sum like this, in expectation of his delivering it to another, when my death would cover the transaction with impenetrable secrecy, would be, indeed, a proof of that infatuation which he thought proper to impute to me.

These thoughts influenced my resolutions, but they were revolved in silence. To state them verbally was useless. They would not justify my conduct in his eyes. They would only exasperate dispute, and impel him to those acts of violence which I was desirous of preventing. The sooner this controversy should end, and my measure be freed from the obstruction of his company, the better.

Mr. Welbeck, said I, my regard to your safety compels me to wish that this interview should terminate. At a different time, I should not be unwilling to discuss this matter. Now it will be fruitless. My conscience points out to me too clearly the path I should pursue for me to mistake it. As long as I have power over this money I shall keep it for the use of the unfortunate lady, whom I have seen in this house. I shall exert myself to find her, but if that be impossible, I shall appropriate it in a way, in which you shall have no participation.

I will not repeat the contest that succeeded between my forbearance and his passions. I listened to the dictates of his rage and his avarice in silence. Astonishment, at my inflexibility, was blended with his anger. By turns he commented on the guilt and on the folly of my resolutions. Sometimes his emotions would mount into fury, and he would approach me in a menacing attitude, and lift his hand as if he would exterminate me at a blow. My languid eyes, my cheeks glowing, and my temples throbbing with fever, and my total passiveness, attracted his attention and arrested his stroke. Compassion would take place of rage, and the belief be revived that remonstrances and arguments would answer his purpose.

Chapter XXIII

T HIS SCENE lasted, I know not how long. Insensibly the
passions and reasonings of Welbeck assumed a new form.
A grief, mingled with perplexity, overspread his countenance.
He ceased to contend or to speak. His regards were withdrawn from me, on whom they had hitherto been fixed; and
wandering or vacant, testified a conflict of mind, terrible beyond any that my young imagination had ever conceived.

For a time, he appeared to be unconscious of my presence.
He moved to and fro with unequal steps, and with gesticulations, that possessed an horrible but indistinct significance.
Occasionally he struggled for breath, and his efforts were directed to remove some choking impediment.

No test of my fortitude had hitherto occurred equal to that
to which it was now subjected. The suspicion which this deportment suggested was vague and formless. The tempest
which I witnessed was the prelude of horror. These were
throes which would terminate in the birth of some gigantic
and sanguinary purpose. Did he meditate to offer a bloody
sacrifice? Was his own death or was mine to attest the magnitude of his despair, or the impetuosity of his vengeance?

Suicide was familiar to his thoughts. He had consented to
live but on one condition: that of regaining possession of this
money. Should I be justified in driving him, by my obstinate
refusal, to this fatal consummation of his crimes? Yet my fear
of this catastrophe was groundless. Hitherto he had argued
and persuaded, but this method was pursued because it was
more eligible than the employment of force, or than procrastination.

No. These were tokens that pointed to me. Some unknown
instigation was at work within him, to tear away his remnant
of humanity, and fit him for the office of my murderer. I knew
not how the accumulation of guilt could contribute to his
gratification or security. His actions had been partially exhibited and vaguely seen. What extenuations or omissions had
vitiated his former or recent narrative; how far his actual per-

formances were congenial with the deed which was now to be perpetrated, I knew not.

These thoughts lent new rapidity to my blood. I raised my head from the pillow, and watched the deportment of this man, with deeper attention. The paroxysm which controlled him, at length, in some degree subsided. He muttered, Yes. It must come. My last humiliation must cover me. My last confession must be made. To die, and leave behind me this train of enormous perils, must not be.

O Clemenza! O Mervyn! Ye have not merited that I should leave you a legacy of persecution and death. Your safety must be purchased at what price my malignant destiny will set upon it. The cord of the executioner, the note of everlasting infamy, is better than to leave you beset by the consequences of my guilt. It must not be.

Saying this, Welbeck cast fearful glances at the windows and door. He examined every avenue and listened. Thrice he repeated this scrutiny. Having, as it seemed, ascertained that no one lurked within audience, he approached the bed. He put his mouth close to my face. He attempted to speak, but once more examined the apartment with suspicious glances.

He drew closer, and at length, in a tone, scarcely articulate and suffocated with emotion, he spoke: Excellent but fatally obstinate youth! Know at least the cause of my importunity. Know at least the depth of my infatuation and the enormity of my guilt.

The bills—Surrender them to me, and save yourself from persecution and disgrace. Save the woman whom you wish to benefit, from the blackest imputations; from hazard to her life and her fame; from languishing in dungeons; from expiring on the gallows!—

The bills—O save me from the bitterness of death. Let the evils, to which my miserable life has given birth terminate here and in myself. Surrender them to me, for—

There he stopped. His utterance was choaked by terror. Rapid glances were again darted at the windows and door. The silence was uninterrupted except by far-off sounds, produced by some moving carriage. Once more, he summoned resolution, and spoke:

Surrender them to me, for—*they are forged*.

Formerly I told you, that a scheme of forgery had been conceived. Shame would not suffer me to add, that my scheme was carried into execution. The bills were fashioned, but my fears contended against my necessities, and forbade me to attempt to exchange them. The interview with Lodi saved me from the dangerous experiment. I enclosed them in that volume, as the means of future opulence, to be used when all other, and less hazardous resources should fail.

In the agonies of my remorse, at the death of Watson, they were forgotten. They afterwards recurred to recollection. My wishes pointed to the grave; but the stroke that should deliver me from life, was suspended only till I could hasten hither, get possession of these papers, and destroy them.

When I thought upon the chances that should give them an owner; bring them into circulation; load the innocent with suspicion; and lead them to trial, and, perhaps, to death, my sensations were fraught with agony: earnestly as I panted for death, it was necessarily deferred till I had gained possession of and destroyed these papers.

What now remains? You have found them. Happily they have not been used. Give them, therefore, to me, that I may crush at once the brood of mischiefs which they could not but generate.

This disclosure was strange. It was accompanied with every token of sincerity. How had I tottered on the brink of destruction! If I had made use of this money, in what a labyrinth of misery might I not have been involved! My innocence could never have been proved. An alliance with Welbeck could not have failed to be inferred. My career would have found an ignominious close; or, if my punishment had been transmuted into slavery and toil, would the testimony of my conscience have supported me?

I shuddered at the view of those disasters from which I was rescued by the miraculous chance which led me to this house. Welbeck's request was salutary to me, and honourable to himself. I could not hesitate a moment in compliance. The notes were enclosed in paper, and deposited in a fold of my clothes. I put my hand upon them.

My motion and attention was arrested at the instant, by a

noise which arose in the street. Foot-steps were heard upon the pavement before the door, and voices, as if busy in discourse. This incident was adapted to infuse the deepest alarm into myself and my companion. The motives of our trepidation were, indeed, different, and were infinitely more powerful in my case than in his. It portended to me nothing less than the loss of my asylum, and condemnation to an hospital.

Welbeck hurried to the door, to listen to the conversation below. This interval was pregnant with thought. That impulse which led my reflections from Welbeck to my own state, past away in a moment, and suffered me to meditate anew upon the terms of that confession which had just been made.

Horror at the fate which this interview had enabled me to shun, was uppermost in my conceptions. I was eager to surrender these fatal bills. I held them for that purpose in my hand, and was impatient for Welbeck's return. He continued at the door; stooping, with his face averted, and eagerly attentive to the conversation in the street.

All the circumstances of my present situation tended to arrest the progress of thought, and chain my contemplations to one image; but even now there was room for foresight and deliberation. Welbeck intended to destroy these bills. Perhaps he had not been sincere; or, if his purpose had been honestly disclosed, this purpose might change when the bills were in his possession. His poverty and sanguineness of temper, might prompt him to use them.

That this conduct was evil and would only multiply his miseries, could not be questioned. Why should I subject his frailty to this temptation? The destruction of these bills was the loudest injunction of my duty; was demanded by every sanction which bound me to promote the welfare of mankind.

The means of destruction were easy. A lighted candle stood on a table, at the distance of a few yards. Why should I hesitate a moment to annihilate so powerful a cause of error and guilt? A passing instant was sufficient. A momentary lingering might change the circumstances that surrounded me, and frustrate my project.

My languors were suspended by the urgencies of this occasion. I started from my bed and glided to the table. Seizing the notes with my right hand, I held them in the flame of the candle, and then threw them, blazing, on the floor.

The sudden illumination was perceived by Welbeck. The cause of it appeared to suggest itself as soon. He turned, and marking the paper where it lay, leaped to the spot, and extinguished the fire with his foot. His interposition was too late. Only enough of them remained to inform him of the nature of the sacrifice.

Welbeck now stood, with limbs trembling, features aghast, and eyes glaring upon me. For a time he was without speech. The storm was gathering in silence, and at length burst upon me. In a tone menacing and loud, he exclaimed:

Wretch! What have you done?

I have done justly. These notes were false. You desired to destroy them that they might not betray the innocent. I applauded your purpose, and have saved you from the danger of temptation by destroying them myself.

Maniac! Miscreant! To be fooled by so gross an artifice! The notes were genuine. The tale of their forgery was false, and meant only to wrest them from you. Execrable and perverse idiot! Your deed has sealed my perdition. It has sealed your own. You shall pay for it with your blood. I will slay you by inches. I will stretch you as you have stretched me, on the rack.

During this speech, all was frenzy and storm in the countenance and features of Welbeck. Nothing less could be expected than that the scene would terminate in some bloody catastrophe. I bitterly regretted the facility with which I had been deceived, and the precipitation of my sacrifice. The act, however lamentable, could not be revoked. What remained, but to encounter or endure its consequences with unshrinking firmness?

The contest was too unequal. It is possible that the frenzy which actuated Welbeck might have speedily subsided. It is more likely that his passions would have been satiated with nothing but my death. This event was precluded by loud knocks at the street-door, and calls by some one on the pavement without, of—Who is within? Is any one within?

These noises gave a new direction to Welbeck's thoughts. They are coming, said he. They will treat you as a sick man and a theif. I cannot desire you to suffer a worse evil than they will inflict. I leave you to your fate. So saying, he rushed out of the room.

Though confounded and stunned by this rapid succession of events, I was yet able to pursue measures for eluding these detested visitants. I first extinguished the light, and then, observing that the parley in the street continued and grew louder, I sought an asylum in the remotest corner of the house. During my former abode here, I noticed, that a trap door opened in the ceiling of the third story, to which you were conducted by a movable stair or ladder. I considered that this, probably, was an opening into a narrow and darksome nook, formed by the angle of the roof. By ascending, drawing after me the ladder, and closing the door, I should escape the most vigilant search.

Enfeebled as I was by my disease, my resolution rendered me strenuous. I gained the uppermost room, and mounting the ladder, found myself at a sufficient distance from suspicion. The stair was hastily drawn up, and the door closed. In a few minutes, however, my new retreat proved to be worse than any for which it was possible to change it. The air was musty, stagnant, and scorchingly hot. My breathing became difficult, and I saw that to remain here ten minutes, would unavoidably produce suffocation.

My terror of intruders had rendered me blind to the consequences of immuring myself in this chearless recess. It was incumbent on me to extricate myself as speedily as possible. I attempted to lift the door. My first effort was successless. Every inspiration was quicker, and more difficult than the former. As my terror, so my strength and my exertions increased. Finally my trembling hand lighted on a nail that was imperfectly driven into the wood, and which by affording me a firmer hold, enabled me at length to raise it, and to inhale the air from beneath.

Relieved from my new peril, by this situation, I bent an attentive ear through the opening with a view to ascertain if the house had been entered or if the outer door was still beset, but could hear nothing. Hence I was authorized to conclude, that the people had departed, and that I might resume my former station without hazard.

Before I descended, however, I cast a curious eye over this recess—It was large enough to accommodate an human being. The means by which it was entered were easily concealed. Though narrow and low, it was long, and were it possible to contrive some inlet for the air, one studious of concealment, might rely on its protection with unbounded confidence.

My scrutiny was imperfect by reason of the faint light which found its way through the opening, yet it was sufficient to set me afloat on a sea of new wonders and subject my fortitude to a new test—

Here Mervyn paused in his narrative. A minute passed in silence and seeming indecision. His perplexities gradually disappeared, and he continued.

I have promised to relate the momentous incidents of my life, and have hitherto been faithful in my enumeration. There is nothing which I more detest than equivocation and mystery. Perhaps, however, I shall now incur some imputation of that kind. I would willingly escape the accusation, but confess that I am hopeless of escaping it.

I might indeed have precluded your guesses and surmises by omitting to relate what befel me from the time of my leaving my chamber till I regained it. I might deceive you by asserting that nothing remarkable occurred, but this would be false, and every sacrifice is trivial which is made upon the altar of sincerity. Beside, the time may come when no inconvenience will arise from minute descriptions of the objects which I now saw and of the reasonings and inferences which they suggested to my understanding. At present, it appears to be my duty to pass them over in silence, but it would be needless to conceal from you that the interval, though short, and the scrutiny, though hasty, furnished matter which my curiosity devoured with unspeakable eagerness, and from which consequences may hereafter flow, deciding on my peace and my life.

Nothing however occurred which could detain me long in this spot. I once more sought the lower story and threw myself on the bed which I had left. My mind was thronged with the images flowing from my late adventures. My fever had gradually increased, and my thoughts were deformed by inaccuracy and confusion.

My heart did not sink when I reverted to my own condition. That I should quickly be disabled from moving, was readily perceived. The fore-sight of my destiny was stedfast and clear. To linger for days in this comfortless solitude; to ask in vain, not for powerful restoratives or alleviating cordials, but for water to moisten my burning lips, and abate the torments of thirst; ultimately, to expire in torpor or phrenzy, was the fate to which I looked forward, yet I was not terrified. I seemed to be sustained by a preternatural energy. I felt as if the opportunity of combating such evils was an enviable privilege, and though none would witness my victorious magnanimity, yet to be conscious that praise was my due, was all that my ambition required.

These sentiments were doubtless tokens of delirium. The excruciating agonies which now seized upon my head, and the cord which seemed to be drawn across my breast, and which, as my fancy imagined, was tightened by some forcible hand, with a view to strangle me, were incompatible with sober and coherent views.

Thirst was the evil which chiefly oppressed me. The means of relief were pointed out by nature and habit. I rose and determined to replenish my pitcher at the well. It was easier, however, to descend than to return. My limbs refused to bear me, and I sat down upon the lower step of the stair-case. Several hours had elapsed since my entrance into this dwelling, and it was now night.

My imagination now suggested a new expedient. Medlicote was a generous and fearless spirit. To put myself under his protection, if I could walk as far as his lodgings, was the wisest proceeding which I could adopt. From this design, my incapacity to walk thus far, and the consequences of being discovered in the street, had hitherto deterred me. These impediments were now, in the confusion of my understanding, overlooked or despised, and I forthwith set out upon this hopeless expedition.

The doors communicating with the court, and through the court, with the street, were fastened by inside bolts. These were easily withdrawn, and I issued forth with alacrity and confidence. My perturbed senses and the darkness hindered me from discerning the right way. I was conscious of this difficulty, but was not disheartened. I proceeded, as I have since discovered, in a direction different from the true, but hesitated not, till my powers were exhausted, and I sunk upon the ground. I closed my eyes, and dismissed all fear, and all fore-sight of futurity. In this situation I remained some hours, and should probably have expired on this spot, had not I attracted your notice, and been provided under this roof, with all that medical skill, and the tenderest humanity could suggest.

In consequence of your care, I have been restored to life and to health. Your conduct was not influenced by the prospect of pecuniary recompence, of service, or of gratitude. It is only in one way that I am able to heighten the gratification which must flow from reflection on your conduct—by shewing that the being whose life you have prolonged, though uneducated, ignorant and poor, is not profligate and worthless, and will not dedicate that life which your bounty has given, to mischievous or contemptible purposes.

Chapter I

H ERE ENDED the narrative of Mervyn. Surely its incidents were of no common kind. During this season of pestilence, my opportunities of observation had been numerous, and I had not suffered them to pass unimproved. The occurrences which fell within my own experience bore a general resemblance to those which had just been related, but they did not hinder the latter from striking on my mind with all the force of novelty. They served no end, but as vouchers for the truth of the tale.

Surely the youth had displayed inimitable and heroic qualities. His courage was the growth of benevolence and reason, and not the child of insensibility and the nursling of habit. He had been qualified for the encounter of gigantic dangers by no laborious education. He stept forth upon the stage, unfurnished, by anticipation or experience, with the means of security against fraud; and yet, by the aid of pure intentions, had frustrated the wiles of an accomplished and veteran deceiver.

I blessed the chance which placed the youth under my protection. When I reflected on that tissue of nice contingences which led him to my door, and enabled me to save from death a being of such rare endowments, my heart overflowed with joy, not unmingled with regrets and trepidation. How many have been cut off by this disease, in their career of virtue and their blossom-time of genius! How many deeds of heroism and self-devotion are ravished from existence, and consigned to hopeless oblivion!

I had saved the life of this youth. This was not the limit of my duty or my power. Could I not render that life profitable to himself and to mankind? The gains of my profession were slender; but these gains were sufficient for his maintenance as well as my own. By residing with me, partaking my instructions, and reading my books, he would, in a few years, be fitted for the practice of physic. A science, whose truths are so conducive to the welfare of mankind, and which comprehends the whole system of nature, could not but gratify a mind so beneficent and strenuous as his.

This scheme occurred to me as soon as the conclusion of his tale allowed me to think. I did not immediately mention it; since the approbation of my wife, of whose concurrence, however, I entertained no doubt, was previously to be obtained. Dismissing it, for the present, from my thoughts, I reverted to the incidents of his tale.

The lady whom Welbeck had betrayed and deserted, was not unknown to me. I was but too well acquainted with her fate. If she had been single in calamity, her tale would have been listened to with insupportable sympathy; but the frequency of the spectacle of distress, seems to lessen the compassion with which it is reviewed. Now that those scenes are only remembered, my anguish is greater than when they were witnessed. Then every new day was only a repetition of the disasters of the foregoing. My sensibility, if not extinguished, was blunted; and I gazed upon the complicated ills of poverty and sickness with a degree of unconcern, on which I should once have reflected with astonishment.

The fate of Clemenza Lodi was not, perhaps, more signal than many which have occurred. It threw detestable light upon the character of Welbeck, and showed him to be more inhuman than the tale of Mervyn had evinced him to be. That man, indeed, was hitherto imperfectly seen. The time had not come which should fully unfold the enormity of his transgressions and the complexity of his frauds.

There lived in a remote quarter of the city a woman, by name Villars, who passed for the widow of an English officer. Her manners and mode of living were specious. She had three daughters, well trained in the school of fashion, and elegant in person, manners and dress. They had lately arrived from Europe, and for a time, received from their neighbors that respect to which their education and fortune appeared to lay claim.

The fallacy of their pretensions slowly appeared. It began to be suspected that their subsistence was derived not from pension or patrimony, but from the wages of pollution. Their

habitation was clandestinely frequented by men who were unfaithful to their secret; one of these was allied to me by ties,
which authorized me in watching his steps and detecting his
errors, with a view to his reformation. From him I obtained
a knowledge of the genuine character of these women.

A man like Welbeck, who was the slave of depraved appetites, could not fail of being quickly satiated with innocence
and beauty. Some accident introduced him to the knowledge
of this family, and the youngest daughter found him a proper
subject on which to exercise her artifices. It was to the frequent demands made upon his purse, by this woman, that part
of the embarrassments in which Mervyn found him involved,
are to be ascribed.

To this circumstance must likewise be imputed his anxiety
to transfer to some other the possession of the unhappy
stranger. Why he concealed from Mervyn his connection with
Lucy Villars, may be easily imagined. His silence, with regard
to Clemenza's asylum, will not create surprise, when it is
told that she was placed with Mrs. Villars. On what conditions
she was received under this roof, cannot be so readily conjectured. It is obvious, however, to suppose, that advantage was
to be taken of her ignorance and weakness, and that they
hoped, in time, to make her an associate in their profligate
schemes.

The appearance of pestilence, meanwhile, threw them into
panick, and they hastened to remove from danger. Mrs. Villars
appears to have been a woman of no ordinary views. She
stooped to the vilest means of amassing money; but this
money was employed to secure to herself and her daughters
the benefits of independence. She purchased the house which
she occupied in the city, and a mansion in the environs, well
built and splendidly furnished. To the latter, she and her family, of which the Italian girl was now a member, retired at the
close of July.

I have mentioned that the source of my intelligence was a
kinsman, who had been drawn from the paths of sobriety and
rectitude, by the impetuosity of youthful passions. He had
power to confess and deplore, but none to repair his errors.
One of these women held him by a spell which he struggled
in vain to dissolve, and by which, in spite of resolutions and

remorses, he was drawn to her feet, and made to sacrifice to her pleasure, his reputation and his fortune.

My house was his customary abode during those intervals in which he was persuaded to pursue his profession. Some time before the infection began its progress, he had disappeared. No tidings was received of him, till a messenger arrived intreating my assistance. I was conducted to the house of Mrs. Villars, in which I found no one but my kinsman. Here it seems he had immured himself from my enquiries, and on being seized by the reigning malady, had been deserted by the family, who, ere they departed, informed me by a messenger of his condition.

Despondency combined with his disease to destroy him. Before he died, he informed me fully of the character of his betrayers. The late arrival, name and personal condition of Clemenza Lodi were related. Welbeck was not named, but was described in terms, which, combined with the narrative of Mervyn, enabled me to recognize the paramour of Lucy Villars in the man whose crimes had been the principal theme of our discourse.

Mervyn's curiosity was greatly roused when I intimated my acquaintance with the fate of Clemenza. In answer to his eager interrogations, I related what I knew. The tale plunged him into reverie. Recovering, at length, from his thoughtfulness, he spoke.

Her condition is perilous. The poverty of Welbeck will drive him far from her abode. Her profligate protectors will entice her or abandon her to ruin. Cannot she be saved?

I know not, answered I, by what means.

The means are obvious. Let her remove to some other dwelling. Let her be apprized of the vices of those who surround her. Let her be intreated to fly. The will need only be inspired, the danger need only be shown, and she is safe, for she will remove beyond its reach.

Thou art an adventurous youth. Who wilt thou find to undertake the office? Who will be persuaded to enter the house of a stranger, seek without an introduction the presence of this girl, tell her that the house she inhabits is an house of prostitution, prevail on her to believe the tale, and persuade her to accompany him? Who will open his house to the fugitive? Whom will you convince that her illicit intercourse with Welbeck, of which the opprobrious tokens cannot be concealed, has not fitted her for the company of prostitutes, and made her unworthy of protection? Who will adopt into their family, a stranger, whose conduct has incurred infamy, and whose present associates have, no doubt, made her worthy of the curse?

True. These are difficulties which I did not foresee. Must she then perish! Shall not something be done to rescue her from infamy and guilt?

It is neither in your power nor in mine to do any thing.

The lateness of the hour put an end to our conversation and summoned us to repose. I seized the first opportunity of imparting to my wife the scheme which had occurred, relative to our guest; with which, as I expected, she readily concurred. In the morning, I mentioned it to Mervyn. I dwelt upon the benefits that adhered to the medical profession, the power which it confers of lightening the distresses of our neighbors, the dignity which popular opinion annexes to it, the avenue which it opens to the acquisition of competence, the freedom from servile cares which attends it, and the means of intellectual gratification with which it supplies us.

As I spoke, his eyes sparkled with joy. Yes, said he with vehemence, I willingly embrace your offer. I accept this benefit, because I know that if my pride should refuse it, I should prove myself less worthy than you think, and give you pain, instead of that pleasure which I am bound to confer. I would enter on the duties and studies of my new profession immediately, but somewhat is due to Mr. Hadwin and his daughters. I cannot vanquish my inquietudes respecting them, but by returning to Malverton and ascertaining their state with my own eyes. You know in what circumstances I parted with Wallace and Mr. Hadwin. I am not sure, that either of them ever reached home, or that they did not carry the infection along with them. I now find myself sufficiently strong to perform the journey, and proposed to have acquainted you, at this interview, with my intentions. An hour's delay is superfluous, and I hope you will consent to my setting out immediately. Rural exercise and air, for a week or fortnight, will greatly contribute to my health.

No objection could be made to this scheme. His narrative had excited no common affection in our bosoms for the Hadwins. His visit could not only inform us of their true state, but would dispel that anxiety which they could not but entertain respecting our guest. It was a topic of some surprize that neither Wallace nor Hadwin had returned to the city, with a view to obtain some tidings of their friend. It was more easy to suppose them to have been detained by some misfortune, than by insensibility or indolence. In a few minutes Mervyn bade us adieu, and set out upon his journey, promising to acquaint us with the state of affairs, as soon as possible after his arrival. We parted from him with reluctance, and found no consolation but in the prospect of his speedy return.

During his absence, conversation naturally turned upon those topics which were suggested by the narrative and deportment of this youth. Different conclusions were formed by his two auditors. They had both contracted a deep interest in his welfare, and an ardent curiosity as to those particulars which his unfinished story had left in obscurity. The true character and actual condition of Welbeck, were themes of much speculation. Whether he were dead or alive, near or distant from his ancient abode, was a point on which neither Mervyn, nor any of those with whom I had means of intercourse, afforded any information. Whether he had shared the common fate, and had been carried by the collectors of the dead from the highway or the hovel to the pits opened alike for the rich and the poor, the known and the unknown; whether he had escaped to a foreign shore, or were destined to re-appear upon this stage, were questions involved in uncertainty.

The disappearance of Watson would, at a different time, have excited much enquiry and suspicion; but as this had taken place on the eve of the epidemic, his kindred and friends would acquiesce, without scruple, in the belief that he had been involved in the general calamity, and was to be numbered among the earliest victims. Those of his profession usually resided in the street where the infection began, and where its ravages had been most destructive; and this circumstance would corroborate the conclusions of his friends.

I did not perceive any immediate advantage to flow from imparting the knowledge I had lately gained to others. Shortly after Mervyn's departure to Malverton, I was visited by Wortley. Enquiring for my guest, I told him that, having recovered his health, he had left my house. He repeated his invectives against the villainy of Welbeck, his suspicions of Mervyn, and his wishes for another interview with the youth. Why had I suffered him to depart, and whither had he gone?

He has gone for a short time into the country. I expect him to return in less than a week, when you will meet with him here as often as you please, for I expect him to take up his abode in this house.

Much astonishment and disapprobation were expressed by my friend. I hinted that the lad had made disclosures to me, which justified my confidence in his integrity. These proofs of his honesty were not of a nature to be indiscriminately unfolded. Mervyn had authorized me to communicate so much of his story to Wortley, as would serve to vindicate him from the charge of being Welbeck's copartner in fraud; but this end would only be counteracted by an imperfect tale, and the full recital, though it might exculpate Mervyn, might produce inconveniences by which this advantage would be outweighed.

Wortley, as might be naturally expected, was by no means satisfied with this statement. He suspected that Mervyn was a wily imposter; that he had been trained in the arts of fraud, under an accomplished teacher; that the tale which he had told to me, was a tissue of ingenious and plausible lies; that the mere assertions, however plausible and solemn, of one like him, whose conduct had incurred such strong suspicions, were unworthy of the least credit.

It cannot be denied, continued my friend, that he lived with Welbeck at the time of his elopement; that they disappeared together; that they entered a boat, at Pine-street wharf, at midnight; that this boat was discovered by the owner in the possession of a fisherman at Red-bank, who affirmed that he had found it stranded near his door, the day succeeding that on which they disappeared. Of all this, I can supply you with incontestible proof. If, after this proof, you can give credit to his story, I shall think you made of very perverse and credulous materials.

The proof you mention, said I, will only enhance his credibility. All the facts which you have stated, have been admitted by him. They constitute an essential portion of his narrative.

What then is the inference? Are not these evidences of a compact between them? Has he not acknowledged this compact in confessing that he knew Welbeck was my debtor; that he was apprized of his flight, but that, (what matchless effrontery!) he had promised secrecy, and would, by no means, betray him? You say he means to return; but of that I doubt. You will never see his face more. He is too wise to thrust himself again into the noose: but I do not utterly despair of lighting upon Welbeck. Old Thetford, Jamieson and I, have sworn to hunt him through the world. I have strong hopes that he has not strayed far. Some intelligence has lately been received, which has enabled us to place our hounds upon the scent. He may double and skulk; but if he does not fall into our toils at last, he will have the agility and cunning, as well as the malignity of devils.

The vengeful disposition thus betrayed by Wortley, was not without excuse. The vigor of his days had been spent in acquiring a slender capital: his diligence and honesty had succeeded, and he had lately thought his situation such as to justify marriage with an excellent woman, to whom he had for years been betrothed, but from whom his poverty had hitherto compelled him to live separate. Scarcely had this alliance taken place, and the full career of nuptial enjoyments begun, when his ill fate exposed him to the frauds of Welbeck, and brought him, in one evil hour, to the brink of insolvency.

Jamieson and Thetford, however, were rich, and I had not till now been informed that they had reasons for pursuing Welbeck with peculiar animosity. The latter was the uncle of him whose fate had been related by Mervyn, and was one of those who employed money, not as the medium of traffic, but as in itself a commodity. He had neither wines nor cloths, to transmute into silver. He thought it a tedious process to exchange to day, one hundred dollars for a cask or bale, and to-morrow exchange the bale or cask for an hundred *and ten* dollars. It was better to give the hundred for a piece of paper, which, carried forthwith to the money changers, he could procure an hundred twenty-three and three-fourths. In short, this man's coffers were supplied by the despair of honest men and the stratagems of rogues. I did not immediately suspect how this man's prudence and indefatigable attention to his own interest should allow him to become the dupe of Welbeck.

What, said I, is old Thetford's claim upon Welbeck?

It is a claim, he replied, that, if it ever be made good, will doom Welbeck to imprisonment and wholsome labor for life.

How? Surely it is nothing more than debt.

Have you not heard? But that is no wonder. Happily you are a stranger to mercantile anxieties and revolutions. Your fortune does not rest on a basis which an untoward blast may sweep away, or four strokes of a pen may demolish. That hoary dealer in suspicions was persuaded to put his hand to three notes for eight hundred dollars each. The *eight* was then dextrously prolonged to eigh*teen*; they were duly deposited in time and place, and the next day Welbeck was credited for fifty-three hundred and seventy-three, which an hour after, were *told out* to his messenger. Hard to say whether the old man's grief, shame or rage be uppermost. He disdains all comfort but revenge, and that he will procure at any price. Jamieson, who deals in the same *stuff* with Thetford, was outwitted in the same manner, to the same amount, and on the same day.

This Welbeck must have powers above the common rate of mortals. Grown grey in studying the follies and the stratagems of men, these veterans were overreached. No one pities them. 'Twere well if his artifices had been limited to such, and he had spared the honest and the poor. It is for his injuries to men who have earned their scanty subsistence without forfeiting their probity, that I hate him, and shall exult to see him suffer all the rigors of the law. Here Wortley's engagements compelled him to take his leave.

Chapter II

WHILE MUSING upon these facts, I could not but reflect with astonishment on the narrow escapes which Mervyn's virtue had experienced. I was by no means certain that his fame or his life was exempt from all danger, or that the suspicions which had already been formed respecting him, could possibly be wiped away. Nothing but his own narrative, repeated with that simple but nervous eloquence, which we had witnessed, could rescue him from the most heinous charges. Was there any tribunal that would not acquit him on merely hearing his defence?

Surely the youth was honest. His tale could not be the fruit of invention; and yet, what are the bounds of fraud? Nature has set no limits to the combinations of fancy. A smooth exterior, a show of virtue, and a specious tale, are, a thousand times, exhibited in human intercourse by craft and subtlety. Motives are endlessly varied, while actions continue the same; and an acute penetration may not find it hard to select and arrange motives, suited to exempt from censure any action that an human being can commit.

Had I heard Mervyn's story from another, or read it in a book, I might, perhaps, have found it possible to suspect the truth; but, as long as the impression, made by his tones, gestures and looks, remained in my memory, this suspicion was impossible. Wickedness may sometimes be ambiguous, its mask may puzzle the observer; our judgment may be made to faulter and fluctuate, but the face of Mervyn is the index of an honest mind. Calm or vehement, doubting or confident, it is full of benevolence and candor. He that listens to his words may question their truth, but he that looks upon his countenance when speaking, cannot withhold his faith.

It was possible, however, to find evidence, supporting or confuting his story. I chanced to be acquainted with a family, by name Althorpe, who were natives of that part of the country where his father resided. I paid them a visit, and, after a few preliminaries, mentioned, as if by accident, the name of Mervyn. They immediately recognized this name as belonging

436

to one of their ancient neighbors. The death of the wife and sons, and the seduction of the only daughter by Colvil, with many pathetic incidents connected with the fate of this daughter, were mentioned.

This intelligence induced me to inquire of Mrs. Althorpe, a sensible and candid woman, if she were acquainted with the recent or present situation of this family.

I cannot say much, she answered, of my own knowledge. Since my marriage, I am used to spend a few weeks of summer, at my father's, but am less inquisitive than I once was into the concerns of my old neighbors. I recollect, however, when there, last year, during *the fever*, to have heard that Sawny Mervyn had taken a second wife; that his only son, a youth of eighteen, had thought proper to be highly offended with his father's conduct, and treated the new mistress of the house with insult and contempt. I should not much wonder at this, seeing children are so apt to deem themselves unjustly treated by a second marriage of their parent, but it was hinted that the boy's jealousy and discontent was excited by no common cause. The new mother was not much older than himself, had been a servant of the family, and a criminal intimacy had subsisted between her, while in that condition, and the son. Her marriage with his father was justly accounted by their neighbors, a most profligate and odious transaction. The son, perhaps, had, in such a case, a right to scold, but he ought not to have carried his anger to such extremes as have been imputed to him. He is said to have grinned upon her with contempt, and even to have called her *strumpet* in the presence of his father and of strangers.

It was impossible for such a family to keep together. Arthur took leave one night to possess himself of all his father's cash, mount the best horse in his meadow, and elope. For a time, no one knew whither he had gone. At last, one was said to have met with him in the streets of this city, metamorphosed from a rustic lad into a fine gentleman. Nothing could be quicker than this change, for he left the country on a Saturday morning, and was seen in a French frock and silk stockings, going into Christ's Church the next day. I suppose he kept it up with an high hand, as long as his money lasted.

My father paid us a visit last week, and among other country news, told us that Sawny Mervyn had sold his place. His wife had persuaded him to try his fortune in the Western Country. The price of his hundred acres here would purchase a thousand there, and the man being very gross and ignorant, and withall, quite a simpleton, found no difficulty in perceiving that a thousand are ten times more than an hundred. He was not aware that a rood of ground upon Schuylkill is ten fold better than an acre on the Tenessee.

The woman turned out to be an artful profligate. Having sold his ground and gotten his money, he placed it in her keeping, and she, to enjoy it with the more security, ran away to the city; leaving him to prosecute his journey to Kentucky, moneyless and alone. Sometime after, Mr. Althorpe and I were at the play, when he pointed out to me a groupe of females in an upper box, one of whom was no other than Betty Laurence. It was not easy to recognize, in her present gaudy trim, all flaunting with ribbons and shining with trinkets, the same Betty who used to deal out pecks of potatoes and superintend her basket of cantilopes in the Jersey market, in paste-board bonnet and linsey petticoat. Her companions were of the infamous class. If Arthur were still in the city, there is no doubt that the mother and son might renew the ancient terms of their acquaintance.

The old man, thus robbed and betrayed, sought consolation in the bottle, of which he had been at all times overfond. He wandered from one tavern to another till his credit was exhausted, and then was sent to jail, where, I believe, he is likely to continue till his death. Such, my friend, is the history of the Mervyns.

What proof, said I, have you of the immoral conduct of the son? of his mistreatment of his mother, and his elopement with his father's horse and money?

I have no proof but the unanimous report of Mervyn's neighbors. Respectable and honest men have affirmed, in my hearing, that they have been present when the boy treated his mother in the way that I have described. I was, besides, once in company with the old man, and heard him bitterly inveigh against his son, and charge him with the fact of stealing his horse and money. I well remember that tears rolled from his eyes while talking on the subject. As to his being seen in the city the next day after his elopement, dressed in a most costly and fashionable manner, I can doubt that as little as the rest, for he that saw him was my father, and you who know my father, know what credit is due to his eyes and his word. He had seen Arthur often enough not to be mistaken, and described his appearance with great exactness. The boy is extremely handsome, give him his due; has dark hazle eyes, auburn hair, and very elegant proportions. His air and gate have nothing of the clown in them. Take away his jacket and trowsers, and you have as spruce a fellow as ever came from dancing-school or college. He is the exact picture of his mother, and the most perfect contrast to the sturdy legs, squat figure, and broad, unthinking, sheepish face of the father that can be imagined. You must confess that his appearance here is a pretty strong proof of the father's assertions. The money given for these clothes could not possibly have been honestly acquired. It is to be presumed that they were bought or stolen, for how else should they have been gotten?

What was this lad's personal deportment during the life of his mother, and before his father's second marriage?

Very little to the credit of his heart or his intellects. Being the youngest son, the only one who at length survived, and having a powerful resemblance to herself, he became the mother's favorite. His constitution was feeble, and he loved to stroll in the woods more than to plow or sow. This idleness was much against the father's inclination and judgment; and, indeed, it was the foundation of all his vices. When he could be prevailed upon to do any thing it was in a bungling manner, and so as to prove that his thoughts were fixed on any thing except his business. When his assistance was wanted he was never to be found at hand. They were compelled to search for him among the rocks and bushes, and he was generally discovered sauntering along the bank of the river, or lolling in the shade of a tree. This disposition to inactivity and laziness, in so young a man, was very strange. Persons of his age are rarely fond of work, but then they are addicted to company, and sports, and exercises. They ride, or shoot, or frolic; but this being moped away his time in solitude, never associated with other young people, never mounted an horse but when he could not help it, and never fired a gun or angled for a fish in his life. Some people supposed him to be half an idiot, or, at least, not to be in his right mind; and, indeed, his conduct was so very perverse and singular, that I do not wonder at those who accounted for it in this way.

But, surely, said I, he had some object of pursuit. Perhaps he was addicted to books.

Far from it. On the contrary, his aversion to school was as great as his hatred of the plough. He never could get his lessons or bear the least constraint. He was so much indulged by his mother at home, that tasks and discipline of any kind were intolerable. He was a perpetual truant; till the master one day attempting to strike him, he ran out of the room and never entered it more. The mother excused and countenanced his frowardness, and the foolish father was obliged to give way. I do not believe he had two months' schooling in his life.

Perhaps, said I, he preferred studying by himself, and at liberty. I have known boys endowed with great curiosity and aptitude to learning, who never could endure set tasks, and spurned at the pedagogue and his rod.

I have known such likewise, but this was not one of them. I know not whence he could derive his love of knowledge or the means of acquiring it. The family were totally illiterate. The father was a Scotch peasant, whose ignorance was so great that he could not sign his name. His wife, I believe, could read, and might sometimes decypher the figures in an almanac, but that was all. I am apt to think, that the son's ability was not much greater. You might as well look for silver platters or marble tables in his house, as for a book or a pen.

I remember calling at their house one evening in the winter before last. It was intensely cold; and my father, who rode with me, having business with Sawney Mervyn, we stopped a minute at his gate; and, while the two old men were engaged in conversation, I begged leave to warm myself by the kitchen fire. Here, in the chimney-corner, seated on a block, I found Arthur busily engaged in *knitting stockings*! I thought this a whimsical employment for a young active man. I told him so, for I wanted to put him to the blush; but he smiled in my face, and answered, without the least discomposure, just as whimsical a business for a young active woman. Pray, did you never knit a stocking?

Yes; but that was from necessity. Were I of a different sex, or did I possess the strength of a man, I should rather work in my field or study my book.

Rejoice that you are a woman, then, and are at liberty to pursue that which costs least labor and demands most skill. You see, though a man, I use your privilege, and prefer knitting yarn to threshing my brain with a book or the barn-floor with a flail.

I wonder, said I contemptuously, you do not put on the petticoat as well as handle the needle.

Do not wonder, he replied: it is because I hate a petticoat incumbrance as much as I love warm feet. Look there (offering the stocking to my inspection) is it not well done?

I did not touch it, but sneeringly said, excellent! I wonder you do not apprentice yourself to a taylor.

He looked at me with an air of ridiculous simplicity and said, how prone the woman is to *wonder*. You call the work excellent, and yet *wonder* that I do not make myself a slave to improve my skill! Did you learn needle-work from seven years' squatting on a taylor's board? Had you come to me, I would have taught you in a day.

I was taught at school.

And paid your instructor?

To be sure.

'Twas liberty and money thrown away. Send your sister, if you have one, to me, and I will teach her without either rod or wages. Will you?

You have an old and a violent antipathy, I believe, to any thing like a school.

True. It was early and violent. Had not you?

No. I went to school with pleasure; for I thought to read and write were accomplishments of some value.

Indeed? Then I misunderstood you just now. I thought you said, that, had you the strength of a man, you should prefer the plough and the book to the needle. Whence, supposing you a female, I inferred that you had a woman's love for the needle and a fool's hatred of books.

My father calling me from without, I now made a motion to go. Stay, continued he with great earnestness, throwing aside his knitting apparatus, and beginning in great haste to pull off his stockings. Draw these stockings over your shoes. They will save your feet from the snow while walking to your horse.

Half angry, and half laughing, I declined the offer. He had drawn them off, however, and holding them in his hand, be persuaded, said he; only lift your feet, and I will slip them on in a trice.

Finding me positive in my refusal, he dropped the stockings; and, without more ado, caught me up in his arms, rushed out of the room, and, running barefoot through the snow, set me fairly on my horse. All was done in a moment, and before I had time to reflect on his intentions. He then seized my hand, and, kissing it with great fervor, exclaimed, a thousand thanks to you for not accepting my stockings. You have thereby saved yourself and me the time and toil of drawing on and drawing off. Since you have taught me to wonder, let me practice the lesson in wondering at your folly, in wearing worsted shoes and silk stockings at a season like this. Take my counsel, and turn your silk to worsted and your worsted to leather. Then may you hope for warm feet and dry. What! Leave the gate without a blessing on your counsellor?

I spurred my horse into a gallop, glad to escape from so strange a being. I could give you many instances of behaviour equally singular, and which betrayed a mixture of shrewdness and folly, of kindness and impudence, which justified, perhaps, the common notion that his intellects were unsound. Nothing was more remarkable than his impenetrability to ridicule and censure. You might revile him for hours, and he would listen to you with invincible composure. To awaken anger or shame in him was impossible. He would answer, but in such a way as to show him totally unaware of your true meaning. He would afterwards talk to you with all the smiling affability and freedom of an old friend. Every one despised him for his idleness and folly, no less conspicuous in his words than his actions; but no one feared him, and few were angry with him, till after the detection of his commerce with *Betty*, and his inhuman treatment of his father.

Have you good reasons for supposing him to have been illicitly connected with that girl?

Yes. Such as cannot be discredited. It would not be proper for me to state these proofs. Nay, he never denied it. When reminded, on one occasion, of the inference which every impartial person would draw from appearances, he acknowledged, with his usual placid effrontery, that the inference was unavoidable. He even mentioned other concurring and contemporary incidents, which had eluded the observation of his censurer, and which added still more force to the conclusion. He was studious to palliate the vices of this woman as long as he was her only paramour; but after her marriage with his father, the tone was changed. He confessed that she was tidy, notable, industrious; but, then, she was a prostitute. When charged with being instrumental in making her such, and when his companions dwelt upon the depravity of reviling her for vices which she owed to him: True, he would say, there is depravity and folly in the conduct you describe. Make me out, if you please, to be a villain. What then? I was talking not of myself, but of Betty. Still this woman is a prostitute. If it were I that made her such, with more confidence may I make the charge. But think not that I blame Betty. Place me in her situation, and I should have acted just so. I should have formed just such notions of my interest, and pursued it by the same means. Still, say I, I would fain have a different woman for my father's wife, and the mistress of this family.

Chapter III

THIS CONVERSATION was interrupted by a messenger from my wife, who desired my return immediately. I had some hopes of meeting with Mervyn, some days having now elapsed since his parting from us, and not being conscious of any extraordinary motives for delay. It was Wortley, however, and not Mervyn, to whom I was called.

My friend came to share with me his suspicions and inquietudes respecting Welbeck and Mervyn. An accident had newly happened which had awakened these suspicions afresh. He desired a patient audience while he explained them to me. These were his words.

To-day a person presented me a letter from a mercantile friend at Baltimore. I easily discerned the bearer to be a sea captain. He was a man of sensible and pleasing aspect, and was recommended to my friendship and counsel in the letter which he brought. The letter stated, that a man, by name Amos Watson, by profession a mariner, and a resident at Baltimore, had disappeared in the summer of last year, in a mysterious and incomprehensible manner. He was known to have arrived in this city from Jamaica, and to have intended an immediate journey to his family, who lived at Baltimore; but he never arrived there, and no trace of his existence has since been discovered. The bearer had come to investigate, if possible, the secret of his fate, and I was earnestly intreated to afford him all the assistance and advice in my power, in the prosecution of his search. I expressed my willingness to serve the stranger, whose name was Williams; and, after offering him entertainment at my house, which was thankfully accepted, he proceeded to unfold to me the particulars of this affair. His story was this.

On the 20th of last June, I arrived, said he, from the West-Indies, in company with captain Watson. I commanded the ship in which he came as a passenger, his own ship being taken and confiscated by the English. We had long lived in habits of strict friendship, and I loved him for his own sake, as well as because he had married my sister. We landed in the morning, and went to dine with Mr. Keysler, since dead, but who then lived in Water-street. He was extremely anxious to visit his family, and having a few commissions to perform in the city, which would not demand more than a couple of hours, he determined to set out next morning in the stage. Meanwhile, I had engagements which required me to repair with the utmost expedition to New-York. I was scarcely less anxious than my brother to reach Baltimore, where my friends also reside, but there was an absolute necessity of going eastward. I expected, however, to return hither in three days, and then to follow Watson home. Shortly after dinner we parted; he to execute his commissions, and I to embark in the mail-stage.

In the time prefixed I returned. I arrived early in the morning, and prepared to depart again at noon. Meanwhile, I called at Keysler's. This is an old acquaintance of Watson's and mine; and, in the course of talk, he expressed some surprize that Watson had so precipitately deserted his house. I stated the necessity there was for Watson's immediate departure *southward*, and added, that no doubt my brother had explained this necessity.

Why, said Keysler, it is true, Captain Watson mentioned his intention of leaving town early next day; but then he gave me reason to expect that he would sup and lodge with me that night, whereas he has not made his appearance since. Beside his trunk was brought to my house. This, no doubt, he intended to carry home with him, but here it remains still. It is not likely that in the hurry of departure his baggage was forgotten. Hence, I inferred that he was still in town, and have been puzzling myself these three days with conjectures, as to what is become of him. What surprizes me more is, that, on enquiring among the few friends which he has in this city, I find them as ignorant of his motions as myself. I have not, indeed, been wholly without apprehensions that some accident or other has befallen him.

I was not a little alarmed by this intimation. I went myself, agreeably to Keysler's directions, to Watson's friends, and made anxious enquiries, but none of them had seen my brother since his arrival. I endeavored to recollect the commissions which he designed to execute, and, if possible, to trace him to the spot where he last appeared. He had several packets to deliver, one of which was addressed to Walter Thetford. Him, after some enquiry, I found out, but unluckily he chanced to be in the country. I found, by questioning a clerk who transacted his business in his absence, that a person, who answered the minute description which I gave of Watson, had been there on the day on which I parted with him, and had left papers relative to the capture of one of Thetford's vessels by the English. This was the sum of the information he was able to afford me.

I then applied to three merchants for whom my brother had letters. They all acknowledged the receipt of these letters, but they were delivered through the medium of the post-office.

I was extremely anxious to reach home. Urgent engagements compelled me to go on without delay. I had already exhausted all the means of enquiry within my reach, and was obliged to acquiesce in the belief, that Watson had proceeded homeward at the time appointed, and left, by forgetfulness or accident, his trunk behind him. On examining the books kept at the stage offices, his name no where appeared, and no conveyance by water had occurred during the last week. Still the only conjecture I could form, was that he had gone homeward.

Arriving at Baltimore, I found that Watson had not yet made his appearance. His wife produced a letter, which, by the post mark, appeared to have been put into the office at Philadelphia, on the morning after our arrival, and on which he had designed to commence his journey. This letter had been written by my brother, in my presence, but I had dissuaded him from sending it, since the same coach that should bear the letter, was likewise to carry himself. I had seen him put it unwafered in his pocket-book, but this letter, unaltered in any part, and containing money which he had at first intended to enclose in it, was now conveyed to his wife's hand. In this letter he mentioned his design of setting out for Baltimore, on the *twenty-first*, yet, on that day the letter itself had been put into the office.

We hoped that a short time would clear up this mystery, and bring the fugitive home, but from that day till the present, no atom of intelligence has been received concerning him. The yellow-fever, which quickly followed, in this city, and my own engagements, have hindered me, till now, from coming hither and resuming the search.

My brother was one of the most excellent of men. His wife loved him to distraction, and, together with his children, depended for subsistence upon his efforts. You will not, therefore, be surprized that his disappearance excited, in us, the deepest consternation and distress; but I have other, and peculiar reasons for wishing to know his fate. I gave him several bills of exchange on merchants of Baltimore, which I had received in payment of my cargo, in order that they might, as soon as possible, be presented and accepted. These have disappeared with the bearer. There is likewise another circumstance that makes his existence of no small value.

There is an English family, who formerly resided in Jamaica, and possessed an estate of great value, but who, for some years, have lived in the neighborhood of Baltimore. The head of this family died a year ago, and left a widow and three daughters. The lady tho't it eligible to sell her husband's property in Jamaica, the Island becoming hourly more exposed to the chances of war and revolution, and transfer it to the United States, where she purposes henceforth to reside. Watson had been her husband's friend, and his probity and disinterestedness being well known, she entrusted him with legal powers to sell this estate. This commission was punctually performed, and the purchase money was received. In order to confer on it the utmost possible security, he rolled up four bills of exchange, drawn upon opulent merchants of London, in a thin sheet of lead, and depositing this roll in a leathern girdle, fastened it round his waist, and under his clothes; a second set he gave to me, and a third he dispatched to Mr. Keysler, by a vessel which sailed a few days before him. On our arrival in this city, we found that Keysler had received those transmitted to him, and which he had been charged to keep till our arrival. They were now produced, and, together with those which I had carried, were delivered to Watson. By him they were joined to those in the girdle, which he still wore, conceiving this method of conveyance to be safer than any other, and, at the same time, imagining it needless, in so short a journey as remained to be performed, to resort to other expedients.

The sum which he thus bore about him, was no less than ten thousand pounds sterling. It constituted the whole patrimony of a worthy and excellent family, and the loss of it reduces them to beggary. It is gone with Watson, and whither Watson has gone, it is impossible even to guess.

You may now easily conceive, Sir, the dreadful disasters which may be connected with this man's fate, and with what immeasurable anxiety his family and friends have regarded his disappearance. That he is alive, can scarcely be believed, for in what situation could he be placed in which he would not be able and willing to communicate some tidings of his fate to his family?

Our grief has been unspeakably aggravated by the suspicions which Mrs. Maurice and her friends have allowed themselves to admit. They do not scruple to insinuate, that Watson, tempted by so great a prize, has secretly embarked for England, in order to obtain payment for these bills, and retain the money for his own use.

No man was more impatient of poverty than Watson, but no man's honesty was more inflexible. He murmured at the destiny that compelled him to sacrifice his ease, and risk his life upon the ocean in order to procure the means of subsistence; and all the property which he had spent the best part of his life in collecting, had just been ravished away from him by the English; but if he had yielded to this temptation at any time, it would have been on receiving these bills at Jamaica. Instead of coming hither, it would have been infinitely more easy and convenient to have embarked directly for London; but none, who thoroughly knew him, can, for a moment, harbor a suspicion of his truth.

If he be dead, and if the bills are not to be recovered, yet, to ascertain this, will, at last, serve to vindicate his character. As long as his fate is unknown, his fame will be loaded with the most flagrant imputations, and if these bills be ever paid in London, these imputations will appear to be justified. If he has been robbed, the robber will make haste to secure the payment, and the Maurices may not unreasonably conclude that the robber was Watson himself. Many other particulars were added by the stranger, to show the extent of the evils flowing from the death of his brother, and the loss of the papers which he carried with him.

I was greatly at a loss, continued Wortley, what directions or advice to afford this man. Keysler, as you know, died early of the pestilence; but Keysler was the only resident in this city with whom Williams had any acquaintance. On mentioning the propriety of preventing the sale of these bills in America, by some public notice, he told me that this caution had been early taken; and I now remembered seeing the advertisement, in which the bills had been represented as having been lost or stolen in this city, and a reward of a thousand dollars was offered to any one who should restore them. This caution had been published in September, in all the trading towns from Portsmouth to Savannah, but had produced no satisfaction.

I accompanied Williams to the mayor's office, in hopes of finding in the records of his proceedings, during the last six months, some traces of Watson, but neither these records nor the memory of the magistrate, afforded us any satisfaction. Watson's friends had drawn up, likewise, a description of the person and dress of the fugitive, an account of the incidents attending his disappearance, and of the papers which he had in his possession, with the manner in which these papers had been secured. These had been already published in the Southern newspapers, and have been just re-printed in our own. As the former notice had availed nothing, this second expedient was thought necessary to be employed.

After some reflection, it occurred to me that it might be proper to renew the attempt which Williams had made to trace the footsteps of his friend to the moment of his final disappearance. He had pursued Watson to Thetford's, but Thetford himself had not been seen, and he had been contented with the vague information of his clerk. Thetford and his family, including his clerk, had perished, and it seemed as if this source of information was dried up. It was possible, however, that old Thetford might have some knowledge of his nephew's transactions, by which some light might chance to be thrown upon this obscurity. I therefore called on him, but found him utterly unable to afford me the light that I wished. My mention of the packet which Watson had brought to Thetford, containing documents respecting the capture of a certain ship, reminded him of the injuries which he had received from Welbeck, and excited him to renew his menaces and imputations on that wretch. Having somewhat exhausted this rhetoric, he proceeded to tell me what connection there was between the remembrance of his injuries and the capture of this vessel.

This vessel and its cargo were, in fact, the property of Welbeck. They had been sent to a good market and had been secured by an adequate insurance. The value of this ship and cargo, and the validity of the policy he had taken care to ascertain by means of his two nephews, one of whom had gone out supercargo. This had formed his inducement to lend his three notes to Welbeck, in exchange for three other notes, the whole amount of which included the *equitable interest* of *five per cent. per month* on his own loan. For the payment of these notes, he by no means relied, as the world foolishly imagined, on the seeming opulence and secret funds of Welbeck. These were illusions too gross to have any influence on him. He was too old a bird to be decoyed into the net by *such* chaff. No; his nephew, the supercargo, would of course receive the produce of the voyage, and so much of this produce as would pay his debt. He had procured the owner's authority to intercept its passage from the pocket of his nephew to that of Welbeck. In case of loss, he had obtained a similar security upon the policy. Jamieson's proceedings had been the same with his own, and no affair in which he had ever engaged, had appeared to be more free from hazard than this. Their calculations, however, though plausible, were defeated. The ship was taken and condemned, for a cause which rendered the insurance ineffectual.

I bestowed no time in reflecting on this tissue of extortions and frauds, and on that course of events which so often disconcerts the stratagems of cunning. The names of Welbeck and Watson were thus associated together, and filled my thoughts with restlessness and suspicion. Welbeck was capable of any wickedness. It was possible an interview had happened between these men, and that the fugitive had been someway instrumental in Watson's fate. These thoughts were mentioned to Williams, whom the name of Welbeck threw into the utmost perturbation. On finding that one of this name had dwelt in this city, and, that he had proved a villain, he instantly admitted the most dreary forebodings.

I have heard, said Williams, the history of this Welbeck a score of times from my brother. There formerly subsisted a very intimate connection between them. My brother had conferred upon one whom he thought honest, innumerable benefits, but all his benefits had been repaid by the blackest treachery. Welbeck's character and guilt had often been made the subject of talk between us, but, on these occasions, my brother's placid and patient temper forsook him. His grief for the calamities which had sprung from this man, and his desire of revenge, burst all bounds, and transported him to a pitch of temporary frenzy. I often enquired in what manner he intended to act, if a meeting should take place between them. He answered, that doubtless he should act like a maniac, in defiance of his sober principles, and of the duty which he owed his family.

What, said I, would you stab or pistol him?

No! I was not born for an assassin. I would upbraid him in such terms as the furious moment might suggest, and then challenge him to a meeting, from which either he or I should not part with life. I would allow time for him to make his peace with Heaven, and for me to blast his reputation upon earth, and to make such provision for my possible death, as duty and discretion would prescribe.

Now, nothing is more probable than that Welbeck and my brother have met. Thetford would of course mention his name and interest in the captured ship, and hence the residence of this detested being in this city, would be made known. Their meeting could not take place without some dreadful consequence. I am fearful that to that meeting we must impute the disappearance of my brother.

Chapter IV

HERE WAS new light thrown upon the character of Welbeck, and new food administered to my suspicions. No conclusion could be more plausible than that which Williams had drawn; but how should it be rendered certain? Walter Thetford, or some of his family, had possibly been witnesses of something, which, added to our previous knowledge, might strengthen or prolong that clue, one end of which seemed now to be put into our hands; but Thetford's father-in-law was the only one of his family, who, by seasonable flight from the city, had escaped the pestilence. To him, who still resided in the country, I repaired with all speed, accompanied by Williams.

The old man being reminded, by a variety of circumstances, of the incidents of that eventful period, was, at length, enabled to relate that he had been present at the meeting which took place between Watson and his son Walter, when certain packets were delivered by the former, relative, as he quickly understood, to the condemnation of a ship in which Thomas Thetford had gone supercargo. He had noticed some emotion of the stranger, occasioned by his son's mentioning the concern which Welbeck had in the vessel. He likewise remembered the stranger's declaring his intention of visiting Welbeck, and requesting Walter to afford him directions to his house.

Next morning at the breakfast table, continued the old man, I adverted to yesterday's incidents, and asked my son how Welbeck had borne the news of the loss of his ship. He bore it, says Walter, as a man of his wealth ought to bear so trivial a loss. But there was something very strange in his behaviour, says my son, when I mentioned the name of the captain who brought the papers; and when I mentioned the captain's design of paying him a visit, he stared upon me, for a moment, as if he were frighted out of his wits, and then, snatching up his hat, ran furiously out of the house. This was all my son said upon that occasion; but, as I have since heard, it was on that very night, that Welbeck absconded from his creditors.

I have this moment returned from this interview with old Thetford. I come to you, because I thought it possible that Mervyn, agreeably to your expectations, had returned, and I wanted to see the lad once more. My suspicions with regard to him have been confirmed, and a warrant was this day issued for apprehending him as Welbeck's accomplice.

I was startled by this news. My friend, said I, be cautious how you act, I beseech you. You know not in what evils you may involve the innocent. Mervyn I know to be blameless; but Welbeck is indeed, a villain. The latter I shall not be sorry to see brought to justice, but the former, instead of meriting punishment, is entitled to rewards.

So you believe, on the mere assertion of the boy; perhaps, his plausible lies might produce the same effect upon me, but I must stay till he thinks proper to exert his skill. The suspicions to which he is exposed will not easily be obviated; but if he has any thing to say in his defence, his judicial examination will afford him the suitable opportunity. Why are you so much afraid to subject his innocence to this test? It was not till you heard his tale, that your own suspicions were removed. Allow me the same privilege of unbelief.

But you do me wrong, in deeming me the cause of his apprehension. It is Jamieson and Thetford's work, and they have not proceeded on shadowy surmises and the impulses of mere revenge. Facts have come to light of which you are wholly unaware, and which, when known to you, will conquer even your incredulity as to the guilt of Mervyn.

Facts? Let me know them, I beseech you. If Mervyn has deceived me, there is an end to my confidence in human nature. All limits to dissimulation, and all distinctions between vice and virtue will be effaced. No man's word, no force of collateral evidence shall weigh with me an hair.

It was time, replied my friend, that your confidence in smooth features and fluent accents should have ended long ago. Till I gained from my present profession, some knowledge of the world, a knowledge which was not gained in a moment, and has not cost a trifle, I was equally wise in my own conceit; and, in order to decide upon the truth of any one's pretensions, needed only a clear view of his face and a distinct hearing of his words. My folly, in that respect, was only to be cured, however, by my own experience, and I suppose your credulity will yield to no other remedy. These are the facts.

Mrs. Wentworth, the proprietor of the house in which Welbeck lived, has furnished some intelligence respecting Mervyn, whose truth cannot be doubted, and which furnishes the strongest evidence of a conspiracy between this lad and his employer. It seems, that, some years since, a nephew of this lady left his father's family clandestinely, and has not been heard of since. This nephew was intended to inherit her fortunes, and her anxieties and enquiries respecting him have been endless and incessant. These, however, have been fruitless. Welbeck, knowing these circumstances, and being desirous of substituting a girl whom he had moulded for his purpose, in place of the lost youth, in the affections of the lady while living, and in her testament when dead, endeavored to persuade her that the youth had died in some foreign country. For this end, Mervyn was to personate a kinsman of Welbeck who had just arrived from Europe, and who had been a witness of her nephew's death. A story was, no doubt, to be contrived, where truth should be copied with the most exquisite dexterity, and the lady, being prevailed upon to believe the story, the way was cleared for accomplishing the remainder of the plot.

In due time, and after the lady's mind had been artfully prepared by Welbeck, the pupil made his appearance; and, in a conversation full of studied ambiguities, assured the lady, that her nephew was dead. For the present he declined relating the particulars of his death, and displayed a constancy and intrepidity in resisting her intreaties, that would have been admirable in a better cause. Before she had time to fathom this painful mystery, Welbeck's frauds were in danger of detection, and he and his pupil suddenly disappeared.

While the plot was going forward, there occurred an incident which the plotters had not foreseen or precluded, and which possibly might have created some confusion or impediment in their designs. A bundle was found one night in the street, consisting of some coarse clothes, and containing, in the midst of it, the miniature portrait of Mrs. Wentworth's nephew. It fell into the hands of one of that lady's friends, who immediately dispatched the bundle to her. Mervyn, in his interview with this lady, spied the portrait on the mantle-piece. Led by some freak of fancy, or some web of artifice, he introduced the talk respecting her nephew, by boldly claiming it as his; but, when the mode in which it had been found was mentioned, he was disconcerted and confounded, and precipitately withdrew.

This conduct, and the subsequent flight of the lad, afforded ground enough to question the truth of his intelligence respecting her nephew; but it has since been confuted, in a letter just received from her brother in England. In this letter she is informed, that her nephew had been seen by one who knew him well, in Charleston; that some intercourse took place between the youth and the bearer of the news, in the course of which the latter had persuaded the nephew to return to his family, and that the youth had given some tokens of compliance. The letter-writer, who was father to the fugitive, had written to certain friends at Charleston, intreating them to use their influence with the runaway to the same end, and, at any rate, to cherish and protect him. Thus, I hope you will admit that the duplicity of Mervyn is demonstrated.

The facts which you have mentioned, said I, after some pause, partly correspond with Mervyn's story; but the last particular is irreconcileably repugnant to it. Now, for the first time, I begin to feel that my confidence is shaken. I feel my mind bewildered and distracted by the multitude of new discoveries which have just taken place. I want time to revolve them slowly, to weigh them accurately, and to estimate their consequences fully. I am afraid to speak; fearing, that, in the present trouble of my thoughts, I may say something which I may afterwards regret. I want a counsellor; but you, Wortley, are unfit for the office. Your judgment is unfurnished with the same materials; your sufferings have soured your humanity and biassed your candor. The only one qualified to divide with me these cares, and aid in selecting the best mode of action, is my wife. She is mistress of Mervyn's history; an observer of his conduct during his abode with us; and is hindered, by her

education and temper, from deviating into rigor and malevolence. Will you pardon me, therefore, if I defer commenting
on your narrative till I have had an opportunity of reviewing
it and comparing it with my knowledge of the lad, collected
from himself and from my own observation.

Wortley could not but admit the justice of my request, and
after some desultory conversation we parted. I hastened to
communicate to my wife the various intelligence which I had
lately received. Mrs. Althorpe's portrait of the Mervyns contained lineaments which the summary detail of Arthur did not
enable us fully to comprehend. The treatment which the
youth is said to have given to his father; the illicit commerce
that subsisted between him and his father's wife; the pillage
of money and his father's horse, but ill accorded with the tale
which we had heard, and disquieted our minds with doubts,
though far from dictating our belief.

What, however, more deeply absorbed our attention, was
the testimony of Williams and of Mrs. Wentworth. That which
was mysterious and inscrutable to Wortley and the friends of
Watson, was luminous to us. The coincidence between the
vague hints, laboriously collected by these enquirers, and the
narrative of Mervyn, afforded the most cogent attestation of
the truth of that narrative.

Watson had vanished from all eyes, but the spot where
rested his remains was known to us. The girdle spoken of by
Williams, would not be suspected to exist by his murderer. It
was unmolested, and was doubtless buried with him. That
which was so earnestly sought, and which constituted the subsistence of the Maurices, would probably be found adhering
to his body. What conduct was incumbent upon me who possessed this knowledge?

It was just to restore these bills to their true owner; but
how could this be done without hazardous processes and tedious disclosures? To whom ought these disclosures to be
made? By what authority or agency could these half-decayed
limbs be dug up, and the lost treasure be taken from amidst
the horrible corruption in which it was immersed?

This ought not to be the act of a single individual. This act
would entangle him in a maze of perils and suspicions, of
concealments and evasions, from which he could not hope to

escape with his reputation inviolate. The proper method was through the agency of the law. It is to this that Mervyn must submit his conduct. The story which he told to me he must tell to the world. Suspicions have fixed themselves upon him, which allow him not the privilege of silence and obscurity. While he continued unknown and unthought of, the publication of his story would only give unnecessary birth to dangers; but now dangers are incurred which it may probably contribute to lessen, if not to remove.

Meanwhile the return of Mervyn to the city was anxiously expected. Day after day passed and no tidings were received. I had business of an urgent nature which required my presence in Jersey, but which, in the daily expectation of the return of my young friend, I postponed a week longer than rigid discretion allowed. At length I was obliged to comply with the exigence, and left the city, but made such arrangements that I should be apprized by my wife of Mervyn's return with all practicable expedition.

These arrangements were superfluous, for my business was dispatched, and my absence at an end, before the youth had given us any tokens of his approach. I now remembered the warnings of Wortley, and his assertions that Mervyn had withdrawn himself forever from our view. The event had hitherto unwelcomely coincided with these predictions, and a thousand doubts and misgivings were awakened.

One evening, while preparing to shake off gloomy thoughts by a visit to a friend, some one knocked at my door, and left a billet containing these words:

"Dr. Stevens is requested to come immediately to the Debtors' Apartments in Prune Street."

This billet was without signature. The hand writing was unknown, and the precipitate departure of the bearer, left me wholly at a loss with respect to the person of the writer, or the end for which my presence was required. This uncertainty only hastened my compliance with the summons.

The evening was approaching—a time when the prison doors are accustomed to be shut and strangers to be excluded. This furnished an additional reason for dispatch. As I walked swiftly along, I revolved the possible motives that might have prompted this message. A conjecture was soon formed, which led to apprehension and inquietude.

One of my friends, by name Carlton, was embarrassed with debts which he was unable to discharge. He had lately been menaced with arrest, by a creditor not accustomed to remit any of his claims. I dreaded that this catastrophe had now happened, and called to mind the anguish with which this untoward incident would overwhelm his family. I knew his incapacity to take away the claim of his creditor by payment, or to soothe him into clemency by supplication.

So prone is the human mind to create for itself distress, that I was not aware of the uncertainty of this evil till I arrived at the prison. I checked myself at the moment when I opened my lips to utter the name of my friend, and was admitted without particular enquiries. I supposed that he by whom I had been summoned hither would meet me in the common room.

The apartment was filled with pale faces and withered forms. The marks of negligence and poverty were visible in all; but few betrayed, in their features or gestures, any symptoms of concern on account of their condition. Ferocious gaiety, or stupid indifference, seemed to sit upon every brow. The vapour from an heated stove, mingled with the fumes of beer and tallow that were spilled upon it, and with the tainted breath of so promiscuous a crowd, loaded the stagnant atmosphere. At my first transition from the cold and pure air without, to this noxious element, I found it difficult to breathe. A moment, however, reconciled me to my situation, and I looked anxiously round to discover some face which I knew.

Almost every mouth was furnished with a segar, and every hand with a glass of porter. Conversation, carried on with much emphasis of tone and gesture, was not wanting. Sundry groupes, in different corners, were beguiling the tedious hours at whist. Others, unemployed, were strolling to and fro, and testified their vacancy of thought and care by humming or whistling a tune.

I fostered the hope, that my prognostics had deceived me. This hope was strengthened by reflecting that the billet received was written in a different hand from that of my friend.

Meanwhile I continued my search. Seated on a bench, silent and aloof from the crowd, his eyes fixed upon the floor, and his face half concealed by his hand, a form was at length discovered which verified all my conjectures and fears. Carlton was he.

My heart drooped, and my tongue faultered, at this sight. I surveyed him for some minutes in silence. At length, approaching the bench on which he sat, I touched his hand and awakened him from his reverie. He looked up. A momentary gleam of joy and surprize was succeeded by a gloom deeper than before.

It was plain that my friend needed consolation. He was governed by an exquisite sensibility to disgrace. He was impatient of constraint. He shrunk, with fastidious abhorrence, from the contact of the vulgar and the profligate. His constitution was delicate and feeble. Impure airs, restraint from exercise, unusual aliment, unwholesome or incommodious accommodations, and perturbed thoughts, were, at any time, sufficient to generate disease and to deprive him of life.

To these evils he was now subjected. He had no money wherewith to purchase food. He had been dragged hither in the morning. He had not tasted a morsel since his entrance. He had not provided a bed on which to lie; or enquired in what room, or with what companions, the night was to be spent.

Fortitude was not among my friend's qualities. He was more prone to shrink from danger than encounter it, and to yield to the flood rather than sustain it; but it is just to observe, that his anguish, on the present occasion, arose not wholly from selfish considerations. His parents were dead, and two sisters were dependent on him for support. One of these was nearly of his own age. The other was scarcely emerged from childhood. There was an intellectual as well as a personal resemblance between my friend and his sisters. They possessed his physical infirmities, his vehement passions, and refinements of taste; and the misery of his condition was tenfold increased, by reflecting on the feelings which would be awakened in them by the knowledge of his state, and the hardships to which the loss of his succour would expose them.

Chapter V

IT WAS NOT in my power to release my friend by the payment of his debt; but, by contracting with the keeper of the prison for his board, I could save him from famine; and, by suitable exertions, could procure him lodging as convenient as the time would admit. I could promise to console and protect his sisters, and, by cheerful tones and frequent visits, dispel some part of the evil which encompassed him.

After the first surprize had subsided, he enquired by what accident this meeting had been produced. Conscious of my incapacity to do him any essential service, and unwilling to make me a partaker in his miseries, he had forborne to inform me of his condition.

This assurance was listened to with some wonder. I showed him the billet. It had not been written by him. He was a stranger to the penmanship. None but the attorney and officer were apprized of his fate. It was obvious to conclude, that this was the interposition of some friend, who, knowing my affection for Carlton, had taken this mysterious method of calling me to his succour.

Conjectures, as to the author and motives of this interposition, were suspended by more urgent considerations. I requested an interview with the keeper, and enquired how Carlton could be best accommodated.

He said, that all his rooms were full but one, which, in consequence of the dismission of three persons in the morning, had at present but one tenant. This person had lately arrived, was sick, and had with him, at this time, one of his friends. Carlton might divide the chamber with this person. No doubt his consent would be readily given; though this arrangement, being the best, must take place whether he consented or not.

This consent I resolved immediately to seek, and, for that purpose, desired to be led to the chamber. The door of the apartment was shut. I knocked for admission. It was instantly opened, and I entered. The first person who met my view was—Arthur Mervyn.

460

I started with astonishment. Mervyn's countenance betrayed nothing but satisfaction at the interview. The traces of fatigue and anxiety gave place to tenderness and joy. It readily occurred to me that Mervyn was the writer of the note which I had lately received. To meet him within these walls, and at this time, was the most remote and undesirable of all contingences. The same hour had thus made me acquainted with the kindred and unwelcome fate of two beings whom I most loved.

I had scarcely time to return his embrace, when, taking my hand, he led me to a bed that stood in one corner. There was stretched upon it one whom a second glance enabled me to call by his name, though I had never before seen him. The vivid portrait which Mervyn had drawn was conspicuous in the sunken and haggard visage before me. This face had, indeed, proportions and lines which could never be forgotten or mistaken. Welbeck, when once seen or described, was easily distinguished from the rest of mankind. He had stronger motives than other men for abstaining from guilt, the difficulty of concealment or disguise being tenfold greater in him than in others, by reason of the indelible and eye-attracting marks which nature had set upon him.

He was pallid and emaciated. He did not open his eyes on my entrance. He seemed to be asleep; but, before I had time to exchange glances with Mervyn, or to enquire into the nature of the scene, he awoke. On seeing me he started, and cast a look of upbraiding on my companion. The latter comprehended his emotion and endeavored to appease him.

This person, said he, is my friend. He is likewise a physician; and, perceiving your state to require medical assistance, I ventured to send for him.

Welbeck replied, in a contemptuous and indignant tone, thou mistakest my condition, boy. My disease lies deeper than his scrutiny will ever reach. I had hoped thou wert gone. Thy importunities are well meant, but they aggravate my miseries.

He now rose from the bed, and continued, in a firm and resolute tone, you are intruders into this apartment. It is mine, and I desire to be left alone.

Mervyn returned, at first, no answer to this address. He was immersed in perplexity. At length, raising his eyes from the floor, he said, my intentions are indeed honest, and I am grieved that I want the power of persuasion. To-morrow, perhaps, I may reason more cogently with your despair, or your present mood may be changed. To aid my own weakness I will entreat the assistance of this friend.

These words roused a new spirit in Welbeck. His confusion and anger encreased. His tongue faultered as he exclaimed, good God! what mean you? Headlong and rash as you are, you will not share with this person your knowledge of me? —Here he checked himself, conscious that the words he had already uttered tended to the very end which he dreaded. This consciousness, added to the terror of more ample disclosures, which the simplicity and rectitude of Mervyn might prompt him to make, chained up his tongue, and covered him with dismay.

Mervyn was not long in answering—I comprehend your fears and your wishes. I am bound to tell you the truth. To this person your story has already been told. Whatever I have witnessed under your roof, whatever I have heard from your lips, have been faithfully disclosed to him.

The countenance of Welbeck now betrayed a mixture of incredulity and horror. For a time his utterance was stifled by his complicated feelings.

It cannot be. So enormous a deed is beyond thy power. Thy qualities are marvellous. Every new act of thine outstrips the last, and belies the newest calculations. But this—this perfidy exceeds—This outrage upon promises, this violation of faith, this blindness to the future is incredible. There he stopped; while his looks seemed to call upon Mervyn for a contradiction of his first assertion.

I know full well how inexpiably stupid or wicked my act will appear to you, but I will not prevaricate or lie. I repeat, that every thing is known to him. Your birth; your early fortunes; the incidents at Charleston and Wilmington; your treatment of the brother and sister; your interview with Watson, and the fatal issue of that interview—I have told him all, just as it was told to me.

Here the shock that was felt by Welbeck overpowered his caution and his strength. He sunk upon the side of the bed.

His air was still incredulous, and he continued to gaze upon Mervyn. He spoke in a tone less vehement.

And hast thou then betrayed me? Hast thou shut every avenue to my return to honor? Am I known to be a seducer and assassin? To have meditated all crimes, and to have perpetrated the worst?

Infamy and death are my portion. I know they are reserved for me; but I did not think to receive them at thy hands, that under that innocent guise there lurked a heart treacherous and cruel. But go; leave me to myself. This stroke has exterminated my remnant of hope. Leave me to prepare my neck for the halter, and my lips for this last, and bitterest cup.

Mervyn struggled with his tears and replied, all this was foreseen, and all this I was prepared to endure. My friend and I will withdraw, as you wish; but to-morrow I return; not to vindicate my faith or my humanity; not to make you recant your charges, or forgive the faults which I seem to have committed, but to extricate you from your present evil, or to arm you with fortitude.

So saying he led the way out of the room. I followed him in silence. The strangeness and abruptness of this scene left me no power to assume a part in it. I looked on with new and indescribable sensations. I reached the street before my recollection was perfectly recovered. I then reflected on the purpose that had led me to Welbeck's chamber. This purpose was yet unaccomplished. I desired Mervyn to linger a moment while I returned into the house. I once more enquired for the keeper, and told him I should leave to him the province of acquainting Welbeck with the necessity of sharing his apartment with a stranger. I speedily rejoined Mervyn in the street.

I lost no time in requiring an explanation of the scene that I had witnessed. How became you once more the companion of Welbeck? Why did you not inform me by letter of your arrival at Malverton, and of what occurred during your absence? What is the fate of Mr. Hadwin and of Wallace?

Alas! said he, I perceive, that, though I have written, you have never received my letters. The tale of what has occurred since we parted is long and various. I am not only willing but eager to communicate the story, but this is no suitable place.

Have patience till we reach your house. I have involved myself in perils and embarrassments from which I depend upon your counsel and aid to release me.

I had scarcely reached my own door, when I was overtaken by a servant, whom I knew to belong to the family in which Carlton and his sisters resided. Her message, therefore, was readily guessed. She came, as I expected, to enquire for my friend, who had left his home in the morning with a stranger, and had not yet returned. His absence had occasioned some inquietude, and his sister had sent this message to me, to procure what information respecting the cause of his detention I was able to give.

My perplexity hindered me, for some time, from answering. I was willing to communicate the painful truth with my own mouth. I saw the necessity of putting an end to her suspence, and of preventing the news from reaching her with fallacious aggravations or at an unseasonable time.

I told the messenger, that I had just parted with Mr. Carlton, that he was well, and that I would speedily come and acquaint his sister with the cause of his absence.

Though burning with curiosity respecting Mervyn and Welbeck, I readily postponed its gratification till my visit to Miss Carlton was performed. I had rarely seen this lady; my friendship for her brother, though ardent, having been lately formed, and chiefly matured by interviews at my house. I had designed to introduce her to my wife, but various accidents had hindered the execution of my purpose. Now consolation and counsel was more needed than ever, and delay or reluctance in bestowing it would have been, in an high degree, unpardonable.

I therefore parted with Mervyn, requesting him to await my return, and promising to perform the engagement which compelled me to leave him with the utmost dispatch. On entering Miss Carlton's apartment, I assumed an air of as much tranquillity as possible. I found the lady seated at a desk, with pen in hand and parchment before her. She greeted me with affectionate dignity, and caught from my countenance that cheerfulness of which on my entrance she was destitute.

You come, said she, to inform me what has made my brother a truant to-day. Till your message was received I was somewhat anxious. This day he usually spends in rambling through the fields, but so bleak and stormy an atmosphere I suppose would prevent his excursion. I pray, sir, what is it detains him?

To conquer my embarrassment, and introduce the subject by indirect and cautious means, I eluded her question, and casting an eye at the parchment, how now? said I; this is strange employment for a lady. I knew that my friend pursued this trade, and lived by binding fast the bargains which others made, but I knew not that the pen was ever usurped by his sister.

The usurpation was prompted by necessity. My brother's impatient temper and delicate frame unfitted him for this trade. He pursued it with no less reluctance than diligence, devoting to the task three nights in the week and the whole of each day. It would long ago have killed him, if I had not bethought myself of sharing his tasks. The pen was irksome and toilsome at first, but use has made it easy, and far more eligible than the needle, which was formerly my only tool.

This arrangement affords my brother opportunities of exercise and recreation, without diminishing our profits; and my time, though not less constantly, is more agreeably, as well as more lucratively, employed than formerly.

I admire your reasoning. By this means provision is made against untoward accidents. If sickness should disable him, you are qualified to pursue the same means of support.

At these words the lady's countenance changed. She put her hand on my arm, and said, in a fluttering and hurried accent, is my brother sick?

No. He is in perfect health. My observation was an harmless one. I am sorry to observe your readiness to draw alarming inferences. If I were to say, that your scheme is useful to supply deficiencies, not only when your brother is disabled by sickness, but when thrown, by some inhuman creditor, into jail, no doubt you would perversely and hastily infer that he is now in prison.

I had scarcely ended the sentence, when the piercing eyes of the lady were anxiously fixed upon mine. After a moment's pause, she exclaimed—The inference, indeed, is too plain. I know his fate. It has long been foreseen and expected, and I have summoned up my equanimity to meet it. Would to Heaven he may find the calamity as light as I should find it; but I fear his too irritable spirit.

When her fears were confirmed, she started out into no vehemence of exclamation. She quickly suppressed a few tears which would not be withheld, and listened to my narrative of what had lately occurred, with tokens of gratitude.

Formal consolation was superfluous. Her mind was indeed more fertile than my own in those topics which take away its keenest edge from affliction. She observed that it was far from being the heaviest calamity which might have happened. The creditor was perhaps vincible by arguments and supplications. If these should succeed, the disaster would not only be removed, but that security from future molestation, be gained, to which they had for a long time been strangers.

Should he be obdurate, their state was far from being hopeless. Carlton's situation allowed him to pursue his profession. His gains would be equal, and his expences would not be augmented. By their mutual industry they might hope to amass sufficient to discharge the debt at no very remote period.

What she chiefly dreaded was the pernicious influence of dejection and sedentary labor on her brother's health. Yet this was not to be considered as inevitable. Fortitude might be inspired by exhortation and example, and no condition precluded us from every species of bodily exertion. The less inclined he should prove to cultivate the means of deliverance and happiness within his reach, the more necessary it became for her to stimulate and fortify his resolution.

If I were captivated by the charms of this lady's person and carriage, my reverence was excited by these proofs of wisdom and energy. I zealously promised to concur with her in every scheme she should adopt for her own or her brother's advantage; and after spending some hours with her, took my leave.

I now regretted the ignorance in which I had hitherto remained respecting this lady. That she was, in an eminent degree, feminine and lovely, was easily discovered; but intellectual weakness had been rashly inferred from external frailty. She was accustomed to shrink from observation, and reserve was mistaken for timidity. I called on Carlton only when numerous engagements would allow, and when by some accident, his customary visits had been intermitted. On those occasions, my stay was short, and my attention chiefly confined to her brother. I now resolved to atone for my ancient negligence, not only by my own assiduities, but by those of my wife.

On my return home, I found Mervyn and my wife in earnest discourse. I anticipated the shock which the sensibility of the latter would receive from the tidings which I had to communicate respecting Carlton. I was unwilling, and yet perceived the necessity, of disclosing the truth. I desired to bring these women, as soon as possible, to the knowledge of each other, but the necessary prelude to this was an acquaintance with the disaster that had happened.

Scarcely had I entered the room, when Mervyn turned to me and said, with an air of anxiety and impatience—Pray, my friend, have you any knowledge of Francis Carlton?

The mention of this name by Mervyn, produced some surprize. I acknowledged my acquaintance with him.

Do you know in what situation he now is?

In answer to this question, I stated by what singular means his situation had been made known to me, and the purpose, from the accomplishment of which, I had just returned. I enquired, in my turn, whence originated this question?

He had overheard the name of Carlton in the prison. Two persons were communing in a corner, and accident enabled him to catch this name, though uttered by them in an half whisper, and to discover that the person talked about, had lately been conveyed thither.

This name was not now heard for the first time. It was connected with remembrances that made him anxious for the fate of him to whom it belonged. In discourse with my wife, this name chanced to be again mentioned, and his curiosity was roused afresh. I was willing to communicate all that I knew, but Mervyn's own destiny was too remarkable not to absorb all my attention, and I refused to discuss any other theme till that were fully explained. He postponed his own gratification to mine, and consented to relate the incidents that had happened from the moment of our separation till the present.

Chapter VI

AT PARTING with you, my purpose was to reach the abode of the Hadwins as speedily as possible. I travelled therefore with diligence. Setting out so early, I expected, though on foot, to reach the end of my journey before noon. The activity of muscles is no obstacle to thought. So far from being inconsistent with intense musing, it is, in my own case, propitious to that state of mind.

Probably no one had stronger motives for ardent meditation than I. My second journey to the city was prompted by reasons, and attended by incidents, that seemed to have a present existence. To think upon them, was to view, more deliberately and thoroughly, objects and persons that still hovered in my sight. Instead of their attributes being already seen, and their consequences at an end, it seemed as if a series of numerous years and unintermitted contemplation were requisite to comprehend them fully, and bring into existence their most momentous effects.

If men be chiefly distinguished from each other by the modes in which attention is employed, either on external and sensible objects, or merely on abstract ideas and the creatures of reflection, I may justly claim to be enrolled in the second class. My existence is a series of thoughts rather than of motions. Ratiocination and deduction leave my senses unemployed. The fulness of my fancy renders my eye vacant and inactive. Sensations do not precede and suggest, but follow and are secondary to the acts of my mind.

There was one motive, however, which made me less inattentive to the scene that was continually shifting before and without me than I am wont to be. The loveliest form which I had hitherto seen, was that of Clemenza Lodi. I recalled her condition as I had witnessed it, as Welbeck had described, and as you had painted it. The past was without remedy; but the future was, in some degree, within our power to create and to fashion. Her state was probably dangerous. She might already be forlorn, beset with temptation or with anguish; or danger might only be approaching her, and the worst evils be impending ones.

I was ignorant of her state. Could I not remove this ignorance? Would not some benefit redound to her from beneficent and seasonable interposition?

You had mentioned that her abode had lately been with Mrs. Villars, and that this lady still resided in the country. The residence had been sufficiently described, and I perceived that I was now approaching it. In a short time I spied its painted roof and five chimneys through an avenue of *catalpas.*

When opposite the gate which led into this avenue, I paused. It seemed as if this moment were to decide upon the liberty and innocence of this being. In a moment I might place myself before her, ascertain her true condition, and point out to her the path of honor and safety. This opportunity might be the last. Longer delay might render interposition fruitless.

But how was I to interpose? I was a stranger to her language, and she was unacquainted with mine. To obtain access to her, it was necessary only to demand it. But how should I explain my views and state my wishes when an interview was gained? And what expedient was it in my power to propose?

Now, said I, I perceive the value of that wealth which I have been accustomed to despise. The power of eating and drinking, the nature and limits of existence and physical enjoyment, are not changed or enlarged by the increase of wealth. Our corporeal and intellectual wants are supplied at little expence; but our own wants are the wants of others, and that which remains, after our own necessities are obviated, it is always easy and just to employ in relieving the necessities of others.

There are no superfluities in my store. It is not in my power to supply this unfortunate girl with decent rayment and honest bread. I have no house to which to conduct her. I have no means of securing her from famine and cold.

Yet, though indigent and feeble, I am not destitute of friends and of home. Cannot she be admitted to the same asylum to which I am now going? This thought was sudden and new. The more it was revolved, the more plausible it seemed. This was not merely the sole expedient, but the best that could have been suggested.

The Hadwins were friendly, hospitable, unsuspicious. Their board, though simple and uncouth, was wholesome and plenteous. Their residence was sequestered and obscure, and not obnoxious to impertinent enquiries and malignant animadversion. Their frank and ingenuous temper would make them easy of persuasion, and their sympathies were prompt and overflowing.

I am nearly certain, continued I, that they will instantly afford protection to this desolate girl. Why shall I not anticipate their consent, and present myself to their embraces and their welcomes in her company?

Slight reflection showed me, that this precipitation was improper. Whether Wallace had ever arrived at Malverton? Whether Mr. Hadwin had escaped infection? whether his house were the abode of security and quiet, or a scene of desolation? were questions yet to be determined. The obvious and best proceeding was to hasten forward, to afford the Hadwins, if in distress, the feeble consolations of my friendship; or, if their state were happy, to procure their concurrence to my scheme respecting Clemenza.

Actuated by these considerations, I resumed my journey. Looking forward, I perceived a chaise and horse standing by the left hand fence, at the distance of some hundred yards. This object was not uncommon or strange, and, therefore, it was scarcely noticed. When I came near, however, methought I recognized in this carriage the same in which my importunities had procured a seat for the languishing Wallace, in the manner which I have formerly related.

It was a crazy vehicle and old fashioned. When once seen it could scarcely be mistaken or forgotten. The horse was held by his bridle to a post, but the seat was empty. My solicitude with regard to Wallace's destiny, of which he to whom the carriage belonged might possibly afford me some knowledge, made me stop and reflect on what measures it was proper to pursue.

The rider could not be at a great distance from this spot. His absence would probably be short. By lingering a few minutes an interview might be gained, and the uncertainty and suspence of some hours be thereby precluded. I therefore waited, and the same person whom I had formerly encountered made his appearance, in a short time, from under a copse that skirted the road.

He recognized me with more difficulty than attended my recognition of him. The circumstances, however, of our first meeting were easily recalled to his remembrance. I eagerly enquired when and where he had parted with the youth who had been, on that occasion, entrusted to his care.

He answered, that, on leaving the city and inhaling the purer air of the fields and woods, Wallace had been, in a wonderful degree, invigorated and refreshed. An instantaneous and total change appeared to have been wrought in him. He no longer languished with fatigue or fear, but became full of gaiety and talk.

The suddenness of this transition; the levity with which he related and commented on his recent dangers and evils, excited the astonishment of his companion, to whom he not only communicated the history of his disease, but imparted many anecdotes of a humorous kind. Some of these my companion repeated. I heard them with regret and dissatisfaction. They betokened a mind vitiated by intercourse with the thoughtless and depraved of both sexes, and particularly with infamous and profligate women.

My companion proceeded to mention, that Wallace's exhiliration lasted but for a short time, and disappeared as suddenly as it had appeared. He was seized with deadly sickness, and insisted upon leaving the carriage, whose movements shocked his stomach and head to an insupportable degree. His companion was not void of apprehensions on his own account, but was unwilling to desert him, and endeavored to encourage him. His efforts were vain. Though the nearest house was at the distance of some hundred yards, and though it was probable that the inhabitants of this house would refuse to accommodate one in his condition, yet Wallace could not be prevailed on to proceed; and, in spite of persuasion and remonstrance, left the carriage and threw himself on the grassy bank beside the road.

This person was not unmindful of the hazard which he incurred by contact with a sick man. He conceived himself to have performed all that was consistent with duty to himself and to his family; and Wallace, persisting in affirming that, by attempting to ride farther, he should merely hasten his death, was at length left to his own guidance.

These were unexpected and mournful tidings. I had fondly imagined, that his safety was put beyond the reach of untoward accidents. Now, however, there was reason to suppose him to have perished by a lingering and painful disease, rendered fatal by the selfishness of mankind, by the want of seasonable remedies, and exposure to inclement airs. Some uncertainty, however, rested on his fate. It was my duty to remove it, and to carry to the Hadwins no mangled and defective tale. Where, I asked, had Wallace and his companion parted?

It was about three miles further onward. The spot and the house within view from the spot, were accurately described. In this house it was possible that Wallace had sought an asylum, and some intelligence respecting him might be gained from its inhabitants. My informant was journeying to the city, so that we were obliged to separate.

In consequence of this man's description of Wallace's deportment, and the proofs of a dissolute and thoughtless temper which he had given, I began to regard his death as an event less deplorable. Such an one was unworthy of a being so devoutly pure, so ardent in fidelity and tenderness as Susan Hadwin. If he loved, it was probable that in defiance of his vows, he would seek a different companion. If he adhered to his first engagements, his motives would be sordid, and the disclosure of his latent defects might produce more exquisite misery to his wife, than his premature death or treacherous desertion.

The preservation of this man, was my sole motive for entering the infected city, and subjecting my own life to the hazards, from which my escape may almost be esteemed miraculous. Was not the end disproportioned to the means? Was there arrogance in believing my life a price too great to be given for his?

I was not, indeed, sorry for the past. My purpose was just, and the means which I selected, were the best my limited knowledge applied. My happiness should be drawn from reflection on the equity of my intentions. That these intentions were frustrated by the ignorance of others, or my own, was the consequence of human frailty. Honest purposes, though they may not bestow happiness on others, will, at least, secure it to him who fosters them.

By these reflections my regrets were dissipated, and I prepared to rejoice alike, whether Wallace should be found to have escaped or to have perished. The house to which I had been directed was speedily brought into view. I enquired for the master or mistress of the mansion, and was conducted to a lady of a plain and housewifely appearance.

My curiosity was fully gratified. Wallace, whom my description easily identifed, had made his appearance at her door on the evening of the day on which he left the city. The dread of *the fever* was descanted on with copious and rude eloquence. I supposed her eloquence on this theme to be designed to apologize to me for her refusing entrance to the sick man. The peroration, however, was different. Wallace was admitted, and suitable attention paid to his wants.

Happily, the guest had nothing to struggle with but extreme weakness. Repose, nourishing diet, and salubrious airs restored him in a short time to health. He lingered under this roof for three weeks, and then, without any professions of gratitude, or offers of pecuniary remuneration, or information of the course which he determined to take, he left them.

These facts, added to that which I had previously known, threw no advantageous light upon the character of Wallace. It was obvious to conclude, that he had gone to Malverton, and thither there was nothing to hinder me from following him.

Perhaps, one of my grossest defects is a precipitate temper. I chuse my path suddenly, and pursue it with impetuous expedition. In the present instance, my resolution was conceived with unhesitating zeal, and I walked the faster that I might the sooner execute it. Miss Hadwin deserved to be happy. Love was in her heart the all-absorbing sentiment. A disappointment there was a supreme calamity. Depravity and folly must assume the guise of virtue before it can claim her affection. This disguise might be maintained for a time, but its detection must inevitably come, and the sooner this detection takes place the more beneficial it must prove.

I resolved to unbosom myself, with equal and unbounded confidence, to Wallace and his mistress. I would chuse for this end not the moment when they were separate, but that in which they were together. My knowledge, and the sources of my knowledge, relative to Wallace, should be unfolded to the lady with simplicity and truth. The lover should be present, to confute, to extenuate, or to verify the charges.

During the rest of the day these images occupied the chief place in my thoughts. The road was miry and dark, and my journey proved to be more tedious and fatiguing than I expected. At length, just as the evening closed, the well-known habitation appeared in view. Since my departure, winter had visited the world, and the aspect of nature was desolate and dreary. All around this house was vacant, negligent, forlorn. The contrast between these appearances and those which I had noticed on my first approach to it, when the ground and the trees were decked with the luxuriance and vivacity of summer, was mournful, and seemed to foretoken ill. My spirits drooped as I noticed the general inactivity and silence.

I entered, without warning, the door that led into the parlour. No face was to be seen or voice heard. The chimney was ornamented, as in summer, with evergreen shrubs. Though it was now the second month of frost and snow, fire did not appear to have been lately kindled on this hearth.

This was a circumstance from which nothing good could be deduced. Had there been those to share its comforts, who had shared them on former years, this was the place and hour at which they commonly assembled. A door on one side led, through a narrow entry, into the kitchen. I opened this door, and passed towards the kitchen.

No one was there but an old man, squatted in the chimney-corner. His face, though wrinkled, denoted undecayed health and an unbending spirit. An homespun coat, leathern breeches wrinkled with age, and blue yarn hose, were well suited to his lean and shrivelled form. On his right knee was a wooden bowl, which he had just replenished from a pipkin of hasty-pudding still smoking on the coals; and in his left hand a spoon, which he had, at that moment, plunged into a bottle of molasses that stood beside him.

This action was suspended by my entrance. He looked up and exclaimed, hey day! who's this that comes into other people's houses without so much as saying "by your leave?" What's thee business? Who's thee want?

I had never seen this personage before. I supposed it to be some new domestic, and enquired for Mr. Hadwin.

Ah! replied he with a sigh, William Hadwin. Is it him thee wants? Poor man! He is gone to rest many days since.

My heart sunk within me at these tidings. Dead, said I, do you mean that he is dead?—This exclamation was uttered in a tone of some vehemence. It attracted the attention of some one who was standing without, who immediately entered the kitchen. It was Eliza Hadwin. The moment she beheld me she shrieked aloud, and, rushing into my arms, fainted away.

The old man dropped his bowl; and, starting from his seat, stared alternately at me and at the breathless girl. My emotion, made up of joy, and sorrow, and surprize, rendered me for a moment powerless as she. At length, he said, I understand this. I know who thee is, and will tell her thee's come. So saying he hastily left the room.

Chapter VII

IN A SHORT TIME this gentle girl recovered her senses. She did not withdraw herself from my sustaining arm, but, leaning on my bosom, she resigned herself to passionate weeping. I did not endeavor to check this effusion, believing that its influence would be salutary.

I had not forgotten the thrilling sensibility and artless graces of this girl. I had not forgotten the scruples which had formerly made me check a passion whose tendency was easily discovered. These new proofs of her affection were, at once, mournful and delightful. The untimely fate of her father and my friend pressed with new force upon my heart, and my tears, in spite of my fortitude, mingled with hers.

The attention of both was presently attracted by a faint scream, which proceeded from above. Immediately tottering footsteps were heard in the passage, and a figure rushed into the room, pale, emaciated, haggard, and wild. She cast a piercing glance at me, uttered a feeble exclamation, and sunk upon the floor without signs of life.

It was not difficult to comprehend this scene. I now conjectured, what subsequent enquiry confirmed, that the old man had mistaken me for Wallace, and had carried to the elder sister the news of his return. This fatal disappointment of hopes that had nearly been extinct, and which were now so powerfully revived, could not be endured by a frame verging to dissolution.

This object recalled all the energies of Eliza, and engrossed all my solicitude. I lifted the fallen girl in my arms; and, guided by her sister, carried her to her chamber. I had now leisure to contemplate the changes which a few months had made in this lovely frame. I turned away from the spectacle with anguish, but my wandering eyes were recalled by some potent fascination, and fixed in horror upon a form which evinced the last stage of decay. Eliza knelt on one side, and, leaning her face upon the bed, endeavored in vain to smother her sobs. I sat on the other motionless, and holding the passive and withered hand of the sufferer.

I watched with ineffable solicitude the return of life. It returned, at length, but merely to betray symptoms that it would speedily depart forever. For a time my faculties were palsied, and I was made an impotent spectator of the ruin that environed me. This pusillanimity quickly gave way to resolutions and reflections better suited to the exigencies of the time.

The first impulse was to summon a physician, but it was evident that the patient had been sinking by slow degrees to this state, and that the last struggle had begun. Nothing remained but to watch her while expiring, and perform for her, when dead, the rites of interment. The survivor was capable of consolation and of succour. I went to her and drew her gently into another apartment. The old man, tremulous and wonderstruck, seemed anxious to perform some service. I directed him to kindle a fire in Eliza's chamber. Meanwhile I persuaded my gentle friend to remain in this chamber, and resign to me the performance of every office which her sister's condition required. I sat beside the bed of the dying till the mortal struggle was past.

I perceived that the house had no inhabitant beside the two females and the old man. I went in search of the latter, and found him crouched as before, at the kitchen fire, smoking his pipe. I placed myself on the same bench, and entered into conversation with him.

I gathered from him that he had, for many years, been Mrs. Hadwin's servant. That lately he had cultivated a small farm in this neighborhood for his own advantage. Stopping one day in October, at the tavern, he heard that his old master had lately been in the city, had caught *the fever*, and after his return had died with it. The moment he became sick, his servants fled from the house, and the neighbors refused to approach it. The task of attending his sick bed, was allotted to his daughters, and it was by their hands that his grave was dug, and his body covered with earth. The same terror of infection existed after his death as before, and these hapless females were deserted by all mankind.

Old Caleb was no sooner informed of these particulars, than he hurried to the house, and had since continued in their service. His heart was kind, but it was easily seen that his skill extended only to execute the directions of another. Grief for the death of Wallace, and her father, preyed upon the health of the elder daughter. The younger became her nurse, and Caleb was always at hand to execute any orders, the performance of which was on a level with his understanding. Their neighbors had not withheld their good offices, but they were still terrified and estranged by the phantoms of pestilence.

During the last week Susan had been too weak to rise from her bed, yet such was the energy communicated by the tidings that Wallace was alive, and had returned, that she leaped upon her feet and rushed down stairs. How little did that man deserve so strenuous and immortal an affection.

I would not allow myself to ponder on the sufferings of these women. I endeavored to think only of the best expedients for putting an end to these calamities. After a moment's deliberation, I determined to go to an house at some miles distance; the dwelling of one, who, though not exempt from the reigning panic, had shewn more generosity towards these unhappy girls than others. During my former abode in this district, I had ascertained his character, and found him to be compassionate and liberal.

Overpowered by fatigue and watching, Eliza was no sooner relieved by my presence, of some portion of her cares, than she sunk into profound slumber. I directed Caleb to watch the house till my return, which should be before midnight, and then set out for the dwelling of Mr. Ellis.

The weather was temperate and moist, and rendered the footing of the meadows extremely difficult. The ground that had lately been frozen and covered with snow, was now changed into gullies and pools, and this was no time to be fastidious in the choice of paths. A brook, swelled by the recent *thaw*, was likewise to be passed. The rail which I had formerly placed over it by way of bridge, had disappeared, and I was obliged to wade through it. At length I approached the house to which I was going.

At so late an hour, farmers and farmers' servants are usually abed, and their threshold is entrusted to their watch-dogs. Two belonged to Mr. Ellis, whose ferocity and vigilance were truly formidable to a stranger, but I hoped that in me they would recognize an old acquaintance, and suffer me to approach. In this I was not mistaken. Though my person could not be distinctly seen by star-light, they seemed to scent me from afar, and met me with a thousand caresses.

Approaching the house, I perceived that its tenants were retired to their repose. This I expected, and hastened to awaken Mr. Ellis, by knocking briskly at the door. Presently he looked out of a window above, and in answer to his enquiries, in which impatience at being so unseasonably disturbed, was mingled with anxiety, I told him my name, and entreated him to come down and allow me a few minutes conversation. He speedily dressed himself, and opening the kitchen door, we seated ourselves before the fire.

My appearance was sufficiently adapted to excite his wonder; he had heard of my elopement from the house of Mr. Hadwin, he was a stranger to the motives that prompted my departure, and to the events that had befallen me, and no interview was more distant from his expectations than the present. His curiosity was written in his features, but this was no time to gratify his curiosity. The end that I now had in view, was to procure accommodation for Eliza Hadwin in this man's house. For this purpose it was my duty to describe with simplicity and truth, the inconveniences which at present surrounded her, and to relate all that had happened since my arrival.

I perceived that my tale excited his compassion, and I continued with new zeal to paint to him the helplessness of this girl. The death of her father and sister left her the property of this farm. Her sex and age disqualified her for superintending the harvest-field and the threshing-floor; and no expedient was left, but to lease the land to another, and, taking up her abode in the family of some kinsman or friend, to subsist, as she might easily do, upon the rent. Meanwhile her continuance in this house was equally useless and dangerous, and I insinuated to my companion the propriety of immediately removing her to his own.

Some hesitation and reluctance appeared in him, which I immediately ascribed to an absurd dread of infection. I endeavored, by appealing to his reason, as well as to his pity, to conquer this dread. I pointed out the true cause of the death of the elder daughter, and assured him the youngest knew no indisposition but that which arose from distress. I offered to save him from any hazard that might attend his approaching the house, by accompanying her hither myself. All that her safety required was that his doors should not be shut against her when she presented herself before them.

Still he was fearful and reluctant; and, at length, mentioned that her uncle resided not more than sixteen miles farther; that he was her natural protector, and he dared to say would find no difficulty in admitting her into his house. For his part, there might be reason in what I said, but he could not bring himself to think but that there was still some danger of *the fever*. It was right to assist people in distress, to be sure; but to risk his own life he did not think to be his duty. He was no relation of the family, and it was the duty of relations to help each other. Her uncle was the proper person to assist her, and no doubt he would be as willing as able.

The marks of dubiousness and indecision which accompanied these words, encouraged me in endeavoring to subdue his scruples. The increase of his aversion to my scheme kept pace with my remonstrances, and he finally declared that he would, on no account, consent to it.

Ellis was by no means hard of heart. His determination did not prove the coldness of his charity, but merely the strength of his fears. He was himself an object more of compassion than of anger; and he acted like the man, whose fear of death prompts him to push his companion from the plank which saved him from drowning, but which is unable to sustain both. Finding him invincible to my entreaties, I thought upon the expedient which he suggested of seeking the protection of her uncle. It was true, that the loss of parents had rendered her uncle her legal protector. His knowledge of the world; his house, and property, and influence would, perhaps, fit him for this office in a more eminent degree than I was fitted. To seek a different asylum might, indeed, be unjust to both, and, after some reflection, I not only dismissed the regret which Ellis's refusal had given me, but even thanked him for the intelligence and counsel which he had afforded me. I took leave of him, and hastened back to Hadwin's.

Eliza, by Caleb's report, was still asleep. There was no urgent necessity for awakening her; but something was forthwith to be done with regard to the unhappy girl that was dead. The proceeding incumbent on us was obvious. All that remained was to dig a grave, and to deposit the remains with as much solemnity and decency as the time would permit. There were two methods of doing this. I might wait till the next day; till a coffin could be made and conveyed hither; till the woman, whose trade it was to make and put on the habiliments assigned by custom to the dead, could be sought out and hired to attend; till kindred, friends, and neighbors could be summoned to the obsequies; till a carriage were provided to remove the body to a burying-ground, belonging to a meeting-house, and five miles distant; till those, whose trade it was to dig graves, had prepared one, within the sacred inclosure, for her reception; or, neglecting this toilsome, tedious, and expensive ceremonial, I might seek the grave of Hadwin, and lay the daughter by the side of her parent.

Perhaps I was wrong in my preference of the latter mode. The customs of burial may, in most cases, be in themselves proper. If the customs be absurd, yet it may be generally proper to adhere to them: but, doubtless, there are cases in which it is our duty to omit them. I conceived the present case to be such an one.

The season was bleak and inclement. Much time, labor, and expence would be required to go through the customary rites. There was none but myself to perform these, and I had not the suitable means. The misery of Eliza would only be prolonged by adhering to these forms; and her fortune be needlesly diminished, by the expences unavoidably to be incurred.

After musing upon these ideas for some time, I rose from my seat, and desired Caleb to follow me. We proceeded to an outer shed where farmers' tools used to be kept. I supplied him and myself with a spade, and requested him to lead me to the spot where Mr. Hadwin was laid.

He betrayed some hesitation to comply, and appeared struck with some degree of alarm, as if my purpose had been to molest, instead of securing, the repose of the dead. I removed his doubts by explaining my intentions, but he was scarcely less shocked, on discovering the truth, than he had been alarmed by his first suspicions. He stammered out his objections to my scheme. There was but one mode of burial he thought that was decent and proper, and he could not be free to assist me in pursuing any other mode.

Perhaps Caleb's aversion to the scheme might have been easily overcome, but I reflected that a mind like his was at once flexible and obstinate. He might yield to arguments and entreaties, and act by their immediate impulse; but the impulse passed away in a moment, old and habitual convictions were resumed, and his deviation from the beaten track would be merely productive of compunction. His aid, on the present occasion, though of some use, was by no means indispensible. I forbore to solicit his concurrence, or even to vanquish the scruples he entertained against directing me to the grave of Hadwin. It was a groundless superstition that made one spot more suitable for this purpose than another. I desired Caleb, in a mild tone, to return to the kitchen, and leave me to act as I thought proper. I then proceeded to the orchard.

One corner of this field was somewhat above the level of the rest. The tallest tree of the groupe grew there, and there I had formerly placed a bench, and made it my retreat at periods of leisure. It had been recommended by its sequestered situation, its luxuriant verdure, and profound quiet. On one side was a potatoe field, on the other a *melon-patch*; and before me, in rows, some hundreds of apple trees. Here I was accustomed to seek the benefits of contemplation, and study the manuscripts of Lodi. A few months had passed since I had last visited this spot. What revolutions had since occurred, and how gloomily contrasted was my present purpose with what had formerly led me hither!

In this spot I had hastily determined to dig the grave of Susan. The grave was dug. All that I desired was a cavity of sufficient dimensions to receive her. This being made, I returned to the house, lifted the corpse in my arms, and bore it without delay to the spot. Caleb seated in the kitchen, and Eliza asleep in her chamber, were wholly unapprised of my motions. The grave was covered, the spade reposited under the shed, and my seat by the kitchen fire resumed in a time apparently too short for so solemn and momentous a transaction.

I look back upon this incident with emotions not easily described. It seems as if I acted with too much precipitation;

as if insensibility, and not reason, had occasioned that clearness of conceptions, and bestowed that firmness of muscles, which I then experienced. I neither trembled nor wavered in my purpose. I bore in my arms the being whom I had known and loved, through the whistling gale and intense darkness of a winter's night; I heaped earth upon her limbs, and covered them from human observation, without fluctuations or tremors, though not without feelings that were awful and sublime.

Perhaps some part of my stedfastness was owing to my late experience, and some minds may be more easily inured to perilous emergencies than others. If reason acquires strength only by the diminution of sensibility, perhaps it is just for sensibility to be diminished.

Chapter VIII

T HE SAFETY of Eliza was the object that now occupied my cares. To have slept, after her example, had been most proper, but my uncertainty with regard to her fate, and my desire to conduct her to some other home, kept my thoughts in perpetual motion. I waited with impatience till she should awake and allow me to consult with her on plans for futurity.

Her sleep terminated not till the next day had arisen. Having recovered the remembrance of what had lately happened, she enquired for her sister. She wanted to view once more the face, and kiss the lips, of her beloved Susan. Some relief to her anguish she expected to derive from this privilege.

When informed of the truth, when convinced that Susan had disappeared forever, she broke forth into fresh passion. It seemed as if her loss was not hopeless or compleat as long as she was suffered to behold the face of her friend and to touch her lips. She accused me of acting without warrant and without justice; of defrauding her of her dearest and only consolation; and of treating her sister's sacred remains with barbarous indifference and rudeness.

I explained in the gentlest terms the reasons of my conduct. I was not surprized or vexed, that she, at first, treated them as futile, and as heightening my offence. Such was the impulse of a grief, which was properly excited by her loss. To be tranquil and stedfast, in the midst of the usual causes of impetuosity and agony, is either the prerogative of wisdom that sublimes itself above all selfish considerations, or the badge of giddy and unfeeling folly.

The torrent was at length exhausted. Upbraiding was at an end; and gratitude, and tenderness, and implicit acquiescence in any scheme which my prudence should suggest, succeeded. I mentioned her uncle as one to whom it would be proper, in her present distress, to apply.

She started and betrayed uneasiness at this name. It was evident that she by no means concurred with me in my notions of propriety; that she thought with aversion of seeking her uncle's protection. I requested her to state her objections to this scheme, or to mention any other which she thought preferable.

She knew no body. She had not a friend in the world but myself. She had never been out of her father's house. She had no relation but her uncle Philip, and he—she could not live with him. I must not insist upon her going to his house. It was not the place for her. She should never be happy there.

I was, at first, inclined to suspect in my friend some capricious and groundless antipathy. I desired her to explain what in her uncle's character made him so obnoxious. She refused to be more explicit, and persisted in thinking that his house was no suitable abode for her.

Finding her, in this respect, invincible, I sought for some other expedient. Might she not easily be accommodated as a boarder in the city, or some village, or in a remote quarter of the country? Ellis, her nearest and most opulent neighbor, had refused to receive her; but there were others who had not his fears. There were others, within the compass of a day's journey, who were strangers to the cause of Hadwin's death; but would it not be culpable to take advantage of that ignorance? Their compliance ought not to be the result of deception.

While thus engaged, the incidents of my late journey recurred to my remembrance, and I asked, is not the honest woman, who entertained Wallace, just such a person as that of whom I am in search? Her treatment of Wallace shews her to be exempt from chimerical fears, proves that she has room in her house for an occasional inmate.

Encouraged by these views, I told my weeping companion, that I had recollected a family in which she would be kindly treated; and that, if she chose, we would not lose a moment in repairing thither. Horses, belonging to the farm, grazed in the meadows, and a couple of these would carry us in a few hours to the place which I had selected for her residence. On her eagerly assenting to this proposal, I enquired in whose care, and in what state, our present habitation should be left.

The father's property now belonged to the daughter. Eliza's mind was quick, active, and sagacious; but her total inexperience gave her sometimes the appearance of folly. She was eager to fly from this house, and to resign herself and her property, without limitation or condition, to my controul.

Our intercourse had been short, but she relied on my protection and counsel as absolutely as she had been accustomed to do upon her father's.

She knew not what answer to make to my enquiry. Whatever I pleased to do was the best. What did I think ought to be done?

Ah! thought I, sweet, artless, and simple girl! how wouldst thou have fared, if Heaven had not sent me to thy succour? There are beings in the world who would make a selfish use of thy confidence; who would beguile thee at once of innocence and property. Such am not I. Thy welfare is a precious deposit, and no father or brother could watch over it with more solicitude than I will do.

I was aware that Mr. Hadwin might have fixed the destination of his property, and the guardianship of his daughters, by will. On suggesting this to my friend, it instantly reminded her of an incident that took place after his last return from the city. He had drawn up his will, and gave it into Susan's possession, who placed it in a drawer, whence it was now taken by my friend.

By this will his property was now found to be bequeathed to his two daughters; and his brother, Philip Hadwin, was named executor, and guardian to his daughters till they should be twenty years old. This name was no sooner heard by my friend, than she exclaimed, in a tone of affright, executor! My uncle! What is that? What power does that give him?

I know not exactly the power of executors. He will, doubtless, have possession of your property till you are twenty years of age. Your person will likewise be under his care till that time.

Must he decide where I am to live?

He is vested with all the power of a father.

This assurance excited the deepest consternation. She fixed her eyes on the ground, and was lost, for a time, in the deepest reverie. Recovering, at length, she said, with a sigh, what if my father had made no will?

In that case, a guardian could not be dispensed with, but the right of naming him would belong to yourself.

And my uncle would have nothing to do with my affairs?

I am no lawyer, said I; but I presume all authority over your person and property would devolve upon the guardian of your own choice.

Then I am free. Saying this, with a sudden motion, she tore in several pieces the will, which, during this dialogue, she had held in her hand, and threw the fragments into the fire.

No action was more unexpected to me than this. My astonishment hindered me from attempting to rescue the paper from the flames. It was consumed in a moment. I was at a loss in what manner to regard this sacrifice. It denoted a force of mind little in unison with that simplicity and helplessness which this girl had hitherto displayed. It argued the deepest apprehensions of mistreatment from her uncle. Whether his conduct had justified this violent antipathy, I had no means of judging. Mr. Hadwin's choice of him, as his executor, was certainly one proof of his integrity.

My abstraction was noticed by Eliza, with visible anxiety. It was plain, that she dreaded the impression which this act of seeming temerity had made upon me. Do not be angry with me, said she; perhaps I have been wrong, but I could not help it. I will have but one guardian and one protector.

The deed was irrevocable. In my present ignorance of the domestic history of the Hadwins, I was unqualified to judge how far circumstances might extenuate or justify the act. On both accounts, therefore, it was improper to expatiate upon it.

It was concluded to leave the care of the house to honest Caleb; to fasten closets and drawers, and, carrying away the money which was found in one of them, and which amounted to no inconsiderable sum, to repair to the house formerly mentioned. The air was cold; an heavy snow began to fall in the night; the wind blew tempestuously; and we were compelled to confront it.

In leaving her dwelling, in which she had spent her whole life, the unhappy girl gave way afresh to her sorrow. It made her feeble and helpless. When placed upon the horse, she was scarcely able to maintain her seat. Already chilled by the cold, blinded by the drifting snow, and cut by the blast, all my remonstrances were needed to inspire her with resolution.

I am not accustomed to regard the elements, or suffer them to retard or divert me from any design that I have formed. I had overlooked the weak and delicate frame of my companion, and made no account of her being less able to support cold and fatigue than myself. It was not till we had made some progress in our way, that I began to view, in their true light, the obstacles that were to be encountered. I conceived it, however, too late to retreat, and endeavored to push on with speed.

My companion was a skilful rider, but her steed was refractory and unmanageable. She was able, however, to curb his spirit till we had proceeded ten or twelve miles from Malverton. The wind and the cold became too violent to be longer endured, and I resolved to stop at the first house which should present itself to my view, for the sake of refreshment and warmth.

We now entered a wood of some extent, at the termination of which I remembered that a dwelling stood. To pass this wood, therefore, with expedition, was all that remained before we could reach an hospitable asylum. I endeavored to sustain, by this information, the sinking spirits of my companion. While busy in conversing with her, a blast of irresistible force twisted off the highest branch of a tree before us. It fell in the midst of the road, at the distance of a few feet from her horse's head. Terrified by this accident, the horse started from the path, and, rushing into the wood, in a moment threw himself and his rider on the ground, by encountering the rugged stock of an oak.

I dismounted and flew to her succour. The snow was already dyed with the blood which flowed from some wound in her head, and she lay without sense or motion. My terrors did not hinder me from anxiously searching for the hurt which was received, and ascertaining the extent of the injury. Her forehead was considerably bruised; but, to my unspeakable joy, the blood flowed from the nostrils, and was, therefore, to be regarded as no mortal symptom.

I lifted her in my arms, and looked around me for some means of relief. The house at which I proposed to stop was upwards of a mile distant. I remembered none that was nearer. To place the wounded girl on my own horse, and proceed gently to the house in question, was the sole expedient; but, at present, she was senseless, and might, on recovering, be too feeble to sustain her own weight.

To recall her to life was my first duty; but I was powerless, or unacquainted with the means. I gazed upon her features, and endeavored, by pressing her in my arms, to inspire her with some warmth. I looked towards the road, and listened for the wished-for sound of some carriage that might be prevailed on to stop and receive her. Nothing was more improbable than that either pleasure or business would induce men to encounter so chilling and vehement a blast. To be lighted on by some traveller was, therefore, an hopeless event.

Meanwhile, Eliza's swoon continued, and my alarm increased. What effect her half-frozen blood would have in prolonging this condition, or preventing her return to life, awakened the deepest apprehensions. I left the wood, still bearing her in my arms, and re-entered the road, from the desire of descrying, as soon as possible, the coming passenger. I looked this way and that, and again listened. Nothing but the sweeping blast, rent and falling branches, and snow that filled and obscured the air, were perceivable. Each moment retarded the course of my own blood and stiffened my sinews, and made the state of my companion more desperate. How was I to act? To perish myself or see her perish, was an ignoble fate: courage and activity were still able to avert it. My horse stood near, docile and obsequious; to mount him and to proceed on my way, holding my lifeless burthen in my arms, was all that remained.

At this moment my attention was called by several voices, issuing from the wood. It was the note of gaiety and glee: presently a sleigh, with several persons of both sexes, appeared, in a road which led through the forest into that in which I stood. They moved at a quick pace, but their voices were hushed and they checked the speed of their horses on discovering us. No occurrence was more auspicious than this; for I relied with perfect confidence on the benevolence of these persons, and as soon as they came near, claimed their assistance.

My story was listened to with sympathy, and one of the young men, leaping from the sleigh, assisted me in placing

Eliza in the place which he had left. A female, of sweet aspect and engaging manners, insisted upon turning back and hastening to the house, where it seems her father resided, and which the party had just left. I rode after the sleigh, which in a few minutes arrived at the house.

The dwelling was spacious and neat, and a venerable man and woman, alarmed by the quick return of the young people, came forth to know the cause. They received their guest with the utmost tenderness, and provided her with all the accommodations which her condition required. Their daughter relinquished the scheme of pleasure in which she had been engaged, and, compelling her companions to depart without her, remained to nurse and console the sick.

A little time shewed that no lasting injury had been suffered. Contusions, more troublesome than dangerous, and easily curable by such applications as rural and traditional wisdom has discovered, were the only consequences of the fall. My mind, being relieved from apprehensions on this score, had leisure to reflect upon the use which might be made of the present state of things.

When I marked the structure of this house, and the features and deportment of its inhabitants, methought I discerned a powerful resemblance between this family and Hadwin's. It seemed as if some benignant power had led us hither as to the most suitable asylum that could be obtained; and in order to supply, to the forlorn Eliza, the place of those parents and that sister she had lost, I conceived, that, if their concurrence could be gained, no abode was more suitable than this. No time was to be lost in gaining this concurrence. The curiosity of our host and hostess, whose name was Curling, speedily afforded me an opportunity to disclose the history and real situation of my friend. There were no motives to reserve or prevarication. There was nothing which I did not faithfully and circumstantially relate. I concluded with stating my wishes that they would admit my friend as a boarder into their house.

The old man was warm in his concurrence. His wife betrayed some scruples; which, however, her husband's arguments and mine removed. I did not even suppress the tenor and destruction of the will, and the antipathy which Eliza had conceived for her uncle, and which I declared myself unable to explain. It presently appeared that Mr. Curling had some knowledge of Philip Hadwin, and that the latter had acquired the repute of being obdurate and profligate. He employed all means to accomplish his selfish ends, and would probably endeavor to usurp the property which his brother had left. To provide against his power and his malice would be particularly incumbent on us, and my new friend readily promised his assistance in the measures which we should take to that end.

Chapter IX

THE STATE of my feelings may be easily conceived to consist of mixed, but on the whole, of agreeable sensations. The death of Hadwin and his elder daughter could not be thought upon without keen regrets. These it were useless to indulge, and were outweighed by reflections on the personal security in which the survivor was now placed. It was hurtful to expend my unprofitable cares upon the dead, while there existed one to whom they could be of essential benefit, and in whose happiness they would find an ample compensation.

This happiness, however, was still incomplete. It was still exposed to hazard, and much remained to be done before adequate provision was made against the worst of evils, poverty. I now found that Eliza, being only fifteen years old, stood in need of a guardian, and that the forms of law required that some one should make himself her father's administrator. Mr. Curling being tolerably conversant with these subjects, pointed out the mode to be pursued, and engaged to act on this occasion as Eliza's friend.

There was another topic on which my happiness, as well as that of my friend, required us to form some decision. I formerly mentioned, that during my abode at Malverton, I had not been insensible to the attractions of this girl. An affection had stolen upon me, for which, it was easily discovered, that I should not have been denied a suitable return. My reasons for stifling these emotions, at that time, have been mentioned. It may now be asked, what effect subsequent events had produced on my feelings, and how far partaking and relieving her distresses, had revived a passion which may readily be supposed to have been, at no time, entirely extinguished.

The impediments which then existed, were removed. Our union would no longer risk the resentment or sorrow of her excellent parent. She had no longer a sister to divide with her the property of the farm, and make what was sufficient for both, when living together, too little for either separately. Her youth and simplicity required, beyond most others, a legal protector, and her happiness was involved in the success of those hopes which she took no pains to conceal.

As to me, it seemed at first view, as if every incident conspired to determine my choice. Omitting all regard to the happiness of others, my own interest could not fail to recommend a scheme by which the precious benefits of competence and independence might be honestly obtained. The excursions of my fancy had sometimes carried me beyond the bounds prescribed by my situation, but they were, nevertheless, limited to that field to which I had once some prospect of acquiring a title. All I wanted for the basis of my gaudiest and most dazzling structures, was an hundred acres of plough-land and meadow. Here my spirit of improvement, my zeal to invent and apply new maxims of household luxury and convenience, new modes and instruments of tillage, new arts connected with orchard, garden and cornfield, were supplied with abundant scope. Though the want of these would not benumb my activity, or take away content, the possession would confer exquisite and permanent enjoyments.

My thoughts have ever hovered over the images of wife and children with more delight than over any other images. My fancy was always active on this theme, and its reveries sufficiently extatic and glowing; but since my intercourse with this girl, my scattered visions were collected and concentered. I had now a form and features before me, a sweet and melodious voice vibrated in my ear, my soul was filled, as it were, with her lineaments and gestures, actions and looks. All ideas, possessing any relation to beauty or sex, appeared to assume this shape. They kept an immoveable place in my mind, they diffused around them an ineffable complacency. Love is merely of value as a prelude to a more tender, intimate and sacred union. Was I not in love, and did I not pant after the irrevocable bonds, the boundless privileges of wedlock?

The question which others might ask, I have asked myself. Was I not in love? I am really at a loss for an answer. There seemed to be irresistible weight in the reasons why I should refuse to marry, and even forbear to foster love in my friend. I considered my youth, my defective education and my limited views. I had passed from my cottage into the world. I had acquired even in my transient sojourn among the busy haunts

of men, more knowledge than the lucubrations and employments of all my previous years had conferred. Hence I might
infer the childlike immaturity of my understanding, and the
rapid progress I was still capable of making. Was this an age
to form an irrevocable contract; to chuse the companion of
my future life, the associate of my schemes of intellectual and
benevolent activity?

I had reason to contemn my own acquisitions; but were not
those of Eliza still more slender? Could I rely upon the permanence of her equanimity and her docility to my instructions? What qualities might not time unfold, and how little
was I qualified to estimate the character of one, whom no
vicissitude or hardship had approached before the death of
her father? Whose ignorance was, indeed, great, when it could
justly be said even to exceed my own.

Should I mix with the world; enrol myself in different
classes of society; be a witness to new scenes, might not my
modes of judging undergo essential variations? Might I not
gain the knowledge of beings whose virtue was the gift of
experience and the growth of knowledge? Who joined to the
modesty and charms of woman, the benefits of education, the
maturity and steadfastness of age, and with whose character
and sentiments my own would be much more congenial than
they could possibly be with the extreme youth, rustic simplicity and mental imperfections of Eliza Hadwin?

To say truth, I was now conscious of a revolution in my
mind. I can scarcely assign its true cause. No tokens of it
appeared during my late retreat to Malverton. Subsequent incidents, perhaps, joined with the influence of meditation, had
generated new views. On my first visit to the city, I had met
with nothing but scenes of folly, depravity and cunning. No
wonder that the images connected with the city, were disastrous and gloomy; but my second visit produced somewhat
different impressions. Maravegli, Estwick, Medlicote and you,
were beings who inspired veneration and love. Your residence
appeared to beautify and consecrate this spot, and gave birth
to an opinion that if cities are the chosen seats of misery and
vice, they are likewise the soil of all the laudable and strenuous
productions of mind.

My curiosity and thirst of knowledge had likewise received

a new direction. Books and inanimate nature were cold and lifeless instructors. Men, and the works of men, were the objects of rational study, and our own eyes only could communicate just conceptions of human performances. The influence of manners, professions and social institutions, could be thoroughly known only by direct inspection.

Competence, fixed property and a settled abode, rural occupations and conjugal pleasures, were justly to be prized; but their value could be known, and their benefits fully enjoyed only by those who have tried all scenes; who have mixed with all classes and ranks; who have partaken of all conditions; and who have visited different hemispheres and climates and nations. The next five or eight years of my life, should be devoted to activity and change: it should be a period of hardship, danger and privation: it should be my apprenticeship to fortitude and wisdom, and be employed to fit me for the tranquil pleasures and steadfast exertions of the remainder of my life.

In consequence of these reflections, I determined to suppress that tenderness which the company of Miss Hadwin produced, to remove any mistakes into which she had fallen, and to put it out of my power to claim from her more than the dues of friendship. All ambiguities, in a case like this, and all delays were hurtful. She was not exempt from passion, but this passion I thought was young, and easily extinguished.

In a short time her health was restored, and her grief melted down into a tender melancholy. I chose a suitable moment, when not embarrassed by the presence of others, to reveal my thoughts. My disclosure was ingenuous and perfect. I laid before her the whole train of my thoughts, nearly in the order, though in different and more copious terms than those in which I have just explained them to you. I concealed nothing. The impression which her artless lovelines had made upon me at Malverton; my motives for estranging myself from her society; the nature of my present feelings with regard to her, and my belief of the state of her heart; the reasonings into which I had entered; the advantages of wedlock and its inconveniences; and, finally, the resolution I had formed of seeking the city, and perhaps, of crossing the ocean, were minutely detailed.

She interrupted me not, but changing looks, blushes, flutterings and sighs, shewed her to be deeply and variously affected by my discourse. I paused for some observation or comment. She seemed conscious of my expectation, but had no power to speak. Overpowered, at length, by her emotions, she burst into tears.

I was at a loss in what manner to construe these symptoms. I waited till her vehemence was somewhat subsided, and then said—what think you of my schemes? Your approbation is of some moment: do you approve of them or not?

This question excited some little resentment, and she answered—you have left me nothing to say. Go and be happy: no matter what becomes of me. I hope I shall be able to take care of myself.

The tone in which this was said, had something in it of upbraiding. Your happiness, said I, is too dear to me to leave it in danger. In this house you will not need my protection, but I shall never be so far from you, as to be disabled from hearing how you fared, by letter, and of being active for your good. You have some money which you must husband well. Any rent from your farm cannot be soon expected; but what you have got, if you remain with Mr. Curling, will pay your board and all other expences for two years: but you must be a good economist. I shall expect, continued I, with a serious smile, a punctual account of all your sayings and doings. I must know how every minute is employed, and every penny is expended, and if I find you erring, I must tell you so in good round terms.

These words did not dissipate the sullenness which her looks had betrayed. She still forebore to look at me, and said—I do not know how I should tell you every thing. You care so little about me that—I should only be troublesome. I am old enough to think and act for myself, and shall advise with no body but myself.

That is true, said I. I shall rejoice to see you independent and free. Consult your own understanding, and act according to its dictates. Nothing more is wanting to make you useful and happy. I am anxious to return to the city; but, if you will allow me, will go first to Malverton, see that things are in due order, and that old Caleb is well. From thence, if you please,

I will call at your uncle's, and tell him what has happened. He may, otherwise, entertain pretensions and form views, erroneous in themselves and injurious to you. He may think himself entitled to manage your estate. He may either suppose a will to have been made, or may actually have heard from your father, or from others, of that which you burnt, and in which he was named executor. His boisterous and sordid temper may prompt him to seize your house and goods, unless seasonably apprised of the truth; and, when he knows the truth, he may start into rage, which I shall be more fitted to encounter than you. I am told that anger transforms him into a ferocious madman. Shall I call upon him?

She shuddered at the picture which I had drawn of her uncle's character; but this emotion quickly gave place to self-upbraiding, for the manner in which she had repelled my proffers of service. She melted once more into tears and exclaimed:

I am not worthy of the pains you take for me. I am unfeeling and ungrateful. Why should I think ill of you for despising me, when I despise myself?

You do yourself injustice, my friend. I think I see your most secret thoughts; and these, instead of exciting anger or contempt, only awaken compassion and tenderness. You love; and must, therefore, conceive my conduct to be perverse and cruel. I counted on your harboring such thoughts. Time only and reflection will enable you to see my motives in their true light. Hereafter you will recollect my words, and find them sufficient to justify my conduct. You will acknowledge the propriety of my engaging in the cares of the world, before I sit down in retirement and ease.

Ah! how much you mistake me! I admire and approve of your schemes. What angers and distresses me is, that you think me unworthy to partake of your cares and labors; that you regard my company as an obstacle and incumbrance; that assistance and counsel must all proceed from you; and that no scene is fit for me, but what you regard as slothful and inglorious.

Have I not the same claims to be wise, and active, and courageous as you? If I am ignorant and weak, do I not owe it to the same cause that has made you so; and will not the same means which promote your improvement be likewise useful to me? You desire to obtain knowledge, by travelling and conversing with many persons, and studying many scenes; but you desire it for yourself alone. Me, you think poor, weak, and contemptible; fit for nothing but to spin and churn. Provided I exist, am screened from the weather, have enough to eat and drink, you are satisfied. As to strengthening my mind and enlarging my knowledge, these things are valuable to you, but on me they are thrown away. I deserve not the gift.

This strain, simple and just as it was, was wholly unexpected. I was surprized and disconcerted. In my previous reasonings I had certainly considered her sex as utterly unfitting her for those scenes and pursuits, to which I had destined myself. Not a doubt of the validity of my conclusion had insinuated itself; but now my belief was shaken, though it was not subverted. I could not deny, that human ignorance was curable by the same means in one sex as in the other; that fortitude and skill was of no less value to one than to the other.

Questionless, my friend was rendered, by her age and inexperience, if not by sex, more helpless and dependent than I; but had I not been prone to overrate the difficulties which I should encounter? Had I not deemed unjustly of her constancy and force of mind? Marriage would render her property joint, and would not compel me to take up my abode in the woods, to abide forever in one spot, to shackle my curiosity, or limit my excursions.

But marriage was a contract awful and irrevocable. Was this the woman with whom my reason enjoined me to blend my fate, without the power of dissolution? Would not time unfold qualities in her which I did not at present suspect, and which would evince an incurable difference in our minds? Would not time lead me to the feet of one who more nearly approached that standard of ideal excellence which poets and romancers had exhibited to my view?

These considerations were powerful and delicate. I knew not in what terms to state them to my companion, so as to preclude the imputation of arrogance or indecorum. It became me, however, to be explicit, and to excite her resentment rather than mislead her judgment. She collected my meaning from a few words, and, interrupting me, said:

How very low is the poor Eliza in your opinion! We are, indeed, both too young to be married. May I not see you, and talk with you, without being your wife? May I not share your knowledge, relieve your cares, and enjoy your confidence, as a sister might do? May I not accompany you in your journeys and studies, as one friend accompanies another? My property may be yours; you may employ it for your benefit and mine; not because you are my husband, but my friend. You are going to the city. Let me go along with you. Let me live where you live. The house that is large enough to hold you, will hold me. The fare that is good enough for you will be luxury to me. Oh! let it be so, will you? You cannot think how studious, how thoughtful, how inquisitive I will be. How tenderly I will nurse you when sick: it is possible you may be sick, you know, and no one in the world will be half so watchful and affectionate as I shall be. Will you let me?

In saying this, her earnestness gave new pathos to her voice. Insensibly she put her face close to mine, and, transported beyond the usual bounds of reserve, by the charms of that picture which her fancy contemplated, she put her lips to my cheek, and repeated, in a melting accent, will you let me?

You, my friends, who have not seen Eliza Hadwin, cannot conceive what effect this entreaty was adapted to produce in me. She has surely the sweetest voice, the most speaking features, and most delicate symetry, that ever woman possessed. Her guileless simplicity and tenderness made her more enchanting. To be the object of devotion to an heart so fervent and pure, was, surely, no common privilege. Thus did she tender me herself; and was not the gift to be received with eagerness and gratitude?

No. I was not so much a stranger to mankind as to acquiesce in this scheme. As my sister or my wife, the world would suffer us to reside under the same roof; to apply, to common use, the same property; and daily to enjoy the company of each other: but she was not my sister, and marriage would be an act of the grossest indiscretion. I explained to her, in few words, the objections to which her project was liable.

Well, then, said she, let me live in the next house, in the neighborhood, or, at least, in the same city. Let me be where I may see you once a day, or once a week, or once a month. Shut me not wholly from your society, and the means of becoming, in time, less ignorant and foolish than I now am.

After a pause, I replied, I love you too well not to comply with this request. Perhaps the city will be as suitable a residence as any other for you, as it will, for some time, be most convenient to me. I shall be better able to watch over your welfare, and supply you with the means of improvement, when you are within a small distance. At present, you must consent to remain here, while I visit your uncle, and afterwards go to the city. I shall look out for you a suitable lodging, and inform you when it is found. If you then continue in the same mind, I will come, and, having gained the approbation of Mr. Curling, will conduct you to town. Here ended our dialogue.

Chapter X

THOUGH I had consented to this scheme, I was conscious that some hazards attended it. I was afraid of calumny, which might trouble the peace or destroy the reputation of my friend. I was afraid of my own weakness, which might be seduced into an indiscreet marriage, by the charms or sufferings of this bewitching creature. I felt that there was no price too dear to save her from slander. A fair fame is of the highest importance to a young female, and the loss of it but poorly supplied by the testimony of her own conscience. I had reason for tenfold solicitude on this account, since I was her only protector and friend. Hence, I cherished some hopes, that time might change her views, and suggest less dangerous schemes. Meanwhile, I was to lose no time in visiting Malverton and Philip Hadwin.

About ten days had elapsed since we had deserted Malverton. These were days of successive storms, and travelling had been rendered inconvenient. The weather was now calm and clear, and, early in the morning that ensued the dialogue which I have just related, I set out on horseback.

Honest Caleb was found, eating his breakfast, nearly in the spot where he had been first discovered. He answered my enquiries by saying, that, two days after our departure, several men had come to the house, one of whom was Philip Hadwin. They had interrogated him as to the condition of the farm, and the purpose of his remaining on it. William Hadwin they knew to have been sometime dead, but where were the girls, his daughters?

Caleb answered that Susy, the eldest, was likewise dead.

These tidings excited astonishment. When died she, and how, and where was she buried?

It happened two days before, and she was buried, he believed, but could not tell where.

Not tell where? By whom then was she buried?

Really, he could not tell. Some strange man came there just as she was dying. He went to the room, and when she was dead, took her away, but what he did with the body, was more than he could say, but he had a notion that he buried it. The man staid till the morning, and then went off with Lizzy, leaving him to keep house by himself. He had not seen either of them, nor indeed, a single soul since.

This was all the information that Caleb could afford the visitants. It was so lame and incredible, that they began to charge the man with falsehood, and to threaten him with legal animadversion. Just then, Mr. Ellis entered the house, and being made acquainted with the subject of discourse, told all that he himself knew. He related the midnight visit which I had paid him, explained my former situation in the family, and my disappearance in September. He stated the advice he had given me to carry Eliza to her uncle's, and my promise to comply with his counsel. The uncle declared he had seen nothing of his niece, and Caleb added, that when she set out, she took the road that led to town.

These hints afforded grounds for much conjecture and suspicion. Ellis now mentioned some intelligence that he had gathered respecting me in a late journey to ——. It seems I was the son of an honest farmer in that quarter, who married a tidy girl of a milk maid, that lived with him. My father had detected me in making some atrocious advances to my mother-in-law, and had turned me out of doors. I did not go off, however, without rifling his drawer of some hundreds of dollars, which he had laid up against a rainy day. I was noted for such pranks, and was hated by all the neighbors for my pride and laziness. It was easy by comparison of circumstances, for Ellis to ascertain that Hadwin's servant Mervyn, was the same against whom such hearty charges were laid.

Previously to this journey, he had heard of me from Hadwin, who was loud in praise of my diligence, sobriety and modesty. For his part, he had always been cautious of giving countenance to vagrants, that came from nobody knew where, and worked their way with a plausible tongue. He was not surprised to hear it whispered that Betsey Hadwin had fallen in love with the youth, and now, no doubt, he had persuaded her to run away with him. The heiress of a fine farm was a prize not to be met with every day.

Philip broke into rage at this news; swore that if it turned out so, his niece should starve upon the town, and that he would take good care to baulk the lad. His brother he well knew had left a will, to which he was executor, and that this will, would in good time, be forth coming. After much talk and ransacking the house, and swearing at his truant niece, he and his company departed, charging Caleb to keep the house and its contents for his use. This was all that Caleb's memory had retained of that day's proceedings.

Curling had lately commented on the character of Philip Hadwin. This man was totally unlike his brother, was a noted brawler and bully, a tyrant to his children, a plague to his neighbors, and kept a rendezvous for drunkards and idlers, at the sign of the Bull's Head, at ———. He was not destitute of parts, and was no less dreaded for cunning than malignity. He was covetous, and never missed an opportunity of overreaching his neighbor. There was no doubt that his niece's property would be embezzled, should it ever come into his hands, and any power which he might obtain over her person, would be exercised to her destruction. His children were tainted with the dissoluteness of their father, and marriage had not repaired the reputation of his daughters, or cured them of depravity: this was the man whom I now proposed to visit.

I scarcely need to say that the calumny of Betty Lawrence gave me no uneasiness. My father had no doubt been deceived, as well as my father's neighbors, by the artifices of this woman. I passed among them for a thief and a profligate, but their error had hitherto been harmless to me. The time might come which should confute the tale, without my efforts. Betty, sooner or later would drop her mask, and afford the antidote to her own poisons, unless some new incident should occur to make me hasten the catastrophe.

I arrived at Hadwin's house. I was received with some attention as a guest. I looked among the pimpled visages that filled the piazza, for that of the landlord, but found him in an inner apartment with two or three more, seated round a table. On intimating my wish to speak with him alone, the others withdrew.

Hadwin's visage had some traces of resemblance to his brother; but the meek, placid air, pale cheeks and slender form of the latter, were powerfully contrasted with the bloated arrogance, imperious brow and robust limbs of the former. This man's rage was awakened by a straw; it impelled him in an instant to oaths and buffetings, and made his life an eternal brawl. The sooner my interview with such a personage should be at an end, the better. I therefore explained the purpose of my coming as fully and in as few words as possible.

Your name, Sir, is Philip Hadwin. Your brother William, of Malverton, died lately and left two daughters. The youngest only is now alive, and I come, commissioned from her, to inform you, that as no will of her father's is extant, she is preparing to administer to his estate. As her father's brother, she thought you entitled to this information.

The change which took place in the countenance of this man, during this address, was remarkable, but not easily described. His cheeks contracted a deeper crimson, his eyes sparkled, and his face assumed an expression in which curiosity was mingled with rage. He bent forwards and said, in an hoarse and contemptuous tone, pray, is your name Mervyn?

I answered, without hesitation, and as if the question were wholly unimportant, yes: my name is Mervyn.

God damn it! You then are the damn'd rascal—(but permit me to repeat his speech without the oaths, with which it was plentifully interlarded. Not three words were uttered without being garnished with a—God damn it! damnation! I'll be damn'd to hell if—and the like energetic expletives.) You then are the rascal that robbed Billy's house; that ran away with the fool his daughter; persuaded her to burn her father's will, and have the hellish impudence to come into this house! But I thank you for it. I was going to look for you—youv'e saved me trouble. I'll settle all accounts with you here. Fair and softly, my good lad! If I don't bring you to the gallows—If I let you escape without such a dressing! Damned impudence! Fellow! I've been at Malverton. I've heard of your tricks: so! finding the will not quite to your mind, knowing that the executor would baulk your schemes, you threw the will into the fire; you robbed the house of all the cash, and made off with the girl!—The old fellow saw it all, and will swear to the truth.

These words created some surprize. I meant not to conceal from this man the tenor and destruction of the will, nor even the measures which his niece had taken or intended to take.

What I supposed to be unknown to him, appeared to have been communicated by the talkative Caleb, whose mind was more inquisitive and less sluggish than first appearances had led me to imagine. Instead of moping by the kitchen fire, when Eliza and I were conversing in an upper room, it now appeared that he had reconnoitred our proceedings through some key hole or crevice, and had related what he had seen to Hadwin.

Hadwin proceeded to exhaust his rage in oaths and menaces. He frequently clenched his fist, and thrust it in my face, drew it back as if to render his blow more deadly; ran over the same series of exclamations on my impudence and villainy, and talked of the gallows and the whipping-post; enforced each word by the epithets—*damnable* and *hellish*—closed each sentence with—and be curst to you!

There was but one mode for me to pursue: all forcible opposition to a man of his strength was absurd. It was my province to make his anger confine itself to words, and patiently to wait till the paroxism should end or subside of itself. To effect this purpose, I kept my seat, and carefully excluded from my countenance every indication of timidity and panick on the one hand, and of scorn and defiance on the other. My look and attitude were those of a man who expected harsh words, but who entertained no suspicion that blows would be inflicted.

I was indebted for my safety to an inflexible adherence to this medium. To have strayed, for a moment, to either side, would have brought upon me his blows. That he did not instantly resort to violence, inspired me with courage, since it depended on myself whether food should be supplied to his passion. Rage must either progress or decline, and since it was in total want of provocation, it could not fail of gradually subsiding.

My demeanor was calculated to damp the flame, not only by its direct influence, but by diverting his attention from the wrongs which he had received, to the novelty of my behaviour. The disparity in size and strength between us, was too evident to make him believe that I confided in my sinews for my defence; and since I betrayed neither contempt nor fear, he could not but conclude that I trusted to my own integrity or to his moderation. I seized the first pause in his rhetorick to enforce this sentiment.

You are angry, Mr. Hadwin, and are loud in your threats, but they do not frighten me. They excite no apprehension or alarm, because I know myself able to convince you that I have not injured you. This is an inn, and I am your guest. I am sure I shall find better entertainment than blows. Come, continued I, smiling, it is possible that I am not so mischievous a wretch as your fancy paints me. I have no claims upon your niece but that of friendship, and she is now in the house of an honest man, Mr. Curling, where she proposes to continue as long as is convenient.

It is true that your brother left a will, which his daughter burnt in my presence, because she dreaded the authority which that will gave you, not only over her property, but person. It is true that on leaving the house, she took away the money which was now her own, and which was necessary to subsistence. It is true that I bore her company, and have left her in an honest man's keeping. I am answerable for nothing more. As to you, I meant not to injure you; I advised not the burning of the will. I was a stranger till after that event, to your character. I knew neither good nor ill of you. I came to tell you all this, because, as Eliza's uncle, you had a right to the information.

So! you come to tell me that she burnt the will, and is going to administer—to what, I beseech you? To her father's property? Aye, I warrant you; but take this along with you, that property is mine; land, house, stock, every thing. All is safe and snug under cover of a mortgage, to which Billy was kind enough to add a bond. One was sued, and the other *entered up*, a week ago. So that all is safe under my thumb, and the girl may whistle or starve for me. I shall give myself no concern about the strumpet. You thought to get a prize; but, damn me, you've met with your match in me. Phil. Haddin's not so easily choused, I promise you. I intended to give you this news, and a drubbing into the bargain; but you may go, and make haste. She burnt the will, did she; because I was named in it—and sent you to tell me so? Good souls! It was kind of you, and I am bound to be thankful. Take her back news of the mortgage; and, as for you, leave my house. You may go scot free this time; but I pledge my word for a sound beating when you next enter these doors. I'll pay it you with interest. Leave my house, I say!

A mortgage, said I, in a low voice, and affecting not to hear his commands, that will be sad news for my friend. Why, sir, you are a fortunate man. Malverton is an excellent spot; well watered and manured; newly and completely fenced: not a larger barn in the county: oxen, and horses, and cows in the best order: I never sat eyes on a finer orchard. By my faith, sir, you are a fortunate man. But, pray, what have you for dinner? I am hungry as a wolf. Order me a beef-steak, and some potation or other. The bottle there—it is cyder, I take it; pray, push it to this side. Saying this, I stretched out my hand towards the bottle which stood before him.

I confided in the power of a fearless and sedate manner. Methought that as anger was the food of anger, it must unavoidably subside in a contest with equability. This opinion was intuitive, rather than the product of experience, and perhaps, I gave no proof of my sagacity in hazarding my safety on its truth. Hadwin's character made him dreaded and obeyed by all. He had been accustomed to ready and tremulous submission from men far more brawny and robust than I was, and to find his most vehement menaces and gestures, totally ineffectual on a being so slender and diminutive, at once wound up his rage and excited his astonishment. One motion counteracted and suspended the other. He lifted his hand, but delayed to strike. One blow, applied with his usual dexterity, was sufficient to destroy me. Though seemingly careless, I was watchful of his motions, and prepared to elude the stroke by shrinking or stooping. Meanwhile, I stretched my hand far enough to seize the bottle, and pouring its contents into a tumbler, put it to my lips.

Come, sir, I drink your health, and wish you speedy possession of Malverton. I have some interest with Eliza, and will prevail on her to forbear all opposition and complaint. Why should she complain? While I live, she shall not be a beggar. No doubt, your claim is legal, and therefore ought to be admitted. What the law gave, the law has taken away. Blessed be the dispensers of law—excellent cyder! open another bottle, will you, and I beseech hasten dinner, if you would not see me devour the table.

It was just, perhaps, to conjure up the demon avarice to fight with the demon anger. Reason alone, would, in such a contest, be powerless, but, in truth, I spoke without artifice or disguise. If his claim were legal, opposition would be absurd and pernicious. I meant not to rely upon his own assertions, and would not acknowledge the validity of his claim, till I had inspected the deed. Having instituted suits, this was now in a public office, and there the inspection should be made. Meanwhile, no reason could be urged why I should part from him in anger, while his kindred to Eliza, and his title to her property, made it useful to secure his favor. It was possible to obtain a remission of his claims, even when the law enforced them: it would be imprudent at least to diminish the chances of remission by fostering his wrath and provoking his enmity.

What, he exclaimed, in a transport of fury, a'n't I master of my own house? Out, I say!

These were harsh terms, but they were not accompanied by gestures and tones so menacing as those which had before been used. It was plain that the tide, which so lately threatened my destruction, had begun to recede. This encouraged me to persist.

Be not alarmed, my good friend, said I, placidly and smiling. A man of your bone need not fear a pigmy like me. I shall scarcely be able to dethrone you in your own castle, with an army of hostlers, tapsters, and cooks at your beck. You shall still be master here, provided you use your influence to procure me a dinner.

His acquiescence in a pacific system, was extremely reluctant and gradual. He laid aside one sullen tone and wrathful look after the other; and, at length, consented not only to supply me with a dinner, but to partake of it with me. Nothing was more a topic of surprize to himself, than his forbearance. He knew not how it was. He had never been treated so before. He was not proof against entreaty and submission; but I had neither supplicated nor submitted. The stuff that I was made of was at once damnably tough and devilishly pliant. When he thought of my impudence, in staying in his house after he had bade me leave it, he was tempted to resume his passion. When he reflected on my courage, in making light of his anger, notwithstanding his known impetuosity and my personal inferiority, he could not withhold his esteem. But my patience under his rebukes, my unalterable equanimity, and my ready consent to the validity of his claims, soothed and propitiated him.

An exemption from blows and abuse was all that I could gain from this man. I told him the truth, with regard to my own history, so far as it was connected with the Hadwins. I exhibited, in affecting colours, the helpless condition of Eliza; but could extort from him nothing but his consent, that, if she chose, she might come and live with him. He would give her victuals and clothes for so much house-work as she was able to do. If she chose to live elsewhere, he promised not to molest her, or intermeddle in her concerns. The house and land were his by law, and he would have them.

It was not my province to revile, or expostulate with him. I stated what measures would be adopted by a man who regarded the interest of others more than his own; who was anxious for the welfare of an innocent girl, connected with him so closely by the ties of kindred, and who was destitute of what is called natural friends. If he did not cancel, for her sake, his bond and mortgage, he would, at least, afford her a frugal maintainance. He would extend to her, in all emergencies, his counsel and protection.

All that, he said, was sheer nonsense. He could not sufficiently wonder at my folly, in proposing to him to make a free gift of an hundred rich acres, to a girl too who scarcely knew her right hand from her left; whom the first cunning young rogue, like myself, would *chouse* out of the whole, and take herself into the bargain. But my folly was even surpassed by my impudence, since, as the *friend* of this girl, I was merely petitioning on my own account. I had come to him, whom I never saw before, on whom I had no claim, and who, as I well knew, had reason to think me a sharper, and modestly said—"Here's a girl who has no fortune. I am greatly in want of one. Pray, give her such an estate that you have in your possession. If you do, I'll marry her, and take it into my own hands." I might be thankful that he did not answer such a petition with an horse-whipping. But if he did not give her his estate, he might extend to her, forsooth, his counsel and protection. That I've offered to do, continued he. She may come and live in my house, if she will. She may do some of the family work. I'll discharge the chamber-maid to make room for her. Lizzy, if I remember right, has a pretty face. She can't have a better market for it than as chamber-maid to an inn. If she minds her p's and q's she may make up a handsome sum at the year's end.

I thought it time to break off the conference; and, my dinner being finished, took my leave; leaving behind me the character of *a queer sort of chap.* I speeded to the prothonotary's office, which was kept in the village, and quickly ascertained the truth of Hadwin's pretensions. There existed a mortgage, with bond and warrant of attorney, to so great an amount as would swallow up every thing at Malverton. Furnished with these tidings, I prepared, with a drooping heart, to return to Mr. Curling's.

Chapter XI

THIS INCIDENT necessarily produced a change in my views with regard to my friend. Her fortune consisted of a few hundreds of dollars, which, frugally administered, might procure decent accommodation in the country. When this was consumed, she must find subsistence in tending the big-wheel or the milk-pail, unless fortune should enable me to place her in a more favorable situation. This state was, in some respects, but little different from that in which she had spent the former part of her life; but, in her father's house, these employments were dignified by being, in some degree, voluntary, and relieved by frequent intervals of recreation and leisure. Now they were likely to prove irksome and servile, in consequence of being performed for hire, and imposed by necessity. Equality, parental solicitudes, and sisterly endearments would be wanting to lighten the yoke.

These inconveniences, however, were imaginary. This was the school in which fortitude and independence were to be learned. Habit, and the purity of rural manners, would, likewise, create a-new those ties which death had dissolved. The affections of parent and sister would be supplied by the fonder and more rational attachments of friendship. These toils were not detrimental to beauty or health. What was to be dreaded from them, was, their tendency to quench the spirit of liberal curiosity; to habituate the person to bodily, rather than intellectual, exertions; to supersede, and create indifference or aversion to the only instruments of rational improvement, the pen and the book.

This evil, however, was at some distance from Eliza. Her present abode was quiet and serene. Here she might enjoy domestic pleasures and opportunities of mental improvement, for the coming twelvemonth at least. This period would, perhaps, be sufficient for the formation of studious habits. What schemes should be adopted, for this end, would be determined by the destiny to which I myself should be reserved.

My path was already chalked out, and my fancy now pursued it with uncommon pleasure. To reside in your family; to study your profession; to pursue some subordinate or casual mode of industry, by which I might purchase leisure for medical pursuits, for social recreations, and for the study of mankind on your busy and thronged stage, was the scope of my wishes. This destiny would not hinder punctual correspondence and occasional visits to Eliza. Her pen might be called into action, and her mind be awakened by books, and every hour be made to add to her stores of knowledge and enlarge the bounds of her capacity.

I was spiritless and gloomy when I left ——, but reflections on my future lot, and just views of the situation of my friend, insensibly restored my cheerfulness. I arrived at Mr. Curling's in the evening, and hastened to impart to Eliza the issue of my commission. It gave her uneasiness, merely as it frustrated the design, on which she had fondly mused, of residing in the city. She was somewhat consoled by my promises of being her constant correspondent and occasional visitor.

Next morning I set out on my journey hither, on foot. The way was not long; the weather, though cold, was wholesome and serene. My spirits were high, and I saw nothing in the world before me but sunshine and prosperity. I was conscious that my happiness depended not on the revolutions of nature or the caprice of man. All without was, indeed, vicissitude and uncertainty; but within my bosom was a centre not to be shaken or removed. My purposes were honest and steadfast. Every sense was the inlet of pleasure, because it was the avenue to knowledge; and my soul brooded over the world of ideas, and glowed with exultation at the grandeur and beauty of its own creations.

This felicity was too rapturous to be of long duration. I gradually descended from these heights; and the remembrance of past incidents, connected with the images of your family, to which I was returning, led my thoughts into a different channel. Welbeck and the unhappy girl whom he had betrayed; Mrs. Villars and Wallace were recollected a-new. The views which I had formed, for determining the fate and affording assistance to Clemenza, were recalled. My former resolutions, with regard to her, had been suspended by the uncertainty in which the fate of the Hadwins was, at that time, wrapped. Had it not become necessary wholly to lay aside these resolutions?

That, indeed, was an irksome conclusion. No wonder that I struggled to repel it: that I fostered the doubt whether money was the only instrument of benefit: whether caution, and fortitude, and knowledge were not the genuine preservatives from evil. Had I not the means in my hands of dispelling her fatal ignorance of Welbeck and of those with whom she resided? Was I not authorized by my previous, though slender, intercourse, to seek her presence?

Suppose I should enter Mrs. Villars' house, desire to be introduced to the lady, accost her with affectionate simplicity, and tell her the truth? Why be anxious to smooth the way; why deal in apologies, circuities and inuendoes? All these are feeble and perverse refinements, unworthy of an honest purpose and an erect spirit. To believe her inaccessible to my visit, was absurd. To wait for the permission of those whose interest it might be to shut out visitants, was cowardice. This was an infringement of her liberty, which equity and law equally condemned. By what right could she be restrained from intercourse with others? Doors and passages may be between her and me. With a purpose such as mine, no one had a right to close the one or obstruct the other. Away with cowardly reluctances and clownish scruples, and let me hasten this moment to her dwelling.

Mrs. Villars is the portress of the mansion. She will probably present herself before me, and demand the reason of my visit. What shall I say to her? The truth. To faulter, or equivocate, or dissemble to this woman, would be wicked. Perhaps her character has been misunderstood and maligned. Can I render her a greater service than to apprize her of the aspersions that have rested on it, and afford her the opportunity of vindication? Perhaps she is indeed selfish and profligate; the betrayer of youth and the agent of lasciviousness. Does she not deserve to know the extent of her errors and the ignominy of her trade? Does she not merit the compassion of the good and the rebukes of the wise? To shrink from the task, would prove me cowardly and unfirm. Thus far, at least, let my courage extend.

Alas! Clemenza is unacquainted with my language. My thoughts cannot make themselves apparent but by words, and to my words she will be able to affix no meaning. Yet is not that an hasty decision? The version from the dramas of Zeno which I found in her toilet, was probably hers, and proves her to have a speculative knowledge of our tongue. Near half a year has since elapsed, during which she has dwelt with talkers of English, and consequently could not fail to have acquired it. This conclusion is somewhat dubious, but experiment will give it certainty.

Hitherto I had strolled along the path at a lingering pace. Time enough, methought, to reach your threshold between sun-rise and moonlight, if my way had been three times longer than it was. Yon were the pleasing phantoms that hovered before me, and beckoned me forward. What a total revolution had occurred in the course of a few seconds, for thus long did my reasonings with regard to Clemenza and the Villars require to pass through my understanding, and escape, in half muttered soliloquy, from my lips. My muscles trembled with eagerness, and I bounded forward with impetuosity. I saw nothing but a visto of catalpas, leafless, loaded with icicles, and terminating in four chimneys and a painted roof. My fancy outstripped my footsteps, and was busy in picturing faces and rehearsing dialogues. Presently I reached this new object of my pursuit, darted through the avenue, noticed that some windows of the house were unclosed, drew thence an hasty inference that the house was not without inhabitants, and knocked, quickly and loudly, for admission.

Some one within crept to the door, opened it with seeming caution, and just far enough to allow the face to be seen. It was the timid, pale and unwashed face of a girl who was readily supposed to be a servant, taken from a cottage, and turned into a bringer of wood and water, and a scourer of tubs and trenchers. She waited in timorous silence the delivery of my message. Was Mrs. Villars at home?

No: she was gone to town.

Were any of her daughters within?

She could not tell; she believed—she thought—which did I want? Miss Hetty or Miss Sally?

Let me see Miss Hetty. Saying this, I pushed gently against

the door. The girl, half reluctant, yielded way: I entered the passage, and putting my hand on the lock of a door that seemed to lead into a parlour—is Miss Hetty in this room?

No: there was nobody there.

Go call her then. Tell her there is one who wishes to see her on important business. I will wait for her coming in this room. So saying, I opened the door, and entered the apartment, while the girl withdrew to perform my message.

The parlour was spacious and expensively furnished, but an air of negligence and disorder was every where visible. The carpet was wrinkled and unswept; a clock on the table, in a glass frame, so streaked and spotted with dust as scarcely to be transparent, and the index motionless, and pointing at four instead of nine; embers scattered on the marble hearth, and tongs lying on the fender with the handle in the ashes; an harpsicord, uncovered, one end loaded with *scores*, tumbled together in a heap, and the other with volumes of novels and plays, some on their edges, some on their backs, gaping open by the scorching of their covers; rent; blurred; stained; blotted; dog-eared; tables awry; chairs crouding each other; in short, no object but indicated the neglect or ignorance of domestic neatness and economy.

My leisure was employed in surveying these objects, and in listening for the approach of Miss Hetty. Some minutes elapsed, and no one came. A reason for delay was easily imagined, and I summoned patience to wait. I opened a book; touched the instrument; surveyed the vases on the mantletree; the figures on the hangings, and the print of Apollo and the Sybil, taken from Salvator, and hung over the chimney. I eyed my own shape and garb in the mirror, and asked how my rustic appearance would be regarded by that supercilious and voluptuous being, to whom I was about to present myself.

Presently the latch of the door was softly moved, it opened, and the simpleton, before described, appeared. She spoke, but her voice was so full of hesitation, and so near a whisper, that much attention was needed to make out her words: Miss Hetty was not at home—she was gone to town with her *mistiss.*

This was a tale not to be credited. How was I to act? She persisted in maintaining the truth of it.—Well then, said I, at length, tell Miss Sally that I wish to speak with her. She will answer my purpose just as well.

Miss Sally was not at home neither. She had gone to town too. They would not be back, she did not know when: not till night, she supposed. It was so indeed, none of them wasn't at home: none but she and Nanny in the kitchen—indeed'n there wasn't.

Go tell Nanny to come here—I will leave my message with her. She withdrew, but Nanny did not receive the summons, or thought proper not to obey it. All was vacant and still.

My state was singular and critical. It was absurd to prolong it; but to leave the house with my errand unexecuted, would argue imbecility and folly. To ascertain Clemenza's presence in this house, and to gain an interview, were yet in my power. Had I not boasted of my intrepidity in braving denials and commands, when they endeavored to obstruct my passage to this woman? But here were no obstacles nor prohibitions. Suppose the girl had said truth, that the matron and her daughters were absent, and that Nanny and herself were the only guardians of the mansion. So much the better. My design will not be opposed. I have only to mount the stair, and go from one room to another, till I find what I seek.

There was hazard, as well as plausibility, in this scheme. I thought it best once more to endeavor to extort information from the girl, and persuade her to be my guide to whomsoever the house contained. I put my hand to the bell and rung a brisk peal. No one came. I passed into the entry, to the foot of a stair-case, and to a back window. Nobody was within hearing or sight.

Once more I reflected on the rectitude of my intentions, on the possibility that the girl's assertions might be true, on the benefits of expedition, and of gaining access to the object of my visit without interruption or delay. To these considerations was added a sort of charm, not easily explained, and by no means justifiable, produced by the very temerity and hazardness accompanying this attempt. I thought, with scornful emotions, on the bars and hindrances which pride and caprice, and delusive maxims of decorum, raise in the way of human intercourse. I spurned at these semblances and substitutes of honesty, and delighted to shake such fetters into air, and trample such impediments to dust. I wanted to see an human being, in order to promote her happiness. It was doubtful whether she was within twenty paces of the spot where I stood. The doubt was to be solved. How? By examining the space. I forthwith proceeded to examine it. I reached the second story. I approached a door that was closed. I knocked: after a pause, a soft voice said, who is there?

The accents were as musical as those of Clemenza, but were in other respects, different. I had no topic to discuss with this person. I answered not, yet hesitated to withdraw. Presently the same voice was again heard: what is it you want? Why don't you answer? Come in!—I complied with the command, and entered the room.

It was deliberation and foresight that led me hither, and not chance or caprice. Hence, instead of being disconcerted or vanquished by the objects that I saw, I was tranquil and firm. My curiosity, however, made me a vigilant observer. Two females, arrayed with voluptuous negligence, in a manner adapted to the utmost seclusion, and seated in a careless attitude, on a sofa, were now discovered.

Both darted glances at the door. One, who appeared to be the youngest, no sooner saw me, than she shrieked, and starting from her seat, betrayed, in the looks which she successively cast upon me, on herself and on the chamber, whose apparatus was in no less confusion than that of the apartment below, her consciousness of the unseasonableness of this meeting.

The other shrieked likewise, but on her it seemed to be the token of surprize, rather than that of terror. There was, probably, somewhat in my aspect and garb that suggested an apology for this intrusion, as arising from simplicity and mistake. She thought proper, however, to assume the air of one offended, and looking sternly—How now, fellow, said she, what is this? Why come you hither?

This questioner was of mature age, but had not passed the period of attractiveness and grace. All the beauty that nature had bestowed was still retained, but the portion had never been great. What she possessed was so modelled and embellished by such a carriage and dress, as to give it most power over the senses of the gazer. In proportion, however, as it was intended and adapted to captivate those, who know none but physical pleasures, it was qualified to breed distaste and aversion in me.

I am sensible how much error may have lurked in this decision. I had brought with me the belief of their being unchaste; and seized, perhaps, with too much avidity, any appearance that coincided with my prepossessions. Yet the younger by no means inspired the same disgust; though I had no reason to suppose her more unblemished than the elder. Her modesty seemed unaffected, and was by no means satisfied, like that of the elder, with defeating future curiosity. The consciousness of what had already been exposed filled her with confusion, and she would have flown away, if her companion had not detained her by some degree of force. What ails the girl? There's nothing to be frightened at. Fellow! she repeated, what brings you here?

I advanced and stood before them. I looked steadfastly, but, I believe, with neither effrontery nor anger, on the one who addressed me. I spoke in a tone serious and emphatical. I come for the sake of speaking to a woman, who formerly resided in this house, and probably resides here still. Her name is Clemenza Lodi. If she be here, I request you to conduct me to her instantly.

Methought I perceived some inquietude, a less imperious and more inquisitive air, in this woman, on hearing the name of Clemenza. It was momentary, and gave way to peremptory looks. What is your business with her? And why did you adopt this mode of enquiry? A very extraordinary intrusion! Be good enough to leave the chamber. Any questions proper to be answered, will be answered below.

I meant not to intrude or offend. It was not an idle or impertinent motive that led me hither. I waited below for some time after soliciting an audience of you, through the servant. She assured me you were absent, and laid me under the necessity of searching for Clemenza Lodi myself, and without a guide. I am anxious to withdraw, and request merely to be directed to the room which she occupies.

I direct you, replied she in a more resolute tone, to quit the room and the house.

Impossible, madam, I replied, still looking at her earnestly, leave the house without seeing her! You might as well enjoin me to pull the Andes on my head! To walk barefoot to Peking! Impossible!

Some solicitude was now mingled with her anger. This is strange insolence! unaccountable behaviour!—be gone from my room! will you compel me to call the gentlemen?

Be not alarmed, said I, with augmented mildness. There was indeed compassion and sorrow at my heart, and these must have somewhat influenced my looks. Be not alarmed— I came to confer a benefit, not to perpetrate an injury. I came not to censure or expostulate with you, but merely to counsel and aid a being that needs both: all I want is to see her. In this chamber I sought not you, but her. Only lead me to her, or tell me where she is. I will then rid you of my presence.

Will you compel me to call those who will punish this insolence as it deserves?

Dearest madam! I compel you to nothing. I merely supplicate. I would ask you to lead me to these gentlemen, if I did not know that there are none but females in the house. It is you who must receive and comply with my petition. Allow me a moment's interview with Clemenza Lodi. Compliance will harm you not, but will benefit her. What is your objection?

This is the strangest proceeding! the most singular conduct! Is this a place fit to parley with you? I warn you of the consequence of staying a moment longer. Depend upon it, you will sorely repent it.

You are obdurate, said I, and turned towards the younger, who listened to this discourse in tremors and panick. I took her hand with an air of humility and reverence. Here, said I, there seems to be purity, innocence and condescension. I took this house to be the temple of voluptuousness. Females, I expected to find in it, but such only as traded in licentious pleasures: specious, perhaps not destitute of talents, beauty and address, but dissolute and wanton; sensual and avaricious; yet, in this countenance and carriage there are tokens of virtue. I am born to be deceived, and the semblance of modesty is readily assumed. Under this veil, perhaps, lurk a tainted heart and depraved appetites. Is it so?

She made me no answer, but somewhat in her looks seemed to evince that my favorable prepossessions were just. I noticed likewise that the alarm of the elder was greatly increased by this address to her companion. The thought suddenly occurred that this girl might be in circumstances not unlike those of Clemenza Lodi; that she was not apprized of the character of her associates, and might by this meeting be rescued from similar evils.

This suspicion filled me with tumultuous feelings. Clemenza was for a time forgotten. I paid no attention to the looks or demeanor of the elder, but was wholly occupied in gazing on the younger. My anxiety to know the truth, gave pathos and energy to my tones, while I spoke:

Who, where, what are you? Do you reside in this house? Are you a sister or daughter in this family, or merely a visitant? Do you know the character, profession and views of your companions? Do you deem them virtuous, or know them to be profligate? Speak! tell me, I beseech you!

The maiden confusion which had just appeared in the countenance of this person, now somewhat abated. She lifted her eyes, and glanced by turns at me and at her who sat by her side. An air of serious astonishment overspread her features, and she seemed anxious for me to proceed. The elder, meanwhile, betrayed the utmost alarm, again upbraided my audacity, commanded me to withdraw, and admonished me of the danger I incurred by lingering.

I noticed not her interference, but again entreated to know of the younger her true state. She had no time to answer me, supposing her not to want the inclination, for every pause was filled by the clamorous importunities and menaces of the other. I began to perceive that my attempts were useless to this end, but the chief, and most estimable purpose, was attainable. It was in my power to state the knowledge I possessed, through your means, of Mrs. Villars and her daughters. This information might be superfluous, since she to whom it was given, might be one of this licentious family. The contrary, however, was not improbable, and my tidings, therefore, might be of the utmost moment to her safety.

A resolute, and even impetuous manner, reduced my incessant interruptor to silence. What I had to say I compressed in a few words, and adhered to perspicuity and candor with the utmost care. I still held the hand that I had taken, and fixed my eyes upon her countenance with a steadfastness that hindered her from lifting her eyes.

I know you not; whether you be dissolute or chaste, I cannot tell. In either case, however, what I am going to say will be useful. Let me faithfully repeat what I have heard. It is mere rumor, and I vouch not for its truth. Rumor as it is, I submit it to your judgment, and hope that it may guide you into paths of innocence and honor.

Mrs. Villars and her three daughters are English women, who supported for a time an unblemished reputation, but who, at length, were suspected of carrying on the trade of prostitution. This secret could not be concealed forever. The profligates who frequented their house, betrayed them. One of them who died under their roof, after they had withdrawn from it into the country, disclosed to his kinsman, who attended his death bed, their genuine character.

The dying man likewise related incidents in which I am deeply concerned. I have been connected with one by name Welbeck. In his house I met an unfortunate girl, who was afterwards removed to Mrs. Villars's. Her name was Clemenza Lodi. Residence in this house, under the controul of a woman like Mrs. Villars and her daughters, must be injurious to her innocence, and from this controul I now come to rescue her.

I turned to the elder, and continued: By all that is sacred, I adjure you to tell me whether Clemenza Lodi be under this roof! if she be not, whither has she gone? To know this, I came hither, and any difficulty or reluctance in answering, will be useless; till an answer be obtained, I will not go hence.

During this speech, anger had been kindling in the bosom of this woman. It now burst upon me in a torrent of opprobrious epithets. I was a villain, a calumniator, a thief. I had lurked about the house, till those whose sex and strength enabled them to cope with me, had gone. I had entered these doors by fraud. I was a wretch, guilty of the last excesses of insolence and insult.

To repel these reproaches, or endure them, was equally useless. The satisfaction that I sought was only to be gained by searching the house. I left the room without speaking. Did I act illegally in passing from one story and one room to another? Did I really deserve the imputations of rashness and insolence? My behaviour, I well know, was ambiguous and hazardous, and perhaps wanting in discretion, but my motives were unquestionably pure. I aimed at nothing but the rescue of an human creature from distress and dishonor.

I pretend not to the wisdom of experience and age; to the praise of forethought or subtlety. I chuse the obvious path, and pursue it with headlong expedition. Good intentions, unaided by knowledge, will, perhaps, produce more injury than benefit, and therefore, knowledge must be gained, but the acquisition is not momentary; is not bestowed unasked and untoil'd for: meanwhile, we must not be unactive because we are ignorant. Our good purposes must hurry to performance, whether our knowledge be greater or less.

Chapter XII

To explore the house in this manner was so contrary to ordinary rules, that the design was probably wholly unsuspected by the women whom I had just left. My silence, at parting, might have been ascribed by them to the intimidating influence of invectives and threats. Hence I proceeded in my search without interruption.

Presently I reached a front chamber in the third story. The door was ajar. I entered it on tiptoe. Sitting on a low chair by the fire, I beheld a female figure, dressed in a negligent, but not indecent manner. Her face in the posture in which she sat was only half seen. Its hues were sickly and pale, and in mournful unison with a feeble and emaciated form. Her eyes were fixed upon a babe, that lay stretched upon a pillow at her feet. The child, like its mother, for such she was readily imagined to be, was meagre and cadaverous. Either it was dead, or could not be very distant from death.

The features of Clemenza were easily recognized, though no contrast could be greater, in habit and shape, and complexion, than that which her present bore to her former appearance. All her roses had faded, and her brilliances vanished. Still, however, there was somewhat fitted to awaken the tenderest emotions. There were tokens of inconsolable distress.

Her attention was wholly absorbed by the child. She lifted not her eyes, till I came close to her, and stood before her. When she discovered me, a faint start was perceived. She looked at me for a moment, then putting one spread hand before her eyes, she stretched out the other towards the door, and waving it in silence, as if to admonish me to depart.

This motion, however emphatical, I could not obey. I wished to obtain her attention, but knew not in what words to claim it. I was silent. In a moment she removed her hand from her eyes, and looked at me with new eagerness. Her features bespoke emotions, which, perhaps, flowed from my likeness to her brother, joined with the memory of my connection with Welbeck.

My situation was full of embarrassment. I was by no means

certain that my language would be understood. I knew not in what light the policy and dissimulation of Welbeck might have taught her to regard me. What proposal, conducive to her comfort and her safety, could I make to her?

Once more she covered her eyes, and exclaimed in a feeble voice, go away! be gone!

As if satisfied with this effort, she resumed her attention to her child. She stooped and lifted it in her arms, gazing, meanwhile, on its almost lifeless features with intense anxiety. She crushed it to her bosom, and again looking at me, repeated, go away! go away! be gone!

There was somewhat in the lines of her face, in her tones and gestures, that pierced to my heart. Added to this, was my knowledge of her condition; her friendlessness; her poverty; the pangs of unrequited love; and her expiring infant. I felt my utterance choaked, and my tears struggling for passage. I turned to the window, and endeavored to regain my tranquillity.

What was it, said I, that brought me hither? The perfidy of Welbeck must surely have long since been discovered. What can I tell her of the Villars which she does not already know, or of which the knowledge will be useful? If their treatment has been just, why should I detract from their merit? If it has been otherwise, their own conduct will have disclosed their genuine character. Though voluptuous themselves, it does not follow that they have labored to debase this creature. Though wanton, they may not be inhuman.

I can propose no change in her condition for the better. Should she be willing to leave this house, whither is it in my power to conduct her? O that I were rich enough to provide food for the hungry, shelter for the housless, and raiment for the naked.

I was roused from these fruitless reflections by the lady, whom some sudden thought induced to place the child in its bed, and rising to come towards me. The utter dejection which her features lately betrayed, was now changed for an air of anxious curiosity. Where, said she, in her broken English, where is Signior Welbeck?

Alas! returned I, I know not. That question might, I thought, with more propriety be put to you than me.

I know where he be; I fear where he be.

So saying, the deepest sighs burst from her heart. She turned from me, and going to the child, took it again into her lap. Its pale and sunken cheek was quickly wet with the mother's tears, which, as she silently hung over it, dropped fast from her eyes.

This demeanor could not but awaken curiosity, while it gave a new turn to my thoughts. I began to suspect that in the tokens which I saw, there was not only distress for her child, but concern for the fate of Welbeck. Know you, said I, where Mr. Welbeck is? Is he alive? Is he near? Is he in calamity?

I do not know if he be alive. He be sick. He be in prison. They will not let me go to him. And—Here her attention and mine was attracted by the infant, whose frame, till now motionless, began to be tremulous. Its features sunk into a more ghastly expression. Its breathings were difficult, and every effort to respire produced a convulsion harder than the last.

The mother easily interpreted these tokens. The same mortal struggle seemed to take place in her feature as in those of her child. At length her agony found way in a piercing shriek. The struggle in the infant was past. Hope looked in vain for a new motion in its heart or its eyelids. The lips were closed, and its breath was gone, forever!

The grief which overwhelmed the unhappy parent, was of that outrageous and desperate kind which is wholly incompatible with thinking. A few incoherent motions and screams, that rent the soul, were followed by a deep swoon. She sunk upon the floor, pale and lifeless as her babe.

I need not describe the pangs which such a scene was adapted to produce in me. These were rendered more acute by the helpless and ambiguous situation in which I was placed. I was eager to bestow consolation and succour, but was destitute of all means. I was plunged into uncertainties and doubts. I gazed alternately at the infant and its mother. I sighed. I wept. I even sobbed. I stooped down and took the lifeless hand of the sufferer. I bathed it with my tears, and exclaimed, Ill-fated woman! unhappy mother! what shall I do for thy relief? How shall I blunt the edge of this calamity, and rescue thee from new evils?

At this moment the door of the apartment was opened, and

the youngest of the women whom I had seen below, entered. Her looks betrayed the deepest consternation and anxiety. Her eyes in a moment were fixed by the decayed form and the sad features of Clemenza. She shuddered at this spectacle, but was silent. She stood in the midst of the floor, fluctuating and bewildered. I dropped the hand that I was holding, and approached her.

You have come, said I, in good season. I know you not, but will believe you to be good. You have an heart, it may be, not free from corruption, but it is still capable of pity for the miseries of others. You have an hand that refuses not its aid to the unhappy. See; there is an infant dead. There is a mother whom grief has, for a time, deprived of life. She has been oppressed and betrayed; been robbed of property and reputation—but not of innocence. She is worthy of relief. Have you arms to receive her? Have you sympathy, protection, and a home to bestow upon a forlorn, betrayed and unhappy stranger? I know not what this house is; I suspect it to be no better than a brothel. I know not what treatment this woman has received. If, when her situation and wants are ascertained, will you supply her wants? Will you rescue her from evils that may attend her continuance here?

She was disconcerted and bewildered by this address. At length she said—All that has happened, all that I have heard and seen is so unexpected, so strange, that I am amazed and distracted. Your behaviour I cannot comprehend, nor your motive for making this address to me. I cannot answer you, except in one respect. If this woman has suffered injury, I have had no part in it. I knew not of her existence, nor her situation till this moment; and whatever protection or assistance she may justly claim, I am both able and willing to bestow. I do not live here, but in the city. I am only an occasional visitant in this house.

What then, I exclaimed, with sparkling eyes and a rapturous accent, you are not profligate; are a stranger to the manners of this house, and a detester of these manners? Be not a deceiver, I entreat you. I depend only on your looks and professions, and these may be dissembled.

These questions, which indeed argued a childish simplicity, excited her surprise. She looked at me, uncertain whether I was in earnest or in jest. At length she said, your language is so singular, that I am at a loss how to answer it. I shall take no pains to find out its meaning, but leave you to form conjectures at leisure. Who is this woman, and how can I serve her? After a pause, she continued—I cannot afford her any immediate assistance, and shall not stay a moment longer in this house. There (putting a card in my hand) is my name and place of abode. If you shall have any proposals to make, respecting this woman, I shall be ready to receive them in my own house. So saying, she withdrew.

I looked wistfully after her, but could not but assent to her assertion, that her presence here would be more injurious to her than beneficial to Clemenza. She had scarcely gone, when the elder woman entered. There was rage, sullenness, and disappointment in her aspect. These, however, were suspended by the situation in which she discovered the mother and child. It was plain that all the sentiments of woman were not extinguished in her heart. She summoned the servants and seemed preparing to take such measures as the occasion prescribed. I now saw the folly of supposing that these measures would be neglected, and that my presence could not essentially contribute to the benefit of the sufferer. Still, however, I lingered in the room, till the infant was covered with a cloth, and the still senseless parent was conveyed into an adjoining chamber. The woman then, as if she had not seen me before, fixed scowling eyes upon me, and exclaimed, thief! villain! why do you stay here?

I mean to go, said I, but not till I express my gratitude and pleasure, at the sight of your attention to this sufferer. You deem me insolent and perverse, but I am not such; and hope that the day will come when I shall convince you of my good intentions.

Begone! interrupted she, in a more angry tone. Begone this moment, or I will treat you as a thief. She now drew forth her hand from under her gown, and shewed a pistol. You shall see, she continued, that I will not be insulted with impunity. If you do not vanish, I will shoot you as a robber.

This woman was far from wanting a force and intrepidity worthy of a different sex. Her gestures and tones were full of energy. They denoted an haughty and indignant spirit. It was plain that she conceived herself deeply injured by my conduct; and was it absolutely certain that her anger was without reason? I had loaded her house with atrocious imputations, and these imputations might be false. I had conceived them upon such evidence as chance had provided, but this evidence, intricate and dubious as human actions and motives are, might be void of truth.

Perhaps, said I, in a sedate tone, I have injured you; I have mistaken your character. You shall not find me less ready to repair, than to perpetrate, this injury. My error was without malice, and——

I had not time to finish the sentence, when this rash and enraged woman thrust the pistol close to my head and fired it. I was wholly unaware that her fury would lead her to this excess. It was a sort of mechanical impulse that made me raise my hand, and attempt to turn aside the weapon. I did this deliberately and tranquilly, and without conceiving that any thing more was intended by her movement than to intimidate me. To this precaution, however, I was indebted for life. The bullet was diverted from my forehead to my left ear, and made a slight wound upon the surface, from which the blood gushed in a stream.

The loudness of this explosion, and the shock which the ball produced in my brain, sunk me into a momentary stupor. I reeled backward, and should have fallen had not I supported myself against the wall. The sight of my blood instantly restored her reason. Her rage disappeared, and was succeeded by terror and remorse. She clasped her hands, and exclaimed—Oh! what, what have I done? My frantic passion has destroyed me.

I needed no long time to shew me the full extent of the injury which I had suffered and the conduct which it became me to adopt. For a moment I was bewildered and alarmed, but presently perceived that this was an incident more productive of good than of evil. It would teach me caution in contending with the passions of another, and shewed me that there is a limit which the impetuosities of anger will sometimes overstep. Instead of reviling my companion, I addressed myself to her thus:

Be not frighted. You have done me no injury, and I hope

will derive instruction from this event. Your rashness had like to have sacrificed the life of one who is your friend, and to have exposed yourself to infamy and death, or, at least, to the pangs of eternal remorse. Learn, from hence, to curb your passions, and especially to keep at a distance from every murderous weapon, on occasions when rage is likely to take place of reason.

I repeat that my motives in entering this house were connected with your happiness as well as that of Clemenza Lodi. If I have erred, in supposing you the member of a vile and pernicious trade, that error was worthy of being rectified, but violence and invective tend only to confirm it. I am incapable of any purpose that is not beneficent; but, in the means that I use and in the evidence on which I proceed, I am liable to a thousand mistakes. Point out to me the road by which I can do you good, and I will cheerfully pursue it.

Finding that her fears had been groundless, as to the consequences of her rashness, she renewed, though with less vehemence than before, her imprecations on my intermeddling and audacious folly. I listened till the storm was nearly exhausted, and then, declaring my intention to re-visit the house, if the interest of Clemenza should require it, I resumed my way to the city.

Chapter XIII

WHY, said I, as I hasted forward, is my fortune so abundant in unforeseen occurrences? Is every man, who leaves his cottage and the impressions of his infancy behind him, ushered into such a world of revolutions and perils as have trammelled my steps? or, is my scene indebted for variety and change to my propensity to look into other people's concerns, and to make their sorrows and their joys mine?

To indulge an adventurous spirit, I left the precincts of the barn-door, enlisted in the service of a stranger, and encountered a thousand dangers to my virtue under the disastrous influence of Welbeck. Afterwards my life was set at hazard in the cause of Wallace, and now am I loaded with the province of protecting the helpless Eliza Hadwin and the unfortunate Clemenza. My wishes are fervent, and my powers shall not be inactive in their defence, but how slender are these powers!

In the offers of the unknown lady there is, indeed, some consolation for Clemenza. It must be my business to lay before my friend Stevens the particulars of what has befallen me, and to entreat his directions how this disconsolate girl may be most effectually succoured. It may be wise to take her from her present abode, and place her under some chaste and humane guardianship, where she may gradually lose remembrance of her dead infant and her specious betrayer. The barrier that severs her from Welbeck must be high as heaven and insuperable as necessity.

But, soft! Talked she not of Welbeck? Said she not that he was in prison and was sick? Poor wretch! I thought thy course was at an end; that the penalty of guilt no longer weighed down thy heart. That thy misdeeds and thy remorses were buried in a common and obscure grave; but it seems thou art still alive.

Is it rational to cherish the hope of thy restoration to innocence and peace? Thou art no obdurate criminal; hadst thou less virtue, thy compunctions would be less keen. Wert thou deaf to the voice of duty, thy wanderings into guilt and folly would be less fertile of anguish. The time will perhaps come, when the measure of thy transgressions and calamities will overflow, and the folly of thy choice will be too conspicuous to escape thy discernment. Surely, even for such transgressors as thou, there is a salutary power in the precepts of truth and the lessons of experience.

But, thou art imprisoned and art sick. This, perhaps, is the crisis of thy destiny. Indigence and dishonour were the evils, to shun which thy integrity and peace of mind have been lightly forfeited. Thou hast found that the price was given in vain; that the hollow and deceitful enjoyments of opulence and dignity were not worth the purchase; and that, frivolous and unsubstantial as they are, the only path that leads to them is that of honesty and diligence. Thou art in prison and art sick; and there is none to cheer thy hour with offices of kindness, or uphold thy fainting courage by the suggestions of good counsel. For such as thou the world has no compassion. Mankind will pursue thee to the grave with execrations. Their cruelty will be justified or palliated, since they know thee not. They are unacquainted with the goadings of thy conscience and the bitter retributions which thou art daily suffering: they are full of their own wrongs, and think only of those tokens of exultation and complacency which thou wast studious of assuming in thy intercourse with them. It is I only that thoroughly know thee, and can rightly estimate thy claims to compassion.

I have somewhat partaken of thy kindness, and thou meritest some gratitude at my hands. Shall I not visit and endeavor to console thee in thy distress? Let me, at least, ascertain thy condition, and be the instrument in repairing the wrongs which thou hast inflicted. Let me gain, from contemplation of thy misery, new motives to sincerity and rectitude.

While occupied by these reflections, I entered the city. The thoughts which engrossed my mind related to Welbeck. It is not my custom to defer till to-morrow what can be done to-day. The destiny of man frequently hangs upon the lapse of a minute. I will stop, said I, at the prison; and, since the moment of my arrival may not be indifferent, I will go thither with all possible haste. I did not content myself with walking, but, regardless of the comments of passengers, hurried along the way at full speed.

Having enquired for Welbeck, I was conducted through a dark room, crouded with beds, to a stair-case. Never before had I been in a prison. Never had I smelt so noisome an odour, or surveyed faces so begrimed with filth and misery. The walls and floors were alike squallid and detestable. It seemed that in this house existence would be bereaved of all its attractions; and yet those faces, which could be seen through the obscurity that encompassed them, were either void of care or distorted with mirth.

This, said I, as I followed my conductor, is the residence of Welbeck. What contrasts are these to the repose and splendor, pictured walls, glossy hangings, gilded sofas, mirrors that occupied from cieling to floor, carpets of Tauris, and the spotless and transcendent brilliancy of coverlets and napkins, in thy former dwelling? Here brawling and the shuffling of rude feet are eternal. The air is loaded with the exhalations of disease and the fumes of debauchery. Thou art cooped up in airless space, and, perhaps, compelled to share thy narrow cell with some stupid ruffian. Formerly, the breezes were courted by thy lofty windows. Aromatic shrubs were scattered on thy hearth. Menials, splendid in apparel, shewed their faces with diffidence in thy apartment, trod lightly on thy marble floor, and suffered not the sanctity of silence to be troubled by a whisper. Thy lamp shot its rays through the transparency of alabaster, and thy fragrant lymph flowed from vases of porcelain. Such were formerly the decorations of thy hall, the embellishments of thy existence; but now—alas!—

We reached a chamber in the second story. My conductor knocked at the door. No one answered. Repeated knocks were unheard or unnoticed by the person within. At length, lifting a latch, we entered together.

The prisoner lay upon the bed, with his face turned from the door. I advanced softly, making a sign to the keeper to withdraw. Welbeck was not asleep, but merely buried in reverie. I was unwilling to disturb his musing, and stood with my eyes fixed upon his form. He appeared unconscious that any one had entered.

At length, uttering a deep sigh, he changed his posture, and perceived me in my motionless and gazing attitude. Recollect in what circumstances we had last parted. Welbeck had, no doubt, carried away with him, from that interview, a firm belief, that I should speedily die. His prognostic, however, was fated to be contradicted.

His first emotions were those of surprise. These gave place to mortification and rage. After eyeing me for some time, he averted his glances, and that effort which is made to dissipate some obstacle to breathing, shewed me that his sensations were of the most excruciating kind. He laid his head upon the pillow, and sunk into his former musing. He disdained, or was unable, to utter a syllable of welcome or contempt.

In the opportunity that had been afforded me to view his countenance, I had observed tokens of a kind very different from those which used to be visible. The gloomy and malignant were more conspicuous. Health had forsaken his cheeks, and taken along with it those flexible parts, which formerly enabled him to cover his secret torments and insidious purposes, beneath a veil of benevolence and cheerfulness. Alas! said I, loud enough for him to hear me, here is a monument of ruin. Despair and mischievous passions are too deeply rooted in this heart for me to tear them away.

These expressions did not escape his notice. He turned once more and cast sullen looks upon me. There was somewhat in his eyes that made me shudder. They denoted that his reverie was not that of grief, but of madness. I continued, in a less steadfast voice than before:

Unhappy Clemenza! I have performed thy message. I have visited him that is sick and in prison. Thou hadst cause for anguish and terror, even greater cause than thou imaginedst. Would to God that thou wouldst be contented with the report which I shall make; that thy misguided tenderness would consent to leave him to his destiny, would suffer him to die alone; but that is a forbearance which no eloquence that I possess will induce thee to practise. Thou must come, and witness for thyself.

In speaking thus, I was far from foreseeing the effects which would be produced on the mind of Welbeck. I was far from intending to instil into him a belief that Clemenza was near at hand, and was preparing to enter his apartment: yet no other images but these would, perhaps, have roused him from his lethargy, and awakened that attention which I wished to awaken. He started up, and gazed fearfully at the door.

What! he cried. What! Is she here? Ye powers, that have scattered woes in my path, spare me the sight of her! But from this agony I will rescue myself. The moment she appears I will pluck out these eyes and dash them at her feet.

So saying, he gazed with augmented eagerness upon the door. His hands were lifted to his head, as if ready to execute his frantic purpose. I seized his arm, and besought him to lay aside his terror, for that Clemenza was far distant. She had no intention, and besides was unable, to visit him.

Then I am respited. I breathe again. No; keep her from a prison. Drag her to the wheel or to the scaffold; mangle her with stripes; torture her with famine; strangle her child before her face, and cast it to the hungry dogs that are howling at the gate; but—keep her from a prison. Never let her enter these doors.—There he stopped; his eyes being fixed on the floor, and his thoughts once more buried in reverie. I resumed:

She is occupied with other griefs than those connected with the fate of Welbeck. She is not unmindful of you: she knows you to be sick and in prison; and I came to do for you whatever office your condition might require, and I came at her suggestion. She, alas! has full employment for her tears in watering the grave of her child.

He started. What! dead? Say you that the child is dead?

It is dead. I witnessed its death. I saw it expire in the arms of its mother; that mother whom I formerly met under your roof blooming and gay, but whom calamity has tarnished and withered. I saw her in the rayment of poverty, under an accursed roof; desolate; alone; unsolaced by the countenance or sympathy of human beings; approached only by those who mock at her distress, set snares for her innocence, and push her to infamy. I saw her leaning over the face of her dying babe.

Welbeck put his hands to his head and exclaimed: curses on thy lips, infernal messenger! Chant elsewhere thy rueful ditty! Vanish! if thou wouldst not feel in thy heart fangs red with blood less guilty than thine.

Till this moment the uproar in Welbeck's mind appeared to hinder him from distinctly recognizing his visitant. Now it seemed as if the incidents of our last interview suddenly sprung up in his remembrance.

What! This is the villain that rifled my cabinet, the maker of my poverty and of all the evils which it has since engendered! That has led me to a prison! Execrable fool! you are the author of the scene that you describe, and of horrors without number and name. To whatever crimes I have been urged since that interview, and the fit of madness that made you destroy my property, they spring from your act; they flowed from necessity, which, had you held your hand at that fateful moment, would never have existed.

How dare you thrust yourself upon my privacy? Why am I not alone? Fly! and let my miseries want, at least, the aggravation of beholding their author. My eyes loathe the sight of thee! My heart would suffocate thee with its own bitterness! Begone!

I know not, I answered, why innocence should tremble at the ravings of a lunatic; why it should be overwhelmed by unmerited reproaches! Why it should not deplore the errors of its foe, labor to correct those errors, and——

Thank thy fate, youth, that my hands are tied up by my scorn; thank thy fate that no weapon is within reach. Much has passed since I saw thee, and I am a new man. I am no longer inconstant and cowardly. I have no motives but contempt to hinder me from expiating the wrongs which thou hast done me in thy blood. I disdain to take thy life. Go; and let thy fidelity, at least, to the confidence which I have placed in thee, be inviolate. Thou hast done me harm enough, but canst do, if thou wilt, still more. Thou canst betray the secrets that are lodged in thy bosom, and rob me of the comfort of reflecting that my guilt is known but to one among the living.

This suggestion made me pause, and look back upon the past. I had confided this man's tale to you. The secrecy, on which he so fondly leaned, was at an end. Had I acted culpably or not?

But why should I ruminate, with anguish and doubt, upon the past? The future was within my power, and the road of my duty was too plain to be mistaken. I would disclose to

Welbeck the truth, and cheerfully encounter every consequence. I would summon my friend to my aid, and take his
counsel in the critical emergency in which I was placed. I
ought not to rely upon myself alone in my efforts to benefit
this being, when another was so near whose discernment, and
benevolence, and knowledge of mankind, and power of affording relief were far superior to mine.

Influenced by these thoughts, I left the apartment without
speaking; and, procuring pen and paper, dispatched to you
the billet which brought about our meeting.

Chapter XIV

MERVYN'S AUDITORS allowed no pause in their attention to this story. Having ended, a deep silence took place. The clock which stood upon the mantle, had sounded twice the customary *larum*, but had not been heard by us. It was now struck a third time. It was *one*. Our guest appeared somewhat startled at this signal, and looked, with a mournful sort of earnestness, at the clock. There was an air of inquietude about him, which I had never observed in an equal degree before.

I was not without much curiosity respecting other incidents than those which had just been related by him; but after so much fatigue as he had undergone, I thought it improper to prolong the conversation.

Come, said I, my friend, let us to bed. This is a drowsy time, and after so much exercise of mind and body, you cannot but need some repose. Much has happened in your absence, which is proper to be known to you, but our discourse will be best deferred till to-morrow. I will come into your chamber by day-dawn, and unfold to you my particular.

Nay, said he, withdraw not on my account. If I go to my chamber, it will not be to sleep, but to meditate, especially after your assurance that something of moment has occurred in my absence. My thoughts, independently of any cause of sorrow or fear, have received an impulse which solitude and darkness will not stop. It is impossible to know too much for our safety and integrity, or to know it too soon. What has happened?

I did not hesitate to comply with his request, for it was not difficult to conceive that, however tired the limbs might be, the adventures of this day would not be easily expelled from the memory at night. I told him the substance of the conversation with Mrs. Althorpe. He smiled at those parts of the narrative which related to himself; but when his father's depravity and poverty were mentioned, he melted into tears.

Poor wretch! I that knew thee in thy better days, might have easily divined this consequence. I foresaw thy poverty and degradation in the same hour that I left thy roof. My soul drooped at the prospect, but I said, it cannot be prevented, and this reflection was an antidote to grief, but now that thy ruin is complete, it seems as if some of it were imputable to me, who forsook thee when the succour and counsel of a son were most needed. Thou art ignorant and vicious, but thou art my father still. I see that the sufferings of a better man than thou art would less afflict me than thine. Perhaps it is still in my power to restore thy liberty and good name, and yet—that is a fond wish. Thou art past the age when the ignorance and groveling habits of a human being are susceptible of cure—— There he stopt, and after a gloomy pause, continued:

I am not surprized or afflicted at the misconceptions of my neighbors, with relation to my own character. Men must judge from what they see: they must build their conclusions on their knowledge. I never saw in the rebukes of my neighbors, any thing but laudable abhorrence of vice. They were not eager to blame, to collect materials of censure rather than of praise. It was not me whom they hated and despised. It was the phantom that passed under my name, which existed only in their imagination, and which was worthy of all their scorn and all their enmity.

What I appeared to be in their eyes, was as much the object of my own disapprobation as of theirs. Their reproaches only evinced the rectitude of their decisions, as well as of my own. I drew from them new motives to complacency. They fortified my perseverance in the path which I had chosen as best; they raised me higher in my own esteem; they hightened the claims of the reproachers themselves to my respect and my gratitude.

They thought me slothful, incurious, destitute of knowledge, and of all thirst of knowledge, insolent and profligate. They say that in the treatment of my father, I have been ungrateful and inhuman. I have stolen his property, and deserted him in his calamity. Therefore they hate and revile me. It is well: I love them for these proofs of their discernment and integrity. Their indignation at wrong is the truest test of their virtue.

It is true that they mistake me, but that arises from the circumstances of our mutual situation. They examined what was exposed to their view: they grasped at what was placed within their reach. To decide contrary to appearances; to judge from what they know not, would prove them to be brutish and not rational, would make their decision of no worth, and render them, in their turn, objects of neglect and contempt.

It is true that I hated school; that I sought occasions of absence, and finally, on being struck by the master, determined to enter his presence no more. I loved to leap, to run, to swim, to climb trees, and to clamber up rocks, to shroud myself in thickets, and stroll among woods, to obey the impulse of the moment, and to prate or be silent, just as my humor prompted me. All this I loved more than to go to and fro in the same path, and at stated hours, to look off and on a book, to read just as much, and of such a kind, to stand up and be seated, just as another thought proper to direct. I hated to be classed, cribbed, rebuked and feruled at the pleasure of one, who, as it seemed to me, knew no guide in his rewards but caprice, and no prompter in his punishments but passion.

It is true that I took up the spade and the hoe as rarely, and for as short a time, as possible. I preferred to ramble in the forest and loiter on the hill: perpetually to change the scene; to scrutinize the endless variety of objects; to compare one leaf and pebble with another; to pursue those trains of thought which their resemblances and differences suggested; to enquire what it was that gave them this place, structure, and form, were more agreeable employments than plowing and threshing.

My father could well afford to hire labor. What my age and my constitution enabled me to do could be done by a sturdy boy, in half the time, with half the toil, and with none of the reluctance. The boy was a bond servant, and the cost of his clothing and food was next to nothing. True it is, that my service would have saved him even this expence, but my motives for declining the effort were not hastily weighed or superficially examined. These were my motives:

My frame was delicate and feeble. Exposure to wet blasts and vertical suns was sure to make me sick. My father was insensible to this consequence; and no degree of diligence would please him, but that which would destroy my health. My health was dearer to my mother than to me. She was more anxious to exempt me from possible injuries than reason justified; but anxious she was, and I could not save her from anxiety, but by almost wholly abstaining from labor. I thought her peace of mind was of some value, and that, if the inclination of either of my parents must be gratified at the expence of the other, the preference was due to the woman who bore me; who nursed me in disease; who watched over my safety with incessant tenderness; whose life and whose peace were involved in mine. I should have deemed myself brutish and obdurately wicked to have loaded her with fears and cares merely to smooth the brow of a froward old man, whose avarice called on me to sacrifice my ease and my health, and who shifted to other shoulders the province of sustaining me when sick, and of mourning for me when dead.

I likewise believed, that it became me to reflect upon the influence of my decision on my own happiness; and to weigh the profits flowing to my father from my labor, against the benefits of mental exercise, the pleasures of the woods and streams, healthful sensations, and the luxury of musing. The pecuniary profit was petty and contemptible. It obviated no necessity. It purchased no rational enjoyment. It merely provoked, by furnishing the means of indulgence, an appetite from which my father was not exempt. It cherished the seeds of depravity in him, and lessened the little stock of happiness belonging to my mother.

I did not detain you long, my friends, in pourtraying my parents, and recounting domestic incidents, when I first told you my story. What had no connection with the history of Welbeck and with the part that I have acted upon this stage, I thought it proper to omit. My omission was likewise prompted by other reasons. My mind is ennervated and feeble like my body. I cannot look upon the sufferings of those I love without exquisite pain. I cannot steel my heart by the force of reason, and by submission to necessity; and, therefore, too frequently employ the cowardly expedient of endeavoring to forget what I cannot remember without agony.

I told you that my father was sober and industrious by habit, but habit is not uniform. There were intervals when his plodding and tame spirit gave place to the malice and fury of a demon. Liquors were not sought by him, but he could not withstand entreaty, and a potion that produced no effect upon others changed him into a maniac.

I told you that I had a sister, whom the arts of a villain destroyed. Alas! the work of her destruction was left unfinished by him. The blows and contumelies of a misjudging and implacable parent, who scrupled not to thrust her, with her new-born infant, out of doors; the curses and taunts of unnatural brothers left her no alternative but death—But I must not think of this; I must not think of the wrongs which my mother endured in the person of her only and darling daughter.

My brothers were the copyists of the father, whom they resembled in temper and person. My mother doated on her own image in her daughter and in me. This daughter was ravished from her by self-violence, and her other children by disease. I only remained to appropriate her affections and fulfil her hopes. This alone had furnished a sufficient reason why I should be careful of my health and my life, but my father's character supplied me with a motive infinitely more cogent.

It is almost incredible, but, nevertheless, true, that the only being whose presence and remonstrances had any influence on my father, at moments when his reason was extinct, was myself. As to my personal strength, it was nothing; yet my mother's person was rescued from brutal violence: he was checked, in the midst of his ferocious career, by a single look or exclamation from me. The fear of my rebukes had even some influence in enabling him to resist temptation. If I entered the tavern, at the moment when he was lifting the glass to his lips, I never weighed the injunctions of decorum, but, snatching the vessel from his hand, I threw it on the ground. I was not deterred by the presence of others; and their censures, on my want of filial respect and duty, were listened to with unconcern. I chose not to justify myself by expatiating on domestic miseries, and by calling down that pity on my mother, which I knew would only have increased her distress.

The world regarded my deportment as insolent and perverse to a degree of insanity. To deny my father an indulgence which they thought harmless, and which, indeed, was harmless in its influence on other men; to interfere thus publicly with his social enjoyments, and expose him to mortification and shame, was loudly condemned; but my duty to my mother debarred me from eluding this censure on the only terms on which it could have been eluded. Now it has ceased to be necessary to conceal what passed in domestic retirements, and I should willingly confess the truth before any audience.

At first my father imagined, that threats and blows would intimidate his monitor. In this he was mistaken, and the detection of this mistake impressed him with an involuntary reverence for me, which set bounds to those excesses which disdained any other controul. Hence, I derived new motives for cherishing a life which was useful, in so many ways, to my mother.

My condition is now changed. I am no longer on that field to which the law, as well as reason, must acknowledge that I had some right, while there was any in my father. I must hazard my life, if need be, in the pursuit of the means of honest subsistence. I never spared myself while in the service of Mr. Hadwin; and, at a more inclement season, should probably have incurred some hazard by my diligence.

These were the motives of my *idleness*—for, my abstaining from the common toils of the farm passed by that name among my neighbors; though, in truth, my time was far from being wholly unoccupied by manual employments, but these required less exertion of body or mind, or were more connected with intellectual efforts. They were pursued in the seclusion of my chamber or the recesses of a wood. I did not labor to conceal them, but neither was I anxious to attract notice. It was sufficient that the censure of my neighbors was unmerited, to make me regard it with indifference.

I sought not the society of persons of my own age, not from sullen or unsociable habits, but merely because those around me were totally unlike myself. Their tastes and occupations were incompatible with mine. In my few books, in my pen, in the vegetable and animal existences around me, I found companions who adapted their visits and intercourse to my convenience and caprice, and with whom I was never tired of communing.

I was not unaware of the opinion which my neighbors had formed of my being improperly connected with Betty Lawrence. I am not sorry that I fell into company with that girl. Her intercourse has instructed me in what some would think impossible to be attained by one who had never haunted the impure recesses of licentiousness in a city. The knowledge, which residence in this town for ten years gave her audacious and inquisitive spirit, she imparted to me. Her character, profligate and artful, libidinous and impudent, and made up of the impressions which a city life had produced on her coarse but active mind, was open to my study, and I studied it.

I scarcely know how to repel the charge of illicit conduct, and to depict the exact species of intercourse subsisting between us. I always treated her with freedom, and sometimes with gaiety. I had no motives to reserve. I was so formed that a creature like her had no power over my senses. That species of temptation adapted to entice me from the true path, was widely different from the artifices of Betty. There was no point at which it was possible for her to get possession of my fancy. I watched her while she practised all her tricks and blandishments, just as I regarded a similar deportment in the *animal salax ignavumque* who inhabits the stye. I made efforts to pursue my observations unembarrassed; but my efforts were made, not to restrain desire, but to suppress disgust. The difficulty lay, not in withholding my caresses, but in forbearing to repulse her with rage.

Decorum, indeed, was not outraged, and all limits were not overstept, at once. Dubious advances were employed; but, when found unavailing, were displaced by more shameless and direct proceedings. She was too little versed in human nature to see that her last expedient was always worse than the preceding; and that, in proportion as she lost sight of decency, she multiplied the obstacles to her success.

Betty had many enticements in person and air. She was ruddy, smooth, and plump. To these she added—I must not say what, for it is strange to what lengths a woman destitute of modesty will sometimes go. But all her artifices availing her not at all in the contest with my insensibilities, she resorted to extremes which it would serve no good purpose to describe in this audience. They produced not the consequences she wished, but they produced another which was by no means displeasing to her. An incident one night occurred, from which a sagacious observer deduced the existence of an intrigue. It was useless to attempt to rectify his mistake, by explaining appearances, in a manner consistent with my innocence. This mode of explication implied a *continence* in me which he denied to be possible. The standard of possibilities, especially in vice and virtue, is fashioned by most men after their own character. A temptation which this judge of human nature knew that *he* was unable to resist, he sagely concluded to be irresistible by any other man, and quickly established the belief among my neighbors, that the woman who married the father had been prostituted to the son. Though I never admitted the truth of this aspersion, I believe it useless to deny, because no one would credit my denial, and because I had no power to disprove it.

Chapter XV

WHAT OTHER ENQUIRIES were to be resolved by our young friend, we were now, at this late hour, obliged to postpone till the morrow. I shall pass over the reflections which a story like this would naturally suggest, and hasten to our next interview.

After breakfast next morning, the subject of last night's conversation was renewed. I told him that something had occurred in his absence, in relation to Mrs. Wentworth and her nephew, that had perplexed us not a little. My information is obtained, continued I, from Wortley; and it is nothing less, than that young Clavering, Mrs. Wentworth's nephew, is, at this time, actually alive.

Surprise, but none of the embarrassment of guilt, appeared in his countenance at these tidings. He looked at me as if desirous that I should proceed.

It seems, added I, that a letter was lately received by this lady from the father of Clavering, who is now in Europe. This letter reports that this son was lately met with in Charleston, and relates the means which old Mr. Clavering had used to prevail upon his son to return home; means, of the success of which he entertained well grounded hopes. What think you?

I can only reject it, said he, after some pause, as untrue. The father's correspondent may have been deceived. The father may have been deceived, or the father may conceive it necessary to deceive the aunt, or some other supposition, as to the source of the error, may be true; but an error it surely is. Clavering is not alive. I know the chamber where he died, and the withered pine under which he lies buried.

If she be deceived, said I, it will be impossible to rectify her error.

I hope not. An honest front and a straight story will be sufficient.

How do you mean to act?

Visit her without doubt, and tell her the truth. My tale will be too circumstantial and consistent to permit her to disbelieve.

She will not hearken to you. She is too strongly prepossessed against you to admit you even to an hearing.

She cannot help it. Unless she lock her door against me, or stuff her ears with wool, she must hear me. Her prepossessions are reasonable, but are easily removed by telling the truth. Why does she suspect me of artifice? Because I seemed to be allied to Welbeck, and because I disguised the truth. That she thinks ill of me is not her fault, but my misfortune; and, happily for me, a misfortune easily removed.

Then you will try to see her.

I will see her, and the sooner the better. I will see her to-day; this morning; as soon as I have seen Welbeck, whom I shall immediately visit in his prison.

There are other embarrassments and dangers of which you are not aware. Welbeck is pursued by many persons whom he has defrauded of large sums. By these persons you are deemed an accomplice in his guilt, and a warrant is already in the hands of officers for arresting you wherever you are found.

In what way, said Mervyn, sedately, do they imagine me a partaker of his crime?

I know not. You lived with him. You fled with him. You aided and connived at his escape.

Are these crimes?

I believe not, but they subject you to suspicion.

To arrest and to punishment?

To detention for a while, perhaps. But these alone cannot expose you to punishment.

I thought so. Then I have nothing to fear.

You have imprisonment and obloquy, at least, to dread.

True; but they cannot be avoided but by my exile and skulking out of sight—evils infinitely more formidable. I shall, therefore, not avoid them. The sooner my conduct be subjected to scrutiny, the better. Will you go with me to Welbeck?

I will go with you.

Enquiring for Welbeck of the keeper of the prison, we were informed that he was in his own apartment very sick. The physician, attending the prison, had been called, but the prisoner had preserved an obstinate and scornful silence; and had neither explained his condition, nor consented to accept any aid.

We now went, alone, into his apartment. His sensibility seemed fast ebbing, yet an emotion of joy was visible in his eyes at the appearance of Mervyn. He seemed likewise to recognize in me his late visitant, and made no objection to my entrance.

How are you this morning? said Arthur, seating himself on the bed-side, and taking his hand. The sick man was scarcely able to articulate his reply—I shall soon be well. I have longed to see you. I want to leave with you a few words. He now cast his languid eyes on me. You are his friend, he continued. You know all. You may stay.—

There now succeeded a long pause, during which he closed his eyes, and resigned himself as if to an oblivion of all thought. His pulse under my hand was scarcely perceptible. From this in some minutes he recovered, and fixing his eyes on Mervyn, resumed, in a broken and feeble accent:

Clemenza! You have seen her. Weeks ago, I left her in an accursed house: yet she has not been mistreated. Neglected and abandoned indeed, but not mistreated. Save her Mervyn. Comfort her. Awaken charity for her sake.

I cannot tell you what has happened. The tale would be too long—too mournful. Yet, in justice to the living, I must tell you something. My woes and my crimes will be buried with me. Some of them, but not all.

Ere this, I should have been many leagues upon the ocean, had not a newspaper fallen into my hands while on the eve of embarkation. By that I learned that a treasure was buried with the remains of the ill-fated Watson. I was destitute. I was unjust enough to wish to make this treasure my own. Prone to think I was forgotten, or numbered with the victims of pestilence, I ventured to return under a careless disguise. I penetrated to the vaults of that deserted dwelling by night. I dug up the bones of my friend, and found the girdle and its valuable contents, according to the accurate description that I had read.

I hastened back with my prize to Baltimore, but my evil destiny overtook me at last. I was recognized by emissaries of Jamieson, arrested and brought hither, and here shall I consummate my fate and defeat the rage of my creditors by death. But first——

Here Welbeck stretched out his left hand to Mervyn, and, after some reluctance, shewed a roll of lead.

Receive this, said he. In the use of it, be guided by your honesty and by the same advertisement that furnished me the clue by which to recover it. That being secured, the world and I will part forever. Withdraw, for your presence can help me nothing.

We were unwilling to comply with his injunction, and continued some longer time in his chamber, but our kind intent availed nothing. He quickly relapsed into insensibility, from which he recovered not again, but next day expired. Such, in the flower of his age, was the fate of Thomas Welbeck.

Whatever interest I might feel in accompanying the progress of my young friend, a sudden and unforeseen emergency compelled me again to leave the city. A kinsman, to whom I was bound by many obligations, was suffering a lingering disease, and imagining, with some reason, his dissolution to be not far distant, he besought my company and my assistance, to sooth, at least, the agonies of his last hour. I was anxious to clear up the mysteries which Arthur's conduct had produced, and to shield him, if possible, from the evils which I feared awaited him. It was impossible, however, to decline the invitation of my kinsman, as his residence was not a day's journey from the city. I was obliged to content myself with occasional information, imparted by Mervyn's letters, or those of my wife.

Meanwhile, on leaving the prison, I hasted to inform Mervyn of the true nature of the scene which had just passed. By this extraordinary occurrence, the property of the Maurices was now in honest hands. Welbeck, stimulated by selfish motives, had done that which any other person would have found encompassed with formidable dangers and difficulties. How this attempt was suggested or executed, he had not informed us, nor was it desirable to know. It was sufficient that the means of restoring their own to a destitute and meritorious family, were now in our possession.

Having returned home, I unfolded to Mervyn all the particulars respecting Williams and the Maurices, which I had lately learned from Wortley. He listened with deep attention, and my story being finished, he said: In this small compass, then, is the patrimony and subsistence of a numerous family. To restore it to them is the obvious proceeding—but how? Where do they abide?

Williams and Watson's wife live in Baltimore, and the Maurices live near that town. The advertisements alluded to by Wortley, and which are to be found in any newspaper, will inform us; but first, are we sure that any or all of these bills are contained in this covering?

The lead was now unrolled, and the bills which Williams had described, were found inclosed. Nothing appeared to be deficient. Of this, however, we were scarcely qualified to judge. Those that were the property of Williams might not be entire, and what would be the consequence of presenting them to him, if any had been embezzled by Welbeck?

This difficulty was obviated by Mervyn, who observed that the advertisement, describing these bills, would afford us ample information on this head. Having found out where the Maurices and Mrs. Watson live, nothing remains but to visit them, and put an end, as far as lies in my power, to their inquietudes.

What! Would you go to Baltimore?

Certainly. Can any other expedient be proper? How shall I otherwise insure the safe conveyance of these papers?

You may send them by post.

But why not go myself?

I can hardly tell, unless your appearance on such an errand, may be suspected likely to involve you in embarrassments.

What embarrassments? If they receive their own, ought they not to be satisfied?

The enquiry will naturally be made as to the manner of gaining possession of these papers. They were lately in the hands of Watson, but Watson has disappeared. Suspicions are awake respecting the cause of his disappearance. These suspicions are connected with Welbeck, and Welbeck's connection with you is not unknown.

These are evils, but I see not how an ingenuous and open conduct is adapted to increase these evils. If they come, I must endure them.

I believe your decision is right. No one is so skilful an advocate in a cause, as he whose cause it is. I rely upon your skill and address, and shall leave you to pursue your own way. I must leave you for a time, but shall expect to be punctually informed of all that passes. With this agreement we parted, and I hastened to perform my intended journey.

Chapter XVI

I AM GLAD, my friend, thy nimble pen has got so far upon its journey. What remains of my story may be dispatched in a trice. I have just now some vacant hours, which might possibly be more usefully employed, but not in an easier manner or more pleasant. So, let me carry on thy thread.

First, let me mention the resolutions I had formed at the time I parted with my friend. I had several objects in view. One was a conference with Mrs. Wentworth: another was an interview with her whom I met with at Villars's. My heart melted when I thought upon the desolate condition of Clemenza, and determined me to direct my first efforts for her relief. For this end I was to visit the female who had given me a direction to her house. The name of this person is Achsa Fielding, and she lived, according to her own direction, at No. 40, Walnut-street.

I went thither without delay. She was not at home. Having gained information from the servant, as to when she might be found, I proceeded to Mrs. Wentworth's. In going thither my mind was deeply occupied in meditation; and, with my usual carelessness of forms, I entered the house and made my way to the parlour, where an interview had formerly taken place between us.

Having arrived, I began, though somewhat unseasonably, to reflect upon the topics with which I should introduce my conversation, and particularly the manner in which I should introduce myself. I had opened doors without warning, and traversed passages without being noticed. This had arisen from my thoughtlessness. There was no one within hearing or sight. What was next to be done? Should I not return softly to the outer door, and summon the servant by knocking?

Preparing to do this, I heard a footstep in the entry which suspended my design. I stood in the middle of the floor, attentive to these movements, when presently the door opened, and there entered the apartment Mrs. Wentworth herself! She came, as it seemed, without expectation of finding any one there. When, therefore, the figure of a man caught her vagrant attention, she started and cast an hasty look towards me.

Pray! (in a peremptory tone) how came you here, sir? and what is your business?

Neither arrogance, on the one hand; nor humility, upon the other, had any part in modelling my deportment. I came not to deprecate anger, or exult over distress. I answered, therefore, distinctly, firmly, and erectly.

I came to see you, madam, and converse with you; but, being busy with other thoughts, I forgot to knock at the door. No evil was intended by my negligence, though propriety has certainly not been observed. Will you pardon this intrusion, and condescend to grant me your attention?

To what? What have you to say to me? I know you only as the accomplice of a villain in an attempt to deceive me. There is nothing to justify your coming hither, and I desire you to leave the house with as little ceremony as you entered it.

My eyes were lowered at this rebuke, yet I did not obey the command. Your treatment of me, madam, is such as I appear to you to deserve. Appearances are unfavorable to me, but those appearances are false. I have concurred in no plot against your reputation or your fortune. I have told you nothing but the truth. I came hither to promote no selfish or sinister purpose. I have no favor to entreat, and no petition to offer, but that you will suffer me to clear up those mistakes which you have harbored respecting me.

I am poor. I am destitute of fame and of kindred. I have nothing to console me in obscurity and indigence, but the approbation of my own heart and the good opinion of those who know me as I am. The good may be led to despise and condemn me. Their aversion and scorn shall not make me unhappy; but it is my interest and my duty to rectify their error if I can. I regard your character with esteem. You have been mistaken in condemning me as a liar and impostor, and I came to remove this mistake. I came, if not to procure your esteem, at least, to take away hatred and suspicion.

But this is not all my purpose. You are in an error in relation not only to my character, but to the situation of your nephew Clavering. I formerly told you, that I saw him die; that I assisted at his burial; but my tale was incoherent and imperfect, and you have since received intelligence to which you think proper to trust, and which assures you that he is still living. All I now ask is your attention, while I relate the particulars of my knowledge.

Proof of my veracity or innocence may be of no value in your eyes, but the fate of your nephew ought to be known to you. Certainty, on this head, may be of much importance to your happiness, and to the regulation of your future conduct. To hear me patiently can do you no injury, and may benefit you much. Will you permit me to go on?

During this address, little abatement of resentment and scorn was visible in my companion.

I will hear you, she replied. Your invention may amuse if it does not edify. But, I pray you, let your story be short.

I was obliged to be content with this ungraceful concession, and proceeded to begin my narration. I described the situation of my father's dwelling. I mentioned the year, month, day, and hour of her nephew's appearance among us. I expatiated minutely on his form, features, dress, sound of his voice, and repeated his words. His favorite gestures and attitudes were faithfully described.

I had gone but a little way in my story, when the effects were visible in her demeanor which I expected from it. Her knowledge of the youth, and of the time and manner of his disappearance, made it impossible for me, with so minute a narrative, to impose upon her credulity. Every word, every incident related, attested my truth, by their agreement with what she herself previously knew.

Her suspicions and angry watchfulness was quickly exchanged for downcast looks, and stealing tears, and sighs difficultly repressed. Meanwhile, I did not pause, but described the treatment he received from my mother's tenderness, his occupations, the freaks of his insanity, and, finally, the circumstances of his death and funeral.

Thence I hastened to the circumstances which brought me to the city; which placed me in the service of Welbeck, and obliged me to perform so ambiguous a part in her presence. I left no difficulty to be solved and no question unanticipated.

I have now finished my story, I continued, and accomplished my design in coming hither. Whether I have vindicated my integrity from your suspicions, I know not. I have done what in me lay to remove your error; and, in that, have done my duty.—What more remains? Any enquiries you are pleased to make, I am ready to answer. If there be none to make, I will comply with your former commands, and leave the house with as little ceremony as I entered it.

Your story, she replied, has been unexpected. I believe it fully, and am sorry for the hard thoughts which past appearances have made me entertain concerning you.

Here she sunk into mournful silence. The information, she at length resumed, which I have received from another quarter respecting that unfortunate youth, astonishes and perplexes me. It is inconsistent with your story, but it must be founded on some mistake, which I am, at present, unable to unravel. Welbeck, whose connection has been so unfortunate to you——

Unfortunate! Dear Madam! How unfortunate? It has done away a part of my ignorance of the world in which I live. It has led me to the situation in which I am now placed. It has introduced me to the knowledge of many good people. It has made me the witness and the subject of many acts of beneficence and generosity. My knowledge of Welbeck has been useful to me. It has enabled me to be useful to others. I look back upon that allotment of my destiny which first led me to his door, with gratitude and pleasure.

Would to Heaven, continued I, somewhat changing my tone, intercourse with Welbeck had been as harmless to all others as it has been to me: that no injury to fortune and fame, and innocence and life, had been incurred by others greater than has fallen upon my head. There is one being, whose connection with him has not been utterly dissimilar in its origin and circumstances to mine, though the catastrophe has, indeed, been widely and mournfully different.

And yet, within this moment, a thought has occurred from which I derive some consolation and some hope. You, dear madam, are rich. These spacious apartments, this plentiful accommodation are yours. You have enough for your own gratification and convenience, and somewhat to spare. Will you take to your protecting arms, to your hospitable roof, an unhappy girl whom the arts of Welbeck have robbed of fortune, reputation and honor, who is now languishing in poverty, weeping over the lifeless remains of her babe, surrounded by the agents of vice, and trembling on the verge of infamy?

What can this mean? replied the lady. Of whom do you speak?

You shall know her. You shall be apprized of her claims to your compassion. Her story, as far as is known to me, I will faithfully repeat to you. She is a stranger; an Italian; her name is Clemenza Lodi.—

Clemenza Lodi! Good Heaven! exclaimed Mrs. Wentworth; why, surely—it cannot be. And yet—Is it possible that you are that person?

I do not comprehend you, madam.

A friend has related a transaction of a strange sort. It is scarcely an hour since she told it me. The name of Clemenza Lodi was mentioned in it, and a young man of most singular deportment was described.—But tell me how you were engaged on Thursday morning?

I was coming to this city from a distance. I stopped ten minutes at the house of——

Mrs. Villars?

The same. Perhaps you know her and her character. Perhaps you can confirm or rectify my present opinions concerning her. It is there that the unfortunate Clemenza abides. It is thence that I wish her to be speedily removed.

I have heard of you; of your conduct upon that occasion.

Of me? answered I eagerly. Do you know that woman? So saying, I produced the card which I had received from her, and in which her name was written.

I know her well. She is my countrywoman and my friend.

Your friend? Then she is good—she is innocent—she is generous. Will she be a sister, a protectress to Clemenza? Will you exhort her to a deed of charity? Will you be, yourself, an example of beneficence? Direct me to Miss Fielding, I beseech you. I have called on her already, but in vain, and there is no time to be lost.

Why are you so precipitate? What would you do?

Take her away from that house instantly—bring her hither—place her under your protection—give her Mrs. Wentworth for a counsellor—a friend—a mother. Shall I do this?

Shall I hie thither to-day, this very hour—now? Give me your consent, and she shall be with you before noon.

By no means, replied she, with earnestness. You are too hasty. An affair of so much importance cannot be dispatched in a moment. There are many difficulties and doubts to be first removed.

Let them be reserved for the future. Withhold not your helping hand till the struggler has disappeared forever. Think on the gulph that is already gaping to swallow her. This is no time to hesitate and faulter. I will tell you her story, but not now; we will postpone it till to-morrow; and first secure her from impending evils. She shall tell it you herself. In an hour I will bring her hither, and she herself shall recount to you her sorrows. Will you let me?

Your behaviour is extraordinary. I can scarcely tell whether this simplicity be real or affected. One would think that your common sense would shew you the impropriety of your request. To admit under my roof a woman, notoriously dishonoured, and from an infamous house——

My dearest madam! How can you reflect upon the situation without irresistible pity? I see that you are thoroughly aware of her past calamity and her present danger. Do not these urge you to make haste to her relief? Can any lot be more deplorable than hers? Can any state be more perilous? Poverty is not the only evil that oppresses, or that threatens her. The scorn of the world, and her own compunction, the death of the fruit of her error and the witness of her shame, are not the worst. She is exposed to the temptations of the profligate; while she remains with Mrs. Villars, her infamy accumulates; her further debasement is facilitated; her return to reputation and to virtue is obstructed by new bars.

How know I that her debasement is not already complete and irremediable? She is a mother but not a wife. How came she thus? Is her being Welbeck's prostitute no proof of her guilt?

Alas! I know not. I believe her not very culpable; I know her to be unfortunate; to have been robbed and betrayed. You are a stranger to her history. I am myself imperfectly acquainted with it.

But let me tell you the little that I know. Perhaps my narrative may cause you to think of her as I do.

She did not object to this proposal, and I immediately recounted all that I had gained from my own observations, or from Welbeck himself, respecting this forlorn girl. Having finished my narrative, I proceeded thus:—

Can you hesitate to employ that power which was given you for good ends, to rescue this sufferer? Take her to your home; to your bosom; to your confidence. Keep aloof those temptations which beset her in her present situation. Restore her to that purity which her desolate condition, her ignorance, her misplaced gratitude and the artifices of a skilful dissembler, have destroyed, if it be destroyed; for how know we under what circumstances her ruin was accomplished? With what pretences or appearances, or promises she was won to compliance?

True. I confess my ignorance; but ought not that ignorance to be removed before she makes a part of my family?

O no! It may be afterwards removed. It cannot be removed before. By bringing her hither you shield her, at least, from future and possible evils. Here you can watch her conduct and sift her sentiments conveniently and at leisure. Should she prove worthy of your charity, how justly may you congratulate yourself on your seasonable efforts in her cause? If she prove unworthy, you may then demean yourself according to her demerits.

I must reflect upon it.—To-morrow——

Let me prevail on you to admit her at once, and without delay. This very moment may be the critical one. To-day, we may exert ourselves with success, but to-morrow, all our efforts may be fruitless. Why fluctuate, why linger, when so much good may be done, and no evil can possibly be incurred? It requires but a word from you; you need not move a finger. Your house is large. You have chambers vacant and convenient. Consent only that your door shall not be barred against her; that you will treat her with civility; to carry your kindness into effect; to persuade her to attend me hither and to place herself in your care, shall be my province.

These, and many similar entreaties and reasonings, were ineffectual. Her general disposition was kind, but she was un-accustomed to strenuous or sudden exertions. To admit the persuasions of such an advocate to so uncommon a scheme as that of sharing her house with a creature, thus previously un-known to her, thus loaded with suspicion and with obloquy, was not possible.

I at last forbore importunity, and requested her to tell me when I might expect to meet with Miss Fielding at her lodg-ings? Enquiry was made to what end I sought an interview? I made no secret of my purpose.

Are you mad, young man? she exclaimed. Mrs. Fielding has already been egregiously imprudent. On the faith of an an-cient slight acquaintance with Mrs. Villars in Europe, she suf-fered herself to be decoyed into a visit. Instead of taking warning by numerous tokens of the real character of that woman, in her behaviour, and in that of her visitants, she consented to remain there one night. The next morning took place that astonishing interview with you which she has since described to me. She is now warned against the like indiscre-tion. And pray, what benevolent scheme would you propose to her?

Has she property? Is she rich?

She is. Unhappily, perhaps, for her, she is absolute mistress of her fortune, and has neither guardian nor parent to con-troul her in the use of it.

Has she virtue? Does she know the value of affluence and a fair fame? And will not she devote a few dollars to rescue a fellow-creature from indigence and infamy and vice? Surely she will. She will hazard nothing by the boon. I will be her almoner. I will provide the wretched stranger with food and raiment and dwelling, I will pay for all, if Miss Fielding, from her superfluity will supply the means. Clemenza shall owe life and honor to your friend, till I am able to supply the needful sum from my own stock.

While thus speaking, my companion gazed at me with steadfastness—I know not what to make of you. Your lan-guage and ideas are those of a lunatic. Are you acquainted with Mrs. Fielding?

Yes. I have seen her two days ago, and she has invited me to see her again.

And on the strength of this acquaintance, you expect to be her almoner? To be the medium of her charity?

I desire to save her trouble; to make charity as light and easy as possible. 'Twill be better if she perform those offices herself. 'Twill redound more to the credit of her reason and her virtue. But I solicit her benignity only in the cause of Clemenza. For her only do I wish at present to call forth her generosity and pity.

And do you imagine she will entrust her money to one of your age and sex, whom she knows so imperfectly, to administer to the wants of one whom she found in such an house as Mrs. Villars's? She never will. She mentioned her imprudent engagement to meet you, but she is now warned against the folly of such confidence.

You have told me plausible stories of yourself and of this Clemenza. I cannot say that I disbelieve them, but I know the ways of the world too well to bestow implicit faith so easily. You are an extraordinary young man. You may possibly be honest. Such an one as you, with your education and address, may possibly have passed all your life in an hovel; but it is scarcely credible, let me tell you. I believe most of the facts respecting my nephew, because my knowledge of him before his flight, would enable me to detect your falsehood; but there must be other proofs besides an innocent brow and a voluble tongue, to make me give full credit to your pretensions.

I have no claim upon Welbeck which can embarrass you. On that score, you are free from any molestation from me or my friends. I have suspected you of being an accomplice in some vile plot, and am now inclined to acquit you, but that is all that you must expect from me, till your character be established by other means than your own assertions. I am engaged at present, and must therefore request you to put an end to your visit.

This strain was much unlike the strain which preceded it. I imagined, by the mildness of her tone and manners, that her unfavorable prepossessions were removed, but they seemed to have suddenly regained their pristine force. I was somewhat disconcerted by this unexpected change. I stood for a minute silent and irresolute.

Just then a knock was heard at the door, and presently entered that very female whom I had met with at Villars's. I caught her figure as I glanced through the window. Mrs. Wentworth darted at me many significant glances, which commanded me to withdraw; but with this object in view, it was impossible.

As soon as she entered, her eyes were fixed upon me. Certain recollections naturally occurred at that moment, and made her cheeks glow. Some confusion reigned for a moment, but was quickly dissipated. She did not notice me, but exchanged salutations with her friend.

All this while I stood near the window, in a situation not a little painful. Certain tremors which I had not been accustomed to feel, and which seemed to possess a mystical relation to the visitant, disabled me at once from taking my leave, or from performing any useful purpose by staying. At length, struggling for composure, I approached her, and shewing her the card she had given me, said:—

Agreeably to this direction, I called, an hour ago, at your lodgings. I found you not. I hope you will permit me to call once more. When shall I expect to meet you at home?

Her eyes were cast on the floor. A kind of indirect attention was fixed on Mrs. Wentworth, serving to intimidate and check her. At length she said, in an irresolute voice, I shall be at home this evening.

And this evening, replied I, I will call to see you. So saying, I left the house.

This interval was tedious; but was to be endured with equanimity. I was impatient to be gone to Baltimore, and hoped to be able to set out by the dawn of next day. Meanwhile, I was necessarily to perform something with respect to Clemenza.

After dinner I accompanied Mrs. Stevens to visit Miss Carlton. I was eager to see a woman who could bear adversity in the manner which my friend had described.

She met us at the door of her apartment. Her seriousness was not abated by her smiles of affability and welcome.—My friend! whispered I, How truly lovely is this Miss Carlton! Are the heart and the intelligence within worthy of these features? Yes, they are. Your account of her employments; of her resignation to the ill fate of the brother whom she loves, proves that they are.

My eyes were rivetted to her countenance and person. I felt uncontroulable eagerness to speak to her, and to gain her good opinion.

You must know this young man, my dear Miss Carlton, said my friend, looking at me: He is my husband's friend, and professes a great desire to be yours. You must not treat him as a mere stranger, for he knows your character and situation already, as well as that of your brother.

She looked at me with benignity.—I accept his friendship willingly and gratefully, and shall endeavor to convince him that his good opinion is not misplaced.

There now ensued a conversation somewhat general, in which this young woman shewed a mind vigorous from exercise and unembarrassed by care. She affected no concealment of her own condition, of her wants, or her comforts. She laid no stress upon misfortunes, but contrived to deduce some beneficial consequence to herself, and some motive for gratitude to Heaven, from every wayward incident that had befallen her.

This demeanor emboldened me, at length, to enquire into the cause of her brother's imprisonment, and the nature of his debt.

She answered frankly and without hesitation. It is a debt of his father's, for which he made himself responsible during his father's life. The act was generous but imprudent, as the event has shewn; though, at the time, the unhappy effects could not be foreseen.

My father, continued she, was arrested by his creditor, at a time when the calmness and comforts of his own dwelling were necessary to his health. The creditor was obdurate, and would release him upon no condition but that of receiving a bond from my brother, by which he engaged to pay the debt at several successive times and in small portions. All these instalments were discharged with great difficulty indeed, but with sufficient punctuality, except the last, to which my brother's earnings were not adequate.

How much is the debt?

Four hundred dollars.

And is the state of the creditor such as to make the loss of four hundred dollars of more importance to him than the loss of liberty to your brother?

She answered, smiling, that is a very abstract view of things. On such a question, you and I might, perhaps, easily decide in favor of my brother; but would there not be some danger of deciding partially? His conduct is a proof of his decision, and there is no power to change it.

Will not argument change it? Methinks in so plain a case I should be able to convince him. You say he is rich and childless. His annual income is ten times more than this sum. Your brother cannot pay the debt while in prison; whereas, if at liberty, he might slowly and finally discharge it. If his humanity would not yield, his avarice might be brought to acquiesce.

But there is another passion which you would find it somewhat harder to subdue, and that is his vengeance. He thinks himself wronged, and imprisons my brother, not to enforce payment, but to inflict misery. If you could persuade him, that there is no hardship in imprisonment, you would speedily gain the victory; but that could not be attempted consistently with truth. In proportion to my brother's suffering is his gratification.

You draw an odious and almost incredible portrait.

And yet such an one as would serve for the likeness of almost every second man we meet.

And is such your opinion of mankind? Your experience must surely have been of a rueful tenor to justify such hard thoughts of the rest of your species.

By no means. It has been what those whose situation disables them from looking further than the surface of things, would regard as unfortunate; but if my goods and evils were equitably balanced, the former would be the weightiest. I have found kindness and goodness in great numbers, but have likewise met prejudice and rancor in many. My opinion of Farquhar is not lightly taken up. I have seen him yesterday, and the nature of his motives in the treatment of my brother was plain enough.

Here this topic was succeeded by others, and the conversation ceased not till the hour had arrived on which I had preconcerted to visit Mrs. Fielding. I left my two friends for this purpose.

I was admitted to Mrs. Fielding's presence without scruple or difficulty. There were two females in her company, and one of the other sex, well dressed, elderly, and sedate persons. Their discourse turned upon political topics, with which, as you know, I have but slight acquaintance. They talked of fleets and armies, of Robespierre and Pitt, of whom I had only a newspaper knowledge.

In a short time the women rose, and, huddling on their cloaks, disappeared, in company with the gentleman. Being thus left alone with Mrs. Fielding, some embarrassment was mutually betrayed. With much hesitation, which, however, gradually disappeared, my companion, at length, began the conversation.

You met me lately, in a situation, sir, on which I look back with trembling and shame, but not with any self-condemnation. I was led into it without any fault, unless a too hasty confidence may be stiled a fault. I had known Mrs. Villars in England, where she lived with an untainted reputation, at least; and the sight of my countrywoman, in a foreign land, awakened emotions, in the indulgence of which I did not imagine there was either any guilt or any danger. She invited me to see her at her house with so much urgency and warmth, and solicited me to take a place immediately in a chaise in which she had come to the city, that I too incautiously complied.

You are a stranger to me, and I am unacquainted with your character. What little I have seen of your deportment, and what little I have lately heard concerning you from Mrs. Wentworth, do not produce unfavorable impressions; but the apology I have made was due to my own reputation, and should have been offered to you whatever your character had been. There she stopped.

I came not hither, said I, to receive an apology. Your demeanor, on our first interview, shielded you sufficiently from any suspicions or surmises that I could form. What you have now mentioned was likewise mentioned by your friend, and was fully believed upon her authority. My purpose, in coming, related not to you but to another. I desired merely to interest your generosity and justice on behalf of one, whose destitute and dangerous condition may lay claim to your compassion and your succour.

I comprehend you, said she, with an air of some perplexity. I know the claims of that person.

And will you comply with them?

In what manner can I serve her?

By giving her the means of living.

Does she not possess them already?

She is destitute. Her dependence was wholly placed upon one that is dead, by whom her person was dishonored and her fortune embezzled.

But she still lives. She is not turned into the street. She is not destitute of home.

But what an home!

Such as she may chuse to remain in.

She cannot chuse it. She must not chuse it. She remains through ignorance, or through the incapacity of leaving it.

But how shall she be persuaded to a change?

I will persuade her. I will fully explain her situation. I will supply her with a new home.

You would persuade her to go with you, and to live at a home of your providing, and on your bounty?

Certainly.

Would that change be worthy of a cautious person? Would it benefit her reputation? Would it prove her love of independence?

My purposes are good. I know not why she should suspect them. But I am only anxious to be the instrument. Let her be indebted to one of her own sex, of unquestionable reputation. Admit her into this house. Invite her to your arms. Cherish and console her as your sister.

Before I am convinced that she deserves it? And even then, what regard shall I, young, unmarried, independent, affluent, pay to my own reputation in harboring a woman in these circumstances?

But you need not act yourself. Make me your agent and almoner. Only supply her with the means of subsistence through me.

Would you have me act a clandestine part? Hold meetings with one of your sex, and give him money for a purpose which I must hide from the world? Is it worth while to be a dissembler and impostor? And will not such conduct incur more dangerous surmises and suspicions, than would arise from acting openly and directly? You will forgive me for reminding you likewise, that it is particularly incumbent upon those in my situation, to be circumspect in their intercourse with men and with strangers. This is the second time that I have seen you. My knowledge of you is extremely dubious and imperfect, and such as would make the conduct you prescribe to me, in an high degree, rash and culpable. You must not, therefore, expect me to pursue it.

These words were delivered with an air of firmness and dignity. I was not insensible to the truth of her representations. I confess, said I, what you have said makes me doubt the propriety of my proposal: yet I would fain be of service to her. Cannot you point out some practicable method?

She was silent and thoughtful, and seemed indisposed to answer my question.

I had set my heart upon success in this negociation, continued I, and could not imagine any obstacle to its success; but I find my ignorance of the world's ways much greater than I had previously expected. You defraud yourself of all the happiness redounding from the act of making others happy. You sacrifice substance to shew, and are more anxious to prevent unjust aspersions from lighting on yourself, than to rescue a fellow-creature from guilt and infamy.

You are rich, and abound in all the conveniences and luxuries of life. A small portion of your superfluity would obviate the wants of a being not less worthy than yourself. It is not avarice or aversion to labor that makes you withhold your hand. It is dread of the sneers and surmises of malevolence and ignorance.

I will not urge you further at present. Your determination to be wise should not be hasty. Think upon the subject calmly and sedately, and form your resolution in the course of three days. At the end of that period I will visit you again. So saying, and without waiting for comment or answer, I withdrew.

Chapter XVII

I MOUNTED the stage-coach at day-break the next day, in company with a sallow Frenchman from Saint Domingo, his fiddle-case, an ape, and two female blacks. The Frenchman, after passing the suburbs, took out his violin and amused himself with humming to his own *tweedle-tweedle*. The monkey now and then mounched an apple, which was given to him from a basket by the blacks, who gazed with stupid wonder, and an exclamatory *La! La!* upon the passing scenery; or chattered to each other in a sort of open-mouthed, half-articulate, monotonous, and sing-song jargon.

The man looked seldom either on this side or that; and spoke only to rebuke the frolicks of the monkey, with a Tenez! Dominique! Prenez garde! Diable noir!

As to me my thought was busy in a thousand ways. I sometimes gazed at the faces of my *four* companions, and endeavored to discern the differences and samenesses between them. I took an exact account of the features, proportions, looks, and gestures of the monkey, the Congolese, and the Creole-Gaul. I compared them together, and examined them apart. I looked at them in a thousand different points of view, and pursued, untired and unsatiated, those trains of reflections which began at each change of tone, feature, and attitude.

I marked the country as it successively arose before me, and found endless employment in examining the shape and substance of the fence, the barn and the cottage, the aspect of earth and of heaven. How great are the pleasures of health and of mental activity.

My chief occupation, however, related to the scenes into which I was about to enter. My imaginations were, of course, crude and inadequate; and I found an uncommon gratification in comparing realities, as they successively occurred, with the pictures which my wayward fancy had depicted.

I will not describe my dreams. My proper task is to relate the truth. Neither shall I dwell upon the images suggested by the condition of the country through which I passed. I will confine myself to mentioning the transactions connected with the purpose of my journey.

I reached Baltimore at night. I was not so fatigued, but that I could ramble through the town. I intended, at present, merely the gratification of a stranger's curiosity. My visit to Mrs. Watson and her brother I designed should take place on the morrow. The evening of my arrival I deemed an unseasonable time.

While roving about, however, it occurred to me, that it might not be impolitic to find the way to their habitation even now. My purposes of general curiosity would equally be served whichever way my steps were bent; and, to trace the path to their dwelling, would save me the trouble of enquiries and interrogations to-morrow.

When I looked forward to an interview with the wife of Watson, and to the subject which would be necessarily discussed at that interview, I felt a trembling and misgiving at my heart. Surely, thought I, it will become me to exercise immeasurable circumspection and address; and yet how little are these adapted to the impetuosity and candor of my nature.

How am I to introduce myself? What am I to tell her? That I was a sort of witness to the murder of her husband? That I received from the hand of his assassin the letter which I afterwards transmitted to her? and, from the same hands, the bills contained in his girdle?

How will she start and look aghast? What suspicions will she harbor? What enquiries shall be made of me? How shall they be disarmed and eluded, or answered? Deep consideration will be necessary before I trust myself to such an interview. The coming night shall be devoted to reflection upon this subject.

From these thoughts I proceeded to enquiries for the street mentioned in the advertisement, where Mrs. Watson was said to reside. The street, and, at length, the habitation, was found. Having reached a station opposite, I paused and surveyed the mansion. It was a wooden edifice of two stories; humble, but neat. You ascended to the door by several stone steps. Of the two lower windows, the shutters of one were closed, but those of the other were open. Though late in the evening, there was no appearance of light or fire within.

Beside the house was a painted fence, through which was a gate leading to the back of the building. Guided by the impulse of the moment, I crossed the street to the gate, and, lifting the latch, entered the paved alley, on one side of which was a paled fence, and on the other the house, looking through two windows into the alley.

The first window was dark like those in front; but at the second a light was discernible. I approached it, and, looking through, beheld a plain but neat apartment, in which parlour, kitchen, and nursery seemed to be united. A fire burnt cheerfully in the chimney, over which was a tea-kettle. On the hearth sat a smiling and playful cherub of a boy, tossing something to a black girl who sat opposite, and whose innocent and regular features wanted only a different hue to make them beautiful. Near it, in a rocking-chair, with a sleeping babe in her lap, sat a female figure in plain but neat and becoming attire. Her posture permitted half her face to be seen, and saved me from any danger of being observed.

This countenance was full of sweetness and benignity, but the sadness that veiled its lustre was profound. Her eyes were now fixed upon the fire and were moist with the tears of remembrance, while she sung, in low and scarcely audible strains, an artless lullaby.

This spectacle exercised a strange power over my feelings. While occupied in meditating on the features of the mother, I was unaware of my conspicuous situation. The black girl having occasion to change her situation, in order to reach the ball which was thrown at her, unluckily caught a glance of my figure through the glass. In a tone of half surprize and half terror she cried out—O! see dare! a man!

I was tempted to draw suddenly back, but a second thought shewed me the impropriety of departing thus abruptly, and leaving behind me some alarm. I felt a sort of necessity for apologizing for my intrusion into these precincts, and hastened to a door that led into the same apartment. I knocked. A voice somewhat confused bade me enter. It was not till I opened the door and entered the room, that I fully saw in what embarrassments I had incautiously involved myself.

I could scarcely obtain sufficient courage to speak, and gave a confused assent to the question—"Have you business with me, sir?" She offered me a chair, and I sat down. She put the child, not yet awakened, into the arms of the black, who kissed it and rocked it in her arms with great satisfaction, and, re-suming her seat, looked at me with inquisitiveness mingled with complacency.

After a moment's pause, I said—I was directed to this house as the abode of Mr. Ephraim Williams. Can he be seen, madam?

He is not in town at present. If you will leave a message with me, I will punctually deliver it.

The thought suddenly occurred, whether any more was needful than merely to leave the bills suitably enclosed, as they already were, in a pacquet. Thus all painful explanations might be avoided, and I might have reason to congratulate myself on his seasonable absence. Actuated by these thoughts, I drew forth the pacquet, and put it into her hand, saying, I will leave this in your possession, and must earnestly request you to keep it safe until you can deliver it into his own hands.

Scarcely had I said this before new suggestions occurred. Was it right to act in this clandestine and mysterious manner? Should I leave these persons in uncertainty respecting the fate of an husband and a brother? What perplexities, misunder-standings, and suspences might not grow out of this uncer-tainty; and ought they not to be precluded at any hazard to my own safety or good name?

These sentiments made me involuntarily stretch forth my hand to retake the pacquet. This gesture, and other signifi-cances in my manners, joined to a trembling consciousness in herself, filled my companion with all the tokens of confusion and fear. She alternately looked at me and at the paper. Her trepidation increased, and she grew pale. These emotions were counteracted by a strong effort.

At length she said faulteringly, I will take good care of them, and will give them to my brother.

She rose and placed them in a drawer, after which she re-sumed her seat.

On this occasion all my wariness forsook me. I cannot ex-plain why my perplexity and the trouble of my tho'ts were greater upon this than upon similar occasions. However it be, I was incapable of speaking, and fixed my eyes upon the floor. A sort of electrical sympathy pervaded my companion, and terror and anguish were strongly manifested in the glances which she sometimes stole at me. We seemed fully to understand each other without the aid of words.

This imbecility could not last long. I gradually recovered my composure and collected my scattered thoughts. I looked at her with seriousness, and steadfastly spoke—Are you the wife of Amos Watson?

She started.—I am, indeed. Why do you ask? Do you know any thing of——? There her voice failed.

I replied with quickness, yes. I am fully acquainted with his destiny.

Good God! she exclaimed in a paroxysm of surprize, and bending eagerly forward, my husband is then alive. This pacquet is from him. Where is he? When have you seen him?

'Tis a long time since.

But where, where is he now? Is he well? Will he return to me?

Never.

Merciful Heaven! looking upwards and clasping her hands, I thank thee at least for his life! But why has he forsaken me? Why will he not return?

For a good reason, said I with augmented solemnity, he will never return to thee. Long ago was he laid in the cold grave.

She shrieked; and, at the next moment, sunk in a swoon upon the floor. I was alarmed. The two children shrieked, and ran about the room terrified and unknowing what they did. I was overwhelmed with somewhat like terror, yet I involuntarily raised the mother in my arms, and cast about for the means of recalling her from this fit.

Time to effect this had not elapsed, when several persons, apparently Mrs. Watson's neighbors, and raised by the outcries of the girls, hastily entered the room. They looked at me with mingled surprize and suspicion; but my attitude, being that not of an injurer but helper; my countenance, which shewed the pleasure their entrance, at this critical moment, afforded me; and my words, in which I besought their assistance, and explained, in some degree, and briefly, the cause of those appearances, removed their ill thoughts.

Presently, the unhappy woman, being carried by the newcomers into a bed-room adjoining, recovered her sensibility. I only waited for this. I had done my part. More information would be useless to her, and not to be given by me, at least, in the present audience, without embarrassment and peril. I suddenly determined to withdraw, and this, the attention of the company being otherwise engaged, I did without notice. I returned to my inn, and shut myself up in my chamber. Such was the change which, undesigned, unforeseen, an half an hour had wrought in my situation. My cautious projects had perished in their conception. That which I had deemed so arduous, to require such circumspect approaches, such well concerted speeches, was done.

I had started up before this woman as if from the pores of the ground. I had vanished with the same celerity, but had left her in possession of proofs sufficient that I was neither spectre nor demon. I will visit her, said I, again. I will see her brother, and know the full effect of my disclosure. I will tell them all that I myself know. Ignorance would be no less injurious to them than to myself; but, first, I will see the Maurices.

Chapter XVIII

NEXT MORNING I arose betimes, and equipped myself without delay. I had eight or ten miles to walk, so far from the town being the residence of these people; and I forthwith repaired to their dwelling. The persons whom I desired to see were known to me only by name, and by their place of abode. It was a mother and her three daughters to whom I now carried the means not only of competence but riches; means which they, no doubt, had long ago despaired of regaining, and which, among all possible messengers, one of my age and guise would be the least suspected of being able to restore.

I arrived, through intricate ways, at eleven o'clock, at the house of Mrs. Maurice. It was a neat dwelling, in a very fanciful and rustic style, in the bosom of a valley, which, when decorated by the verdure and blossoms of the coming season, must possess many charms. At present it was naked and dreary.

As I approached it, through a long avenue, I observed two female figures, walking arm-in-arm and slowly to and fro, in the path in which I now was. These, said I, are daughters of the family. Graceful, well-dressed, fashionable girls they seem at this distance. May they be deserving of the good tidings which I bring.—Seeing them turn towards the house, I mended my pace, that I might overtake them and request their introduction of me to their mother.

As I more nearly approached, they again turned; and, perceiving me, they stood as if in expectation of my message. I went up to them.

A single glance, cast at each, made me suspect that they were not sisters; but, somewhat to my disappointment, there was nothing highly prepossessing in the countenance of either. They were what is every day met with, though less embellished by brilliant drapery and turban, in markets and streets. An air, somewhat haughty, somewhat supercilious, lessened still more their attractions. These defects, however, were nothing to me.

I enquired, of her that seemed to be the elder of the two, for Mrs. Maurice.

She is indisposed, was the cold reply.

That is unfortunate. Is it not possible to see her?

No—with still more gravity.

I was somewhat at a loss how to proceed. A pause ensued. At length, the same lady resumed—What's your business? You can leave your message with me.

With no body but her. If she be not *very* indisposed——

She is very indisposed, interrupted she peevishly. If you cannot leave your message, you may take it back again, for she must not be disturbed.

This was a singular reception. I was disconcerted and silent. I knew not what to say. Perhaps, I at last observed, some other time——

No, with increasing heat, no other time. She is more likely to be worse than better. Come, Betsy, said she, taking hold of her companion's arm; and, hieing into the house, shut the door after her, and disappeared. I stood, at the bottom of the steps, confounded at such strange and unexpected treatment. I could not withdraw till my purpose was accomplished. After a moment's pause, I stepped to the door, and pulled the bell. A Negro came, of a very unpropitious aspect, and opening the door, looked at me in silence. To my question, was Mrs. Maurice to be seen? he made some answer, in a jargon which I could not understand; but his words were immediately followed by an unseen person within the house—Mrs. Maurice can't be seen by any body. Come in, Cato, and shut the door. This injunction was obeyed by Cato without ceremony.

Here was a dilemma! I came with ten thousand pounds in my hands, to bestow freely on these people, and such was the treatment I received. I must adopt, said I, a new mode.

I lifted the latch, without a second warning, and, Cato having disappeared, went into a room, the door of which chanced to be open, on my right hand. I found within the two females whom I had accosted in the portico. I now addressed myself to the younger—This intrusion, when I have explained the reason of it, will, I hope, be forgiven. I come, madam——

Yes, interrupted the other, with a countenance suffused by indignation, I know very well whom you come from, and what it is that prompts this insolence, but your employer shall see that we have not sunk so low as he imagines. Cato! Bob! I say.

My employer, madam! I see you labor under some great mistake. I have no employer. I come from a great distance. I come to bring intelligence of the utmost importance to your family. I come to benefit and not to injure you.

By this time, Bob and Cato, two sturdy blacks, entered the room. Turn this person, said the imperious lady, regardless of my explanations, out of the house. Don't you hear me? she continued, observing that they looked one upon the other and hesitated.

Surely, madam, said I, you are precipitate. You are treating like an enemy one who will prove himself your mother's best friend.

Will you leave the house? she exclaimed, quite beside herself with anger. Villains! why don't you do as I bid you?

The blacks looked upon each other, as if waiting for an example. Their habitual deference for every thing *white*, no doubt, held their hands from what they regarded as a profanation. At last Bob said, in a whining, beseeching tone—Why, missee, massa buckra wanna go for doo, dan he wanna go fo' wee.

The lady now burst into tears of rage. She held out her hand, menacingly. Will you leave the house?

Not willingly, said I, in a mild tone. I came too far to return with the business that brought me unperformed. I am persuaded, madam, you mistake my character and my views. I have a message to deliver your mother which deeply concerns her and your happiness, if you are her daughter. I merely wished to see her, and leave with her a piece of important news; news in which her fortune is deeply interested.

These words had a wonderful effect upon the young lady. Her anger was checked. Good God! she exclaimed, are you Watson?

No: I am only Watson's representative, and come to do all that Watson could do if he were present.

She was now importunate to know my business.

My business lies with Mrs. Maurice. Advertisements, which

I have seen, direct me to her, and to this house, and to her only shall I deliver my message.

Perhaps, said she, with a face of apology, I have mistaken you. Mrs. Maurice is my mother. She is really indisposed, but I can stand in her place on this occasion.

You cannot represent her in this instance. If I cannot have access to her now, I must go; and shall return when you are willing to grant it.

Nay, replied she, she is not, perhaps, so very sick but that—I will go, and see if she will admit you.—So saying, she left me for three minutes; and returning said, her mother wished to see me.

I followed up stairs, at her request; and, entering an ill-furnished chamber, found, seated in an arm-chair, a lady seemingly in years, pale and visibly infirm. The lines of her countenance were far from laying claim to my reverence. It was too much like the daughter's.

She looked at me, at my entrance, with great eagerness, and said, in a sharp tone, pray, friend, what is it you want with me? Make haste; tell your story, and begone.

My story is a short one, and easily told. Amos Watson was your agent in Jamaica. He sold an estate belonging to you, and received the money.

He did, said she, attempting ineffectually to rise from her seat, and her eyes beaming with a significance that shocked me—He did, the villain, and purloined the money, to the ruin of me and my daughters. But if there be justice on earth it will overtake him. I trust, I shall have the pleasure one day—I hope to hear he's hanged. Well, but go on, friend. He *did* sell it, I tell you.

He sold it for ten thousand pounds, I resumed, and invested this sum in bills of exchange. Watson is dead. These bills came into my hands. I was lately informed, by the public papers, who were the real owners, and have come from Philadelphia with no other view than to restore them to you. There they are, continued I, placing them in her lap, entire and untouched.

She seized the papers, and looked at me and at her daughter, by turns, with an air of one suddenly bewildered. She seemed speechless, and growing suddenly more ghastly pale, leaned her head back upon the chair. The daughter screamed, and hastened to support the languid parent, who difficultly articulated—O! I am sick; sick to death. Put me on the bed.

I was astonished and affrighted at this scene. Some of the domestics, of both colours, entered, and gazed at me with surprise. Involuntarily I withdrew, and returned to the room below into which I had first entered, and which I now found deserted.

I was for some time at a loss to guess at the cause of these appearances. At length it occurred to me, that joy was the source of the sickness that had seized Mrs. Maurice. The abrupt recovery of what had probably been deemed irretrievable, would naturally produce this effect upon a mind of a certain texture.

I was deliberating, whether to stay or go, when the daughter entered the room, and, after expressing some surprise at seeing me, whom she supposed to have retired, told me that her mother wished to see me again before my departure. In this request there was no kindness. All was cold, supercilious, and sullen. I obeyed the summons without speaking.

I found Mrs. Maurice seated in her arm-chair, much in her former guise. Without desiring me to be seated, or relaxing ought in her asperity of looks and tones—Pray, friend, how did you *come by* these papers?

I assure you, madam, they were honestly *come by*, answered I, sedately and with half a smile; but, if the whole is there that was missing, the mode and time in which they came to me is matter of concern only to myself. Is there any deficiency?

I'm not sure. I don't know much of these matters. There may be less. I dare say there is. I shall know that soon. I expect a friend of mine every minute who will look them over. I don't doubt you can give a good account of yourself.

I doubt not but I can—to those who have a right to demand it. In this case, curiosity must be very urgent indeed, before I shall consent to gratify it.

You must know this is a suspicious case. Watson, to be sure, embezzled the money: to be sure, you are his accomplice.

Certainly, said I, my conduct, on this occasion, proves that.

What I have brought to you, of my own accord; what I have restored to you, fully and unconditionally, it is plain Watson embezzled, and that I was aiding in the fraud. To restore what was never stolen always betrays the thief. To give what might be kept without suspicion, is, without doubt, arrant knavery. —To be serious, madam, in coming thus far, for this purpose, I have done enough; and must now bid you farewel.

Nay, don't go yet. I have something more to say to you. My friend I'm sure will be here presently. There he is, noticing a peal upon the bell. Polly, go down, and see if that's Mr. Somers. If it is, bring him up. The daughter went.

I walked to the window absorbed in my own reflections. I was disappointed and dejected. The scene before me was the unpleasing reverse of all that my fancy, while coming hither, had foreboded. I expected to find virtuous indigence and sorrow lifted, by my means, to affluence and exultation. I expected to witness the tears of gratitude and the caresses of affection. What had I found? Nothing but sordidness, stupidity, and illiberal suspicion.

The daughter staid much longer than the mother's patience could endure. She knocked against the floor with her heel. A servant came up.—Where's Polly, you slut? It was not you, hussey, that I wanted. It was her.

She is talking in the parlour with a gentleman.

Mr. Somers, I suppose; hay! fool! Run with my compliments to him, wench. Tell him, please walk up.

It is not Mr. Somers, ma'am.

No! Who then, saucebox? What gentleman can have any thing to do with Polly?

I don't know, ma'am.

Who said you did, impertinence? Run, and tell her I want her this instant.

The summons was not delivered, or Polly did not think proper to obey it. Full ten minutes of thoughtful silence on my part, and of muttered vexation and impatience on that of the old lady, elapsed before Polly's entrance. As soon as she appeared, the mother began to complain bitterly of her inattention and neglect; but Polly, taking no notice of her, addressed herself to me, and told me, that a gentleman below wished to see me. I hastened down, and found a stranger, of a plain appearance, in the parlour. His aspect was liberal and ingenuous; and I quickly collected from his discourse, that this was the brother-in-law of Watson, and the companion of his last voyage.

Chapter XIX

M<small>Y EYES</small> sparkled with pleasure at this unexpected interview, and I willingly confessed my desire to commu-
nicate all the knowledge of his brother's destiny which I
possessed. He told me, that, returning late to Baltimore on
the last evening, he found his sister in much agitation and
distress, which, after a time, she explained to him. She likewise
put the pacquets I had left into his hands.

I leave you to imagine, continued he, my surprize and curiosity at this discovery. I was, of course, impatient to see the
bearer of such extraordinary tidings. This morning, enquiring
for one of your appearance at the taverns, I was, at length,
informed of your arrival yesterday in the stage; of your going
out alone in the evening; of your subsequent return; and of
your early departure this morning. Accidentally I lighted on
your footsteps; and, by suitable enquiries on the road, have
finally traced you hither.

You told my sister her husband was dead. You left with her
papers that were probably in his possession at the time of his
death. I understand from Miss Maurice that the bills belonging to her mother, have just been delivered to her. I presume
you have no objection to clear up this mystery.

To you I am anxious to unfold every thing. At this moment,
or at any time, but the sooner, the more agreeable to me, I
will do it.

This, said he, looking around him, is no place; there is an
inn not an hundred yards from this gate, where I have left my
horse; will you go thither? I readily consented, and calling for
a private apartment, I laid before this man every incident of
my life connected with Welbeck and Watson; my full, circumstantial and explicit story, appeared to remove every doubt
which he might have entertained of my integrity.

In Williams, I found a plain good man, of a temper confiding and affectionate. My narration being finished, he expressed, by unaffected tokens, his wonder and his grief on
account of Watson's destiny. To my enquiries, which were
made with frankness and fervor, respecting his own and his

sister's condition, he said, that the situation of both was deplorable till the recovery of this property. They had been saved from utter ruin, from beggary and a jail, only by the generosity and lenity of his creditors, who did not suffer the suspicious circumstances attending Watson's disappearance to outweigh former proofs of his probity. They had never relinquished the hopes of receiving some tidings of their kinsman.

I related what had just passed in the house of Mrs. Maurice, and requested to know from him the history and character of this family.

They have treated you, he answered, exactly as any one who knew them would have predicted. The mother is narrow, ignorant, bigotted, and avaricious. The eldest daughter, whom you saw, resembles the old lady in many things. Age, indeed, may render the similitude complete. At present, pride and ill-humor are her chief characteristics.

The youngest daughter has nothing in mind or person in common with her family. Where they are irrascible, she is patient; where they are imperious, she is humble; where they are covetous, she is liberal; where they are ignorant and indolent, she is studious and skilful. It is rare, indeed, to find a young lady more amiable than Miss Fanny Maurice, or who has had more crosses and afflictions to sustain.

The eldest daughter always extorted the supply of her wants, from her parents, by threats and importunities; but the younger could never be prevailed upon to employ the same means, and, hence, she suffered inconveniences which, to any other girl, born to an equal rank, would have been, to the last degree, humiliating and vexatious. To her they only afforded new opportunities for the display of her most shining virtues—fortitude and charity. No instance of their sordidness or tyranny ever stole a murmur from her. For what they had given, existence and a virtuous education, she said they were entitled to gratitude. What they withheld was their own, in the use of which they were not accountable to her. She was not ashamed to owe her subsistence to her own industry, and was only held, by the pride of her family—in this instance their pride was equal to their avarice—from seeking out some lucrative kind of employment. Since the shock which their fortune sustained, by Watson's disappearance, she has been permitted to pursue this plan, and she now teaches music in Baltimore for a living. No one, however, in the highest rank, can be more generally respected and caressed than she is.

But will not the recovery of this money make a favorable change in her condition?

I can hardly tell; but I am inclined to think it will not. It will not change her mother's character. Her pride may be awakened anew, and she may oblige Miss Fanny to relinquish her new profession, and that will be a change to be deplored.

What good has been done, then, by restoring this money?

If pleasure be good, you must have conferred a great deal on the Maurices; upon the mother and two of the daughters, at least. The only pleasure, indeed, which their natures can receive. It is less than if you had raised them from absolute indigence, which has not been the case, since they had where-withal to live upon beside their Jamaica property. But how, continued Williams, suddenly recollecting himself, have you claimed the reward promised to him who should restore these bills?

What reward?

No less than a thousand dollars. It was publicly promised under the hands of Mrs. Maurice and of Hemming, her husband's executor.

Really, said I, that circumstance escaped my attention, and I wonder that it did; but is it too late to repair the evil?

Then you have no scruple to accept the reward?

Certainly not. Could you suspect me of so strange a punctilio as that?

Yes; but I know not why. The story you have just finished taught me to expect some unreasonable refinement upon that head.—To be hired, to be bribed to do our duty is supposed by some to be degrading.

This is no such bribe to me. I should have acted just as I have done, had no recompence been promised. In truth, this has been my conduct, for I never once thought of the reward; but now that you remind me of it, I would gladly see it bestowed. To fulfil their engagements, in this respect, is no more than justice in the Maurices. To one, in my condition, the money will be highly useful. If these people were poor, or generous and worthy, or if I myself were already rich, I might less repine at their withholding it; but, things being as they are with them and with me, it would, I think, be gross injustice in them to withhold, and in me to refuse.

That injustice, said Williams, will, on their part, I fear, be committed. 'Tis pity you first applied to Mrs. Maurice. Nothing can be expected from her avarice, unless it be wrested from her by a lawsuit.

That is a force which I shall never apply.

Had you gone first to Hemming's, you might, I think, have looked for payment. He is not a mean man. A thousand dollars he must know is not much to give for forty thousand. Perhaps, indeed, it may not yet be too late. I am well known to him, and if you please, will attend you to him in the evening, and state your claim.

I thankfully accepted this offer, and went with him accordingly. I found that Hemmings had been with Mrs. Maurice in the course of the day; had received from her intelligence of this transaction, and had entertained the expectation of a visit from me for this very purpose.

While Williams explained to him the nature of my claim, he scanned me with great intentness. His austere and inflexible brow, afforded me little room to hope for success, and this hopelessness was confirmed by his silence and perplexity, when Williams had made an end.

To be sure, said he, after some pause, the contract was explicit. To be sure, the conditions on Mr. Mervyn's side have been performed. Certain it is, the bills are entire and complete, but Mrs. Maurice will not consent to do her part, and Mrs. Maurice, to whom the papers were presented, is the person, by whom, according to the terms of the contract, the reward must be paid.

But Mrs. Maurice, you know, sir, may be legally compelled to pay, said Williams.

Perhaps she may; but I tell you plainly, that she never will do the thing without compulsion. Legal process, however, in this case, will have other inconveniences besides delay. Some curiosity will naturally be excited, as to the history of these papers. Watson disappeared a twelve month ago. Who can avoid asking, where have these papers been deposited all this while, and how came this person in possession of them?

That kind of curiosity, said I, is natural and laudable, and gladly would I gratify it. Disclosure or concealment in that case, however, would no wise affect my present claim. Whether a bond, legally executed, shall be paid, does not depend upon determining whether the payer is fondest of boiled mutton or roast beef. Truth, in the first case, has no connection with truth in the second. So far from eluding this curiosity; so far from studying concealment, I am anxious to publish the truth.

You are right, to be sure, said Hemmings. Curiosity is a natural, but only an incidental consequence in this case. I have no reason for desiring that it should be an unpleasant consequence to you.

Well, sir, said Williams, you think that Arthur Mervyn has no remedy in this case but the law.

Mrs. Maurice, to be sure, will never pay but on compulsion. Mervyn should have known his own interest better. While his left hand was stretched out to give, his right should have been held forth to receive. As it is, he must be contented with the aid of law. Any attorney will prosecute on condition of receiving *half the sum* when recovered.

We now rose to take our leave, when, Hemmings desiring us to pause a moment, said, to be sure, in the utmost strictness of the terms of our promise, the reward was to be paid by the person who received the papers; but it must be owned that your claim, at any rate, is equitable. I have money of the deceased Mr. Maurice in my hands. These very bills are now in my possession. I will therefore pay you your due, and take the consequences of an act of justice on myself. I was prepared for you. Sign that receipt, and there is a *check* for the amount.

Chapter XX

THIS UNEXPECTED and agreeable decision was accompanied by an invitation to supper, at which we were treated by our host with much affability and kindness. Finding me the author of Williams's good fortune, as well as Mrs. Maurice's, and being assured by the former of his entire conviction of the rectitude of my conduct, he laid aside all reserve and distance with regard to me. He enquired into my prospects and wishes, and professed his willingness to serve me.

I dealt with equal unreserve and frankness. I am poor, said I. Money for my very expences hither, I have borrowed from a friend, to whom I am, in other respects, much indebted, and whom I expect to compensate only by gratitude and future services.

In coming hither, I expected only an increase of my debts; to sink still deeper into poverty; but happily the issue has made me rich. This hour has given me competence, at least.

What! call you a thousand dollars competence?

More than competence. I call it an abundance. My own ingenuity, while I enjoy health, will enable me to live. This I regard as a fund, first to pay my debts, and next to supply deficiencies occasioned by untoward accidents or ill health, during the ensuing three or four years, at least.

We parted with this new acquaintance at a late hour, and I accepted Williams's invitation to pass the time I should spend at Baltimore, under his sister's roof. There were several motives for prolonging this stay. What I had heard of Miss Fanny Maurice, excited strong wishes to be personally acquainted with her. This young lady was affectionately attached to Mrs. Watson, by whose means my wishes were easily accomplished.

I never was in habits of reserve, even with those whom I had no reason to esteem. With those who claimed my admiration and affection, it was impossible to be incommunicative. Before the end of my second interview, both these women were mistresses of every momentous incident of my life, and of the whole chain of my feelings and opinions, in relation to every subject, and particularly in relation to themselves. Every topic disconnected with these, is comparatively lifeless and inert.

I found it easy to win their attention, and to render them communicative in their turn. As full disclosures as I had made without condition or request, my enquiries and example easily obtained from Mrs. Watson and Miss Maurice. The former related every event of her youth, and the circumstances leading to her marriage. She depicted the character of her husband, and the whole train of suspenses and inquietudes occasioned by his disappearance. The latter did not hide from me her opinions upon any important subject, and made me thoroughly acquainted with her actual situation.

This intercourse was strangely fascinating. My heart was buoyed up by a kind of intoxication. I now found myself exalted to my genial element, and began to taste the delights of existence. In the intercourse of ingenious and sympathetic minds, I found a pleasure which I had not previously conceived.

The time flew swiftly away, and a fortnight passed almost before I was aware that a day had gone by. I did not forget the friends whom I had left behind, but maintained a punctual correspondence with Stevens, to whom I imparted all occurrences.

The recovery of my friend's kinsman, allowed him in a few days to return home. His first object was the consolation and relief of Carlton, whom, with much difficulty, he persuaded to take advantage of the laws in favor of insolvent debtors. Carlton's only debt was owing to his uncle, and by rendering up every species of property, except his clothes and the implements of his trade, he obtained a full discharge. In conjunction with his sister, he once more assumed the pen, and being no longer burthened with debts he was unable to discharge, he resumed, together with his pen, his cheerfulness. Their mutual industry was sufficient for their decent and moderate subsistence.

The chief reason for my hasty return, was my anxiety respecting Clemenza Lodi. This reason was removed by the activity and benevolence of my friend. He paid this unfortunate stranger a visit at Mrs. Villars's. Access was easily obtained, and he found her sunk into the deepest melancholy. The recent loss of her child, the death of Welbeck, of which she was soon apprized, her total dependence upon those with whom she was placed, who, however, had always treated her without barbarity or indecorum, were the calamities that weighed down her spirit.

My friend easily engaged her confidence and gratitude, and prevailed upon her to take refuge under his own roof. Mrs. Wentworth's scruples, as well as those of Mrs. Fielding, were removed by his arguments and entreaties, and they consented to take upon themselves, and divide between them, the care of her subsistence and happiness. They condescended to express much curiosity respecting me, and some interest in my welfare, and promised to receive me on my return, on the footing of a friend.

With some reluctance, I at length bade my new friends farewel, and returned to Philadelphia. Nothing remained, before I should enter on my projected scheme of study and employment, under the guidance of Stevens, but to examine the situation of Eliza Hadwin with my own eyes, and if possible, to extricate my father from his unfortunate situation.

My father's state had given me the deepest concern. I figured to myself his condition, besotted by brutal appetites, reduced to beggary, shut up in a noisome prison, and condemned to that society which must foster all his depraved propensities. I revolved various schemes for his relief. A few hundreds would take him from prison, but how should he be afterwards disposed of? How should he be cured of his indolent habits? How should he be screened from the contagion of vicious society? By what means, consistently with my own wants, and the claims of others, should I secure to him an acceptable subsistence?

Exhortation and example were vain. Nothing but restraint would keep him at a distance from the haunts of brawling and debauchery. The want of money would be no obstacle to prodigality and waste. Credit would be resorted to as long as it would answer his demand. When that failed, he would once more be thrown into a prison; the same means to extricate him would be to be repeated, and money be thus put into the pockets of the most worthless of mankind, the agents of drunkenness and blasphemy, without any permanent advantage to my father, the principal object of my charity.

Though unable to fix on any plausible mode of proceeding, I determined, at least, to discover his present condition. Perhaps, something might suggest itself, upon the spot, suited to my purpose. Without delay I proceeded to the village of Newtown, and alighting at the door of the prison, enquired for my father.

Sawny Mervyn you want, I suppose, said the keeper. Poor fellow! He came into limbo in a crazy condition, and has been a burthen on my hands ever since. After lingering along for some time, he was at last kind enough to give us the slip. It is just a week since he drank his last pint—and *died*.

I was greatly shocked at this intelligence. It was some time before my reason came to my aid, and shewed me that this was an event, on the whole, and on a disinterested and dispassionate view, not unfortunate. The keeper knew not my relation to the deceased, and readily recounted the behaviour of the prisoner and the circumstances of his last hours.

I shall not repeat the narrative. It is useless to keep alive the sad remembrance. He was now beyond the reach of my charity or pity; and since reflection could answer no beneficial end to him, it was my duty to divert my thoughts into different channels, and live henceforth for my own happiness and that of those who were within the sphere of my influence.

I was now alone in the world, so far as the total want of kindred creates solitude. Not one of my blood, nor even of my name, were to be found in this quarter of the world. Of my mother's kindred I knew nothing. So far as friendship or service might be claimed from them, to me they had no existence. I was destitute of all those benefits which flow from kindred, in relation to protection, advice or property. My inheritance was nothing. Not a single relique or trinket in my possession constituted a memorial of my family. The scenes of my childish and juvenile days were dreary and desolate. The fields which I was wont to traverse, the room in which I was born, retained no traces of the past. They were the property and residence of strangers, who knew nothing of the former tenants, and who, as I was now told, had hastened to new-model and transform every thing within and without the habitation.

These images filled me with melancholy, which, however, disappeared in proportion as I approached the abode of my beloved girl. Absence had endeared the image of my *Bess*—I loved to call her so—to my soul. I could not think of her without a melting softness at my heart, and tears in which pain and pleasure were unaccountably mingled. As I approached Curling's house, I strained my sight, in hopes of distinguishing her form through the evening dusk.

I had told her of my purpose, by letter. She expected my approach at this hour, and was stationed, with a heart throbbing with impatience, at the road side, near the gate. As soon as I alighted, she rushed into my arms.

I found my sweet friend less blithsome and contented than I wished. Her situation, in spite of the parental and sisterly regards which she received from the Curlings, was mournful and dreary to her imagination. Rural business was irksome, and insufficient to fill up her time. Her life was tiresome, and uniform and heavy.

I ventured to blame her discontent, and pointed out the advantages of her situation. Whence, said I, can these dissatisfactions and repinings arise?

I cannot tell, said she; I don't know how it is with me. I am always sorrowful and thoughtful. Perhaps, I think too much of my poor father and of Susan, and yet that can't be it neither, for I think of them but seldom; not half as much as I ought, perhaps. I think of nobody almost, but you. Instead of minding my business, or chatting and laughing with Peggy Curling, I love to get by myself—to read, over and over, your letters, or to think how you are employed just then, and how happy I should be if I were in Fanny Maurice's place.

But it is all over now; this visit rewards me for every thing. I wonder how I could ever be sullen or mopeful. I will behave better, indeed I will, and be always, as now, a most happy girl.

The greater part of three days was spent in the society of my friend, in listening to her relation of all that had happened during my absence, and in communicating, in my turn, every incident which had befallen myself. After this I once more returned to the city.

Chapter XXI

I NOW set about carrying my plan of life into effect. I began with ardent zeal and unwearied diligence the career of medical study. I bespoke the counsels and instructions of my friend; attended him on his professional visits, and acted, in all practicable cases, as his substitute. I found this application of time more pleasurable than I had imagined. My mind gladly expanded itself, as it were, for the reception of new ideas. My curiosity grew more eager, in proportion as it was supplied with food, and every day added strength to the assurance that I was no insignificant and worthless being; that I was destined to be *something* in this scene of existence, and might sometime lay claim to the gratitude and homage of my fellow-men.

I was far from being, however, monopolized by these pursuits. I was formed on purpose for the gratification of social intercourse. To love and to be loved; to exchange hearts, and mingle sentiments with all the virtuous and amiable, whom my good fortune had placed within the circuit of my knowledge, I always esteemed my highest enjoyment and my chief duty.

Carlton and his sister, Mrs. Wentworth and Achsa Fielding, were my most valuable associates beyond my own family. With all these my correspondence was frequent and unreserved, but chiefly with the latter. This lady had dignity and independence, a generous and enlightened spirit beyond what her education had taught me to expect. She was circumspect and cautious in her deportment, and was not prompt to make advances or accept them. She withheld her esteem and confidence until she had full proof of their being deserved.

I am not sure that her treatment of me was fully conformable to her rules. My manners, indeed, as she once told me, she had never met with in another. Ordinary rules were so totally overlooked in my behaviour, that it seemed impossible for any one who knew me to adhere to them. No option was left but to admit my claims to friendship and confidence, instantly, or to reject them altogether.

I was not conscious of this singularity. The internal and undiscovered character of another, weighed nothing with me in the question, whether they should be treated with frankness or reserve. I felt no scruple on any occasion, to disclose every feeling and every event. Any one who could listen, found me willing to talk. Every talker found me willing to listen. Every one had my sympathy and kindness, *without* claiming it, but I *claimed* the kindness and sympathy of every one.

Achsa Fielding's countenance bespoke, I thought, a mind worthy to be known and to be loved. The first moment I engaged her attention, I told her so. I related the little story of my family, spread out before her all my reasonings and determinations, my notions of right and wrong, my fears and wishes. All this was done with sincerity and fervor, with gestures, actions and looks, in which I felt as if my whole soul was visible. Her superior age, sedateness and prudence, gave my deportment a filial freedom and affection, and I was fond of calling her *"mamma."*

I particularly dwelt upon the history of my dear country girl; painted her form and countenance; recounted our dialogues, and related all my schemes for making her wise and good and happy. On these occasions my friend would listen to me with the mutest attention. I shewed her the letters I received, and offered her for her perusal, those which I wrote in answer, before they were sealed and sent.

On these occasions she would look by turns on my face and away from me. A varying hue would play upon her cheek, and her eyes were fuller than was common of meaning.

Such and such, I once said, are my notions; now what do *you* think?

Think! emphatically, and turning somewhat aside, she answered, that you are the most—*strange* of human creatures.

But tell me, I resumed, following and searching her averted eyes, am I right; would you do thus? Can you help me to improve my girl? I wish you knew the bewitching little creature. How would that heart overflow with affection and with gratitude towards you. She should be your daughter. No— you are too nearly of an age for that. A sister: her *elder* sister you should be. *That*, when there is no other relation, includes them all. Fond sisters you would be, and I the fond brother of you both.

My eyes glistened as I spoke. In truth, I am in that respect, a mere woman. My friend was more powerfully moved. After a momentary struggle, she burst into tears.

Good Heaven! said I, what ails you? Are you not well?

Her looks betrayed an unaccountable confusion, from which she quickly recovered—it was folly to be thus affected. Something ailed me I believe, but it is past—But come; you want some lines of finishing the description of the *Boa* in Lacepede.

True. And I have twenty minutes to spare. Poor Franks is very ill indeed, but he cannot be seen till nine. We'll read till then.

Thus on the wings of pleasure and improvement past my time; not without some hues, occasionally of a darker tinct. My heart was now and then detected in sighing. This occurred when my thoughts glanced at the poor Eliza, and measured, as it were, the interval between us. We are too—*too* far apart, thought I.

The best solace on these occasions was the company of Mrs. Fielding; her music, her discourse, or some book which she set me to rehearsing to her. One evening, when preparing to pay her a visit, I received the following letter from my Bess.

To A. Mervyn.

Curling's, May 6, 1794.

Where does this letter you promised me, stay all this while? Indeed, Arthur, you torment me more than I deserve, and more than I could ever find it in my heart to do you. You treat me cruelly. I must say so, though I offend you. I must write, though you do not deserve that I should, and though I fear I am in a humor not very fit for writing. I had better go to my chamber and weep: weep at your—*unkindness*, I was going to say; but, perhaps, it is only forgetfulness: and yet what can be more unkind than forgetfulness? I am sure I have never forgotten you. Sleep itself, which wraps all other images in forgetfulness, only brings you nearer, and makes me see you more distinctly.

But where can this letter stay?—O! that—hush! foolish girl! If a word of that kind escape thy lips, Arthur will be angry with thee; and then, indeed, thou mightst weep in earnest. *Then* thou wouldst have some cause for thy tears. More than once already has he almost broken thy heart with his reproaches. Sore and weak as it now is, any new reproaches would assuredly break it quite.

I *will* be content. I will be as good an housewife and dairy-woman, stir about as briskly, and sing as merrily as Peggy Curling. Why not? I am as young, as innocent, and enjoy as good health.—Alas! she has reason to be merry. She has father, mother, brothers; but I have none.—And he that was all these, and more than all these, to me, has—*forgotten* me.

But, perhaps, it is some accident that hinders. Perhaps Oliver left the market earlier than he used to do; or you mistook the house; or, perhaps, some poor creature was sick, was taken suddenly ill, and you were busy in chafing his clay-cold limbs; it fell to you to wipe the clammy drops from his brow. Such things often happen; don't they, Arthur, to people of your trade, and some such thing has happened now; and that was the reason you did not write.

And if so, shall I repine at your silence? O no! At such a time the poor Bess might easily be, and ought to be forgotten. She would not deserve your love, if she could repine at a silence brought about this way.

And O! May it be so! May there be nothing worse than this. If the sick man—see, Arthur, how my hand trembles. Can you read this scrawl? What is always bad, my fears make worse than ever.

I must not think that. And yet, if it be so, if my friend himself be sick, what will become of me? Of me, that ought to cherish you and comfort you; that ought to be your nurse. Endure for you your sickness, when she cannot remove it.

O! that—I *will* speak out—O! that this strange scruple had never possessed you. Why should I *not* be with you? Who can love you and serve you as well as I? In sickness and health, I will console and assist you. Why will you deprive yourself of such a comforter, and such an aid as I would be to you?

Dear Arthur, think better of it. Let me leave this dreary spot, where, indeed, as long as I am thus alone, I can enjoy no comfort. Let me come to you. I will put up with any thing for the sake of seeing you, tho' it be but once a day. Any garret or cellar in the dirtiest lane or darkest alley, will be good enough for me. I will think it a palace, so that I can *but* see you now and then.

Do not refuse—do not argue with me, so fond you always are of arguing! My heart is set upon your compliance. And yet, dearly as I prize your company, I would not ask it, if I thought there was any thing improper. You say there is, and you talk about it in a way that I do not understand. For my sake, you tell me, you refuse, but let me entreat you to comply for my sake.

Your pen cannot teach me like your tongue. You write me long letters, and tell me a great deal in them, but my soul droops when I call to mind your voice and your looks, and think how long a time must pass before I see you and hear you again. I have no spirit to think upon the words and paper before me. My eye and my thought wander far away.

I bethink me how many questions I might ask you; how many doubts you might clear up if you were but within hearing. If you were but close to me; but I cannot ask them here. I am too poor a creature at the pen, and, some how or another, it always happens, I can only write about myself or about you. By the time I have said all this, I have tired my fingers, and when I set about telling you how this poem and that story have affected me, I am at a loss for words; I am bewildered and bemazed as it were.

It is not so when we talk to one another. With your arm about me, and your sweet face close to mine, I can prattle forever. Then my heart overflows at my lips. After hours thus spent, it seems as if there were a thousand things still to be said. Then I can tell you what the book has told me. I can repeat scores of verses by heart, though I heard them only once read, but it is because *you* have read them to me.

Then there is nobody here to answer my questions. They never look into books. They hate books. They think it waste of time to read. Even Peggy, who you say has naturally a strong mind, wonders what I can find to amuse myself in a book. In her playful mood, she is always teazing me to lay it aside.

I do not mind her, for I like to read; but if I did not like it before, I could not help doing so ever since you told me that nobody could gain your love who was not fond of books. And yet, though I like it on that account, more than I did, I don't read somehow so earnestly, and understand so well as I use to do, when my mind was all at ease; always frolicksome, and ever upon *tiptoe*, as I may say.

How strangely, (have you not observed it?) I am altered of late; I that was ever light of heart, the very soul of gaiety, brim full of glee—am now, demure as our old *tabby*—and not half as wise. Tabby had wit enough to keep her paws out of the coals, whereas poor I have—but no matter what. It will never come to pass, I see that. So many reasons for every thing! Such looking forward! Arthur, are not men sometimes too *wise* to be happy?

I am now *so* grave. Not one smile can Peggy sometimes get from me, though she tries for it the whole day. But I know how it comes. Strange, indeed, if losing father and sister, and thrown upon the wide world, pennyless and *friendless* too, now that *you* forget me, I should continue to smile. No. I never shall smile again. At least, while I stay here, I never shall, I believe.

If a certain somebody suffer me to live with him—*near* him, I mean: perhaps the sight of him as he enters the door, perhaps the sound of his voice, asking—"where is my Bess?"—might produce a smile. Such a one as the very thought produces now—yet not, I hope, so transient, and so quickly followed by a tear. Women are born, they say, to trouble, and tears are given them for their relief. 'Tis all very true.

Let it be as I wish, will you? If Oliver bring not back good tidings, if he bring not a letter from thee, or thy letter still refuses my request—I don't know what may happen. Consent, if you love your poor girl.

E. H.

Chapter XXII

THE READING of this letter, though it made me mournful, did not hinder me from paying the visit I intended. My friend noticed my discomposure.

What, Arthur, thou art quite the "penseroso" to night. Come, let me cheer thee with a song. Thou shalt have thy favorite ditty:—She stepped to the instrument, and with more than airy lightness, touched and sung:

> Now knit hands and beat the ground
> In a light, fantastic round,
> Till the tell-tale sun descry
> Our conceal'd solemnity.

Her music, though blithsome and aerial, was not sufficient for the end. My cheerfulness would not return even at her bidding. She again noticed my sedateness, and enquired into the cause.

This girl of mine, said I, has infected me with her own sadness. There is a letter I have just received—she took it and began to read.

Meanwhile, I placed myself before her, and fixed my eyes steadfastly upon her features. There is no book in which I read with more pleasure, than the face of woman. *That* is generally more full of meaning, and of better meaning too, than the hard and inflexible lineaments of man, and *this* woman's face has no parallel.

She read it with visible emotion. Having gone through it, she did not lift her eye from the paper, but continued silent, as if buried in thought. After some time, for I would not interrupt the pause, she addressed me thus:

This girl seems to be very anxious to be with you.

As much as I am that she should be so.—My friend's countenance betrayed some perplexity. As soon as I perceived it, I said, why are you thus grave? Some little confusion appeared as if she would not have her gravity discovered. There again, said I, new tokens in your face, my good mamma, of something which you will not mention. Yet, sooth to say, this is not your first perplexity. I have noticed it before, and wondered. It happens only when my *Bess* is introduced. Something in relation to her it must be, but what I cannot imagine. Why does *her* name, particularly, make you thoughtful; disturbed; dejected?—There now—but I must know the reason. You don't agree with me in my notions of this girl, I fear, and you will not disclose your thoughts.

By this time, she had gained her usual composure, and without noticing my comments on her looks, said: Since you are both of one mind, why does she not leave the country?

That cannot be, I believe. Mrs. Stevens says it would be disreputable. I am no proficient in etiquette, and must, therefore, in affairs of this kind, be guided by those who are. But would to Heaven, I were truly her father or brother. Then all difficulties would be done away.

Can you seriously wish that?

Why no. I believe it would be more rational to wish that the world would suffer me to act the fatherly or brotherly part, without the relationship.

And is that the only part you wish to act towards this girl?

Certainly, the only part.

You surprize me. Have you not confessed your love for her?

I *do* love her. There is nothing upon earth more dear to me than my *Bess*.

But love is of different kinds. She was loved by her father——

Less than by me. He was a good man, but not of lively feelings. Besides, he had another daughter, and they shared his love between them, but she has no sister to share *my* love. Calamity too, has endeared her to me; I am all her consolation, dependence and hope, and nothing, surely, can induce me to abandon her.

Her reliance upon you, for happiness, replied my friend, with a sigh, is plain enough.

It is: but why that sigh? And yet I understand it. It remonstrates with me on my incapacity for her support. I know it well, but it is wrong to be cast down. I have youth, health and spirits, and ought not to despair of living for my own benefit and hers; but you sigh again, and it is impossible to keep my courage when *you* sigh. Do tell me what you mean by it?

You partly guessed the cause. She trusts to you for happiness, but I somewhat suspect she trusts in vain.

In vain! I beseech you tell me why you think so.

You say you love her—why then not make her your wife?

My wife! Surely her extreme youth, and my destitute condition, will account for that.

She is fifteen: the age of delicate fervor; of inartificial love, and suitable enough for marriage. As to your condition, you may live more easily together than apart. She has no false taste or perverse desires to gratify. She has been trained in simple modes and habits. Besides, that objection can be removed another way. But are these all your objections?

Her youth I object to, merely in connection with her mind. She is too little improved to be my wife. She wants that solidity of mind; that maturity of intelligence which ten years more may possibly give her, but which she cannot have at this age.

You are a very prudential youth; then you are willing to wait ten years for a wife?

Does that follow? Because my Bess will not be qualified for wedlock, in less time, does it follow that I must wait for her?

I spoke on the supposition that you loved her.

And that is true; but love is satisfied with studying her happiness as her father or brother. Some years hence, perhaps in half a year, for this passion, called wedded, or *marriage-wishing* love, is of sudden growth, my mind may change, and nothing may content me but to have Bess for my wife. Yet I do not expect it.

Then you are determined against marriage with this girl.

Of course; until that love comes which I feel not now; but which, no doubt, will come, when Bess has had the benefit of five or eight years more, unless previously excited by another.

All this is strange, Arthur. I have heretofore supposed that you actually loved (I mean with the *marriage-seeking* passion) your *Bess*.

I believe I once did; but it happened at a time when marriage was improper; in the life of her father and sister, and when I had never known in what female excellence consisted. Since that time my happier lot has cast me among women so far above Eliza Hadwin; so far above, and so widely different from any thing which time is likely to make her, that I own, nothing appears more unlikely than that I shall ever love her.

Are you not a little capricious in that respect, my good friend? You have praised your *Bess* as rich in natural endowments; as having an artless purity and rectitude of mind, which somewhat supersedes the use of formal education; as being full of sweetness and tenderness, and in her person a very angel of loveliness.

All that is true. I never saw features and shape so delicately beautiful; I never knew so young a mind so quick sighted and so firm; but, nevertheless, she is not the creature whom I would call my *wife*. My bosom slave; counsellor; friend; the mother; the pattern; the tutress of my children must be a different creature.

But what are the attributes of this *desirable* which Bess wants?

Every thing she wants. Age, capacity, acquirements, person, features, hair, complexion, all, all are different from this girl's.

And pray of what kind may they be?

I cannot pourtray them in words—but yes, I can:—The creature whom I shall worship:—it sounds oddly, but, I verily believe, the sentiment which I shall feel for my wife, will be more a kin to worship than any thing else. I shall never love, but such a creature as I now image to myself, and *such* a creature will deserve, or almost deserve, worship—but this creature, I was going to say, must be the exact counterpart, my good mamma—of *yourself*.

This was said very earnestly, and with eyes and manners that fully expressed my earnestness: perhaps my expressions were unwittingly strong and emphatic, for she started and blushed, but the cause of her discomposure, whatever it was, was quickly removed, and she said:

Poor Bess! This will be sad news to thee!

Heaven forbid! said I, of what moment can my opinions be to her?

Strange questioner that thou art. Thou knowest that her gentle heart is touched with love. See how it shews itself in

the tender and inimitable strain of this epistle. Does not this
sweet ingenuousness bewitch you?

It does so, and I love, beyond expression, the sweet girl;
but my love is in some inconceivable way, different from the
passion which that *other* creature will produce. She is no
stranger to my thoughts. I will impart every thought over and
over to her. I question not but I shall make her happy without
forfeiting my own.

Would marriage with her, be a forfeiture of your happiness?

Not absolutely, or forever, I believe. I love her company.
Her absence for a long time is irksome. I cannot express the
delight with which I see and hear her. To mark her features,
beaming with vivacity; playful in her pleasures; to hold her in
my arms, and listen to her prattle; always musically voluble;
always sweetly tender, or artlessly intelligent—and this you
will say is the dearest privilege of marriage: and so it is; and
dearly should I prize it; and yet, I fear my heart would droop
as often as that *other* image should occur to my fancy. For
then, you know, it would occur as something never to be
possessed by me.

Now this image might, indeed, seldom occur. The intervals,
at least, would be serene. It would be my interest to prolong
these intervals as much as possible, and my endeavors to this
end, would, no doubt, have some effect. Besides, the bitterness of this reflection would be lessened by contemplating, at
the same time, the happiness of my beloved girl.

I should likewise have to remember, that to continue unmarried, would not necessarily secure me the possession of
the *other* good——

But these reflections, my friend (broke she in upon me) are
of as much force to induce you to marry, as to reconcile you
to marriage already contracted.

Perhaps they are. Assuredly, I have not a hope that the *fancied* excellence will ever be mine. Such happiness is not the
lot of humanity, and is, least of all, within my reach.

Your diffidence, replied my friend, in a timorous accent, has
not many examples; but your character, without doubt, is all
your own; possessing all and disclaiming all, is, in few words,
your picture.

I scarcely understand you. Do you think I ever shall be

happy to that degree which I have imagined. Think you I shall ever meet with an exact copy of *yourself*!

Unfortunate you will be, if you do not meet with many better. Your Bess, in personals, is, beyond measure, *my* superior, and in mind, allowing for difference in years, quite as much so.

But that, returned I, with quickness and fervor, is not the object. The very counterpart of *you* I want; neither worse nor better, nor different in any thing. Just such form, such features, such hues. Just that melting voice, and above all, the same habits of thinking and conversing. In thought, word and deed; gesture, look and form, that rare and precious creature whom I shall love, must be your resemblance. Your——

Have done with these comparisons, interrupted she, in some hurry, and let us return to the country girl, thy Bess.

You once, my friend, wished me to treat this girl of yours as my sister. Do you know what the duties of a sister are?

They imply no more kindness or affection than you already feel toward my Bess. Are you not her sister?

I ought to have been so. I ought to have been proud of the relation you ascribe to me, but I have not performed any of its duties. I blush to think upon the coldness and perverseness of my heart. With such means as I possess, of giving happiness to others, I have been thoughtless and inactive to a strange degree; perhaps, however, it is not yet too late. Are you still willing to invest me with all the rights of an elder sister over this girl? And will she consent, think you?

Certainly, she will; she has.

Then the first act of sistership, will be to take her from the country; from persons on whose kindness she has no natural claim, whose manners and characters are unlike her own, and with whom no improvement can be expected, and bring her back to her sister's house and bosom, to provide for her subsistence and education, and watch over her happiness.

I will not be a nominal sister. I will not be a sister by halves. *All* the rights of that relation I will have, or none. As for you, you have claims upon her, on which I must be permitted to judge, as becomes the elder sister, who, by the loss of all other relations, must occupy the place, possess the rights, and fulfil the duties of father, mother and brother.

She has now arrived at an age, when longer to remain in a cold and churlish soil, will stunt her growth and wither her blossoms. We must hasten to transplant her to a genial element, and a garden well enclosed. Having so long neglected this charming plant, it becomes me henceforth to take her wholly to myself.

And now, for it is no longer in her or your power to take back the gift, since she is fully mine, I will charge you with the office of conducting her hither. I grant it to you as a favor. Will you go?

Go! I will fly! I exclaimed, in an extacy of joy, on pinions swifter than the wind. Not the lingering of an instant will I bear. Look! one, two, three—thirty minutes after nine. I will reach Curling's gate by the morn's dawn. I will put my girl into a chaise, and by noon, she shall throw herself into the arms of her sister. But first, shall I not, in some way, manifest my gratitude?

My senses were bewildered, and I knew not what I did. I intended to kneel, as to my mother or my deity, but, instead of that, I clasped her in my arms, and kissed her lips fervently. I staid not to discover the effects of this insanity, but left the room and the house, and calling for a moment at Stevens's, left word with the servant, my friend being gone abroad, that I should not return till the morrow.

Never was a lighter heart, a gaiety more overflowing, and more buoyant than mine. All cold from a boisterous night, at a chilly season, all weariness from a rugged and miry road, were charmed away. I might have ridden, but I could not brook delay, even the delay of enquiring for and equipping an horse. I might thus have saved myself fatigue, and have lost no time, but my mind was in too great a tumult for deliberation and forecast. I saw nothing but the image of my girl, whom my tidings would render happy.

The way was longer than my fond imagination had foreseen. I did not reach Curling's till an hour after sun-rise. The distance was full thirty-five miles. As I hastened up the green lane leading to the house, I spied my Bess passing through a covered way, between the dwelling and kitchen. I caught her eye. She stopped and held up her hands, and then ran into my arms.

What means my girl? Why this catching of the breath? Why this sobbing? Look at me my love. It is Arthur, he who has treated you with forgetfulness, neglect and cruelty.

O! do not, she replied, hiding her face with her hand. One single reproach, added to my own, will kill me. That foolish, wicked letter—I could tear my fingers for writing it.

But, said I, I will kiss them—and put them to my lips. They have told me the wishes of my girl. They have enabled me to gratify her wishes. I have come to carry thee this very moment to town.

Lord bless me, Arthur—said she, lost in a sweet confusion, and her cheeks, always glowing, glowing still more deeply—indeed, I did not mean—I meant only—I will stay here—I would rather stay——

It grieves me to hear that, said I, with earnestness, I thought I was studying our mutual happiness.

It grieves you? Don't say so. I would not grieve you for the world—but, indeed, indeed, it is too soon. Such a girl as I, am not yet fit to—live in your city. Again she hid her glowing face in my bosom.

Sweet consciousness! Heavenly innocence! thought I; may Achsa's conjectures prove false!—You have mistaken my design, for I do not intend to carry you to town with such a view as you have hinted—but merely to place you with a beloved friend; with Achsa Fielding, of whom already you know so much, where we shall enjoy each other's company without restraint or intermission.

I then proceeded to disclose to her the plan suggested by my friend, and to explain all the consequences that would flow from it. I need not say that she assented to the scheme. She was all rapture and gratitude. Preparations for departure were easily and speedily made. I hired a chaise of a neighboring farmer, and, according to my promise, by noon the same day, delivered the timid and bashful girl into the arms of her new sister.

She was received with the utmost tenderness, not only by Mrs. Fielding, but by all my friends. Her affectionate heart was encouraged to pour forth all its feeling as into the bosom of a mother. She was reinspired with confidence. Her want of experience was supplied by the gentlest admonitions and instructions. In every plan for her improvement, suggested by her new *mamma*, for she never called her by any other name, she engaged with docility and eagerness; and her behaviour and her progress exceeded the most sanguine hopes that I had formed, as to the softness of her temper and the acuteness of her genius.

Those graces which a polished education, and intercourse with the better classes of society, are adapted to give, my girl possessed, in some degree, by a native and intuitive refinement and sagacity of mind. All that was to be obtained from actual observation and instruction, was obtained without difficulty; and in a short time, nothing but the affectionate simplicity and unperverted feelings of the country girl, bespoke the original condition.—

What art so busy about, Arthur? Always at thy pen of late. Come, I must know the fruit of all this toil and all this meditation. I am determined to scrape acquaintance with Haller and Lineus. I will begin this very day. All one's friends you know should be our's. Love has made many a patient, and let me see if it cannot, in my case, make a physician. But first, what is all this writing about?

Mrs. Wentworth has put me upon a strange task—not disagreeable, however, but such as I should, perhaps, have declined, had not the absence of my Bess, and her mamma, made the time hang somewhat heavy. I have, oftener than once, and far more circumstantially than now, told her my adventures, but she is not satisfied. She wants a written narrative, for some purpose which she tells me she will disclose to me hereafter.

Luckily, my friend Stevens has saved me more than half the trouble. He has done me the favor to compile much of my history with his own hand. I cannot imagine what could prompt him to so wearisome an undertaking; but he says that adventures and a destiny so singular as mine, ought not to be abandoned to forgetfulness like any vulgar and *every-day* existence. Besides, when he wrote it, he suspected that it might be necessary to the safety of my reputation and my life, from the consequences of my connection with Welbeck. Time has annihilated that danger. All enmities and all suspicions are buried with that ill-fated wretch. Wortley has been won by my behaviour, and confides in my integrity now as much as he formerly suspected it. I am glad, however, that the task was performed. It has saved me a world of writing. I had only to take up the broken thread, and bring it down to the period of my present happiness, and this was done, just as you tripped along the entry this morning.

To bed, my friend, it is late, and this delicate frame is not half so able to encounter fatigue as a youth spent in the hay-field and the dairy might have been expected to be.

I will, but let me take these sheets along with me. I will read them, that I am determined, before I sleep, and watch if you have told the whole truth.

Do so, if you please; but remember one thing. Mrs. Wentworth requested me to write not as if it were designed for her perusal, but for those who have no previous knowledge of her or of me. 'Twas an odd request. I cannot imagine what she means by it, but she never acts without good reason, and I have done so. And now withdraw, my dear, and farewel.

Chapter XXIII

M OVE ON, my quill! wait not for my guidance. Reanimated with thy master's spirit, all-airy light! An hey day rapture! A mounting impulse sways him: lifts him from the earth.

I must, cost what it will, rein in this upward-pulling, forward-urging—what shall I call it? But there are times, and now is one of them, when words are poor.

It will not do—Down this hill, up that steep; thro' this thicket, over that hedge—I have *labored* to fatigue myself: To reconcile me to repose; to lolling on a sofa; to poring over a book; to any thing that might win for my heart a respite from these throbs; to deceive me into a few *tolerable* moments of forgetfulness.

Let me see: they tell me this is Monday night. Only three days yet to come! If thus restless to day; if my heart thus bounds till its mansion scarcely can hold it, what must be my state to morrow! What next day! What as the hour hastens on; as the sun descends; as my hand touches her in sign of wedded unity, of love without interval; of concord without end.

I must quell these tumults. They will disable me else. They will wear out all my strength. They will drain away life itself. But who could have thought! So soon! Not three months since I first set eyes upon her. Not three weeks since our plighted love, and only three days to terminate suspense and give me *all*.

I must compel myself to quiet: to sleep. I must find some refuge from anticipations so excruciating. All extremes are agonies. A joy like this is too big for this narrow tenement. I must thrust it forth; I must bar and bolt it out for a time, or these frail walls will burst asunder. The pen is a pacifyer. It checks the mind's career; it circumscribes her wanderings. It traces out, and compels us to adhere to one path. It ever was my friend. Often it has blunted my vexations; hushed my stormy passions; turned my peevishness to soothing; my fierce revenge to heart-dissolving pity.

Perhaps it will befriend me now. It may temper my impetuous wishes; lull my intoxication; and render my happiness supportable: And, indeed, it has produced partly this effect already. My blood, within the few minutes thus employed, flows with less destructive rapidity. My thoughts range themselves in less disorder—And now that the conquest is effected, what shall I say? I must continue at the pen, or shall immediately relapse.

What shall I say? Let me look back upon the steps that led me hither. Let me recount preliminaries. I cannot do better.

And first as to Achsa Fielding—to describe this woman.

To recount, in brief, so much of her history as has come to my knowledge, will best account for that zeal, almost to idolatry, with which she has, ever since I thoroughly knew her, been regarded by me.

Never saw I one to whom the term *lovely* more truly belonged: And yet, in stature she is too low; in complection, dark and almost sallow; and her eyes, though black and of piercing lustre, has a cast, which I cannot well explain. It lessens without destroying their lustre and their force to charm; but all personal defects are outweighed by her heart and her intellect. There is the secret of her power to entrance the soul of the listener and beholder. It is not only when she sings that her utterance is musical. It is not only when the occasion is urgent and the topic momentous that her eloquence is rich and flowing. They are always so.

I had vowed to love her and serve her, and been her frequent visitant, long before I was acquainted with her past life. I had casually picked up some intelligence, from others, or from her own remarks. I knew very soon that she was English by birth, and had been only a year and an half in America; that she had scarcely passed her twenty-fifth year, and was still embellished with all the graces of youth; that she had been a wife; but was uninformed whether the knot had been untied by death or divorce: That she possessed considerable, and even splendid fortune; but the exact amount, and all beside these particulars, were unknown to me till some time after our acquaintance was begun.

One evening, she had been talking very earnestly on the influence annexed, in Great Britain, to birth, and had given me some examples of this influence. Meanwhile, my eyes were fixed steadfastly on hers. The peculiarity in their expression never before affected me so strongly. A vague resemblance to something seen elsewhere, on the same day, occurred, and occasioned me to exclaim, suddenly in a pause of her discourse—

As I live, my good mamma, those eyes of yours have told me a secret. I almost think they spoke to me; and I am not less amazed at the strangeness than at the distinctness of their story.

And pry'thee what have they said?

Perhaps I was mistaken. I might have been deceived by a fancied voice, or have confounded one word with another near akin to it; but let me die, if I did not think they said that you were—*a Jew*.

At this sound, her features were instantly veiled with the deepest sorrow and confusion. She put her hand to her eyes, the tears started and she sobbed. My surprise at this effect of my words, was equal to my contrition. I besought her to pardon me, for having thus unknowingly, alarmed and grieved her.

After she had regained some composure, she said, you have not offended, Arthur. Your surmise was just and natural, and could not always have escaped you. Connected with that word are many sources of anguish, which time has not, and never will, dry up; and the less I think of past events, the less will my peace be disturbed. I was desirous that you should know nothing of me, but what you see; nothing but the present and the future, merely that no allusions might occur in our conversation, which will call up sorrows and regrets that will avail nothing.

I now perceive the folly of endeavoring to keep you in ignorance, and shall therefore, once for all, inform you of what has befallen me, that your enquiries and suggestions may be made, and fully satisfied at once, and your curiosity have no motive for calling back my thoughts to what I ardently desire to bury in oblivion.

My father was indeed a *jew*, and one of the most opulent of his nation in London. A Portuguese by birth, but came to London when a boy. He had few of the moral or external qualities of jews. For I suppose there is some justice in the obloquy that follows them so closely. He was frugal without meanness, and cautious in his dealings, without extortion. I need not fear to say this, for it was the general voice.

Me, an only child, and of course, the darling of my parents, they trained up in the most liberal manner. My education was purely English. I learned the same things and of the same masters with my neighbors. Except frequenting their church and repeating their creed, and partaking of the same food, I saw no difference between them and me. Hence I grew more indifferent, perhaps, than was proper to the distinctions of religion. They were never enforced upon me. No pains were taken to fill me with scruples and antipathies. They never stood, as I may say, upon the threshold: They were often thought upon but were vague, and easily eluded or forgotten.

Hence it was that my heart too readily admitted impressions, that more zeal and more parental caution would have saved me from. They could scarcely be avoided, as my society was wholly English; and my youth, my education and my father's wealth made me an object of much attention. And the same causes that lulled to sleep my own watchfulness, had the same effect upon that of others. To regret or to praise this remissness, is now too late. Certain it is, that my destiny, and not a happy destiny, was fixed by it.

The fruit of this remissness was a passion for one, who fully returned it. Almost as young as I, who was only sixteen, he knew as little as myself, what obstacles the difference of our births was likely to raise between us. His father, Sir Ralph Fielding, a man nobly born, high in office, splendidly allied, could not be expected to consent to the marriage of his eldest son, in such green youth, to the daughter of an alien, a Portuguese, a Jew; but these impediments were not seen by my ignorance, and were overlooked by the youth's passion.

But strange to tell, what common prudence would have so confidently predicted, did not happen. Sir Ralph had a numerous family, likely to be still more so; had but slender patrimony: the income of his offices nearly made up his all. The young man was head-strong, impetuous, and would probably disregard the inclinations of his family. Yet the father would not consent but on one condition, that of my admission to the English church.

No very strenuous opposition to these terms could be expected from me. At so thoughtless an age, with an education so unfavorable to religious impressions; swayed likewise, by the strongest of human passions; made somewhat impatient by the company I kept, of the disrepute and scorn to which the Jewish nation are every where condemned, I could not be expected to be very averse to the scheme.

My fears, as to what my father's decision would be, were soon at an end. He loved his child too well to thwart her wishes in so essential a point. Finding in me no scruples, no unwillingness, he thought it absurd to be scrupulous for me. My own heart having abjured my religion, it was absurd to make any difficulty about a formal renunciation. These were his avowed reasons for concurrence, but time shewed that he had probably other reasons, founded, indeed, in his regard for my happiness, but such as, if they had been known, would probably have strengthened into invincible, the reluctance of my lover's family.

No marriage was ever attended with happier presages. The numerous relations of my husband, admitted me with the utmost cordiality, among them. My father's tenderness was unabated by this change, and those humiliations to which I had before been exposed, were now no more; and every tie was strengthened, at the end of a year, by the feelings of a *mother*. I had need, indeed, to know a season of happiness, that I might be fitted to endure the sad reverses that succeeded. One after the other my disasters came, each one more heavy than the last, and in such swift succession, that they hardly left me time to breathe.

I had scarcely left my chamber, I had scarcely recovered my usual health, and was able to press with true fervor, the new and precious gift to my bosom, when melancholy tidings came—I was in the country, at the seat of my father-in-law, when the messenger arrived.

A shocking tale it was! and told abruptly, with every unpitying aggravation. I hinted to you once, my father's death. The *kind* of death—O! my friend! It was horrible. He was then a placid venerable old man; though many symptoms of disquiet had long before been discovered by my mother's watchful tenderness. Yet none could suspect him capable of such a deed; for none, so carefully had he conducted his affairs, suspected the havock that mischance had made of his property.

I, that had so much reason to love my father—I will leave you to imagine how I was affected by a catastrophe so dreadful, so unlooked-for. Much less could I suspect the cause of his despair; yet he had foreseen his ruin before my marriage; had resolved to defer it for his daughter's and his wife's sake, as long as possible, but had still determined not to survive the day that should reduce him to indigence. The desperate act was thus preconcerted—thus deliberate.

The true state of his affairs was laid open by his death. The failure of great mercantile houses at Frankfort and Liege was the cause of his disasters. Thus were my prospects shut in. That wealth, which no doubt, furnished the chief inducement with my husband's family to concur in his choice, was now suddenly exchanged for poverty.

Bred up, as I had been, in pomp and luxury; conscious that my wealth was my chief security from the contempt of the proud and bigotted, and my chief title to the station to which I had been raised, and which I the more delighted in because it enabled me to confer so great obligations on my husband, what reverse could be harder than this, and how much bitterness was added by it to the grief, occasioned by the violent end of my father!

Yet, loss of fortune, though it mortified my pride, did not prove my worst calamity. Perhaps it was scarcely to be ranked with evils, since it furnished a touchstone by which my husband's affections were to be tried; especially as the issue of the trial was auspicious; for my misfortune seemed only to heighten the interest which my character had made for me in the hearts of all that knew me. The paternal regards of Sir Ralph had always been tender, but that tenderness seemed now to be redoubled.

New events made this consolation still more necessary. My unhappy mother!—She was nearer to the dreadful scene when it happened. Had no surviving object to beguile her sorrow;

was rendered, by long habit, more dependent upon fortune than her child.

A melancholy always mute was the first effect upon my mother. Nothing could charm her eye, or her ear. Sweet sounds that she once loved, and especially when her darling child was the warbler, were heard no longer. How, with streaming eyes, have I sat and watched the dear lady, and endeavored to catch her eye, to rouse her attention!—But I must not think of these things.

But even this distress was little in comparison with what was to come. A frenzy thus mute, motionless and vacant, was succeeded by fits, talkative, outrageous, requiring incessant superintendance, restraint, and even violence.

Why led you me thus back to my sad remembrances? Excuse me for the present. I will tell you the rest some other time; to-morrow.

To-morrow, accordingly, my friend resumed her story.

Let me now make an end, said she, of my mournful narrative, and never, I charge you, do any thing to revive it again.

Deep as was my despondency, occasioned by these calamities, I was not destitute of some joy. My husband and my child were lovely and affectionate. In their caresses, in their welfare, I found peace; and might still have found it, had there not been—But why should I open afresh, wounds which time has imperfectly closed? But the story must have sometime been told to you, and the sooner it is told and dismissed to forgetfulness, the better.

My ill fate led me into company with a woman too well known in the idle and dissipated circles. Her character was not unknown to me. There was nothing in her features or air to obviate disadvantageous prepossessions. I sought not her intercourse; I rather shunned it, as unpleasing and discreditable, but she would not be repulsed. Self invited, she made herself my frequent guest; took unsolicited part in my concerns; did me many kind offices; and, at length, in spite of my counter inclination, won upon my sympathy and gratitude.

No one in the world, did I fondly think, had I less reason to fear than Mrs. Waring. Her character excited not the slightest apprehension for my own safety. She was upwards of forty, no wise remarkable for grace or beauty; tawdry in her dress; accustomed to render more conspicuous the traces of age by her attempts to hide them; the mother of a numerous family, with a mind but slenderly cultivated; always careful too to save appearances; studiously preserving distance with my husband, and he, like myself, enduring, rather than wishing her society. What could I fear from the arts of such an one?

But alas! the woman had consummate address.—Patience too, that nothing could tire. Watchfulness that none could detect. Insinuation the wiliest and most subtle. Thus wound she herself into my affections, by an unexampled perseverance in seeming kindness; by tender confidence; by artful glosses of past misconduct; by self-rebukes and feigned contritions.

Never were stratagems so intricate, dissimulation so profound! But still, that such an one should seduce my husband; young; generous; ambitious; impatient of contumely and reproach, and surely not indifferent; before this fatal intercourse, not indifferent to his wife and child!—Yet, so it was!

I saw his discontents; his struggles; I heard him curse this woman, and the more deeply for my attempts, unconscious as I was of her machinations, to reconcile them to each other, to do away what seemed a causeless indignation, or antipathy against her. How little I suspected the nature of the conflict in his heart, between a new passion and the claims of pride; of conscience and of humanity; the claims of a child and a wife; a wife already in affliction, and placing all that yet remained of happiness, in the firmness of his virtue; in the continuance of his love; a wife, at the very hour of his meditated flight, full of terrors at the near approach of an event, whose agonies demand a double share of an husband's supporting, encouraging love—

Good Heaven! For what evils are some of thy creatures reserved! Resignation to thy decree, in the last, and most cruel distress, was, indeed, an hard task.

He was gone. Some unavoidable engagement calling him to Hamburgh was pleaded. Yet to leave me at such an hour! I dared not upbraid, nor object. The tale was so specious! The fortunes of a friend depended on his punctual journey. The falsehood of his story too soon made itself known. He was gone, in company with his detested paramour!

Yet, though my vigilance was easily deceived, it was not so

with others. A creditor, who had his bond for three thousand pounds, pursued, and arrested him at Harwich. He was thrown into prison, but his companion, let me, at least, say that in her praise, would not desert him. She took lodging near the place of his confinement, and saw him daily. That, had she not done it, and had my personal condition allowed, should have been my province.

Indignation and grief hastened the painful crisis with me. I did not weep that the second fruit of this unhappy union saw not the light. I wept only that this hour of agony, was not, to its unfortunate mother, the last.

I felt not anger; I had nothing but compassion for Fielding. Gladly would I have recalled him to my arms and to virtue: I wrote, adjuring him by all our past joys, to return; vowing only gratitude for his new affection, and claiming only the recompence of seeing him restored to his family; to liberty; to reputation.

But alas! Fielding had a good, but a proud, heart. He looked upon his error with remorse, with self-detestation, and with the fatal belief that it could not be retrieved; shame made him withstand all my reasonings and persuasions, and in the hurry of his feelings, he made solemn vows that he would, in the moment of restored liberty, abjure his country and his family forever. He bore indignantly the yoke of his new attachment, but he strove in vain to shake it off. Her behaviour, always yielding, doating, supplicative, preserved him in her fetters. Though upbraided, spurned and banished from his presence, she would not leave him, but by new efforts and new artifices, soothed, appeased, and won again, and kept his tenderness.

What my entreaties were unable to effect, his father could not hope to accomplish. He offered to take him from prison; the creditor offered to cancel the bond, if he would return to me; but this condition he refused. All his kindred, and one who had been his bosom friend from childhood, joined in beseeching his compliance with these conditions; but his pride, his dread of my merited reproaches, the merits and dissuasions of his new companion, whose sacrifices for his sake had not been small, were obstacles which nothing could subdue.

Far, indeed, was I from imposing these conditions. I waited only till, by certain arrangements, I could gather enough to pay his debts, to enable him to execute his vow; empty would have been my claims to his affection, if I could have suffered, with the means of his deliverance in my hands, my husband to remain a moment in prison.

The remains of my father's vast fortune, was a jointure of a thousand pounds a year, settled on my mother, and after her death, on me. My mother's helpless condition put this revenue into my disposal. By this means was I enabled, without the knowledge of my father-in-law, or my husband, to purchase the debt, and dismiss him from prison. He set out instantly, in company with his paramour, to France.

When somewhat recovered from the shock of this calamity, I took up my abode with my mother. What she had was enough, as you, perhaps, will think, for plentiful subsistence, but to us, with habits of a different kind, it was little better than poverty. That reflection, my father's memory, my mother's deplorable state, which every year grew worse, and the late misfortune, were the chief companions of my thoughts.

The dear child, whose smiles were uninterrupted by his mother's afflictions, was some consolation in my solitude. To his instruction and to my mother's wants, all my hours were devoted. I was sometimes not without the hope of better days. Full as my mind was of Fielding's merits, convinced by former proofs of his ardent and generous spirit, I trusted that time and reflection would destroy that spell by which he was now bound.

For some time, the progress of these reflections was not known. In leaving England, Fielding dropped all correspondence and connection with his native country. He parted with the woman at Rouen, leaving no trace behind him by which she might follow him, as she wished to do. She never returned to England, but died a twelve month afterwards in Switzerland.

As to me, I had only to muse day and night upon the possible destiny of this beloved fugitive. His incensed father cared not for him. He had cast him out of his paternal affections, ceased to make enquiries respecting him, and even wished never to hear of him again. My boy succeeded to my husband's place in his grand-father's affections, and in the hopes and views of the family; and his mother wanted nothing which their compassionate and respectful love could bestow.

Three long and tedious years passed away, and no tidings were received. Whether he were living or dead, nobody could tell. At length, an English traveller, going out of the customary road from Italy, met with Fielding, in a town in the Venaissin. His manners, habit and language, had become French. He seemed unwilling to be recognized by an old acquaintance, but not being able to avoid this, and becoming gradually familiar, he informed the traveller of many particulars in his present situation. It appeared that he had made himself useful to a neighboring *Seigneur*, in whose *chateau* he had long lived on the footing of a brother. France he had resolved to make his future country, and among other changes for that end, he had laid aside his English name, and taken that of his patron, which was *Perrin*. He had endeavored to compensate himself for all other privations, by devoting himself to rural amusements and to study.

He carefully shunned all enquiries respecting me, but when my name was mentioned by his friend, who knew well all that had happened, and my general welfare, together with that of his son, asserted, he shewed deep sensibility, and even consented that I should be made acquainted with his situation.

I cannot describe the effect of this intelligence on me. My hopes of bringing him back to me, were suddenly revived. I wrote him a letter, in which I poured forth my whole heart; but his answer contained avowals of all his former resolutions, to which time had only made his adherence more easy. A second and third letter were written, and an offer made to follow him to his retreat, and share his exile; but all my efforts availed nothing. He solemnly and repeatedly renounced all the claims of an husband over me, and absolved me from every obligation as a wife.

His part in this correspondence, was performed without harshness or contempt. A strange mixture there was of pathos and indifference; of tenderness and resolution. Hence I continually derived hope, which time, however, brought no nearer to certainty.

At the opening of the revolution, the name of Perrin appeared among the deputies to the constituent assembly, for the district in which he resided. He had thus succeeded in gaining all the rights of a French citizen; and the hopes of his return became almost extinct; but that, and every other hope, respecting him, has since been totally extinguished by his marriage with Marguerite D'Almont, a young lady of great merit and fortune, and a native of Avignon.

A long period of suspence was now at an end, and left me in a state almost as full of anguish as that which our first separation produced. My sorrows were increased by my mother's death, and this incident freeing me from those restraints upon my motions which before existed, I determined to come to America.

My son was now eight years old, and his grandfather claiming the province of his instruction, I was persuaded to part with him, that he might be sent to a distant school. Thus was another tie removed, and in spite of the well meant importunities of my friends, I persisted in my scheme of crossing the ocean.

I could not help, at this part of her narration, expressing my surprise, that any motives were strong enough to recommend this scheme.

It was certainly a freak of despair. A few months would, perhaps, have allayed the fresh grief, and reconciled me to my situation; but I would not pause or deliberate. My scheme was opposed by my friends, with great earnestness. During my voyage, affrighted by the dangers which surrounded me, and to which I was wholly unused, I heartily repented of my resolution; but now, methinks, I have reason to rejoice at my perseverance. I have come into a scene and society so new, I have had so many claims made upon my ingenuity and fortitude, that my mind has been diverted in some degree from former sorrows. There are even times when I wholly forget them, and catch myself indulging in cheerful reveries.

I have often reflected with surprise on the nature of my own mind. It is eight years since my father's violent death. How few of my hours since that period, have been blessed with serenity! How many nights and days, in hateful and lingering succession, have been bathed in tears and tormented with regrets! That I am still alive with so many causes of death, and with such a slow consuming malady, is surely to be wondered at.

I believe the worst foes of man, at least of men in grief, are solitude and idleness. The same eternally occurring round of objects, feeds his disease, and the effects of mere vacancy and uniformity, is sometimes mistaken for those of grief. Yes, I am glad I came to America. My relations are importunate for my return, and till lately, I had some thoughts of it; but I think now, I shall stay where I am, for the rest of my days.

Since I arrived, I am become more of a student than I used to be. I always loved literature, but never, till of late, had a mind enough at ease, to read with advantage. I now find pleasure in the occupation which I never expected to find.

You see in what manner I live. The letters which I brought secured me a flattering reception from the best people in your country; but scenes of gay resort had nothing to attract me, and I quickly withdrew to that seclusion in which you now find me. Here, always at leisure, and mistress of every laudable means of gratification, I am not without the belief of serene days yet to come.

I now ventured to enquire what were her latest tidings of her husband.

At the opening of the revolution, I told you he became a champion of the people. By his zeal and his efforts he acquired such importance as to be deputed to the National Assembly. In this post he was the adherent of violent measures, till the subversion of monarchy; and then, when too late for his safety, he checked his career.

And what has since become of him?

She sighed deeply. You were yesterday reading a list of the proscribed under Robespierre. I checked you. I had good reason. But this subject grows too painful, let us change it.

Some time after I ventured to renew this topic; and discovered that Fielding, under his new name of Perrin d'Almont, was among the outlawed deputies of last year*, and had been slain in resisting the officers, sent to arrest him. My friend had been informed that his *wife* Philippine d'Almont, whom she

*1793.

had reason to believe, a woman of great merit, had eluded persecution, and taken refuge in some part of America. She had made various attempts, but in vain, to find out her retreat. Ah! said I, you must commission me to find her. I will hunt her through the continent from Penobscot to Savanna. I will not leave a nook unsearched.

Chapter XXIV

NONE will be surprized, that to a woman thus unfortunate and thus deserving, my heart willingly rendered up all its sympathies; that as I partook of all her grief, I hailed, with equal delight, those omens of felicity which now, at length, seemed to play in her fancy.

I saw her often, as often as my engagements would permit, and oftener than I allowed myself to visit any other. In this I was partly selfish. So much entertainment, so much of the best instruction did her conversation afford me, that I never had enough of it.

Her experience had been so much larger than mine, and so wholly different, and she possessed such unbounded facility of recounting all she had seen and felt, and absolute sincerity and unreserve in this respect, were so fully established between us, that I can imagine nothing equally instructive and delightful with her conversation.

Books are cold, jejune, vexatious in their sparingness of information at one time, and their impertinent loquacity at another. Besides, all they chuse to give, they give at once; they allow no questions; offer no further explanations, and bend not to the caprices of our curiosity. They talk to us behind a screen. Their tone is lifeless and monotonous. They charm not our attention by mute significances of gesture and looks. They spread no light upon their meaning by cadences and emphasis and pause.

How different was Mrs. Fielding's discourse! So versatile; so bending to the changes of occasion; so obsequious to my curiosity, and so abundant in that very knowledge in which I was most deficient, and on which I set the most value, the knowledge of the human heart; of society as it existed in another world, more abundant in the varieties of customs and characters, than I had ever had the power to witness.

Partly selfish I have said my motives were, but not wholly so, as long as I saw that my friend derived pleasure, in her turn, from my company. Not that I could add directly to her knowledge or pleasure, but that expansion of heart, that ease of utterance and flow of ideas which always were occasioned by my approach, were sources of true pleasure of which she had been long deprived, and for which her privation had given her a higher relish than ever.

She lived in great affluence and independence, but made use of her privileges of fortune chiefly to secure to herself the command of her own time. She had been long ago tired and disgusted with the dull and fulsome uniformity and parade of the play-house and ball-room. Formal visits were endured as mortifications and penances, by which the delights of privacy and friendly intercourse were by contrast increased. Music she loved, but never sought it in place of public resort, or from the skill of mercenary performers, and books were not the least of her pleasures.

As to me, I was wax in her hand. Without design and without effort, I was always of that form she wished me to assume. My own happiness became a secondary passion, and her gratification the great end of my being. When with her, I thought not of myself. I had scarcely a separate or independent existence, since my senses were occupied by her, and my mind was full of those ideas which her discourse communicated. To meditate on her looks and words, and to pursue the means suggested by my own thoughts, or by her, conducive, in any way, to her good, was all my business.

What a fate, said I, at the conclusion of one of our interviews, has been yours. But, thank Heaven, the storm has disappeared before the age of sensibility has gone past, and without drying up every source of happiness. You are still young: all your powers unimpaired; rich in the compassion and esteem of the world; wholly independent of the claims and caprices of others; amply supplied with that mean of usefulness, called money; wise in that experience which only adversity can give. Past evils and sufferings, if incurred and endured without guilt, if called to view without remorse, make up the materials of present joy. They cheer our most dreary hours with the whispered accents of "well done," and they heighten our pleasures into somewhat of celestial brilliancy, by furnishing a deep, a ruefully deep contrast.

From this moment, I will cease to weep for you. I will call

you the happiest of women. I will share with you your happiness by witnessing it—but that shall not content me. I must someway contribute to it. Tell me how I shall serve you? What can I do to make you happier? Poor am I in every thing but zeal, but still I may do something. What—pray tell me what can I do?

She looked at me with sweet and solemn significance. What it was exactly, I could not divine, yet I was strangely affected by it. It was but a glance, instantly withdrawn. She made me no answer.

You must not be silent; you *must* tell me what I can do for you. Hitherto I have done nothing. All the service is on your side. Your conversation has been my study, a delightful study, but the profit has only been mine. Tell me how I can be grateful—my voice and manner, I believe, seldom belye my feelings. At this time, I had almost done what a second thought made me suspect to be unauthorized. Yet I cannot tell why. My heart had nothing in it but reverence and admiration. Was she not the substitute of my lost mamma. Would I not have clasped that beloved shade? Yet the two beings were not just the same, or I should not, as now, have checked myself, and only pressed her hand to my lips.

Tell me, repeated I, what can I do to serve you? I read to you a little now, and you are pleased with my reading. I copy for you when you want the time. I guide the reins for you when you chuse to ride. Humble offices, indeed, though, perhaps, all that a raw youth like me can do for you; but I can be still more assiduous. I can read several hours in the day, instead of one. I can write ten times as much as now.

Are you not my lost mamma come back again? And yet, not *exactly* her, I think. Something different; something better, I believe, if that be possible. At any rate, methinks I would be wholly yours. I shall be impatient and uneasy till every act, every thought, every minute, someway does you good.

How! said I—her eye still averted, seemed to hold back the tear with difficulty, and she made a motion as if to rise—have I grieved you? Have I been importunate? Forgive me if I have offended you.

Her eyes now overflowed without restraint. She articulated

with difficulty—Tears are too prompt with me of late; but they did not upbraid you. Pain has often caused them to flow, but now it—is—*pleasure*.

What an heart must yours be, I resumed. When susceptible of such pleasures, what pangs must formerly have rent it!—But you are not displeased, you say, with my importunate zeal. You will accept me as your own in every thing. Direct me: prescribe to me. There must be *something* in which I can be of still more use to you: some way in which I can be wholly yours——

Wholly mine! she repeated, in a smothered voice, and rising—leave me, Arthur. It is too late for you to be here. It was wrong to stay so late.

I have been wrong, but how too late! I entered but this moment. It is twilight still: Is it not?

No—it is almost twelve. You have been here a long four hours; short ones, I would rather say—but indeed you must go.

What made me so thoughtless of the time! But I will go, yet not till you forgive me. I approached her with a confidence, and for a purpose at which, upon reflection, I am not a little surprized, but the being called Mervyn is not the same in her company and in that of another. What is the difference, and whence comes it? Her words and looks engross me. My mind wants room for any other object. But why enquire whence the difference? The superiority of her merits and attractions to all those whom I knew, would surely account for my fervor. Indifference, if I felt it, would be the only just occasion of wonder.

The hour was, indeed too late, and I hastened home. Stevens was waiting my return with some anxiety. I apologized for my delay, and recounted to him what had just passed. He listened with more than usual interest. When I had finished,

Mervyn, said he, you seem not to be aware of your present situation. From what you now tell me, and from what you have formerly told me, one thing seems very plain to me.

Pry'thee, what is it?

Eliza Hadwin—do you wish—could you bear to see her the wife of another?

Five years hence I will answer you. Then my answer may

be—"No: I wish her only to be mine." Till then, I wish her only to be my pupil, my ward, my sister.

But these are remote considerations: they are bars to marriage, but not to love. Would it not molest and disquiet you to observe in her a passion for another?

It would, but only on her own account: not on mine. At a suitable age it is very likely I may love her, because, it is likely, if she holds on in her present career, she will then be worthy, but, at present, though I would die to ensure her happiness, I have no wish to ensure it by marriage with her.

Is there no other whom you love?

No. There is one worthier than all others: one whom I wish the woman who shall be my wife to resemble in all things.

And who is this model?

You know I can only mean Achsa Fielding.

If you love her likeness, why not love herself?

I felt my heart leap.—What a thought is that! Love her I *do* as I love my God; as I love virtue. To love her in another sense, would brand me for a lunatic.

To love her as a woman, then, appears to you an act of folly.

In me it would be worse than folly. 'Twould be frenzy.

And why?

Why? Really, my friend, you astonish me. Nay, you startle me—for a question like that implies a doubt in you whether I have not actually harbored the tho't.

No, said he, smiling, presumtuous though you be, you have not, to be sure, reached so high a pitch. But still, though I think you innocent of so heinous an offence, there is no harm in asking why you might not love her, and even seek her for a wife.

Achsa Fielding *my wife!* Good Heaven!—The very sound threw my soul into unconquerable tumults.—Take care, my friend, continued I, in beseeching accents, you may do me more injury than you conceive, by even starting such a thought.

True, said he, as long as such obstacles exist to your success; so many incurable objections; for instance, she is six years older than you——

That is an advantage. Her age is what it ought to be.

But she has been a wife and mother already.

That is likewise an advantage. She has wisdom, because she has experience. Her sensibilities are stronger, because they have been exercised and chastened. Her first marriage was unfortunate. The purer is the felicity she will taste in a second! If her second choice be propitious, the greater her tenderness and gratitude.

But she is a foreigner: independent of controul, and rich.

All which, are blessings to herself and to him for whom her hand is reserved; especially if like me, he is indigent.

But then she is unsightly as a *night-hag*, tawney as a moor, the eye of a gypsy, low in stature, contemptibly diminutive, scarcely bulk enough to cast a shadow as she walks, less luxuriance than a charred log, fewer elasticities than a sheet pebble.

Hush! hush! blasphemer!—and I put my hand before his mouth—have I not told you that in mind, person and condition, she is the type after which my enamored fancy has modelled my wife.

O ho! Then the objection does not lie with you. It lies with her, it seems. She can find nothing in you to esteem! And pray, for what faults do you think she would reject you?

I cannot tell. That she can ever balance for a moment, on such a question, is incredible. *Me! me!* That Achsa Fielding should think of me!

Incredible, indeed! You who are loathsome in your person, an ideot in your understanding, a villain in your morals! deformed! withered! vain, stupid and malignant. That such an one should chuse *you* for an idol!

Pray, my friend, said I, anxiously, jest not. What mean you by an hint of this kind?

I will not jest then, but will soberly enquire, what faults are they which make this lady's choice of you so incredible? You are younger than she, though no one, who merely observed your manners, and heard you talk, would take you to be under thirty. You are poor; are these impediments?

I should think not. I have heard her reason with admirable eloquence, against the vain distinctions of property and nation and rank. They were once of moment in her eyes; but the sufferings, humiliations and reflections of years, have cured her of the folly. Her nation has suffered too much by the inhuman antipathies of religious and political faction; she, herself, has felt so often the contumelies of the rich, the highborn, and the bigotted, that——

Pry'thee then, what dost imagine her objections to be?

Why—I don't know. The thought was so aspiring; to call her *my wife*, was an height of bliss, the very far-off view of which made my head dizzy.

An height, however, to attain which you suppose only her consent, her love, to be necessary?

Without doubt, her love is indispensible.

Sit down, Arthur, and let us no longer treat this matter lightly. I clearly see the importance of this moment to this lady's happiness and yours. It is plain that you love this woman. How could you help it? A brilliant skin is not her's; nor elegant proportions; nor majestic stature; yet no creature had ever more power to bewitch. Her manners have grace and dignity that flow from exquisite feeling, delicate taste, and the quickest and keenest penetration. She has the wisdom of men and of books. Her sympathies are enforced by reason, and her charities regulated by knowledge. She has a woman's age, fortune more than you wish, and a spotless fame. How could you fail to love her?

You, who are her chosen friend, who partake her pleasures, and share her employments, on whom she almost exclusively bestows her society and confidence, and to whom she thus affords the strongest of all indirect proofs of impassioned esteem. How could you, with all that firmness to love, joined with all that discernment of her excellence, how could you escape the enchantment?

You have not thought of marriage. You have not suspected your love. From the purity of your mind, from the idolatry with which this woman has inspired you, you have imaged no delight beyond that of enjoying her society as you now do, and have never fostered an hope beyond this privilege.

How quickly would this tranquillity vanish, and the true state of your heart be evinced, if a rival should enter the scene and be entertained with preference; then would the seal be removed, the spell be broken, and you would awaken to terror and to anguish.

Of this, however, there is no danger. Your passion is not

felt by you alone. From her treatment of you, your diffidence disables you from seeing, but nothing can be clearer to me than, that she loves you.

I started on my feet. A flush of scorching heat flowed to every part of my frame. My temples began to throb like my heart. I was half delirious, and my delirium was strangely compounded of fear and hope, of delight and of terror.

What have you done, my friend? You have overturned my peace of mind. Till now the image of this woman has been followed by complacency and sober rapture; but your words have dashed the scene with dismay and confusion. You have raised up wishes and dreams and doubts, which possess me in spite of my reason, in spite of a thousand proofs.

Good God! You say she loves; loves *me!* me, a boy in age; bred in clownish ignorance; scarcely ushered into the world; more than childishly unlearned and raw; a barn-door simpleton; a plow-tail, kitchen-hearth, turnip-hoeing novice! She, thus splendidly endowed; thus allied to nobles; thus gifted with arts, and adorned with graces; that she should chuse me, me for the partner of her fortune; her affections; and her life! It cannot be. Yet, if it were; if your guesses should— prove—Oaf! madman! To indulge so fatal a chimera! So rash a dream!

My friend! my friend! I feel that you have done me an irreparable injury. I can never more look her in the face. I can never more frequent her society. These new thoughts will beset and torment me. My disquiet will chain up my tongue. That overflowing gratitude; that innocent joy, unconscious of offence, and knowing no restraint, which have hitherto been my titles to her favor, will fly from my features and manners. I shall be anxious, vacant and unhappy in her presence. I shall dread to look at her, or to open my lips lest my mad and unhallowed ambition should betray itself.

Well, replied Stevens, this scene is quite new. I could almost find it in my heart to pity you. I did not expect this; and yet from my knowledge of your character, I ought, perhaps, to have foreseen it. This is a necessary part of the drama. A joyous certainty, on these occasions, must always be preceded by suspenses and doubts, and the close will be joyous in proportion as the preludes are excruciating. Go to bed, my good friend, and think of this. Time and a few more interviews with Mrs. Fielding, will, I doubt not, set all to rights.

Chapter XXV

I WENT to my chamber, but what different sensations did I carry into it, from those with which I had left it a few hours before. I stretched myself on the mattress and put out the light; but the swarm of new images that rushed on my mind, set me again instantly in motion. All was rapid, vague and undefined, wearying and distracting my attention. I was roused as by a divine voice, that said:—"Sleep no more: Mervyn shall sleep no more."

What chiefly occupied me was a nameless sort of terror. What shall I compare it to? Methinks, that one falling from a tree, overhanging a torrent, plunged into the whirling eddy, and gasping and struggling while he sinks to rise no more, would feel just as I did then. Nay, some such image actually possessed me. Such was one of my reveries, in which suddenly I stretched my hand, and caught the arm of a chair. This act called me back to reason, or rather gave my soul opportunity to roam into a new track equally wild.

Was it the abruptness of this vision that thus confounded me! was it a latent error in my moral constitution, which this new conjuncture drew forth into influence? These were all the tokens of a mind lost to itself; bewildered; unhinged; plunged into a drear insanity.

Nothing less could have prompted so phantastically—for midnight as it was, my chamber's solitude was not to be supported. After a few turns across the floor, I left the room, and the house. I walked without design and in an hurried pace. I posted straight to the house of Mrs. Fielding. I lifted the latch, but the door did not open. It was, no doubt, locked.

How comes this, said I, and looked around me. The hour and occasion were unthought of. Habituated to this path, I had taken it spontaneously. How comes this? repeated I. Locked upon *me!* but I will summon them, I warrant me—and rung the bell, not timidly or slightly, but with violence. Some one hastened from above. I saw the glimmer of a candle through the key-hole.

Strange, thought I, a candle at noon day!—The door was

opened, and my poor Bess, robed in a careless and a hasty manner, appeared. She started at sight of me, but merely because she did not, in a moment, recognize me.—Ah! Arthur, is it you? Come in. My mamma has wanted you these two hours. I was just going to dispatch Philip to tell you to come.

Lead me to her, said I.

She led the way into the parlor.—Wait a moment here: I will tell her you are come—and she tripped away.

Presently a step was heard. The door opened again, and then entered a man. He was tall, elegant, sedate to a degree of sadness: Something in his dress and aspect that bespoke the foreigner; the Frenchman.

What, said he, mildly, is your business with my wife? She cannot see you instantly, and has sent me to receive your commands.

Your *wife!* I want Mrs. Fielding.

True; and Mrs. Fielding is my wife. Thank Heaven I have come in time to discover her, and claim her as such.

I started back. I shuddered. My joints slackened, and I stretched my hand to catch something by which I might be saved from sinking on the floor. Meanwhile, Fielding changed his countenance into rage and fury. He called me villain! bad me avaunt! and drew a shining steel from his bosom, with which he stabbed me to the heart. I sunk upon the floor, and all, for a time, was darkness and oblivion! At length, I returned as it were to life. I opened my eyes. The mists disappeared, and I found myself stretched upon the bed in my own chamber. I remembered the fatal blow I had received. I put my hand upon my breast; the spot where the dagger entered. There were no traces of a wound. All was perfect and entire. Some miracle had made me whole.

I raised myself up. I re-examined my body. All around me was hushed, till a voice from the pavement below, proclaimed that it was "past three o'clock."

What, said I, has all this miserable pageantry, this midnight wandering, and this ominous interview, been no more than—*a dream!*

It may be proper to mention, in explanation of this scene, and to shew the thorough perturbation of my mind, during this night, intelligence gained some days after from Eliza. She said, that about two o'clock, on this night, she was roused by a violent ringing of the bell. She was startled by so unseasonable a summons. She slept in a chamber adjoining Mrs. Fielding's, and hesitated whether she should alarm her friend, but the summons not being repeated, she had determined to forbear.

Added to this, was the report of Mrs. Stevens, who, on the same night, about half an hour after I and her husband had retired, imagined that she heard the street-door opened and shut, but this being followed by no other consequence, she supposed herself mistaken. I have little doubt, that, in my feverish and troubled sleep, I actually went forth, posted to the house of Mrs. Fielding, rung for admission, and shortly after, returned to my own apartment.

This confusion of mind was somewhat allayed by the return of light. It gave way to more uniform, but not less rueful and despondent perceptions. The image of Achsa filled my fancy, but it was the harbinger of nothing but humiliation and sorrow. To outroot the conviction of my own unworthiness, to persuade myself that I was regarded with the tenderness that Stevens had ascribed to her, that the discovery of my thoughts would not excite her anger and grief, I felt to be impossible.

In this state of mind, I could not see her. To declare my feelings would produce indignation and anguish; to hide them from her scrutiny was not in my power: yet, what would she think of my estranging myself from her society? What expedient could I honestly adopt to justify my absence, and what employments could I substitute for those precious hours hitherto devoted to her.

This afternoon, thought I, she has been invited to spend at Stedman's country house on Schuylkill. She consented to go, and I was to accompany her. I am fit only for solitude. My behaviour, in her presence, will be enigmatical, capricious and morose. I must not go: Yet, what will she think of my failure? Not to go will be injurious and suspicious.

I was undetermined. The appointed hour arrived. I stood at my chamber window, torn by variety of purposes, and swayed alternately by repugnant arguments. I several times went to the door of my apartment, and put my foot upon the first step of the stair-case, but as often paused, reconsidered and returned to my room.

In these fluctuations the hour passed. No messenger arrived from Mrs. Fielding, enquiring into the cause of my delay. Was she offended at my negligence? Was she sick and disabled from going, or had she changed her mind? I now remember her parting words at our last interview. Were they not susceptible of two constructions? She said my visit was too long, and bad me begone. Did she suspect my presumption, and is she determined thus to punish me?

This terror added anew to all my former anxieties. It was impossible to rest in this suspense. I would go to her. I would lay before her all the anguish of my heart: I would not spare myself. She shall not reproach me more severely than I will reproach myself. I will hear my sentence from her own lips, and promise unlimited submission to the doom of separation and exile, which she will pronounce.

I went forthwith to her house. The drawing-room and summer-house was empty. I summoned Philip the footman—his mistress was gone to Mr. Stedman's.

How?—To Stedman's?—In whose company?

Miss Stedman and her brother called for her in the carriage, and persuaded her to go with them.

Now my heart sunk, indeed! Miss Stedman's *brother*! A youth, forward, gallant and gay! Flushed with prosperity, and just returned from Europe, with all the confidence of him, though pre-engaged to me! Poor Arthur, how art thou despised!

This information only heightened my impatience. I went away, but returned in the evening. I waited till eleven, but she came not back. I cannot justly paint the interval that passed till next morning. It was void of sleep. On leaving her house, I wandered into the fields. Every moment increased my impatience. She will probably spend the morrow at Stedman's, said I, and possibly the next day. Why should I wait for her return? Why not seek her there, and rid myself at once of this agonizing suspense? Why not go thither now? This night, wherever I spend it, will be unacquainted with repose. I will go, it is already near twelve, and the distance is more than eight miles. I will hover near the house till morning, and then, as early as possible, demand an interview.

I was well acquainted with Stedman's Villa, having formerly been there with Mrs. Fielding. I quickly entered its precincts. I went close to the house; looked mournfully at every window. At one of them a light was to be seen, and I took various stations to discover, if possible, the persons within. Methought once I caught a glimpse of a female, whom my fancy easily imagined to be Achsa. I sat down upon the lawn, some hundred feet from the house, and opposite the window whence the light proceeded. I watched it, till at length some one came to the window, lifted it, and leaning on her arms, continued to look out.

The preceding day had been a very sultry one; the night, as usual after such a day, and the fall of a violent shower, was delightfully serene and pleasant. Where I stood, was enlightened by the moon. Whether she saw me or not, I could hardly tell, or whether she distinguished any thing but a human figure.

Without reflecting on what was due to decorum and punctilio, I immediately drew near the house. I quickly perceived that her attention was fixed. Neither of us spoke, till I had placed myself directly under her; I then opened my lips, without knowing in what manner to address her. She spoke first, and in a startled and anxious voice—

Arthur Mervyn: he that was two days ago your friend.

Mervyn! What is it that brings you here at this hour? What is the matter? What has happened? Is any body sick?

All is safe—all are in good health.

What then do you come hither for at such an hour?

I meant not to disturb you: I meant not to be seen.

Good Heavens! How you frighten me. What can be the reason of so strange——

Be not alarmed. I meant to hover near the house till morning, that I might see you as early as possible.

For what purpose?

I will tell you when we meet, and let that be at five o'clock; the sun will then be risen; in the cedar grove under the bank; till when, farewell.

Having said this, I prevented all expostulation, by turning

the angle of the house, and hastening towards the shore of the river. I roved about the grove that I have mentioned. In one part of it is a rustic seat and table, shrouded by trees and shrubs, and an intervening eminence, from the view of those in the house. This I designed to be the closing scene of my destiny.

Presently, I left this spot and wandered upward through embarrassed and obscure paths, starting forward or checking my pace, according as my wayward meditations governed me. Shall I describe my thoughts?—Impossible! It was certainly a temporary loss of reason; nothing less than madness could lead into such devious tracts, drag me down to so hopeless, helpless, panickful a depth, and drag me down so suddenly; lay waste, as at a signal, all my flourishing structures, and reduce them in a moment to a scene of confusion and horror.

What did I fear? What did I hope? What did I design? I cannot tell; my glooms were to retire with the night. The point to which every tumultuous feeling was linked, was the coming interview with Achsa. That was the boundary of fluctuation and suspense. Here was the sealing and ratification of my doom.

I rent a passage through the thicket, and struggled upward till I reached the edge of a considerable precipice; I laid me down at my length upon the rock, whose cold and hard surface I pressed with my bared and throbbing breast. I leaned over the edge; fixed my eyes upon the water and wept—plentifully; but why?

May *this* be my heart's last beat, if I can tell why.

I had wandered so far from Stedman's, that when roused by the light, I had some miles to walk before I could reach the place of meeting. Achsa was already there. I slid down the rock above, and appeared before her. Well might she be startled at my wild and abrupt appearance.

I placed myself, without uttering a word, upon a seat opposite to her, the table between, and crossing my arms upon the table, leaned my head upon them. While my face was turned towards and my eyes fixed upon hers, I seemed to have lost the power and the inclination to speak.

She regarded me, at first, with anxious curiosity; after examining my looks, every emotion was swallowed up in terrified sorrow. For God's sake!—what does all this mean? Why am I called to this place? What tidings, what fearful tidings do you bring?

I did not change my posture or speak. What, she resumed, could inspire all this woe? Keep me not in this suspense, Arthur; these looks and this silence shocks and afflicts me too much.

Afflict you? said I, at last: I come to tell you, what, now that I am here, I cannot tell——there I stopped.

Say what, I entreat you. You seem to be very unhappy— such a change—from yesterday!

Yes! From yesterday: all then was a joyous calm, and now all is—but then I knew not my infamy, my guilt——

What words are these, and from you Arthur? Guilt is to you impossible. If purity is to be found on earth, it is lodged in your heart. What have you done?

I have dared—how little you expect the extent of my daring. That such as I should look upwards with this ambition.

I now stood up, and taking her hands in mine, as she sat, looked earnestly in her face—I come only to beseech your pardon. To tell you my crime, and then disappear forever; but first let me see if there be any omen of forgiveness. Your looks—they are kind; heavenly; compassionate still. I will trust them, I believe: and yet—letting go her hands, and turning away.—This offence is beyond the reach even of *your* mercy.

How beyond measure these words and this deportment distress me! Let me know the worst; I cannot bear to be thus perplexed.

Why, said I, turning quickly round, and again taking her hands, that Mervyn, whom you have honored and confided in, and blessed with your sweet regards, has been——

What has he been? Divinely amiable, heroic in his virtue, I am sure. What else has he been?

This Mervyn has imagined, has dared—Will you forgive him?

Forgive you what? Why don't you speak? Keep not my soul in this suspense.

He has dared—But do not think that I am he. Continue to look as now, and reserve your killing glances, the vengeance of those eyes as for one that is absent.—Why, what—You weep, then, at last. That is a propitious sign. When pity drops from the eyes of our judge, then should the suppliant approach. Now, in confidence of pardon, I will tell you: This Mervyn, not content with all you have hitherto granted him, has dared—to *love* you; nay, to think of you, as of *his wife!*

Her eye sunk beneath mine, and disengaging her hands, covered her face with them.

I see my fate, said I, in a tone of despair. Too well did I predict the effect of this confession; but I will go— *and unforgiven.*

She now partly uncovered her face. The hand withdrawn from her cheek, was stretched towards me. She looked at me.

Arthur! I *do* forgive thee.—With what accents was this uttered! With what looks! The cheek that was before pale with terror, was now crimsoned over by a different emotion, and delight swam in her eye.

Could I mistake? My doubts, my new-born fears made me tremble, while I took the offered hand.

Surely—faultered I, I am not—I cannot be—so blessed.

There was no need of words. The hand that I held, was sufficiently eloquent. She was still silent.

Surely, said I, my senses deceive me. A bliss like this cannot be reserved for me. Tell me, once more—set my doubting heart at rest.—

She now gave herself to my arms—I have not words—Let your own heart tell you, you have made your Achsa——

At this moment, a voice from without, it was Miss Stedman's, called—Mrs. Fielding! where are you?

My friend started up, and in a hasty voice, bade me begone! You must not be seen by this giddy girl. Come hither this evening, as if by my appointment, and I will return with you.—She left me in a kind of trance. I was immoveable. My reverie was too delicious;—but let me not attempt the picture. If I can convey no image of my state, previous to this interview, my subsequent feelings are still more beyond the reach of my powers to describe.

Agreeably to the commands of my mistress, I hastened away, evading paths which might expose me to observation. I speedily made my friends partake of my joy, and passed the day in a state of solemn but confused rapture. I did not accurately pourtray the various parts of my felicity. The whole rushed upon my soul at once. My conceptions were too rapid, and too comprehensive to be distinct.

I went to Stedman's in the evening. I found in the accents and looks of my Achsa new assurances that all which had lately past, was more than a dream. She made excuses for leaving the Stedmans sooner than ordinary, and was accompanied to the city by her friend. We dropped Mrs. Fielding at her own house, and thither, after accompanying Miss Stedman to her own home, I returned, upon the wings of tremulous impatience.—

Now could I repeat every word of every conversation that has since taken place between us; but why should I do that on paper? Indeed it could not be done. All is of equal value, and all could not be comprized but in many volumes. There needs nothing more deeply to imprint it on my memory; and while thus reviewing the past, I should be iniquitously neglecting the present. What is given to the pen, would be taken from her; and that, indeed, would be—but no need of saying what it would be, since it is impossible.

I merely write to allay those tumults which our necessary separation produces; to aid me in calling up a little patience, till the time arrives, when our persons, like our minds, shall be united forever. That time—may nothing happen to prevent—but nothing can happen. But why this ominous misgiving just now? My love has infected me with these unworthy terrors, for she has them too.

This morning I was relating my dream to her. She started, and grew pale. A sad silence ensued the cheerfulness that had reigned before—why thus dejected, my friend?

I hate your dream. It is a horrid thought. Would to God it had never occurred to you.

Why surely you place no confidence in dreams.

I know not where to place confidence; not in my present promises of joy—and she wept. I endeavored to soothe or console her. Why, I asked, did she weep.

My heart is sore. Former disappointments were so heavy; the hopes which were blasted, were so like my present ones, that the dread of a like result, will intrude upon my thoughts. And now your dream! Indeed, I know not what to do. I believe I ought still to retract—ought, at least, to postpone an act so irrevocable.

Now was I obliged again to go over in my catalogue of arguments to induce her to confirm her propitious resolution to be mine within the week. I, at last, succeeded, even in restoring her serenity and beguiling her fears by dwelling on our future happiness.

Our houshold, while we staid in America—in a year or two we hie to Europe—should be *thus* composed. Fidelity and skill and pure morals, should be sought out, and enticed, by generous recompences, into our domestic service. Duties should be light and regular.—Such and such should be our amusements and employments abroad and at home, and would not this be true happiness?

O yes—If it may be so.

It shall be so; but this is but the humble outline of the scene; something is still to be added to complete our felicity.

What more can be added?

What more? Can Achsa ask what more? She who has not been *only* a wife——

But why am I indulging this pen-prattle? The hour she fixed for my return to her is come, and now take thyself away, quill. Lie there, snug in thy leathern case, till I call for thee, and that will not be very soon. I believe I will abjure thy company till all is settled with my love. Yes: I *will* abjure thee, so let *this* be thy last office, till Mervyn has been made the happiest of men.

THE END

EDGAR HUNTLY

OR

MEMOIRS OF A SLEEP-WALKER

TO THE PUBLIC

THE FLATTERING RECEPTION that has been given, by the public, to Arthur Mervyn, has prompted the writer to solicit a continuance of the same favour, and to offer to the world a new performance.

America has opened new views to the naturalist and politician, but has seldome furnished themes to the moral painter. That new springs of action, and new motives to curiosity should operate; that the field of investigation, opened to us by our own country, should differ essentially from those which exist in Europe, may be readily conceived. The sources of amusement to the fancy and instruction to the heart, that are peculiar to ourselves, are equally numerous and inexhaustible. It is the purpose of this work to profit by some of these sources; to exhibit a series of adventures, growing out of the condition of our country, and connected with one of the most common and most wonderful diseases or affections of the human frame.

One merit the writer may at least claim; that of calling forth the passions and engaging the sympathy of the reader, by means hitherto unemployed by preceding authors. Puerile superstition and exploded manners; Gothic castles and chimeras, are the materials usually employed for this end. The incidents of Indian hostility, and the perils of the western wilderness, are for more suitable; and, for a native of America to overlook these, would admit of no apology. These, therefore, are, in part, the ingredients of this tale, and these he has been ambitious of depicting in vivid and faithful colours. The success of his efforts must be estmated by the liberal and candid reader.

C.B.B.

Chapter I

I SIT DOWN, my friend, to comply with thy request. At length does the impetuosity of my fears, the transports of my wonder permit me to recollect my promise and perform it. At length am I somewhat delivered from suspence and from tremors. At length the drama is brought to an imperfect close, and the series of events, that absorbed my faculties, that hurried away my attention, has terminated in repose.

Till now, to hold a steadfast pen was impossible; to disengage my senses from the scene that was passing or approaching; to forbear to grasp at futurity; to suffer so much thought to wander from the purpose which engrossed my fears and my hopes, could not be.

Yet am I sure that even now my perturbations are sufficiently stilled for an employment like this? That the incidents I am going to relate can be recalled and arranged without indistinctness and confusion? That emotions will not be reawakened by my narrative, incompatible with order and coherence? Yet when I shall be better qualified for this task I know not. Time may take away these headlong energies, and give me back my ancient sobriety: but this change will only be effected by weakening my remembrance of these events. In proportion as I gain power over words, shall I lose dominion over sentiments. In proportion as my tale is deliberate and slow, the incidents and motives which it is designed to exhibit will be imperfectly revived and obscurely pourtrayed.

O! why art thou away at a time like this? Wert thou present, the office to which my pen is so inadequate would easily be executed by my tongue. Accents can scarcely be too rapid, or that which words should fail to convey, my looks and gestures would suffice to communicate. But I know thy coming is impossible. To leave this spot is equally beyond my power. To keep thee in ignorance of what has happened would justly offend thee. There is no method of informing thee except by letter, and this method, must I, therefore, adopt.

How short is the period that has elapsed since thou and I parted, and yet how full of tumult and dismay has been my

soul during that period! What light has burst upon my ignorance of myself and of mankind! How sudden and enormous the transition from uncertainty to knowledge!—

But let me recall my thoughts: let me struggle for so much
composure as will permit my pen to trace intelligible characters. Let me place in order the incidents that are to compose
my tale. I need not call on thee to listen. The fate of Waldegrave was as fertile of torment to thee as to me. His bloody
and mysterious catastrophe equally awakened thy grief, thy
revenge, and thy curiosity. Thou wilt catch from my story
every horror and every sympathy which it paints. Thou wilt
shudder with my forboding and dissolve with my tears. As the
sister of my friend, and as one who honours me with her
affection, thou wilt share in all my tasks and all my dangers.

You need not be reminded with what reluctance I left you.
To reach this place by evening was impossible, unless I had
set out early in the morning, but your society was too precious
not to be enjoyed to the last moment. It was indispensable to
be here on Tuesday, but my duty required no more than that
I should arrive by sun-rise on that day. To travel during the
night, was productive of no formidable inconvenience. The
air was likely to be frosty and sharp, but these would not
incommode one who walked with speed. A nocturnal journey
in districts so romantic and wild as these, through which lay
my road, was more congenial to my temper than a noon-day
ramble.

By night-fall I was within ten miles of my uncle's house. As
the darkness increased, and I advanced on my way, my sensations sunk into melancholy. The scene and the time reminded me of the friend whom I had lost. I recalled his
features, and accents, and gestures, and mused with unutterable feelings on the circumstances of his death.

My recollections once more plunged me into anguish and
perplexity. Once more I asked, who was his assassin? By what
motives could he be impelled to a deed like this? Waldegrave
was pure from all offence. His piety was rapturous. His benevolence was a stranger to remisness or torpor. All who came
within the sphere of his influence experienced and acknowledged his benign activity. His friends were few, because his

habits were timid and reserved, but the existence of an enemy was impossible.

I recalled the incidents of our last interview, my importunities that he should postpone his ill-omened journey till the morning, his inexplicable obstinacy; his resolution to set out on foot, during a dark and tempestuous night, and the horrible disaster that befel him.

The first intimation I received of this misfortune, the insanity of vengeance and grief into which I was hurried, my fruitless searches for the author of this guilt, my midnight wanderings and reveries beneath the shade of that fatal Elm, were revived and re-acted. I heard the discharge of the pistol, I witnessed the alarm of Inglefield, I heard his calls to his servants, and saw them issue forth, with lights and hasten to the spot whence the sound had seemed to proceed. I beheld my friend, stretched upon the earth, ghastly with a mortal wound, alone, with no traces of the slayer visible, no tokens by which his place of refuge might be sought, the motives of his enmity or his instruments of mischief might be detected.

I hung over the dying youth, whose insensibility forbade him to recognize his friend, or unfold the cause of his destruction. I accompanied his remains to the grave, I tended the sacred spot where he lay, I once more exercised my penetration and my zeal in pursuit of his assassin. Once more my meditations and exertions were doomed to be disappointed.

I need not remind thee of what is past. Time and reason seemed to have dissolved the spell which made me deaf to the dictates of duty and discretion. Remembrances had ceased to agonize, to urge me to headlong acts, and foster sanguinary purposes. The gloom was half dispersed and a radiance had succeeded sweeter than my former joys.

Now, by some unseen concurrence of reflections, my thoughts reverted into some degree of bitterness. Methought that to ascertain the hand who killed my friend, was not impossible, and to punish the crime was just. That to forbear inquiry or withold punishment was to violate my duty to my God and to mankind. The impulse was gradually awakened that bade me once more to seek the Elm; once more to explore the ground; to scrutinize its trunk. What could I expect to find? Had it not been an hundred times examined? Had I not extended my search to the neighbouring groves and precipices? Had I not pored upon the brooks, and pryed into the pits and hollows, that were adjacent to the scene of blood?

Lately I had viewed this conduct with shame and regret; but in the present state of my mind, it assumed the appearance of conformity with prudence, and I felt myself irresistably prompted to repeat my search. Some time had elapsed since my departure from this district. Time enough for momentous changes to occur. Expedients that formerly were useless, might now lead instantaneously to the end which I sought. The tree which had formerly been shunned by the criminal, might, in the absence of the avenger of blood, be incautiously approached. Thoughtless or fearless of my return, it was possible that he might, at this moment, be detected hovering near the scene of his offences.

Nothing can be pleaded in extenuation of this relapse into folly. My return, after an absence of some duration, into the scene of these transactions and sufferings, the time of night, the glimmering of the stars, the obscurity in which external objects were wrapped, and which, consequently, did not draw my attention from the images of fancy, may, in some degree, account for the revival of those sentiments and resolutions which immediately succeeded the death of Waldegrave, and which, during my visit to you, had been suspended.

You know the situation of the Elm, in the midst of a private road, on the verge of Norwalk, near the habitation of Inglefield, but three miles from my uncle's house. It was now my intention to visit it. The road in which I was travelling, led a different way. It was requisite to leave it, therefore, and make a circuit through meadows and over steeps. My journey would, by these means, be considerably prolonged, but on that head I was indifferent, or rather, considering how far the night had already advanced, it was desirable not to reach home till the dawn.

I proceeded in this new direction with speed. Time, however, was allowed for my impetuosities to subside, and for sober thoughts to take place. Still I persisted in this path. To linger a few moments in this shade; to ponder on objects connected with events so momentous to my happiness, promised me a mournful satisfaction. I was familiar with the way, though trackless and intricate, and I climbed the steeps, crept through the brambles, leapt the rivulets and fences with undeviating aim, till at length I reached the craggy and obscure path, which led to Inglefield's house.

In a short time, I descried through the dusk the wide-spread branches of the Elm. This tree, however faintly seen, cannot be mistaken for another. The remarkable bulk and shape of its trunk, its position in the midst of the way, its branches spreading into an ample circumference, made it conspicuous from afar. My pulse throbbed as I approached it.

My eyes were eagerly bent to discover the trunk and the area beneath the shade. These, as I approached, gradually became visible. The trunk was not the only thing which appeared in view. Somewhat else, which made itself distinguishable by its motions, was likewise noted. I faultered and stopt.

To a casual observer this appearance would have been unnoticed. To me, it could not but possess a powerful significance. All my surmises and suspicions, instantly returned. This apparition was human, it was connected with the fate of Waldegrave, it led to a disclosure of the author of that fate. What was I to do? To approach unwarily would alarm the person. Instant flight would set him beyond discovery and reach.

I walked softly to the road-side. The ground was covered with rocky masses, scattered among shrub-oaks and dwarf-cedars, emblems of its sterile and uncultivated state. Among these it was possible to elude observation and yet approach near enough to gain an accurate view of this being.

At this time, the atmosphere was somewhat illuminated by the moon, which, though it had already set, was yet so near the horizon, as to benefit me by its light. The shape of a man, tall and robust, was now distinguished. Repeated and closer scrutiny enabled me to perceive that he was employed in digging the earth. Something like flannel was wrapt round his waist and covered his lower limbs. The rest of his frame was naked. I did not recognize in him any one whom I knew.

A figure, robust and strange, and half naked, to be thus employed, at this hour and place, was calculated to rouse up my whole soul. His occupation was mysterious and obscure.

Was it a grave that he was digging? Was his purpose to explore or to hide? Was it proper to watch him at a distance, unobserved and in silence, or to rush upon him and extort from him by violence or menaces, an explanation of the scene?

Before my resolution was formed, he ceased to dig. He cast aside his spade and sat down in the pit that he had dug. He seemed wrapt in meditation; but the pause was short, and succeeded by sobs, at first low, and at wide intervals, but presently louder and more vehement. Sorely charged was indeed that heart whence flowed these tokens of sorrow. Never did I witness a scene of such mighty anguish, such heart-bursting grief.

What should I think? I was suspended in astonishment. Every sentiment, at length, yielded to my sympathy. Every new accent of the mourner struck upon my heart with additional force, and tears found their way spontaneously to my eyes. I left the spot where I stood, and advanced within the verge of the shade. My caution had forsaken me, and instead of one whom it was duty to persecute, I beheld, in this man, nothing but an object of compassion.

My pace was checked by his suddenly ceasing to lament. He snatched the spade, and rising on his feet began to cover up the pit with the utmost diligence. He seemed aware of my presence, and desirous of hiding something from my inspection. I was prompted to advance nearer and hold his hand, but my uncertainty as to his character and views, the abruptness with which I had been ushered into this scene, made me still hesitate; but though I hesitated to advance, there was nothing to hinder me from calling.

What, ho! said I. Who is there? What are you doing?

He stopt, the spade fell from his hand, he looked up and bent forward his face towards the spot where I stood. An interview and explanation were now methought unavoidable. I mustered up my courage to confront and interrogate this being.

He continued for a minute in his gazing and listening attitude. Where I stood I could not fail of being seen, and yet he acted as if he saw nothing. Again he betook himself to his spade, and proceeded with new diligence to fill up the pit.

This demeanour confounded and bewildered me. I had no power but to stand and silently gaze upon his motions.

The pit being filled, he once more sat upon the ground, and resigned himself to weeping and sighs with more vehemence than before. In a short time the fit seemed to have passed. He rose, seized the spade, and advanced to the spot where I stood.

Again I made preparation as for an interview which could not but take place. He passed me, however, without appearing to notice my existence. He came so near as almost to brush my arm, yet turned not his head to either side. My nearer view of him, made his brawny arms and lofty stature more conspicuous; but his imperfect dress, the dimness of the light, and the confusion of my own thoughts, hindered me from discerning his features. He proceeded with a few quick steps, along the road, but presently darted to one side and disappeared among the rocks and bushes.

My eye followed him as long as he was visible, but my feet were rooted to the spot. My musing was rapid and incongruous. It could not fail to terminate in one conjecture, that this person was *asleep*. Such instances were not unknown to me, through the medium of conversation and books. Never, indeed, had it fallen under my own observation till now, and now it was conspicuous and environed with all that could give edge to suspicion, and vigour to inquiry. To stand here was no longer of use, and I turned my steps toward my uncle's habitation.

Chapter II

I HAD food enough for the longest contemplation. My steps partook, as usual, of the vehemence of my thoughts, and I reached my uncle's gate before I believed myself to have lost sight of the Elm. I looked up and discovered the well-known habitation. I could not endure that my reflections should so speedily be interrupted. I, therefore, passed the gate, and stopped not till I had reached a neighbouring summit, crowned with chesnut-oaks and poplars.

Here I more deliberately reviewed the incidents that had just occurred. The inference was just, that the man, half-clothed and digging, was a sleeper: But what was the cause of this morbid activity? What was the mournful vision that dissolved him in tears, and extorted from him tokens of inconsolable distress? What did he seek, or what endeavour to conceal in this fatal spot? The incapacity of sound sleep denotes a mind sorely wounded. It is thus that atrocious criminals denote the possession of some dreadful secret. The thoughts, which considerations of safety enables them to suppress or disguise during wakefulness, operate without impediment, and exhibit their genuine effects, when the notices of sense are partly excluded, and they are shut out from a knowledge of their intire condition.

This is the perpetrator of some nefarious deed. What but the murder of Waldegrave could direct his steps hither? His employment was part of some fantastic drama in which his mind was busy. To comprehend it, demands penetration into the recesses of his soul. But one thing is sure; an incoherent conception of his concern in that transaction, bewitches him hither. This it is that deluges his heart with bitterness and supplies him with ever-flowing tears.

But whence comes he? He does not start from the bosom of the earth, or hide himself in airy distance. He must have a name and a terrestrial habitation. It cannot be at an immeasurable distance from the haunted Elm. Inglefield's house is the nearest. This may be one of its inhabitants. I did not recognize his features, but this was owing to the dusky atmos-

phere and to the singularity of his garb. Inglefield has two
servants, one of whom was a native of this district, simple,
guileless and incapable of any act of violence. He was, more-
over devoutly attached to his sect. He could not be the
criminal.

The other was a person of a very different cast. He was an
emigrant from Ireland, and had been six months in the family
of my friend. He was a pattern of sobriety and gentleness. His
mind was superior to his situation. His natural endowments
were strong, and had enjoyed all the advantage of cultivation.
His demeanour was grave, and thoughtful, and compassionate. He appeared not untinctured with religion, but his devotion, though unostentatious, was of a melancholy tenor.

There was nothing in the first view of his character calculated to engender suspicion. The neighbourhood was populous. But as I conned over the catalogue, I perceived that the
only foreigner among us was Clithero. Our scheme was, for
the most part, a patriarchal one. Each farmer was surrounded
by his sons and kinsmen. This was an exception to the rule.
Clithero was a stranger, whose adventures and character, previously to his coming hither, were unknown to us. The Elm
was surrounded by his master's domains. An actor there must
be, and no one was equally questionable.

The more I revolved the pensive and reserved deportment
of this man, the ignorance in which we were placed respecting
his former situation, his possible motives for abandoning his
country and chusing a station so much below the standard of
his intellectual attainments, the stronger my suspicions became. Formerly, when occupied with conjectures relative to
the same topic, the image of this man did not fail to occur;
but the seeming harmlessness of his ordinary conduct, had
raised him to a level with others, and placed him equally beyond the reach of suspicion. I did not, till now, advert to the
recentness of his appearance among us, and to the obscurity
that hung over his origin and past life. But now these considerations appeared so highly momentous, as almost to decide
the question of his guilt.

But how were these doubts to be changed into absolute
certainty? Henceforth this man was to become the subject of
my scrutiny. I was to gain all the knowledge, respecting him,

which those with whom he lived, and were the perpetual witnesses of his actions, could impart. For this end I was to make
minute inquiries, and to put seasonable interrogatories. From
this conduct I promised myself an ultimate solution of my
doubts.

I acquiesced in this view of things with considerable satisfaction. It seemed as if the maze was no longer inscrutable. It
would be quickly discovered who were the agents and insti-
gators of the murder of my friend.

But it suddenly occurred to me, For what purpose shall I
prosecute this search? What benefit am I to reap from this
discovery? How shall I demean myself when the criminal is
detected? I was not insensible, at that moment, of the impulses of vengeance, but they were transient. I detested the
sanguinary resolutions that I had once formed. Yet I was fearful of the effects of my hasty rage, and dreaded an encounter,
in consequence of which, I might rush into evils which no
time could repair, nor penitence expiate.

But why, said I, should it be impossible to arm myself with
firmness? If forbearance be the dictate of wisdom, cannot it
be so deeply engraven on my mind as to defy all temptation,
and be proof against the most abrupt surprise? My late experience has been of use to me. It has shewn me my weakness
and my strength. Having found my ancient fortifications insufficient to withstand the enemy, what should I learn from
thence but that it becomes me to strengthen and enlarge
them?

No caution indeed can hinder the experiment from being
hazardous. Is it wise to undertake experiments by which nothing can be gained, and much may be lost? Curiosity is vicious,
if undisciplined by reason, and inconducive to benefit.

I was not, however, to be diverted from my purpose. Curiosity, like virtue, is its own reward. Knowledge is of value
for its own sake, and pleasure is annexed to the acquisition,
without regard to any thing beyond. It is precious even when
disconnected with moral inducements and heart-felt sympathies, but the knowledge which I sought by its union with
these was calculated to excite the most complex and fiery sentiment in my bosom.

Hours were employed in revolving these thoughts. At

length I began to be sensible of fatigue, and returning home, explored the way to my chamber without molesting the repose of the family. You know that our doors are always unfastened, and are accessible at all hours of the night.

My slumbers were imperfect, and I rejoiced when the morning light permitted me to resume my meditations. The day glided away, I scarcely know how, and as I had rejoiced at the return of morning, I now hailed, with pleasure, the approach of night.

My uncle and sisters having retired, I betook myself, instead of following their example, to the *Chesnut-hill*. Concealed among its rocks, or gazing at the prospect, which stretched so far and so wide around it, my fancy has always been accustomed to derive its highest enjoyment from this spot. I found myself again at leisure to recall the scene which I had witnessed during the last night, to imagine its connection with the fate of Waldegrave, and to plan the means of discovering the secret that was hidden under these appearances.

Shortly, I began to feel insupportable disquiet at the thoughts of postponing this discovery. Wiles and stratagems were practicable, but they were tedious and of dubious success. Why should I proceed like a plotter? Do I intend the injury of this person? A generous purpose will surely excuse me from descending to artifices. There are two modes of drawing forth the secrets of another, by open and direct means and by circuitous and indirect. Why scruple to adopt the former mode? Why not demand a conference, and state my doubts, and demand a solution of them, in a manner worthy of a beneficent purpose? Why not hasten to the spot? He may be, at this moment, mysteriously occupied under this shade. I may note his behaviour; I may ascertain his person, if not by the features that belong to him, yet by tracing his footsteps when he departs, and pursuing him to his retreats.

I embraced this scheme, which was thus suggested, with eagerness. I threw myself, with headlong speed, down the hill and pursued my way to the Elm. As I approached the tree, my palpitations increased, though my pace slackened. I looked forward with an anxious glance. The trunk of the tree was hidden in the deepest shade. I advanced close up to it. No one was visible, but I was not discouraged. The hour of his coming was, perhaps, not arrived. I took my station at a small distance, beside a fence, on the right hand.

An hour elapsed before my eyes lighted on the object of which they were in search. My previous observation had been roving from one quarter to another. At last, it dwelt upon the tree. The person whom I before described was seated on the ground. I had not perceived him before, and the means by which he placed himself in this situation had escaped my notice. He seemed like one, whom an effort of will, without the exercise of locomotion, had transported hither, or made visible. His state of disarray, and the darkness that shrouded him, prevented me, as before, from distinguishing any peculiarities in his figure or countenance.

I continued watchful and mute. The appearances already described took place, on this occasion, except the circumstance of digging in the earth. He sat musing for a while, then burst into sighs and lamentations.

These being exhausted, he rose to depart. He stalked away with a solemn and deliberate pace. I resolved to tread, as closely as possible, in his footsteps, and not to lose sight of him till the termination of his career.

Contrary to my expectation, he went in a direction opposite to that which led to Inglefield's. Presently, he stopped at bars, which he cautiously removed, and, when he had passed through them, as deliberately replaced. He then proceeded along an obscure path, which led across stubble fields, to a wood. The path continued through the wood, but he quickly struck out of it, and made his way, seemingly at random, through a most perplexing undergrowth of bushes and briars.

I was, at first, fearful that the noise, which I made behind him, in trampling down the thicket, would alarm him; but he regarded it not. The way that he had selected, was always difficult; sometimes considerable force was requisite to beat down obstacles; sometimes, it led into a deep glen, the sides of which were so steep as scarcely to afford a footing; sometimes, into fens, from which some exertions were necessary to extricate the feet, and sometimes, through rivulets, of which the water rose to the middle.

For some time I felt no abatement of my speed or my resolution. I thought I might proceed, without fear, through breaks and dells, which my guide was able to penetrate. He was perpetually changing his direction. I could form no just opinion as to my situation or distance from the place at which we had set out.

I began at length to be weary. A suspicion, likewise, suggested itself to my mind, whether my guide did not perceive that he was followed, and thus prolonged his journey in order to fatigue or elude his pursuer. I was determined, however, to baffle his design. Though the air was frosty, my limbs were bedewed with sweat and my joints were relaxed with toil, but I was obstinately bent upon proceeding.

At length a new idea occurred to me. On finding me indefatigable in pursuit, this person might resort to more atrocious methods of concealment. But what had I to fear? It was sufficient to be upon my guard. Man to man, I needed not to dread his encounter.

We, at last, arrived at the verge of a considerable precipice. He kept along the edge. From this height, a dreary vale was discoverable, embarrassed with the leafless stocks of bushes, and encumbered with rugged and pointed rocks. This scene reminded me of my situation. The desert tract called Norwalk, which I have often mentioned to you, my curiosity had formerly induced me to traverse in various directions. It was in the highest degree, rugged, picturesque and wild. This vale, though I had never before viewed it by the glimpses of the moon, suggested the belief that I had visited it before. Such an one I knew belonged to this uncultivated region. If this opinion were true, we were at no inconsiderable distance from Inglefield's habitation. Where, said I, is this singular career to terminate?

Though occupied with these reflections, I did not slacken my pursuit. The stranger kept along the verge of the cliff, which gradually declined till it terminated in the valley. He then plunged into its deepest thickets. In a quarter of an hour he stopped under a projecture of the rock which formed the opposite side of the vale. He then proceeded to remove the stalks, which, as I immediately perceived, concealed the mouth of a cavern. He plunged into the darkness, and in a few moments, his steps were heard no more!

Hitherto my courage had supported me, but here it failed.

Was this person an assassin, who was acquainted with the windings of the grotto, and who would take advantage of the dark, to execute his vengeance upon me, who had dared to pursue him to these forlorn retreats; or was he maniac, or walker in his sleep? Whichever supposition were true, it would be rash in me to follow him. Besides, he could not long remain in these darksome recesses, unless some fatal accident should overtake him.

I seated myself at the mouth of the cave, determined patiently to wait till he should think proper to emerge. This opportunity of rest was exceedingly acceptable after so toilsome a pilgrimage. My pulse began to beat more slowly, and the moisture that incommoded me ceased to flow. The coolness which, for a little time, was delicious, presently increased to shivering, and I found it necessary to change my posture, in order to preserve my blood from congealing.

After I had formed a path before the cavern's mouth, by the removal of obstructions, I employed myself in walking to and fro. In this situation I saw the moon gradually decline to the horizon, and, at length, disappear. I marked the deepenings of the shade, and the mutations which every object successively underwent. The vale was narrow, and hemmed in on all sides by lofty and precipitous cliffs. The gloom deepened as the moon declined, and the faintness of star-light was all that preserved my senses from being useless to my own guidance.

I drew nearer the cleft at which this mysterious personage had entered. I stretched my hands before it, determined that he should not emerge from his den without my notice. His steps would, necessarily, communicate the tidings of his approach. They could not move without a noise which would be echoed to, on all sides, by the abruptnesses by which this valley was surrounded. Here, then, I continued till the day began to dawn, in momentary expectation of the stranger's reappearance.

My attention was at length excited by a sound that seemed to issue from the cave. I imagined that the sleeper was returning, and prepared therefore to seize him. I blamed myself for neglecting the opportunities that had already been afforded, and was determined that another should not escape.

My eyes were fixed upon the entrance. The rustling increased, and presently an animal leapt forth, of what kind I was unable to discover. Heart-struck by this disappointment, but not discouraged, I continued to watch, but in vain. The day was advancing apace. At length the sun arose, and its beams glistened on the edges of the cliffs above, whose sapless stalks and rugged masses were covered with hoar-frost. I began to despair of success, but was unwilling to depart, until it was no longer possible to hope for the return of this extraordinary personage. Whether he had been swallowed up by some of the abysses of this grotto, or lurked near the entrance, waiting my departure, or had made his exit at another and distant aperture, was unknown to me.

Exhausted and discouraged, I prepared, at length, to return. It was easy to find my way out of this wilderness by going forward in one direction, regardless of impediments and cross-paths. My absence I believed to have occasioned no alarm to my family, since they knew not of my intention to spend the night abroad. Thus unsatisfactorily terminated this night's adventures.

Chapter III

THE ENSUING DAY was spent, partly in sleep, and partly in languor and disquietude. I incessantly ruminated on the incidents of the last night. The scheme that I had formed was defeated. Was it likely that this unknown person would repeat his midnight visits to the Elm? If he did, and could again be discovered, should I resolve to undertake a new pursuit, which might terminate abortively, or in some signal disaster? But what proof had I that the same rout would be taken, and that he would again inter himself alive in the same spot? Or, if he did, since his reappearance would sufficiently prove that the cavern was not dangerous, and that he who should adventure in, might hope to come out again in safety, why not enter it after him? What could be the inducements of this person to betake himself to subterranean retreats? The basis of all this region is *limestone*; a substance that eminently abounds in rifts and cavities. These, by the gradual decay of their cementing parts, frequently make their appearance in spots where they might have been least expected. My attention has often been excited by the hollow sound which was produced by my casual footsteps, and which shewed me that I trod upon the roof of caverns. A mountain-cave and the rumbling of an unseen torrent, are appendages of this scene, dear to my youthful imagination. Many of romantic structure were found within the precincts of Norwalk.

These I had industriously sought out; but this had hitherto escaped my observation, and I formed the resolution of sometime exploring it. At present I determined to revisit the Elm, and dig in the spot where this person had been employed in a similar way. It might be that something was here deposited which might exhibit this transaction in a new light. At the suitable hour, on the ensuing night, I took my former stand. The person again appeared. My intention to dig was to be carried into effect on condition of his absence, and was, consequently, frustrated.

Instead of rushing on him, and breaking at once the spell by which his senses were bound, I concluded, contrary to my first design, to wait his departure, and allow myself to be conducted whithersoever he pleased. The track into which he now led me was different from the former one. It was a maze, oblique, circuitous, upward and downward, in a degree which only could take place in a region so remarkably irregular in surface, so abounding with hillocks and steeps, and pits and brooks as *Solebury*. It seemed to be the sole end of his labours to bewilder or fatigue his pursuer, to pierce into the deepest thickets, to plunge into the darkest cavities, to ascend the most difficult heights, and approach the slippery and tremulous verge of the dizziest precipices.

I disdained to be outstripped in this career. All dangers were overlooked, and all difficulties defied. I plunged into obscurities, and clambered over obstacles, from which, in a different state of mind, and with a different object of pursuit, I should have recoiled with invincible timidity. When the scene had passed, I could not review the perils I had undergone without shuddering.

At length my conductor struck into a path which, compared with the ruggedness of that which we had lately trodden, was easy and smooth. This track led us to the skirt of the wilderness, and at no long time we reached an open field, when a dwelling appeared, at a small distance, which I speedily recognized to be that belonging to Inglefield. I now anticipated the fulfilment of my predictions. My conductor directed his steps towards the barn, into which he entered by a small door.

How were my doubts removed! This was no other than Clithero Edny. There was nothing in his appearance incompatible with this conclusion. He and his fellow servant occupied an apartment in the barn as a lodging room. This arduous purpose was accomplished, and I retired to the shelter of a neighbouring shed, not so much to repose myself after the fatigues of my extraordinary journey, as to devise farther expedients.

Nothing now remained but to take Clithero to task; to repeat to him the observations of the two last nights; to unfold to him my conjectures and suspicions; to convince him of the rectitude of my intentions, and to extort from him a disclosure of all the circumstances connected with the death of Waldegrave, which it was in his power to communicate.

In order to obtain a conference, I resolved to invite him to my uncle's, to perform a certain piece of work for me under my own eyes. He would, of course, spend the night with us, and in the evening I would make an opportunity of entering into conversation with him.

A period of the deepest deliberation was necessary to qualify myself for performing suitably my part in this projected interview. I attended to the feelings that were suggested in this new state of my knowledge. I found reason to confide in my newly acquired equanimity. Remorse, said I, is an ample and proper expiation for all offences. What does vengeance desire but to inflict misery? If misery come, its desires are accomplished. It is only the obdurate and exulting criminal that is worthy of our indignation. It is common for pity to succeed the bitterest suggestions of resentment. If the vengeful mind be delighted with the spectacle of woes of its own contriving, at least its canine hunger is appeased, and thenceforth, its hands are inactive.

On the evening of the next day, I paid a visit to Inglefield. I wished to impart to him the discoveries that I had made, and to listen to his reflections on the subject. I likewise desired to obtain all possible information from the family respecting the conduct of Clithero.

My friend received me with his usual kindness. Thou art no stranger to his character; thou knowest with what paternal affection I have ever been regarded by this old man; with what solicitude the wanderings of my reason and my freaks of passion, have been noted and corrected by him. Thou knowest his activity to save the life of thy brother, and the hours that have been spent by him, in aiding my conjectures as to the cause of his death, and inculcating the lessons of penitence and duty.

The topics which could not but occur at such a meeting, were quickly discussed, and I hastily proceeded to that subject which was nearest my heart. I related the adventures of the two preceding nights, and mentioned the inference to which they irresistably led.

He said that this inference coincided with suspicions he had formed, since our last interview, in consequence of certain communications from his house-keeper. It seems the character of Clithero, had, from the first, exercised the inquisitiveness of this old lady. She had carefully marked his musing and melancholy deportment. She had tried innumerable expedients for obtaining a knowledge of his past life, and particularly of his motives for coming to America. These expedients, however profound and addressful, had failed. He took no pains to elude them. He contented himself with turning a deaf ear to all indirect allusions and hints, and, when more explicitly questioned, with simply declaring that he had nothing to communicate worthy of her notice.

During the day he was a sober and diligent workman. His evenings he spent in incommunicative silence. On sundays, he always rambled away, no one knew whither, and without a companion. I have already observed that he and his fellow servant occupied the same apartment in the barn. This circumstance was not unattended to by Miss Inglefield. The name of Clithero's companion was Ambrose. This man was copiously interrogated by his mistress, and she found him by no means so refractory as the other.

Ambrose, in his tedious and confused way, related that soon after Clithero and he had become bed-fellows, the former was considerably disturbed by restlessness and talking in his sleep. His discourse was incoherent. It was generally in the tone of expostulation, and appeared to be intreating to be saved from some great injury. Such phrases as these, "have pity"; "have mercy," were frequently intermingled with groans, and accompanied with weeping. Sometimes he seemed to be holding conferences with some one, who was making him considerable offers on condition of his performing some dangerous service. What he said, in his own person, and in answer to his imaginary tempter, testified the utmost reluctance.

Ambrose had no curiosity on the subject. As this interruption prevented him at first from sleeping, it was his custom to put an end to the dialogue, by awakening his companion, who betrayed tokens of great alarm and dejection. On discovering how he had been employed, he would solicitously inquire what were the words that he had uttered; but Ambrose's report was seldom satisfactory, because he had attended to them but little, and because he begrudged every moment in which he was deprived of his accustomed repose.

Whether Clithero had ceased from this practice, or habit had reconciled his companion to the sounds, they no longer occasioned any interruption to his slumber.

No one appeared more shocked than he at the death of Waldegrave. After this event his dejection suddenly increased. This symptom was observed by the family, but none but the house-keeper took the trouble to notice it to him, or build conjectures on the incident. During nights, however, Ambrose experienced a renewal of his ancient disturbances. He remarked that Clithero, one night, had disappeared from his side. Ambrose's range of reflection was extremely narrow. Quickly falling asleep, and finding his companion beside him when he awoke, he dismissed it from his mind.

On several ensuing nights he awakened in like manner, and always found his companion's place empty. The repetition of so strange an incident at length incited him to mention it to Clithero. The latter was confounded at this intelligence. He questioned Ambrose with great anxiety as to the particulars of this event, but he could gain no satisfaction from the stupid inattention of the other. From this time there was a visible augmentation of his sadness. His fits of taciturnity became more obstinate, and a deeper gloom sat upon his brow.

There was one other circumstance, of particular importance, mentioned by the house-keeper. One evening some one on horseback, stopped at this gate. He rattled at the gate, with an air of authority, in token of his desire that some one would come from the house. Miss Inglefield was employed in the kitchen, from a window of which she perceived who it was that made the signal. Clithero happened, at the same moment, to be employed near her. She, therefore, desired him to go and see whom the stranger wanted. He laid aside his work and went. The conference lasted above five minutes. The length of it excited in her a faint degree of surprise, inducing her to leave her employment, and pay an unintermitted attention to the scene. There was nothing, however, but its duration that rendered it remarkable.

Clithero at length entered, and the traveller proceeded. The countenance of the former betrayed a degree of perturbation which she had never witnessed before. The muscles of his face was distorted and tremulous. He immediately sat down to his work, but he seemed, for some time, to have lost all power over his limbs. He struggled to avoid the sight of the lady, and his gestures, irresolute, or misdirected, betokened the deepest dismay. After some time, he recovered, in some degree, his self-possession; but, while the object was viewed through a new medium, and the change existed only in the imagination of the observer, a change was certainly discovered.

These circumstances were related to me by Inglefield and corroborated by his house-keeper. One consequence inevitably flowed from them. The sleep-walker, he who had led me through so devious a tract, was no other than Clithero. There was, likewise, a strong relation between this person and him who stopped at the gate. What was the subject of discourse between them? In answer to Miss Inglefield's interrogatories, he merely said that the traveller inquired whither the road led, which at a small distance forward, struck out of the principal one. Considering the length of the interview it was not likely that this was the only topic.

My determination to confer with him in private acquired new force from these reflections. Inglefield assented to my proposal. His own affairs would permit the absence of his servant for one day. I saw no necessity for delay, and immediately made my request to Clithero. I was fashioning an implement, I told him, with respect to which I could not wholly depend upon my own skill. I was acquainted with the dexterity of his contrivances, and the neatness of his workmanship. He readily consented to assist me on this occasion. Next day he came. Contrary to my expectation, he prepared to return home in the evening. I urged him to spend the night with us; but no: It was equally convenient, and more agreeable to him, to return.

I was not aware of this resolution. I might, indeed, have foreseen, that, being conscious of his infirmity, he would desire to avoid the scrutiny of strangers. I was painfully disconcerted, but it occurred to me, that the best that could be done, was to bear him company, and seize some opportunity, during this interval, of effecting my purpose. I told him, that since he would not remain, I cared not if, for the sake of recreation, and of a much more momentous purpose, I went along with him. He tacitly, and without apparent reluctance, consented to my scheme, and accordingly, we set off together. This was an awful crisis. The time had now come, that was to dissipate my uncertainty. By what means should I introduce a topic so momentous and singular? I had been qualified by no experience for rightly conducting myself on so critical an emergency. My companion preserved a mournful and inviolable silence. He afforded me no opening, by which I might reach the point in view. His demeanour was sedate, while I was almost disabled, by the confusion of my thoughts, to utter a word.

It was a dreadful charge that I was about to insinuate. I was to accuse my companion of nothing less than murder. I was to call upon him for an avowal of his guilt. I was to state the grounds of my suspicions, and desire him to confute, or confirm them. In doing this, I was principally stimulated by an ungovernable curiosity; yet, if I intended not the conferring of a benefit, I did not, at least, purpose the infliction of evil. I persuaded myself, that I was able to exclude from my bosom, all sanguinary or vengeful impulses; and that, whatever should be the issue of this conversation, my equanimity would be unsubdued.

I revolved various modes of introducing the topic, by which my mind was engaged. I passed rapidly from one to another. None of them were sufficiently free from objection, to allow me to adopt it. My perplexity became, every moment, more painful, and my ability to extricate myself, less.

In this state of uncertainty, so much time elapsed, that the Elm at length appeared in sight. This object had somewhat of a mechanical influence upon me. I stopped short, and seized the arm of my companion. Till this moment, he appeared to have been engrossed by his own reflections, and not to have heeded those emotions, which must have been sufficiently conspicuous in my looks.

This action recalled him from his reverie. The first idea that occurred to him, when he had noticed my behaviour, was, that I was assailed by some sudden indisposition.

What is the matter, said he, in a tone of anxiety: Are you not well?

Yes, replied I, perfectly well; but stop a moment; I have something to say to you.

To me? answered he, with surprise.

Yes, said I, let us turn down this path, pointing at the same time, to that along which I had followed him the preceding night.

He now partook, in some degree, of my embarrassment.

Is there any thing particular? said he, in a doubting accent. There he stopped.

Something, I answered, of the highest moment. Go with me down this path. We shall be in less danger of interruption.

He was irresolute and silent, but seeing me remove the bars and pass through them, he followed me. Nothing more was said till we entered the wood. I trusted to the suggestions of the moment. I had now gone too far to recede, and the necessity that pressed upon me, supplied me with words. I continued.

This is a remarkable spot. You may wonder why I have led you to it. I ought not to keep you in suspence. There is a tale connected with it, which I am desirous of telling you. For this purpose I have brought you hither. Listen to me.

I then recapitulated the adventures of the two preceding nights. I added nothing, nor retrenched any thing. He listened in the deepest silence. From every incident, he gathered new cause of alarm. Repeatedly he wiped his face with his handkerchief, and sighed deeply. I took no verbal notice of these symptoms. I deemed it incumbent on me to repress nothing. When I came to the concluding circumstance, by which his person was identified, he heard me, without any new surprise. To this narrative, I subjoined the inquiries that I had made at Inglefield's, and the result of those inquiries. I then continued in these words.

You may ask why I subjected myself to all this trouble? The mysteriousness of these transactions would have naturally suggested curiosity in any one. A transient passenger would probably have acted as I have done. But I had motives peculiar to myself. Need I remind you of a late disaster? That it happened beneath the shade of this tree? Am I not justified in drawing certain inferences from your behaviour? What they are, I leave you to judge. Be it your task, to confute, or confirm them. For this end I have conducted you hither.

My suspicions are vehement. How can they be otherwise? I call upon you to say whether they be just.

The spot where we stood was illuminated by the moon, that had now risen, though all around was dark. Hence his features and person were easily distinguished. His hands hung at his side. His eyes were downcast, and he was motionless as a statue. My last words seemed scarcely to have made any impression on his sense. I had no need to provide against the possible suggestions of revenge. I felt nothing but the tenderness of compassion. I continued, for some time, to observe him in silence, and could discover no tokens of a change of mood. I could not forbear, at last, to express my uneasiness at the fixedness of his features and attitude.

Recollect yourself. I mean not to urge you too closely. This topic is solemn, but it need not divest you of the fortitude becoming a man.

The sound of my voice startled him. He broke from me, looked up, and fixed his eyes upon me with an expression of affright. He shuddered and recoiled as from a spectre. I began to repent of my experiment. I could say nothing suitable to this occasion. I was obliged to stand a silent and powerless spectator, and to suffer this paroxysm to subside of itself. When its violence appeared to be somewhat abated, I resumed.

I can feel for you. I act not thus, in compliance with a temper that delights in the misery of others. The explanation that I have solicited is no less necessary for your sake than for mine. You are no stranger to the light in which I viewed this man. You have witnessed the grief which his fate occasioned, and the efforts that I made to discover, and drag to punishment his murderer. You heard the execrations that I heaped upon him, and my vows of eternal revenge. You expect that, having detected the offender, I will hunt him to infamy and death. You are mistaken. I consider the deed as sufficiently expiated.

I am no stranger to your gnawing cares. To the deep and incurable despair that haunts you, to which your waking thoughts are a prey, and from which sleep cannot secure you.

I know the enormity of your crime, but I know not your inducements. Whatever they were, I see the consequences with regard to yourself. I see proofs of that remorse which must ever be attendant on guilt.

This is enough. Why should the effects of our misdeeds be inexhaustible? Why should we be debarred from a comforter? An opportunity of repairing our errors may, at least, be demanded from the rulers of our destiny.

I once imagined, that he who killed Waldegrave inflicted the greatest possible injury on me. That was an error, which reflection has cured. Were futurity laid open to my view, and events, with their consequences unfolded, I might see reason to embrace the assassin as my best friend. Be comforted.

He was still incapable of speaking; but tears came to his relief. Without attending to my remonstrances, he betrayed a disposition to return. I had, hitherto, hoped for some disclosure, but now feared that it was designed to be withheld. He stopped not till we reached Inglefield's piazza. He then spoke, for the first time, but in an hollow and tremulous voice.

You demand of me a confession of crimes. You shall have it. Some time you shall have it. When it will be, I cannot tell. Something must be done, and shortly.

He hurried from me into the house, and after a pause, I turned my steps homewards. My reflections, as I proceeded, perpetually revolved round a single point. These were scarcely more than a repetition, with slight variations, of a single idea.

When I awoke in the morning, I hied, in fancy, to the wilderness. I saw nothing but the figure of the wanderer before me. I traced his footsteps anew, retold my narrative, and pondered on his gestures and words. My condition was not destitute of enjoyment. My stormy passions had subsided into a calm, portentous and awful. My soul was big with expectation. I seemed as if I were on the eve of being ushered into a world, whose scenes were tremendous, but sublime. The suggestions of sorrow and malice had, for a time, taken their flight, and yielded place to a generous sympathy, which filled my eyes with tears, but had more in it of pleasure than of pain. That Clithero was instrumental to the death of Waldegrave, that he could furnish the clue, explanatory of every bloody and mysterious event, that had hitherto occurred, there was no longer the possibility of doubting. He, indeed, said I, is the murderer of excellence, and yet it shall be my province to emulate a father's clemency, and restore this unhappy man to purity, and to peace.

Day after day passed, without hearing any thing of Clithero. I began to grow uneasy and impatient. I had gained so much, and by means so unexpected, that I could more easily endure uncertainty, with respect to what remained to be known. But my patience had its limits. I should, doubtless, have made use of new means to accelerate this discovery, had not his timely appearance made them superfluous.

Sunday being at length arrived, I resolved to go to Ingle-field's, seek an interview with his servant, and urge him, by new importunities, to confide to me the secret. On my way thither, Clithero appeared in sight. His visage was pale and wan, and his form emaciated and shrunk. I was astonished at the alteration, which the lapse of a week had made in his appearance. At a small distance I mistook him for a stranger. As soon as I perceived who it was, I greeted him with the utmost friendliness. My civilities made little impression on him, and he hastened to inform me, that he was coming to my uncle's, for the purpose of meeting and talking with me. If I thought proper, we would go into the wood together: and find some spot, where we might discourse at our leisure, and be exempt from interruption.

You will easily conceive with what alacrity I accepted his invitation. We turned from the road into the first path, and proceeded in silence, till the wildness of the surrounding scenery informed us, that we were in the heart of Norwalk. We lighted on a recess, to which my companion appeared to be familiar, and which had all the advantages of solitude, and was suitable to rest. Here we stopped. Hitherto my companion had displayed a certain degree of composure. Now his countenance betokened a violent internal struggle. It was a considerable time before he could command his speech. When he had so far effected the conquest of his feelings, he began.

Chapter IV

YOU CALL upon me for a confession of my offences. What a strange fortune is mine! That an human being, in the present circumstances, should make this demand, and that I should be driven, by an irresistible necessity to comply with it! That here should terminate my calamitous series! That my destiny should call upon me to lie down and die, in a region so remote from the scene of my crimes; at a distance, so great, from all that witnessed and endured their consequences!

You believe me to be an assassin. You require me to explain the motives that induced me to murder the innocent. While this is your belief, and this the scope of your expectations, you may be sure of my compliance. I could resist every demand but this.

For what purpose have I come hither? Is it to relate my story? Shall I calmly sit here, and rehearse the incidents of my life? Will my strength be adequate to this rehearsal? Let me recollect the motives that governed me, when I formed this design. Perhaps, a strenuousness may be imparted by them, which, otherwise, I cannot hope to obtain. For the sake of those, I consent to conjure up the ghost of the past, and to begin a tale that, with a fortitude like mine, I am not sure that I shall live to finish.

You are unacquainted with the man before you. The inferences which you have drawn, with regard to my designs, and my conduct, are a tissue of destructive errors. You, like others, are blind to the most momentous consequences of your own actions. You talk of imparting consolation. You boast the benificence of your intentions. You set yourself to do me a benefit. What are the effects of your misguided zeal, and random efforts? They have brought my life to a miserable close. They have shrouded the last scene of it in blood. They have put the seal to my perdition.

My misery has been greater than has fallen to the lot of mortals. Yet it is but beginning. My present path, full as it is of asperities, is better than that into which I must enter, when this is abandoned. Perhaps, if my pilgrimage had been longer,

I might, at some future day, have lighted upon hope. In consequence of your interference, I am forever debarred from it. My existence is henceforward to be invariable. The woes that are reserved for me, are incapable alike of alleviation or intermission.

But I came not hither to recriminate. I came not hither to accuse others but myself. I know the retribution that is appointed for guilt like mine. It is just. I may shudder at the foresight of my punishment and shrink in the endurance of it; but I shall be indebted for part of my torment to the vigour of my understanding, which teaches me that my punishment is just. Why should I procrastinate my doom and strive to render my burthen more light? It is but just that it should crush me. Its procrastination is impossible. The stroke is already felt. Even now I drink of the cup of retribution. A change of being cannot aggravate my woe. Till consciousness itself be extinct, the worm that gnaws me will never perish.

Fain would I be relieved from this task. Gladly would I bury in oblivion the transactions of my life: but no. My fate is uniform. The dæmon that controuled me at first is still in the fruition of power. I am entangled in his fold, and every effort that I make to escape only involves me in deeper ruin. I need not conceal, for all the consequences of disclosure are already experienced. I cannot endure a groundless imputation, though to free me from it, I must create and justify imputations still more atrocious. My story may at least be brief. If the agonies of remembrance must be awakened afresh, let me do all that in me lies to shorten them.

I was born in the county of Armagh. My parents were of the better sort of peasants, and were able to provide me with the rudiments of knowledge. I should doubtless have trodden in their footsteps, and have spent my life in the cultivation of their scanty fields, if an event had not happened, which, for a long time, I regarded as the most fortunate of my life; but which I now regard as the scheme of some infernal agent and as the primary source of all my calamities.

My father's farm was a portion of the demesne of one who resided wholly in the metropolis, and consigned the management of his estates to his stewards and retainers. This person married a lady, who brought him great accession of fortune.

Her wealth was her only recommendation in the eyes of her husband, whose understanding was depraved by the prejudices of luxury and rank, but was the least of her attractions in the estimate of reasonable beings.

They passed some years together. If their union were not a source of misery to the lady, she was indebted for her tranquility to the force of her mind. She was, indeed, governed, in every action of her life by the precepts of duty, while her husband listened to no calls but those of pernicious dissipation. He was immersed in all the vices that grow out of opulence and a mistaken education.

Happily for his wife his career was short. He was enraged at the infidelity of his mistress, to purchase whose attachment, he had lavished two thirds of his fortune. He called the paramour, by whom he had been supplanted, to the field. The contest was obstinate, and terminated in the death of the challenger.

This event freed the lady from many distressful and humiliating obligations. She determined to profit by her newly acquired independence, to live thenceforward conformable to her notions of right, to preserve and improve, by schemes of economy, the remains of her fortune, and to employ it in the diffusion of good. Her plans made it necessary to visit her estates in the distant provinces.

During her abode in the manor of which my father was a vassal, she visited his cottage. I was at that time a child. She was pleased with my vivacity and promptitude, and determined to take me under her own protection. My parents joyfully acceded to her proposal, and I returned with her to the capital.

She had an only son of my own age. Her design, in relation to me, was, that I should be educated with her child, and that an affection, in this way, might be excited in me towards my young master, which might render me, when we should attain to manhood, one of his most faithful and intelligent dependents. I enjoyed, equally with him, all the essential benefits of education. There were certain accomplishments, from which I was excluded, from the belief that they were unsuitable to my rank and station. I was permitted to acquire others, which, had she been actuated by true discernment, she would, perhaps, have discovered to be far more incompatible with a servile station. In proportion as my views were refined and enlarged by history and science, I was likely to contract a thirst of independence, and an impatience of subjection and poverty.

When the period of childhood and youth was past, it was thought proper to send her son, to improve his knowledge and manners, by a residence on the continent. This young man was endowed with splendid abilities. His errors were the growth of his condition. All the expedients that maternal solicitude and wisdom could suggest, were employed to render him an useful citizen. Perhaps this wisdom was attested by the large share of excellence which he really possessed; and, that his character was not unblemished, proved only, that no exertions could preserve him from the vices that are inherent in wealth and rank, and which flow from the spectacle of universal depravity.

As to me, it would be folly to deny, that I had benefited by my opportunities of improvement. I fulfilled the expectation of my mistress, in one respect. I was deeply imbued with affection for her son, and reverence for herself. Perhaps the force of education was evinced in those particulars, without reflecting any credit on the directors of it. Those might merit the name of defects, which were regarded by them as accomplishments. My unfavorable qualities, like those of my master, were imputed to my condition, though, perhaps, the difference was advantageous to me, since the vices of servitude are less hateful than those of tyranny.

It was resolved that I should accompany my master in his travels, in quality of favourite domestic. My principles, whatever might be their rectitude, were harmonious and flexible. I had devoted my life to the service of my patron. I had formed conceptions of what was really conducive to his interest, and was not to be misled by specious appearances. If my affection had not stimulated my diligence, I should have found sufficient motives in the behaviour of his mother. She condescended to express her reliance on my integrity and judgment. She was not ashamed to manifest, at parting, the tenderness of a mother, and to acknowledge that, all her tears were not shed on her son's account. I had my part in the regrets that called them forth.

During our absence, I was my master's constant attendant. I corresponded with his mother, and made the conduct of her son the principal theme of my letters. I deemed it my privilege, as well as duty, to sit in judgment on his actions, to form my opinions without regard to selfish considerations, and to avow them whenever the avowal tended to benefit. Every letter which I wrote, particularly those in which his behaviour was freely criticised, I allowed him to peruse. I would, on no account, connive at, or participate in the slightest irregularity. I knew the duty of my station, and assumed no other controul than that which resulted from the avoiding of deceit, and the open expression of my sentiments. The youth was of a noble spirit, but his firmness was wavering. He yielded to temptations which a censor less rigorous than I would have regarded as venial, or, perhaps laudable. My duty required me to set before him the consequences of his actions, and to give impartial and timely information to his mother.

He could not brook a monitor. The more he needed reproof, the less supportable it became. My company became every day less agreeable, till at length, there appeared a necessity of parting. A seperation took place, but not as enemies. I never lost his respect. In his representations to his mother, he was just to my character and services. My dismission was not allowed to injure my fortune, and his mother considered this event merely as a new proof of the inflexible consistency of my principles.

On this change in my situation, she proposed to me to become a member of her own family. No proposal could be more acceptable. I was fully acquainted with the character of this lady, and had nothing to fear from injustice and caprice. I did not regard her with filial familiarity, but my attachment and reverence would have done honour to that relation. I performed for her the functions of a steward. Her estates in the city were put under my direction. She placed boundless confidence in my discretion and integrity, and consigned to me the payment, and in some degree, the selection and government of her servants. My station was a servile one, yet most of the evils of servitude were unknown to me. My personal ease and independence were less infringed than that of those who are accounted the freest members of society. I derived a

sort of authority and dignity from the receipt and disburse-
ment of money. The tenants and debtors of the lady were, in
some respects, mine. It was, for the most part, on my justice
and lenity that they depended for their treatment. My lady's
household establishment was large and opulent. Her servants
were my inferiors and menials. My leisure was considerable,
and my emoluments large enough to supply me with every
valuable instrument of improvement or pleasure.

These were reasons why I should be contented with my lot.
These circumstances alone would have rendered it more eligible than any other, but it had additional, and far more powerful recommendations, arising from the character of Mrs.
Lorimer, and from the relation in which she allowed me to
stand to her.

How shall I enter upon this theme? How shall I expatiate
upon excellencies, which it was my fate to view in their genuine colours, to adore with an immeasurable and inextinguish-
able ardour, and which, nevertheless, it was my hateful task
to blast and destroy? Yet I will not be spared. I shall find in
the rehearsal, new incitements to sorrow. I deserve to be supreme in misery, and will not be denied the full measure of a
bitter retribution.

No one was better qualified to judge of her excellencies. A
casual spectator might admire her beauty, and the dignity of
her demeanour. From the contemplation of those, he might
gather motives for loving or revering her. Age was far from
having withered her complexion, or destroyed the evenness of
her skin; but no time could rob her of the sweetness and
intelligence which animated her features. Her habitual beneficence was bespoken in every look. Always in search of occasions for doing good, always meditating scenes of happiness,
of which she was the author, or of distress, for which she was
preparing relief, the most torpid insensibility was, for a time,
subdued, and the most depraved smitten by charms, of which,
in another person, they would not perhaps have been sensible.

A casual visitant might enjoy her conversation, might applaud the rectitude of her sentiments, the richness of her elocution, and her skill in all the offices of politeness. But it was
only for him, who dwelt constantly under the same roof, to
mark the inviolable consistency of her actions and opinions,

the ceaseless flow of her candour, her cheerfulness, and her benevolence. It was only for one who witnessed her behaviour at all hours, in sickness and in health, her management of that great instrument of evil and good, money, her treatment of her son, her menials, and her kindred, rightly to estimate her merits.

The intercourse between us was frequent, but of a peculiar kind. My office in her family required me often to see her, to submit schemes to her considerations, and receive her directions. At these times she treated me in a manner, in some degree, adapted to the difference of rank, and the inferiority of my station, and yet widely dissimilar from that, which a different person would have adopted, in the same circumstances. The treatment was not that of an equal and a friend, but still more remote was it from that of a mistress. It was merely characterised by affability and condescention, but as such it had no limits.

She made no scruple to ask my council in every pecuniary affair, to listen to my arguments, and decide conformably to what, after sufficient canvassings and discussions, should appear to be right. When the direct occasions of our interview were dismissed, I did not of course withdraw. To detain or dismiss me was indeed at her option, but, if no engagement interfered, she would enter into general conversation. There was none who could with more safety to herself have made the world her confessor; but the state of society in which she lived, imposed certain limitations on her candour. In her intercourse with me there were fewer restraints than on any other occasion. My situation had made me more intimately acquainted with domestic transactions, with her views respecting her son, and with the terms on which she thought proper to stand with those whom old acquaintance or kindred gave some title to her good offices. In addition to all those motives to a candid treatment of me, there were others which owed their efficacy to her maternal regard for me, and to the artless and unsuspecting generosity of her character.

Her hours were distributed with the utmost regularity, and appropriated to the best purposes. She selected her society without regard to any qualities but probity and talents. Her associates were numerous, and her evening conversations embellished with all that could charm the senses or instruct the understanding. This was a chosen field for the display of her magnificence, but her grandeur was unostentatious, and her gravity unmingled with hautiness. From these my station excluded me, but I was compensated by the freedom of her communications in the intervals. She found pleasure in detailing to me the incidents that passed on those occasions, in rehearsing conversations and depicting characters. There was an uncommon portion of dramatic merit in her recitals, besides valuable and curious information. One uniform effect was produced in me by this behaviour. Each day, I thought it impossible for my attachment to receive any new accessions, yet the morrow was sure to produce some new emotion of respect or of gratitude, and to set the unrivalled accomplishments of this lady in a new and more favourable point of view. I contemplated no change in my condition. The necessity of change, whatever were the alternative, would have been a subject of piercing regret. I deemed my life a cheap sacrifice in her cause. No time would suffice to discharge the debt of gratitude that was due to her. Yet it was continually accumulating. If an anxious thought ever invaded my bosom it arose from this source.

It was no difficult task faithfully to execute the functions assigned to me. No merit could accrue to me from this source. I was exposed to no temptation. I had passed the feverish period of youth. No contagious example had contaminated my principles. I had resisted the allurements of sensuality and dissipation incident to my age. My dwelling was in pomp and splendour. I had amassed sufficient to secure me, in case of unforeseen accidents, in the enjoyment of competence. My mental resources were not despicable, and the external means of intellectual gratification were boundless. I enjoyed an unsullied reputation. My character was well known in that sphere which my lady occupied, not only by means of her favourable report, but in numberless ways in which it was my fortune to perform personal services to others.

Chapter V

MRS. LORIMER had a twin brother. Nature had impressed the same image upon them, and had modelled them after the same pattern. The resemblance between them was exact to a degree almost incredible. In infancy and childhood they were perpetually liable to be mistaken for each other. As they grew up nothing to a superficial examination appeared to distinguish them but the sexual characteristics. A sagacious observer would, doubtless, have noted the most essential differences. In all those modifications of the features which are produced by habits and sentiments, no two persons were less alike. Nature seemed to have intended them as examples of the futility of those theories, which ascribe every thing to conformation and instinct, and nothing to external circumstances; in what different modes the same materials may be fashioned, and to what different purposes the same materials may be applied. Perhaps the rudiments of their intellectual character as well as of their form, were the same; but the powers, that in one case, were exerted in the cause of virtue, were, in the other, misapplied to sordid and flagitious purposes.

Arthur Wiatte, that was his name, had ever been the object of his sister's affection. As long as he existed she never ceased to labour in the promotion of his happiness. All her kindness was repaid by a stern and inexorable hatred. This man was an exception to all the rules which govern us in our judgments of human nature. He exceeded in depravity all that has been imputed to the arch-foe of mankind. His wickedness was without any of those remorseful intermissions from which it has been supposed that the deepest guilt is not entirely exempt. He seemed to relish no food but pure unadulterated evil. He rejoiced in proportion to the depth of that distress of which he was the author.

His sister, by being placed most within the reach of his enmity, experienced its worst effects. She was the subject on which, by being acquainted with the means of influencing her happiness, he could try his malignant experiments with most hope of success. Her parents being high in rank and wealth, the marriage of their daughter was, of course, an object of anxious attention. There is no event on which our felicity and usefulness more materially depends, and with regard to which, therefore, the freedom of choice and the exercise of our own understanding ought to be less infringed, but this maxim is commonly disregarded in proportion to the elevation of our rank and extent of our property.

The lady made her own election, but she was one of those who acted on a comprehensive plan, and would not admit her private inclination to dictate her decision. The happiness of others, though founded on mistaken views, she did not consider as unworthy of her regard. The choice was such as was not likely to obtain the parental sanction, to whom the moral qualities of their son-in-law, though not absolutely weightless in the balance, were greatly inferior to the considerations of wealth and dignity.

The brother set no value on any thing but the means of luxury and power. He was astonished at that perverseness which entertained a different conception of happiness from himself. Love and friendship he considered as groundless and chimerical, and believed that those delusions, would, in people of sense, be rectified by experience; but he knew the obstinacy of his sister's attachment to these phantoms, and that to bereave her of the good they promised was the most effectual means of rendering her miserable. For this end he set himself to thwart her wishes. In the imbecility and false indulgence of his parents he found his most powerful auxiliaries. He prevailed upon them to forbid that union which wanted nothing but their concurrence, and their consent to endow her with a small portion of their patrimony to render completely eligible. The cause was that of her happiness and the happiness of him on whom she had bestowed her heart. It behoved her, therefore, to call forth all her energies in defence of it, to weaken her brother's influence on the minds of her parents, or to win him to be her advocate. When I reflect upon her mental powers, and the advantages which should seem to flow from the circumstance of pleading in the character of daughter and sister, I can scarcely believe that her attempts miscarried. I should have imagined that all obstacles would yield before her, and particularly in a case like this, in which she must have summoned all her forces, and never have believed that she had struggled sufficiently.

Certain it is that her lot was fixed. She was not only denied the husband of her choice, but another was imposed upon her, whose recommendations were irresistible in every one's apprehension but her own. The discarded lover was treated with every sort of contumely. Deceit and violence were employed by her brother to bring his honour, his liberty, and even his life into hazard. All these iniquities produced no considerable effect on the mind of the lady. The machinations to which her love was exposed, would have exasperated him into madness, had not her most strenuous exertions been directed to appease him.

She prevailed on him at length to abandon his country, though she thereby merely turned her brother's depravity into a new channel. Her parents died without consciousness of the evils they inflicted, but they experienced a bitter retribution in the conduct of their son. He was the darling and stay of an ancient and illustrious house, but his actions reflected nothing but disgrace upon his ancestry, and threatened to bring the honours of their line to a period in his person. At their death the bulk of their patrimony devolved upon him. This he speedily consumed in gaming and riot. From splendid, he descended to meaner vices. The efforts of his sister to recall him to virtue were unintermitted and fruitless. Her affection for him he converted into a means of prolonging his selfish gratifications. She decided for the best. It was no argument of weakness that she was so frequently deceived. If she had judged truly of her brother, she would have judged not only without example, but in opposition to the general experience of mankind. But she was not to be forever deceived. Her tenderness was subservient to justice. And when his vices had led him from the gaming table to the highway, when seized at length by the ministers of law, when convicted and sentenced to transportation, her intercession was solicited, when all the world knew that pardon would readily be granted to a supplicant of her rank, fortune, and character, when the criminal himself, his kindred, his friends, and even indifferent persons implored her interference, her justice was inflexible: She knew full well the incurableness of his depravity; that banishment was the mildest destiny that would befall him; that estrangement from ancient haunts and associates was the condition from which his true friends had least to fear.

Finding intreaties unavailing, the wretch delivered himself to the suggestions of his malice, and he vowed to be bloodily revenged on her inflexibility. The sentence was executed. That character must indeed be monstrous from which the execution of such threats was to be dreaded. The event sufficiently shewed that our fears on this head were well grounded. This event, however, was at a great distance. It was reported that the fellons, of whom he was one, mutinied on board the ship in which they had been embarked. In the affray that succeeded it was said that he was killed.

Among the nefarious deeds which he perpetrated was to be numbered the seduction of a young lady, whose heart was broken by the detection of his perfidy. The fruit of this unhappy union was a daughter. Her mother died shortly after her birth. Her father was careless of her destiny. She was consigned to the care of an hireling, who, happily for the innocent victim, performed the maternal offices for her own sake, and did not allow the want of a stipulated recompence to render her cruel or neglectful.

This orphan was sought out by the benevolence of Mrs. Lorimer and placed under her own protection. She received from her the treatment of a mother. The ties of kindred, corroborated by habit, was not the only thing that united them. That resemblance to herself, which had been so deplorably defective in her brother, was completely realized in his offspring. Nature seemed to have precluded every difference between them but that of age. This darling object excited in her bosom more than maternal sympathies. Her soul clung to the happiness of her *Clarice*, with more ardour than to that of her own son. The latter was not only less worthy of affection, but their separation necessarily diminished their mutual confidence.

It was natural for her to look forward to the future destiny of *Clarice*. On these occasions she could not help contemplating the possibility of a union between her son and niece. Considerable advantages belonged to this scheme, yet it was the subject of hope rather than the scope of a project. The contingencies were numerous and delicate on which the ultimate desirableness of this union depended. She was far from certain that her son would be worthy of this benefit, or that, if he were worthy, his propensities would not select for themselves a different object. It was equally dubious whether the young lady would not think proper otherwise to dispose of her affections. These uncertainties could be dissipated only by time. Meanwhile she was chiefly solicitous to render them virtuous and wise.

As they advanced in years, the hopes that she had formed were annihilated. The youth was not exempt from egregious errors. In addition to this, it was manifest that the young people were disposed to regard each other in no other light than that of brother and sister. I was not unapprised of her views. I saw that their union was impossible. I was near enough to judge of the character of Clarice. My youth and intellectual constitution made me peculiarly susceptible to female charms. I was her play-fellow in childhood, and her associate in studies and amusements at a maturer age. This situation might have been suspected of a dangerous tendency. This tendency, however, was obviated by motives of which I was, for a long time, scarcely conscious.

I was habituated to consider the distinctions of rank as indelible. The obstructions that existed, to any wish that I might form, were like those of time and space, and as, in their own nature, insuperable.

Such was the state of things previous to our setting out upon our travels. Clarice was indirectly included in our correspondence. My letters were open to her inspection, and I was sometimes honoured with a few complimentary lines under her own hand. On returning to my ancient abode, I was once more exposed to those sinister influences which absence had, at least, suspended. Various suitors had, meanwhile, been rejected. Their character, for the most part, had been such as to account for her refusal, without resorting to the supposition of a lurking or unavowed attachment.

On our meeting she greeted me in a respectful but dignified manner. Observers could discover in it nothing not corresponding to that difference of fortune which subsisted between us. If her joy, on that occasion, had in it some portion of tenderness, the softness of her temper, and the peculiar circumstances in which we had been placed, being considered, the most rigid censor could find no occasion for blame or suspicion.

A year passed away, but not without my attention being solicited by something new and inexplicable in my own sensations. At first I was not aware of their true cause; but the gradual progress of my feelings left me not long in doubt as to their origin. I was alarmed at the discovery, but my courage did not suddenly desert me. My hopes seemed to be extinguished the moment that I distinctly perceived the point to which they led. My mind had undergone a change. The ideas with which it was fraught were varied. The sight, or recollection of Clarice, was sure to occasion my mind to advert to the recent discovery, and to revolve the considerations naturally connected with it. Some latent glows and secret trepidations were likewise experienced, when, by some accident, our meetings were abrupt or our interviews unwitnessed; yet my usual tranquility was not as yet sensibly diminished. I could bear to think of her marriage with another without painful emotions, and was anxious only that her choice should be judicious and fortunate.

My thoughts could not long continue in this state. They gradually became more ardent and museful. The image of Clarice occurred with unseasonable frequency. Its charms were enhanced by some nameless and indefinable additions. When it met me in the way I was irresistibly disposed to stop and survey it with particular attention. The pathetic cast of her features, the deep glow of her cheek, and some catch of melting music, she had lately breathed, stole incessantly upon my fancy. On recovering from my thoughtful moods, I sometimes found my cheeks wet with tears, that had fallen unperceived, and my bosom heaved with involuntary sighs.

These images did not content themselves with invading my wakeful hours; but, likewise, incroached upon my sleep. I could no longer resign myself to slumber with the same ease as before. When I slept, my visions were of the same impassioned tenor.

There was no difficulty in judging rightly of my situation. I knew what it was that duty exacted from me. To remain in my present situation was a chimerical project. That time and reflection would suffice to restore me to myself was a notion equally falacious. Yet I felt an insupportable reluctance to change it. This reluctance was owing, not wholly or chiefly to my growing passion, but to the attachment which bound me to the service of my lady. All my contemplations had hitherto been modelled on the belief of my remaining in my present situation during my life. My mildest anticipations had never fashioned an event like this. Any misfortune was light in comparison with that which tore me from her presence and service. But should I ultimately resolve to separate, how should I communicate my purpose? The pain of parting would scarcely be less on her side than on mine. Could I consent to be the author of disquietude to her? I had consecrated all my faculties to her service. This was the recompence which it was in my power to make for the benefits that I had received. Would not this procedure bear the appearance of the basest ingratitude? The shaddow of an imputation like this was more excruciating than the rack.

What motive could I assign for my conduct? The truth must not be told. This would be equivalent to supplicating for a new benefit. It would more become me to lessen than increase my obligations. Among all my imaginations on this subject, the possibility of a mutual passion never occurred to me. I could not be blind to the essential distinctions that subsist among men. I could expatiate, like others, on the futility of ribbonds and titles, and on the dignity that was annexed to skill and virtue; but these, for the most part, were the incoherences of speculation, and in no degree influenced the stream of my actions, and practical sentiments. The barrier that existed in the present case, I deemed insurmountable. This was not even the subject of doubt. In disclosing the truth, I should be conceived to be soliciting my lady's mercy and intercession; but this would be the madness of presumption. Let me impress her with any other opinion than that I go in search of the happiness that I have lost under her roof. Let me save her generous heart from the pangs which this persuasion would infallibly produce.

I could form no stable resolutions. I seemed unalterably convinced of the necessity of separation, and yet could not execute my design. When I had wrought up my mind to the intention of explaining myself on the next interview, when the next interview took place my tongue was powerless. I admitted any excuse for postponing my design, and gladly admitted any topic, however foreign to my purpose.

It must not be imagined that my health sustained no injury from this conflict of my passions. My patroness perceived this alteration. She inquired with the most affectionate solicitude, into the cause. It could not be explained. I could safely make light of it, and represented it as something which would probably disappear of itself, as it originated without any adequate cause. She was obliged to acquiesce in my imperfect account.

Day after day passed in this state of fluctuation. I was conscious of the dangers of delay, and that procrastination, without rendering the task less necessary, augmented its difficulties. At length, summoning my resolution, I demanded an audience. She received me with her usual affability. Common topics were started; but she saw the confusion and trepidation of my thoughts, and quickly relinquished them. She then noticed to me what she had observed, and mentioned the anxiety which these appearances had given her. She reminded me of the maternal regard which she had always manifested towards me, and appealed to my own heart whether any thing could be said in vindication of that reserve with which I had lately treated her, and urged me as I valued her good opinion, to explain the cause of a dejection *that was too visible.*

To all this I could make but one answer: Think me not, Madam, perverse or ungrateful. I came just now to apprise you of a resolution that I had formed. I cannot explain the motives that induce me. In this case, to lie to you would be unpardonable, and since I cannot assign my true motives, I will not mislead you by false representations. I came to inform you of my intention to leave your service, and to retire with the fruits of your bounty, to my native village, where I shall spend my life, I hope, in peace.

Her surprise at this declaration was beyond measure. She could not believe her ears. She had not heard me rightly. She compelled me to repeat it. Still I was jesting. I could not possibly mean what my words imported.

I assured her, in terms still more explicit, that my resolution was taken and was unalterable, and again intreated her to spare me the task of assigning my motives.

This was a strange determination. What could be the grounds of this new scheme? What could be the necessity of hiding them from her? This mystery was not to be endured. She could by no means away with it. She thought it hard that I should abandon her at this time, when she stood in particular need of my assistance and advice. She would refuse nothing to make my situation eligible. I had only to point out where she was deficient in her treatment of me and she would endeavour to supply it. She was willing to augment my emoluments in any degree that I desired. She could not think of parting with me; but, at any rate, she must be informed of my motives.

It is an hard task, answered I, that I have imposed upon myself. I foresaw its difficulties, and this foresight has hitherto prevented me from undertaking it; but the necessity by which I am impelled, will no longer be withstood. I am determined to go; but to say why, is impossible. I hope I shall not bring upon myself the imputation of ingratitude; but this imputation, more intolerable than any other, must be borne, if it cannot be avoided but by this disclosure.

Keep your motives to yourself, said she. I have too good an opinion of you to suppose that you would practice concealment without good reason. I merely desire you to remain where you are. Since you will not tell me why you take up this new scheme, I can only say that it is impossible there should be any advantage in this scheme. I will not hear of it I tell you. Therefore, submit to my decree with a good grace.

Notwithstanding this prohibition I persisted in declaring that my determination was fixed, and that the motives that governed me would allow of no alternative.

So, you will go, will you, whether I will or no? I have no power to detain you? You will regard nothing that I can say?

Believe me, madam, no resolution ever was formed after a more vehement struggle. If my motives were known, you would not only cease to oppose, but would hasten my departure. Honour me so far with your good opinion, as to believe that, in saying this, I say nothing but the truth, and render my duty less burthensome by cheerfully acquiescing in its dictates.

I would, replied my lady, I could find somebody that has more power over you than I have. Whom shall I call in to aid me in this arduous task?

Nay, dear madam, if I can resist your intreaties, surely no other can hope to succeed.

I am not sure of that, said my friend, archly: there is one person in the world whose supplications, I greatly suspect, you would not withstand.

Whom do you mean? said I, in some trepidation.

You will know presently. Unless I can prevail upon you, I shall be obliged to call for assistance.

Spare me the pain of repeating that no power on earth can change my resolution.

That's a fib, she rejoined, with increased archness. You know it is. If a certain person intreat you to stay, you will easily comply. I see I cannot hope to prevail by my own strength. That is a mortifying consideration, but we must not part, that is a point settled. If nothing else will do, I must go and fetch my advocate. Stay here a moment.

I had scarcely time to breathe, before she returned, leading in Clarice. I did not yet comprehend the meaning of this ceremony. The lady was overwhelmed with sweet confusion. Averted eyes and reluctant steps, might have explained to me the purpose of this meeting, if I had believed that purpose to be possible. I felt the necessity of new fortitude, and struggled to recollect the motives that had hitherto sustained me.

There, said my patroness, I have been endeavouring to persuade this young man to live with us a little longer. He is determined, it seems, to change his abode. He will not tell why, and I do not care to know, unless I could shew his reasons to be groundless. I have merely remonstrated with him on the folly of his scheme, but he has proved refractory to all I can say. Perhaps your efforts may meet with better success.

Clarice said not a word. My own embarrassment equally disabled me from speaking. Regarding us both, for some time, with a benign aspect, Mrs. Lorimer resumed, taking an hand of each and joining them together.

I very well know what it was that suggested this scheme. It is strange that you should suppose me so careless an observer as not to note, or not to understand your situation. I am as well acquainted with what is passing in your heart as you yourself are, but why are you so anxious to conceal it? You know less of the adventurousness of love than I should have suspected. But I will not trifle with your feelings.

You, Clithero, know the wishes that I once cherished. I had hoped that my son would have found, in this darling child, an object worthy of his choice, and that my girl would have preferred him to all others. But I have long since discovered that this could not be. They are nowise suited to each other. There is one thing in the next place desirable, and now my wishes are accomplished. I see that you love each other, and never, in my opinion, was a passion more rational and just. I should think myself the worst of beings if I did not contribute all in my power to your happiness. There is not the shadow of objection to your union. I know your scruples, Clithero, and am sorry to see that you harbour them for a moment. Nothing is more unworthy of your good sense.

I found out this girl long ago. Take my word for it, young man, she does not fall short of you in the purity and tenderness of her attachment. What need is there of tedious preliminaries? I will leave you together, and hope you will not be long in coming to a mutual understanding. Your union cannot be completed too soon for my wishes. Clarice is my only and darling daughter. As to you Clithero, expect henceforth that treatment from me, not only to which your own merit intitles you, but which is due to the husband of my daughter.—With these words she retired and left us together.

Great God! deliver me from the torments of this remembrance. That a being by whom I was snatched from penury and brutal ignorance, exalted to some rank in the intelligent creation, reared to affluence and honour, and thus, at last, spontaneously endowed with all that remained to complete the sum of my felicity, that a being like this—but such thoughts must not yet be—I must shut them out, or I shall never arrive at the end of my tale. My efforts have been thus far successful. I have hitherto been able to deliver a coherent narrative. Let the last words that I shall speak afford some glimmering of my better days. Let me execute without faltering the only task that remains for me.

Chapter VI

How propitious, how incredible was this event! I could scarcely confide in the testimony of my senses. Was it true that Clarice was before me, that she was prepared to countenance my presumption, that she had slighted obstacles which I had deemed insurmountable, that I was fondly beloved by her, and should shortly be admitted to the possession of so inestimable a good? I will not repeat the terms in which I poured forth, at her feet, the raptures of my gratitude. My impetuosity soon extorted from Clarice, a confirmation of her mother's declaration. An unrestrained intercourse was thenceforth established between us. Dejection and languor gave place, in my bosom, to the irradiations of joy and hope. My flowing fortunes seemed to have attained their utmost and immutable height.

Alas! They were destined to ebb with unspeakably greater rapidity, and to leave me, in a moment, stranded and wrecked.

Our nuptials would have been solemnised without delay, had not a melancholy duty interferred. Clarice had a friend in a distant part of the kingdom. Her health had long been the prey of a consumption. She was now evidently tending to dissolution. In this extremity she intreated her friend to afford her the consolation of her presence. The only wish that remained was to die in her arms.

This request could not but be willingly complied with. It became me patiently to endure the delay that would thence arise to the completion of my wishes. Considering the urgency and mournfulness of the occasion, it was impossible for me to murmur, and the affectionate Clarice would suffer nothing to interfere with the duty which she owed to her dying friend. I accompanied her on this journey, remained with her a few days, and then parted from her to return to the metropolis. It was not imagined that it would be necessary to prolong her absence beyond a month. When I bade her farewell, and informed her on what day I proposed to return for her, I felt no decay of my satisfaction. My thoughts were bright and full of exultation. Why was not some intimation afforded me of the snares that lay in my path? In the train laid for my de-struction, the agent had so skilfully contrived that my security was not molested by the faintest omen.

I hasten to the crisis of my tale. I am almost dubious of my strength. The nearer I approach to it, the stronger is my aver-sion. My courage, instead of gathering force as I proceed, decays. I am willing to dwell still longer on preliminary cir-cumstances. There are other incidents without which my story would be lame. I retail them because they afford me a kind of respite from horrors, at the thought of which every joint in my frame trembles. They must be endured, but that infir-mity may be forgiven, which makes me inclined to procrasti-nate my suffering.

I mentioned the lover whom my patroness was compelled, by the machinations of her brother, to discard. More than twenty years had passed since their separation. His birth was mean and he was without fortune. His profession was that of a surgeon. My lady not only prevailed upon him to abandon his country, but enabled him to do this by supplying his ne-cessities from her own purse. His excellent understanding was, for a time, obscured by passion; but it was not difficult for my lady ultimately to obtain his concurrence to all her schemes. He saw and adored the rectitude of her motives, did not disdain to accept her gifts, and projected means for main-taining an epistolary intercourse during their separation.

Her interest procured him a post in the service of the East-India company. She was, from time to time, informed of his motions. A war broke out between the Company and some of the native powers. He was present at a great battle in which the English were defeated. She could trace him by his letters and by other circumstances thus far, but here the thread was discontinued, and no means which she employed could pro-cure any tidings of him. Whether he was captive, or dead, continued, for several years, to be merely matter of conjecture.

On my return to Dublin, I found my patroness engaged in conversation with a stranger. She introduced us to each other in a manner that indicated the respect which she entertained for us both. I surveyed and listened to him with considerable attention. His aspect was noble and ingenuous, but his sun-burnt and rugged features bespoke a various and boisterous pilgrimage. The furrows of his brow were the products of vicissitude and hardship, rather than of age. His accents were fiery and energetic, and the impassioned boldness of his address, as well as the tenor of his discourse, full of allusions to the past, and regrets that the course of events had not been different, made me suspect something extraordinary in his character.

As soon as he left us, my lady explained who he was. He was no other than the object of her youthful attachment, who had, a few days before, dropped among us as from the skies. He had a long and various story to tell. He had accounted for his silence by enumerating the incidents of his life. He had escaped from the prisons of Hyder, had wandered on foot, and under various disguises, through the northern district of Hindoostaun. He was sometimes a scholar of Benares, and sometimes a disciple of the Mosque. According to the exigencies of the times, he was a pilgrim to Mecca or to Jagunaut. By a long, circuitous, and perilous route, he at length arrived at the Turkish capital. Here he resided for several years, deriving a precarious subsistence from the profession of a surgeon. He was obliged to desert this post, in consequence of a duel between two Scotsmen. One of them had embraced the Greek religion, and was betrothed to the daughter of a wealthy trader of that nation. He perished in the conflict, and the family of the lady not only procured the execution of his antagonist, but threatened to involve all those who were known to be connected with him in the same ruin.

His life being thus endangered, it became necessary for him to seek a new residence. He fled from Constantinople with such precipitation as reduced him to the lowest poverty. He had traversed the Indian conquests of Alexander, as a mendicant. In the same character, he now wandered over the native country of Philip and Philopoemen. He passed safely through multiplied perils, and finally, embarking at Salonichi, he reached Venice. He descended through the passes of the Apennine into Tuscany. In this journey he suffered a long detention from banditti, by whom he was waylaid. In consequence of his harmless deportment, and a seasonable display of his chirurgical skill, they granted him his life, though they, for a time restrained him of his liberty, and compelled him to endure their society. The time was not misemployed which he spent immured in caverns and carousing with robbers. His details were eminently singular and curious, and evinced the acuteness of his penetration, as well the steadfastness of his courage.

After emerging from these wilds, he found his way along the banks of the Arno to Leghorn. Thence he procured a passage to America, whence he had just returned, with many additions to his experience, but none to his fortune.

This was a remarkable event. It did not at first appear how far its consequences would extend. The lady was, at present, disengaged and independent. Though the passion which clouded her early prosperity was extinct, time had not diminished the worth of her friend, and they were far from having reached that age when love becomes chimerical and marriage folly. A confidential intercourse was immediately established between them. The bounty of Mrs. Lorimer soon divested her friend of all fear of poverty. At any rate, said she, he shall wander no further, but shall be comfortably situated for the rest of his life. All his scruples were vanquished by the reasonableness of her remonstrances and the vehemence of her solicitations.

A cordial intimacy grew between me and the newly arrived. Our interviews were frequent, and our communications without reserve. He detailed to me the result of his experience, and expatiated without end on the history of his actions and opinions. He related the adventures of his youth, and dwelt upon all the circumstances of his attachment to my patroness. On this subject I had heard only general details. I continually found cause, in the course of his narrative, to revere the illustrious qualities of my lady, and to weep at the calamities to which the infernal malice of her brother had subjected her.

The tale of that man's misdeeds, amplified and dramatised, by the indignant eloquence of this historian, oppressed me with astonishment. If a poet had drawn such a portrait I should have been prone to suspect the soundness of his judgment. Till now I had imagined that no character was uniform and unmixed, and my theory of the passions did not enable me to account for a propensity gratified merely by evil, and delighting in shrieks and agony for their own sake.

It was natural to suggest to my friend, when expatiating on this theme, an inquiry as to how far subsequent events had obliterated the impressions that were then made, and as to the plausibility of reviving, at this more auspicious period, his claims on the heart of his friend. When he thought proper to notice these hints, he gave me to understand that time had made no essential alteration in his sentiments in this respect, that he still fostered an hope, to which every day added new vigour, that whatever was the ultimate event, he trusted in his fortitude to sustain it, if adverse, and in his wisdom to extract from it the most valuable consequences, if it should prove prosperous.

The progress of things was not unfavourable to his hopes. She treated his insinuations and professions with levity; but her arguments seemed to be urged, with no other view than to afford an opportunity of confutation; and, since there was no abatement of familiarity and kindness, there was room to hope that the affair would terminate agreeably to his wishes.

Chapter VII

C LARICE, meanwhile, was absent. Her friend seemed, at the end of a month, to be little less distant from the grave than at first. My impatience would not allow me to wait till her death. I visited her, but was once more obliged to return alone. I arrived late in the city, and being greatly fatigued, I retired almost immediately to my chamber.

On hearing of my arrival, Sarsefield hastened to see me. He came to my bed-side, and such, in his opinion, was the importance of the tidings which he had to communicate, that he did not scruple to rouse me from a deep sleep. . . .

At this period of his narrative, Clithero stopped. His complexion varied from one degree of paleness to another. His brain appeared to suffer some severe constriction. He desired to be excused, for a few minutes, from proceeding. In a short time he was relieved from this paroxysm, and resumed his tale with an accent tremulous at first, but acquiring stability and force as he went on.

On waking, as I have said, I found my friend seated at my bed-side. His countenance exhibited various tokens of alarm. As soon as I perceived who it was, I started, exclaiming, What is the matter?

He sighed. Pardon, said he, this unseasonable intrusion. A light matter would not have occasioned it. I have waited, for two days past, in an agony of impatience, for your return. Happily, you are, at last, come. I stand in the utmost need of your council and aid.

Heaven defend! cried I. This is a terrible prelude. You may, of course, rely upon my assistance and advice. What is it that you have to propose?

Tuesday evening, he answered, I spent here. It was late before I returned to my lodgings. I was in the act of lifting my hand to the bell, when my eye was caught by a person standing close to the wall, at the distance of ten paces. His attitude was that of one employed in watching my motions. His face was turned towards me, and happened, at that moment, to be fully illuminated by the rays of a globe-lamp that hung over the door. I instantly recognized his features. I was petrified. I had no power to execute my design, or even to move, but stood, for some seconds gazing upon him. He was, in no degree, disconcerted by the eagerness of my scrutiny. He seemed perfectly indifferent to the consequences of being known. At length he slowly turned his eyes to another quarter, but without changing his posture, or the sternness of his looks. I cannot describe to you the shock which this encounter produced in me. At last I went into the house, and have ever since been excessively uneasy.

I do not see any ground for uneasiness.

You do not then suspect who this person is?

No. . . .

It is Arthur Wiatte. . . .

Good heaven! It is impossible. What, my lady's brother?

The same. . . .

It cannot be. Were we not assured of his death? That he perished in a mutiny on board the vessel in which he was embarked for transportation?

Such was rumour, which is easily mistaken. My eyes cannot be deceived in this case. I should as easily fail to recognize his sister, when I first met her, as him. This is the man; whether once dead or not, he is, at present, alive, and in this city.

But has any thing since happened to confirm you in this opinion?

Yes, there has. As soon as I had recovered from my first surprise, I began to reflect upon the measures proper to be taken. This was the identical Arthur Wiatte. You know his character. No time was likely to change the principles of such a man, but his appearance sufficiently betrayed the incurableness of his habits. The same sullen and atrocious passions were written in his visage. You recollect the vengeance which Wiatte denounced against his sister. There is every thing to dread from his malignity. How to obviate the danger, I know not. I thought, however, of one expedient. It might serve a present purpose, and something better might suggest itself on your return.

I came hither early the next day. Old Gowan the porter is well acquainted with Wiatte's story. I mentioned to him that I had reason to think that he had returned. I charged him to have a watchful eye upon every one that knocked at the gate, and that if this person should come, by no means to admit him. The old man promised faithfully to abide by my directions. His terrors, indeed, were greater than mine, and he knew the importance of excluding Wiatte from these walls.

Did you not inform my lady of this?

No. In what way could I tell it to her? What end could it answer? Why should I make her miserable? But I have not done. Yesterday morning Gowan took me aside, and informed me that Wiatte had made his appearance, the day before, at the gate. He knew him, he said, in a moment. He demanded to see the lady, but the old man told him she was engaged, and could not be seen. He assumed peremtory and haughty airs, and asserted that his business was of such importance as not to endure a moment's delay. Gowan persisted in his first refusal. He retired with great reluctance, but said he should return to-morrow, when he should insist upon admission to the presence of the lady. I have inquired, and find that he has not repeated his visit. What is to be done?

I was equally at a loss with my friend. This incident was so unlooked for. What might not be dreaded from the monstrous depravity of Wiatte? His menaces of vengeance against his sister still rung in my ears. Some means of eluding them were indispensable. Could law be resorted to? Against an evil like this, no legal provision had been made. Nine years had elapsed since his transportation. Seven years was the period of his exile. In returning, therefore, he had committed no crime. His person could not be lawfully molested. We were justified, merely, in repelling an attack. But suppose we should appeal to law, could this be done without the knowledge and concurrence of the lady? She would never permit it. Her heart was incapable of fear from this quarter. She would spurn at the mention of precautions against the hatred of her brother. Her inquietude would merely be awakened on his own account.

I was overwhelmed with perplexity. Perhaps if he were sought out, and some judgment formed of the kind of danger to be dreaded from him, by a knowledge of his situation and views, some expedient might be thence suggested.

But how should his haunts be discovered? This was easy.

He had intimated the design of applying again for admission to his sister. Let a person be stationed near at hand, who, being furnished with an adequate description of his person and dress, shall mark him when he comes, and follow him, when he retires, and shall forthwith impart to us the information on that head which he shall be able to collect.

My friend concurred in this scheme. No better could, for the present, be suggested. Here ended our conference.

I was thus supplied with a new subject of reflection. It was calculated to fill my mind with dreary forbodings. The future was no longer a scene of security and pleasure. It would be hard for those to partake of our fears, who did not partake of our experience. The existence of Wiatte, was the canker that had blasted the felicity of my patroness. In his reappearance on the stage, there was something portentous. It seemed to include in it, consequences of the utmost moment, without my being able to discover what these consequences were.

That Sarsefield should be so quickly followed by his Arch-foe; that they started anew into existence, without any previous intimation, in a manner wholly unexpected, and at the same period. It seemed as if there lurked, under those appearances, a tremendous significance, which human sagacity could not uncover. My heart sunk within me when I reflected that this was the father of my Clarice. He by whose cruelty her mother was torn from the injoyment of untarnished honour, and consigned to infamy and an untimely grave: He by whom herself was abandoned in the helplessness of infancy, and left to be the prey of obdurate avarice, and the victim of wretches who traffic in virgin innocence: Who had done all that in him lay to devote her youth to guilt and misery. What were the limits of his power? How may he exert the parental prerogatives?

To sleep, while these images were haunting me, was impossible. I passed the night in continual motion. I strode, without ceasing, across the floor of my apartment. My mind was wrought to an higher pitch than I had ever before experienced. The occasion, accurately considered, was far from justifying the ominous inquietudes which I then felt. How then should I account for them?

Sarsefield probably enjoyed his usual slumber. His repose

might not be perfectly serene, but when he ruminated on impending or possible calamities, his tongue did not cleave to his mouth, his throat was not parched with unquenchable thirst, he was not incessantly stimulated to employ his superfluous fertility of thought in motion. If I trembled for the safety of her whom I loved, and whose safety was endangered by being the daughter of this miscreant, had he not equal reason to fear for her whom he also loved, and who, as the sister of this ruffian, was encompassed by the most alarming perils? Yet he probably was calm while I was harassed by anxieties.

Alas! The difference was easily explained. Such was the beginning of a series ordained to hurry me to swift destruction. Such were the primary tokens of the presence of that power by whose accursed machinations I was destined to fall. You are startled at this declaration. It is one to which you have been little accustomed. Perhaps you regard it merely as an effusion of phrenzy. I know what I am saying. I do not build upon conjectures and surmises. I care not indeed for your doubts. Your conclusion may be fashioned at your pleasure. Would to heaven that my belief were groundless, and that I had no reason to believe my intellects to have been perverted by diabolical instigations.

I could procure no sleep that night. After Sarsefield's departure I did not even lie down. It seemed to me that I could not obtain the benefits of repose otherwise than by placing my lady beyond the possibility of danger.

I met Sarsefield the next day. In pursuance of the scheme which had been adopted by us on the preceding evening, a person was selected and commissioned to watch the appearance of Wiatte. The day passed as usual with respect to the lady. In the evening she was surrounded by a few friends. Into this number I was now admitted. Sarsefield and myself made a part of this company. Various topics were discussed with ease and sprightliness. Her societies were composed of both sexes, and seemed to have monopolized all the ingenuity and wit that existed in the metropolis.

After a slight repast the company dispersed. This separation took place earlier than usual on account of a slight indisposition in *Mrs. Lorimer*. Sarsefield and I went out together. We took that opportunity of examining our agent, and receiving no satisfaction from him, we dismissed him, for that night, enjoining him to hold himself in readiness for repeating the experiment to-morrow. My friend directed his steps homeward, and I proceeded to execute a commission, with which I had charged myself.

A few days before, a large sum had been deposited in the hands of a banker, for the use of my lady. It was the amount of a debt which had lately been recovered. It was lodged here for the purpose of being paid on demand of her or her agents. It was my present business to receive this money. I had deferred the performance of this engagement to this late hour, on account of certain preliminaries which were necessary to be adjusted.

Having received this money, I prepared to return home. The inquietude which had been occasioned by Sarsefield's intelligence, had not incapacitated me from performing my usual daily occupations. It was a theme, to which, at every interval of leisure from business or discourse, I did not fail to return. At those times I employed myself in examining the subject on all sides; in supposing particular emergencies, and delineating the conduct that was proper to be observed on each. My daily thoughts were, by no means, so fear-inspiring as the meditations of the night had been.

As soon as I left the banker's door, my meditations fell into this channel. I again reviewed the recent occurrences, and imagined the consequences likely to flow from them. My deductions were not, on this occasion, peculiarly distressful. The return of darkness had added nothing to my apprehensions. I regarded Wiatte merely as one against whose malice it was wise to employ the most vigilant precautions. In revolving these precautions nothing occurred that was new. The danger appeared without unusual aggravations, and the expedients that offered themselves to my choice, were viewed with a temper not more sanguine or despondent than before.

In this state of mind I began and continued my walk. The distance was considerable between my own habitation and that which I had left. My way lay chiefly through populous and well frequented streets. In one part of the way, however, it was at the option of the passenger either to keep along the large streets, or considerably to shorten the journey, by turning into a dark, crooked, and narrow lane. Being familiar with every part of this metropolis, and deeming it advisable to take the shortest and obscurest road, I turned into the alley. I proceeded without interruption to the next turning. One night officer, distinguished by his usual ensigns, was the only person who passed me. I had gone three steps beyond when I perceived a man by my side. I had scarcely time to notice this circumstance, when an hoarse voice exclaimed, "Damn ye villain, ye're a dead man!"

At the same moment a pistol flashed at my ear, and a report followed. This, however, produced no other effect, than, for a short space, to overpower my senses. I staggered back, but did not fall.

The ball, as I afterwards discovered, had grazed my forehead, but without making any dangerous impression. The assassin, perceiving that his pistol had been ineffectual, muttered, in an enraged tone,—This shall do your business —At the same time, he drew a knife forth from his bosom.

I was able to distinguish this action by the rays of a distant lamp, which glistened on the blade. All this passed in an instant. The attack was so abrupt that my thoughts could not be suddenly recalled from the confusion into which they were thrown. My exertions were mechanical. My will might be said to be passive, and it was only by retrospect and a contemplation of consequences, that I became fully informed of the nature of the scene.

If my assailant had disappeared as soon as he had discharged the pistol, my state of extreme surprise might have slowly given place to resolution and activity. As it was, my sense was no sooner struck by the reflection from the blade, than my hand, as if by spontaneous energy, was thrust into my pocket. I drew forth a pistol—

He lifted up his weapon to strike, but it dropped from his powerless fingers. He fell and his groans informed me that I had managed my arms with more skill than my adversary. The noise of this encounter soon attracted spectators. Lights were brought and my antagonist discovered bleeding at my feet. I explained, as briefly as I was able, the scene which they witnessed. The prostrate person was raised by two men, and carried into a public house, nigh at hand.

I had not lost my presence of mind. I, at once, perceived the propriety of administering assistance to the wounded man. I dispatched, therefore, one of the by-standers for a surgeon of considerable eminence, who lived at a small distance, and to whom I was well known. The man was carried into an inner apartment and laid upon the floor. It was not till now that I had a suitable opportunity of ascertaining who it was with whom I had been engaged. I now looked upon his face. The paleness of death could not conceal his well known features. It was Wiatte himself who was breathing his last groans at my feet! . . .

The surgeon, whom I had summoned, attended; but immediately perceived the condition of his patient to be hopeless. In a quarter of an hour he expired. During this interval, he was insensible to all around him. I was known to the surgeon, the landlord and some of the witnesses. The case needed little explanation. The accident reflected no guilt upon me. The landlord was charged with the care of the corse till the morning, and I was allowed to return home, without further impediment.

Chapter VIII

TILL NOW my mind had been swayed by the urgencies of this occasion. Those reflections were excluded, which rushed tumultuously upon me, the moment I was at leisure to receive them. Without foresight of a previous moment, an entire change had been wrought in my condition.

I had been oppressed with a sense of the danger that flowed from the existence of this man. By what means the peril could be annihilated, and we be placed in security from his attempts, no efforts of mind could suggest. To devise these means, and employ them with success, demanded, as I conceived, the most powerful sagacity and the firmest courage. Now the danger was no more. The intelligence in which plans of mischief might be generated, was extinguished or flown. Lifeless were the hands ready to execute the dictates of that intelligence. The contriver of enormous evil, was, in one moment, bereft of the power and the will to injure. Our past tranquility had been owing to the belief of his death. Fear and dismay had resumed their dominion when the mistake was discovered. But now we might regain possession of our wonted confidence. I had beheld with my own eyes the lifeless corpse of our implacable adversary. Thus, in a moment, had terminated his long and flagitious career. His restless indignation, his malignant projects, that had so long occupied the stage, and been so fertile of calamity, were now at an end!

In the course of my meditations, the idea of the death of this man had occurred, and it bore the appearance of a desirable event. Yet it was little qualified to tranquilise my fears. In the long catalogue of contingencies, this, indeed, was to be found; but it was as little likely to happen as any other. It could not happen without a series of anterior events paving the way for it. If his death came from us, it must be the theme of design. It must spring from laborious circumvention and deep laid stratagems.

No. He was dead. I had killed him. What had I done? I had meditated nothing. I was impelled by an unconscious necessity. Had the assailant been my father the consequence would have been the same. My understanding had been neutral. Could it be? In a space so short, was it possible that so tremendous a deed had been executed? Was I not deceived by some portentous vision? I had witnessed the convulsions and last agonies of Wiatte. He was no more, and I was his destroyer!

Such was the state of my mind for some time after this dreadful event. Previously to it I was calm, considerate, and self-collected. I marked the way that I was going. Passing objects were observed. If I adverted to the series of my own reflections, my attention was not seized and fastened by them. I could disengage myself at pleasure, and could pass, without difficulty, from attention to the world within, to the contemplation of that without.

Now my liberty, in this respect, was at an end. I was fettered, confounded, smitten with excess of thought, and laid prostrate with wonder! I no longer attended to my steps. When I emerged from my stupor, I found that I had trodden back the way which I had lately come, and had arrived within sight of the banker's door. I checked myself, and once more turned my steps homeward.

This seemed to be an hint for entering into new reflections. The deed, said I, is irretrievable. I have killed the brother of my patroness, the father of my love.

This suggestion was new. It instantly involved me in terror and perplexity. How shall I communicate the tidings? What effect will they produce? My lady's sagacity is obscured by the benevolence of her temper. Her brother was sordidly wicked. An hoary ruffian, to whom the language of pity was as unintelligible as the gabble of monkeys. His heart was fortified against compunction, by the atrocious habits of forty years: he lived only to interrupt her peace, to confute the promises of virtue, and convert to rancour and reproach the fair fame of fidelity.

He was her brother still. As an human being, his depravity was never beyond the health-restoring power of repentance. His heart, so long as it beat, was accessible to remorse. The singularity of his birth had made her regard this being as more intimately her brother, than would have happened in different circumstances. It was her obstinate persuasion that their fates

were blended. The rumour of his death she had never credited. It was a topic of congratulation to her friends, but of
mourning and distress to her. That he would one day re-
appear upon the stage, and assume the dignity of virtue, was
a source of consolation with which she would never consent
to part.

Her character was now known. When the doom of exile
was pronounced upon him, she deemed it incumbent on her
to vindicate herself from aspersions founded on misconceptions of her motives in refusing her interference. The manuscript, though unpublished, was widely circulated. None could
resist her simple and touching eloquence, nor rise from the
perusal without resigning his heart to the most impetuous
impulses of admiration, and enlisting himself among the eulogists of her justice and her fortitude. This was the only monument, in a written form, of her genius. As such it was
engraven on my memory. The picture that it described was
the perpetual companion of my thoughts.

Alas! It had, perhaps, been well for me if it had been buried
in eternal oblivion. I read in it the condemnation of my deed,
the agonies she was preparing to suffer, and the indignation
that would overflow upon the author of so signal a calamity.

I had rescued my life by the sacrifice of his. Whereas I
should have died. Wretched and precipitate coward! What had
become of my boasted gratitude? Such was the zeal that I had
vowed to her. Such the services which it was the business of
my life to perform. I had snatched her brother from existence.
I had torn from her the hope which she so ardently and indefatigably cherished. From a contemptible and dastardly regard to my own safety I had failed in the moment of trial, and
when called upon by heaven to evince the sincerity of my
professions.

She had treated my professions lightly. My vows of eternal
devotion she had rejected with lofty disinterestedness. She had
arraigned my impatience of obligation as criminal, and condemned every scheme I had projected for freeing myself from
the burthen which her beneficence had laid upon me. The
impassioned and vehement anxiety with which, in former
days, she had deprecated the vengeance of her lover against
Wiatte, rung in my ears. My senses were shocked anew by the

dreadful sounds "Touch not my brother. Wherever you meet with him, of whatever outrage he be guilty, suffer him to pass in safety. Despise me: abandon me: kill me. All this I can bear even from you, but spare, I implore you, my unhappy brother. The stroke that deprives him of life will not only have the same effect upon me, but will set my portion in everlasting misery."

To these supplications I had been deaf. It is true I had not rushed upon him unarmed, intending no injury nor expecting any. Of that degree of wickedness I was, perhaps, incapable. Alas! I have immersed myself sufficiently deep in crimes. I have trampled under foot every motive dear to the heart of honour. I have shewn myself unworthy the society of men.

Such were the turbulent suggestions of that moment. My pace slackened. I stopped and was obliged to support myself against a wall. The sickness that had seized my heart penetrated every part of my frame. There was but one thing wanting to complete my distraction. . . . My lady, said I, believed her fate to be blended with that of Wiatte. Who shall affirm that the persuasion is a groundless one? She had lived and prospered, notwithstanding the general belief that her brother was dead. She would not hearken to the rumour. Why? Because nothing less than indubitable evidence would suffice to convince her? Because the counter-intimation flowed from an infallible source? How can the latter supposition be confuted? Has she not predicted the event?

The period of terrible fulfilment has arrived. The same blow that bereaved *him* of life, has likewise ratified her doom.

She has been deceived. It is nothing more, perhaps, than a fond imagination. . . . It matters not. Who knows not the cogency of faith? That the pulses of life are at the command of the will? The bearer of these tidings will be the messenger of death. A fatal sympathy will seize her. She will shrink, and swoon, and perish at the news!

Fond and short-sighted wretch! This is the price thou hast given for security. In the rashness of thy thought thou said'st, Nothing is wanting but his death to restore us to confidence and safety. Lo! the purchase is made. Havock and despair, that were restrained during his life, were let loose by his last sigh. Now only is destruction made sure. Thy lady, thy Clarice, thy

friend, and thyself, are, by this act, involved in irretreivable
and common ruin!

I started from my attitude. I was scarcely conscious of any
transition. The interval was fraught with stupor and amazement. It seemed as if my senses had been hushed in sleep,
while the powers of locomotion were unconsciously exerted
to bear me to my chamber. By whatever means the change
was effected, there I was. . . .

I have been able to proceed thus far. I can scarcely believe
the testimony of my memory that assures me of this. My task
is almost executed, but whence shall I obtain strength enough
to finish it? What I have told is light as gossamer, compared
with the insupportable and crushing horrors of that which is
to come. Heaven, in token of its vengeance, will enable me
to proceed. It is fitting that my scene should thus close.

My fancy began to be infected with the errors of my understanding. The mood into which my mind was plunged was
incapable of any propitious intermission. All within me was
tempestuous and dark. My ears were accessible to no sounds
but those of shrieks and lamentations. It was deepest midnight, and all the noises of a great metropolis were hushed.
Yet I listened as if to catch some strain of the dirge that was
begun. Sable robes, sobs and a dreary solemnity encompassed
me on all sides. I was haunted to despair by images of death,
imaginary clamours, and the train of funeral pageantry. I
seemed to have passed forward to a distant era of my life. The
effects which were to come were already realized. The foresight of misery created it, and set me in the midst of that hell
which I feared.

From a paroxysm like this the worst might reasonably be
dreaded, yet the next step to destruction was not suddenly
taken. I paused on the brink of the precipice, as if to survey
the depth of that phrensy that invaded me; was able to ponder
on the scene, and deliberate, in a state that partook of calm,
on the circumstances of my situation. My mind was harrassed
by the repetition of one idea. Conjecture deepened into certainty. I could place the object in no light which did not corroborate the persuasion that, in the act committed, I had
ensured the destruction of my lady. At length my mind, some-

what relieved from the tempest of my fears, began to trace and analize the consequences which I dreaded.

The fate of Wiatte would inevitably draw along with it that of his sister. In what way would this effect be produced? Were they linked together by a sympathy whose influence was independent of sensible communication? Could she arrive at a knowledge of his miserable end by other than verbal means? I had heard of such extraordinary co-partnerships in being and modes of instantaneous intercourse among beings locally distant. Was this a new instance of the subtlety of mind? Had she already endured his agonies, and like him already ceased to breathe?

Every hair bristled at this horrible suggestion. But the force of sympathy might be chimerical. Buried in sleep, or engaged in careless meditation, the instrument by which her destiny might be accomplished, was the steel of an assassin. A series of events, equally beyond the reach of foresight, with those which had just happened, might introduce, with equal abruptness, a similar disaster. What, at that moment, was her condition? Reposing in safety in her chamber, as her family imagined. But were they not deceived? Was she not a mangled corse? Whatever were her situation, it could not be ascertained, except by extraordinary means, till the morning. Was it wise to defer the scrutiny till then? Why not instantly investigate the truth?

These ideas passed rapidly through my mind. A considerable portion of time and amplification of phrase are necessary to exhibit, verbally, ideas contemplated in a space of incalculable brevity. With the same rapidity I conceived the resolution of determining the truth of my suspicions. All the family, but myself, were at rest. Winding passages would conduct me, without danger of disturbing them, to the hall from which double staircases ascended. One of these led to a saloon above, on the east side of which was a door that communicated with a suit of rooms, occupied by the lady of the mansion. The first was an antichamber, in which a female servant usually lay. The second was the lady's own bed-chamber. This was a sacred recess, with whose situation, relative to the other apartments of the building, I was well acquainted, but of which I knew nothing from my own examination, having never been admitted into it.

Thither I was now resolved to repair. I was not deterred by the sanctity of the place and hour. I was insensible to all consequences but the removal of my doubts. Not that my hopes were balanced by my fears. That the same tragedy had been performed in her chamber and in the street, nothing hindered me from believing with as much cogency as if my own eyes had witnessed it, but the reluctance with which we admit a detestable truth.

To terminate a state of intolerable suspense, I resolved to proceed forthwith to her chamber. I took the light and paced, with no interruption, along the galleries. I used no precaution. If I had met a servant or robber, I am not sure that I should have noticed him. My attention was too perfectly engrossed to allow me to spare any to a casual object. I cannot affirm that no one observed me. This, however, was probable from the distribution of the dwelling. It consisted of a central edifice and two wings, one of which was appropriated to domestics, and the other, at the extremity of which my apartment was placed, comprehended a library, and rooms for formal, and social, and literary conferences. These, therefore, were deserted at night, and my way lay along these. Hence it was not likely that my steps would be observed.

I proceeded to the hall. The principal parlour was beneath her chamber. In the confusion of my thoughts I mistook one for the other. I rectified, as soon as I detected my mistake. I ascended, with a beating heart, the staircase. The door of the antichamber was unfastened. I entered, totally regardless of disturbing the girl who slept within. The bed which she occupied was concealed by curtains. Whether she were there, I did not stop to examine. I cannot recollect that any tokens were given of wakefulness or alarm. It was not till I reached the door of her own apartment that my heart began to falter.

It was now that the momentousness of the question I was about to decide, rushed with its genuine force, upon my apprehension. Appaled and aghast, I had scarcely power to move the bolt. If the imagination of her death was not to be supported, how should I bear the spectacle of wounds and blood? Yet this was reserved for me. A few paces would set me in the midst of a scene, of which I was the abhorred contriver. Was it right to proceed? There were still the remnants of doubt. My forebodings might possibly be groundless. All within might be safety and serenity. A respite might be gained from the execution of an irrevocable sentence. What could I do? Was not any thing easy to endure in comparison with the agonies of suspense? If I could not obviate the evil I must bear it, but the torments of suspense were susceptible of remedy.

I drew back the bolt, and entered with the reluctance of fear, rather than the cautiousness of guilt. I could not lift my eyes from the ground. I advanced to the middle of the room. Not a sound like that of the dying saluted my ear. At length, shaking off the fetters of hopelesness, I looked up. . . .

I saw nothing calculated to confirm my fears. Every where there reigned quiet and order. My heart leaped with exultation. Can it be, said I, that I have been betrayed with shadows? . . . But this is not sufficient. . . .

Within an alcove was the bed that belonged to her. If her safety were inviolate, it was here that she reposed. What remained to convert tormenting doubt into ravishing certainty? I was insensible to the perils of my present situation. If she, indeed, were there, would not my intrusion awaken her? She would start and perceive me, at this hour, standing at her bedside. How should I account for an intrusion so unexampled and audacious? I could not communicate my fears. I could not tell her that the blood with which my hands were stained had flowed from the wounds of her brother.

My mind was inaccessible to such considerations. They did not even modify my predominant idea. Obstacles like these, had they existed, would have been trampled under foot.

Leaving the lamp, that I bore, on the table, I approached the bed. I slowly drew aside the curtain and beheld her tranquilly slumbering. I listened, but so profound was her sleep that not even her breathings could be overheard. I dropped the curtain and retired.

How blissful and mild were the illuminations of my bosom at this discovery. A joy that surpassed all utterance succeeded the fierceness of desperation. I stood, for some moments, wrapt in delightful contemplation. Alas! It was a luminous but transient interval. The madness, to whose black suggestions it bore so strong a contrast, began now to make sensible approaches on my understanding.

True, said I, she lives. Her slumber is serene and happy. She is blind to her approaching destiny. Some hours will at least be rescued from anguish and death. When she wakes the phantom that soothed her will vanish. The tidings cannot be withheld from her. The murderer of thy brother cannot hope to enjoy thy smiles. Those ravishing accents, with which thou hast used to greet me, will be changed. Scouling and reproaches, the invectives of thy anger and the maledictions of thy justice will rest upon my head.

What is the blessing which I made the theme of my boastful arrogance? This interval of being and repose is momentary. She will awake but only to perish at the spectacle of my ingratitude. She will awake only to the consciousness of instantly impending death. When she again sleeps she will wake no more. I her son, I, whom the law of my birth doomed to poverty and hardship, but whom her unsolicited beneficence snatched from those evils, and endowed with the highest good known to intelligent beings, the consolations of science and the blandishments of affluence; to whom the darling of her life, the offspring in whom are faithfully preserved the lineaments of its angelic mother, she has not denied! . . . What is the recompense that I have made? How have I discharged the measureless debt of gratitude to which she is entitled? Thus! . . .

Cannot my guilt be extenuated? Is there not a good that I can do thee? Must I perpetrate unmingled evil? Is the province assigned me that of an infernal emissary, whose efforts are concentred in a single purpose and that purpose a malignant one? I am the author of thy calamities. Whatever misery is reserved for thee, I am the source whence it flows. Can I not set bounds to the stream? Cannot I prevent thee from returning to a consciousness which, till it ceases to exist, will not cease to be rent and mangled?

Yes. It is in my power to screen thee from the coming storm: to accelerate thy journey to rest. I will do it. . . .

The impulse was not to be resisted. I moved with the suddenness of lightning. Armed with a pointed implement that lay . . . it was a dagger. As I set down the lamp, I struck the edge. Yet I saw it not, or noticed it not till I needed its assistance. By what accident it came hither, to what deed of darkness it had already been subservient, I had no power to inquire. I stepped to the table and seized it.

The time which this action required was insufficient to save me. My doom was ratified by powers which no human energies can counterwork. . . . Need I go farther? Did you entertain any imagination of so frightful a catastrophe? I am overwhelmed by turns with dismay and with wonder. I am prompted by turns to tear my heart from my breast, and deny faith to the verdict of my senses.

Was it I that hurried to the deed? No. It was the dæmon that possessed me. My limbs were guided to the bloody office by a power foreign and superior to mine. I had been defrauded, for a moment, of the empire of my muscles. A little moment for that sufficed.

If my destruction had not been decreed why was the image of Clarice so long excluded? Yet why do I say long? The fatal resolution was conceived, and I hastened to the execution, in a period too brief for more than itself to be viewed by the intellect.

What then? Were my hands embrued in this precious blood? Was it to this extremity of horror that my evil genius was determined to urge me? Too surely this was his purpose; too surely I was qualified to be its minister.

I lifted the weapon. Its point was aimed at the bosom of the sleeper. The impulse was given. . . .

At the instant a piercing shriek was uttered behind me, and a stretched-out hand, grasping the blade, made it swerve widely from its aim. It descended, but without inflicting a wound. Its force was spent upon the bed.

O! for words to paint that stormy transition! I loosed my hold of the dagger. I started back, and fixed eyes of frantic curiosity on the author of my rescue. He that interposed to arrest my deed, that started into being and activity at a moment so pregnant with fate, without tokens of his purpose or his coming being previously imparted, could not, methought, be less than divinity.

The first glance that I darted on this being corroborated

my conjecture. It was the figure and the lineaments of Mrs. Lorimer. Negligently habited in flowing and brilliant white, with features bursting with terror and wonder, the likeness of that being who was stretched upon the bed, now stood before me.

All that I am able to conceive of angel was comprised in the moral constitution of this woman. That her genius had overleaped all bounds, and interposed to save her, was no audacious imagination. In the state in which my mind then was no other belief than this could occupy the first place.

My tongue was tied. I gazed by turns upon her who stood before me, and her who lay upon the bed, and who, awakened by the shriek that had been uttered, now opened her eyes. She started from her pillow, and, by assuming a new and more distinct attitude, permitted me to recognize *Clarice herself!*

Three days before, I had left her, beside the bed of a dying friend, at a solitary mansion in the mountains of Donnegal. Here it had been her resolution to remain till her friend should breathe her last. Fraught with this persuasion; knowing this to be the place and hour of repose of my lady, hurried forward by the impetuosity of my own conceptions, deceived by the faint gleam which penetrated through the curtain and imperfectly irradiated features which bore, at all times, a powerful resemblance to those of Mrs. Lorimer, I had rushed to the brink of this terrible precipice!

Why did I linger on the verge? Why, thus perilously situated, did I not throw myself headlong? The steel was yet in my hand. A single blow would have pierced my heart, and shut out from my remembrance and foresight the past and the future.

The moment of insanity had gone by, and I was once more myself. Instead of regarding the act which I had meditated as the dictate of compassion or of justice, it only added to the sum of my ingratitude, and gave wings to the whirlwind that was sent to bear me to perdition.

Perhaps I was influenced by a sentiment which I had not leisure to distribute into parts. My understanding was, no doubt, bewildered in the maze of consequences which would spring from my act. How should I explain my coming hither in this murderous guise, my arm lifted to destroy the idol of my soul, and the darling child of my patroness? In what words should I unfold the tale of Wiatte, and enumerate the motives that terminated in the present scene? What penalty had not my infatuation and cruelty deserved? What could I less than turn the dagger's point against my own bosom?

A second time, the blow was thwarted and diverted. Once more this beneficent interposer held my arm from the perpetration of a new iniquity. Once more frustrated the instigations of that dæmon, of whose malice a mysterious destiny had consigned me to be the sport and the prey.

Every new moment added to the sum of my inexpiable guilt. Murder was succeeded, in an instant, by the more detestable enormity of suicide. She, to whom my ingratitude was flagrant in proportion to the benefits of which she was the author, had now added to her former acts, that of rescuing me from the last of mischiefs.

I threw the weapon on the floor. The zeal which prompted her to seize my arm, this action occasioned to subside, and to yield place to those emotions which this spectacle was calculated to excite. She watched me in silence, and with an air of ineffable solicitude. Clarice, governed by the instinct of modesty, wrapt her bosom and face in the bed-clothes, and testified her horror by vehement, but scarcely articulate exclamations.

I moved forward, but my steps were random and tottering. My thoughts were fettered by reverie, and my gesticulations destitute of meaning. My tongue faltered without speaking, and I felt as if life and death were struggling within me for the mastery.

My will, indeed, was far from being neutral in this contest. To such as I, annihilation is the supreme good. To shake off the ills that fasten on us by shaking off existence, is a lot which the system of nature has denied to man. By escaping from life, I should be delivered from this scene, but should only rush into a world of retribution, and be immersed in new agonies.

I was yet to live. No instrument of my deliverance was within reach. I was powerless. To rush from the presence of these women, to hide me forever from their scrutiny, and their upbraiding, to snatch from their minds all traces of the existence of Clithero, was the scope of unutterable longings.

Urged to flight by every motive of which my nature was susceptible, I was yet rooted to the spot. Had the pause been only to be interrupted by me, it would have lasted forever.

At length, the lady, clasping her hands and lifting them, exclaimed, in a tone melting into pity and grief:

Clithero! what is this? How came you hither and why?

I struggled for utterance: I came to murder you. Your brother has perished by my hands. Fresh from the commission of this deed, I have hastened hither, to perpetrate the same crime upon you.

My brother! replied the lady, with new vehemence, O! say not so! I have just heard of his return from Sarsefield and that he lives.

He is dead, repeated I, with fierceness: I know it. It was I that killed him.

Dead! she faintly articulated. And by thee Clithero? O! cursed chance that hindered thee from killing me also! Dead! Then is the omen fulfilled! Then am I undone! Lost forever!

Her eyes now wandered from me, and her countenance sunk into a wild and rueful expression. Hope was utterly extinguished in her heart, and life forsook her at the same moment. She sunk upon the floor pallid and breathless. . . .

How she came into possession of this knowledge I know not. It is possible that Sarsefield had repented of concealment, and, in the interval that passed between our separation and my encounter with Wiatte, had returned, and informed her of the reappearance of this miscreant.

Thus then was my fate consummated. I was rescued from destroying her by a dagger, only to behold her perish by the tidings which I brought. Thus was every omen of mischief and misery fulfilled. Thus was the enmity of Wiatte, rendered efficacious, and the instrument of his destruction, changed into the executioner of his revenge.

Such is the tale of my crimes. It is not for me to hope that the curtain of oblivion will ever shut out the dismal spectacle. It will haunt me forever. The torments that grow out of it, can terminate only with the thread of my existence, but that I know full well will never end. Death is but a shifting of the scene, and the endless progress of eternity, which, to the good, is merely the perfection of felicity, is, to the wicked, an accumulation of woe. The self-destroyer is his own enemy; this has ever been my opinion. Hitherto it has influenced my action. Now, though the belief continues, its influence on my conduct is annihilated. I am no stranger to the depth of that abyss, into which I shall plunge. No matter. Change is precious for its own sake.

Well: I was still to live. My abode must be somewhere fixed. My conduct was henceforth the result of a perverse and rebellious principle. I banished myself forever from my native soil. I vowed never more to behold the face of my Clarice, to abandon my friends, my books, all my wonted labours, and accustomed recreations.

I was neither ashamed nor afraid. I considered not in what way the justice of the country would affect me. It merely made no part of my contemplations. I was not embarrassed by the choice of expedients, for trammeling up the visible consequences and for eluding suspicion. The idea of abjuring my country, and flying forever from the hateful scene, partook, to my apprehension, of the vast, the boundless, and strange: of plunging from the height of fortune to obscurity and indigence, corresponded with my present state of mind. It was of a piece with the tremendous and wonderful events that had just happened.

These were the images that haunted me, while I stood speechlessly gazing at the ruin before me. I heard a noise from without, or imagined that I heard it. My reverie was broken, and my muscular power restored. I descended into the street, through doors of which I possessed one set of keys, and hurried by the shortest way beyond the precincts of the city. I had laid no plan. My conceptions, with regard to the future, were shapeless and confused. Successive incidents supplied me with a clue, and suggested, as they rose, the next step to be taken.

I threw off the garb of affluence, and assumed a beggar's attire. That I had money about me for the accomplishment of my purposes was wholly accidental. I travelled along the coast, and when I arrived at one town, knew not why I should go further; but my restlessness was unabated, and change was some relief. I at length arrived at Belfast. A vessel was preparing for America. I embraced eagerly the opportunity of passing into a new world. I arrived at Philadelphia. As soon as I landed I wandered hither, and was content to wear out my few remaining days in the service of Inglefield.

I have no friends. Why should I trust my story to another? I have no solicitude about concealment; but who is there who will derive pleasure or benefit from my rehearsal? And why should I expatiate on so hateful a theme? Yet now have I consented to this. I have confided in you the history of my disasters. I am not fearful of the use that you may be disposed to make of it. I shall quickly set myself beyond the reach of human tribunals. I shall relieve the ministers of law from the trouble of punishing. The recent events which induced you to summon me to this conference, have likewise determined me to make this disclosure.

I was not aware, for some time, of my perturbed sleep. No wonder that sleep cannot soothe miseries like mine: that I am alike infested by memory in wakefulness and slumber. Yet I was anew distressed at the discovery that my thoughts found their way to my lips, without my being conscious of it, and that my steps wandered forth unknowingly and without the guidance of my will.

The story you have told is not incredible. The disaster to which you allude did not fail to excite my regret. I can still weep over the untimely fall of youth and worth. I can no otherwise account for my frequenting this shade than by the distant resemblance which the death of this man bore to that of which I was the perpetrator. This resemblance occurred to me at first. If time were able to weaken the impression which was produced by my crime, this similitude was adapted to revive and inforce them.

The wilderness, and the cave to which you followed me, were familiar to my sunday rambles. Often have I indulged in audible griefs on the cliffs of that valley. Often have I brooded over my sorrows in the recesses of that cavern. This scene is adapted to my temper. Its mountainous asperities supply me with images of desolation and seclusion, and its headlong streams lull me into temporary forgetfulness of mankind.

I comprehend you. You suspect me of concern in the death

of Waldegrave. You could not do otherwise. The conduct that you have witnessed was that of a murderer. I will not upbraid you for your suspicions, though I have bought exemption from them at an high price.

Chapter IX

THERE ENDED his narrative. He started from the spot where he stood, and, without affording me any opportunity of replying or commenting, disappeared amidst the thickest of the wood. I had no time to exert myself for his detention. I could have used no arguments for this end, to which it is probable he would have listened. The story I had heard was too extraordinary, too completely the reverse of all my expectations, to allow me to attend to the intimations of self-murder which he dropped.

The secret, which I imagined was about to be disclosed, was as inscrutable as ever. Not a circumstance, from the moment when Clithero's character became the subject of my meditations, till the conclusion of his tale, but served to confirm my suspicion. Was this error to be imputed to credulity? Would not any one, from similar appearances, have drawn similar conclusions? Or is there a criterion by which truth can always be distinguished? Was it owing to my imperfect education that the inquietudes of this man were not traced to a deed performed at the distance of a thousand leagues, to the murder of his patroness and friend?

I had heard a tale which apparently related to scenes and persons far distant, but though my suspicions have appeared to have been misplaced, what should hinder but that the death of my friend was, in like manner, an act of momentary insanity and originated in a like spirit of mistaken benevolence?

But I did not consider this tale merely in relation to myself. My life had been limited and uniform. I had communed with romancers and historians, but the impression made upon me by this incident was unexampled in my experience. My reading had furnished me with no instance, in any degree, parallel to this, and I found that to be a distant and second-hand spectator of events was widely different from witnessing them myself and partaking in their consequences. My judgement was, for a time, sunk into imbecility and confusion. My mind was full of the images unavoidably suggested by this tale, but they existed in a kind of chaos, and not otherwise, than gradually, was I able to reduce them to distinct particulars, and subject them to a deliberate and methodical inspection.

How was I to consider this act of Clithero? What a deplorable infatuation! Yet it was the necessary result of a series of ideas mutually linked and connected. His conduct was dictated by a motive allied to virtue. It was the fruit of an ardent and grateful spirit.

The death of Wiatte could not be censured. The life of Clithero was unspeakably more valuable than that of his antagonist. It was the instinct of self-preservation that swayed him. He knew not his adversary in time enough, to govern himself by that knowledge. Had the assailant been an unknown ruffian, his death would have been followed by no remorse. The spectacle of his dying agonies would have dwelt upon the memory of his assassin like any other mournful sight, in the production of which he bore no part.

It must at least be said that his will was not concerned in this transaction. He acted in obedience to an impulse which he could not controul, nor resist. Shall we impute guilt where there is no design? Shall a man extract food for self-reproach from an action to which it is not enough to say that he was actuated by no culpable intention, but that he was swayed by no intention whatever? If consequences arise that cannot be foreseen, shall we find no refuge in the persuasion of our rectitude and of human frailty? Shall we deem ourselves criminal because we do not enjoy the attributes of deity? Because our power and our knowledge are confined by impassable boundaries?

But whence arose the subsequent intention? It was the fruit of a dreadful mistake. His intents were noble and compassionate. But this is of no avail to free him from the imputation of guilt. No remembrance of past beneficence can compensate for this crime. The scale, loaded with the recriminations of his conscience, is immovable by any counter-weight.

But what are the conclusions to be drawn by dispassionate observers? Is it possible to regard this person with disdain or with enmity? The crime originated in those limitations which nature has imposed upon human faculties. Proofs of a just intention are all that are requisite to exempt us from blame. He is thus in consequence of a double mistake. The light in which he views this event is erroneous. He judges wrong and is therefore miserable.

How imperfect are the grounds of all our decisions! Was it of no use to superintend his childhood, to select his instructors and examples, to mark the operations of his principles, to see him emerging into youth, to follow him through various scenes and trying vicissitudes, and mark the uniformity of his integrity? Who would have predicted his future conduct? Who would not have affirmed the impossibility of an action like this?

How mysterious was the connection between the fate of Wiatte and his sister! By such circuitous, and yet infallible means, were the prediction of the lady and the vengeance of the brother accomplished! In how many cases may it be said, as in this, that the prediction was the cause of its own fulfilment? That the very act, which considerate observers, and even himself, for a time, imagined to have utterly precluded the execution of Wiatte's menaces, should be that inevitably leading to it? That the execution should be assigned to him, who, abounding in abhorrence, and in the act of self-defence, was the slayer of the menacer?

As the obstructor of his designs, Wiatte way-laid and assaulted Clithero. He perished in the attempt. Were his designs frustrated? . . . No. It was thus that he secured the gratification of his vengeance. His sister was cut off in the bloom of life and prosperity. By a refinement of good fortune, the voluntary minister of his malice had entailed upon himself exile without reprieve and misery without end.

But what chiefly excited my wonder was the connection of this tale with the destiny of Sarsefield. This was he whom I have frequently mentioned to you as my preceptor. About four years previous to this era, he appeared in this district without fortune or friend. He desired, one evening, to be accomodated at my uncle's house. The conversation turning on the objects of his journey, and his present situation, he professed himself in search of lucrative employment. My uncle proposed to him to become a teacher, there being a sufficient number of young people in this neighbourhood to afford him occupation and subsistence. He found it his interest to embrace this proposal.

I, of course, became his pupil, and demeaned myself in such a manner as speedily to grow into a favourite. He communicated to us no part of his early history, but informed us sufficiently of his adventures in Asia and Italy, to make it plain that this was the same person alluded to by Clithero. During his abode among us his conduct was irreproachable. When he left us, he manifested the most poignant regret, but this originated chiefly in his regard to me. He promised to maintain with me an epistolary intercourse. Since his departure, however, I had heard nothing respecting him. It was with unspeakable regret that I now heard of the disappointment of his hopes, and was inquisitive respecting the measures which he would adopt in his new situation. Perhaps he would once more return to America, and I should again be admitted to the enjoyment of his society. This event I anticipated with the highest satisfaction.

At present, the fate of the unhappy Clithero was the subject of abundant anxiety. On his suddenly leaving me, at the conclusion of his tale, I supposed that he had gone upon one of his usual rambles, and that it would terminate only with the day. Next morning a message was received from Inglefield inquiring if any one knew what had become of his servant. I could not listen to this message with tranquility. I recollected the hints that he had given of some design upon his life, and admitted the most dreary forebodings. I speeded to Inglefield's. Clithero had not returned, they told me, the preceding evening. He had not apprized them of any intention to change his abode. His boxes, and all that composed his slender property, were found in their ordinary state. He had expressed no dissatisfaction with his present condition.

Several days passed, and no tidings could be procured of him. His absence was a topic of general speculation, but was a source of particular anxiety to no one but myself. My apprehensions were surely built upon sufficient grounds. From the moment that we parted, no one had seen or heard of him. What mode of suicide he had selected, he had disabled us from discovering, by the impenetrable secrecy in which he had involved it.

In the midst of my reflections upon this subject, the idea of the wilderness occurred. Could he have executed his design in the deepest of its recesses? These were unvisited by human footsteps, and his bones might lie for ages in this solitude without attracting observation. To seek them where they lay, to gather them together and provide for them a grave, was a duty which appeared incumbent on me, and of which the performance was connected with a thousand habitual sentiments and mixed pleasures.

Thou knowest my devotion to the spirit that breathes its inspiration in the gloom of forests and on the verge of streams. I love to immerse myself in shades and dells, and hold converse with the solemnities and secrecies of nature in the rude retreats of Norwalk. The disappearance of Clithero had furnished new incitements to ascend its cliffs and pervade its thickets, as I cherished the hope of meeting in my rambles, with some traces of this man. But might he not still live? His words had imparted the belief that he intended to destroy himself. This catastrophe, however, was far from certain. Was it not in my power to avert it? Could I not restore a mind thus vigorous, to tranquil and wholesome existence? Could I not subdue his perverse disdain and immeasurable abhorrence of himself? His upbraiding and his scorn were unmerited and misplaced. Perhaps they argued phrensy rather than prejudice; but phrensy, like prejudice, was curable. Reason was no less an antidote to the illusions of insanity like his, than to the illusions of error.

I did not immediately recollect that to subsist in this desert was impossible. Nuts were the only fruits it produced, and these were inadequate to sustain human life. If it were haunted by Clithero, he must occasionally pass its limits and beg or purloin victuals. This deportment was too humiliating and flagitious to be imputed to him. There was reason to suppose him smitten with the charms of solitude, of a lonely abode in the midst of mountainous and rugged nature; but this could not be uninterruptedly enjoyed. Life could be supported only by occasionally visiting the haunts of men, in the guise of a thief or a mendicant. Hence, since Clithero was not known to have reappeared, at any farm-house in the neighbourhood, I was compelled to conclude, either that he had retired far from this district, or that he was dead.

Though I designed that my leisure should chiefly be con-

sumed in the bosom of Norwalk, I almost dismissed the hope
of meeting with the fugitive. There were indeed two sources
of my hopelessness on this occasion. Not only was it probable
that Clithero had fled far away, but, should he have concealed
himself in some nook or cavern, within these precincts, his
concealment was not to be traced. This arose from the nature
of that sterile region.

It would not be easy to describe the face of this district, in
a few words. Half of Solebury, thou knowest, admits neither
of plough nor spade. The cultivable space lies along the river,
and the desert, lying on the north, has gained, by some
means, the apellation of Norwalk. Canst thou imagine a space,
somewhat circular, about six miles in diameter, and exhibiting
a perpetual and intricate variety of craggy eminences and deep
dells?

The hollows are single, and walled around by cliffs, ever
varying in shape and height, and have seldom any perceptible
communication with each other. These hollows are of all dimensions, from the narrowness and depth of a well, to the
amplitude of one hundred yards. Winter's snow is frequently
found in these cavities at mid-summer. The streams that burst
forth from every crevice, are thrown, by the irregularities of
the surface, into numberless cascades, often disappear in mists
or in chasms, and emerge from subterranean channels, and,
finally, either subside into lakes, or quietly meander through
the lower and more level grounds.

Wherever nature left a flat it is made rugged and scarcely
passable by enormous and fallen trunks, accumulated by the
storms of ages, and forming, by their slow decay, a moss-
covered soil, the haunt of rabbets and lizards. These spots are
obscured by the melancholy umbrage of pines, whose eternal
murmurs are in unison with vacancy and solitude, with the
reverberations of the torrents and the whistling of the blasts.
Hiccory and poplar, which abound in the low-lands, find here
no fostering elements.

A sort of continued vale, winding and abrupt, leads into the
midst of this region and through it. This vale serves the purpose of a road. It is a tedious maze, and perpetual declivity,
and requires, from the passenger, a cautious and sure foot.
Openings and ascents occasionally present themselves on each

side, which seem to promise you access to the interior region, but always terminate, sooner or later, in insuperable difficulties, at the verge of a precipice, or the bottom of a steep.

Perhaps no one was more acquainted with this wilderness than I, but my knowledge was extremely imperfect. I had traversed parts of it, at an early age, in pursuit of berries and nuts, or led by a roaming disposition. Afterwards the sphere of my rambles was enlarged and their purpose changed. When Sarsefield came among us, I became his favourite scholar and the companion of all his pedestrian excursions. He was fond of penetrating into these recesses, partly from the love of picturesque scenes, partly to investigate its botanical and mineral productions, and, partly to carry on more effectually that species of instruction which he had adopted with regard to me, and which chiefly consisted in moralizing narratives or synthetical reasonings. These excursions had familiarized me with its outlines and most accessible parts; but there was much which, perhaps, could never be reached without wings, and much the only paths to which I might forever overlook.

Every new excursion indeed added somewhat to my knowledge. New tracks were pursued, new prospects detected, and new summits were gained. My rambles were productive of incessant novelty, though they always terminated in the prospect of limits that could not be overleaped. But none of these had led me wider from my customary paths than that which had taken place when in pursuit of Clithero. I had faint remembrance of the valley, into which I had descended after him, but till then I had viewed it at a distance, and supposed it impossible to reach the bottom but by leaping from a precipice some hundred feet in height. The opposite steep seemed no less inaccessible, and the cavern at the bottom was impervious to any views which my former positions had enabled me to take of it.

My intention to re-examine this cave and ascertain whither it led, had, for a time, been suspended by different considerations. It was now revived with more energy than ever. I reflected that this had formerly been haunted by Clithero, and might possibly have been the scene of the desperate act which he had meditated. It might at least conceal some token of his past existence. It might lead into spaces hitherto unvisited, and to summits from which wider landscapes might be seen.

One morning I set out to explore this scene. The road which Clithero had taken was laboriously circuitous. On my return from the first pursuit of him, I ascended the cliff in my former footsteps, but soon lighted on the beaten track which I had already described. This enabled me to shun a thousand obstacles, which had lately risen before me, and opened an easy passage to the cavern.

I once more traversed this way. The brow of the hill was gained. The ledges of which it consisted, afforded sufficient footing, when the attempt was made, though viewed at a distance they seemed to be too narrow for that purpose. As I descended the rugged stair, I could not but wonder at the temerity and precipitation with which this descent had formerly been made. It seemed as if the noon-day-light and the tardiest circumspection would scarcely enable me to accomplish it, yet then it had been done with headlong speed, and with no guidance but the moon's uncertain rays.

I reached the mouth of the cave. Till now I had forgotten that a lamp or a torch might be necessary to direct my subterranean footsteps. I was unwilling to defer the attempt. Light might possibly be requisite, if the cave had no other outlet. Somewhat might present itself within to the eyes, which might forever elude the hands, but I was more inclined to consider it merely as an avenue, terminating in an opening on the summit of the steep, or on the opposite side of the ridge. Caution might supply the place of light, or, having explored the cave as far as possible at present, I might hereafter return, better furnished for the scrutiny.

Chapter X

WITH these determinations, I proceeded. The entrance was low, and compelled me to resort to hands as well as feet. At a few yards from the mouth the light disappeared, and I found myself immersed in the dunnest obscurity. Had I not been persuaded that another had gone before me, I should have relinquished the attempt. I proceeded with the utmost caution, always ascertaining, by out-stretched arms, the height and breadth of the cavity before me. In a short time the dimensions expanded on all sides, and permitted me to resume my feet.

I walked upon a smooth and gentle declivity. Presently the wall, on one side, and the ceiling receded beyond my reach. I began to fear that I should be involved in a maze, and should be disabled from returning. To obviate this danger it was requisite to adhere to the nearest wall, and conform to the direction which it should take, without straying through the palpable obscurity. Whether the ceiling was lofty or low, whether the opposite wall of the passage was distant or near, this, I deemed no proper opportunity to investigate.

In a short time, my progress was stopped by an abrupt descent. I set down the advancing foot with caution, being aware that I might at the next step encounter a bottomless pit. To the brink of such an one I seemed now to have arrived. I stooped, and stretched my hand forward and downward, but all was vacuity.

Here it was needful to pause. I had reached the brink of a cavity whose depth it was impossible to ascertain. It might be a few inches beyond my reach, or hundreds of feet. By leaping down I might incur no injury, or might plunge into a lake or dash myself to pieces on the points of rocks.

I now saw with new force the propriety of being furnished with a light. The first suggestion was to return upon my footsteps, and resume my undertaking on the morrow. Yet, having advanced thus far, I felt reluctance to recede without accomplishing my purposes. I reflected likewise that Clithero had boldly entered this recess, and had certainly come forth at a different avenue from that at which he entered.

At length it occurred to me, that though I could not go forward, yet I might proceed along the edge of this cavity. This edge would be as safe a guidance, and would serve as well for a clue by which I might return, as the wall which it was now necessary to forsake.

Intense dark is always the parent of fears. Impending injuries cannot in this state be descried, nor shunned, nor repelled. I began to feel some faltering of my courage and seated myself, for a few minutes, on a stoney mass which arose before me. My situation was new. The caverns I had hitherto met with, in this desert, were chiefly formed of low-browed rocks. They were chambers, more or less spacious, into which twilight was at least admitted; but here it seemed as if I was surrounded by barriers that would forever cut off my return to air and to light.

Presently I resumed my courage and proceeded. My road appeared now to ascend. On one side I seemed still upon the verge of a precipice, and, on the other, all was empty and waste. I had gone no inconsiderable distance, and persuaded myself that my career would speedily terminate. In a short time, the space on the left hand, was again occupied, and I cautiously proceeded between the edge of the gulf and a rugged wall. As the space between them widened I adhered to the wall.

I was not insensible that my path became more intricate and more difficult to retread in proportion as I advanced. I endeavoured to preserve a vivid conception of the way which I had already passed, and to keep the images of the left, and right-hand wall, and the gulf, in due succession in my memory.

The path which had hitherto been considerably smooth, now became rugged and steep. Chilling damps, the secret trepidation which attended me, the length and difficulties of my way, enhanced by the ceaseless caution and the numerous expedients which the utter darkness obliged me to employ, began to overpower my strength. I was frequently compelled to stop and recruit myself by rest. These respites from toil were of use, but they could not enable me to prosecute an endless journey, and to return was scarcely a less arduous task than to proceed.

I looked anxiously forward in the hope of being comforted by some dim ray, which might assure me that my labours were approaching an end. At last this propitious token appeared, and I issued forth into a kind of chamber, one side of which was open to the air and allowed me to catch a portion of the checquered sky. This spectacle never before excited such exquisite sensations in my bosom. The air, likewise, breathed into the cavern, was unspeakably delicious.

I now found myself on the projecture of a rock. Above and below the hill-side was nearly perpendicular. Opposite, and at the distance of fifteen or twenty yards, was a similar ascent. At the bottom was a glen, cold, narrow and obscure. The projecture, which served as a kind of vestibule to the cave, was connected with a ledge, by which, though not without peril and toil, I was conducted to the summit.

This summit was higher than any of those which were interposed between itself and the river. A large part of this chaos of rocks and precipices was subjected, at one view, to the eye. The fertile lawns and vales which lay beyond this, the winding course of the river, and the slopes which rose on its farther side, were parts of this extensive scene. These objects were at any time fitted to inspire rapture. Now my delight was enhanced by the contrast which this lightsome and serene element bore to the glooms from which I had lately emerged. My station, also, was higher, and the limits of my view, consequently more ample than any which I had hitherto enjoyed.

I advanced to the outer verge of the hill, which I found to overlook a steep, no less inaccessible, and a glen equally profound. I changed frequently my station in order to diversify the scenery. At length it became necessary to inquire by what means I should return. I traversed the edge of the hill, but on every side it was equally steep and always too lofty to permit me to leap from it. As I kept along the verge, I perceived that it tended in a circular direction, and brought me back, at last, to the spot from which I had set out. From this inspection, it seemed as if return was impossible by any other way than that through the cavern.

I now turned my attention to the interior space. If you imagine a cylindrical mass, with a cavity dug in the centre, whose edge conforms to the exterior edge; and, if you place in this cavity another cylinder, higher than that which surrounds it, but so small as to leave between its sides and those of the cavity, an hollow space, you will gain as distinct an image of this hill as words can convey. The summit of the inner rock was rugged and covered with trees of unequal growth. To reach this summit would not render my return easier; but its greater elevation would extend my view, and perhaps furnish a spot from which the whole horizon was conspicuous.

As I had traversed the outer, I now explored the inner edge of this hill. At length I reached a spot where the chasm, separating the two rocks, was narrower than at any other part. At first view, it seemed as if it were possible to leap over it, but a nearer examination shewed me that the passage was impracticable. So far as my eye could estimate it, the breadth was thirty or forty feet. I could scarcely venture to look beneath. The height was dizzy, and the walls, which approached each other at top, receded at the bottom, so as to form the resemblance of an immense hall, lighted from a rift, which some convulsion of nature had made in the roof. Where I stood there ascended a perpetual mist, occasioned by a torrent that dashed along the rugged pavement below.

From these objects I willingly turned my eye upon those before and above me, on the opposite ascent. A stream, rushing from above, fell into a cavity, which its own force seemed gradually to have made. The noise and the motion equally attracted my attention. There was a desolate and solitary grandeur in the scene, enhanced by the circumstances in which it was beheld, and by the perils through which I had recently passed, that had never before been witnessed by me.

A sort of sanctity and awe environed it, owing to the consciousness of absolute and utter loneliness. It was probable that human feet had never before gained this recess, that human eyes had never been fixed upon these gushing waters. The aboriginal inhabitants had no motives to lead them into caves like this, and ponder on the verge of such a precipice. Their successors were still less likely to have wandered hither.

Since the birth of this continent, I was probably the first who had deviated thus remotely from the customary paths of men.

While musing upon these ideas, my eye was fixed upon the foaming current. At length, I looked upon the rocks which confined and embarrassed its course. I admired their phantastic shapes, and endless irregularities. Passing from one to the other of these, my attention lighted, at length, as if by some magical transition, on . . . an human countenance!

My surprise was so abrupt, and my sensations so tumultuous that I forgot for a moment the perilous nature of my situation. I loosened my hold of a pine branch, which had been hitherto one of my supports, and almost started from my seat. Had my station been, in a slight degree nearer the brink than it was, I should have fallen headlong into the abyss.

To meet an human creature, even on that side of the chasm which I occupied, would have been wholly adverse to my expectation. My station was accessible by no other road than that through which I had passed, and no motives were imaginable by which others could be prompted to explore this road. But he whom I now beheld, was seated where it seemed impossible for human efforts to have placed him. . . .

But this affected me but little in comparison with other incidents. Not only the countenance was human, but in spite of shaggy and tangled locks, and an air of melancholy wildness, I speedily recognized the features of the fugitive Clithero.

One glance was not sufficient to make me acquainted with this scene. I had come hither partly in pursuit of this man, but some casual appendage of his person, something which should indicate his past rather than his present existence, was all that I hoped to find. That he should be found alive in this desert; that he should have gained this summit, access to which was apparently impossible, were scarcely within the boundaries of belief.

His scanty and coarse garb, had been nearly rent away by brambles and thorns, his arms, bosom and cheek were overgrown and half-concealed by hair. There was somewhat in his attitude and looks denoting more than anarchy of thoughts and passions. His rueful, ghastly, and immoveable eyes, testified not only that his mind was ravaged by despair, but that he was pinched with famine.

These proofs of his misery thrilled to my inmost heart. Horror and shuddering invaded me as I stood gazing upon him, and, for a time, I was without the power of deliberating on the measures which it was my duty to adopt for his relief. The first suggestion was, by calling, to inform him of my presence. I knew not what counsel or comfort to offer. By what words to bespeak his attention, or by what topics to molify his direful passions I knew not. Though so near, the gulf by which we were separated was impassable. All that I could do was to speak.

My surprise and my horror were still strong enough to give a shrill and piercing tone to my voice. The chasm and the rocks loudened and reverberated my accents while I exclaimed . . . *Man! Clithero!*

My summons was effectual. He shook off his trance in a moment. He had been stretched upon his back, with his eyes fixed upon a craggy projecture above, as if he were in momentary expectation of its fall, and crushing him to atoms. Now he started on his feet. He was conscious of the voice, but not of the quarter whence it came. He was looking anxiously around when I again spoke . . . Look hither: It is I who called.

He looked. Astonishment was now mingled with every other dreadful meaning in his visage. He clasped his hands together and bent forward, as if to satisfy himself that his summoner was real. At the next moment he drew back, placed his hands upon his breast, and fixed his eyes on the ground.

This pause was not likely to be broken but by me. I was preparing again to speak. To be more distinctly heard, I advanced closer to the brink. During this action, my eye was necessarily withdrawn from him. Having gained a somewhat nearer station, I looked again, but . . . he was gone!

The seat which he so lately occupied was empty. I was not forewarned of his disappearance, or directed to the course of his flight by any rustling among leaves. These indeed would have been overpowered by the noise of the cataract. The place where he sat was the bottom of a cavity, one side of which terminated in the verge of the abyss, but the other sides were perpendicular or overhanging. Surely he had not leaped into this gulf, and yet that he had so speedily scaled the steep was impossible.

I looked into the gulf, but the depth and the gloom allowed me to see nothing with distinctness. His cries or groans could not be overheard amidst the uproar of the waters. His fall must have instantly destroyed him, and that he had fallen was the only conclusion I could draw.

My sensations on this incident cannot be easily described. The image of this man's despair, and of the sudden catastrophe to which my inauspicious interference had led, filled me with compunction and terror. Some of my fears were relieved by the new conjecture, that, behind the rock on which he had lain, there might be some aperture or pit into which he had descended, or in which he might be concealed.

I derived consolation from this conjecture. Not only the evil which I dreaded might not have happened, but some alleviation of his misery was possible. Could I arrest his footsteps and win his attention, I might be able to insinuate the lessons of fortitude; but if words were impotent, and arguments were nugatory, yet to set by him in silence, to moisten his hand with tears, to sigh in unison, to offer him the spectacle of sympathy, the solace of believing that his demerits were not estimated by so rigid a standard by others as by himself, that one at least among his fellow men regarded him with love and pity, could not fail to be of benign influence.

These thoughts inspired me with new zeal. To effect my purpose it was requisite to reach the opposite steep. I was now convinced that this was not an impracticable undertaking, since Clithero had already performed it. I once more made the circuit of the hill. Every side was steep and of enormous height, and the gulf was no where so narrow as at this spot. I therefore returned hither, and once more pondered on the means of passing this tremendous chasm in safety.

Casting my eyes upward, I noted the tree at the root of which I was standing. I compared the breadth of the gulf with the length of the trunk of this tree, and it appeared very suitable for a bridge. Happily it grew obliquely, and, if felled by an axe, would probably fall of itself, in such a manner as to be suspended across the chasm. The stock was thick enough to afford me footing, and would enable me to reach the opposite declivity without danger or delay.

A more careful examination of the spot, the scite of the tree, its dimensions and the direction of its growth convinced me fully of the practicability of this expedient, and I determined to carry it into immediate execution. For this end I must hasten home, procure an axe, and return with all expedition hither. I took my former way, once more entered the subterranean avenue, and slowly re-emerged into day. Before I reached home, the evening was at hand, and my tired limbs and jaded spirits obliged me to defer my undertaking till the morrow.

Though my limbs were at rest, my thoughts were active through the night. I carefully reviewed the situation of this hill, and was unable to conjecture by what means Clithero could place himself upon it. Unless he occasionally returned to the habitable grounds, it was impossible for him to escape perishing by famine. He might intend to destroy himself by this means, and my first efforts were to be employed to overcome this fatal resolution. To persuade him to leave his desolate haunts might be a laborious and tedious task; meanwhile all my benevolent intentions would be frustrated by his want of sustenance. It was proper, therefore, to carry bread with me, and to place it before him. The sight of food, the urgencies of hunger, and my vehement intreaties might prevail on him to eat, though no expostulation might suffice to make him seek food at a distance.

Chapter XI

NEXT MORNING I stored a small bag with meat and bread, and throwing an axe on my shoulder, set out, without informing any one of my intentions, for the hill. My passage was rendered more difficult by these incumbrances, but my perseverance surmounted every impediment, and I gained, in a few hours, the foot of the tree, whose trunk was to serve me for a bridge. In this journey I saw no traces of the fugitive.

A new survey of the tree confirmed my former conclusions, and I began my work with diligence. My strokes were repeated by a thousand echoes, and I paused at first somewhat startled by reverberations, which made it appear as if not one, but a score of axes, were employed at the same time on both sides of the gulf.

Quickly the tree fell, and exactly in the manner which I expected and desired. The wide-spread limbs occupied and choaked up the channel of the torrent, and compelled it to seek a new outlet and multiplied its murmurs. I dared not trust myself to cross it in an upright posture, but clung, with hands and feet, to its rugged bark. Having reached the opposite cliff I proceeded to examine the spot where Clithero had disappeared. My fondest hopes were realised, for a considerable cavity appeared, which, on a former day, had been concealed from my distant view by the rock.

It was obvious to conclude that this was his present habitation, or that an avenue, conducting hither and terminating in the unexplored sides of this pit, was that by which he had come hither, and by which he had retired. I could not hesitate long to slide into the pit. I found an entrance through which I fearlessly penetrated. I was prepared to encounter obstacles and perils similar to those which I have already described, but was rescued from them by ascending, in a few minutes, into a kind of passage, open above, but walled by a continued rock on both sides. The sides of this passage conformed with the utmost exactness to each other. Nature, at some former period, had occasioned the solid mass to dispart at this place, and had thus afforded access to the summit of the hill. Loose stones and ragged points formed the flooring of this passage, which rapidly and circuitously ascended.

I was now within a few yards of the surface of the rock. The passage opened into a kind of chamber or pit, the sides of which were not difficult to climb. I rejoiced at the prospect of this termination of my journey. Here I paused, and throwing my weary limbs on the ground, began to examine the objects around me, and to meditate on the steps that were next to be taken.

My first glance lighted on the very being of whom I was in search. Stretched upon a bed of moss, at the distance of a few feet from my station, I beheld Clithero. He had not been roused by my approach, though my footsteps were perpetually stumbling and sliding. This reflection gave birth to the fear that he was dead. A nearer inspection dispelled my apprehensions, and shewed me that he was merely buried in profound slumber. Those vigils must indeed have been long which were at last succeeded by a sleep so oblivious.

This meeting was, in the highest degree, propitious. It not only assured me of his existence, but proved that his miseries were capable to be suspended. His slumber enabled me to pause, to ruminate on the manner by which his understanding might be most successfully addressed; to collect and arrange the topics fitted to rectify his gloomy and disastrous perceptions.

Thou knowest that I am qualified for such tasks neither by my education nor my genius. The headlong and ferocious energies of this man could not be repelled or diverted into better paths by efforts so undisciplined as mine. A despair so stormy and impetuous would drown my feeble accents. How should I attempt to reason with him? How should I outroot prepossessions so inveterate; the fruits of his earliest education, fostered and matured by the observation and experience of his whole life? How should I convince him that since the death of Wiatte was not intended, the deed was without crime; that, if it had been deliberately concerted, it was still a virtue, since his own life could, by no other means, be preserved; that when he pointed a dagger at the bosom of his mistress he was actuated, not by avarice, or ambition, or revenge, or malice? He desired to confer on her the highest and the only benefit of which he believed her capable. He sought to rescue her from tormenting regrets and lingering agonies.

These positions were sufficiently just to my own view, but I was not called upon to reduce them to practice. I had not to struggle with the consciousness of having been rescued by some miraculous contingency, from embruing my hands in the blood of her whom I adored; of having drawn upon myself suspicions of ingratitude and murder too deep to be ever effaced; of having bereft myself of love, and honour, and friends, and spotless reputation; of having doomed myself to infamy and detestation, to hopeless exile, penury, and servile toil. These were the evils which his malignant destiny had made the unalterable portion of Clithero, and how should my imperfect eloquence annihilate these evils? Every man, not himself the victim of irretreivable disasters, perceives the folly of ruminating on the past, and of fostering a grief which cannot reverse or recall the decrees of an immutable necessity; but every man who suffers is unavoidably shackled by the errors which he censures in his neighbour, and his efforts to relieve himself are as fruitless as those with which he attempted the relief of others.

No topic, therefore, could be properly employed by me on the present occasion. All that I could do was to offer him food, and, by pathetic supplications, to prevail on him to eat. Famine, however obstinate, would scarcely refrain when bread was placed within sight and reach. When made to swerve from his resolution in one instance, it would be less difficult to conquer it a second time. The magic of sympathy, the perseverance of benevolence, though silent, might work a gradual and secret revolution, and better thoughts might insensibly displace those desperate suggestions which now governed him.

Having revolved these ideas, I placed the food which I had brought at his right hand, and, seating myself at his feet, attentively surveyed his countenance. The emotions, which were visible during wakefulness, had vanished during this cessation of remembrance and remorse, or were faintly discernible. They served to dignify and solemnize his features, and to embellish those immutable lines which betokened the spirit of his better days. Lineaments were now observed which could never co-exist with folly, or associate with obdurate guilt.

I had no inclination to awaken him. This respite was too sweet to be needlessly abridged. I determined to await the operation of nature, and to prolong, by silence and by keeping interruption at a distance, this salutary period of forgetfulness. This interval permitted new ideas to succeed in my mind.

Clithero believed his solitude to be unapproachable. What new expedients to escape inquiry and intrusion might not my presence suggest! Might he not vanish, as he had done on the former day, and afford me no time to assail his constancy and tempt his hunger? If, however, I withdrew during his sleep, he would awake without disturbance, and be unconscious for a time, that his secrecy had been violated. He would quickly perceive the victuals and would need no foreign inducements to eat. A provision, so unexpected and extraordinary, might suggest new thoughts, and be construed into a kind of heavenly condemnation of his purpose. He would not readily suspect the motives or person of his visitant, would take no precaution against the repetition of my visit, and, at the same time, our interview would not be attended with so much surpise. The more I revolved these reflections, the greater force they acquired. At length, I determined to withdraw, and, leaving the food where it could scarcely fail of attracting his notice, I returned by the way that I had come. I had scarcely reached home, when a messenger from Inglefield arrived, requesting me to spend the succeeding night at his house, as some engagement had occurred to draw him to the city.

I readily complied with this request. It was not necessary, however, to be early in my visit. I deferred going till the evening was far advanced. My way led under the branches of the elm which recent events had rendered so memorable. Hence my reflections reverted to the circumstances which had lately occurred in connection with this tree.

I paused, for some time, under its shade. I marked the spot where Clithero had been discovered digging. It shewed marks of being unsettled, but the sod which had formerly covered it and which had lately been removed, was now carefully replaced. This had not been done by him on that occasion in which I was a witness of his behaviour. The earth was then hastily removed and as hastily thrown again into the hole from which it had been taken.

Some curiosity was naturally excited by this appearance. Either some other person, or Clithero, on a subsequent occasion, had been here. I was now likewise led to reflect on the possible motives that prompted the maniac to turn up this earth. There is always some significance in the actions of a sleeper. Somewhat was, perhaps, buried in this spot, connected with the history of Mrs. Lorimer or of Clarice. Was it not possible to ascertain the truth in this respect?

There was but one method. By carefully uncovering this hole, and digging as deep as Clithero had already dug, it would quickly appear whether any thing was hidden. To do this publickly by day-light was evidently indiscreet. Besides, a moment's delay was superfluous. The night had now fallen, and before it was past this new undertaking might be finished. An interview was, if possible, to be gained with Clithero on the morrow, and for this interview the discoveries made on this spot might eminently qualify me. Influenced by these considerations, I resolved to dig. I was first, however, to converse an hour with the house-keeper, and then to withdraw to my chamber. When the family were all retired, and there was no fear of observation or interruption, I proposed to rise and hasten, with a proper implement, hither.

One chamber, in Inglefield's house, was usually reserved for visitants. In this chamber thy unfortunate brother died, and here it was that I was to sleep. The image of its last inhabitant could not fail of being called up, and of banishing repose; but the scheme which I had meditated was an additional incitement to watchfulness. Hither I repaired, at the due season, having previously furnished myself with candles, since I knew not what might occur to make a light necessary.

I did not go to bed, but either sat musing by a table or walked across the room. The bed before me was that on which my friend breathed his last. To rest my head upon the same pillow, to lie on that pallet which sustained his cold and motionless limbs, were provocations to remembrance and grief that I desired to shun. I endeavoured to fill my mind with more recent incidents, with the disasters of Clithero, my subterranean adventures, and the probable issue of the schemes which I now contemplated.

I recalled the conversation which had just ended with the house-keeper. Clithero had been our theme, but she had dealt chiefly in repetitions of what had formerly been related by her or by Inglefield. I inquired what this man had left behind, and found that it consisted of a square box, put together by himself with uncommon strength, but of rugged workmanship. She proceeded to mention that she had advised her brother, Mr. Inglefield, to break open this box and ascertain its contents, but this he did not think himself justified in doing. Clithero was guilty of no known crime, was responsible to no one for his actions, and might sometime return to claim his property. This box contained nothing with which others had a right to meddle. Somewhat might be found in it, throwing light upon his past or present situation, but curiosity was not to be gratified by these means. What Clithero thought proper to conceal, it was criminal for us to extort from him.

The house-keeper was by no means convinced by these arguments, and at length, obtained her brother's permission to try whether any of her own keys would unlock this chest. The keys were produced, but no lock nor key-hole were discoverable. The lid was fast, but by what means it was fastened, the most accurate inspection could not detect. Hence she was compelled to lay aside her project. This chest had always stood in the chamber which I now occupied.

These incidents were now remembered, and I felt disposed to profit by this opportunity of examining this box. It stood in a corner, and was easily distinguished by its form. I lifted it and found its weight by no means extraordinary. Its structure was remarkable. It consisted of six sides, square and of similar dimensions. These were joined, not by mortice and tennon; not by nails, not by hinges, but the junction was accurate. The means by which they were made to cohere were invisible.

Appearances on every side were uniform, nor were there any marks by which the lid was distinguishable from its other surfaces.

During his residence with Inglefield, many specimens of mechanical ingenuity were given by his servant. This was the workmanship of his own hands. I looked at it, for some time, till the desire insensibly arose of opening and examining its contents.

I had no more right to do this than the Inglefields; perhaps indeed this curiosity was more absurd, and the gratification more culpable in me than in them. I was acquainted with the history of Clithero's past life, and with his present condition. Respecting these, I had no new intelligence to gain, and no doubts to solve. What excuse could I make to the proprietor, should he ever reappear to claim his own, or to Inglefield for breaking open a receptacle which all the maxims of society combine to render sacred?

But could not my end be gained without violence? The means of opening might present themselves on a patient scrutiny. The lid might be raised and shut down again without any tokens of my act; its contents might be examined, and all things restored to their former condition in a few minutes.

I intended not a theft. I intended to benefit myself without inflicting injury on others. Nay, might not the discoveries I should make, throw light upon the conduct of this extraordinary man, which his own narrative had withheld? Was there reason to confide implicitly on the tale which I had heard?

In spite of the testimony of my own feelings, the miseries of Clithero appeared in some degree, phantastic and groundless. A thousand conceivable motives might induce him to pervert or conceal the truth. If he were thoroughly known, his character might assume a new appearance, and what is now so difficult to reconcile to common maxims, might prove perfectly consistent with them. I desire to restore him to peace, but a thorough knowledge of his actions is necessary, both to shew that he is worthy of compassion, and to suggest the best means of extirpating his errors. It was possible that this box contained the means of this knowledge.

There were likewise other motives which, as they possessed some influence, however small, deserve to be mentioned. Thou knowest that I also am a mechanist. I had constructed a writing desk and cabinet, in which I had endeavoured to combine the properties of secrecy, security, and strength, in the highest possible degree. I looked upon this therefore with the eye of an artist, and was solicitous to know the principles on which it was formed. I determined to examine, and if possible to open it.

Chapter XII

I SURVEYED IT with the utmost attention. All its parts appeared equally solid and smooth. It could not be doubted that one of its sides served the purpose of a lid, and was possible to be raised. Mere strength could not be applied to raise it, because there was no projecture which might be firmly held by the hand, and by which force could be exerted. Some spring, therefore, secretly existed which might forever elude the senses, but on which the hand, by being moved over it, in all directions, might accidentally light.

This process was effectual. A touch, casually applied at an angle, drove back a bolt, and a spring, at the same time, was set in action, by which the lid was raised above half an inch. No event could be supposed more fortuitous than this. An hundred hands might have sought in vain for this spring. The spot in which a certain degree of pressure was sufficient to produce this effect, was of all, the last likely to attract notice or awaken suspicion.

I opened the trunk with eagerness. The space within was divided into numerous compartments, none of which contained any thing of moment. Tools of different and curious constructions, and remnants of minute machinery, were all that offered themselves to my notice.

My expectations being thus frustrated, I proceeded to restore things to their former state. I attempted to close the lid; but the spring which had raised it refused to bend. No measure that I could adopt, enabled me to place the lid in the same situation in which I had found it. In my efforts to press down the lid, which were augmented in proportion to the resistance that I met with, the spring was broken. This obstacle being removed, the lid resumed its proper place; but no means, within the reach of my ingenuity to discover, enabled me to push forward the bolt, and thus to restore the fastening.

I now perceived that Clithero had provided not only against the opening of his cabinet, but likewise against the possibility of concealing that it had been opened. This discovery threw me into some confusion. I had been tempted thus far, by the belief that my action was without witnesses, and might be forever concealed. This opinion was now confuted. If Clithero should ever reclaim his property, he would not fail to detect the violence of which I had been guilty. Inglefield would disapprove in another what he had not permitted to himself, and the unauthorized and clandestine manner in which I had behaved, would aggravate, in his eyes, the heinousness of my offence.

But now there was no remedy. All that remained was to hinder suspicion from lighting on the innocent, and to confess, to my friend, the offence which I had committed. Meanwhile my first project was resumed, and, the family being now wrapt in profound sleep, I left my chamber, and proceeded to the elm. The moon was extremely brilliant, but I hoped that this unfrequented road and unseasonable hour would hinder me from being observed. My chamber was above the kitchen, with which it communicated by a small stair-case, and the building to which it belonged was connected with the dwelling by a gallery. I extinguished the light, and left it in the kitchen, intending to relight it, by the embers that still glowed on the hearth, on my return.

I began to remove the sod, and cast out the earth, with little confidence in the success of my project. The issue of my examination of the box humbled and disheartened me. For some time I found nothing that tended to invigorate my hopes. I determined, however, to descend, as long as the unsettled condition of the earth shewed me that some one had preceded me. Small masses of stone were occasionally met with, which served only to perplex me with groundless expectations. At length my spade struck upon something which emitted a very different sound. I quickly drew it forth, and found it to be wood. Its regular form, and the crevices which were faintly discernible, persuaded me that it was human workmanship, and that there was a cavity within. The place in which it was found, easily suggested some connection between this and the destiny of Clithero. Covering up the hole with speed, I hastened with my prize to the house. The door, by which the kitchen was entered, was not to be seen from the road. It opened on a field, the farther limit of which was a ledge of rocks, which formed, on this side, the boundary of Inglefield's estate and the westernmost barrier of Norwalk.

As I turned the angle of the house, and came in view of this door, methought I saw a figure issue from it. I was startled at this incident, and, stopping, crouched close to the wall, that I might not be discovered. As soon as the figure passed beyond the verge of the shade, it was easily distinguished to be that of Clithero! He crossed the field with a rapid pace, and quickly passed beyond the reach of my eye.

This appearance was mysterious. For what end he should visit this habitation, could not be guessed. Was the contingency to be lamented, in consequence of which an interview had been avoided? Would it have compelled me to explain the broken condition of his trunk? I knew not whether to rejoice at having avoided this interview, or to deplore it.

These thoughts did not divert me from examining the nature of the prize which I had gained. I relighted my candle and hied once more to the chamber. The first object which, on entering it, attracted my attention, was the cabinet broken into twenty fragments, on the hearth. I had left it on a low table, at a distant corner of the room.

No conclusion could be formed, but that Clithero had been here, had discovered the violence which had been committed on his property, and, in the first transport of his indignation, had shattered it to pieces. I shuddered on reflecting how near I had been to being detected by him in the very act, and by how small an interval I had escaped that resentment, which, in that case, would have probably been wreaked upon me.

My attention was withdrawn, at length, from this object, and fixed upon the contents of the box which I had dug up. This was equally inaccessible with the other. I had not the same motives for caution and forbearance. I was somewhat desperate, as the consequences of my indiscretion could not be aggravated, and my curiosity was more impetuous, with regard to the smaller than to the larger cabinet. I placed it on the ground and crushed it to pieces with my heel.

Something was within. I brought it to the light, and, after loosing numerous folds, at length drew forth a volume. No object, in the circle of nature, was more adapted than this, to rouse up all my faculties. My feelings were anew excited on observing that it was a manuscript. I bolted the door, and, drawing near the light, opened and began to read.

A few pages was sufficient to explain the nature of the work. Clithero had mentioned that his lady had composed a vindication of her conduct towards her brother, when her intercession in his favour was solicited and refused. This performance had never been published, but had been read by many, and was preserved by her friends as a precious monument of her genius and her virtue. This manuscript was now before me.

That Clithero should preserve this manuscript, amidst the wreck of his hopes and fortunes, was apparently conformable to his temper. That, having formed the resolution to die, he should seek to hide this volume from the profane curiosity of survivors, was a natural proceeding. To bury it rather than to burn, or disperse it into fragments, would be suggested by the wish to conceal, without committing what his heated fancy would regard as sacrilege. To bury it beneath the elm, was dictated by no fortuitous or inexplicable caprice. This event could scarcely fail of exercising some influence on the perturbations of his sleep, and thus, in addition to other causes, might his hovering near this trunk, and throwing up this earth, in the intervals of slumber, be accounted for. Clithero, indeed, had not mentioned this proceeding in the course of his narrative; but that would have contravened the end for which he had provided a grave for this book.

I read this copious tale with unspeakable eagerness. It essentially agreed with that which had been told by Clithero. By drawing forth events into all their circumstances, more distinct impressions were produced on the mind, and proofs of fortitude and equanimity were here given, to which I had hitherto known no parallel. No wonder that a soul like Clithero's, pervaded by these proofs of inimitable excellence, and thrillingly alive to the passion of virtuous fame, and the value of that existence which he had destroyed, should be overborne by horror at the view of the past.

The instability of life and happiness was forcibly illustrated, as well as the perniciousness of error. Exempt as this lady was from almost every defect, she was indebted for her ruin to absurd opinions of the sacredness of consanguinity, to her anxiety for the preservation of a ruffian, because that ruffian was her brother. The spirit of Clithero was enlightened and erect, but he weakly suffered the dictates of eternal justice to be swallowed up by gratitude. The dread of unjust upbraiding hurried him to murder and to suicide, and the imputation of imaginary guilt, impelled him to the perpetration of genuine and enormous crimes.

The perusal of this volume ended not but with the night. Contrary to my hopes, the next day was stormy and wet. This did not deter me from visiting the mountain. Slippery paths and muddy torrents were no obstacles to the purposes which I had adopted. I wrapt myself, and a bag of provisions, in a cloak of painted canvass and speeded to the dwelling of Clithero.

I passed through the cave and reached the bridge which my own ingenuity had formed. At that moment, torrents of rain poured from above, and stronger blasts thundered amidst these desolate recesses and profound chasms. Instead of lamenting the prevalence of this tempest, I now began to regard it with pleasure. It conferred new forms of sublimity and grandeur on this scene.

As I crept with hands and feet, along my imperfect bridge, a sudden gust had nearly whirled me into the frightful abyss below. To preserve myself, I was oblidged to loose my hold of my burthen and it fell into the gulf. This incident disconcerted and distressed me. As soon as I had effected my dangerous passage, I screened myself behind a cliff, and gave myself up to reflection.

The purpose of this arduous journey was defeated, by the loss of the provisions I had brought. I despaired of winning the attention of the fugitive to supplications, or arguments tending to smother remorse, or revive his fortitude. The scope of my efforts was to consist in vanquishing his aversion to food; but these efforts would now be useless, since I had no power to supply his cravings.

This deficiency, however, was easily supplied. I had only to return home and supply myself anew. No time was to be lost in doing this; but I was willing to remain under this shelter, till the fury of the tempest had subsided. Besides, I was not certain that Clithero had again retreated hither. It was requisite to explore the summit of this hill, and ascertain whether it had any inhabitant. I might likewise discover what had been the success of my former experiment, and whether the food, which had been left here on the former day, was consumed or neglected.

While occupied with these reflections, my eyes were fixed upon the opposite steeps. The tops of the trees, waving to and fro, in the wildest commotion, and their trunks, occasionally bending to the blast, which, in these lofty regions, blew with a violence unknown in the tracts below, exhibited an awful spectacle. At length, my attention was attracted by the trunk which lay across the gulf, and which I had converted into a bridge. I perceived that it had already somewhat swerved from its original position, that every blast broke or loosened some of the fibres by which its root was connected with the opposite bank, and that, if the storm did not speedily abate, there was imminent danger of its being torn from the rock and precipitated into the chasm. Thus my retreat would be cut off, and the evils, from which I was endeavouring to rescue another, would be experienced by myself.

I did not just then reflect that Clithero had found access to this hill by other means, and that the avenue by which he came, would be equally commodious to me. I believed my destiny to hang upon the expedition with which I should re-cross this gulf. The moments that were spent in these deliberations were critical, and I shuddered to observe that the trunk was held in its place by one or two fibres which were already stretched almost to breaking.

To pass along the trunk, rendered slippery by the wet, and unsteadfast by the wind, was eminently dangerous. To maintain my hold, in passing, in defiance of the whirlwind, required the most vigorous exertions. For this end it was necessary to discommode myself of my cloak, and of the volume, which I carried in the pocket of my cloak. I believed there was no reason to dread their being destroyed or purloined, if left, for a few hours or a day, in this recess. If laid beside a stone, under shelter of this cliff, they would, no doubt, remain unmolested till the disappearance of the storm should permit me to revisit this spot in the afternoon or on the morrow.

Just as I had disposed of these incumbrances, and had risen from my seat, my attention was again called to the opposite steep, by the most unwelcome object that, at this time, could possibly occur. Something was perceived moving among the bushes and rocks, which, for a time, I hoped was no more than a racoon or oppossum; but which presently appeared to be a panther. His grey coat, extended claws, fiery eyes, and a cry which he at that moment uttered, and which, by its resemblance to the human voice, is peculiarly terrific, denoted him to be the most ferocious and untamable of that detested race*.

The industry of our hunters has nearly banished animals of prey from these precincts. The fastnesses of Norwalk, however, could not but afford refuge to some of them. Of late I had met them so rarely, that my fears were seldom alive, and I trod, without caution, the ruggedest and most solitary haunts. Still, however, I had seldom been unfurnished in my rambles with the means of defence.

My temper never delighted in carnage and blood. I found no pleasure in plunging into bogs, wading through rivulets, and penetrating thickets, for the sake of dispatching woodcocks and squirrels. To watch their gambols and flittings, and invite them to my hand, was my darling amusement when loitering among the woods and the rocks. It was much otherwise, however, with regard to rattlesnakes and panthers. These I thought it no breach of duty to exterminate wherever they could be found. These judicious and sanguinary spoilers were equally the enemies of man and of the harmless race that sported in the trees, and many of their skins are still preserved by me as trophies of my juvenile prowess.

As hunting was never my trade or my sport, I never loaded myself with fowling-piece or rifle. Assiduous exercise had made me master of a weapon of much easier carriage, and, within a moderate distance, more destructive and unerring. This was the tom-hawk. With this I have often severed an oak branch and cut the sinews of a cat-o'mountain, at the distance of sixty feet.

*The grey Cougar. This animal has all the essential characteristics of a tyger. Though somewhat inferior in size and strength, these are such as to make him equally formidable to man.

The unfrequency with which I had lately encountered this foe, and the incumbrance of provision, made me neglect, on this occasion, to bring with me my usual arms. The beast that was now before me, when stimulated by hunger, was accustomed to assail whatever could provide him with a banquet of blood. He would set upon the man and the deer with equal and irresistible ferocity. His sagacity was equal to his strength, and he seemed able to discover when his antagonist was armed and prepared for defence.

My past experience enabled me to estimate the full extent of my danger. He sat on the brow of the steep, eyeing the bridge, and apparently deliberating whether he should cross it. It was probable that he had scented my footsteps thus far, and should he pass over, his vigilance could scarcely fail of detecting my assylum. The pit into which Clithero had sunk from my view was at some distance. To reach it was the first impulse of my fear, but this could not be done without exciting the observation and pursuit of this enemy. I deeply regretted the untoward chance that had led me, when I first came over, to a different shelter.

Should he retain his present station, my danger was scarcely lessened. To pass over in the face of a famished tyger was only to rush upon my fate. The falling of the trunk, which had lately been so anxiously deprecated, was now, with no less solicitude, desired. Every new gust, I hoped, would tear asunder its remaining bands, and, by cutting off all communication between the opposite steeps, place me in security.

My hopes, however, were destined to be frustrated. The fibres of the prostrate tree, were obstinately tenacious of their hold, and presently the animal scrambled down the rock and proceeded to cross it.

Of all kinds of death, that which now menaced me was the most abhorred. To die by disease, or by the hand of a fellow-creature, was propitious and lenient in comparison with being rent to pieces by the fangs of this savage. To perish, in this obscure retreat, by means so impervious to the anxious curiosity of my friends, to lose my portion of existence by so untoward and ignoble a destiny, was insupportable. I bitterly deplored my rashness in coming hither unprovided for an encounter like this.

The evil of my present circumstances consisted chiefly in suspense. My death was unavoidable, but my imagination had leisure to torment itself by anticipations. One foot of the savage was slowly and cautiously moved after the other. He struck his claws so deeply into the bark that they were with difficulty withdrawn. At length he leaped upon the ground. We were now separated by an interval of scarcely eight feet. To leave the spot where I crouched, was impossible. Behind and beside me, the cliff rose perpendicularly, and before me was this grim and terrific visage. I shrunk still closer to the ground and closed my eyes.

From this pause of horror I was roused by the noise occasioned by a second spring of the animal. He leaped into the pit, in which I had so deeply regretted that I had not taken refuge, and disappeared. My rescue was so sudden, and so much beyond my belief or my hope, that I doubted, for a moment, whether my senses did not deceive me. This opportunity of escape was not to be neglected. I left my place, and scrambled over the trunk with a precipitation which had liked to have proved fatal. The tree groaned and shook under me, the wind blew with unexampled violence, and I had scarcely reached the opposite steep when the roots were severed from the rock and the whole fell thundering to the bottom of the chasm.

My trepidations were not speedily quieted. I looked back with wonder on my hair-breadth escape, and on that singular concurrence of events, which had placed me, in so short a period, in absolute security. Had the trunk fallen a moment earlier, I should have been imprisoned on the hill or thrown headlong. Had its fall been delayed another moment I should have been pursued; for the beast now issued from his den, and testified his surprise and disappointment by tokens the sight of which made my blood run cold.

He saw me, and hastened to the verge of the chasm. He squatted on his hind-legs and assumed the attitude of one preparing to leap. My consternation was excited afresh by these appearances. It seemed at first as if the rift was too wide for any power of muscles to carry him in safety over; but I knew the unparalleled agility of this animal, and that his experience had made him a better judge of the practicability of this exploit than I was.

Still there was hope that he would relinquish this design as desperate. This hope was quickly at an end. He sprung, and his fore-legs touched the verge of the rock on which I stood. In spite of vehement exertions, however, the surface was too smooth and too hard to allow him to make good his hold. He fell, and a piercing cry, uttered below, shewed that nothing had obstructed his descent to the bottom.

Thus was I again rescued from death. Nothing but the pressure of famine could have prompted this savage to so audacious and hazardous an effort; but, by yeilding to this impulse, he had made my future visits to this spot exempt from peril. Clithero was, likewise, relieved from a danger that was imminent and unforeseen. Prowling over these grounds the panther could scarcely have failed to meet with this solitary fugitive.

Had the animal lived, my first duty would have been to have sought him out, and assailed him with my tom-hawk; but no undertaking would have been more hazardous. Lurking in the grass, or in the branches of a tree, his eye might have descried my approach, he might leap upon me unperceived, and my weapon would be useless.

With an heart beating with unwonted rapidity, I once more descended the cliff, entered the cavern, and arrived at Huntly farm, drenched with rain, and exhausted by fatigue.

By night the storm was dispelled; but my exhausted strength would not allow me to return to the mountain. At the customary hour I retired to my chamber. I incessantly ruminated on the adventures of the last day, and inquired into the conduct which I was next to pursue.

The bridge being destroyed, my customary access was cut off. There was no possibility of restoring this bridge. My strength would not suffice to drag a fallen tree from a distance, and there was none whose position would abridge or supersede that labour. Some other expedient must, therefore, be discovered to pass this chasm.

I reviewed the circumstances of my subterranean journey. The cavern was imperfectly explored. Its branches might be numerous. That which I had hitherto pursued, terminated in an opening at a considerable distance from the bottom. Other branches might exist, some of which might lead to the foot of the precipice, and thence a communication might be found with the summit of the interior hill.

The danger of wandering into dark and untried paths, and the commodiousness of that road which had at first been taken, were sufficient reasons for having hitherto suspended my examination of the different branches of this labyrinth. Now my customary road was no longer practicable, and another was to be carefully explored. For this end, on my next journey to the mountain, I determined to take with me a lamp, and unravel this darksome maze: This project I resolved to execute the next day.

I now recollected what, if it had more seasonably occurred, would have taught me caution. Some months before this a farmer, living in the skirts of Norwalk, discovered two marauders in his field, whom he imagined to be a male and female panther. They had destroyed some sheep, and had been hunted by the farmer, with long and fruitless diligence. Sheep had likewise been destroyed in different quarters; but the owners had fixed the imputation of the crime upon dogs, many of whom had atoned for their supposed offences by their death. He who had mentioned his discovery of panthers, received little credit from his neighbours; because a long time had elapsed since these animals were supposed to have been exiled from this district, and because no other person had seen them. The truth of this seemed now to be confirmed by the testimony of my own senses; but, if the rumour were true, there still existed another of these animals, who might harbour in the obscurities of this desert, and against whom it was necessary to employ some precaution. Henceforth I resolved never to traverse the wilderness unfurnished with my tomhawk.

These images, mingled with those which the contemplation of futurity suggested, floated, for a time, in my brain; but at length gave place to sleep.

Chapter XIII

SINCE my return home, my mind had been fully occupied by schemes and reflections relative to Clithero. The project suggested by thee, and to which I had determined to devote my leisure, was forgotten, or remembered for a moment and at wide intervals. What, however, was nearly banished from my waking thoughts, occurred, in an incongruous and half-seen form, to my dreams. During my sleep, the image of Waldegrave flitted before me. Methought the sentiment that impelled him to visit me, was not affection or complacency, but inquietude and anger. Some service or duty remained to be performed by me, which I had culpably neglected: to inspirit my zeal, to awaken my remembrance, and incite me to the performance of this duty, did this glimmering messenger, this half indignant apparition, come.

I commonly awake soon enough to mark the youngest dawn of the morning. Now, in consequence perhaps of my perturbed sleep, I opened my eyes before the stars had lost any of their lustre. This circumstance produced some surprise, until the images that lately hovered in my fancy, were recalled, and furnished somewhat like a solution of the problem. Connected with the image of my dead friend, was that of his sister. The discourse that took place at our last interview; the scheme of transcribing, for thy use, all the letters which, during his short but busy life, I received from him; the nature of this correspondence, and the opportunity which this employment would afford me of contemplating these ample and precious monuments of the intellectual existence and moral pre-eminence of my friend, occurred to my thoughts.

The resolution to prosecute the task was revived. The obligation of benevolence, with regard to Clithero, was not discharged. This, neither duty nor curiosity would permit to be overlooked or delayed; but why should my whole attention and activity be devoted to this man? The hours which were spent at home and in my chamber, could not be more usefully employed than in making my intended copy.

In a few hours after sun-rise I purposed to resume my way

to the mountain. Could this interval be appropriated to a better purpose than in counting over my friend's letters, setting them apart from my own, and preparing them for that transcription from which I expected so high and yet so mournful a gratification?

This purpose, by no violent union, was blended with the recollection of my dream. This recollection infused some degree of wavering and dejection into my mind. In transcribing these letters I should violate pathetic and solemn injunctions frequently repeated by the writer. Was there some connection between this purpose and the incidents of my vision? Was the latter sent to enforce the interdictions which had been formerly imposed?

Thou art not fully acquainted with the intellectual history of thy brother. Some information on that head will be necessary to explain the nature of that reluctance which I now feel to comply with thy request, and which had formerly so much excited thy surprise.

Waldegrave, like other men, early devoted to meditation and books, had adopted, at different periods, different systems of opinion, on topics connected with religion and morals. His earliest creeds, tended to efface the impressions of his education; to deify necessity and universalize matter; to destroy the popular distinctions between soul and body, and to dissolve the supposed connection between the moral condition of man, anterior and subsequent to death.

This creed he adopted with all the fulness of conviction, and propagated with the utmost zeal. Soon after our friendship commenced, fortune placed us at a distance from each other, and no intercourse was allowed but by the pen. Our letters, however, were punctual and copious. Those of Waldegrave were too frequently devoted to the defence of his favourite tenets.

Thou art acquainted with the revolution that afterwards took place in his mind. Placed within the sphere of religious influence, and listening daily to the reasonings and exhortations of Mr. S——, whose benign temper and blameless deportment was a visible and constant lesson, he insensibly resumed the faith which he had relinquished, and became the vehement opponent of all that he had formerly defended. The chief object of his labours, in this new state of his mind, was to counteract the effect of his former reasonings on my opinions.

At this time, other changes took place in his situation, in consequence of which we were once more permitted to reside under the same roof. The intercourse now ceased to be by letter, and the subtle and laborious argumentations which he had formerly produced against religion, and which were contained in a permanent form, were combatted in transient conversation. He was not only eager to subvert those opinions, which he had contributed to instil into me, but was anxious that the letters and manuscripts, which had been employed in their support, should be destroyed. He did not fear wholly or chiefly on my own account. He believed that the influence of former reasonings on my faith would be sufficiently eradicated by the new; but he dreaded lest these manuscripts might fall into other hands, and thus produce mischiefs which it would not be in his power to repair. With regard to me, the poison had been followed by its antidote; but with respect to others, these letters would communicate the poison when the antidote could not be administered.

I would not consent to this sacrifice. I did not entirely abjure the creed which had, with great copiousness and eloquence, been defended in these letters. Beside, mixed up with abstract reasonings, were numberless passages which elucidated the character and history of my friend. These were too precious to be consigned to oblivion, and to take them out of their present connection and arrangement, would be to mutilate and deform them.

His intreaties and remonstrances were earnest and frequent, but always ineffectual. He had too much purity of motives to be angry at my stubbornness, but his sense of the mischievous tendency of these letters, was so great, that my intractability cost him many a pang.

He was now gone, and I had not only determined to preserve these monuments, but had consented to copy them for the use of another: for the use of one whose present and eternal welfare had been the chief object of his cares and efforts. Thou, like others of thy sex, art unaccustomed to metaphysical refinements. Thy religion is the growth of sensibility and not of argument. Thou art not fortified and prepossessed against the subtleties, with which the being and attributes of the deity have been assailed. Would it be just to expose thee to pollution and depravity from this source? To make thy brother the instrument of thy apostacy, the author of thy fall? That brother, whose latter days were so ardently devoted to cherishing the spirit of devotion in thy heart?

These ideas now occurred with more force than formerly. I had promised, not without reluctance, to give thee the entire copy of his letters; but I now receded from this promise. I resolved merely to select for thy perusal such as were narrative or descriptive. This could not be done with too much expedition. It was still dark, but my sleep was at an end, and, by a common apparatus, that lay beside my bed, I could instantly produce a light.

The light was produced, and I proceeded to the cabinet where all my papers and books are deposited. This was my own contrivance and workmanship, undertaken by the advice of Sarsefield, who took infinite pains to foster that mechanical genius, which displayed itself so early and so forcibly in thy friend. The key belonging to this, was, like the cabinet itself, of singular structure. For greater safety, it was constantly placed in a closet, which was likewise locked.

The key was found as usual, and the cabinet opened. The letters were bound together in a compact form, lodged in a parchment case, and placed in a secret drawer. This drawer would not have been detected by common eyes, and it opened by the motion of a spring, of whose existence none but the maker was conscious. This drawer I had opened before I went to sleep and the letters were then safe.

Thou canst not imagine my confusion and astonishment, when, on opening the drawer, I perceived that the pacquet was gone. I looked with more attention, and put my hand within it, but the space was empty. Whither had it gone, and by whom was it purloined? I was not conscious of having taken it away, yet no hands but mine could have done it. On the last evening I had doubtless removed it to some other corner, but had forgotten it. I tasked my understanding and my memory. I could not conceive the possibility of any motives inducing me to alter my arrangements in this respect, and was unable to recollect that I had made this change.

What remained? This invaluable relique had disappeared. Every thought and every effort must be devoted to the single purpose of regaining it. As yet I did not despair. Until I had opened and ransacked every part of the cabinet in vain, I did not admit the belief that I had lost it. Even then this persuasion was tumultuous and fluctuating. It had vanished to my senses, but these senses were abused and depraved. To have passed, of its own accord, through the pores of this wood, was impossible; but if it were gone, thus did it escape.

I was lost in horror and amazement. I explored every nook a second and a third time, but still it eluded my eye and my touch. I opened my closets and cases. I pryed every where, unfolded every article of cloathing, turned and scrutinized every instrument and tool, but nothing availed.

My thoughts were not speedily collected or calmed. I threw myself on the bed and resigned myself to musing. That my loss was irretreivable, was a supposition not to be endured. Yet ominous terrors haunted me. A whispering intimation that a relique which I valued more than life was torn forever away by some malignant and inscrutable destiny. The same power that had taken it from this receptacle, was able to waft it over the ocean or the mountains, and condemn me to a fruitless and eternal search.

But what was he that committed the theft? Thou only, of the beings who live, wast acquainted with the existence of these manuscripts. Thou art many miles distant, and art utterly a stranger to the mode or place of their concealment. Not only access to the cabinet, but access to the room, without my knowledge and permission, was impossible. Both were locked during this night. Not five hours had elapsed since the cabinet and drawer had been opened, and since the letters had been seen and touched, being in their ordinary position. During this interval, the thief had entered, and despoiled me of my treasure.

This event, so inexplicable and so dreadful, threw my soul into a kind of stupor or distraction, from which I was suddenly roused by a footstep, softly moving in the entry near my door.

I started from my bed, as if I had gained a glimpse of the robber. Before I could run to the door, some one knocked. I did not think upon the propriety of answering the signal, but hastened with tremulous fingers and throbbing heart to open the door. My uncle, in his night-dress, and apparently just risen from his bed, stood before me!

He marked the eagerness and perturbation of my looks, and inquired into the cause. I did not answer his inquiries. His appearance in my chamber and in this guise, added to my surprise. My mind was full of the late discovery, and instantly conceived some connection between this unseasonable visit and my lost manuscript. I interrogated him in my turn as to the cause of his coming.

Why, said he, I came to ascertain whether it was you or not who amused himself so strangely at this time of night. What is the matter with you? Why are you up so early?

I told him that I had been roused by my dreams, and finding no inclination to court my slumber back again, I had risen, though earlier by some hours than the usual period of my rising.

Buy why did you go up stairs? You might easily imagine that the sound of your steps would alarm those below, who would be puzzled to guess who it was that had thought proper to amuse himself in this manner.

Up stairs? I have not left my room this night. It is not ten minutes since I awoke, and my door has not since been opened.

Indeed! That is strange. Nay, it is impossible. It was your feet surely that I heard pacing so solemnly and indefatigably across the *long-room* for near an hour. I could not for my life conjecture, for a time, who it was, but finally concluded that it was you. There was still, however, some doubt, and I came hither to satisfy myself.

These tidings were adapted to raise all my emotions to a still higher pitch. I questioned him with eagerness as to the circumstances he had noticed. He said he had been roused by a sound, whose power of disturbing him arose, not from its loudness, but from its uncommonness. He distinctly heard some one pacing to and fro with bare feet, in the long room: This sound continued, with little intermission, for an hour.

He then noticed a cessation of the walking, and a sound as if some one were lifting the lid of the large cedar chest, that stood in the corner of this room. The walking was not resumed, and all was silent. He listened for a quarter of an hour, and busied himself in conjecturing the cause of this disturbance. The most probable conclusion was, that the walker was his nephew, and his curiosity had led him to my chamber to ascertain the truth.

This dwelling has three stories. The two lower stories are divided into numerous apartments. The upper story constitutes a single room whose sides are the four walls of the house, and whose ceiling is the roof. This room is unoccupied, except by lumber, and imperfectly lighted by a small casement at one end. In this room, were footsteps heard by my uncle.

The stair-case leading to it terminated in a passage near my door. I snatched the candle, and desiring him to follow me, added, that I would ascertain the truth in a moment. He followed, but observed that the walking had ceased long enough for the person to escape.

I ascended to the room, and looked behind and among the tables, and chairs, and casks, which were confusedly scattered through it, but found nothing in the shape of man. The cedar chest, spoken of by Mr. Huntly, contained old books, and remnants of maps and charts, whose worthlessness unfitted them for accommodation elsewhere. The lid was without hinges or lock. I examined this repository, but there was nothing which attracted my attention.

The way between the kitchen door, and the door of the long-room, had no impediments. Both were usually unfastened but the motives by which any stranger to the dwelling, or indeed any one within it, could be prompted to chuse this place and hour, for an employment of this kind, were wholly incomprehensible.

When the family rose, inquiries were made but no satisfaction was obtained. The family consisted only of four persons, my uncle, my two sisters, and myself. I mentioned to them the loss I had sustained, but their conjectures were no less unsatisfactory on this than on the former incident.

There was no end to my restless meditations. Waldegrave was the only being, beside myself, acquainted with the secrets of my cabinet. During his life these manuscripts had been the objects of perpetual solicitude; to gain possession, to destroy, or secrete them, was the strongest of his wishes. Had he retained his sensibility on the approach of death, no doubt he would have renewed, with irresistable solemnity, his injunctions to destroy them.

Now, however, they had vanished. There were no materials of conjecture; no probabilities to be weighed, or suspicions to revolve. Human artifice or power was unequal to this exploit. Means less than preternatural would not furnish a conveyance for this treasure.

It was otherwise with regard to this unseasonable walker. His inducements indeed were beyond my power to conceive, but to enter these doors and ascend these stairs, demanded not the faculties of any being more than human.

This intrusion, and the pillage of my cabinet were contemporary events. Was there no more connection between them than that which results from time? Was not the purloiner of my treasure and the wanderer the same person? I could not reconcile the former incident with the attributes of man, and yet a secret faith, not to be outrooted or suspended, swayed me, and compelled me to imagine that the detection of this visitant, would unveil the thief.

These thoughts were pregnant with dejection and reverie. Clithero, during the day, was forgotten. On the succeeding night, my intentions, with regard to this man, returned. I derived some slender consolation from reflecting, that time, in its long lapse and ceaseless revolutions, might dissipate the gloom that environed me. Meanwhile I struggled to dismiss the images connected with my loss and to think only of Clithero.

My impatience was as strong as ever to obtain another interview with this man. I longed with vehemence for the return of day. I believed that every moment added to his sufferings, intellectual and physical, and confided in the efficacy of my presence to alleviate or suspend them. The provisions I had left would be speedily consumed, and the abstinence of three days was sufficient to undermine the vital energies. I, sometimes, hesitated whether I ought not instantly to depart. It was night indeed, but the late storm had purified the air, and the radiance of a full moon was universal and dazling.

From this attempt I was deterred by reflecting that my own frame needed the repairs of sleep. Toil and watchfulness, if prolonged another day, would deeply injure a constitution by no means distinguished for its force. I must, therefore, compel, if it were possible, some hours of repose. I prepared to retire to bed, when a new incident occurred to divert my attention for a time from these designs.

Chapter XIV

WHILE sitting alone by the parlour fire, marking the effects of moon-light, I noted one on horseback coming towards the gate. At first sight, methought his shape and guise were not wholly new to me; but all that I could discern was merely a resemblance to some one whom I had before seen. Presently he stopped, and, looking towards the house, made inquiries of a passenger who chanced to be near. Being apparently satisfied with the answers he received, he rode with a quick pace, into the court and alighted at the door. I started from my seat, and, going forth, waited with some impatience to hear his purpose explained.

He accosted me with the formality of a stranger, and asked if a young man, by name Edgar Huntly, resided here. Being answered in the affirmative, and being requested to come in, he entered, and seated himself, without hesitation, by the fire. Some doubt and anxiety were visible in his looks. He seemed desirous of information upon some topic, and yet betrayed terror lest the answers he might receive should subvert some hope, or confirm some foreboding.

Meanwhile I scrutinized his features with much solicitude. A nearer and more deliberate view convinced me that the first impression was just; but still I was unable to call up his name or the circumstances of our former meeting. The pause was at length ended by his saying, in a faltering voice:

My name is Weymouth. I came hither to obtain information on a subject in which my happiness is deeply concerned.

At the mention of his name, I started. It was a name too closely connected with the image of thy brother, not to call up affecting and vivid recollections. Weymouth thou knowest, was thy brother's friend. It is three years since this man left America, during which time no tidings had been heard of him, at least, by thy brother. He had now returned, and was probably unacquainted with the fate of his friend.

After an anxious pause, he continued. . . . Since my arrival I have heard of an event which has, on many accounts, given me the deepest sorrow. I loved Waldegrave, and know not any person in the world whose life was dearer to me than his. There were considerations, however, which made it more precious to me than the life of one whose merits might be greater. With his life, my own existence and property were, I have reason to think, inseparably united.

On my return to my country, after a long absence, I made immediate inquiries after him. I was informed of his untimely death. I had questions, of infinite moment to my happiness, to decide with regard to the state and disposition of his property. I sought out those of his friends who had maintained with him the most frequent and confidential intercourse, but they could not afford me any satisfaction. At length, I was informed that a young man of your name, and living in this district, had enjoyed more of his affection and society than any other, had regulated the property which he left behind, and was best qualified to afford the intelligence which I sought. You, it seems, are this person, and of you I must make inquiries to which I conjure you to return sincere and explicit answers.

That, said I, I shall find no difficulty in doing. Whatever questions you shall think proper to ask, I will answer with readiness and truth.

What kind of property and to what amount was your friend possessed of at his death?

It was money, and consisted of deposits at the bank of North America. The amount was little short of eight thousand dollars.

On whom has this property devolved?

His sister was his only kindred, and she is now in possession of it.

Did he leave any will by which he directed the disposition of his property? While thus speaking, Weymouth fixed his eyes upon my countenance, and seemed anxious to pierce into my inmost soul. I was somewhat surprised at his questions, but much more at the manner in which they were put. I answered him, however, without delay. . . . He left no will, nor was any paper discovered, by which we could guess at his intentions. No doubt, indeed, had he made a will his sister would have been placed precisely in the same condition in which she now is. He was not only bound to her by the strongest ties of kindred, but by affection and gratitude.

Weymouth now withdrew his eyes from my face, and sunk into a mournful reverie. He sighed often and deeply. This deportment and the strain of his inquiries excited much surprise. His interest in the fate of Waldegrave ought to have made the information he had received, a source of satisfaction rather than of regret. The property which Waldegrave left was much greater than his mode of life, and his own professions had given us reason to expect, but it was no more than sufficient to insure to thee an adequate subsistence. It ascertained the happiness of those who were dearest to Waldegrave, and placed them forever beyond the reach of that poverty which had hitherto beset them. I made no attempt to interrupt the silence, but prepared to answer any new interrogatory. At length, Weymouth resumed:

Waldegrave was a fortunate man, to amass so considerable a sum in so short a time. I remember, when we parted, he was poor. He used to lament that his scrupulous integrity precluded him from all the common roads to wealth. He did not contemn riches, but he set the highest value upon competence; and imagined that he was doomed forever to poverty. His religious duty compelled him to seek his livelihood by teaching a school of blacks. The labour was disproportioned to his feeble constitution, and the profit was greatly disproportioned to the labour. It scarcely supplied the necessities of nature, and was reduced sometimes even below that standard by his frequent indisposition. I rejoice to find that his scruples had somewhat relaxed their force, and that he had betaken himself to some more profitable occupation. Pray, what was his new way of business?

Nay, said I, his scruples continued as rigid, in this respect, as ever. He was teacher of the Negro free-school when he died.

Indeed! How then came he to amass so much money? Could he blend any more lucrative pursuit with his duty as a school-master?

So it seems.

What was his pursuit?

That question, I believe, none of his friends are qualified to answer. I thought myself acquainted with the most secret transactions of his life, but this had been carefully concealed from me. I was not only unapprised of any other employment of his time, but had not the slightest suspicion of his possessing any property beside his clothes and books. Ransacking his papers, with a different view, I lighted on his bank-book, in which was a regular receipt for seven thousand five hundred dollars. By what means he acquired this money, and even the acquisition of it, till his death put us in possession of his papers, was wholly unknown to us.

Possibly he might have held it in trust for another. In this case some memorandums or letters would be found explaining this affair.

True. This supposition could not fail to occur, in consequence of which the most diligent search was made among his papers, but no shred or scrap was to be found which countenanced our conjecture.

You may reasonably be surprised, and perhaps offended, said Weymouth, at these inquiries; but it is time to explain my motives for making them. Three years ago I was, like Waldegrave, indigent, and earned my bread by daily labour. During seven years service in a public office, I saved, from the expences of subsistence, a few hundred dollars. I determined to strike into a new path, and, with this sum, to lay the foundation of better fortune. I turned it into a bulky commodity, freighted and loaded a small vessel, and went with it to Barcelona in Spain. I was not unsuccessful in my projects, and, changing my abode to England, France and Germany, according as my interest required, I became finally possessed of sufficient for the supply of all my wants. I then resolved to return to my native country, and, laying out my money in land, to spend the rest of my days in the luxury and quiet of an opulent farmer. For this end I invested the greatest part of my property in a cargo of wine from Madeira. The remainder I turned into a bill of exchange for seven thousand five hundred dollars. I had maintained a friendly correspondence with Waldegrave during my absence. There was no one with whom I had lived on terms of so much intimacy, and had boundless confidence in his integrity. To him therefore I determined to transmit this bill, requesting him to take the money into safe keeping until my return. In this manner I endeavoured to provide against the accidents that might befall my person or my cargo in crossing the ocean.

It was my fate to encounter the worst of these disasters. We were overtaken by a storm, my vessel was driven ashore on the coast of Portugal, my cargo was utterly lost, and the greater part of the crew and passengers were drowned. I was rescued from the same fate by some fishermen. In consequence of the hardships to which I had been exposed, having laboured for several days at the pumps, and spent the greater part of a winter night, hanging from the rigging of the ship, and perpetually beaten by the waves, I contracted a severe disease, which bereaved me of the use of my limbs. The fishermen who rescued me, carried me to their huts, and there I remained three weeks helpless and miserable.

That part of the coast on which I was thrown, was, in the highest degree, sterile and rude. Its few inhabitants subsisted precariously on the produce of the ocean. Their dwellings were of mud, low, filthy, dark, and comfortless. Their fuel was the stalks of shrubs, sparingly scattered over a sandy desert. Their poverty scarcely allowed them salt and black bread with their fish, which was obtained in unequal and sometimes insufficient quantities, and which they ate with all its impurities and half cooked.

My former habits as well as my present indisposition required very different treatment from what the ignorance and penury of these people obliged them to bestow. I lay upon the moist earth, imperfectly sheltered from the sky, and with neither raiment or fire to keep me warm. My hosts had little attention or compassion to spare to the wants of others. They could not remove me to a more hospitable district, and here, without doubt, I should have perished had not a monk chanced to visit their hovels. He belonged to a convent of St. Jago, some leagues farther from the shore, who used to send one of its members annually to inspect the religious concerns of those outcasts. Happily this was the period of their visitations.

My abode in Spain had made me somewhat conversant with its language. The dialect of this monk did not so much differ from Castilian, but that, with the assistance of Latin, we were able to converse. The jargon of the fishermen was unintelligible, and they had vainly endeavoured to keep up my spirits by informing me of this expected visit.

This monk was touched with compassion at my calamity, and speedily provided the means of my removal to his convent. Here I was charitably entertained, and the aid of a physician was procured for me. He was but poorly skilled in his profession, and rather confirmed than alleviated my disease. The Portuguese of his trade, especially in remoter districts, are little more than dealers in talismans and nostrums. For a long time I was unable to leave my pallet, and had no prospect before me but that of consuming my days in the gloom of this cloister.

All the members of this convent, but he who had been my first benefactor, and whose name was Chaledro, were bigotted and sordid. Their chief motive for treating me with kindness, was the hope of obtaining a convert from heresy. They spared no pains to subdue my errors, and were willing to prolong my imprisonment, in the hope of finally gaining their end. Had my fate been governed by those, I should have been immured in this convent, and compelled, either to adopt their fanatical creed or to put an end to my own life, in order to escape their well meant persecutions. Chaledro, however, though no less sincere in his faith and urgent in his intreaties, yet finding me invincible, exerted his influence to obtain my liberty.

After many delays, and strenuous exertions of my friend, they consented to remove me to Oporto. The journey was to be performed in an open cart over a mountainous country, in the heats of summer. The monks endeavoured to dissuade me from the enterprize, for my own sake, it being scarcely possible that one in my feeble state, should survive a journey like this; but I despaired of improving my condition by other means. I preferred death to the imprisonment of a Portuguese monastery, and knew that I could hope for no alleviation of my disease, but from the skill of Scottish or French physicians, whom I expected to meet with in that city. I adhered to my purpose with so much vehemence and obstinacy, that they finally yielded to my wishes.

My road lay through the wildest and most rugged districts.

It did not exceed ninety miles, but seven days were consumed on the way. The motion of the vehicle racked me with the keenest pangs, and my attendants concluded that every stage would be my last. They had been selected without due regard to their characters. They were knavish and inhuman, and omitted nothing, but actual violence, to hasten my death. They purposely retarded the journey, and protracted to seven, what might have been readily performed in four days. They neglected to execute the orders which they had received, respecting my lodging and provisions, and from them, as well as from the peasants, who were sure to be informed that I was an heretic, I suffered every species of insult and injury. My constitution, as well as my frame, possessed a fund of strength of which I had no previous conception. In spite of hardship and exposure and abstinence, I, at last, arrived at Oporto.

Instead of being carried, agreeably to Chaledro's direction, to a convent of St. Jago, I was left, late in the evening, in the porch of a common hospital. My attendants, having laid me on the pavement and loaded me with imprecations, left me to obtain admission by my own efforts. I passed the live-long night in this spot, and in the morning was received into the house, in a state which left it uncertain whether I was alive or dead.

After recovering my sensibility, I made various efforts to procure a visit from some English merchant. This was no easy undertaking for one in my deplorable condition. I was too weak to articulate my words distinctly, and these words were rendered by my foreign accent, scarcely intelligible. The likelihood of my speedy death made the people about me more indifferent to my wants and petitions.

I will not dwell upon my repeated disappointments, but content myself with mentioning that I gained the attention of a French gentleman, whose curiosity brought him to view the hospital. Through him, I obtained a visit from an English merchant, and finally gained the notice of a person, who formerly resided in America, and of whom I had imperfect knowledge. By their kindness I was removed from the hospital to a private house. A Scottish surgeon was summoned to my assistance, and in seven months, I was restored to my present state of health.

At Oporto, I embarked, in an American ship, for New-York. I was destitute of all property, and relied, for the payment of the debts which I was obliged to contract, as well as for my future subsistence, on my remittance to Waldegrave. I hastened to Philadelphia, and was soon informed that my friend was dead. His death had taken place a long time since my remittance to him, hence this disaster was a subject of regret chiefly on his own account. I entertained no doubt but that my property had been secured, and that either some testamentary directions, or some papers had been left behind respecting this affair.

I sought out those who were formerly our mutual acquaintance, I found that they were wholly strangers to his affairs. They could merely relate some particulars of his singular death, and point out the lodgings which he formerly occupied. Hither I forthwith repaired, and discovered that he lived in this house with his sister, disconnected with its other inhabitants. They described his mode of life in terms that shewed them to be very imperfectly acquainted with it. It was easy indeed to infer, from their aspect and manners, that little sympathy or union could have subsisted between them and their co-tenants, and this inference was confirmed by their insinuations, the growth of prejudice and envy. They told me that Waldegrave's sister had gone to live in the country, but whither or for how long, she had not condescended to inform them, and they did not care to ask. She was a topping dame whose notions were much too high for her station. Who was more nice than wise, and yet was one who could stoop, when it most became her to stand upright. It was no business of theirs, but they could not but mention their suspicions that she had good reasons for leaving the city, and for concealing the place of her retreat. Some things were hard to be disguised. They spoke for themselves, and the only way to hinder disagreeable discoveries, was to keep out of sight.

I was wholly a stranger to Waldegrave's sister. I knew merely that he had such a relation. There was nothing therefore to outbalance this unfavourable report, but the apparent malignity and grossness of those who gave it. It was not, however, her character about which I was solicitous, but merely the place where she might be found, and the suitable inquiries respecting her deceased brother, be answered. On this head, these people professed utter ignorance and were either unable or unwilling to direct me to any person in the city who knew more than themselves. After much discourse they, at length, let fall an intimation that if any one knew her place of retreat, it was probably a country lad, by name Huntly, who lived near the *Forks* of Delaware. After Waldegrave's death, this lad had paid his sister a visit, and seemed to be admitted on a very confidential footing. She left the house, for the last time, in his company, and he, therefore, was most likely to know what had become of her.

The name of Huntly was not totally unknown to me. I myself was born and brought up in the neighbouring township of Chetasco. I had some knowledge of your family, and your name used often to be mentioned by Waldegrave, as that of one who, at a maturer age, would prove himself useful to his country. I determined therefore to apply to you for what information you could give. I designed to visit my father who lives in Chetasco and relieve him from that disquiet which his ignorance of my fate could not fail to have inspired, and both these ends could be thus, at the same time, accomplished.

Before I left the city, I thought it proper to apply to the merchant on whom my bill had been drawn. If this bill had been presented and paid, he had doubtless preserved some record of it, and hence a clue might be afforded, though every other expedient should fail. My usual ill fortune pursued me upon this occasion, for the merchant had lately become insolvent, and, to avoid the rage of his creditors, had fled, without leaving any vestige of this or similar transactions behind him. He had, some years since, been an adventurer from Holland, and was suspected to have returned thither.

Chapter XV

I CAME hither with an heart desponding of success. Adversity had weakened my faith in the promises of the future, and I was prepared to receive just such tidings as you have communicated. Unacquainted with the secret motives of Waldegrave and his sister, it is impossible for me to weigh the probabilities of their rectitude. I have only my own assertion to produce in support of my claim. All other evidence, all vouchers and papers, which might attest my veracity, or sanction my claim in a court of law, are buried in the ocean. The bill was transmitted just before my departure from Madeira, and the letters by which it was accompanied, informed Waldegrave of my design to follow it immediately. Hence he did not, it is probable, acknowledge the receipt of my letters. The vessels in which they were sent, arrived in due season. I was assured that all letters were duly deposited in the post-office, where, at present, mine are not to be found.

You assure me that nothing has been found among his papers, hinting at any pecuniary transaction between him and me. Some correspondence passed between us previous to that event. Have no letters, with my signature, been found? Are you qualified, by your knowledge of his papers, to answer me explicitly? Is it not possible for some letters to have been mislaid?

I am qualified, said I, to answer your inquiries beyond any other person in the world. Waldegrave maintained only general intercourse with the rest of mankind. With me his correspondence was copious, and his confidence, as I imagined, without bounds. His books and papers were contained in a single chest, at his lodgings, the keys of which he had about him when he died. These keys I carried to his sister, and was authorized by her to open and examine the contents of this chest. This was done with the utmost care. These papers are now in my possession. Among them no paper, of the tenor you mention, was found, and no letter with your signature. Neither Mary Waldegrave nor I are capable of disguising the truth or committing an injustice. The moment she receives conviction of your right she will restore this money to you. The moment I imbibe this conviction, I will exert all my influence, and it is not small, to induce her to restore it. Permit me, however, to question you in your turn. Who was the merchant on whom your bill was drawn, what was the date of it, and when did the bill and its counterparts arrive?

I do not exactly remember the date of the bills. They were made out, however, six days before I myself embarked which happened on the tenth of August 1784. They were sent by three vessels, one of which was bound to Charleston and the others to New-York. The last arrived within two days of each other, and about the middle of November in the same year. The name of the payer was Monteith.

After a pause of recollection, I answered, I will not hesitate to apprise you of every thing which may throw light upon this transaction, and whether favourable or otherwise to your claim. I have told you among my friend's papers your name is not to be found. I must likewise repeat that the possession of this money by Waldegrave was wholly unknown to us till his death. We are likewise unacquainted with any means by which he could get possession of so large a sum in his own right. He spent no more than his scanty stipend as a teacher, though this stipend was insufficient to supply his wants. This Bank-receipt is dated in December 1784, a fortnight, perhaps, after the date that you have mentioned. You will perceive how much this coincidence, which could scarcely have taken place by chance, is favourable to your claim.

Mary Waldegrave resides, at present, at Abingdon. She will rejoice, as I do, to see one who, as her brother's friend, is entitled to her affection. Doubt not but that she will listen with impartiality and candour to all that you can urge in defence of your title to this money. Her decision will not be precipitate, but it will be generous and just, and founded on such reasons that, even if it be adverse to your wishes, you will be compelled to approve it.

I can entertain no doubt, he answered, as to the equity of my claim. The coincidences you mention are sufficient to convince me, that this sum was received upon my bill, but this conviction must necessarily be confined to myself. No one but I can be conscious to the truth of my own story. The evidence on which I build my faith, in this case, is that of my own memory and senses; but this evidence cannot make itself conspicuous to you. You have nothing but my bare assertion, in addition to some probabilities flowing from the conduct of Waldegrave. What facts may exist to corroborate my claim, which you have forgotten, or which you may think proper to conceal, I cannot judge. I know not what is passing in the secret of your hearts; I am unacquainted with the character of this lady and with yours. I have nothing on which to build surmises and suspicions of your integrity, and nothing to generate unusual confidence. The frailty of your virtue and the strength of your temptations I know not. However she decides in this case, and whatever opinion I shall form as to the reasonableness of her decision, it will not become me either to upbraid her, or to nourish discontentment and repinings.

I know that my claim has no legal support: that, if this money be resigned to me, it will be the impulse of spontaneous justice, and not the coercion of law to which I am indebted for it. Since, therefore, the justice of my claim is to be measured not by law, but by simple equity, I will candidly acknowledge that, as yet it is uncertain whether I ought to receive, even should Miss Waldegrave be willing to give it. I know my own necessities and schemes, and in what degree this money would be subservient to these; but I know not the views and wants of others, and cannot estimate the usefulness of this money to them. However I decide upon your conduct in withholding or retaining it, I shall make suitable allowance for my imperfect knowledge of your motives and wants, as well as for your unavoidable ignorance of mine.

I have related my sufferings from shipwreck and poverty, not to bias your judgment or engage your pity, but merely because the impulse to relate them chanced to awake; because my heart is softened by the remembrance of Waldegrave, who has been my only friend, and by the sight of one whom he loved.

I told you that my father lived in Chetasco. He is now aged, and I am his only child. I should have rejoiced in being able to relieve his grey hairs from labour to which his failing strength cannot be equal. This was one of my inducements in coming to America. Another was, to prepare the way for a woman whom I married in Europe and who is now awaiting intelligence from me in London. Her poverty is not less than my own, and by marrying against the wishes of her kindred, she has bereaved herself of all support but that of her husband. Whether I shall be able to rescue her from indigence, whether I shall alleviate the poverty of my father, or increase it by burthening his scanty funds by my own maintenance as well as his, the future alone can determine.

I confess that my stock of patience and hope has never been large, and that my misfortunes have nearly exhausted it. The flower of my years has been consumed in struggling with adversity, and my constitution has received a shock, from sickness and mistreatment in Portugal, which I cannot expect long to survive. . . . But I make you sad (he continued.) I have said all that I meant to say in this interview. I am impatient to see my father, and night has already come. I have some miles yet to ride to his cottage and over a rough road. I will shortly visit you again, and talk to you at greater leisure on these and other topics. At present I leave you.

I was unwilling to part so abruptly with this guest, and intreated him to prolong his visit, but he would not be prevailed upon. Repeating his promise of shortly seeing me again, he mounted his horse and disappeared. I looked after him with affecting and complex emotions. I reviewed the incidents of this unexpected and extraordinary interview, as if it had existed in a dream. An hour had passed, and this stranger had alighted among us as from the clouds, to draw the veil from those obscurities which had bewildered us so long, to make visible a new train of disastrous consequences flowing from the untimely death of thy brother, and to blast that scheme of happiness on which thou and I had so fondly meditated.

But what wilt thou think of this new born claim? The story, hadst thou observed the features and guize of the relater, would have won thy implicit credit. His countenance exhibited deep traces of the afflictions he had endured and the fortitude which he had exercised. He was sallow and emaciated, but his countenance was full of seriousness and dignity. A sort of ruggedness of brow, the token of great mental exertion and varied experience, argued a premature old age.

What a mournful tale! Is such the lot of those who wander

from their rustic homes in search of fortune? Our countrymen are prone to enterprize, and are scattered over every sea and every land in pursuit of that wealth which will not screen them from disease and infirmity, which is missed much oftener than found, and which, when gained, by no means compensates them for the hardships and vicissitudes endured in the pursuit.

But what if the truth of these pretentions be admitted? The money must be restored to its right owner. I know that whatever inconveniences may follow the deed, thou wilt not hesitate to act justly. Affluence and dignity, however valuable, may be purchased too dear. Honesty will not take away its keenness from the winter-blast, its ignominy and unwholesomeness from servile labour, or strip of its charms the life of elegance and leisure; but these, unaccompanied with self-reproach, are less deplorable than wealth and honour, the possession of which is marred by our own disapprobation.

I know the bitterness of this sacrifice. I know the impatience with which your poverty has formerly been borne, how much your early education is at war with that degradation and obscurity to which your youth has been condemned. How earnestly your wishes panted after a state, which might exempt you from dependence upon daily labour and on the caprices of others, and might secure to you leisure to cultivate and indulge your love of knowledge and your social and beneficent affections.

Your motive for desiring a change of fortune has been greatly enforced since we have become known to each other. Thou hast honoured me with thy affection, but that union, on which we rely for happiness, could not take place while both of us were poor. My habits, indeed, have made labour and rustic obscurity less painful than they would prove to my friend, but my present condition is wholly inconsistent with marriage. As long as my exertions are insufficient to maintain us both, it would be unjustifiable to burthen you with new cares and duties. Of this you are more thoroughly convinced than I am. The love of independence and ease, and impatience of drudgery are woven into your constitution. Perhaps they are carried to an erroneous extreme, and derogate from that uncommon excellence by which your character is, in other respects, distinguished, but they cannot be removed.

This obstacle was unexpectedly removed by the death of your brother. However justly to be deplored was this catastrophe, yet like every other event, some of its consequences were good. By giving you possession of the means of independence and leisure, by enabling us to complete a contract which poverty alone had thus long delayed, this event has been, at the same time, the most disastrous and propitious which could have happened.

Why thy brother should have concealed from us the possession of this money; why, with such copious means of indulgence and leisure, he should still pursue his irksome trade, and live in so penurious a manner, has been a topic of endless and unsatisfactory conjecture between us. It was not difficult to suppose that this money was held in trust for another, but in that case it was unavoidable that some document or memorandum, or at least some claimant would appear. Much time has since elapsed, and you have thought yourself at length justified in appropriating this money to your own use.

Our flattering prospects are now shut in. You must return to your original poverty, and once more depend for precarious subsistence on your needle. You cannot restore the whole, for unavoidable expenses and the change of your mode of living, has consumed some part of it. For so much you must consider yourself as Weymouth's debtor.

Repine not, my friend, at this unlooked-for reverse. Think upon the merits and misfortunes of your brother's friend, think upon his aged father whom we shall enable him to rescue from poverty; think upon his desolate wife, whose merits are, probably, at least equal to your own, and whose helplessness is likely to be greater. I am not insensible to the evils which have returned upon us with augmented force, after having, for a moment, taken their flight. I know the precariousness of my condition and that of my sisters, that our subsistence hangs upon the life of an old man. My uncle's death will transfer this property to his son, who is a stranger and an enemy to us, and the first act of whose authority will unquestionably be to turn us forth from these doors. Marriage with thee was anticipated with joyous emotions, not merely on my own account or on thine, but likewise for the sake of those beloved girls, to whom that event would enable me to furnish an asylum.

But wedlock is now more distant than ever. My heart bleeds to think of the sufferings which my beloved Mary is again fated to endure, but regrets are only aggravations of calamity. They are pernicious, and it is our duty to shake them off.

I can entertain no doubts as to the equity of Weymouth's claim. So many coincidences could not have happened by chance. The non-appearance of any letters or papers connected with it is indeed a mysterious circumstance, but why should Waldegrave be studious of preserving these? They were useless paper, and might, without impropriety, be cast away or made to serve any temporary purpose. Perhaps, indeed, they still lurk in some unsuspected corner. To wish that time may explain this mystery in a different manner, and so as to permit our retention of this money, is, perhaps, the dictate of selfishness. The transfer to Weymouth will not be productive of less benefit to him and to his family, than we should derive from the use of it.

These considerations, however, will be weighed when we meet. Meanwhile I will return to my narrative.

Chapter XVI

HERE, my friend, thou must permit me to pause. The following incidents are of a kind to which the most ardent invention has never conceived a parallel. Fortune, in her most wayward mood, could scarcely be suspected of an influence like this. The scene was pregnant with astonishment and horror. I cannot, even now, recall it without reviving the dismay and confusion which I then experienced.

Possibly, the period will arrive when I shall look back without agony on the perils I have undergone. That period is still distant. Solitude and sleep are now no more than the signals to summon up a tribe of ugly phantoms. Famine, and blindness, and death, and savage enemies, never fail to be conjured up by the silence and darkness of the night. I cannot dissipate them by any efforts of reason. My cowardice requires the perpetual consolation of light. My heart droops when I mark the decline of the sun, and I never sleep but with a candle burning at my pillow. If, by any chance, I should awake and find myself immersed in darkness, I know not what act of desperation I might be suddenly impelled to commit.

I have delayed this narrative, longer than my duty to my friend enjoined. Now that I am able to hold a pen, I will hasten to terminate that uncertainty with regard to my fate, in which my silence has involved thee. I will recall that series of unheard of and disastrous vicissitudes which has constituted the latest portion of my life.

I am not certain, however, that I shall relate them in an intelligible manner. One image runs into another, sensations succeed in so rapid a train, that I fear, I shall be unable to distribute and express them with sufficient perspicuity. As I look back, my heart is sore and aches within my bosom. I am conscious to a kind of complex sentiment of distress and forlornness that cannot be perfectly pourtrayed by words; but I must do as well as I can. In the utmost vigour of my faculties, no eloquence that I possess would do justice to the tale. Now in my languishing and feeble state, I shall furnish thee with little more than a glimpse of the truth. With these glimpses, transient and faint as they are, thou must be satisfied.

I have said that I slept. My memory assures me of this: It informs of the previous circumstances of my laying aside my clothes, of placing the light upon a chair within reach of my pillow, of throwing myself upon the bed, and of gazing on the rays of the moon reflected on the wall, and almost obscured by those of the candle. I remember my occasional relapses into fits of incoherent fancies, the harbingers of sleep: I remember, as it were, the instant when my thoughts ceased to flow, and my senses were arrested by the leaden wand of forgetfulness.

My return to sensation and to consciousness took place in no such tranquil scene. I emerged from oblivion by degrees so slow and so faint, that their succession cannot be marked. When enabled at length to attend to the information which my senses afforded, I was conscious, for a time, of nothing but existence. It was unaccompanied with lassitude or pain, but I felt disinclined to stretch my limbs, or raise my eye-lids. My thoughts were wildering and mazy, and though consciousness were present, it was disconnected with the loco-motive or voluntary power.

From this state a transition was speedily effected. I perceived that my posture was supine, and that I lay upon my back. I attempted to open my eyes. The weight that oppressed them was too great for a slight exertion to remove. The exertion which I made cost me a pang more acute than any which I ever experienced. My eyes, however, were opened; but the darkness that environed me was as intense as before.

I attempted to rise, but my limbs were cold, and my joints had almost lost their flexibility. My efforts were repeated, and at length I attained a sitting posture. I was now sensible of pain in my shoulders and back. I was universally in that state to which the frame is reduced by blows of a club, mercilessly and endlessly repeated; my temples throbbed and my face was covered with clamy and cold drops, but that which threw me into deepest consternation was, my inability to see. I turned my head to different quarters, I stretched my eye-lids, and exerted every visual energy, but in vain. I was wrapt in the murkiest and most impenetrable gloom.

The first effort of reflection was to suggest the belief that I was blind; that disease is known to assail us in a moment and

without previous warning. This surely was the misfortune that
had now befallen me. Some ray, however fleeting and uncertain, could not fail to be discerned, if the power of vision were
not utterly extinguished. In what circumstances could I possibly be placed, from which every particle of light should, by
other means, be excluded?

This led my thoughts into a new train. I endeavoured to
recall the past, but the past was too much in contradiction to
the present, and my intellect was too much shattered by external violence, to allow me accurately to review it.

Since my sight availed nothing to the knowledge of my condition, I betook myself to other instruments. The element
which I breathed was stagnant and cold. The spot where I lay
was rugged and hard. I was neither naked nor clothed. A shirt
and trossers composed my dress, and the shoes and stockings,
which always accompanied these, were now wanting. What
could I infer from this scanty garb, this chilling atmosphere,
this stony bed?

I had awakened as from sleep. What was my condition when
I fell asleep? Surely it was different from the present. Then I
inhabited a lightsome chamber, and was stretched upon a
down bed. Now I was supine upon a rugged surface and immersed in palpable obscurity. Then I was in perfect health;
now my frame was covered with bruises and every joint was
racked with pain. What dungeon or den had received me, and
by whose command was I transported hither?

After various efforts I stood upon my feet. At first I tottered
and staggered. I stretched out my hands on all sides but met
only with vacuity. I advanced forward. At the third step my
foot moved something which lay upon the ground. I stooped
and took it up, and found, on examination, that it was an
Indian tom-hawk. This incident afforded me no hint from
which I might conjecture my state.

Proceeding irresolutely and slowly forward, my hands at
length touched a wall. This, like the flooring, was of stone,
and was rugged and impenetrable. I followed this wall. An
advancing angle occurred at a short distance, which was followed by similar angles. I continued to explore this clue, till
the suspicion occurred that I was merely going round the
walls of a vast and irregular apartment.

The utter darkness disabled me from comparing directions and distances. This discovery, therefore, was not made on a sudden and was still entangled with some doubt. My blood recovered some warmth, and my muscles some elasticity, but in proportion as my sensibility returned my pains augmented. Overpowered by my fears and my agonies I desisted from my fruitless search, and sat down, supporting my back against the wall.

My excruciating sensations for a time occupied my attention. These, in combination with other causes, gradually produced a species of delirium. I existed as it were in a wakeful dream. With nothing to correct my erroneous perceptions, the images of the past occurred in capricious combinations, and vivid hues. Methought I was the victim of some tyrant who had thrust me into a dungeon of his fortress, and left me no power to determine whether he intended I should perish with famine, or linger out a long life in hopeless imprisonment: Whether the day was shut out by insuperable walls, or the darkness that surrounded me, was owing to the night and to the smallness of those cranies through which day-light was to be admitted, I conjectured in vain.

Sometimes I imagined myself buried alive. Methought I had fallen into seeming death and my friends had consigned me to the tomb, from which a resurrection was impossible. That in such a case, my limbs would have been confined to a coffin, and my coffin to a grave, and that I should instantly have been suffocated, did not occur to destroy my supposition: Neither did this supposition overwhelm me with terror or prompt my efforts at deliverance. My state was full of tumult and confusion, and my attention was incessantly divided between my painful sensations and my feverish dreams.

There is no standard by which time can be measured, but the succession of our thoughts, and the changes that take place in the external world. From the latter I was totally excluded. The former made the lapse of some hours appear like the tediousness of weeks and months. At length, a new sensation, recalled my rambling meditations, and gave substance to my fears. I now felt the cravings of hunger, and perceived that unless my deliverance were speedily effected, I must suffer a tedious and lingering death.

I once more tasked my understanding and my senses, to discover the nature of my present situation and the means of escape. I listened to catch some sound. I heard an unequal and varying echo, sometimes near and sometimes distant, sometimes dying away and sometimes swelling into loudness. It was unlike any thing I had before heard, but it was evident that it arose from wind sweeping through spacious halls and winding passages. These tokens were incompatible with the result of the examination I had made. If my hands were true I was immured between walls, through which there was no avenue.

I now exerted my voice, and cried as loud as my wasted strength would admit. Its echoes were sent back to me in broken and confused sounds and from above. This effort was casual, but some part of that uncertainty in which I was involved, was instantly dispelled by it. In passing through the cavern on the former day, I have mentioned the verge of the pit at which I arrived. To acquaint me as far as was possible, with the dimensions of the place, I had hallooed with all my force, knowing that sound is reflected according to the distance and relative positions of the substances from which it is repelled.

The effect produced by my voice on this occasion resembled, with remarkable exactness, the effect which was then produced. Was I then shut up in the same cavern? Had I reached the brink of the same precipice and been thrown headlong into that vacuity? Whence else could arise the bruises which I had received, but from my fall? Yet all remembrance of my journey hither was lost. I had determined to explore this cave on the ensuing day, but my memory informed me not that this intention had been carried into effect. Still it was only possible to conclude that I had come hither on my intended expedition and had been thrown by another, or had, by some ill chance, fallen into the pit.

This opinion was conformable to what I had already observed. The pavement and walls were rugged like those of the footing and sides of the cave through which I had formerly passed.

But if this were true, what was the abhorred catastrophe to which I was now reserved? The sides of this pit were inaccessible: human footsteps would never wander into these recesses. My friends were unapprised of my forlorn state. Here I should continue till wasted by famine. In this grave should I linger out a few days, in unspeakable agonies, and then perish forever.

The inroads of hunger were already experienced, and this knowledge of the desperateness of my calamity, urged me to phrenzy. I had none but capricious and unseen fate to condemn. The author of my distress and the means he had taken to decoy me hither, were incomprehensible. Surely my senses were fettered or depraved by some spell. I was still asleep, and this was merely a tormenting vision, or madness had seized me, and the darkness that environed and the hunger that afflicted me, existed only in my own distempered imagination.

The consolation of these doubts could not last long. Every hour added to the proofs that my perceptions were real. My hunger speedily became ferocious. I tore the linen of my shirt between my teeth and swallowed the fragments. I felt a strong propensity to bite the flesh from my arm. My heart overflowed with cruelty, and I pondered on the delight I should experience in rending some living animal to pieces, and drinking its blood and grinding its quivering fibres between my teeth.

This agony had already passed beyond the limits of endurance. I saw that time, instead of bringing respite or relief, would only aggravate my wants, and that my only remaining hope was to die before I should be assaulted by the last extremes of famine. I now recollected that a tom-hawk was at hand, and rejoiced in the possession of an instrument by which I could so effectually terminate my sufferings.

I took it in my hand, moved its edge over my fingers, and reflected on the force that was required to make it reach my heart. I investigated the spot where it should enter, and strove to fortify myself with resolution to repeat the stroke a second or third time, if the first should prove insufficient. I was sensible that I might fail to inflict a mortal wound, but delighted to consider that the blood which would be made to flow, would finally release me, and that meanwhile my pains would be alleviated by swallowing this blood.

You will not wonder that I felt some reluctance to employ so fatal though indispensable a remedy. I once more ruminated on the possibility of rescuing myself by other means. I now reflected that the upper termination of the wall could not be at an immeasurable distance from the pavement. I had fallen from an height, but if that height had been considerable, instead of being merely bruised, should I not have been dashed into pieces?

Gleams of hope burst anew upon my soul. Was it not possible, I asked, to reach the top of this pit? The sides were rugged and uneven. Would not their projectures and abruptnesses serve me as steps by which I might ascend in safety? This expedient was to be tried without delay. Shortly my strength would fail and my doom would be irrevocably sealed.

I will not enumerate my laborious efforts, my alternations of despondency and confidence, the eager and unwearied scrutiny with which I examined the surface, the attempts which I made, and the failures which, for a time, succeeded each other. An hundred times, when I had ascended some feet from the bottom, I was compelled to relinquish my undertaking by the *untenable* smoothness of the spaces which remained to be gone over. An hundred times I threw myself, exhausted by fatigue and my pains, on the ground. The consciousness was gradually restored that till I had attempted every part of the wall, it was absurd to despair, and I again drew my tottering limbs and aching joints to that part of the wall which had not been surveyed.

At length, as I stretched my hand upward, I found somewhat that seemed like a recession in the wall. It was possible that this was the top of the cavity, and this might be the avenue to liberty. My heart leaped with joy, and I proceeded to climb the wall. No undertaking could be conceived more arduous than this. The space between this verge and the floor was nearly smooth. The verge was higher from the bottom than my head. The only means of ascending that were offered me were by my hands, with which I could draw myself upward so as, at length, to maintain my hold with my feet.

My efforts were indefatigable, and at length I placed myself on the verge; when this was accomplished my strength was nearly gone. Had I not found space enough beyond this brink to stretch myself at length, I should unavoidably have fallen

backward into the pit, and all my pains had served no other
end than to deepen my despair and hasten my destruction.

What impediments and perils remained to be encountered
I could not judge. I was now inclined to forbode the worst.
The interval of repose which was necessary to be taken, in
order to recruit my strength, would accelerate the ravages of
famine, and leave me without the power to proceed.

In this state, I once more consoled myself that an instrument of death was at hand. I had drawn up with me the
tom-hawk, being sensible that should this impediment be
overcome others might remain that would prove insuperable.
Before I employed it, however, I cast my eyes wildly and languidly around. The darkness was no less intense than in the
pit below, and yet two objects were distinctly seen.

They resembled a fixed and obscure flame. They were motionless. Though lustrous themselves they created no illumination around them. This circumstance, added to others,
which reminded me of similar objects, noted on former occasions, immediately explained the nature of what I beheld.
These were the eyes of a panther.

Thus had I struggled to obtain a post where a savage was
lurking, and waited only till my efforts should place me within
reach of his fangs. The first impulse was to arm myself against
this enemy. The desperateness of my condition was, for a moment, forgotten. The weapon which was so lately lifted against
my own bosom, was now raised to defend my life against the
assault of another.

There was no time for deliberation and delay. In a moment
he might spring from his station and tear me to pieces. My
utmost speed might not enable me to reach him where he sat,
but merely to encounter his assault. I did not reflect how far
my strength was adequate to save me. All the force that remained was mustered up and exerted in a throw.

No one knows the powers that are latent in his constitution.
Called forth by imminent dangers, our efforts frequently exceed our most sanguine belief. Though tottering on the verge
of dissolution, and apparently unable to crawl from this spot,
a force was exerted in this throw, probably greater than I had
ever before exerted. It was resistless and unerring. I aimed at

the middle space between these glowing orbs. It penetrated the scull and the animal fell, struggling and shrieking, on the ground.

My ears quickly informed me when his pangs were at an end. His cries and his convulsions lasted for a moment and then ceased. The effect of his voice, in these subterranean abodes, was unspeakably rueful.

The abruptness of this incident, and the preternatural exertion of my strength, left me in a state of languor and sinking from which slowly and with difficulty I recovered. The first suggestion that occurred was to feed upon the carcass of this animal. My hunger had arrived at that pitch where all fastidiousness and scruples are at an end. I crept to the spot. . . . I will not shock you by relating the extremes to which dire necessity had driven me. I review this scene with loathing and horror. Now that it is past I look back upon it as on some hideous dream. The whole appears to be some freak of insanity. No alternative was offered, and hunger was capable to be appeased, even by a banquet so detestable.

If this appetite has sometimes subdued the sentiments of nature, and compelled the mother to feed upon the flesh of her offspring, it will not excite amazement that I did not turn from the yet warm blood and reeking fibres of a brute.

One evil was now removed, only to give place to another. The first sensations of fullness had scarcely been felt when my stomach was seized by pangs whose acuteness exceeded all that I ever before experienced. I bitterly lamented my inordinate avidity. The excruciations of famine were better than the agonies which this abhorred meal had produced. Death was now impending with no less proximity and certainty, though in a different form. Death was a sweet relief for my present miseries, and I vehemently longed for its arrival. I stretched myself on the ground. I threw myself into every posture that promised some alleviation of this evil. I rolled along the pavement of the cavern, wholly inattentive to the dangers that environed me. That I did not fall into the pit, whence I had just emerged, must be ascribed to some miraculous chance.

How long my miseries endured, it is not possible to tell. I cannot even form a plausible conjecture. Judging by the lingering train of my sensations, I should conjecture that some days elapsed in this deplorable condition, but nature could not have so long sustained a conflict like this.

Gradually my pains subsided and I fell into a deep sleep. I was visited by dreams of a thousand hues. They led me to flowing streams and plenteous banquets, which, though placed within my view, some power forbade me to approach. From this sleep I recovered to the fruition of solitude and darkness, but my frame was in a state less feeble than before. That which I had eaten had produced temporary distress, but on the whole had been of use. If this food had not been provided for me I should scarcely have avoided death. I had reason therefore to congratulate myself on the danger that had lately occurred.

I had acted without foresight, and yet no wisdom could have prescribed more salutary measures. The panther was slain, not from a view to the relief of my hunger, but from the self-preserving and involuntary impulse. Had I foreknown the pangs to which my ravenous and bloody meal would give birth, I should have carefully abstained, and yet these pangs were a useful effort of nature to subdue and convert to nourishment the matter I had swallowed.

I was now assailed by the torments of thirst. My invention and my courage were anew bent to obviate this pressing evil. I reflected that there was some recess from this cavern, even from the spot where I now stood. Before, I was doubtful whether in this direction from this pit any avenue could be found, but since the panther had come hither there was reason to suppose the existence of some such avenue.

I now likewise attended to a sound, which, from its invariable tenour, denoted somewhat different from the whistling of a gale. It seemed like the murmur of a running stream. I now prepared to go forward, and endeavoured to move along in that direction in which this sound apparently came.

On either side and above my head, there was nothing but vacuity. My steps were to be guided by the pavement, which, though unequal and rugged, appeared, on the whole, to ascend. My safety required that I should employ both hands and feet in exploring my way.

I went on thus for a considerable period. The murmur, instead of becoming more distinct, gradually died away. My progress was arrested by fatigue, and I began once more to despond. My exertions, produced a perspiration, which, while it augmented my thirst, happily supplied me with imperfect means of appeasing it.

This expedient would, perhaps, have been accidentally suggested, but my ingenuity was assisted by remembering the history of certain English prisoners in Bengal, whom their merciless enemy imprisoned in a small room, and some of whom preserved themselves alive merely by swallowing the moisture that flowed from their bodies. This experiment I now performed with no less success.

This was slender and transitory consolation. I knew that, wandering at random, I might never reach the outlet of this cavern, or might be disabled, by hunger and fatigue, from going farther than the outlet. The cravings which had lately been satiated, would speedily return, and my negligence had cut me off from the resource which had recently been furnished. I thought not till now that a second meal might be indispensable.

To return upon my footsteps to the spot where the dead animal lay was an heartless project. I might thus be placing myself at an hopeless distance from liberty. Besides my track could not be retraced. I had frequently deviated from a straight direction for the sake of avoiding impediments. All of which I was sensible was, that I was travelling up a irregular acclivity. I hoped sometime to reach the summit, but had no reason for adhering to one line of ascent in preference to another.

To remain where I was, was manifestly absurd. Whether I mounted or descended, a change of place was most likely to benefit me. I resolved to vary my direction, and, instead of ascending, keep along the side of what I accounted an hill. I had gone some hundred feet when the murmur, before described, once more saluted my ear.

This sound, being imagined to proceed from a running stream, could not but light up joy in the heart of one nearly perishing with thirst. I proceeded with new courage. The sound approached no nearer nor became more distinct, but as long as it died not away, I was satisfied to listen and to hope.

I was eagerly observant if any the least glimmering of light, should visit this recess. At length, on the right hand a gleam, infinitely faint, caught my attention. It was wavering and unequal. I directed my steps towards it. It became more vivid, and permanent. It was of that kind, however, which proceeded from a fire, kindled with dry sticks, and not from the sun. I now heard the crackling of flames.

This sound made me pause, or at least to proceed with circumspection. At length the scene opened, and I found myself at the entrance of a cave. I quickly reached a station where I saw a fire burning. At first no other object was noted, but it was easy to infer that the fire was kindled by men, and that they who kindled it could be at no great distance.

Chapter XVII

THUS was I delivered from my prison and restored to the enjoyment of the air and the light. Perhaps the chance was almost miraculous that led me to this opening. In any other direction, I might have involved myself in an inextricable maze, and rendered my destruction sure: but what now remained to place me in absolute security? Beyond the fire I could see nothing; but since the smoke rolled rapidly away, it was plain that on the opposite side the cavern was open to the air.

I went forward, but my eyes were fixed upon the fire; presently, in consequence of changing my station, I perceived several feet, and the skirts of blankets. I was somewhat startled at these appearances. The legs were naked, and scored into uncouth figures. The *mocassins* which lay beside them, and which were adorned in a grotesque manner, in addition to other incidents, immediately suggested the suspicion that they were Indians. No spectacle was more adapted than this to excite wonder and alarm. Had some mysterious power snatched me from the earth, and cast me, in a moment, into the heart of the wilderness? Was I still in the vicinity of my paternal habitation, or was I thousands of miles distant?

Were these the permanent inhabitants of this region, or were they wanderers and robbers? While in the heart of the mountain I had entertained a vague belief that I was still within the precincts of Norwalk. This opinion was shaken for a moment by the objects which I now beheld, but it insensibly returned; yet, how was this opinion to be reconciled to appearances so strange and uncouth, and what measure did a due regard to my safety enjoin me to take?

I now gained a view of four brawny and terrific figures, stretched upon the ground. They lay parallel to each other, on their left sides; in consequence of which their faces were turned from me. Between each was an interval where lay a musquet. Their right hands seemed placed upon the stocks of their guns, as if to seize them on the first moment of alarm.

The aperture through which these objects were seen, was

at the back of the cave, and some feet from the ground. It was merely large enough to suffer an human body to pass. It was involved in profound darkness, and there was no danger of being suspected or discovered as long as I maintained silence, and kept out of view.

It was easily imagined that these guests would make but a short sojourn in this spot. There was reason to suppose that it was now night, and that after a short repose, they would start up and resume their journey. It was my first design to remain shrouded in this covert till their departure, and I prepared to endure imprisonment and thirst somewhat longer.

Meanwhile my thoughts were busy in accounting for this spectacle. I need not tell thee that Norwalk is the termination of a sterile and narrow tract, which begins in the Indian country. It forms a sort of rugged and rocky vein, and continues upwards of fifty miles. It is crossed in a few places by narrow and intricate paths, by which a communication is maintained between the farms and settlements on the opposite sides of the ridge.

During former Indian wars, this rude surface was sometimes traversed by the Red-men, and they made, by means of it, frequent and destructive inroads into the heart of the English settlements. During the last war, notwithstanding the progress of population, and the multiplied perils of such an expedition, a band of them had once penetrated into Norwalk, and lingered long enough to pillage and murder some of the neighbouring inhabitants.

I have reason to remember that event. My father's house was placed on the verge of this solitude. Eight of these assassins assailed it at the dead of night. My parents and an infant child were murdered in their beds; the house was pillaged, and then burnt to the ground. Happily, myself and my two sisters were abroad upon a visit. The preceding day had been fixed for our return to our father's house, but a storm occurred, which made it dangerous to cross the river, and by obliging us to defer our journey, rescued us from captivity or death.

Most men are haunted by some species of terror or antipathy, which they are, for the most part, able to trace to some incident which befel them in their early years. You will not be surprized that the fate of my parents, and the sight of the body of one of this savage band, who, in the pursuit that was made after them, was overtaken and killed, should produce lasting and terrific images in my fancy. I never looked upon, or called up the image of a savage without shuddering.

I knew that, at this time, some hostilities had been committed on the frontier; that a long course of injuries and encroachments had lately exasperated the Indian tribes; that an implacable and exterminating war was generally expected. We imagined ourselves at an inaccessible distance from the danger, but I could not but remember that this persuasion was formerly as strong as at present, and that an expedition, which had once succeeded, might possibly be attempted again. Here was every token of enmity and bloodshed. Each prostrate figure was furnished with a rifled musquet, and a leathern bag tied round his waist, which was, probably, stored with powder and ball.

From these reflections, the sense of my own danger was revived and enforced, but I likewise ruminated on the evils which might impend over others. I should, no doubt, be safe by remaining in this nook; but might not some means be pursued to warn others of their danger? Should they leave this spot, without notice of their approach being given to the fearless and pacific tenants of the neighbouring district, they might commit, in a few hours, the most horrid and irreparable devastation.

The alarm could only be diffused in one way. Could I not escape, unperceived, and without alarming the sleepers, from this cavern? The slumber of an Indian is broken by the slightest noise; but if all noise be precluded, it is commonly profound. It was possible, I conceived, to leave my present post, to descend into the cave, and issue forth without the smallest signal. Their supine posture assured me that they were asleep. Sleep usually comes at their bidding, and if, perchance, they should be wakeful at an unseasonable moment, they always sit upon their haunches, and, leaning their elbows on their knees, consume the tedious hours in smoking. My peril would be great. Accidents which I could not foresee, and over which I had no command, might occur to awaken some one at the moment I was passing the fire. Should I pass in safety, I might issue forth into a wilderness, of which I had no knowledge, where I might wander till I perished with famine, or where my footsteps might be noted and pursued, and overtaken by these implacable foes. These perils were enormous and imminent; but I likewise considered that I might be at no great distance from the habitations of men, and, that my escape might rescue them from the most dreadful calamities, I determined to make this dangerous experiment without delay.

I came nearer to the aperture, and had, consequently, a larger view of this recess. To my unspeakable dismay, I now caught a glimpse of one, seated at the fire. His back was turned towards me so that I could distinctly survey his gigantic form and fantastic ornaments.

My project was frustrated. This one was probably commissioned to watch and to awaken his companions when a due portion of sleep had been taken. That he would not be unfaithful or remiss in the performance of the part assigned to him was easily predicted. To pass him without exciting his notice, and the entrance could not otherwise be reached, was impossible. Once more I shrunk back and revolved with hopelessness and anguish, the necessity to which I was reduced.

This interval of dreary foreboding did not last long. Some motion in him that was seated by the fire attracted my notice. I looked, and beheld him rise from his place and go forth from the cavern. This unexpected incident led my thoughts into a new channel. Could not some advantage be taken of his absence? Could not this opportunity be seized for making my escape? He had left his gun and hatchet on the ground. It was likely, therefore, that he had not gone far, and would speedily return. Might not these weapons be seized, and some provision be thus made against the danger of meeting him without, or of being pursued?

Before a resolution could be formed, a new sound saluted my ear. It was a deep groan, succeeded by sobs that seemed struggling for utterance, but were vehemently counteracted by the sufferer. This low and bitter lamentation apparently proceeded from some one within the cave. It could not be from one of this swarthy band. It must then proceed from a captive, whom they had reserved for torment or servitude, and who had seized the opportunity afforded by the absence of him that watched, to give vent to his despair.

I again thrust my head forward, and beheld, lying on the ground, apart from the rest, and bound hand and foot, a young girl. Her dress was the coarse russet garb of the country, and bespoke her to be some farmer's daughter. Her features denoted the last degree of fear and anguish, and she moved her limbs in such a manner as shewed that the ligatures by which she was confined, produced, by their tightness, the utmost degree of pain.

My wishes were now bent not only to preserve myself, and to frustrate the future attempts of these savages, but likewise to relieve this miserable victim. This could only be done by escaping from the cavern and returning with seasonable aid. The sobs of the girl were likely to rouse the sleepers. My appearance before her would prompt her to testify her surprise by some exclamation or shriek. What could hence be predicted but that the band would start on their feet, and level their unerring pieces at my head!

I know not why I was insensible to these dangers. My thirst was rendered by these delays intolerable. It took from me, in some degree, the power of deliberation. The murmers which had drawn me hither continued still to be heard. Some torrent or cascade could not be far distant from the entrance of the cavern, and it seemed as if one draught of clear water was a luxury cheaply purchased by death itself. This, in addition to considerations more disinterested, and which I have already mentioned, impelled me forward.

The girl's cheek rested on the hard rock, and her eyes were dim with tears. As they were turned towards me, however, I hoped that my movements would be noticed by her gradually and without abruptness. This expectation was fulfilled. I had not advanced many steps before she discovered me. This moment was critical beyond all others in the course of my existence. My life was suspended, as it were, by a spider's thread. All rested on the effect which this discovery should make upon this feeble victim.

I was watchful of the first movement of her eye, which should indicate a consciousness of my presence. I laboured, by gestures and looks, to deter her from betraying her emotion. My attention was, at the same time, fixed upon the sleepers, and an anxious glance was cast towards the quarter whence the watchful savage might appear.

I stooped and seized the musquet and hatchet. The space beyond the fire was, as I expected, open to the air. I issued forth with trembling steps. The sensations inspired by the dangers which environed me, added to my recent horrors, and the influence of the moon, which had now gained the zenith, and whose lustre dazzled my long benighted senses, cannot be adequately described.

For a minute I was unable to distinguish objects. This confusion was speedily corrected, and I found myself on the verge of a steep. Craggy eminences arose on all sides. On the left hand was a space that offered some footing, and hither I turned. A torrent was below me, and this path appeared to lead to it. It quickly appeared in sight, and all foreign cares were, for a time, suspended.

This water fell from the upper regions of the hill, upon a flat projecture which was continued on either side, and on part of which I was now standing. The path was bounded on the left by an inaccessible wall, and on the right terminated at the distance of two or three feet from the wall, in a precipice. The water was eight or ten paces distant, and no impediment seemed likely to rise between us. I rushed forward with speed.

My progress was quickly checked. Close to the falling water, seated on the edge, his back supported by the rock, and his legs hanging over the precipice, I now beheld the savage who left the cave before me. The noise of the cascade and the improbability of interruption, at least from this quarter, had made him inattentive to my motions.

I paused. Along this verge lay the only road by which I could reach the water, and by which I could escape. The passage was completely occupied by this antagonist. To advance towards him, or to remain where I was, would produce the same effect. I should, in either case, be detected. He was unarmed; but his outcries would instantly summon his companions to his aid. I could not hope to overpower him, and pass him in defiance of his opposition. But if this were effected, pursuit would be instantly commenced. I was unacquainted with the way. The way was unquestionably difficult. My strength was nearly annihilated: I should be overtaken in a moment, or their deficiency in speed would be supplied by the accuracy of their aim. Their bullets, at least, would reach me.

There was one method of removing this impediment. The piece which I held in my hand was cocked. There could be no doubt that it was loaded. A precaution of this kind would never be omitted by a warrior of this hue. At a greater distance than this, I should not fear to reach the mark. Should I not discharge it, and, at the same moment, rush forward to secure the road which my adversary's death would open to me?

Perhaps you will conceive a purpose like this to have argued a sanguinary and murderous disposition. Let it be remembered, however, that I entertained no doubts about the hostile designs of these men. This was sufficiently indicated by their arms, their guise, and the captive who attended them. Let the fate of my parents be, likewise, remembered. I was not certain but that these very men were the assassins of my family, and were those who had reduced me and my sisters to the condition of orphans and dependants. No words can describe the torments of my thirst. Relief to these torments, and safety to my life, were within view. How could I hesitate?

Yet I did hesitate. My aversion to bloodshed was not to be subdued but by the direst necessity. I knew, indeed, that the discharge of a musket would only alarm the enemies which remained behind; but I had another and a better weapon in my grasp. I could rive the head of my adversary, and cast him headlong, without any noise which should be heard, into the cavern.

Still I was willing to withdraw, to re-enter the cave, and take shelter in the darksome recesses from which I had emerged. Here I might remain, unsuspected, till these detested guests should depart. The hazards attending my re-entrance were to be boldly encountered, and the torments of unsatisfied thirst were to be patiently endured, rather than imbrue my hands in the blood of my fellow men. But this expedient would be ineffectual if my retreat should be observed by this savage. Of that I was bound to be incontestibly assured. I retreated, therefore, but kept my eye fixed at the same time upon the enemy.

Some ill fate decreed that I should not retreat unobserved. Scarcely had I withdrawn three paces when he started from his seat, and turning towards me, walked with a quick pace. The shadow of the rock, and the improbability of meeting an enemy here, concealed me for a moment from his observation. I stood still. The slightest motion would have attracted his notice. At present, the narrow space engaged all his vigilance. Cautious footsteps, and attention to the path, were indispensable to his safety. The respite was momentary, and I employed it in my own defence.

How otherwise could I act? The danger that impended aimed at nothing less than my life. To take the life of another was the only method of averting it. The means were in my hand, and they were used. In an extremity like this, my muscles would have acted almost in defiance of my will.

The stroke was quick as lightning, and the wound mortal and deep. He had not time to descry the author of his fate; but, sinking on the path, expired without a groan. The hatchet buried itself in his breast, and rolled with him to the bottom of the precipice.

Never before had I taken the life of an human creature. On this head, I had, indeed, entertained somewhat of religious scruples. These scruples did not forbid me to defend myself, but they made me cautious and reluctant to decide. Though they could not withhold my hand, when urged by a necessity like this, they were sufficient to make me look back upon the deed with remorse and dismay.

I did not escape all compunction in the present instance, but the tumult of my feelings was quickly allayed. To quench my thirst was a consideration by which all others were supplanted. I approached the torrent, and not only drank copiously, but laved my head, neck, and arms, in this delicious element.

Chapter XVIII

NEVER was any delight worthy of comparison with the raptures which I then experienced. Life, that was rapidly ebbing, appeared to return upon me with redoubled violence. My languors, my excruciating heat, vanished in a moment, and I felt prepared to undergo the labours of Hercules. Having fully supplied the demands of nature in this respect, I returned to reflection on the circumstances of my situation. The path winding round the hill was now free from all impediments. What remained but to precipitate my flight? I might speedily place myself beyond all danger. I might gain some hospitable shelter, where my fatigues might be repaired by repose, and my wounds be cured. I might likewise impart to my protectors seasonable information of the enemies who meditated their destruction.

I thought upon the condition of the hapless girl whom I had left in the power of the savages. Was it impossible to rescue her? Might I not relieve her from her bonds, and make her the companion of my flight? The exploit was perilous but not impracticable. There was something dastardly and ignominious in withdrawing from the danger, and leaving an helpless being exposed to it. A single minute might suffice to snatch her from death or captivity. The parents might deserve that I should hazard or even sacrifice my life, in the cause of their child.

After some fluctuation, I determined to return to the cavern, and attempt the rescue of the girl. The success of this project depended on the continuance of their sleep. It was proper to approach with wariness, and to heed the smallest token which might bespeak their condition. I crept along the path, bending my ear forward to catch any sound that might arise. I heard nothing but the half-stifled sobs of the girl.

I entered with the slowest and most anxious circumspection. Every thing was found in its pristine state. The girl noticed my entrance with a mixture of terror and joy. My gestures and looks enjoined upon her silence. I stooped down, and taking another hatchet, cut assunder the deer-skin thongs by which her wrists and ancles were tied. I then made signs for her to rise and follow me. She willingly complied with my directions; but her benumbed joints and lacerated sinews, refused to support her. There was no time to be lost; I therefore, lifted her in my arms, and, feeble and tottering as I was, proceeded with this burthen, along the perilous steep, and over a most rugged path.

I hoped that some exertion would enable her to retrieve the use of her limbs. I set her, therefore, on her feet, exhorting her to walk as well as she was able, and promising her my occasional assistance. The poor girl was not deficient in zeal, and presently moved along with light and quick steps. We speedily reached the bottom of the hill.

No fancy can conceive a scene more wild and desolate than that which now presented itself. The soil was nearly covered with sharp fragments of stone. Between these sprung brambles and creeping vines, whose twigs, crossing and intertwining with each other, added to the roughnesses below, made the passage infinitely toilsome. Scattered over this space were single cedars with their ragged spines and wreaths of moss, and copses of dwarf oaks, which were only new emblems of sterility.

I was wholly unacquainted with the scene before me. No marks of habitation or culture, no traces of the footsteps of men, were discernible. I scarcely knew in what region of the globe I was placed. I had come hither by means so inexplicable, as to leave it equally in doubt, whether I was separated from my paternal abode by a river or an ocean.

I made inquiries of my companion, but she was unable to talk coherently. She answered my questions with weeping, and sobs, and intreaties, to fly from the scene of her distress. I collected from her, at length, that her father's house had been attacked on the preceding evening, and all the family but herself destroyed. Since this disaster she had walked very fast and a great way, but knew not how far or in what direction.

In a wilderness like this, my only hope was to light upon obscure paths, made by cattle. Meanwhile I endeavoured to adhere to one line, and to burst through the vexatious obstacles which encumbered our way. The ground was concealed by the bushes, and we were perplexed and fatigued by a con-

tinual succession of hollows and prominences. At one moment
we were nearly thrown headlong into a pit. At another we
struck our feet against the angles of stones. The branches of
the oak rebounded in our faces or entangled our legs, and the
unseen thorns inflicted on us a thousand wounds.

I was obliged, in these arduous circumstances, to support
not only myself but my companion. Her strength was overpowered by her evening journey, and the terror of being overtaken, incessantly harrassed her.

Sometimes we lighted upon tracks which afforded us an
easier footing, and inspired us with courage to proceed.
These, for a time, terminated at a brook or in a bog, and we
were once more compelled to go forward at random. One of
these tracks insensibly became more beaten, and, at length,
exhibited the traces of wheels. To this I adhered, confident
that it would finally conduct us to a dwelling.

On either side, the undergrowth of shrubs and brambles
continued as before. Sometimes small spaces were observed,
which had lately been cleared by fire. At length a vacant space
of larger dimensions than had hitherto occurred, presented
itself to my view. It was a field of some acres, that had, apparently, been upturned by the hoe. At the corner of this field
was a small house.

My heart leaped with joy at this sight. I hastened toward
it, in the hope that my uncertainties, and toils, and dangers,
were now drawing to a close. This dwelling was suited to the
poverty and desolation which surrounded it. It consisted of a
few unhewn logs laid upon each other, to the height of eight
or ten feet, including a quadrangular space of similar dimensions, and covered by thatch. There was no window, light
being sufficiently admitted into the crevices between the logs.
These had formerly been loosely plastered with clay, but air
and rain had crumbled and washed the greater part of this
rude cement away. Somewhat like a chimney, built of half-
burnt bricks, was perceived at one corner. The door was fastened by a leathern thong, tied to a peg.

All within was silence and darkness. I knocked at the door
and called, but no one moved or answered. The tenant, whoever he was, was absent. His leave could not be obtained, and
I, therefore, entered without it. The autumn had made some

progress, and the air was frosty and sharp. My mind and muscles had been, of late, so strenuously occupied, that the cold
had not been felt. The cessation of exercise, however, quickly
restored my sensibility in this respect, but the unhappy girl
complained of being half frozen.

Fire, therefore, was the first object of my search. Happily,
some embers were found upon the hearth, together with potatoe stalks and dry chips. Of these, with much difficulty, I
kindled a fire, by which some warmth was imparted to our
shivering limbs. The light enabled me, as I sat upon the
ground, to survey the interior of this mansion.

Three saplins, stripped of their branches, and bound together at their ends by twigs, formed a kind of bedstead,
which was raised from the ground by four stones. Ropes
stretched across these, and covered by a blanket, constituted
the bed. A board, of which one end rested on the bedstead,
and the other was thrust between the logs that composed the
wall, sustained the stale fragments of a rye-loaf, and a cedar
bucket kept entire by withs instead of hoops. In the bucket
was a little water, full of droppings from the roof, drowned
insects and sand; a basket or two neatly made, and an hoe,
with a stake thrust into it by way of handle, made up all the
furniture that was visible.

Next to cold, hunger was the most urgent necessity by
which we were now pressed. This was no time to give ear to
scruples. We, therefore, unceremoniously divided the bread
and the water between us. I had now leisure to bestow some
regards upon the future.

These remnants of fire and food convinced me that this
dwelling was usually inhabited, and that it had lately been
deserted. Some engagement had probably carried the tenant
abroad. His absence might be terminated in a few minutes,
or might endure through the night. On his return, I questioned not my power to appease any indignation he might feel
at the liberties which I had taken. I was willing to suppose
him one who would readily afford us all the information and
succour that we needed.

If he should not return till sunrise, I meant to resume my
journey. By the comfortable meal we had made, and the repose of a few hours, we should be considerably invigorated

and refreshed, and the road would lead us to some more hospitable tenement.

My thoughts were too tumultuous, and my situation too precarious, to allow me to sleep. The girl, on the contrary, soon sunk into a sweet oblivion of all her cares. She laid herself, by my advice, upon the bed, and left me to ruminate without interruption.

I was not wholly free from the apprehension of danger. What influence his boisterous and solitary life might have upon the temper of the being who inhabited this hut, I could not predict. How soon the Indians might awake, and what path they would pursue, I was equally unable to guess. It was by no means impossible that they might tread upon my footsteps, and knock, in a few minutes, at the door of this cottage. It behoved me to make all the preparation in my power against untoward incidents.

I had not parted with the gun which I had first seized in the cavern, nor with the hatchet which I had afterwards used to cut the bands of the girl. These were, at once, my trophies and my means of defence, which it had been rash and absurd to have relinquished. My present reliance was placed upon these.

I now, for the first time, examined the prize that I had made. Other considerations had prevented me till now, from examining the structure of the piece, but I could not but observe that it had two barrels, and was lighter and smaller than an ordinary musquet. The light of the fire now enabled me to inspect it with more accuracy.

Scarcely had I fixed my eyes upon the stock, when I perceived marks that were familiar to my apprehension. Shape, ornaments, and cyphers, were evidently the same with those of a piece which I had frequently handled. The marks were of a kind which could not be mistaken. This piece was mine; and when I left my uncle's house, it was deposited, as I believed, in the closet of my chamber.

Thou wilt easily conceive the inference which this circumstance suggested. My hairs rose and my teeth chattered with horror. My whole frame was petrified, and I paced to and fro, hurried from the chimney to the door, and from the door to the chimney, with the misguided fury of a maniac.

I needed no proof of my calamity more incontestible than this. My uncle and my sisters had been murdered; the dwelling had been pillaged, and this had been a part of the plunder. Defenceless and asleep, they were assailed by these inexorable enemies, and I, who ought to have been their protector and champion, was removed to an immeasurable distance, and was disabled, by some accursed chance, from affording them the succour which they needed.

For a time, I doubted whether I had not witnessed and shared this catastrophe. I had no memory of the circumstances that preceded my awaking in the pit. Had not the cause of my being cast into this abyss some connection with the ruin of my family? Had I not been dragged hither by these savages, and reduced, by their malice, to that breathless and insensible condition? Was I born to a malignant destiny never tired of persecuting? Thus had my parents and their infant offspring perished, and thus completed was the fate of all those to whom my affections cleaved, and whom the first disaster had spared.

Hitherto the death of the savage, whom I had dispatched with my hatchet, had not been remembered without some remorse. Now my emotions were totally changed: I was somewhat comforted in thinking that thus much of necessary vengeance had been executed. New and more vehement regrets were excited by reflecting on the forbearance I had practised when so much was in my power. All the miscreants had been at my mercy, and a bloody retribution might, with safety and ease, have been inflicted on their prostrate bodies.

It was now too late. What of consolation or of hope remained to me? To return to my ancient dwelling, now polluted with blood, or perhaps, nothing but a smoking ruin, was abhorred. Life, connected with remembrances of my misfortunes was detestable. I was no longer anxious for flight. No change of the scene but that which terminated all consciousness, could I endure to think of.

Amidst these gloomy meditations the idea was suddenly suggested of returning, with the utmost expedition, to the cavern. It was possible that the assassins were still asleep. He who was appointed to watch and to make, in due season, the signal for resuming their march, was forever silent. Without this signal it was not unlikely that they would sleep till dawn of day. But if they should be roused, they might be overtaken or met, and by choosing a proper station, two victims might at least fall. The ultimate event to myself would surely be fatal; but my own death was an object of desire rather than of dread. To die thus speedily, and after some atonement was made for those who had already been slain, was sweet.

The way to the mountain was difficult and tedious, but the ridge was distinctly seen from the door of the cottage, and I trusted that auspicious chance would lead me to that part of it where my prey was to be found. I snatched up the gun and tom-hawk in a transport of eagerness. On examining the former, I found that both barrels were deeply loaded.

This piece was of extraordinary workmanship. It was the legacy of an English officer, who died in Bengal, to Sarsefield. It was constructed for the purposes not of sport but of war. The artist had made it a congeries of tubes and springs, by which every purpose of protection and offence was effectually served. A dagger's blade was attached to it, capable of being fixed at the end, and of answering the destructive purpose of a bayonet. On his departure from Solebury, my friend left it, as a pledge of his affection, in my possession. Hitherto I had chiefly employed it in shooting at a mark, in order to improve my sight; now was I to profit by the gift in a different way.

Thus armed, I prepared to sally forth on my adventurous expedition. Sober views might have speedily succeeded to the present tempest of my passions. I might have gradually discovered the romantic and criminal temerity of my project, the folly of revenge, and the duty of preserving my life for the benefit of mankind. I might have suspected the propriety of my conclusion, and have admitted some doubts as to the catastrophe which I imagined to have befallen my uncle and sisters. I might, at least, have consented to ascertain their condition with my own eyes; and for this end have returned to the cottage, and have patiently waited till the morning light should permit me to resume my journey.

This conduct was precluded by a new incident. Before I opened the door I looked through a crevice of the wall, and perceived three human figures at the farther end of the field. They approached the house. Though indistinctly seen, something in their port persuaded me that these were the Indians from whom I had lately parted. I was startled but not dismayed. My thirst of vengeance was still powerful, and I believed that the moment of its gratification was hastening. In a short time they would arrive and enter the house. In what manner should they be received?

I studied not my own security. It was the scope of my wishes to kill the whole number of my foes; but that being done, I was indifferent to the consequences. I desired not to live to relate or to exult in the deed.

To go forth was perilous and useless. All that remained was to sit upon the ground opposite the door, and fire at each as he entered. In the hasty survey I had taken of this apartment, one object had been overlooked, or imperfectly noticed. Close to the chimney was an aperture, formed by a cavity partly in the wall and in the ground. It was the entrance of an oven, which resembled, on the outside, a mound of earth, and which was filled with dry stalks of potatoes and other rubbish.

Into this it was possible to thrust my body. A sort of screen might be formed of the brush-wood, and more deliberate and effectual execution be done upon the enemy. I weighed not the disadvantages of this scheme, but precipitately threw myself into this cavity. I discovered, in an instant, that it was totally unfit for my purpose, but it was too late to repair my miscarriage.

This wall of the hovel was placed near the verge of a sand-bank. The oven was erected on the very brink. This bank being of a loose and mutable soil, could not sustain my weight. It sunk, and I sunk along with it. The height of the bank was three or four feet, so that, though disconcerted and embarrassed, I received no injury. I still grasped my gun, and resumed my feet in a moment.

What was now to be done? The bank screened me from the view of the savages. The thicket was hard by, and if I were eager to escape, the way was obvious and sure. But though single, though enfeebled by toil, by abstinence and by disease, and though so much exceeded in numbers and strength, by my foes, I was determined to await and provoke the contest.

In addition to the desperate impulse of passion, I was swayed by thoughts of the danger which beset the sleeping

girl, and from which my flight would leave her without protection. How strange is the destiny that governs mankind!
The consequence of shrouding myself in this cavity had not
been foreseen. It was an expedient which courage, and not
cowardice suggested; and yet it was the only expedient by
which flight had been rendered practicable. To have issued
from the door would only have been to confront, and not to
elude the danger.

The first impulse prompted me to re-enter the cottage by
this avenue, but this could not be done with certainty and
expedition. What then remained? While I deliberated, the men
approached, and, after a moment's hesitation, entered the
house, the door being partly open.

The fire on the hearth enabled them to survey the room.
One of them uttered a sudden exclamation of surprize. This
was easily interpreted. They had noticed the girl who had
lately been their captive lying asleep on the blanket. Their
astonishment at finding her here, and in this condition, may
be easily conceived.

I now reflected that I might place myself, without being
observed, near the entrance, at an angle of the building, and
shoot at each as he successively came forth. I perceived that
the bank conformed to two sides of the house, and that I
might gain a view of the front and of the entrance, without
exposing myself to observation.

I lost no time in gaining this station. The bank was as high
as my breast. It was easy, therefore, to crouch beneath it, to
bring my eye close to the verge, and, laying my gun upon the
top of it among the grass, with its muzzles pointed to the
door, patiently to wait their forth-coming.

My eye and my ear were equally attentive to what was passing. A low and muttering conversation was maintained in the
house. Presently I heard an heavy stroke descend. I shuddered, and my blood ran cold at the sound. I entertained no
doubt but that it was the stroke of an hatchet on the head or
breast of the helpless sleeper.

It was followed by a loud shriek. The continuance of these
shrieks proved that the stroke had not been instantly fatal. I
waited to hear it repeated, but the sounds that now arose were
like those produced by dragging somewhat along the ground.

The shrieks, meanwhile, were incessant and piteous. My heart faltered, and I saw that mighty efforts must be made to preserve my joints and my nerves stedfast. All depended on the strenuous exertions and the fortunate dexterity of a moment.

One now approached the door, and came forth, dragging the girl, whom he held by the hair, after him. What hindered me from shooting at his first appearance, I know not. This had been my previous resolution. My hand touched the trigger, and as he moved, the piece was levelled at his right ear. Perhaps the momentous consequences of my failure, made me wait till his ceasing to move might render my aim more sure.

Having dragged the girl, still piteously shrieking, to the distance of ten feet from the house, he threw her from him with violence. She fell upon the ground, and observing him level his piece at her breast, renewed her supplications in a still more piercing tone. Little did the forlorn wretch think that her deliverance was certain and near. I rebuked myself for having thus long delayed. I fired, and my enemy sunk upon the ground without a struggle.

Thus far had success attended me in this unequal contest. The next shot would leave me nearly powerless. If that, however, proved as unerring as the first, the chances of defeat were lessened. The savages within, knowing the intentions of their associate with regard to the captive girl, would probably mistake the report which they heard for that of his piece. Their mistake, however, would speedily give place to doubts, and they would rush forth to ascertain the truth. It behoved me to provide a similar reception for him that next appeared.

It was as I expected. Scarcely was my eye again fixed upon the entrance, when a tawny and terrific visage was stretched fearfully forth. It was the signal of his fate. His glances cast wildly and swiftly round, lighted upon me, and on the fatal instrument which was pointed at his forehead. His muscles were at once exerted to withdraw his head, and to vociferate a warning to his fellow, but his movement was too slow. The ball entered above his ear: He tumbled headlong to the ground, bereaved of sensation, though not of life, and had power only to struggle and mutter.

Chapter XIX

THINK NOT that I relate these things with exultation or tranquility. All my education and the habits of my life tended to unfit me for a contest and a scene like this. But I was not governed by the soul which usually regulates my conduct. I had imbibed from the unparalleled events which had lately happened a spirit vengeful, unrelenting, and ferocious.

There was now an interval for flight. Throwing my weapons away, I might gain the thicket in a moment. I had no ammunition, nor would time be afforded me to re-load my piece. My antagonist would render my poniard and my speed of no use to me. Should he miss me as I fled, the girl would remain to expiate, by her agonies and death, the fate of his companions.

These thoughts passed through my mind in a shorter time than is demanded to express them. They yielded to an expedient suggested by the sight of the gun that had been raised to destroy the girl, and which now lay upon the ground. I am not large of bone, but am not deficient in agility and strength. All that remained to me of these qualities was now exerted; and dropping my own piece, I leaped upon the bank, and flew to seize my prize.

It was not till I snatched it from the ground, that the propriety of regaining my former post, rushed upon my apprehension. He that was still posted in the hovel would mark me through the seams of the wall, and render my destruction sure. I once more ran towards the bank, with the intention to throw myself below it. All this was performed in an instant; but my vigilant foe was aware of his advantage, and fired through an opening between the logs. The bullet grazed my cheek, and produced a benumbing sensation that made me instantly fall to the earth. Though bereaved of strength, and fraught with the belief that I had received a mortal wound, my caution was not remitted. I loosened not my grasp of the gun, and the posture into which I accidentally fell enabled me to keep an eye upon the house and an hand upon the trigger. Perceiving my condition, the savage rushed from his covert in order to complete his work; but at three steps from the threshold, he received my bullet in his breast. The uplifted tomahawk fell from his hand, and, uttering a loud shriek, he fell upon the body of his companion. His cries struck upon my heart, and I wished that his better fortune had cast this evil from him upon me.

Thus I have told thee a bloody and disastrous tale. When thou reflectest on the mildness of my habits, my antipathy to scenes of violence and bloodshed, my unacquaintance with the use of fire-arms, and the motives of a soldier, thou wilt scarcely allow credit to my story. That one rushing into these dangers, unfurnished with stratagems or weapons, disheartened and enfeebled by hardships and pain, should subdue four antagonists, trained from their infancy to the artifices and exertions of Indian warfare, will seem the vision of fancy, rather than the lesson of truth.

I lifted my head from the ground and pondered upon this scene. The magnitude of this exploit made me question its reality. By attending to my own sensations, I discovered that I had received no wound, or at least, none of which there was reason to complain. The blood flowed plentifully from my cheek, but the injury was superficial. It was otherwise with my antagonists. The last that had fallen now ceased to groan. Their huge limbs, inured to combat and *war-worn*, were useless to their own defence, and to the injury of others.

The destruction that I witnessed was vast. Three beings, full of energy and heroism, endowed with minds strenuous and lofty, poured out their lives before me. I was the instrument of their destruction. This scene of carnage and blood was laid by me. To this havock and horror was I led by such rapid footsteps!

My anguish was mingled with astonishment. In spite of the force and uniformity with which my senses were impressed by external objects, the transition I had undergone was so wild and inexplicable; all that I had performed; all that I had witnessed since my egress from the pit, were so contradictory to precedent events, that I still clung to the belief that my thoughts were confused by delirium. From these reveries I was at length recalled by the groans of the girl, who lay near me on the ground.

I went to her and endeavoured to console her. I found that while lying in the bed, she had received a blow upon the side, which was still productive of acute pain. She was unable to rise or to walk, and it was plain that one or more of her ribs had been fractured by the blow.

I knew not what means to devise for our mutual relief. It was possible that the nearest dwelling was many leagues distant. I knew not in what direction to go in order to find it, and my strength would not suffice to carry my wounded companion thither in my arms. There was no expedient but to remain in this field of blood till the morning.

I had scarcely formed this resolution before the report of a musquet was heard at a small distance. At the same moment, I distinctly heard the whistling of a bullet near me. I now remembered that of the five Indians whom I saw in the cavern, I was acquainted with the destiny only of four. The fifth might be still alive, and fortune might reserve for him the task of avenging his companions. His steps might now be tending hither in search of them.

The musquet belonging to him who was shot upon the threshold, was still charged. It was discreet to make all the provision in my power against danger. I possessed myself of this gun, and seating myself on the ground, looked carefully on all sides, to descry the approach of the enemy. I listened with breathless eagerness.

Presently voices were heard. They ascended from that part of the thicket from which my view was intercepted by the cottage. These voices had something in them that bespoke them to belong to friends and countrymen. As yet I was unable to distinguish words.

Presently my eye was attracted to one quarter, by a sound as of feet trampling down bushes. Several heads were seen moving in succession, and at length, the whole person was conspicuous. One after another leaped over a kind of mound which bordered the field, and made towards the spot where I sat. This band was composed of ten or twelve persons, with each a gun upon his shoulder. Their guise, the moment it was perceived, dissipated all my apprehensions.

They came within the distance of a few paces before they discovered me. One stopped, and bespeaking the attention of his followers, called to know who was there? I answered that I was a friend, who intreated their assistance. I shall not paint their astonishment when, on coming nearer, they beheld me surrounded by the arms and dead bodies of my enemies.

I sat upon the ground, supporting my head with my left hand, and resting on my knee the stock of an heavy musquet. My countenance was wan and haggard, my neck and bosom were died in blood, and my limbs, almost stripped by the brambles of their slender covering, were lacerated by a thousand wounds. Three savages, two of whom were steeped in gore, lay at a small distance, with the traces of recent life on their visages. Hard by was the girl, venting her anguish in the deepest groans, and intreating relief from the new comers.

One of the company, on approaching the girl, betrayed the utmost perturbation. "Good God!" he cried, "is this a dream? Can it be you? Speak!"

"Ah, my father! my father!" answered she, "it is I indeed."

The company, attracted by this dialogue, crowded round the girl, whom her father, clasping in his arms, lifted from the ground, and pressed, in a transport of joy to his breast. This delight was succeeded by solicitude respecting her condition. She could only answer his inquiries by complaining that her side was bruised to pieces. How came you here? . . . Who hurt you? . . . Where did the Indians carry you? were questions to which she could make no reply but by sobs and plaints.

My own calamities were forgotten in contemplating the fondness and compassion of the man for his child. I derived new joy from reflecting that I had not abandoned her, and that she owed her preservation to my efforts. The inquiries which the girl was unable to answer, were now put to me. Every one interrogated who I was, whence I had come, and what had given rise to this bloody contest?

I was not willing to expatiate on my story. The spirit which had hitherto sustained me, began now to subside. My strength ebbed away with my blood. Tremors, lassitude, and deadly cold, invaded me, and I fainted on the ground.

Such is the capricious constitution of the human mind. While dangers were at hand, while my life was to be preserved only by zeal, and vigilance, and courage, I was not wanting to myself. Had my perils continued or even multiplied, no doubt my energies would have kept equal pace with them, but the moment that I was encompassed by protectors, and placed in security, I grew powerless and faint. My weakness was proportioned to the duration and intensity of my previous efforts, and the swoon into which I now sunk, was no doubt, mistaken by the spectators, for death.

On recovering from this swoon, my sensations were not unlike those which I had experienced on awaking in the pit. For a moment a mistiness involved every object, and I was able to distinguish nothing. My sight, by rapid degrees, was restored, my painful dizziness was banished, and I surveyed the scene before me with anxiety and wonder.

I found myself stretched upon the ground. I perceived the cottage and the neighbouring thicket, illuminated by a declining moon. My head rested upon something, which, on turning to examine, I found to be one of the slain Indians. The other two remained upon the earth at a small distance, and in the attitudes in which they had fallen. Their arms, the wounded girl, and the troop who were near me when I fainted, were gone.

My head had reposed upon the breast of him whom I had shot in this part of his body. The blood had ceased to ooze from the wound, but my dishevelled locks were matted and steeped in that gore which had overflowed and choked up the orifice. I started from this detestable pillow, and regained my feet.

I did not suddenly recall what had lately passed, or comprehend the nature of my situation. At length, however, late events were recollected.

That I should be abandoned in this forlorn state by these men, seemed to argue a degree of cowardice or cruelty, of which I should have thought them incapable. Presently, however, I reflected that appearances might have easily misled them into a belief of my death: on this supposition, to have carried me away, or to have stayed beside me, would be useless. Other enemies might be abroad, or their families, now that their fears were somewhat tranquilized, might require their presence and protection.

I went into the cottage. The fire still burned, and afforded me a genial warmth. I sat before it and began to ruminate on the state to which I was reduced, and on the measures I should next pursue. Day-light could not be very distant. Should I remain in this hovel till the morning, or immediately resume my journey? I was feeble, indeed, but by remaining here should I not increase my feebleness? The sooner I should gain some human habitation the better; whereas watchfulness and hunger would render me, at each minute, less able to proceed than on the former.

This spot might be visited on the next day; but this was involved in uncertainty. The visitants, should any come, would come merely to examine and bury the dead, and bring with them neither the clothing nor the food which my necessities demanded. The road was sufficiently discernible, and would, unavoidably, conduct me to some dwelling. I determined, therefore, to set out without delay. Even in this state I was not unmindful that my safety might require the precaution of being armed. Besides the fusil, which had been given me by Sarsefield, and which I had so unexpectedly recovered, had lost none of its value in my eyes. I hoped that it had escaped the search of the troop who had been here, and still lay below the bank, in the spot where I had dropped it.

In this hope I was not deceived. It was found. I possessed myself of the powder and shot belonging to one of the savages, and loaded it. Thus equipped for defence, I regained the road, and proceeded, with alacrity, on my way. For the wound in my cheek, nature had provided a styptic, but the soreness was extreme, and I thought of no remedy but water, with which I might wash away the blood. My thirst likewise incommoded me, and I looked with eagerness for the traces of a spring. In a soil like that of the wilderness around me, nothing was less to be expected than to light upon water. In this respect, however, my destiny was propitious. I quickly perceived water in the ruts. It trickled hither from the thicket on one side, and, pursuing it among the bushes, I reached the bubbling source. Though scanty and brackish, it afforded me unspeakable refreshment.

Thou wilt think, perhaps, that my perils were now at an end; that the blood I had already shed was sufficient for my safety. I fervently hoped that no new exigence would occur, compelling me to use the arms that I bore in my own defence. I formed a sort of resolution to shun the contest with a new enemy, almost at the expense of my own life. I was satiated and gorged with slaughter, and thought upon a new act of destruction with abhorrence and loathing.

But though I dreaded to encounter a new enemy, I was sensible that an enemy might possibly be at hand. I had moved forward with caution, and my sight and hearing were attentive to the slightest tokens. Other troops, besides that which I encountered, might be hovering near, and of that troop, I remembered that one at least had survived.

The gratification which this spring had afforded me was so great, that I was in no haste to depart. I lay upon a rock, which chanced to be shaded by a tree behind me. From this post I could overlook the road to some distance, and, at the same time, be shaded from the observation of others.

My eye was now caught by movements which appeared like those of a beast. In different circumstances, I should have instantly supposed it to be a wolf, or panther, or bear. Now my suspicions were alive on a different account, and my startled fancy figured to itself nothing but an human adversary.

A thicket was on either side of the road. That opposite to my station was discontinued at a small distance by the cultivated field. The road continued along this field, bounded by the thicket on the one side, and the open space on the other. To this space the being who was now descried was cautiously approaching.

He moved upon all fours, and presently came near enough to be distinguished. His disfigured limbs, pendants from his ears and nose, and his shorn locks, were indubitable indications of a savage. Occasionally he reared himself above the bushes, and scanned, with suspicious vigilance, the cottage and the space surrounding it. Then he stooped, and crept along as before.

I was at no loss to interpret these appearances. This was my surviving enemy. He was unacquainted with the fate of his associates, and was now approaching the theatre of carnage, to ascertain their fate.

Once more was the advantage afforded me. From this spot might unerring aim be taken, and the last of this hostile troop be made to share the fate of the rest. Should I fire or suffer him to pass in safety?

My abhorrence of bloodshed was not abated. But I had not foreseen this occurrence. My success hitherto had seemed to depend upon a combination of fortunate incidents, which could not be expected again to take place; but now was I invested with the same power. The mark was near; nothing obstructed or delayed; I incurred no danger, and the event was certain.

Why should he be suffered to live? He came hither to murder and despoil my friends; this work he has, no doubt, performed. Nay, has he not borne his part in the destruction of my uncle and my sisters? He will live only to pursue the same sanguinary trade; to drink the blood and exult in the laments of his unhappy foes, and of my own brethren. Fate has reserved him for a bloody and violent death. For how long a time soever it may be deferred, it is thus that his career will inevitably terminate.

Should he be spared, he will still roam in the wilderness, and I may again be fated to encounter him. Then our mutual situation may be widely different, and the advantage I now possess may be his.

While hastily revolving these thoughts I was thoroughly aware that one event might take place which would render all deliberation useless. Should he spy me where I lay, my fluctuations must end. My safety would indispensably require me to shoot. This persuasion made me keep a stedfast eye upon his motions, and be prepared to anticipate his assault.

It now most seasonably occurred to me that one essential duty remained to be performed. One operation, without which fire arms are useless, had been unaccountably omitted. My piece was uncocked. I did not reflect that in moving the spring, a sound would necessarily be produced, sufficient to alarm him. But I knew that the chances of escaping his notice, should I be perfectly mute and still, were extremely slender, and that, in such a case, his movements would be quicker than the light; it behoved me, therefore, to repair my omission.

The sound struck him with alarm. He turned and darted at me an inquiring glance. I saw that forbearance was no longer in my power; but my heart sunk while I complied with what may surely be deemed an indispensable necessity. This faltering, perhaps it was, that made me swerve somewhat from the fatal line. He was disabled by the wound, but not killed.

He lost all power of resistance, and was, therefore, no longer to be dreaded. He rolled upon the ground, uttering doleful shrieks, and throwing his limbs into those contorsions which bespeak the keenest agonies to which ill-fated man is subject. Horror, and compassion, and remorse, were mingled into one sentiment, and took possession of my heart. To shut out this spectacle, I withdrew from the spot, but I stopped before I had moved beyond hearing of his cries.

The impulse that drove me from the scene was pusillanimous and cowardly. The past, however deplorable, could not be recalled; but could not I afford some relief to this wretch? Could not I, at least, bring his pangs to a speedy close? Thus he might continue, writhing and calling upon death for hours. Why should his miseries by uselessly prolonged?

There was but one way to end them. To kill him outright, was the dictate of compassion and of duty. I hastily returned, and once more levelled my piece at his head. It was a loathsome obligation, and was performed with unconquerable reluctance. Thus to assault and to mangle the body of an enemy, already prostrate and powerless, was an act worthy of abhorrence; yet it was, in this case, prescribed by pity.

My faltering hand rendered this second bullet ineffectual. One expedient, still more detestable, remained. Having gone thus far, it would have been inhuman to stop short. His heart might easily be pierced by the bayonet, and his struggles would cease.

This task of cruel lenity was at length finished. I dropped the weapon and threw myself on the ground, overpowered by the horrors of this scene. Such are the deeds which perverse nature compels thousands of rational beings to perform and to witness! Such is the spectacle, endlessly prolonged and diversified, which is exhibited in every field of battle; of which, habit and example, the temptations of gain, and the illusions of honour, will make us, not reluctant or indifferent, but zealous and delighted actors and beholders!

Thus, by a series of events impossible to be computed or foreseen, was the destruction of a band, selected from their fellows for an arduous enterprise, distinguished by prowess and skill, and equally armed against surprize and force, completed by the hand of a boy, uninured to hostility, unprovided with arms, precipitate and timerous! I have noted men who seemed born for no end but by their achievements to belie experience, and baffle foresight, and outstrip belief. Would to God that I had not deserved to be numbered among these! But what power was it that called me from the sleep of death, just in time to escape the merciless knife of this enemy? Had my swoon continued till he had reached the spot, he would have effectuated my death by new wounds and torn away the skin from my brows. Such are the subtile threads on which hangs the fate of man and of the universe!

While engaged in these reflections, I perceived that the moon-light had began to fade before that of the sun. A dusky and reddish hue spread itself over the east. Cheered by this appearance, I once more resumed my feet and the road. I left the savage where he lay, but made prize of his tom-hawk. I had left my own in the cavern; and this weapon added little to my burthen. Prompted by some freak of fancy, I stuck his musquet in the ground, and left it standing upright in the middle of the road.

Chapter XX

I MOVED forward with as quick a pace as my feeble limbs would permit. I did not allow myself to meditate. The great object of my wishes was a dwelling where food and repose might be procured. I looked earnestly forward, and on each side, in search of some token of human residence; but the spots of cultivation, the *well-pole*, the *worm-fence*, and the hay-rick, were no where to be seen. I did not even meet with a wild hog, or a bewildered cow. The path was narrow, and on either side was a trackless wilderness. On the right and left were the waving lines of mountainous ridges which had no peculiarity enabling me to ascertain whether I had ever before seen them.

At length I noticed that the tracks of wheels had disappeared from the path that I was treading; that it became more narrow, and exhibited fewer marks of being frequented. These appearances were discouraging. I now suspected that I had taken a wrong direction, and instead of approaching, was receding from the habitation of men.

It was wisest, however, to proceed. The road could not but have some origin as well as end. Some hours passed away in this uncertainty. The sun rose, and by noon-day I seemed to be farther than ever from the end of my toils. The path was more obscure, and the wilderness more rugged. Thirst more incommoded me than hunger, but relief was seasonably afforded by the brooks that flowed across the path.

Coming to one of these, and having slaked my thirst, I sat down upon the bank, to reflect on my situation. The circuity of the path had frequently been noticed, and I began to suspect that though I had travelled long, I had not moved far from the spot where I had commenced my pilgrimage.

Turning my eyes on all sides, I noticed a sort of pool, formed by the rivulet, at a few paces distant from the road. In approaching and inspecting it, I observed the footsteps of cattle, who had retired by a path that seemed much beaten; I likewise noticed a cedar bucket, broken and old, lying on the margin. These tokens revived my drooping spirits, and I betook myself to this new track. It was intricate; but, at length, led up a steep, the summit of which was of better soil than that of which the flats consisted. A clover field, and several apple-trees, sure attendants of man, were now discovered. From this space I entered a corn-field, and at length, to my inexpressible joy, caught a glimpse of an house.

This dwelling was far different from that I had lately left. It was as small and as low, but its walls consisted of boards. A window of four panes admitted the light, and a chimney of brick, well burnt, and neatly arranged, peeped over the roof. As I approached I heard the voice of children, and the hum of a spinning-wheel.

I cannot make thee conceive the delight which was afforded me by all these tokens. I now found myself, indeed, among beings like myself, and from whom hospitable entertainment might be confidently expected. I compassed the house, and made my appearance at the door.

A good woman, busy at her wheel, with two children play-ing on the ground before her, were the objects that now pre-sented themselves. The uncouthness of my garb, my wild and weather-worn appearance, my fusil and tom-hawk, could not but startle them. The woman stopt her wheel, and gazed as if a spectre had started into view.

I was somewhat aware of these consequences, and endea-voured to elude them, by assuming an air of supplication and humility. I told her that I was a traveller, who had unfortu-nately lost his way, and had rambled in this wild till nearly famished for want. I intreated her to give me some food; any thing however scanty or coarse, would be acceptable.

After some pause she desired me, though not without some marks of fear, to walk in. She placed before me some brown bread and milk. She eyed me while I eagerly devoured this morsel. It was, indeed, more delicious than any I had ever tasted. At length she broke silence, and expressed her aston-ishment and commiseration at my seemingly forlorn state, adding, that perhaps I was the man whom the men were look-ing after who had been there some hours before.

My curiosity was roused by this intimation. In answer to my interrogations, she said, that three persons had lately stopped, to inquire if her husband had not met, within the last three days, a person of whom their description seemed pretty much to suit my person and dress. He was tall, slender, wore nothing but shirt and trowsers, and was wounded on the cheek.

What, I asked, did they state the rank or condition of the person to be?

He lived in Solebury. He was supposed to have rambled in the mountains, and to have lost his way, or to have met with some mischance. It was three days since he had disappeared, but had been seen, by some one, the last night, at Deb's hut.

What and where was Deb's hut?

It was a hut in the wilderness, occupied by an old Indian woman, known among her neighbours by the name of Old Deb. Some people called her Queen Mab. Her dwelling was eight *long* miles from this house.

A thousand questions were precluded, and a thousand doubts solved by this information. *Queen Mab* were sounds familiar to my ears; for they originated with myself.

This woman originally belonged to the tribe of Delawares or Lennilennapee. All these districts were once comprised within the dominions of that nation. About thirty years ago, in consequence of perpetual encroachments of the English colonists, they abandoned their ancient seats and retired to the banks of the Wabash and Muskingum.

This emigration was concerted in a general council of the tribe, and obtained the concurrence of all but one female. Her birth, talents, and age, gave her much consideration and authority among her countrymen; and all her zeal and eloquence were exerted to induce them to lay aside their scheme. In this, however, she could not succeed. Finding them refractory, she declared her resolution to remain behind, and maintain possession of the land which her countrymen should impiously abandon.

The village inhabited by this clan was built upon ground which now constitutes my uncle's barn yard and orchard. On the departure of her countrymen, this female burnt the empty wigwams and retired into the fastnesses of Norwalk. She selected a spot suitable for an Indian dwelling and a small plantation of maize, and in which she was seldom liable to interruption and intrusion.

Her only companions were three dogs, of the Indian or wolf species. These animals differed in nothing from their kinsmen of the forest, but in their attachment and obedience to their mistress. She governed them with absolute sway: they were her servants and protectors, and attended her person or guarded her threshold, agreeably to her directions. She fed them with corn and they supplied her and themselves with meat, by hunting squirrels, racoons, and rabbits.

To the rest of mankind they were aliens or enemies. They never left the desert but in company with their mistress, and when she entered a farm-house, waited her return at a distance. They would suffer none to approach them, but attacked no one who did not imprudently crave their acquaintance, or who kept at a respectful distance from their wigwam. That sacred asylum they would not suffer to be violated, and no stranger could enter it but at the imminent hazard of his life, unless accompanied and protected by their dame.

The chief employment of this woman, when at home, besides plucking the weeds from among her corn; bruising the grain between two stones, and setting her snares, for rabbits and apossums, was to talk. Though in solitude, her tongue was never at rest but when she was asleep; but her conversation was merely addressed to her dogs. Her voice was sharp and shrill, and her gesticulations were vehement and grotesque. An hearer would naturally imagine that she was scolding; but, in truth, she was merely giving them directions. Having no other object of contemplation or subject of discourse, she always found, in their postures and looks, occasion for praise, or blame, or command. The readiness with which they understood, and the docility with which they obeyed her movements and words, were truly wonderful.

If a stranger chanced to wander near her hut, and overhear her jargon, incessant as it was, and shrill, he might speculate in vain on the reason of these sounds. If he waited in expectation of hearing some reply, he waited in vain. The strain, always voluble and sharp, was never intermitted for a moment, and would continue for hours at a time.

She seldom left the hut but to visit the neighbouring inhabitants, and demand from them food and cloathing, or whatever her necessities required. These were exacted as her due: to have her wants supplied was her prerogative, and to withhold what she claimed was rebellion. She conceived that by remaining behind her countrymen she succeeded to the government, and retained the possession of all this region. The English were aliens and sojourners, who occupied the land merely by her connivance and permission, and whom she allowed to remain on no terms but those of supplying her wants.

Being a woman aged and harmless, her demands being limited to that of which she really stood in need, and which her own industry could not procure, her pretensions were a subject of mirth and good humour, and her injunctions obeyed with seeming deference and gravity. To me she early became an object of curiosity and speculation. I delighted to observe her habits and humour her prejudices. She frequently came to my uncle's house, and I sometimes visited her; insensibly she seemed to contract an affection for me, and regarded me with more complacency and condescension than any other received.

She always disdained to speak English, and custom had rendered her intelligible to most in her native language, with regard to a few simple questions. I had taken some pains to study her jargon, and could make out to discourse with her on the few ideas which she possessed. This circumstance, likewise, wonderfully prepossessed her in my favour.

The name by which she was formerly known was Deb; but her pretensions to royalty, the wildness of her aspect and garb, her shrivelled and diminutive form, a constitution that seemed to defy the ravages of time and the influence of the elements; her age, which some did not scruple to affirm exceeded an hundred years, her romantic solitude and mountainous haunts suggested to my fancy the appellation of *Queen Mab*. There appeared to me some rude analogy between this personage and her whom the poets of old-time have delighted to celebrate: thou perhaps wilt discover nothing but incongruities between them, but, be that as it may, Old Deb and Queen Mab soon came into indiscriminate and general use.

She dwelt in Norwalk upwards of twenty years. She was not forgotten by her countrymen, and generally received from her brothers and sons an autumnal visit; but no solicitations or entreaties could prevail on her to return with them. Two years ago, some suspicion or disgust induced her to forsake her ancient habitation, and to seek a new one. Happily she found a more convenient habitation twenty miles to the westward, and in a spot abundantly sterile and rude.

This dwelling was of logs, and had been erected by a Scottish emigrant, who not being rich enough to purchase land, and entertaining a passion for solitude and independence, cleared a field in the unappropriated wilderness, and subsisted on its produce. After some time he disappeared. Various conjectures were formed as to the cause of his absence. None of them were satisfactory; but that which obtained most credit was, that he had been murdered by the Indians, who, about the same period, paid their annual visit to the *Queen*. This conjecture acquired some force, by observing that the old woman shortly after took possession of his hut, his implements of tillage, and his corn-field.

She was not molested in her new abode, and her life passed in the same quiet tenour as before. Her periodical rambles, her regal claims, her guardian wolfs, and her uncouth volubility, were equally remarkable, but her circuits were new. Her distance made her visit to Solebury more rarely, and had prevented me from ever extending my pedestrian excursions to her present abode.

These recollections were now suddenly called up by the information of my hostess. The hut where I had sought shelter and relief was, it seems, the residence of Queen Mab. Some fortunate occurrence had called her away during my visit. Had she and her dogs been at home, I should have been set upon by these ferocious centinels, and, before their dame could have interfered, have been, together with my helpless companion, mangled or killed. These animals never barked. I should have entered unaware of my danger, and my fate could scarcely have been averted by my fusil.

Her absence at this unseasonable hour was mysterious. It was now the time of year when her countrymen were accustomed to renew their visit. Was there a league between her and the plunderers whom I had encountered?

But who were they by whom my footsteps were so industriously traced? Those whom I had seen at Deb's hut were strangers to me, but the wound upon my face was known only to them. To this circumstance was now added my place of residence and name. I supposed them impressed with the belief that I was dead; but this mistake must have speedily been rectified. Revisiting the spot, finding me gone, and obtaining some intelligence of my former condition, they had instituted a search after me.

But what tidings were these? I was supposed to have been bewildered in the mountains, and three days were said to have passed since my disappearance. Twelve hours had scarcely elapsed since I emerged from the cavern. Had two days and an half been consumed in my subterranean prison?

These reflections were quickly supplanted by others. I now gained a sufficient acquaintance with the region that was spread around me. I was in the midst of a vale, included between ridges that gradually approached each other, and when joined, were broken up into hollows and steeps, and spreading themselves over a circular space, assumed the appellation of Norwalk. This vale gradually widened as it tended to the westward, and was, in this place ten or twelve miles in breadth. My devious footsteps had brought me to the foot of the southern barrier. The outer basis of this was laved by the river, but, as it tended eastward, the mountain and river receded from each other, and one of the cultivable districts lying between them was Solebury, my natal *township*. Hither it was now my duty to return with the utmost expedition.

There were two ways before me. One lay along the interior base of the hill, over a sterile and trackless space, and exposed to the encounter of savages, some of whom might possibly be lurking here. The other was the well frequented road, on the outside and along the river, and which was to be gained by passing over this hill. The practicability of the passage was to be ascertained by inquiries made to my hostess. She pointed out a path that led to the rocky summit and down to the river's brink. The path was not easy to be kept in view or to be trodden, but it was undoubtedly to be preferred to any other.

A route, somewhat circuitous, would terminate in the river road. Thenceforward the way to Solebury was level and direct; but the whole space which I had to traverse was not less than thirty miles. In six hours it would be night, and, to perform the journey in that time would demand the agile boundings of a leopard and the indefatigable sinews of an elk.

My frame was in miserable plight. My strength had been assailed by anguish, and fear, and watchfulness; by toil, and abstinence, and wounds. Still, however, some remnant was left; would it not enable me to reach my home by night-fall? I had delighted, from my childhood, in feats of agility and perseverance. In roving through the maze of thickets and precipices, I had put my energies both moral and physical, frequently to the test. Greater achievements than this had been performed, and I disdained to be out-done in perspicacity by the lynx, in his sure-footed instinct by the roe, or in patience under hardship, and contention with fatigue, by the Mohawk. I have ever aspired to transcend the rest of animals in all that is common to the rational and brute, as well as in all by which they are distinguished from each other.

Chapter XXI

I LIKEWISE burned with impatience to know the condition of my family, to dissipate at once their tormenting doubts and my own, with regard to our mutual safety. The evil that I feared had befallen them was too enormous to allow me to repose in suspense, and my restlessness and ominous forebodings would be more intolerable than any hardship or toils to which I could possibly be subjected during this journey.

I was much refreshed and invigorated by the food that I had taken, and by the rest of an hour. With this stock of recruited force I determined to scale the hill. After receiving minute directions, and returning many thanks for my hospitable entertainment, I set out.

The path was indeed intricate, and deliberate attention was obliged to be exerted in order to preserve it. Hence my progress was slower than I wished. The first impulse was to fix my eye upon the summit, and to leap from crag to crag till I reached it, but this my experience had taught me was impracticable. It was only by winding through gullies, and coasting precipices and bestriding chasms, that I could hope finally to gain the top, and I was assured that by one way only was it possible to accomplish even this.

An hour was spent in struggling with impediments, and I seemed to have gained no way. Hence a doubt was suggested whether I had not missed the true road. In this doubt I was confirmed by the difficulties which now grew up before me. The brooks, the angles and the hollows, which my hostess had described, were not to be seen. Instead of these, deeper dells, more headlong torrents and wider gaping rifts were incessantly encountered.

To return was as hopeles as to proceed. I consoled myself with thinking that the survey which my informant had made of the hill-side, might prove inaccurate, and that in spite of her predictions, the heights might be reached by other means than by those pointed out by her. I will not enumerate my toilsome expedients, my frequent disappointments and my desperate exertions. Suffice it to say that I gained the upper space, not till the sun had dipped beneath the horizon.

My satisfaction at accomplishing thus much was not small, and I hied, with renovated spirits, to the opposite brow. This proved to be a steep that could not be descended. The river flowed at its foot. The opposite bank was five hundred yards distant, and was equally towering and steep as that on which I stood. Appearances were adapted to persuade you that these rocks had formerly joined, but by some mighty effort of nature, had been severed, that the stream might find way through the chasm. The channel, however, was encumbered with asperities over which the river fretted and foamed with thundering impetuosity.

I pondered for a while on these stupendous scenes. They ravished my attention from considerations that related to myself; but this interval was short, and I began to measure the descent, in order to ascertain the practicability of treading it. My survey terminated in bitter disappointment. I turned my eye successively eastward and westward. Solebury lay in the former direction, and thither I desired to go. I kept along the verge in this direction, till I reached an impassable rift. Beyond this I saw that the steep grew lower, but it was impossible to proceed farther. Higher up the descent might be practicable, and though more distant from Solebury, it was better to reach the road, even at that distance, than never to reach it.

Changing my course, therefore, I explored the spaces above. The night was rapidly advancing, the grey clouds gathered in the south-east, and a chilling blast, the usual attendant of a night in October, began to whistle among the pigmy cedars that scantily grew upon these heights. My progress would quickly be arrested by darkness, and it behoved me to provide some place of shelter and repose. No recess, better than an hollow in the rock, presented itself to my anxious scrutiny.

Meanwhile I would not dismiss the hope of reaching the road, which I saw some hundred feet below, winding along the edge of the river, before daylight should utterly fail. Speedily these hopes derived new vigour from meeting a ledge that irregularly declined from the brow of the hill. It was wide enough to allow of cautious footing. On a similar stratum, or ledge, projecting still further from the body of the hill, and close to the surface of the river, was the road. This stratum ascended from the level of the stream, while that on which I trod rapidly descended. I hoped that they would speedily be blended, or at least approach so near as to allow me to leap from one to the other without enormous hazard.

This fond expectation was frustrated. Presently I perceived that the ledge below began to descend, while that above began to tend upward, and was quickly terminated by the uppermost surface of the cliff. Here it was needful to pause. I looked over the brink and considered whether I might not leap from my present station, without endangering my limbs. The road into which I should fall was a rocky pavement far from being smooth. The descent could not be less than forty or fifty feet. Such an attempt was, to the last degree, hazardous, but was it not better to risque my life by leaping from this eminence, than to remain and perish on the top of this inhospitable mountain? The toils which I had endured, in reaching this height appeared to my panic-struck fancy, less easy to be borne again than death.

I know not but that I should have finally resolved to leap, had not different views been suggested by observing that the outer edge of the road was, in like manner, the brow of a steep which terminated in the river. The surface of the road, was twelve or fifteen feet above the level of the stream, which, in this spot was still and smooth. Hence I inferred that the water was not of inconsiderable depth. To fall upon rocky points was, indeed, dangerous, but to plunge into water of sufficient depth, even from an height greater than that at which I now stood, especially to one to whom habit had rendered water almost as congenial an element as air, was scarcely attended with inconvenience. This expedient was easy and safe. Twenty yards from this spot, the channel was shallow, and to gain the road from the stream, was no difficult exploit.

Some disadvantages, however, attended this scheme. The water was smooth, but this might arise from some other cause than its depth. My gun, likewise, must be left behind me, and that was a loss to which I felt invincible repugnance. To let it fall upon the road, would put it in my power to retrieve the possession, but it was likely to be irreparably injured by the fall.

While musing upon this expedient, and weighing injuries with benefits, the night closed upon me. I now considered that should I emerge in safety from the stream, I should have many miles to travel before I could reach an house. My clothes meanwhile would be loaded with wet. I should be heart-pierced by the icy blast that now blew, and my wounds and bruises would be chafed into insupportable pain.

I reasoned likewise on the folly of impatience and the ne-cessity of repose. By thus long continuance in one posture, my sinews began to stiffen, and my reluctance to make new exertions to encrease. My brows were heavy, and I felt an irresistible propensity to sleep. I concluded to seek some shel-ter, and resign myself, my painful recollections, and my mournful presages to sweet forgetfulness. For this end, I once more ascended to the surface of the cliff. I dragged my weary feet forward, till I found somewhat that promised me the shel-ter that I sought.

A cluster of cedars appeared, whose branches over-arched a space that might be called a bower. It was a slight cavity, whose flooring was composed of loose stones and a few faded leaves blown from a distance, and finding a temporary lodge-ment here. On one side was a rock, forming a wall rugged and projecting above. At the bottom of the rock was a rift, some-what resembling a coffin in shape, and not much larger in dimensions. This rift terminated on the opposite side of the rock, in an opening that was too small for the body of a man to pass. The distance between each entrance was twice the length of a man.

This bower was open to the South-east whence the gale now blew. It therefore imperfectly afforded the shelter of which I stood in need; but it was the best that the place and the time afforded. To stop the smaller entrance of the cavity with a stone, and to heap before the other, branches lopped from the trees with my hatchet, might somewhat contribute to my comfort.

This was done, and thrusting myself into this recess, as far as I was able, I prepared for repose. It might have been reasonably suspected to be the den of rattle-snakes or panthers; but my late contention with superior dangers and more formidable enemies made me reckless of these, but another inconvenience remained. In spite of my precautions, my motionless posture and slender covering exposed me so much to the cold that I could not sleep.

The air appeared to have suddenly assumed the temperature of mid-winter. In a short time, my extremities were benumbed, and my limbs shivered and ached as if I had been seized by an ague. My bed likewise was dank and uneven, and the posture I was obliged to assume, unnatural and painful. It was evident that my purpose could not be answered by remaining here.

I, therefore, crept forth, and began to reflect upon the possibility of continuing my journey. Motion was the only thing that could keep me from freezing, and my frame was in that state which allowed me to take no repose in the absence of warmth; since warmth were indispensible. It now occurred to me to ask whether it were not possible to kindle a fire.

Sticks and leaves were at hand. My hatchet and a pebble would enable me to extract a spark. From this, by suitable care and perseverance, I might finally procure sufficient fire to give me comfort and ease, and even enable me to sleep. This boon was delicious and I felt as if I were unable to support a longer deprivation of it.

I proceeded to execute this scheme. I took the dryest leaves, and endeavoured to use them as tinder, but the dryest leaves were moistened by the dews. They were only to be found in the hollows, in some of which were pools of water and others were dank. I was not speedily discouraged, but my repeated attempts failed, and I was finally compelled to relinquish this expedient.

All that now remained was to wander forth and keep myself in motion till the morning. The night was likely to prove tempestuous and long. The gale seemed freighted with ice, and acted upon my body like the points of a thousand needles. There was no remedy, and I mustered my patience to endure it.

I returned again, to the brow of the hill. I ranged along it till I reached a place where the descent was perpendicular, and, in consequence of affording no sustenance to trees or bushes, was nearly smooth and bare. There was no road to be seen, and this circumstance, added to the sounds which the ripling current produced, afforded me some knowledge of my situation.

The ledge, along which the road was conducted, disappeared near this spot. The opposite sides of the chasm through which flowed the river, approached nearer to each other, in the form of jutting promontories. I now stood upon the verge of that on the northern side. The water flowed at the foot, but, for the space of ten or twelve feet from the rock, was so shallow as to permit the traveller and his horse to wade through it, and thus to regain the road which the receding precipice had allowed to be continued on the farther side.

I knew the nature and dimensions of this ford. I knew that, at a few yards from the rock, the channel was of great depth. To leap into it, in this place, was a less dangerous exploit, than at the spot where I had formerly been tempted to leap. There I was unacquainted with the depth, but here I knew it to be considerable. Still there was some ground of hesitation and fear. My present station was loftier, and how deeply I might sink into this gulf, how far the fall and the concussion would bereave me of my presence of mind, I could not determine. This hesitation vanished, and placing my tom-hawk and fusil upon the ground, I prepared to leap.

This purpose was suspended, in the moment of its execution, by a faint sound, heard from the quarter whence I had come. It was the warning of men, but had nothing in common with those which I had been accustomed to hear. It was not the howling of a wolf or the yelling of a panther. These had often been overheard by night during my last year's excursion to the lakes. My fears whispered that this was the vociferation of a savage.

I was unacquainted with the number of the enemies who had adventured into this district. Whether those whom I had encountered at *Deb's hut* were of that band whom I had met with in the cavern, was merely a topic of conjecture. There might be an half-score of troops, equally numerous, spread over the wilderness, and the signal I had just heard might betoken the approach of one of these. Yet by what means they should gain this nook, and what prey they expected to discover, were not easily conceived.

The sounds, somewhat diversified, nearer and rising from different quarters, were again heard. My doubts and apprehensions were increased. What expedient to adopt for my own safety, was a subject of rapid meditation. Whether to remain stretched upon the ground or to rise and go forward. Was it likely the enemy would coast along the edge of the steep? Would they ramble hither to look upon the ample scene which spread on all sides around the base of this rocky pinnacle? In that case, how should I conduct myself? My arms were ready for use. Could I not elude the necessity of shedding more blood? Could I not anticipate their assault by casting myself without delay into the stream?

The sense of danger demanded more attention to be paid to external objects than to the motives by which my future conduct should be influenced. My post was on a circular projecture, in some degree, detached from the body of the hill, the brow of which continued in a streight line, uninterrupted by this projecture, which was somewhat higher than the continued summit of the ridge. This line ran at the distance of a few paces from my post. Objects moving along this line could merely be perceived to move, in the present obscurity.

My scrutiny was entirely directed to this quarter. Presently the treading of many feet was heard, and several figures were discovered, following each other in that streight and regular succession which is peculiar to the Indians. They kept along the brow of the hill joining the promontory. I distinctly marked seven figures in succession.

My resolution was formed. Should any one cast his eye hither, suspect, or discover an enemy, and rush towards me, I determined to start upon my feet, fire on my foe as he advanced, throw my piece on the ground, and then leap into the river.

Happily, they passed unobservant and in silence. I remained, in the same posture, for several minutes. At length, just as my alarms began to subside, the halloos, before heard, arose, and from the same quarter as before. This convinced me that my perils were not at an end. This now appeared to be merely the vanguard, and would speedily be followed by others, against whom the same caution was necessary to be taken.

My eye, anxiously bent the only way by which any one could approach, now discerned a figure, which was indubitably that of a man armed; none other appeared in company, but doubtless others were near. He approached, stood still, and appeared to gaze stedfastly at the spot where I lay.

The optics of a *Lennilennapee* I knew to be far keener than my own. A log or a couched fawn would never be mistaken for a man, nor a man for a couched fawn or a log. Not only a human being would be instantly detected, but a decision be unerringly made whether it were friend or foe. That my prostrate body was the object on which the attention of this vigilant and stedfast gazer was fixed, could not be doubted. Yet, since he continued an inactive gazer, there was ground for a possibility to stand upon, that I was not recognized. My fate, therefore, was still in suspense.

This interval was momentary. I marked a movement, which my fears instantly interpreted to be that of leveling a gun at my head. This action was sufficiently comformable to my prognostics. Supposing me to be detected, there was no need for him to change his post. Aim might too fatally be taken, and his prey be secured, from the distance at which he now stood.

These images glanced upon my thought, and put an end to my suspense. A single effort placed me on my feet. I fired with precipitation that precluded the certainty of hitting my mark, dropped my piece upon the ground, and leaped from this tremendous height into the river. I reached the surface, and sunk in a moment to the bottom.

Plunging endlong into the water, the impetus created by my fall from such an height, would be slowly resisted by this denser element. Had the depth been less, its resistance would not perhaps have hindered me from being mortally injured against the rocky bottom. Had the depth been greater, time enough would not have been allowed me to regain the surface. Had I fallen on my side, I should have been bereaved of life or sensibility by the shock which my frame would have received. As it was, my fate was suspended on a thread. To have lost my presence of mind, to have forborne to counteract my sinking, for an instant, after I had reached the water, would have made all exertions to regain the air, fruitless. To so fortunate a concurrence of events, was thy friend indebted for his safety!

Yet I only emerged from the gulf to encounter new perils. Scarcely had I raised my head above the surface, and inhaled the vital breath, when twenty shots were aimed at me from the precipice above. A shower of bullets fell upon the water. Some of them did not fall further than two inches from my head. I had not been aware of this new danger, and now that it assailed me continued gasping the air, and floundering at random. The means of eluding it did not readily occur. My case seemed desperate and all caution was dismissed.

This state of discomfiting surprise quickly disappeared. I made myself acquainted, at a glance, with the position of surrounding objects. I conceived that the opposite bank of the river would afford me most security, and thither I tended with all the expedition in my power.

Meanwhile, my safety depended on eluding the bullets that continued incessantly to strike the water at an arm's length from my body. For this end I plunged beneath the surface, and only rose to inhale fresh air. Presently the firing ceased, the flashes that lately illuminated the bank disappeared, and a certain bustle and murmur of confused voices gave place to solitude and silence.

Chapter XXII

I REACHED without difficulty the opposite bank, but the steep was inaccessible. I swam along the edge in hopes of meeting with some projection or recess where I might, at least, rest my weary limbs, and if it were necessary to recross the river, to lay in a stock of recruited spirits and strength for that purpose. I trusted that the water would speedily become shoal, or that the steep would afford rest to my feet. In both these hopes I was disappointed.

There is no one to whom I would yield the superiority in swimming, but my strength, like that of other human beings, had its limits. My previous fatigues had been enormous, and my clothes, heavy with moisture, greatly incumbered and retarded my movements. I had proposed to free myself from this imprisonment, but I foresaw the inconveniences of wandering over this scene in absolute nakedness, and was willing therefore, at whatever hazard, to retain them. I continued to struggle with the current and to search for the means of scaling the steeps. My search was fruitless, and I began to meditate the recrossing of the river.

Surely my fate has never been paralleled! Where was this series of hardships and perils to end? No sooner was one calamity eluded, than I was beset by another. I had emerged from abhorred darkness in the heart of the earth, only to endure the extremities of famine and encounter the fangs of a wild beast. From these I was delivered only to be thrown into the midst of savages, to wage an endless and hopeless war with adepts in killing; with appetites that longed to feast upon my bowels and to quaff my heart's-blood. From these likewise was I rescued, but merely to perish in the gulfs of the river, to welter on unvisited shores or to be washed far away from curiosity or pity.

Formerly water was not only my field of sport but my sofa and my bed. I could float for hours on the surface, enjoying its delicious cool, almost without the expense of the slightest motion. It was an element as fitted for repose as for exercise, but now the buoyant spirit seemed to have flown. My muscles were shrunk, the air and water were equally congealed, and my most vehement exertions were requisite to sustain me on the surface.

At first I had moved along with my wonted celerity and ease, but quickly my forces were exhausted. My pantings and efforts were augmented and I saw that to cross the river again was impracticable. I must continue, therefore, to search out some accessible spot in the bank along which I was swimming.

Each moment diminished my stock of strength, and it behoved me to make good my footing before another minute should escape. I continued to swim, to survey the bank, and to make ineffectual attempts to grasp the rock. The shrubs which grew upon it would not uphold me, and the fragments which, for a moment, inspired me with hope, crumbled away as soon as they were touched.

At length, I noticed a pine, which was rooted in a crevice near the water. The trunk, or any part of the root, was beyond my reach, but I trusted that I could catch hold of the branch which hung lowest, and that, when caught, it would assist me in gaining the trunk, and thus deliver me from the death which could not be otherwise averted.

The attempt was arduous. Had it been made when I first reached the bank, no difficulty had attended it, but now, to throw myself some feet above the surface could scarcely be expected from one whose utmost efforts seemed to be demanded to keep him from sinking. Yet this exploit, arduous as it was, was attempted and accomplished. Happily the twigs were strong enough to sustain my weight till I caught at other branches and finally placed myself upon the trunk.

This danger was now past, but I admitted the conviction that others, no less formidable remained to be encountered and that my ultimate destiny was death. I looked upward. New efforts might enable me to gain the summit of this steep, but, perhaps, I should thus be placed merely in the situation from which I had just been delivered. It was of little moment whether the scene of my imprisonment was a dungeon not to be broken, or a summit from which descent was impossible.

The river, indeed, severed me from a road which was level and safe, but my recent dangers were remembered only to make me shudder at the thought of incurring them a second time, by attempting to cross it. I blush at the recollection of this cowardice. It was little akin to the spirit which I had recently displayed. It was, indeed, an alien to my bosom, and was quickly supplanted by intrepidity and perseverance.

I proceeded to mount the hill. From root to root, and from branch to branch, lay my journey. It was finished, and I sat down upon the highest brow to meditate on future trials. No road lay along this side of the river. It was rugged and sterile, and farms were sparingly dispersed over it. To reach one of these was now the object of my wishes. I had not lost the desire of reaching Solebury before morning, but my wet clothes and the coldness of the night seemed to have bereaved me of the power.

I traversed this summit, keeping the river on my right hand. Happily, its declinations and ascents were by no means difficult, and I was cheered in the midst of my vexations, by observing that every mile brought me nearer to my uncle's dwelling. Meanwhile I anxiously looked for some tokens of an habitation. These at length presented themselves. A wild heath, whistled over by October blasts, meagerly adorned with the dry stalks of scented shrubs and the bald heads of the sapless mullen, was succeeded by a fenced field and a corn-stack. The dwelling to which these belonged was eagerly sought.

I was not surprised that all voices were still and all lights extinguished, for this was the hour of repose. Having reached a piazza before the house, I paused. Whether, at this drousy time, to knock for admission, to alarm the peaceful tenants and take from them the rest which their daily toils and their rural innocence had made so sweet, or to retire to what shelter an hay-stack or barn could afford, was the theme of my deliberations.

Meanwhile I looked up at the house. It was the model of cleanliness and comfort. It was built of wood; but the materials had undergone the plane, as well as the axe and the saw. It was painted white, and the windows not only had sashes, but these sashes were supplied, contrary to custom, with glass. In most cases, the aperture where glass should be is stuffed with an old hat or a petticoat. The door had not only all its parts entire, but was embellished with mouldings and a pediment. I gathered from these tokens that this was the abode not only of rural competence and innocence, but of some beings, raised by education and fortune, above the intellectual mediocrity of clowns.

Methought I could claim consanguinity with such beings. Not to share their charity and kindness would be inflicting as well as receiving injury. The trouble of affording shelter, and warmth, and wholesome diet to a wretch destitute as I was, would be eagerly sought by them.

Still I was unwilling to disturb them. I bethought myself that their kitchen might be entered, and all that my necessities required be obtained without interrupting their slumber. I needed nothing but the warmth which their kitchen hearth would afford. Stretched upon the bricks, I might dry my clothes, and perhaps enjoy some unmolested sleep. In spite of presages of ill and the horrid remembrances of what I had performed and endured, I believed that nature would afford a short respite to my cares.

I went to the door of what appeared to be a kitchen. The door was wide open. This circumstance portended evil. Though it be not customary to lock or to bolt, it is still less usual to have entrances unclosed. I entered with suspicious steps, and saw enough to confirm my apprehensions. Several pieces of wood half burned, lay in the midst of the floor. They appeared to have been removed hither from the chimney, doubtless with a view to set fire to the whole building.

The fire had made some progress on the floor, but had been seasonably extinguished by pails-full of water, thrown upon it. The floor was still deluged with wet, the pail not emptied of all its contents stood upon the hearth. The earthen vessels and plates whose proper place was the dresser, were scattered in fragments in all parts of the room. I looked around me for some one to explain this scene, but no one appeared.

The last spark of fire was put out, so that had my curiosity been idle, my purpose could not be accomplished. To retire from this scene, neither curiosity nor benevolence would permit. That some mortal injury had been intended was apparent. What greater mischief had befallen, or whether greater might not, by my interposition, be averted, could only be ascertained by penetrating further into the house. I opened a door on one side which led to the main body of the building and entered to a bed-chamber. I stood at the entrance and knocked, but no one answered my signals.

The sky was not totally clouded, so that some light pervaded the room. I saw that a bed stood in the corner, but whether occupied or not, its curtains hindered me from judging. I stood in suspense a few minutes, when a motion in the bed shewed me that some one was there. I knocked again but withdrew to the outside of the door. This roused the sleeper, who, half-groaning and puffing the air through his nostrils, grumbled out in the hoarsest voice that I ever heard, and in a tone of surly impatience . . . Who is there?

I hesitated for an answer, but the voice instantly continued in the manner of one half-asleep and enraged at being disturbed . . . Is't you Peg? Damn ye, stay away, now; I tell ye stay away, or, by God I will cut your throat . . . I will. . . . He continued to mutter and swear, but without coherence or distinctness.

These were the accents of drunkenness, and denoted a wild and ruffian life. They were little in unison with the external appearances of the mansion, and blasted all the hopes I had formed of meeting under this roof with gentleness and hospitality. To talk with this being, to attempt to reason him into humanity and soberness, was useless. I was at a loss in what manner to address him, or whether it was proper to maintain any parley. Meanwhile, my silence was supplied by the suggestions of his own distempered fancy. Ay, said he, ye will, will ye? well come on, let's see who's the better at the oak-stick. If I part with ye, before I have bared your bones . . . I'll teach ye to be always dipping in my dish, ye devil's dam! ye!

So saying, he tumbled out of bed. At the first step, he struck his head against the bed-post, but setting himself upright, he staggered towards the spot where I stood. Some new obstacle occurred. He stumbled and fell at his length upon the floor.

To encounter or expostulate with a man in this state was plainly absurd. I turned and issued forth, with an aching heart, into the court before the house. The miseries which a debauched husband or father inflicts upon all whom their evil destiny allies to him were pictured by my fancy, and wrung from me tears of anguish. These images, however, quickly yielded to reflections on my own state. No expedient now remained, but to seek the barn, and find a covering and a bed of straw.

I had scarcely set foot within the barn-yard when I heard a sound as of the crying of an infant. It appeared to issue from the barn. I approached softly and listened at the door. The cries of the babe continued, but were accompanied by intreaties of a nurse or a mother to be quiet. These intreaties were mingled with heart-breaking sobs and exclamations of . . . Ah! me, my babe! Canst thou not sleep and afford thy unhappy mother some peace? Thou art cold, and I have not sufficient warmth to cherish thee! What will become of us? Thy deluded father cares not if we both perish.

A glimpse of the true nature of the scene seemed to be imparted by these words. I now likewise recollected incidents that afforded additional light. Somewhere on this bank of the river, there formerly resided one by name Selby. He was an aged person, who united science and taste to the simple and laborious habits of an husbandman. He had a son who resided several years in Europe, but on the death of his father, returned home, accompanied by a wife. He had succeeded to the occupation of the farm, but rumour had whispered many tales to the disadvantage of his morals. His wife was affirmed to be of delicate and polished manners, and much unlike her companion.

It now occurred to me that this was the dwelling of the Selbys, and I seemed to have gained some insight into the discord and domestic miseries by which the unhappy lady suffered. This was no time to waste my sympathy on others. I could benefit her nothing. Selby had probably returned from a carousal, with all his malignant passions raised into phrensy by intoxication. He had driven his desolate wife from her bed and house, and to shun outrage and violence she had fled, with her helpless infant, to the barn. To appease his fury, to console her, to suggest a remedy for this distress, was not in my power. To have sought an interview would be merely to excite her terrors and alarm her delicacy, without contributing to alleviate her calamity. Here then was no asylum for me. A place of rest must be sought at some neighbouring habitation.

It was probable that one would be found at no great distance; the path that led from the spot where I stood, through a gate into a meadow, might conduct me to the nearest dwelling, and this path I immediately resolved to explore.

I was anxious to open the gate without noise, but I could not succeed. Some creaking of its hinges, was unavoidably produced, which I feared would be overheard by the lady and multiply her apprehensions and perplexities. This inconvenience was irremediable. I therefore closed the gate and pursued the foot way before me with the utmost expedition. I had not gained the further end of the meadow when I lighted on something which lay across the path, and which, on being closely inspected, appeared to be an human body. It was the corse of a girl, mangled by an hatchet. Her head gory and deprived of its locks, easily explained the kind of enemies by whom she had been assailed. Here was proof that this quiet and remote habitation had been visited, in their destructive progress by the Indians. The girl had been slain by them, and her scalp, according to their savage custom, had been torn away to be preserved as a trophy.

The fire which had been kindled on the kitchen floor was now remembered, and corroborated the inferences which were drawn from this spectacle. And yet that the mischief had been thus limited, that the besotted wretch who lay helpless on his bed, and careless of impending danger, and that the mother and her infant should escape, excited some degree of surprise. Could the savages have been interrupted in their work, and obliged to leave their vengeance unfinished?

Their visit had been recent. Many hours had not elapsed since they prowled about these grounds. Had they wholly disappeared and meant they not to return? To what new danger might I be exposed in remaining thus guideless and destitute of all defence?

In consequence of these reflections, I proceeded with more caution. I looked with suspicious glances, before and on either side of me. I now approached the fence which, on this side, bounded the meadow. Something was discerned or imagined, stretched close to the fence, on the ground, and filling up the path-way. My apprehensions of a lurking enemy, had been previously awakened, and my fancy instantly figured to itself an armed man, lying on the ground and waiting to assail the unsuspecting passenger.

At first I was prompted to fly, but a second thought shewed me that I had already approached near enough to be endangered. Notwithstanding my pause, the form was motionless. The possibility of being misled in my conjectures was easily supposed. What I saw might be a log or it might be another victim to savage ferocity. This tract was that which my safety required me to pursue. To turn aside or go back would be merely to bewilder myself anew.

Urged by these motives, I went nearer, and at last was close enough to perceive that the figure was human. He lay upon his face; near his right hand was a musquet, unclenched. This circumstance, his death-like attitude and the garb and ornaments of an Indian, made me readily suspect the nature and cause of this catastrophe. Here the invaders had been encountered and repulsed, and one at least of their number had been left upon the field.

I was weary of contemplating these rueful objects. Custom, likewise, even in so short a period, had inured me to spectacles of horror. I was grown callous and immoveable. I staid not to ponder on the scene, but snatching the musquet, which was now without an owner, and which might be indispensable to my defence, I hastened into the wood. On this side the meadow was skirted by a forest, but a beaten road led into it, and might therefore be attempted without danger.

Chapter XXIII

THE ROAD was intricate and long. It seemed designed to pervade the forest in every possible direction. I frequently noticed cut wood, piled in heaps upon either side, and rejoiced in these tokens that the residence of men was near. At length I reached a second fence, which proved to be the boundary of a road still more frequented. I pursued this, and presently beheld, before me, the river and its opposite barriers.

This object afforded me some knowledge of my situation. There was a ford over which travellers used to pass, and in which the road that I was now pursuing terminated. The stream was rapid and tumultuous, but in this place it did not rise higher than the shoulders. On the opposite side was an highway, passable by horses and men, though not carriages, and which led into the midst of Solebury. Should I not rush into the stream, and still aim at reaching my uncle's house before morning? Why should I delay?

Thirty hours of incessant watchfulness and toil, of enormous efforts and perils, preceded and accompanied by abstinence and wounds, were enough to annihilate the strength and courage of ordinary men. In the course of them, I had frequently believed myself to have reached the verge beyond which my force would not carry me, but experience as frequently demonstrated my error. Though many miles were yet to be traversed, though my clothes were once more to be drenched and loaded with moisture, though every hour seemed to add somewhat to the keenness of the blast: yet how should I know, but by trial, whether my stock of energy was not sufficient for this last exploit?

My resolution to proceed was nearly formed, when the figure of a man moving slowly across the road, at some distance before me, was observed. Hard by this ford lived a man by name Bisset, of whom I had slight knowledge. He tended his two hundred acres with a plodding and money-doating spirit, while his son overlooked a Grist-mill, on the river. He was a creature of gain, coarse and harmless. The man whom I saw before me might be he, or some one belonging to his family. Being armed for defence, I less scrupled a meeting with any thing in the shape of man. I therefore called. The figure stopped and answered me, without surliness or anger. The voice was unlike that of Bisset, but this person's information I believed would be of some service.

Coming up to him, he proved to be a clown, belonging to Bisset's habitation. His panic and surprise on seeing me made him aghast. In my present garb I should not have easily been recognized by my nearest kinsman, and much less easily by one who had seldom met me.

It may be easily conceived that my thoughts, when allowed to wander from the objects before me, were tormented with forebodings and inquietudes on account of the ills which I had so much reason to believe had befallen my family. I had no doubt that some evil had happened, but the full extent of it was still uncertain. I desired and dreaded to discover the truth, and was unable to interrogate this person in a direct manner. I could deal only in circuities and hints. I shuddered while I waited for an answer to my inquiries.

Had not Indians, I asked, been lately seen in this neighbourhood? Were they not suspected of hostile designs? Had they not already committed some mischief? Some passenger, perhaps, had been attacked; or fire had been set to some house? On which side of the river had their steps been observed, or any devastation been committed? Above the ford or below it? At what distance from the river?

When his attention could be withdrawn from my person and bestowed upon my questions, he answered that some alarm had indeed been spread about Indians, and that parties from Solebury and Chetasko were out in pursuit of them, that many persons had been killed by them, and that one house in Solebury had been rifled and burnt on the night before the last.

These tidings were a dreadful confirmation of my fears. There scarcely remained a doubt: but still my expiring hope prompted me to inquire to whom did the house belong?

He answered that he had not heard the name of the owner. He was a stranger to the people on the other side of the river.

Were any of the inhabitants murdered?

Yes. All that were at home except a girl whom they carried off. Some said that the girl had been retaken.

What was the name? Was it Huntly?

Huntly? Yes. No. He did not know. He had forgotten.

I fixed my eyes upon the ground. An interval of gloomy meditation succeeded. All was lost, all for whose sake I desired to live, had perished by the hands of these assassins. That dear home, the scene of my sportive childhood, of my studies, labours and recreations, was ravaged by fire and the sword: was reduced to a frightful ruin.

Not only all that embellished and endeared existence was destroyed, but the means of subsistence itself. Thou knowest that my sisters and I were dependants on the bounty of our uncle. His death would make way for the succession of his son, a man fraught with envy and malignity: who always testified a mortal hatred to us, merely because we enjoyed the protection of his father. The ground which furnished me with bread was now become the property of one, who, if he could have done it with security, would gladly have mingled poison with my food.

All that my imagination or my heart regarded as of value had likewise perished. Whatever my chamber, my closets, my cabinets contained, my furniture, my books, the records of my own skill, the monuments of their existence whom I loved, my very cloathing, were involved in indiscriminate and irretreivable destruction. Why should I survive this calamity?

But did not he say that one had escaped? The only females in the family were my sisters. One of these had been reserved for a fate worse than death; to gratify the innate and insatiable cruelty of savages by suffering all the torments their invention can suggest, or to linger out years of dreary bondage and unintermitted hardship in the bosom of the wilderness. To restore her to liberty; to cherish this last survivor of my unfortunate race was a sufficient motive to life and to activity.

But soft! Had not rumour whispered that the captive was retaken? Oh! who was her angel of deliverance? Where did she now abide? Weeping over the untimely fall of her protector and her friend? Lamenting and upbraiding the absence of her brother? Why should I not haste to find her? To mingle my tears with hers, to assure her of my safety and expiate the involuntary crime of my desertion, by devoting all futurity to the task of her consolation and improvement?

The path was open and direct. My new motives, would have trampled upon every impediment and made me reckless of all dangers and all toils. I broke from my reverie, and without taking leave or expressing gratitude to my informant, I ran with frantic expedition towards the river, and plunging into it gained the opposite side in a moment.

I was sufficiently acquainted with the road. Some twelve or fifteen miles remained to be traversed. I did not fear that my strength would fail in the performance of my journey. It was not my uncle's habitation to which I directed my steps. Inglefield was my friend. If my sister had existence, or was snatched from captivity, it was here that an asylum had been afforded to her, and here was I to seek the knowledge of my destiny. For this reason having reached a spot where the road divided into two branches, one of which led to Inglefield's and the other to Huntly's, I struck into the former.

Scarcely had I passed the angle when I noticed a building, on the right hand, at some distance from the road. In the present state of my thoughts, it would not have attracted my attention, had not a light gleamed from an upper window, and told me that all within were not at rest.

I was acquainted with the owner of this mansion. He merited esteem and confidence, and could not fail to be acquainted with recent events. From him I should obtain all the information that I needed, and I should be delivered from some part of the agonies of my suspense. I should reach his door in a few minutes, and the window-light was a proof that my entrance at this hour would not disturb the family, some of whom were stirring.

Through a gate, I entered an avenue of tall oaks, that led to the house. I could not but reflect on the effect which my appearance would produce upon the family. The sleek locks, neat apparel, pacific guise, sobriety and gentleness of aspect by which I was customarily distinguished, would in vain be sought in the apparition which would now present itself before them. My legs, neck and bosom were bare, and their native hue were exchanged for the livid marks of bruises and scarrifications. An horrid scar upon my cheek, and my uncombed locks; hollow eyes, made ghastly by abstinence and cold, and the ruthless passions of which my mind had been the theatre, added to the musquet which I carried in my hand, would prepossess them with the notion of a maniac or ruffian.

Some inconveniences might hence arise, which however could not be avoided. I must trust to the speed with which my voice and my words should disclose my true character and rectify their mistake.

I now reached the principal door of the house. It was open, and I unceremoniously entered. In the midst of the room stood a German stove, well heated. To thaw my half frozen limbs was my first care. Meanwhile, I gazed around me, and marked the appearances of things.

Two lighted candles stood upon the table. Beside them were cyder-bottles and pipes of tobacco. The furniture and room was in that state which denoted it to have been lately filled with drinkers and smokers, yet neither voice, nor visage, nor motion were any where observable. I listened but neither above nor below, within or without, could any tokens of an human being be perceived.

This vacancy and silence must have been lately preceded by noise and concourse and bustle. The contrast was mysterious and ambiguous. No adequate cause of so quick and absolute a transition occurred to me. Having gained some warmth and lingered some ten or twenty minutes in this uncertainty, I determined to explore the other apartments of the building. I knew not what might betide in my absence, or what I might encounter in my search to justify precaution, and, therefore, kept the gun in my hand. I snatched a candle from the table and proceeded into two other apartments on the first floor and the kitchen. Neither was inhabited, though chairs and tables were arranged in their usual order, and no traces of violence or hurry were apparent.

Having gained the foot of the stair-case, I knocked, but my knocking was wholly disregarded. A light had appeared in an upper chamber. It was not, indeed, in one of those apartments which the family permanently occupied, but in that which, according to rural custom, was reserved for guests; but it indubitably betokened the presence of some being by whom my doubts might be solved. These doubts were too tormenting to allow of scruples and delay.—I mounted the stairs.

At each chamber door I knocked, but I knocked in vain. I tried to open, but found them to be locked. I at length reached the entrance of that in which a light had been discovered. Here, it was certain, that some one would be found; but here, as well as elsewhere, my knocking was unnoticed.

To enter this chamber was audacious, but no other expedient was afforded me to determine whether the house had any inhabitants. I, therefore, entered, though with caution and reluctance. No one was within, but there were sufficient traces of some person who had lately been here. On the table stood a travelling escrutoire, open, with pens and ink-stand. A chair was placed before it, and a candle on the right hand. This apparatus was rarely seen in this country. Some traveller it seemed occupied this room, though the rest of the mansion was deserted. The pilgrim, as these appearances testified, was of no vulgar order, and belonged not to the class of periodical and every-day guests.

It now occurred to me that the occupant of this appartment could not be far off, and that some danger and embarrassment could not fail to accrue from being found, thus accoutred and garbed, in a place sacred to the study and repose of another. It was proper, therefore, to withdraw, and either to resume my journey, or wait for the stranger's return, whom perhaps some temporary engagement had called away, in the lower and public room. The former now appeared to be the best expedient, as the return of this unknown person was uncertain, as well as his power to communicate the information which I wanted.

Had paper, as well as the implements of writing, lain upon the desk, perhaps my lawless curiosity would not have scrupled to have pryed into it. On the first glance nothing of that kind appeared, but now, as I turned towards the door, somewhat, lying beside the desk, on the side opposite the candle, caught my attention. The impulse was instantaneous and mechanical, that made me leap to the spot, and lay my hand upon it. Till I felt it between my fingers, till I brought it near my eyes and read frequently the inscriptions that appeared upon it, I was doubtful whether my senses had deceived me.

Few, perhaps, among mankind have undergone vicissitudes of peril and wonder equal to mine. The miracles of poetry, the transitions of enchantment, are beggarly and mean compared with those which I had experienced: Passage into new forms, overleaping the bars of time and space, reversal of the laws of inanimate and intelligent existence had been mine to perform and to witness.

No event had been more fertile of sorrow and perplexity than the loss of thy brother's letters. They went by means invisible, and disappeared at a moment when foresight would have least predicted their disappearance. They now placed themselves before me, in a manner equally abrupt, in a place and by means, no less contrary to expectation. The papers which I now seized were those letters. The parchment cover, the string that tied, and the wax that sealed them, appeared not to have been opened or violated.

The power that removed them from my cabinet, and dropped them in this house, a house which I rarely visited, which I had not entered during the last year, with whose inhabitants I maintained no cordial intercourse, and to whom my occupations and amusements, my joys and my sorrows, were unknown, was no object even of conjecture. But they were not possessed by any of the family. Some stranger was here, by whom they had been stolen, or into whose possession, they had, by some incomprehensible chance, fallen.

That stranger was near. He had left this apartment for a moment. He would speedily return. To go hence, might possibly occasion me to miss him. Here then I would wait, till he should grant me an interview. The papers were mine, and were recovered. I would never part with them. But to know by whose force or by whose stratagems I had been bereaved of them thus long, was now the supreme passion of my soul. I seated myself near a table and anxiously awaited for an interview, on which I was irresistably persuaded to believe that much of my happiness depended.

Meanwhile, I could not but connect this incident with the destruction of my family. The loss of these papers had excited transports of grief, and yet, to have lost them thus, was perhaps the sole expedient, by which their final preservation could be rendered possible. Had they remained in my cabinet, they could not have escaped the destiny which overtook the house and its furniture. Savages are not accustomed to leave their exterminating work unfinished. The house which they have plundered, they are careful to level with the ground. This not only their revenge, but their caution prescribes. Fire may originate by accident as well as by design, and the traces of pillage and murder are totally obliterated by the flames.

These thoughts were interrupted by the shutting of a door below, and by footsteps ascending the stairs. My heart throbbed at the sound. My seat became uneasy and I started on my feet. I even advanced half way to the entrance of the room. My eyes were intensely fixed upon the door. My impatience would have made me guess at the person of this visitant by measuring his shadow, if his shadow were first seen; but this was precluded by the position of the light. It was only when the figure entered, and the whole person was seen, that my curiosity was gratified. He who stood before me was the parent and fosterer of my mind, the companion and instructor of my youth, from whom I had been parted for years; from whom I believed myself to be forever separated;—*Sarsefield* himself!

Chapter XXIV

M Y DEPORTMENT, at an interview so much desired and so wholly unforeseen, was that of a maniac. The petrifying influence of surprise, yielded to the impetuosities of passion. I held him in my arms: I wept upon his bosom, I sobbed with emotion which, had it not found passage at my eyes, would have burst my heart-strings. Thus I who had escaped the deaths that had previously assailed me in so many forms, should have been reserved to solemnize a scene like this by . . . *dying for joy!*

The sterner passions and habitual austerities of my companion, exempted him from pouring out this testimony of his feelings. His feelings were indeed more allied to astonishment and incredulity than mine had been. My person was not instantly recognized. He shrunk from my embrace, as if I were an apparition or impostor. He quickly disengaged himself from my arms, and withdrawing a few paces, gazed upon me as on one whom he had never before seen.

These repulses were ascribed to the loss of his affection. I was not mindful of the hideous guise in which I stood before him, and by which he might justly be misled to imagine me a ruffian or a lunatic. My tears flowed now on a new account, and I articulated in a broken and faint voice—My master! my friend! Have you forgotten? have you ceased to love me?

The sound of my voice made him start and exclaim—Am I alive? am I awake? Speak again I beseech you, and convince me that I am not dreaming or delirious.

Can you need any proof, I answered, that it is Edgar Huntly, your pupil, your child that speaks to you?

He now withdrew his eyes from me and fixed them on the floor. After a pause he resumed, in emphatic accents. Well, I have lived to this age in unbelief. To credit or trust in miraculous agency was foreign to my nature, but now I am no longer sceptical. Call me to any bar, and exact from me an oath that you have twice been dead and twice recalled to life; that you move about invisibly, and change your place by the force, not of muscles, but of thought, and I will give it.

How came you hither? Did you penetrate the wall? Did you rise through the floor?

Yet surely 'tis an error. You could not be he whom twenty witnesses affirmed to have beheld a lifeless and mangled corpse upon the ground, whom my own eyes saw in that condition.

In seeking the spot once more to provide you a grave, you had vanished. Again I met you. You plunged into a rapid stream, from an height from which it was impossible to fall and to live: yet, as if to set the limits of nature at defiance; to sport with human penetration, you rose upon the surface: You floated; you swam: Thirty bullets were aimed at your head, by marks-men celebrated for the exactness of their sight. I myself was of the number, and I never missed what I desired to hit.

My predictions were confirmed by the event. You ceased to struggle; you sunk to rise no more, and yet after these accumulated deaths, you light upon this floor: so far distant from the scene of your catastrophe; over spaces only to be passed, in so short a time as has since elapsed, by those who have wings.

My eyes, my ears bear testimony to your existence now, as they formerly convinced me of your death—What am I to think; What proofs am I to credit?—There he stopped.

Every accent of this speech added to the confusion of my thoughts. The allusions that my friend had made were not unintelligible. I gained a glimpse of the complicated errors by which we had been mutually deceived. I had fainted on the area before Deb's hut. I was found by Sarsefield in this condition, and imagined to be dead.

The man whom I had seen upon the promontory was not an Indian. He belonged to a numerous band of pursuers, whom my hostile and precipitate deportment caused to suspect me for an enemy. They that fired from the steep were friends. The interposition that screened me from so many bullets, was indeed miraculous. No wonder that my voluntary sinking, in order to elude their shots, was mistaken for death, and that, having accomplished the destruction of this foe, they resumed their pursuit of others. But how was Sarsefield apprized that it was I who plunged into the river? No subsequent event was possible to impart to him the incredible truth.

A pause of mutual silence ensued. At length, Sarsefield renewed his expressions of amazement at this interview, and besought me to explain why I had disappeared by night from my Uncle's house, and by what series of unheard of events this interview was brought about. Was it indeed Huntly whom he examined and mourned over at the threshold of Deb's hut? Whom he had sought in every thicket and cave in the ample circuit of Norwalk and Chetasco? Whom he had seen perish in the current of the Delaware?

Instead of noticing his questions, my soul was harrowed with anxiety respecting the fate of my uncle and sisters. Sarsefield could communicate the tidings which would decide on my future lot, and set my portion in happiness or misery. Yet I had not breath to speak my inquiries. Hope tottered, and I felt as if a single word would be sufficient for its utter subversion. At length, I articulated the name of my Uncle.

The single word sufficiently imparted my fears, and these fears needed no verbal confirmation. At that dear name, my companion's features were overspread by sorrow—Your Uncle, said he, is dead.

Dead? Merciful Heaven! And my sisters too? Both?

Your Sisters are alive and well.

Nay, resumed I, in faultering accents, jest not with my feelings. Be not cruel in your pity. Tell me the truth.

I have said the truth. They are well, at Mr. Inglefield's.

My wishes were eager to assent to the truth of these tidings. The better part of me was then safe: but how did they escape the fate that overtook my uncle? How did they evade the destroying hatchet and the midnight conflagration? These doubts were imparted in a tumultuous and obscure manner to my friend. He no sooner fully comprehended them, than he looked at me, with some inquietude and surprise.

Huntly, said he, are you mad—What has filled you with these hideous prepossessions? Much havoc has indeed been committed in Chetasco and the wilderness; and a log hut has been burnt by design or by accident in Solebury, but that is all. Your house has not been assailed by either fire-brand or tom-hawk. Every thing is safe and in its ancient order. The master indeed is gone, but the old man fell a victim to his own temerity and hardihood. It is thirty years since he retired with three wounds, from the field of Braddock; but time, in no degree, abated his adventurous and military spirit. On the first alarm, he summoned his neighbours, and led them in pursuit of the invaders. Alas! he was the first to attack them, and the only one who fell in the contest.

These words were uttered in a manner that left me no room to doubt of their truth. My uncle had already been lamented, and the discovery of the nature of his death, so contrary to my forebodings, and of the safety of my girls, made the state of my mind partake more of exultation and joy, than of grief or regret.

But how was I deceived? Had not my fusil been found in the hands of an enemy? Whence could he have plundered it but from my own chamber? It hung against the wall of a closet; from which no stranger could have taken it except by violence. My perplexities and doubts were not at an end, but those which constituted my chief torment were removed. I listened to my friend's intreaties to tell him the cause of my elopement, and the incidents that terminated in the present interview.

I began with relating my return to consciousness in the bottom of the pit; my efforts to free myself from this abhorred prison; the acts of horror to which I was impelled by famine, and their excruciating consequences; my gaining the outlet of the cavern, the desperate expedient by which I removed the impediment to my escape, and the deliverance of the captive girl; the contest I maintained before Deb's hut; my subsequent wanderings; the banquet which hospitality afforded me; my journey to the river-bank; my meditations on the means of reaching the road; my motives for hazarding my life, by plunging into the stream; and my subsequent perils and fears till I reached the threshold of this habitation.

Thus, continued I, I have complied with your request. I have told all that I, myself, know. What were the incidents between my sinking to rest at my Uncle's, and my awaking in the chambers of the hill; by which means and by whose contrivance, preternatural or human, this transition was effected, I am unable to explain; I cannot even guess.

What has eluded my sagacity may not be beyond the reach of another. Your own reflections on my tale, or some facts that have fallen under your notice, may enable you to furnish a solution. But, meanwhile, how am I to account for your appearance on this spot? This meeting was unexpected and abrupt to you, but it has not been less so to me. Of all mankind, Sarsefield was the farthest from my thoughts, when I saw these tokens of a traveller and a stranger.

You were imperfectly acquainted with my wanderings. You saw me on the ground before Deb's hut. You saw me plunge into the river. You endeavoured to destroy me while swimming; and you knew, before my narrative was heard, that Huntly was the object of your enmity. What was the motive of your search in the desert, and how were you apprized of my condition? These things are not less wonderful than any of those which I have already related.

During my tale the features of Sarsefield betokened the deepest attention. His eye strayed not a moment from my face. All my perils and forebodings, were fresh in my remembrance, they had scarcely gone by; their skirts, so to speak, were still visible. No wonder that my eloquence was vivid and pathetic, that I pourtrayed the past as if it were the present scene; and that not my tongue only, but every muscle and limb, spoke.

When I had finished my relation, Sarsefield sunk into thoughtfulness. From this, after a time, he recovered and said: Your tale, Huntly, is true, yet, did I not see you before me, were I not acquainted with the artlessness and rectitude of your character, and, above all, had not my own experience, during the last three days, confirmed every incident, I should question its truth. You have amply gratified my curiosity, and deserve that your own, should be gratified as fully. Listen to me.

Much has happened since we parted, which shall not be now mentioned. I promised to inform you of my welfare by letter, and did not fail to write, but whether my letters were received, or any were written by you in return, or if written were ever transmitted, I cannot tell; none were ever received.

Some days since, I arrived, in company with a lady who is my wife, in America. You have never been forgotten by me. I knew your situation to be little in agreement with your wishes, and one of the benefits which fortune has lately conferred upon me, is the power of snatching you from a life of labour and obscurity; whose goods, scanty as they are, were transient and precarious; and affording you the suitable leisure and means of intellectual gratification and improvement.

Your silence made me entertain some doubts concerning your welfare, and even your existence. To solve these doubts, I hastened to Solebury; some delays upon the road, hindered me from accomplishing my journey by day-light. It was night before I entered the Norwalk path, but my ancient rambles with you made me familiar with it, and I was not affraid of being obstructed or bewildered.

Just as I gained the southern outlet, I spied a passenger on foot, coming towards me with a quick pace. The incident was of no moment, and yet the time of night, the seeming expedition of the walker, recollection of the mazes and obstacles which he was going to encounter, and a vague conjecture that, perhaps, he was unacquainted with the difficulties that awaited him, made me eye him with attention as he passed.

He came near, and I thought I recognized a friend in this traveller. The form, the gesture, the stature bore a powerful resemblance to those of Edgar Huntly. This resemblance was so strong, that I stopped, and after he had gone by, called him by your name. That no notice was taken of my call proved that the person was mistaken, but even though it were another, that he should not even hesitate or turn at a summons which he could not but perceive to be addressed, though erroneously, to him, was the source of some surprize. I did not repeat my call, but proceeded on my way.

All had retired to repose in your uncle's dwelling. I did not scruple to rouse them, and was received with affectionate and joyous greetings. That you allowed your uncle to rise before you, was a new topic of reflection. To my inquiries concerning you, answers were made that accorded with my wishes. I was told that you were in good health and were then abed. That you had not heard and risen at my knocking, was mentioned with surprise, but your uncle accounted for your indolence by saying that during the last week you had fatigued yourself by rambling night and day, in search of some maniac, or visionary who was supposed to have retreated into Norwalk.

I insisted upon awakening you myself. I anticipated the effect of this sudden and unlooked for meeting, with some emotions of pride as well as of pleasure. To find, in opening your eyes, your old preceptor standing by your bed-side and gazing in your face, would place you, I conceived, in an affecting situation.

Your chamber door was open, but your bed was empty. Your uncle and sisters were made acquainted with this circumstance. Their surprise gave way to conjectures that your restless and romantic spirit, had tempted you from your repose, that you had rambled abroad on some phantastic errand, and would probably return before the dawn. I willingly acquiesced in this opinion, and my feelings being too thoroughly aroused to allow me to sleep, I took possession of your chamber, and patiently awaited your return.

The morning returned but Huntly made not his appearance. Your uncle became somewhat uneasy at this unseasonable absence. Much speculation and inquiry, as to the possible reasons of your flight was made. In my survey of your chamber, I noted that only part of your cloathing remained beside your bed. Coat, hat, stockings and shoes lay upon the spot where they had probably been thrown when you had disrobed yourself, but the pantaloons, which according to Mr. Huntly's report, completed your dress, were no where to be found. That you should go forth on so cold a night so slenderly appareled, was almost incredible. Your reason or your senses had deserted you, before so rash an action could be meditated.

I now remembered the person I had met in Norwalk. His resemblance to your figure, his garb, which wanted hat, coat, stockings and shoes, and your absence from your bed at that hour, were remarkable coincidences: but why did you disregard my call? Your name, uttered by a voice that could not be unknown, was surely sufficient to arrest your steps.

Each hour added to the impatience of your friends; to their recollections and conjectures, I listened with a view to extract from them some solution of this mystery. At length, a story was alluded to, of some one who, on the preceding night, had been heard walking in the long room; to this was added, the tale of your anxieties and wonders occasioned by the loss of certain manuscripts.

While ruminating upon these incidents, and endeavouring to extract from this intelligence a clue, explanatory of your present situation, a single word, casually dropped by your uncle, instantly illuminated my darkness and dispelled my doubts.—After all, said the old man, ten to one, but Edgar himself was the man whom we heard walking, but the lad was asleep, and knew not what he was about.

Surely said I, this inference is just. His manuscripts could not be removed by any hands but his own, since the rest of mankind were unacquainted not only with the place of their concealment, but with their existence. None but a man, insane or asleep, would wander forth so slightly dressed, and none but a sleeper would have disregarded my calls. This conclusion was generally adopted, but it gave birth in my mind, to infinite inquietudes. You had roved into Norwalk, a scene of inequalities, of prominences and pits, among which, thus destitute of the guidance of your senses, you could scarcely fail to be destroyed, or at least, irretreivably bewildered. I painted to myself the dangers to which you were subjected. Your careless feet would bear you into some whirlpool or to the edge of some precipice, some internal revolution or outward shock would recall you to consciousness at some perilous moment. Surprise and fear would disable you from taking seasonable or suitable precautions, and your destruction be made sure.

The lapse of every new hour, without bringing tidings of your state, enhanced these fears. At length, the propriety of searching for you occurred. Mr. Huntly and I determined to set out upon this pursuit, as well as to commission others. A plan was laid by which every accessible part of Norwalk, the wilderness beyond the flats of Solebury, and the valey of Chetasco, should be traversed and explored.

Scarcely had we equipped ourselves for this expedition, when a messenger arrived, who brought the disastrous news of Indians being seen within these precincts, and on the last night a farmer was shot in his fields, a dwelling in Chetasco was burnt to the ground, and its inhabitants murdered or made captives. Rumour and inquiry had been busy, and a plausible conjecture had been formed, as to the course and number of the enemies. They were said to be divided into bands, and to amount in the whole to thirty or forty warriors. This messenger had come to warn us of danger which might impend, and to summon us to join in the pursuit and extirpation of these detestable foes.

Your uncle, whose alacrity and vigour age had not abated, eagerly engaged in this scheme. I was not averse to contribute my efforts to an end like this. The road which we had previously designed to take, in search of my fugitive pupil, was the same by which we must trace or intercept the retreat of the savages. Thus two purposes, equally momentous, would be answered by the same means.

Mr. Huntly armed himself with your fusil; Inglefield supplied me with a gun; during our absence the dwelling was closed and locked, and your sisters placed under the protection of Inglefield, whose age and pacific sentiments unfitted him for arduous and sanguinary enterprises. A troop of rustics was collected, half of whom remained to traverse Solebury and the other, whom Mr. Huntly and I accompanied, hastened to Chetasco.

Chapter XXV

IT WAS noon day before we reached the theatre of action. Fear and revenge combined to make the people of Chetasco diligent and zealous in their own defence. The havock already committed had been mournful. To prevent a repetition of the same calamities, they resolved to hunt out the hostile footsteps and exact a merciless retribution.

It was likely that the enemy, on the approach of day, had withdrawn from the valley and concealed themselves in the thickets, between the parrallel ridges of the mountain. This space, which, according to the object with which it is compared is either a vale or the top of an hill, was obscure and desolate. It was undoubtedly the avenue by which the robbers had issued forth, and by which they would escape to the Ohio. Here they might still remain, intending to emerge from their concealment on the next night, and perpetrate new horrors.

A certain distribution was made of our number, so as to move in all directions at the same time. I will not dwell upon particulars. It will suffice to say that keen eyes and indefatigable feet, brought us at last to the presence of the largest number of these marauders. Seven of them were slain by the edge of a brook, where they sat wholly unconscious of the danger which hung over them. Five escaped, and one of these secured his retreat by wresting your fusil from your uncle, and shooting him dead. Before our companion could be rescued or revenged, the assassin, with the remnant of the troop, disappeared, and bore away with him the fusil as a trophy of his victory.

This disaster was deplored not only on account of that life which had thus been sacrificed, but because a sagacious guide and intrepid leader was lost. His acquaintance with the habits of the Indians, and his experience in their wars made him trace their footsteps with more certainty than any of his associates.

The pursuit was still continued, and parties were so stationed that the escape of the enemy was difficult, if not impossible. Our search was unremitted, but during twelve or fourteen hours, unsuccessful. Queen Mab did not elude all suspicion. Her hut was visited by different parties, but the old woman and her dogs had disappeared.

Meanwhile your situation was not forgotten. Every one was charged to explore your footsteps as well as those of the savages, but this search was no less unsuccessful than the former. None had heard of you or seen you.

This continued till midnight. Three of us, made a pause at a brook, and intended to repair our fatigues by a respite of a few hours, but scarcely had we stretched ourselves on the ground when we were alarmed by a shot which seemed to have been fired at a short distance. We started on our feet and consulted with each other on the measures to be taken. A second, a third and a fourth shot, from the same quarter, excited our attention anew. Mab's hut was known to stand at the distance and in the direction of this sound, and thither we resolved to repair.

This was done with speed but with the utmost circumspection. We shortly gained the road that leads near this hut and at length gained a view of the building. Many persons were discovered, in a sort of bustling inactivity, before the hut. They were easily distinguished to be friends, and were therefore approached without scruple.

The objects that presented themselves to a nearer view were five bodies stretched upon the ground. Three of them were savages. The fourth was a girl, who though alive seemed to have received a mortal wound. The fifth, breathless and mangled and his features almost concealed by the blood that overspread his face, was Edgar; the fugitive for whom I had made such anxious search.

About the same hour on the last night I had met you hastening into Norwalk. Now were you, lying in the midst of savages, at the distance of thirty miles from your home, and in a spot, which it was impossible for you to have reached unless by an immense circuit over rocks and thickets. That you had found a rift at the basis of the hill, and thus permeated its solidities, and thus precluded so tedious and circuitous a journey as must otherwise have been made, was not to be imagined.

But whence arose this scene? It was obvious to conclude that my associates had surprised their enemies in this house,

and exacted from them the forfeit of their crimes, but how
you should have been confounded with their foes, or whence
came the wounded girl was a subject of astonishment.

You will judge how much this surprise was augmented when
I was informed that the party whom we found had been attracted hither by the same signals, by which we had been
alarmed. That on reaching this spot you had been discovered,
alive, seated on the ground and still sustaining the gun with
which you had apparently completed the destruction of so
many adversaries. In a moment after their arrival you sunk
down and expired.

This scene was attended with inexplicable circumstances.
The musquet which lay beside you appeared to have belonged
to one of the savages. The wound by which each had died
was single. Of the four shots we had distinguished at a distance, three of them were therefore fatal to the Indians and
the fourth was doubtless that by which you had fallen, yet
three musquets only were discoverable.

The arms were collected, and the girl carried to the nearest
house in the arms of her father. Her situation was deemed
capable of remedy, and the sorrow and wonder which I felt
at your untimely and extraordinary fate, did not hinder me
from endeavouring to restore the health of this unfortunate
victim. I reflected likewise that some light might be thrown
upon transactions so mysterious, by the information which
might be collected from her story. Numberless questions and
hints were necessary to extract from her a consistent or intelligible tale. She had been dragged, it seems, for miles, at the
heels of her conquerors, who at length, stopped in a cavern
for the sake of some repose; all slept but one, who sat and
watched. Something called him away, and, at the same moment, you appeared at the bottom of the cave half naked and
without arms. You instantly supplied the last deficiency, by
seizing the gun and tom-hawk of him who had gone forth,
and who had negligently left his weapons behind. Then stepping over the bodies of the sleepers, you rushed out of the
cavern.

She then mentioned your unexpected return, her deliverance and flight, and arrival at Deb's hut. You watched upon

the hearth and she fell asleep upon the blanket. From this sleep she was aroused by violent and cruel blows. She looked up:—you were gone and the bed on which she lay was surrounded by the men from whom she had so lately escaped. One dragged her out of the hut and levelled his gun at her breast. At the moment when he touched the trigger, a shot came from an unknown quarter, and he fell at her feet. Of subsequent events she had an incoherent recollection. The Indians were successively slain, and you came to her, and interrogated and consoled her.

In your journey to the hut you were armed. This in some degree accounted for appearances, but where were your arms? Three musquets only were discovered and these undoubtedly belonged to your enemies.

I now had leisure to reflect upon your destiny. I had arrived soon enough on this shore merely to witness the catastrophe of two beings whom I most loved. Both were overtaken by the same fate, nearly at the same hour. The same hand had possibly accomplished the destruction of uncle and nephew.

Now, however, I began to entertain an hope that your state might not be irretreivable. You had walked and spoken after the firing had ceased, and your enemies had ceased to contend with you. A wound had, no doubt, been previously received. I had hastily inferred that the wound was mortal, and that life could not be recalled. Occupied with attention to the wailings of the girl, and full of sorrow and perplexity I had admitted an opinion which would have never been adopted in different circumstances. My acquaintance with wounds would have taught me to regard sunken muscles, lividness and cessation of the pulse as mere indications of a swoon, and not as tokens of death.

Perhaps my error was not irreparable. By hastening to the hut, I might ascertain your condition and at least transport your remains to some dwelling and finally secure to you the decencies of burial.

Of twelve savages, discovered on the preceding day, ten were now killed. Two, at least remained, after whom the pursuit was still zealously maintained. Attention to the wounded girl, had withdrawn me from the party, and I had now leisure to return to the scene of these disasters. The sun had risen, and, accompanied by two others, I repaired thither.

A sharp turn in the road, at the entrance of the field, set before us a starting spectacle. An Indian, mangled by repeated wounds of bayonet and bullet, was discovered. His musquet was stuck in the ground, by way of beacon attracting our attention to the spot. Over this space I had gone a few hours before, and nothing like this was then seen. The parties abroad, had hied away to a distant quarter. Some invisible power seemed to be enlisted in our defence and to preclude the necessity of our arms.

We proceeded to the hut. The savages were there, but Edgar had risen and flown! Nothing now seemed to be incredible. You had slain three foes, and the weapon with which the victory had been achieved, had vanished. You had risen from the dead, had assailed one of the surviving enemies, had employed bullet and dagger in his destruction, with both of which you could only be supplied by supernatural means, and had disappeared. If any inhabitant of Chetasco had done this, we should have heard of it.

But what remained? You were still alive. Your strength was sufficient to bear you from this spot. Why were you still invisible and to what dangers might you not be exposed, before you could disinvolve yourself from the mazes of this wilderness?

Once more I procured indefatigable search to be made after you. It was continued till the approach of evening and was fruitless. Inquiries were twice made at the house where you were supplied with food and intelligence. On the second call I was astonished and delighted by the tidings received from the good woman. Your person and demeanour and arms were described, and mention made of your resolution to cross the southern ridge, and traverse the Solebury road with the utmost expedition.

The greater part of my inquietudes were now removed. You were able to eat and to travel, and there was little doubt that a meeting would take place between us on the next morning. Meanwhile, I determined to concur with those who pursued the remainder of the enemy. I followed you, in the path that you were said to have taken, and quickly joined a numerous party who were searching for those who, on the last night, had attacked a plantation that lies near this, and destroyed the inhabitants.

I need not dwell upon our doublings and circuities. The enemy was traced to the house of Selby. They had entered, they had put fire on the floor, but were compelled to relinquish their prey. Of what number they consisted could not be ascertained, but one, lingering behind his fellows, was shot, at the entrance of the wood, and on the spot where you chanced to light upon him.

Selby's house was empty, and before the fire had made any progress we extinguished it. The drunken wretch whom you encountered, had probably returned from his nocturnal debauch, after we had left the spot.

The flying enemy was pursued with fresh diligence. They were found, by various tokens, to have crossed the river, and to have ascended the mountain. We trod closely on their heels. When we arrived at the promontory, described by you, the fatigues of the night and day rendered me unqualified to proceed. I determined that this should be the bound of my excursions. I was anxious to obtain an interview with you, and unless I paused here, should not be able to gain Inglefield's as early in the morning as I wished. Two others concurred with me in this resolution and prepared to return to this house which had been deserted by its tenants till the danger was past and which had been selected as the place of rendezvous.

At this moment, dejected and weary, I approached the ledge which severed the head-land from the mountain. I marked the appearance of some one stretched upon the ground where you lay. No domestic animal would wander hither and place himself upon this spot. There was something likewise in the appearance of the object that bespoke it to be man, but if it were man, it was, incontrovertibly, a savage and a foe. I determined therefore to rouse you by a bullet.

My decision was perhaps absurd. I ought to have gained more certainty before I hazarded your destruction. Be that as it will, a moment's lingering on your part would have probably been fatal. You started on your feet, and fired. See the hole which your random shot made through my sleeve! This surely was a day destined to be signalized by hair-breadth escapes.

Your action seemed incontestably to confirm my prognostics. Every one hurried to the spot and was eager to destroy an enemy. No one hesitated to believe that some of the shots aimed at you, had reached their mark, and that you had sunk to rise no more.

The gun which was fired and thrown down was taken and examined. It had been my companion in many a toilsome expedition. It had rescued me and my friends from a thousand deaths. In order to recognize it, I needed only to touch and handle it. I instantly discovered that I held in my hand the fusil which I had left with you on parting, with which your uncle had equipped himself, and which had been ravished from him by a savage. What was I hence to infer respecting the person of the last possessor?

My inquiries respecting you of the woman whose milk and bread you had eaten, were minute. You entered, she said, with an hatchet and gun in your hand. While you ate, the gun was laid upon the table. She sat near, and the piece became the object of inquisitive attention. The stock and barrels were described by her in such terms as left no doubt that this was the *Fusil*.

A comparison of incidents enabled me to trace the manner in which you came into possession of this instrument. One of those whom you found in the cavern was the assassin of your uncle. According to the girl's report, on issuing from your hiding place, you seized a gun that was unoccupied, and this gun chanced to be your own.

Its two barrels was probably the cause of your success in that unequal contest at Mab's hut. On recovering from *deliquium*, you found it where it had been dropped by you, out of sight and unsuspected by the party that had afterwards arrived. In your passage to the river had it once more fallen into hostile hands, or, had you missed the way, wandered to this promontory, and mistaken a troop of friends for a band of Indian marauders?

Either supposition was dreadful. The latter was the most plausible. No motives were conceivable by which one of the fugitives could be induced to post himself here, in this conspicuous station: whereas, the road which led you to the summit of the hill, to that spot where descent to the river road was practicable, could not be found but by those who were accustomed to traverse it. The directions which you had exacted from your hostess, proved your previous unacquaintance with these tracts.

I acquiesced in this opinion with an heavy and desponding heart. Fate had led us into a maze, which could only terminate in the destruction of one or of the other. By the breadth of an hair, had I escaped death from your hand. The same fortune had not befriended you. After my tedious search, I had lighted on you, forlorn, bewildered, perishing with cold and hunger. Instead of recognizing and affording you relief, I compelled you to leap into the river, from a perilous height, and had desisted from my persecution only when I had bereaved you of life, and plunged you to the bottom of the gulf.

My motives in coming to America were numerous and mixed. Among these was the parental affection with which you had inspired me. I came with fortune and a better gift than fortune in my hand. I intended to bestow both upon you, not only to give you competence, but one who would endear to you that competence, who would enhance, by participating, every gratification.

My schemes were now at an end. You were gone, beyond the reach of my benevolence and justice. I had robbed your two sisters of a friend and guardian. It was some consolation to think that it was in my power to stand, with regard to them, in your place, that I could snatch them from the poverty, dependence and humiliation, to which your death and that of your uncle had reduced them.

I was now doubly weary of the enterprise in which I was engaged, and returned, with speed, to this rendezvouz. My companions have gone to know the state of the family who resided under this roof and left me to beguile the tedious moments in whatever manner I pleased.

I have omitted mentioning one incident that happened between the detection of your flight and our expedition to Chetasco. Having formed a plausible conjecture as to him who walked in the Long-room, it was obvious to conclude that he who purloined your manuscripts and the walker were the same personage. It was likewise easily inferred that the letters were secreted in the Cedar Chest or in some other part of the room. Instances similar to this have heretofore occurred. Men have employed anxious months in search of that which, in a freak of Noctambulation, was hidden by their own hands.

A search was immediately commenced, and your letters were found, carefully concealed between the rafters and shingles of the roof, in a spot, where, if suspicion had not been previously excited, they would have remained till the vernal rains and the summer heats, had insensibly destroyed them. This pacquet I carried with me, knowing the value which you set upon them, and there being no receptacle equally safe, but your own cabinet, which was locked.

Having, as I said, reached this house, and being left alone, I bethought me of the treasure I possessed. I was unacquainted with the reasons for which these papers were so precious. They probably had some momentous and intimate connection with your own history. As such they could not be of little value to me, and this moment of inoccupation and regrets, was as suitable as any other to the task of perusing them. I drew them forth, therefore, and laid them on the table in this chamber.

The rest is known to you. During a momentary absence you entered. Surely no interview of ancient friends ever took place in so unexpected and abrupt a manner. You were dead. I mourned for you, as one whom I loved, and whom fate had snatched forever from my sight. Now, in a blissful hour, you had risen, and my happiness in thus embracing you, is tenfold greater than would have been experienced, if no uncertainties and perils had protracted our meeting.

Chapter XXVI

H ERE ENDED the tale of Sarsefield. Humiliation and joy were mingled in my heart. The events that preceded my awakening in the cave were now luminous and plain. What explication was more obvious? What but this solution ought to have been suggested by the conduct I had witnessed in Clithero?

Clithero! Was not this the man whom Clithero had robbed of his friend? Was not this the lover of Mrs. Lorimer, the object of the persecutions of Wiatte? Was it not now given me to investigate the truth of that stupendous tale? To dissipate the doubts which obstinately clung to my imagination respecting it?

But soft! Had not Sarsefield said that he was married? Was Mrs. Lorimer so speedily forgotten by him, or was the narrative of Clithero the web of imposture or the raving of insanity?

These new ideas banished all personal considerations from my mind. I looked eagerly into the face of my friend, and exclaimed in a dubious accent—How say you? Married? When? To whom?

Yes, Huntly, I am wedded to the most excellent of women. To her am I indebted for happiness and wealth and dignity and honour. To her do I owe the power of being the benefactor and protector of you and your sisters. She longs to embrace you as a son. To become truly her son, will depend upon your own choice and that of one, who was the companion of our voyage.

Heavens! cried I, in a transport of exultation and astonishment. Of whom do you speak? Of the mother of Clarice? The sister of Wiatte? The sister of the ruffian who laid snares for her life? Who pursued you and the unhappy Clithero, with the bitterest animosity?

My friend started at these sounds as if the earth had yawned at his feet. His countenance was equally significant of terror and rage. As soon as he regained the power of utterance, he spoke—Clithero! Curses light upon thy lips for having uttered

that detested name! Thousands of miles have I flown to shun
the hearing of it. Is the madman here? Have you set eyes upon
him? Does he yet crawl upon the face of the earth? Unhappy?
Unparalleled, unheard of, thankless miscreant! Has he told his
execrable falsehoods here? Has he dared to utter names so
sacred as those of Euphemia Lorimer and Clarice?

He has: He has told a tale, that had all the appearances of
truth—

Out upon the villain! The truth! Truth would prove him to
be unnatural; develish; a thing for which no language has yet
provided a name! He has called himself unhappy? No doubt,
a victim to injustice! Overtaken by unmerited calamity! Say!
Has he fooled thee with such tales?

No. His tale was a catalogue of crimes and miseries of which
he was the author and sufferer. You know not his motives, his
horrors:—

His deeds were monstrous and infernal. His motives were
sordid and flagitious. To display all their ugliness and infamy
was not his province. No: He did not tell you that he stole at
midnight to the chamber of his mistress: a woman who astonished the world by her loftiness and magnanimity; by indefatigable beneficence and unswerving equity; who had lavished
on this wretch, whom she snatched from the dirt, all the
goods of fortune; all the benefits of education; all the treasures
of love; every provocation to gratitude; every stimulant to
justice.

He did not tell you that in recompense for every benefit,
he stole upon her sleep and aimed a dagger at her breast.
There was no room for flight or ambiguity or prevarication.
She whom he meant to murder stood near, saw the lifted
weapon, and heard him confess and glory in his purposes.

No wonder that the shock bereft her, for a time, of life. The
interval was seized by the ruffian to effect his escape. The
rebukes of justice, were shunned by a wretch conscious of his
inexpiable guilt. These things he has hidden from you, and
has supplied their place by a tale specious as false.

No. Among the number of his crimes, hypocrisy is not to be
numbered. These things are already known to me: he spared
himself too little in the narrative. The excellencies of his lady;
her claims to gratitude and veneration, were urged beyond

their true bounds. His attempts upon her life, were related. It is true that he desired and endeavoured to destroy her.

How? Has he told you this?

He has told me all. Alas! the criminal intention has been amply expiated—

What mean you? Whence and how came he hither? Where is he now? I will not occupy the same land, the same world with him. Have this woman and her daughter lighted on the shore haunted by this infernal and implacable enemy?

Alas! It is doubtful whether he exists. If he lives, he is no longer to be feared; but he lives not. Famine and remorse have utterly consumed him.

Famine? Remorse? You talk in riddles.

He has immured himself in the desert. He has abjured the intercourse of mankind. He has shut himself in caverns where famine must inevitably expedite that death for which he longs as the only solace of his woes. To no imagination are his offences blacker and more odious than to his own. I had hopes of rescuing him from this fate, but my own infirmities and errors have afforded me sufficient occupation.

Sarsefield renewed his imprecations on the memory of that unfortunate man: and his inquiries as to the circumstances that led him into this remote district. His inquiries were not to be answered by one in my present condition—My languors and fatigues had now gained a pitch that was insupportable. The wound in my face had been chafed, and inflamed by the cold water and the bleak air; and the pain attending it, would no longer suffer my attention to stray. I sunk upon the floor, and intreated him to afford me the respite of a few hours repose.

He was sensible of the deplorableness of my condition, and chid himself for the negligence of which he had already been guilty. He lifted me to the bed, and deliberated on the mode he should pursue for my relief. Some molifying application to my wound, was immediately necessary; but in our present lonely condition, it was not at hand. It could only be procured from a distance. It was proper therefore to hasten to the nearest inhabited dwelling, which belonged to one, by name Walton, and supply himself with such medicines as could be found.

Meanwhile there was no danger of molestation and intrusion. There was reason to expect the speedy return of those who had gone in pursuit of the savages. This was their place of rendezvous, and hither they appointed to re-assemble before the morrow's dawn. The distance of the neighbouring farm was small, and Sarsefield promised to be expeditious. He left me to myself and my own ruminations.

Harrassed by fatigue and pain, I had yet power to ruminate on that series of unparalleled events, that had lately happened. I wept, but my tears flowed from a double source; from sorrow, on account of the untimely fate of my uncle, and from joy, that my sisters were preserved, that Sarsefield had returned and was not unhappy.

I reflected on the untoward destiny of Clithero. Part of his calamity consisted in the consciousness of having killed his patronness; but it now appeared, though by some infatuation, I had not previously suspected, that the first impulse of sorrow in the lady, had been weakened by reflection and by time. That the prejudice persuading her that her life and that of her brother were to endure and to terminate together, was conquered by experience or by argument. She had come, in company with Sarsefield and Clarice to America. What influence might these events have upon the gloomy meditations of Clithero? Was it possible to bring them together; to win the maniac from his solitude, wrest from him his fatal purposes, and restore him to communion with the beings whose imagined indignation is the torment of his life?

These musings were interrupted by a sound from below which were easily interpreted into tokens of the return of those with whom Sarsefield had parted at the promontory; voices were confused and busy but not turbulent. They entered the lower room and the motion of chairs and tables shewed that they were preparing to rest themselves after their toils.

Few of them were unacquainted with me, since they probably were residents in this district. No inconvenience, therefore, would follow from an interview, though, on their part, wholly unexpected. Besides, Sarsefield would speedily return and none of the present visitants would be likely to withdraw to this apartment.

Meanwhile I lay upon the bed, with my face turned towards the door, and languidly gazing at the ceiling and walls. Just then a musquet was discharged in the room below. The shock affected me mechanically and the first impulse of surprise, made me almost start upon my feet.

The sound was followed by confusion and bustle. Some rushed forth and called on each other to run different ways, and the words "That is he"—"Stop him" were spoken in a tone of eagerness, and rage. My weakness and pain were for a moment forgotten, and my whole attention was bent to discover the meaning of this hubbub. The musquet which I had brought with me to this chamber, lay across the bed. Unknowing of the consequences of this affray, with regard to myself, I was prompted by a kind of self-preserving instinct, to lay hold of the gun, and prepare to repel any attack that might be made upon me.

A few moments elapsed when I thought I heard light footsteps in the entry leading to this room. I had no time to construe these signals, but watching fearfully the entrance, I grasped my weapon with new force, and raised it so as to be ready at the moment of my danger. I did not watch long. A figure cautiously thrust itself forward. The first glance was sufficient to inform me that this intruder was an Indian, and, of consequence, an enemy. He was unarmed. Looking eagerly on all sides, he at last spied me as I lay. My appearance threw him into consternation, and after the fluctuation of an instant, he darted to the window, threw up the sash, and leaped out upon the ground.

His flight might have been easily arrested by my shot, but surprize, added to my habitual antipathy to bloodshed, unless in cases of absolute necessity, made me hesitate. He was gone, and I was left to mark the progress of the drama. The silence was presently broken by firing at a distance. Three shots, in quick succession, were followed by the deepest pause.

That the party, recently arrived, had brought with them one or more captives, and that by some sudden effort, the prisoners had attempted to escape, was the only supposition that I could form. By what motives either of them could be induced to seek concealment in my chamber, could not be imagined.

I now heard a single step on the threshold below. Some one entered the common room. He traversed the floor during a few minutes, and then, ascending the stair-case, he entered my chamber. It was Sarsefield. Trouble and dismay were strongly written on his countenance. He seemed totally unconscious of my presence, his eyes were fixed upon the floor, and as he continued to move across the room, he heaved forth deep sighs.

This deportment was mournful and mysterious. It was little in unison with those appearances which he wore at our parting, and must have been suggested by some event that had since happened. My curiosity impelled me to recall him from his reverie. I rose and seizing him by the arm, looked at him with an air of inquisitive anxiety. It was needless to speak.

He noticed my movement, and turning towards me, spoke in a tone of some resentment—Why did you deceive me? Did you not say Clithero was dead?

I said so because it was my belief. Know you any thing to the contrary? Heaven grant that he is still alive, and that our mutual efforts may restore him to peace.

Heaven grant, replied my friend, with a vehemence that bordered upon fury, Heaven grant that he may live thousands of years, and know not, in their long course, a moment's respite from remorse and from anguish; but this prayer is fruitless. He is not dead, but death hovers over him. Should he live, he will live only to defy justice and perpetrate new horrors. My skill might perhaps save him, but a finger shall not be moved to avert his fate.

Little did I think, that the wretch whom my friends rescued from the power of the savages, and brought wounded and expiring hither was Clithero. They sent for me in haste to afford him surgical assistance. I found him stretched upon the floor below, deserted, helpless and bleeding. The moment I beheld him, he was recognized. The last of evils was to look upon the face of this assassin, but that evil is past, and shall never be endured again.

Rise and come with me. Accommodation is prepared for you at Walcot's. Let us leave this house, and the moment you are able to perform a journey, abandon forever this district.

I could not readily consent to this proposal. Clithero had

been delivered from captivity but was dying for want of that aid which Sarsefield was able to afford. Was it not inhuman to desert him in this extremity? What offence had he committed that deserved such implacable vengeance? Nothing I had heard from Sarsefield was in contradiction to his own story. His deed, imperfectly observed, would appear to be atrocious and detestable, but the view of all its antecedent and accompanying events and motives, would surely place it in the list not of crimes, but of misfortunes.

But what is that guilt which no penitence can expiate? Had not Clithero's remorse been more than adequate to crimes far more deadly and enormous than this? This, however, was no time to argue with the passions of Sarsefield. Nothing but a repetition of Clithero's tale, could vanquish his prepossessions and mollify his rage, but this repetition was impossible to be given by me, till a moment of safety and composure.

These thoughts made me linger, but hindered me from attempting to change the determination of my friend. He renewed his importunities for me to fly with him. He dragged me by the arm, and wavering and reluctant I followed where he chose to lead. He crossed the common-room, with hurried steps and eyes averted from a figure, which instantly fastened my attention.

It was, indeed, Clithero, whom I now beheld, supine, polluted with blood, his eyes closed and apparently insensible. This object was gazed at with emotions that rooted me to the spot. Sarsefield, perceiving me determined to remain where I was, rushed out of the house, and disappeared.

Chapter XXVII

I HUNG over the unhappy wretch whose emaciated form and rueful features, sufficiently bespoke that savage hands had only completed that destruction which his miseries had begun. He was mangled by the tom-hawk in a shocking manner, and there was little hope that human skill could save his life.

I was sensible of nothing but compassion. I acted without design, when seating myself on the floor I raised his head and placed it on my knees. This movement awakened his attention, and opening his eyes he fixed them on my countenance. They testified neither insensibility, nor horror nor distraction. A faint emotion of surprise gave way to an appearance of tranquillity—Having perceived these tokens of a state less hopeless than I at first imagined, I spoke to him:—My friend! How do you feel? Can any thing be done for you?

He answered me, in a tone more firm and with more coherence of ideas than previous appearances had taught me to expect. No, said he, thy kindness good youth, can avail me nothing. The end of my existence here is at hand. May my guilt be expiated by the miseries that I have suffered, and my good deeds only attend me to the presence of my divine judge.

I am waiting, not with trembling or dismay, for this close of my sorrows. I breathed but one prayer, and that prayer has been answered. I asked for an interview with thee, young man, but feeling as I now feel, this interview, so much desired, was beyond my hope. Now thou art come, in due season, to hear the last words that I shall need to utter.

I wanted to assure thee that thy efforts for my benefit were not useless. They have saved me from murdering myself, a guilt more inexpiable than any which it was in my power to commit.

I retired to the innermost recess of Norwalk, and gained the summit of an hill, by subterranean paths. This hill I knew to be on all sides inaccessible to human footsteps, and the subterranean passages was closed up by stones. Here I believed my solitude exempt from interruption and my death, in consequence of famine, sure.

This persuasion was not taken away by your appearance on the opposite steep. The chasm which severed us I knew to be impassable. I withdrew from your sight.

Some time after, awakening from a long sleep, I found victuals beside me. He that brought it was invisible. For a time, I doubted whether some messenger of heaven had not interposed for my salvation. How other than by supernatural means, my retreat should be explored, I was unable to conceive. The summit was encompassed by dizzy and profound gulfs, and the subterranean passages was still closed.

This opinion, though corrected by subsequent reflection, tended to change the course of my desperate thoughts. My hunger, thus importunately urged, would not abstain, and I ate of the food that was provided. Henceforth I determined to live, to resume the path of obscurity and labour, which I had relinquished, and wait till my God should summon me to retribution. To anticipate his call, is only to redouble our guilt.

I designed not to return to Inglefield's service, but to chuse some other and remoter district. Meanwhile, I had left in his possession, a treasure, which my determination to die, had rendered of no value, but which, my change of resolution, restored. Inclosed in a box at Inglefield's, were the memoirs of Euphemia Lorimer, by which in all my vicissitudes, I had been hitherto accompanied, and from which I consented to part only because I had refused to live. My existence was now to be prolonged and this manuscript was once more to constitute the torment and the solace of my being.

I hastened to Inglefield's by night. There was no need to warn him of my purpose. I desired that my fate should be an eternal secret to my ancient master and his neighbours. The apartment, containing my box was well known, and easily accessible.

The box was found but broken and rifled of its treasure. My transports of astonishment, and indignation and grief yielded to the resumption of my fatal purpose. I hastened back to the hill, and determined anew to perish.

This mood continued to the evening of the ensuing day.

Wandering over rocks and pits, I discovered the manuscript, lying under a jutting precipice. The chance that brought it hither was not less propitious and miraculous than that by which I had been supplied with food. It produced a similar effect upon my feelings, and, while in possession of this manuscript I was reconciled to the means of life. I left the mountain, and traversing the wilderness, stopped in Chetasco. That kind of employment which I sought was instantly procured; but my new vocation was scarcely assumed when a band of savages invaded our security.

Rambling in the desert, by moonlight, I encountered these foes. They rushed upon me, and after numerous wounds which, for the present, neither killed nor disabled me, they compelled me to keep pace with them in their retreat. Some hours have passed since the troop was overtaken, and my liberty redeemed. Hardships, and repeated wounds, inflicted at the moment when the invaders were surprised and slain, have brought me to my present condition. I rejoice that my course is about to terminate.

Here the speaker was interrupted by the tumultuous entrance of the party, by whom he had been brought hither. Their astonishment at seeing me, sustaining the head of the dying man, may be easily conceived. Their surprise was more strongly excited by the disappearance of the captive whom they had left in this apartment, bound hand and foot. It now appeared that of the savage troop who had adventured thus far in search of pillage and blood, all had been destroyed but two, who, had been led hither as prisoners. On their entrance into this house, one of the party had been sent to Walcot's to summon Sarsefield to the aid of the wounded man, while others had gone in search of chords to secure the arms and legs of the captives, who had hitherto been manacled imperfectly.

The chords were brought and one of them was bound, but the other, before the same operation was begun upon him, broke, by a sudden effort, the feeble ligatures by which he was at present constrained, and seizing a musquet that lay near him, fired on his enemies, and then rushed out of doors. All eagerly engaged in the pursuit. The savage was fleet as a deer and finally eluded his pursuers.

While their attention was thus engaged abroad, he that remained found means to extricate his wrists and ancles from his bonds and betaking himself to the stairs, escaped, as I before described, through the window of the room which I had occupied. They pestered me with their curiosity and wonder, for I was known to all of them; but waving the discussion of my own concerns I intreated their assistance to carry Clithero to the chamber and the bed which I had just deserted.

I now in spite of pain, fatigue and watchfulness, set out to go to Walton's. Sarsefield was ready to receive me at the door, and the kindness and compassion of the family were active in my behalf. I was conducted to a chamber and provided with suitable attendance and remedies.

I was not unmindful of the more deplorable condition of Clithero. I incessantly meditated on the means for his relief. His case stood in need of all the vigilance and skill of a physician, and Sarsefield was the only one of that profession whose aid could be seasonably administered. Sarsefield therefore must be persuaded to bestow this aid.

There was but one mode of conquering his abhorrence of this man. To prepossess my friend with the belief of the innocence of Clithero, or to soothe him into pity by a picture of remorse and suffering. This could best be done, and in the manner most conformable to truth, by a simple recital of the incidents that had befallen, and by repeating the confession which had been extorted from Clithero.

I requested all but my friend to leave my chamber, and then, soliciting a patient hearing, began the narrative of Waldegrave's death; of the detection of Clithero beneath the shade of the elm; of the suspicions which were thence produced; and of the forest interview to which these suspicions gave birth; I then repeated, without variation or addition, the tale which was then told. I likewise mentioned my subsequent transactions in Norwalk so far as they illustrated the destiny of Clithero.

During this recital, I fixed my eyes upon the countenance of Sarsefield, and watched every emotion as it rose or declined. With the progress of my tale, his indignation and his fury grew less, and at length gave place to horror and compassion.

His seat became uneasy, his pulse throbbed with new vehemence. When I came to the motives which prompted the
unhappy man to visit the chamber of his mistress, he started
from his seat, and sometimes strode across the floor in a troubled mood, and sometimes stood before me, with his breath
almost suspended in the eagerness of his attention. When I
mentioned the lifted dagger, the shriek from behind, and the
apparition that interposed, he shuddered and drew back as if
a dagger had been aimed at his breast.

When the tale was done, some time elapsed in mutual and
profound silence. My friend's thoughts were involved in a
mournful and indefinable reverie. From this he at length recovered and spoke.

It is true. A tale like this could never be the fruit of invention or be invented to deceive. He has done himself injustice.
His character was spotless and fair: All his moral properties
seemed to have resolved themselves into gratitude, fidelity and
honour.

We parted at the door, late in the evening, as he mentioned,
and he guessed truly that subsequent reflection had induced
me to return and to disclose the truth to Mrs. Lorimer. Clarice
relieved by the sudden death of her friend, and unexpectedly
by all, arrived at the same hour.

These tidings, astonished, afflicted, and delighted the lady.
Her brother's death had been long believed by all but herself.
To find her doubts verified, and his existence ascertained was
the dearest consolation that he ever could bestow. She was
afflicted at the proofs that had been noted of the continuance
of his depravity, but she dreaded no danger to herself from
his malignity or vengeance.

The ignorance and prepossessions of this woman were remarkable. On this subject only she was perverse, headlong,
obstinate. Her anxiety to benefit this arch-ruffian occupied her
whole thoughts and allowed her no time to reflect upon the
reasonings or remonstrances of others. She could not be prevailed on to deny herself to his visits, and I parted from her
in the utmost perplexity.

A messenger came to me at mid-night intreating my immediate presence. Some disaster had happened, but of what
kind the messenger was unable to tell. My fears easily conjured

up the image of Wiatte. Terror scarcely allowed me to breathe. When I entered the house of Mrs. Lorimer, I was conducted to her chamber. She lay upon the bed in a state of stupefaction, that rose from some mental cause. Clarice sat by her, wringing her hands and pouring forth her tears without intermission. Neither could explain to me the nature of the scene. I made inquiries of the servants and attendants. They merely said that the family as usual had retired to rest, but their lady's bell rung with great violence, and called them in haste, to her chamber, where they found her in a swoon upon the floor and the young lady in the utmost affright and perturbation.

Suitable means being used Mrs. Lorimer had, at length, recovered, but was still nearly insensible. I went to Clithero's apartments but he was not to be found, and the domestics informed me that since he had gone with me, he had not returned. The doors between this chamber and the court were open; hence that some dreadful interview had taken place, perhaps with Wiatte, was an unavoidable conjecture. He had withdrawn, however, without committing any personal injury.

I need not mention my reflections upon this scene. All was tormenting doubt and suspence till the morning arrived, and tidings were received that Wiatte had been killed in the streets: This event was antecedent to that which had occasioned Mrs. Lorimer's distress and alarm. I now remembered that fatal prepossession by which the lady was governed, and her frantic belief that her death and that of her brother were to fall out at the same time. Could some witness of his death, have brought her tidings of it: Had he penetrated, unexpected and unlicensed to her chamber, and were these the effects produced by the intelligence?

Presently I knew that not only Wiatte was dead, but that Clithero had killed him. Clithero had not been known to return and was no where to be found. He then was the bearer of these tidings, for none but he could have found access or egress without disturbing the servants.

These doubts were at length at an end. In a broken and confused manner, and after the lapse of some days the monstrous and portentous truth was disclosed. After our interview, the lady and her daughter had retired to the same chamber;

the former had withdrawn to her closet and the latter to bed. Some one's entrance alarmed the lady, and coming forth after a moment's pause, the spectacle which Clithero has too faithfully described, presented itself.

What could I think? A life of uniform hypocrisy or a sudden loss of reason were the only suppositions to be formed. Clithero was the parent of fury and abhorrence in my heart. In either case I started at the name. I shuddered at the image of the apostate or the maniac.

What? Kill the brother whose existence was interwoven with that of his benefactress and his friend? Then hasten to her chamber, and attempt her life? Lift a dagger to destroy her who had been the author of his being and his happiness?

He that could meditate a deed like this was no longer man. An agent from Hell had mastered his faculties. He was become the engine of infernal malice against whom it was the duty of all mankind to rise up in arms and never to desist till, by shattering it to atoms, its power to injure was taken away.

All inquiries to discover the place of his retreat were vain. No wonder methought that he wrapt himself in the folds of impenetrable secrecy. Curbed, checked, baffled in the midst of his career, no wonder that he shrunk into obscurity, that he fled from justice and revenge, that he dared not meet the rebukes of that eye which, dissolving in tenderness or flashing with disdain, had ever been irresistible.

But how shall I describe the lady's condition? Clithero she had cherished from his infancy. He was the stay, the consolation, the pride of her life. His projected alliance with her daughter, made him still more dear. Her eloquence was never tired of expatiating on his purity and rectitude. No wonder that she delighted in this theme, for he was her own work. His virtues were the creatures of her bounty.

How hard to be endured was this sad reverse! She can be tranquil, but never more will she be happy. To promote her forgetfulness of him, I persuaded her to leave her country, which contained a thousand memorials of past calamity, and which was lapsing fast into civil broils. Clarice has accompanied us, and time may effect the happiness of others, by her means, though she can never remove the melancholy of her mother.

I have listened to your tale, not without compassion. What would you have me to do? To prolong his life, would be merely to protract his misery.

He can never be regarded with complacency by my wife. He can never be thought of without shuddering by Clarice. Common ills are not without a cure less than death, but here, all remedies are vain. Consciousness itself is the malady; the pest; of which he only is cured who ceases to think.

I could not but assent to this mournful conclusion; yet, though death was better to Clithero than life, could not some of his mistakes be rectified? Euphemia Lorimer, contrary to his belief, was still alive. He dreamed that she was dead, and a thousand evils were imagined to flow from that death. This death and its progeny of ills, haunted his fancy, and added keenness to his remorse. Was it not our duty to rectify this error?

Sarsefield reluctantly assented to the truth of my arguments on this head. He consented to return, and afford the dying man, the consolation of knowing that the being whom he adored as a benefactor and parent, had not been deprived of existence, though bereft of peace by his act.

During Sarsefield's absence my mind was busy in revolving the incidents that had just occurred. I ruminated the last words of Clithero. There was somewhat in his narrative that was obscure and contradictory. He had left the manuscript which he so much and so justly prized, in his cabinet. He entered the chamber in my absence, and found the cabinet unfastened and the manuscript gone. It was I by whom the cabinet was opened, but the manuscript supposed to be contained in it, was buried in the earth beneath the elm. How should Clithero be unacquainted with its situation, since none but Clithero could have dug for it this grave?

This mystery vanished when I reflected on the history of my own manuscript. Clithero had buried his treasure with his own hands as mine had been secreted by myself, but both acts had been performed during sleep. The deed was neither prompted by the will, nor noticed by the senses of him, by whom it was done. Disastrous and humiliating is the state of man! By his own hands, is constructed the mass of misery and error in which his steps are forever involved.

Thus it was with thy friend. Hurried on by phantoms too indistinct to be now recalled, I wandered from my chamber to the desart. I plunged into some unvisited cavern, and easily proceeded till I reached the edge of a pit. There my step was deceived, and I tumbled headlong from the precipice. The fall bereaved me of sense, and I continued breathless and motionless during the remainder of the night and the ensuing day.

How little cognizance have men over the actions and motives of each other! How total is our blindness with regard to our own performances! Who would have sought me in the bowels of this mountain? Ages might have passed away, before my bones would be discovered in this tomb, by some traveller whom curiosity had prompted to explore it.

I was roused from these reflections by Sarsefield's return. Inquiring into Clithero's condition, he answered that the unhappy man was insensible, but that notwithstanding numerous and dreadful gashes, in different parts of his body, it was possible that by submitting to the necessary treatment, he might recover.

Encouraged by this information, I endeavoured to awaken the zeal and compassion of my friend in Clithero's behalf. He recoiled with involuntary shuddering from any task which would confine him to the presence of this man. Time and reflection he said, might introduce different sentiments and feelings, but at present he could not but regard this person as a maniac, whose disease was irremediable, and whose existence could not be protracted, but to his own misery and the misery of others.

Finding him irreconcilably averse to any scheme, connected with the welfare of Clithero, I began to think that his assistance as a surgeon was by no means necessary. He had declared that the sufferer needed nothing more than common treatment, and to this the skill of a score of aged women in this district, furnished with simples culled from the forest, and pointed out, of old time, by Indian *Leeches* was no less adequate than that of Sarsefield. These women were ready and officious in their charity, and none of them were prepossessed against the sufferer by a knowledge of his genuine story.

Sarsefield, meanwhile, was impatient for my removal to

Inglefield's habitation, and that venerable friend was no less impatient to receive me. My hurts were superficial, and my strength sufficiently repaired by a night's repose. Next day, I went thither, leaving Clithero to the care of his immediate neighbours.

Sarsefield's engagements compelled him to prosecute his journey into Virginia, from which he had somewhat deviated, in order to visit Solebury. He proposed to return in less than a month and then to take me in his company to New-York. He has treated me with paternal tenderness, and insists upon the privilege of consulting for my interest, as if he were my real father. Meanwhile, these views have been disclosed to Inglefield, and it is with him that I am to remain, with my sisters, until his return.

My reflections have been various and tumultuous. They have been busy in relation to you, to Weymouth, and especially to Clithero. The latter polluted with gore and weakened by abstinence, fatigue and the loss of blood, appeared in my eyes, to be in a much more dangerous condition than the event proved him to be. I was punctually informed of the progress of his cure, and proposed in a few days to visit him. The duty of explaining the truth, respecting the present condition of Mrs. Lorimer, had devolved upon me. By imparting this intelligence, I hoped to work the most auspicious revolutions in his feelings, and prepared therefore, with alacrity, for an interview.

In this hope I was destined to be disappointed. On the morning on which I intended to visit him, a messenger arrived from the house in which he was entertained, and informed us that the family on entering the sick man's apartment, had found it deserted. It appeared that Clithero, had, during the night, risen from his bed, and gone secretly forth. No traces of his flight have since been discovered.

But, O! my friend! The death of Waldegrave, thy brother, is at length divested of uncertainty and mystery. Hitherto, I had been able to form no conjecture respecting it, but the solution was found shortly after this time.

Queen Mab, three days after my adventure, was seized in her hut on suspicion of having aided and counselled her countrymen, in their late depredations. She was not to be awed or intimidated by the treatment she received, but readily confessed and gloried in the mischief she had done; and accounted for it by enumerating the injuries which she had received from her neighbours.

These injuries consisted in contemptuous or neglectful treatment, and in the rejection of groundless and absurd claims. The people of Chetasco were less obsequious to her humours than those of Solebury, her ancient neighbourhood, and her imagination brooded for a long time, over nothing but schemes of revenge. She became sullen, irascible and spent more of her time in solitude than ever.

A troop of her countrymen at length visited her hut. Their intentions being hostile, they concealed from the inhabitants their presence in this quarter of the country. Some motives induced them to withdraw and postpone, for the present, the violence which they meditated. One of them, however, more sanguinary and audacious than the rest would not depart, without some gratification of his vengeance. He left his associates and penetrated by night into Solebury, resolving to attack the first human being whom he should meet. It was the fate of thy unhappy brother to encounter this ruffian, whose sagacity made him forbear to tear away the usual trophy from the dead, least he should afford grounds for suspicion as to the authors of the evil.

Satisfied with this exploit he rejoined his companions, and after an interval of three weeks returned with a more numerous party, to execute a more extensive project of destruction. They were councelled and guided, in all their movements, by Queen Mab, who now explained these particulars, and boldly defied her oppressors. Her usual obstinacy and infatuation induced her to remain in her ancient dwelling and prepare to meet the consequences.

This disclosure awakened anew all the regrets and anguish which flowed from that disaster. It has been productive, however, of some benefit. Suspicions and doubts, by which my soul was harrassed, and which were injurious to the innocent are now at an end. It is likewise some imperfect consolation to reflect that the assassin has himself been killed and probably by my own hand. The shedder of blood no longer lives to pursue his vocation, and justice is satisfied.

Thus have I fulfilled my promise to compose a minute relation of my sufferings. I remembered my duty to thee, and as soon as I was able to hold a pen, employed it to inform thee of my welfare. I could not at that time enter into particulars, but reserved a more copious narrative till a period of more health and leisure.

On looking back I am surprised at the length to which my story has run. I thought that a few days would suffice to complete it, but one page has insensibly been added to another till I have consumed weeks and filled volumes. Here I will draw to a close; I will send you what I have written, and discuss with you in conversation, my other immediate concerns, and my schemes for the future. As soon as I have seen Sarsefield, I will visit you.

Farewell.

E.H.

Solebury, November, 10.

Letter I

TO MR. SARSEFIELD

Philadelphia.

I CAME hither but ten minutes ago, and write this letter in the bar of the Stagehouse. I wish not to lose a moment in informing you of what has happened. I cannot do justice to my own feelings when I reflect upon the rashness of which I have been guilty.

I will give you the particulars to-morrow. At present, I shall only say that Clithero is alive, is apprised of your wife's arrival and abode in New-York, and has set out, with mysterious intentions to visit her.

May heaven avert the consequences of such a design. May you be enabled by some means to prevent their meeting. If you cannot prevent it—but I must not reason on such an event, nor lengthen out this letter.

E.H.

Letter II

TO THE SAME

I WILL NOW relate the particulars which I yesterday promised to send you. You heard through your niece of my
arrival at Inglefield's in Solebury: My inquiries, you may readily suppose, would turn upon the fate of my friend's servant,
Clithero, whose last disappearance was so strange and abrupt,
and of whom since that time, I had heard nothing. You are
indifferent to his fate and are anxious only that his existence
and misfortunes may be speedily forgotten. I confess that it is
somewhat otherwise with me. I pity him: I wish to relieve
him, and cannot admit the belief that his misery is without a
cure. I want to find him out. I want to know his condition,
and if possible to afford him comfort, and inspire him with
courage and hope.

Inglefield replied to my questions. O yes! He has appeared.
The strange being is again upon the stage. Shortly after he
left his sick bed, I heard from Philip Beddington, of Chetasco,
that Deb's hut had found a new tenant. At first, I imagined
that the Scotsman who built it had returned, but making
closer inquiries, I found that the new tenant was my servant.
I had no inclination to visit him myself, but frequently inquired respecting him of those, who lived or past that way,
and find that he still lives there.

But how, said I. What is his mode of subsistance? The winter has been no time for cultivation, and he found, I presume,
nothing in the ground.

Deb's hut, replied my friend, is his lodging and his place of
retirement, but food and cloathing he procures by labouring
on a neighbouring farm. This farm is next to that of Beddington, who consequently knows something of his present
situation. I find little or no difference in his present deportment, and those appearances which he assumed, while living
with me, except that he retires every night to his hut, and
holds as little intercourse as possible with the rest of mankind.
He dines at his employer's table, but his supper, which is

nothing but rye-bread, he carries home with him, and at all those times when disengaged from employment, he secludes himself in his hut, or wanders nobody knows whither.

This was the substance of Inglefield's intelligence. I gleaned from it some satisfaction. It proved the condition of Clithero to be less deplorable and desperate than I had previously imagined. His fatal and gloomy thoughts seemed to have somewhat yielded to tranquillity.

In the course of my reflections, however, I could not but perceive, that his condition, though eligible when compared with what it once was, was likewise disastrous and humiliating, compared with his youthful hopes and his actual merits. For such an one to mope away his life in this unsocial and savage state, was deeply to be deplored. It was my duty, if possible, to prevail on him to relinquish his scheme. And what would be requisite, for that end, but to inform him of the truth?

The source of his dejection was the groundless belief that he had occasioned the death of his benefactress. It was this alone that could justly produce remorse or grief. It was a distempered imagination both in him and in me, that had given birth to this opinion, since the terms of his narrative, impartially considered, were far from implying that catastrophe. To him, however, the evidence which he possessed was incontestable. No deductions from probability could overthrow his belief. This could only be effected by similar and counter evidence. To apprize him that she was now alive, in possession of some degree of happiness, the wife of Sarsefield, and an actual resident on this shore, would dissipate the sanguinary apparition that haunted him; cure his diseased intellects, and restore him to those vocations for which his talents, and that rank in society for which his education had qualified him. Influenced by these thoughts, I determined to visit his retreat. Being obliged to leave Solebury the next day, I resolved to set out the same afternoon, and stopping in Chetasco, for the night, seek his habitation at the hour when he had probably retired to it.

This was done. I arrived at Beddington's, at night-fall. My inquiries respecting Clithero obtained for me the same intelligence from him, which I had received from Inglefield. Deb's hut was three miles from this habitation, and thither, when the evening had somewhat advanced, I repaired. This was the spot which had witnessed so many perils during the last year, and my emotions, on approaching it, were awful. With palpitating heart and quick steps I traversed the road, skirted on each side by thickets, and the area before the house. The dwelling was by no means in so ruinous a state as when I last visited it. The crannies between the logs had been filled up, and the light within was perceivable only at a crevice in the door.

Looking through this crevice I perceived a fire in the chimney, but the object of my visit was no where to be seen. I knocked and requested admission, but no answer was made. At length I lifted the latch and entered. Nobody was there.

It was obvious to suppose that Clithero had gone abroad for a short time, and would speedily return, or perhaps some engagement had detained him at his labour, later than usual. I therefore seated myself on some straw near the fire, which, with a woollen rug, appeared to constitute his only bed. The rude bedstead which I formerly met with, was gone. The slender furniture, likewise, which had then engaged my attention, had disappeared. There was nothing capable of human use, but a heap of faggots in the corner, which seemed intended for fuel. How slender is the accommodation which nature has provided for man, and how scanty is the portion which our physical necessities require.

While ruminating upon this scene, and comparing past events with the objects before me, the dull whistling of the gale without gave place to the sound of footsteps. Presently the door opened, and Clithero entered the apartment. His aspect and guise were not essentially different from those which he wore when an inhabitant of Solebury.

To find his hearth occupied by another, appeared to create the deepest surprise. He looked at me without any tokens of remembrance! His features assumed a more austere expression, and after scowling on my person for a moment, he withdrew his eyes, and placing in a corner, a bundle which he bore in his hand, he turned and seemed preparing to withdraw.

I was anxiously attentive to his demeanor, and as soon as I perceived his purpose to depart, leaped on my feet to prevent it. I took his hand, and affectionately pressing it, said, do you not know me? Have you so soon forgotten me who is truly your friend?

He looked at me with some attention, but again withdrew his eyes, and placed himself in silence on the seat which I had left. I seated myself near him, and a pause of mutual silence ensued.

My mind was full of the purpose that brought me hither, but I knew not in what manner to communicate my purpose. Several times I opened my lips to speak, but my perplexity continued, and suitable words refused to suggest themselves. At length, I said, in a confused tone:

I came hither with a view to benefit a man, with whose misfortunes his own lips have made me acquainted, and who has awakened in my breast the deepest sympathy. I know the cause and extent of his dejection. I know the event which has given birth to horror and remorse in his heart. He believes that, by his means, his patroness and benefactress has found an untimely death.

These words produced a visible shock in my companion, which evinced that I had at least engaged his attention. I proceeded:

This unhappy lady was cursed with a wicked and unnatural brother. She conceived a disproportionate affection for this brother, and erroneously imagined that her fate was blended with his; that their lives would necessarily terminate at the same period, and that therefore, whoever was the contriver of his death, was likewise, by a fatal and invincible necessity, the author of her own.

Clithero was her servant, but was raised by her bounty, to the station of her son and the rank of her friend. Clithero, in self-defence took away the life of that unnatural brother, and, in that deed, falsely but cogently believed, that he had perpetrated the destruction of his benefactress.

To ascertain the truth, he sought her presence. She was found, the tidings of her brother's death were communicated, and she sunk breathless at his feet.

At these words Clithero started from the ground, and cast upon me looks of furious indignation—And come you hither, he muttered, for this end; to recount my offences, and drive me again to despair?

No, answered I, with quickness, I come to out-root a fatal, but powerful illusion. I come to assure you that the woman, with whose destruction you charge yourself, is *not dead*.

These words, uttered with the most emphatical solemnity, merely produced looks in which contempt was mingled with anger. He continued silent.

I perceive, resumed I, that my words are disregarded. Would to Heaven I were able to conquer your incredulity, could shew you not only the truth, but the probability of my tale. Can you not confide in me; that Euphemia Lorimer is now alive, is happy, is the wife of Sarsefield; that her brother is forgotten and his murderer regarded without enmity or vengeance?

He looked at me with a strange expression of contempt— Come, said he, at length, make out thy assertion to be true. Fall on thy knees and invoke the thunder of heaven to light on thy head if thy words be false. Swear that Euphemia Lorimer is alive; happy; forgetful of Wiatte and compassionate of me. Swear that thou hast seen her; talked with her; received from her own lips the confession of her pity for him who aimed a dagger at her bosom. Swear that she is Sarsefield's wife.

I put my hands together, and lifting my eyes to heaven, exclaimed: I comply with your conditions; I call the omniscient God to witness that Euphemia Lorimer is alive; that I have seen her with these eyes; have talked with her; have inhabited the same house for months.

These asseverations were listened to with shuddering. He laid not aside, however, an air of incredulity and contempt. Perhaps, said he, thou canst point out the place of her abode. Canst guide me to the city, the street, the very door of her habitation?

I can. She rises at this moment in the city of New-York; in Broadway; in an house contiguous to the ——.

'Tis well, exclaimed my companion, in a tone, loud, abrupt, and in the utmost degree, vehement. 'Tis well. Rash and infatuated youth. Thou hast ratified, beyond appeal or forgiveness, thy own doom. Thou hast once more let loose my steps, and sent me on a fearful journey. Thou hast furnished the means of detecting thy imposture. I will fly to the spot which thou describest. I will ascertain thy falsehood with my own eyes. If she be alive then am I reserved for the performance of a new crime. My evil destiny will have it so. If she be dead, I shall make *thee* expiate.

So saying, he darted through the door, and was gone in a moment, beyond my sight and my reach. I ran to the road, looked on every side, and called; but my calls were repeated in vain. He had fled with the swiftness of a deer.

My own embarrassment, confusion and terror were inexpressible. His last words were incoherent. They denoted the tumult and vehemence of phrenzy. They intimated his resolution to seek the presence of your wife. I had furnished a clue, which could not fail to conduct him to her presence. What might not be dreaded from the interview? Clithero is a maniac. This truth cannot be concealed. Your wife can with difficulty preserve her tranquillity, when his image occurs to her remembrance. What must it be when he starts up before her in his neglected and ferocious guise, and armed with purposes, perhaps as terrible as those, which had formerly led him to her secret chamber, and her bed side?

His meaning was obscurely conveyed. He talked of a deed, for the performance of which, his malignant fate had reserved him; which was to ensue their meeting, and which was to afford disastrous testimony of the infatuation which had led me hither.

Heaven grant that some means may suggest themselves to you of intercepting his approach. Yet I know not what means can be conceived. Some miraculous chance may befriend you; yet this is scarcely to be hoped. It is a visionary and fantastic base on which to rest our security.

I cannot forget that my unfortunate temerity has created this evil. Yet who could foresee this consequence of my intelligence? I imagined, that Clithero was merely a victim of erroneous gratitude, a slave of the errors of his education, and the prejudices of his rank, that his understanding was deluded by phantoms in the mask of virtue and duty, and not as you have strenuously maintained, utterly subverted.

I shall not escape your censure, but I shall, likewise, gain your compassion. I have erred, not through sinister or malignant intentions, but from the impulse of misguided, indeed, but powerful benevolence.

E.H.

Letter III

TO EDGAR HUNTLY

New-York.

Edgar,

AFTER the fatigues of the day, I returned home. As I entered, my wife was breaking the seal of a letter, but, on seeing me, she forbore and presented the letter to me.

I saw, said she, by the superscription of this letter, who the writer was. So agreeably to your wishes, I proceeded to open it, but you have come just time enough to save me the trouble.

This letter was from you. It contained information relative to Clithero. See how imminent a chance it was that saved my wife from a knowledge of its contents. It required all my efforts to hide my perturbation from her, and excuse myself from shewing her the letter.

I know better than you the character of Clithero, and the consequences of a meeting between him and my wife. You may be sure that I would exert myself to prevent a meeting.

The method for me to pursue was extremely obvious. Clithero is a madman whose liberty is dangerous, and who requires to be fettered and imprisoned as the most atrocious criminal.

I hastened to the chief Magistrate, who is my friend, and by proper representations, obtained from him authority to seize Clithero wherever I should meet with him, and effectually debar him from the perpetration of new mischiefs.

New-York does not afford a place of confinement for lunatics, as suitable to his case, as Pennsylvania. I was desirous of placing him as far as possible from the place of my wife's residence. Fortunately there was a packet for Philadelphia, on the point of setting out on her voyage. This vessel I engaged to wait a day or two, for the purpose of conveying him to the Pennsylvania hospital. Meanwhile, proper persons were stationed at Powles-hook, and at the quays where the various stageboats from Jersey arrive.

These precautions were effectual. Not many hours after the receipt of your intelligence, this unfortunate man applied for a passage at Elizabeth-town, was seized the moment he set his foot on shore, and was forthwith conveyed to the packet, which immediately set sail.

I designed that all these proceedings should be concealed from the women, but unfortunately neglected to take suitable measures for hindering the letter which you gave me reason to expect on the ensuing day, from coming into their hands. It was delivered to my wife in my absence and opened immediately by her.

You know what is, at present, her personal condition. You know what strong reasons I had to prevent any danger or alarm from approaching her. Terror could not assume a shape, more ghastly than this. The effects have been what might have been easily predicted. Her own life has been imminently endangered and an untimely birth, has blasted my fondest hope. Her infant, with whose future existence so many pleasures were entwined, *is dead*.

I assure you Edgar, my philosophy has not found itself lightsome and active under this burthen. I find it hard to forbear commenting on your rashness in no very mild terms. You acted in direct opposition to my council, and to the plainest dictates of propriety. Be more circumspect and more obsequious for the future.

You knew the liberty that would be taken of opening my letters; you knew of my absence from home, during the greatest part of the day, and the likelihood therefore that your letters would fall into my wife's hands before they came into mine. These considerations should have prompted you to send them under cover to Whitworth or Harvey, with directions to give them immediately to *me*.

Some of these events happened in my absence, for I determined to accompany the packet myself and see the madman safely delivered to the care of the hospital.

I will not torture your sensibility by recounting the incidents of his arrest and detention. You will imagine that his strong, but perverted reason exclaimed loudly against the injustice of his treatment. It was easy for him to outreason his antagonist, and nothing but force could subdue his opposition.

On me devolved the province of his jailor and his tyrant; a province which required an heart more steeled by spectacles of suffering and the exercise of cruelty, than mine had been.

Scarcely had we passed *The Narrows*, when the lunatic, being suffered to walk the deck, as no apprehensions were entertained of his escape in such circumstances, threw himself overboard, with a seeming intention to gain the shore. The boat was immediately manned, the fugitive was pursued, but at the moment, when his flight was overtaken, he forced himself beneath the surface, and was seen no more.

With the life of this wretch, let our regrets and our forebodings terminate. He has saved himself from evils, for which no time would have provided a remedy, from lingering for years in the noisome dungeon of an hospital. Having no reason to continue my voyage, I put myself on board a coasting sloop, and regained this city in a few hours. I persuade myself that my wife's indisposition will be temporary. It was impossible to hide from her the death of Clithero, and its circumstances. May this be the last arrow in the quiver of adversity! Farewell.

END

CHRONOLOGY

NOTE ON THE TEXTS

NOTES

Chronology

1771 Born Charles Brockden Brown on January 17 in Philadelphia, the fifth son of Elijah and Mary Armitt Brown. Father, b. 1740 to James and Miriam Churchman Brown, is
a conveyancer with interests in shipping and real estate.
Mother is the daughter of Elizabeth Lisle Armitt, of a
wealthy Philadelphia family, and the late Joseph Armitt,
who had prospered in commerce and real estate. (Great-
great grandfather James Browne sailed from England to
America in 1677 and helped lay out the town of Burling-
ton, New Jersey; a maternal ancestor helped to establish
Philadelphia. Parents married in 1761 at Arch Street Meeting House; their first son died in infancy.)

1772–81 Lives with parents, brothers Joseph, James, Armitt, and
Elijah Jr., sister Elizabeth, and Grandmother Armitt at her
home on 117 South Second Street. Regularly goes to
Quaker Meeting with family and spends much time reading books from their library.

1782–85 Attends prestigious Friends' Latin School where he studies
Greek, Latin, English, and mathematics and belongs to
Philosophical Society. Considered a precocious student
but physically frail, takes up daily exercise, including long
walks in woods, at suggestion of headmaster Robert
Proud. Begins writing imitations of neoclassical epics in
heroic couplets, including unfinished poem about Colum-
bus titled "The Rising Glory of America" (later expanded
as "The Times"). Brothers begin working in the import
trade.

1786–91 Studies French and reads widely in books at home and
from circulating libraries, including works of Rousseau and
Richard Price. Begins reading law in office of Alexander
Wilcocks, who in 1789 becomes recorder of Philadelphia.
Joins a law society and writes judicial opinions for its moot
court. Finds study of Coke and Blackstone tedious. Keeps
a detailed journal and continues writing poetry, composing up to a hundred lines a day. With friends including
Joseph Bringhurst, forms Belles Lettres club in 1787.

Becomes close friend and confidant of William Wilkins, a
law student from New Jersey whom he introduces to the
club in 1789. Publishes a few poems in newspapers, and
"The Rhapsodist," a series of four essays, appears in *The
Columbian Magazine*, August–November 1789. Around
1790, begins lasting friendship with Elihu Hubbard Smith,
a Deist, poet, and medical student who becomes his literary adviser. Helps form Society for the Attainment of
Useful Knowledge (during his six-year membership, regularly contributes essays and participates in debates). Feels
depressed and dissatisfied with profession of law.

1792–94   Gives up law apprenticeship in early 1792, persuading parents to allow him to pursue a literary career. During yellow
fever epidemic in Philadelphia in 1793, stays for three
months with Smith, who now practices medicine in Weth-
ersfield, Connecticut; during travels with him, meets
Richard Alsop, Theodore Dwight, and others in literary
group known as the "Hartford Wits." In summer of 1794,
travels to New York to visit Smith, who has moved his
practice there; during visit, forms friendships with William
Dunlap, a painter, dramatist, and historian, and William
Johnson, a lawyer, and participates in meetings of the
Friendly Club literary group.

1795   Plans to write "a work equal in extent" to William Godwin's *Caleb Williams* "in less than six weeks"; writes pro-
lifically for a while but then stops (unfinished novel may
be early form of *Arthur Mervyn*). Works on other fiction,
including fragmentary tales "Medway" and "Henry Wallace." Reads Godwin's *Political Justice* and works by Ann
Radcliffe. Friend William Wilkins dies.

1796   Visits Dunlap and his family at their Perth Amboy, New
Jersey, summer home, where they are joined by Smith.
Moves to New York City in September for seven-month
stay; works on a "projected novel" (possibly "Sky-Walk"),
parts of which he has been reading to Smith. Reads
Condorcet's *Outlines of an Historical View of the Progress
of the Human Mind*. Attends meetings of the Friendly
Club and spends much time with Smith, Johnson, and
Dunlap, often discussing moral and social issues. Works
on a "new political romance" (possibly the unfinished
pseudo-historical tale "Sketches of a History of Carsol").

1797   Writes daily, usually on several projects at once, including
a historical piece on the Carolingian dynasty and a dram-
atization of Robert Bage's novel *Hermsprong, Or Man As
He Is Not* (neither is ever finished). Completes first two
parts of *Alcuin*, a dialogue that argues the irrationality of
denying women equality with men in suffrage and access
to education and the professions. Smith expresses enthusiasm for *Alcuin*, reads it at the Friendly Club, and plans
to publish it by subscription. Influenced by reading of
Godwin, Condorcet, and Bage, Brown explores utopian
ideas in "Signior Adini" (never completed). Is concerned
over recurring outbreaks of yellow fever in Philadelphia
and New York through summer and early fall. Completes
first novel, "Sky-Walk; or, The Man Unknown to Himself—An American Tale," based on the theme of somnam-
bulism. Begins courting Susan Potts of Philadelphia, but
is forced to end courtship when his parents disapprove.

1798   *Alcuin; a Dialogue*, parts I and II, are published by Smith
in New York in April; a serialized version, titled "The
Rights of Women," appears in James Watters' new *Weekly
Magazine* in Philadelphia (parts III and IV are completed
by April but are not published in Brown's lifetime).
Brown's work appears regularly in the *Weekly*, including
the first nine chapters of *Arthur Mervyn*; his first published
story, "A Lesson on Sensibility"; the miscellaneous essay
series "Man at Home"; and the first part of an epistolary
novel, "A Series of Original Letters." Brown moves to
New York City in July, where he stays with Smith and
Johnson. Manuscript of "Sky-Walk" is lost after Watters,
who was preparing to publish it, dies in August from yellow fever. Brown composes substantial parts of the stories
"Memoirs of Carwin, the Biloquist" (a sequel to *Wieland*)
and "Memoirs of Stephen Calvert," but does not finish
them. *Wieland; or the Transformation*, Brown's first published novel, appears in September. Smith dies of yellow
fever in late September and Brown, who has been helping
to nurse him, falls ill with the disease. Continues to write
while recuperating, along with Johnson, at Dunlap's Perth
Amboy home. Completes second novel, *Ormond; or, the
Secret Witness*, in about six weeks toward year's end.

1799   *Ormond* published in February and first part of *Arthur
Mervyn; or, Memoirs of the Year 1793* in May. Launches

literary journal *The Monthly Magazine, and American Review*; first number appears in April, containing a fragment from *Edgar Huntly; or, Memoirs of a Sleep-Walker*. Publishes other pieces in the *Monthly* including "Thessalonica: a Roman Story," "Portrait of an Emigrant," and "Walstein's School of History." "Memoirs of Stephen Calvert" begins serialization in *Monthly Magazine* in June. Travels with Johnson in Connecticut during summer, visiting with Alsop and other acquaintances. On return to New York and Philadelphia is apprehensive about resurgence of yellow fever. Composes a monody on the death of George Washington that is recited at the New York Theatre and subsequently published in *Monthly Magazine* (Jan. 1800).

1800   Completes second part of *Arthur Mervyn*, which is published in late summer, and begins novel *Clara Howard*. Serialization of "Calvert" resumes in April after a two-month hiatus. Writes reviews along with many unsigned (or initialed) articles for the *Monthly*. To fill out the third volume of *Edgar Huntly*, adds "Death of Cicero," an unrelated fragment. Travels to Philadelphia in summer to see visiting brother Joseph, now a successful merchant. Meets Elizabeth Linn, daughter of New York Presbyterian minister William Linn and sister of poet John Blair Linn, a friend of Brown. Works on an epistolary novel (never completed), parts of which appear in the *Monthly* as "Friendship" and "The Trials of Arden." The *Monthly* ceases publication with December number.

1801   Begins publishing quarterly, *The American Review and Literary Journal*; in the prospectus, Brown states its purpose as a "repository," where the "intellectual treasure" of the nation may be collected and given encouragement; undertakes to review every native publication. Brown's publisher Hocquet Caritat arranges for the publication of his novels in England by William Lane's Minerva Press, starting with *Ormond*. *Edgar Huntly* is re-issued by the publisher John Conrad and epistolary novels *Clara Howard* and *Jane Talbot* are published. Writes love poems inspired by his courtship of Elizabeth Linn, one of which, "L'Amoroso," appears in Joseph Dennie's magazine *The Port Folio* (April). Develops friendship with Dennie, a fellow member of the literary Tuesday Club. Travels up the

Hudson to Albany, then on to Massachusetts and Connecticut in summer; visits a Shaker village ("a paradise of health and tranquility") and in New Haven hears a sermon by Timothy Dwight.

1802   Grandmother Armitt dies in spring; Brown is named an executor of her will. In dialogues on "Female Accomplishment," published serially in *Port Folio* (Sept.–Oct.), Brown criticizes the exclusion of women from the major professions. Writes numerous book reviews for *The American Review* before it is discontinued after eight numbers are published.

1803   Undertakes another journal, *The Literary Magazine, and American Register*, which begins publication in Philadelphia in October; for the first number, writes essay "Authorship," observing that to be an author by trade necessarily entails poverty. Publishes first installment of "Memoirs of Carwin, the Biloquist" in November number (nine more installments appear, Dec. 1803–March 1805). *Arthur Mervyn* and *Edgar Huntly* are published by Minerva Press; the response of British critics is mainly cursory and negative. Brown writes two polemical pamphlets on the situation in Louisiana, *An Address to the Government of the United States on the Cession of Louisiana to the French* (Jan.) and *Monroe's Embassy, or the Conduct of the Government in Relation to our Claims to the Navigation of the Mississippi* (March), both highly critical of the policies of the Jefferson administration; in the second Brown proposes the immediate seizure of Louisiana as "easy, desirable, necessary and just."

1804   *Jane Talbot* published in a Minerva Press edition. Becomes "principal contributor" to *The Literary Magazine*, writing more than half—and in some cases all—of the material; sometimes uses work he has previously published. Translates C. F. C. Volney's 1803 work *Tableau du climat et du sol des États-Unis d'Amérique*, adding critical commentary in footnotes. John Blair Linn dies in August. Marries Elizabeth Linn in New York on November 19 in Presbyterian ceremony conducted by her father; Brown's parents decline to attend and Brown is censured by the Monthly Meeting of the Philadelphia Society of Friends.

1805   Brown's biographical sketch of John Blair Linn is pub-
            lished as an introduction to Linn's narrative poem *Vale-
            rian*. "Somnabulism: A Fragment" appears in *Literary
            Magazine* (May). Twin sons Charles Brockden Brown Jr.
            and William Linn Brown born August 10.

1806   William Dunlap visits in January, March, and April, and
            paints miniature portraits of Brown and Elizabeth. Suffer-
            ing from symptoms of consumption, Brown journeys "in
            pursuit of health" up the Hudson by sloop in June; visits
            his in-laws in Albany. On the journey meets the 15-year-
            old actor and future playwright John Howard Payne.
            Brown contributes regularly to *The Literary Magazine*,
            which is being published by John Conrad. On grounds
            of "vendability," Conrad urges that the magazine be
            "metamorphosed" into semi-annual *American Register—
            A General Repository of History, Politics & Science*.

1807   The *Register* is launched in November and runs until 1811,
            with Brown editing five of the seven volumes. Although
            the publication is less literary than its predecessor, Brown
            includes poetry and a condensed "Review of Literature";
            reviews Joel Barlow's epic poem *The Columbiad*. Sister
            Elizabeth Horner dies in childbirth on April 6. Brown
            writes *The British Treaty*, criticizing the Jefferson admin-
            istration's negotiations with England with regard to issues
            of maritime navigation, commerce, and impressment. Son
            Eugene Linn Brown born July 26. Minerva Press publishes
            Philip Stanley; or, the Enthusiasm of Love, an edited ver-
            sion of *Clara Howard*. Brother Joseph dies in Holland on
            October 29.

1808–9   Father-in-law William Linn dies January 8. Writes semi-
            annual "Annals of Europe and America" for the four re-
            maining volumes of the *American Register* that he will
            edit. Criticizes Thomas Paine's writing on the Bible for its
            religious irreverence. Writes pamphlet *An Address to the
            Congress of the United States* (1809), arguing the futility of
            Jefferson's Embargo Act. Publishes a series of six "Scrib-
            bler" essays for *Port Folio* (Jan.–Aug. 1809). Works on *Sys-
            tem of General Geography: Containing a Topographical,
            Statistical and Descriptive Survey of the Earth*, projected
            to come out in two 600-page volumes (the manuscript is
            later lost, and only a nine-page Prospectus posthumously

published). Begins final work, "A Sketch of the Life of Horatio Gates" (published in two parts in *Port Folio*, Nov. 1809 and Feb. 1810). Daughter Mary Brown is born.

1810   Brown is confined to his room by worsening pulmonary tuberculosis; suffers pain but remains conscious and is able to receive visitors. Dies on February 22, 1810, and is interred in Friends Burial Ground in Philadelphia.

Note on the Texts

This volume contains three novels of Charles Brockden Brown that were first published from 1798 to 1800: *Wieland: or the Transformation, An American Tale*; *Arthur Mervyn: or, Memoirs of the Year 1793, First and Second Parts*; and *Edgar Huntly: or, Memoirs of a Sleep-Walker*.

The texts of the three novels printed here are those established for Kent State University's Bicentennial Edition of the Novels and Related Works of Charles Brockden Brown under the general editorship of Sydney J. Krause, with S. W. Reid as textual editor, and published by Kent State University Press in, respectively, 1977, 1980, and 1984. These texts were prepared according to the standards established by, and have received the approval of, the Center for Scholarly Editions of the Modern Language Association of America (see *The Center for Scholarly Editions: An Introductory Statement*, 1977).

Brown's manuscripts and prepublication materials, such as page proofs, for the novels printed here are not known to be extant. Brown did not always read proof for his novels; when he did, he often missed errors, including those introduced by the printers. In order to establish texts that represent, as nearly as possible, Brown's final intentions, the editors of the Kent State Edition studied the extant documents pertaining to each work and based their texts on the original printings that could be considered most authoritative, making corrections where necessary.

Brown began writing *Wieland: or the Transformation, An American Tale* by early 1798; an undated outline survives that may have been written as early as 1796. During an extended stay in New York in July 1798, he delivered a manuscript containing most of the novel to Thomas and James Swords, the printers for Brown's publisher, Hocquet Caritat. While it was being set in type, Brown read excerpts of the novel to his friends William Dunlap, Elihu Hubbard Smith, and William Johnson, who made suggestions about the ending of the novel; Smith, in particular, helped Brown with proofreading. Brown completed the novel in New York in August 1798; William Dunlap records in his diary that Brown read final proof for the book. It was published on September 14, 1798, the only edition of *Wieland* published during Brown's lifetime. This volume prints the text of the first 1977 Kent State printing, which is based on Caritat's 1798 printing.

The first nine chapters of *Arthur Mervyn: or, Memoirs of the Year 1793* originally appeared in installments in James Watters' *Weekly*

Magazine, June 16–August 25, 1798. In December 1798, Brown accepted Hugh Maxwell's proposal to publish the first part of the novel; he completed it in early 1799, and it was published as *Arthur Mervyn: or, Memoirs of the Year 1793, First Part* in the spring of that year. Because Brown's manuscript of the first nine chapters was lost when the *Weekly Magazine* was suspended after Watters' death in August 1798, Maxwell based his printing of them on the magazine publication. Brown was in New York when the book was being published and did not read proofs for it. *Arthur Mervyn: or, Memoirs of the Year 1793, Second Part* was published in the summer of 1800 by George Folliot Hopkins, a New York printer. This volume prints the text of the first 1980 Kent State printing of *Arthur Mervyn: or, Memoirs of the Year 1793, First and Second Parts*, which is based on the *Weekly Magazine* printing of the first nine chapters of the novel; the 1799 Maxwell printing for the remainder of the first part of the novel; and the 1800 Hopkins printing for the second part of the novel.

Excerpts from *Edgar Huntly: or, Memoirs of a Sleep-Walker*, corresponding roughly to Chapters 17–20, appeared in April 1799 number of Brown's *Monthly Magazine*. Brown finished the novel in the summer of 1799, and it was printed by Hugh Maxwell in Philadelphia later that year. Brown, who was living in New York during this period and occupied with his duties on the *Monthly Magazine*, did not read proof. This volume prints the text of the first 1984 Kent State printing, which is based on the 1799 Maxwell printing and incorporates corrections from the *Monthly Magazine* text at points where the Maxwell text appears to be erroneous.

The Kent State Edition does not impose a uniform style on the texts or modernize or normalize spelling, punctuation, or grammatical constructions; but it does correct spellings and punctuation that were positively erroneous in Brown's time, restores Brown's habitual usages in instances where the text obviously represents a printer's attempt at styling, and emends printers' errors, such as turned letters or misplaced type. It does not attempt to reproduce features of 18th-century typography, such as the long letter "s." This volume presents the texts of the Kent State printings chosen for inclusion here, but it does not attempt to reproduce features of their typographic design, such as the display capitalization of chapter openings. The texts are presented without change, except for the correction of the following two typographical errors, cited here by page and line number: 276.38, your; 498.21, that.

Notes

In the notes below, the reference numbers denote page and line of this volume. No note is made for material included in standard desk-reference books such as Webster's *Collegiate, Biographical,* and *Geographical* dictionaries. Quotations from Shakespeare are keyed to *The Riverside Shakespeare* (Boston: Houghton Mifflin, 1974), ed. G. Blakemore Evans. Biblical references are keyed to the King James Version. For further background and references to other studies, see: Harry R. Warfel, *Charles Brockden Brown: American Gothic Novelist* (Gainesville: University of Florida Press, 1949); David Lee Clark, *Charles Brockden Brown: Pioneer Voice of America* (Durham: Duke University Press, 1952); Donald A. Ringe, *Charles Brockden Brown* (New York: Twayne Publishers, 1966); Norman S. Grabo, *The Coincidental Art of Charles Brockden Brown* (Chapel Hill: University of North Carolina Press, 1981); and the "Historical Essays" in the individual volumes of The Bicentennial Edition of the Novels and Related Works of Charles Brockden Brown (Kent: Kent State University Press), ed. Sydney J. Krause et. al.: *Wieland and Memoirs of Carwin* (1977), *Arthur Mervyn* (1980), and *Edgar Huntly* (1984).

WIELAND

3.26–27   an authentic case]   Brown's source for Wieland's murder of his family was "An Account of a murder committed by Mr. J— Y—, upon his Family, in December, A.D., 1781," published in the New York *Weekly Magazine* (July 20 & 27, 1796) and the Philadelphia *Minerva* (August 20 & 27, 1796). The account describes how James Yates, of Tomhannock, New York, murdered his wife and four children in response to what he perceived as an angelic command.

6.32–33   My ancestor . . . German Theatre]   This "elder Wieland" (as he is called at 6.36) is Brown's invention.

6.34   modern poet]   German writer and translator Christoph Martin Wieland (1733–1813), from whose translated *Trial of Abraham* (1777) Brown drew source material for *Wieland.* In 1805 Brown's *Literary Magazine* published an account of the poet's life and works.

7.28   Albigenses]   Members of a religious group, also known as Cathars, whose dualistic beliefs and ascetic practices were derived from the teachings of the Persian prophet Mani. Catharism spread widely in southern France beginning in the 11th century; it was denounced as heresy by the Catholic

Church, and its adherents were defeated militarily in the Albigensian Crusade (1208–29).

8.2–3   Seek and ye shall find]   Cf. Matthew 7:7 and Luke 11:9.

8.11   Camissards]   Camisards, a group of Huguenots who remained in France following Louis XIV's 1685 revocation of the Edict of Nantes, and resisted government persecution until their military defeat in 1710.

18.13–14   A case . . . Florence]   The reference is probably to the death of Don G. Maria Bertholi as reported in "Letter respecting an Italian priest, killed by an electrical commotion, the cause of which resided in his own body," published in *The American Museum*, April 1792.

29.3–4   oration for Cluentius]   *Pro Cluentius* (66 BCE), in which Cicero successfully defends his client, Aulus Cluentius Habitus, against a murder charge.

29.13   *"polliceatur"* . . . *"polliceretur"*]   The present and the imperfect subjunctive of the Latin *polliceor* (I promise).

39.24   Della Crusca dictionary]   The *Vocabularia della Crusca* (1612), produced by the Accademia della Crusca, a Florentine literary society; later expanded as *Vocabulario degli Accademia della Crusca* (1697).

44.11   Hollander's creek]   The creek (now filled in) traversed the peninsular meadowland below Philadelphia, bounded by the Delaware and Schuylkill Rivers.

45.28   Dæmon of Socrates]   In Plato's *Phaedo* and *Apology*, the "divine sign" or inner voice that prompted Socrates to seek the truly wise.

52.3   Nice]   Nicaea, now Iznik, Turkey.

62.37   Murviedro]   Present-day Sagunto; called Saguntum under Roman rule.

62.39–40   theatre . . . Saguntum]   The theater was built during the reigns of Septimus Severus (193–211) and his son Caracalla (211–17), against a hill overlooking the town.

63.1   the deacon Marti]   Emmanuel Marti (1663–1737), poet and classicist, who was appointed Dean of Alicante in 1696; he wrote a description of the Sagunto theater.

73.5   Zisca]   Jan Zizka (c. 1358–1424), Bohemian general and Hussite leader, defeated German Crusader armies 1420–21.

148.6   the late war]   The Seven Years War.

165.38   Mania Mutabilis]   In his treatise *Zoonomia* (1794–96), Erasmus Darwin describes those afflicted with this condition as "likely to mistake ideas of sensation for those of irritation, what is imaginations for realities."

183.34   work of the Abbe de la Chappelle] *Le Ventriloque ou L'Engastrimythe* by M. de la Chapelle, published in two volumes in London and Paris in 1772, examines the mechanics and uses of ventriloquism.

189.13–14   —Peeps . . . Hold!] Cf. *Macbeth*, I. v. 53–54.

ARTHUR MERVYN

231.2   evils of pestilence . . . afflicted] Yellow fever appeared in the West Indies in the mid-seventeenth century, and soon reached continental America, where it spread to the major trading ports. It was a chronic problem for Philadelphians throughout the eighteenth century, and reached epidemic proportions in 1732, 1739, 1745, and 1748; the most devastating outbreak was that of 1793.

236.37   Chester County] One of the original three counties of Pennsylvania laid out by William Penn in 1682, encompassing what are now Lancaster, Berks, and Delaware counties.

253.11   Schuylkill . . . bridge] In 1783 there were "floating bridges" at the upper, middle, and lower ferry locations on the Schuylkill.

253.38–40   pendent . . . asphalto."] Cf. John Milton, *Paradise Lost*, I, ll. 727–30.

272.18   Carrara] Center of the Italian marble industry, located in Tuscany.

274.29   "My poverty . . . consents."] Cf. *Romeo and Juliet*, V. i. 75.

280.23–24   fugitives . . . Milanese] Emigré aristocrats from Provence sought refuge in Italian cities like Verona and Milan.

314.2   Portuguese gold] Specie, not bullion. Due to a tight money supply, Congress in 1793 authorized British and Portuguese gold pieces to be passed as legal tender.

337.25   Tuscan] The language of Tuscany, considered the classical form of Italian; it was used by Dante, Petrarch, and Boccaccio, and became the standard literary language of Italy.

446.33   unwafered] Unsealed.

506.30–31   *entered up*] Placed the issue before the court to gain priority for his claim.

509.32   *chouse*] Dupe, swindle.

515.28–29   print . . . Salvator] "Landscape with Apollo and the Cumaean Sibyl," by the Italian baroque landscape painter Salvator Rosa (1615–73).

543.21–22   *animal . . . ignavumque*] Lecherous and slothful animal.

566.12–13   Tenez! . . . Diable noir!] Hold on! Dominique! Watch out! Black devil!

574.22   buckra]   Generic name for "white man" in African-American dialect of the 1790s.

595.9–12   Now knit . . . solemnity.]   Cf. John Milton, "Comus" (1634), ll. 141–44.

615.9   the Venaissin]   The Comtat Venaissin, a former papal possession (1274–1791) in Provence consisting of the region around (but not including) Avignon. It was annexed to France after a plebiscite ordered by the National Assembly and was incorporated into the Vaucluse department in 1793.

624.13–14   sheet pebble]   Should probably read "street pebble."

628.8–9   "Sleep . . . no more."]   Cf. *Macbeth*, II. ii. 32–40.

EDGAR HUNTLY

690.28–30   A war broke out . . . defeated]   The Second Anglo-Mysore War (1780–81), in which Hyder Ali defeated an English detachment near Madras led by Colonel William Baillie.

691.13   Hyder]   Hyder (or Haidar) Ali (1722–82), ruler of Mysore.

691.17   pilgrim to . . . Jagunaut]   Jagannath ("Lord of the World"), or Juggernaut, a form of the Hindu god Vishnu, is celebrated in the Indian city of Puri, where a large wooden image of the god is used in festival processions.

723.11   desert]   Any uninhabited and uncultivated tract of country; a wilderness.

788.8–9   history . . . small room]   After British forces in Calcutta were defeated in 1756 by Siraj-ud-Dowlah, Nawab of Bengal, a militia company under the command of John Z. Holwell was imprisoned over the night of June 20–21 in an 18-by-15-foot cell subsequently known as "the Black Hole of Calcutta." According to Holwell's account, only 23 out of 146 prisoners survived.

789.3–826.14   I was eagerly observant . . . I set out.]   This section of the text was published in somewhat different form in the first issue of Brown's *Monthly Magazine* in April 1799 as "Edgar Huntly, A Fragment." It was prefaced by remarks that the narrative was "extracted from the memoirs of a young man who resided some years since on the upper branches of the Delaware." Brown wrote that "similar events have frequently happened on the Indian borders," and observed: "As to the truth of these incidents, men acquainted with the perils of an Indian war must be allowed to judge."

791.23   the last war]   The French and Indian War (1756–63).

820.14   Queen Mab]   In British folklore, the queen of the fairies.

896.33–34   the Pennsylvania hospital]   Chartered in 1751, the first structure, on Pine Street, had 16 rooms reserved for "lunatics."

896.35   Powles-hook]   Also spelled Paulus-hook (later the site of Jersey City, New Jersey).

897.3   Elizabeth-town]   Elizabeth, New Jersey.

898.4   *The Narrows*]   Mile-wide strait at the entrance to New York Bay, separating Staten Island from Brooklyn.

Library of Congress Cataloging-in-Publication Data

Brown, Charles Brockden, 1771–1810.
  [Novels. Selections]
  Three Gothic novels / Charles Brockden Brown.
      p.   cm. — (The library of America ; 103)
  Contents: Wieland — Arthur Mervyn — Edgar Huntly.
  ISBN 1–883011–57–4 (acid-free paper)
    1. Horror tales, American.   2. Gothic revival (Literature)—
United States.   I. Title.   II. Title: Wieland   III. Title:
Arthur Mervyn.   IV. Title: Edgar Huntly.   V. Series.
PS1132   1998
813'.2—dc21   97–46701
                                                        CIP

THE LIBRARY OF AMERICA SERIES

This book is set in 10 point Linotron Galliard,
a face designed for photocomposition by Matthew Carter
and based on the sixteenth-century face Granjon. The paper is
acid-free Ecusta Nyalite and meets the requirements for permanence
of the American National Standards Institute. The binding
material is Brillianta, a woven rayon cloth made by
Van Heek-Scholco Textielfabrieken, Holland.
The composition is by The Clarinda
Company. Printing and binding by
R.R.Donnelley & Sons Company.
Designed by Bruce Campbell.